**TOKI**
"The Cobalt Kingdom"

**GRIMBO (E)**
"Moss Ocean"

**SALASSANDRA**
"Mystic's Moon"

**MON DOMANI**
"Mother World"

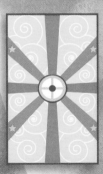

# The Praise for 5 Worlds Is Out of This World!

**A New York Public Library Top Ten Best Books for Kids Selection**

**A *Publishers Weekly* Best Summer Book**

**An NPR Great Read of the Year**

**A Junior Library Guild Selection**

"A bang-zoom start to a series that promises to be epic
in both the classical and internet senses of the word."
—***The New York Times Book Review***

"For kids who love fantasy and other-world adventures,
and for any fans of graphic novels, this book is a must-read."
**—R. J. Palacio, #1 *New York Times* bestselling author of *Wonder***

★ "Sensitive writing, gorgeous artwork, and riveting plot,
this is a series to keep an eye on."
**—*Booklist*, Starred Review**

★ "A dazzling interplanetary fantasy . . . that will easily appeal
to fans of *Naruto* or *Avatar: The Last Airbender*."
**—*Publishers Weekly*, Starred Review**

"Plenty of adventure as truths are uncovered . . .
Give to fans of Judd Winick's Hilo or Kazu Kibuishi's Amulet series."
—***School Library Journal***

"Epic action, adventure, and mystery will draw you in, but the heartfelt characters
and their seemingly impossible journey will keep you turning the pages."
**—Lisa Yee, author of the DC Super Hero Girls™ series**

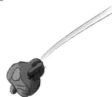

"This stellar team has created a gorgeous and entrancing world like no other!"
—**Noelle Stevenson,**
*New York Times* **bestselling author of** *Nimona*

"The beautiful illustrations will have young readers flying through the pages."
—*Deseret News*

"The adventure continues, growing grander of scale
and if possible even more lavish in visual detail."
—*Kirkus Reviews*

"Ends triumphantly and tantalizingly."
—*The Horn Book Magazine*

"Distinctly unique . . . it oozes with imagination and creativity."
—*Bam! Smack! Pow!*

"An intriguing beginning to what is sure to be a fascinating series."
—*BookRiot*

"I dare you not to get immediately caught up in Oona's epic tale!"
—*MuggleNet*

"Beautiful, with a vast array of characters and creatures from the various worlds."
—*GeekDad*

"A magical adventure full of wisdom, humor, and enough girl power
to make you root for Oona in her quest to light the beacon."
—**Abigail, age 10**

"This book is great! I usually don't like graphic novels,
but this book changed my mind."
—**Lucius, age 9**

# 5 Worlds

## BOOK 3

## THE RED MAZE

Mark
SIEGEL

Alexis
SIEGEL

Xanthe
BOUMA

Boya
SUN

Matt
ROCKEFELLER

Random House 🏠 New York

"Many deaths, and many births,
Windows in and windows out."
—Ancient Felid carving, translation uncertain

# PROLOGUE
# JAX ON SALASSANDRA

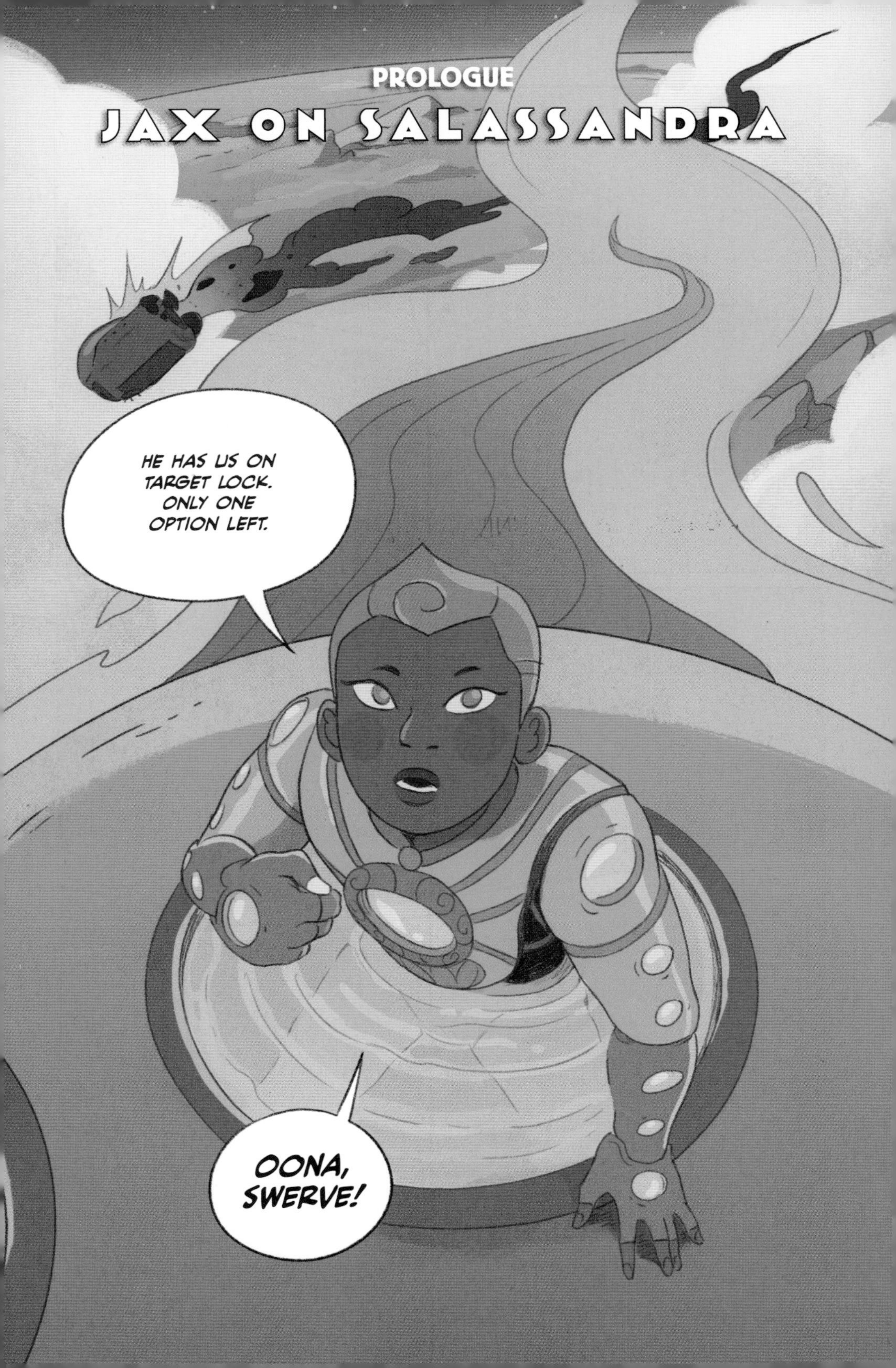

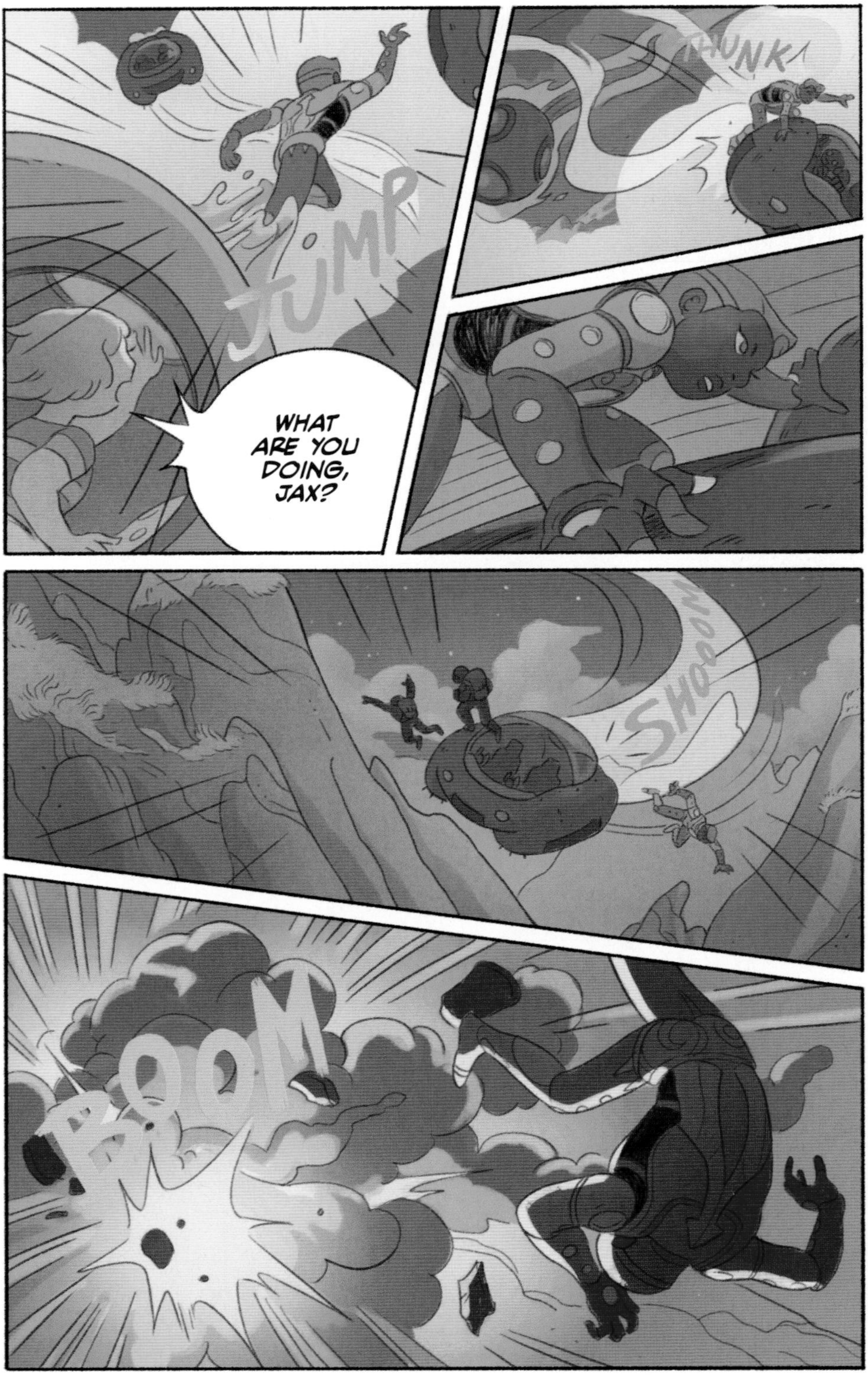
JUMP
THUNK
WHAT ARE YOU DOING, JAX?
SHOOOOM
BOOOM

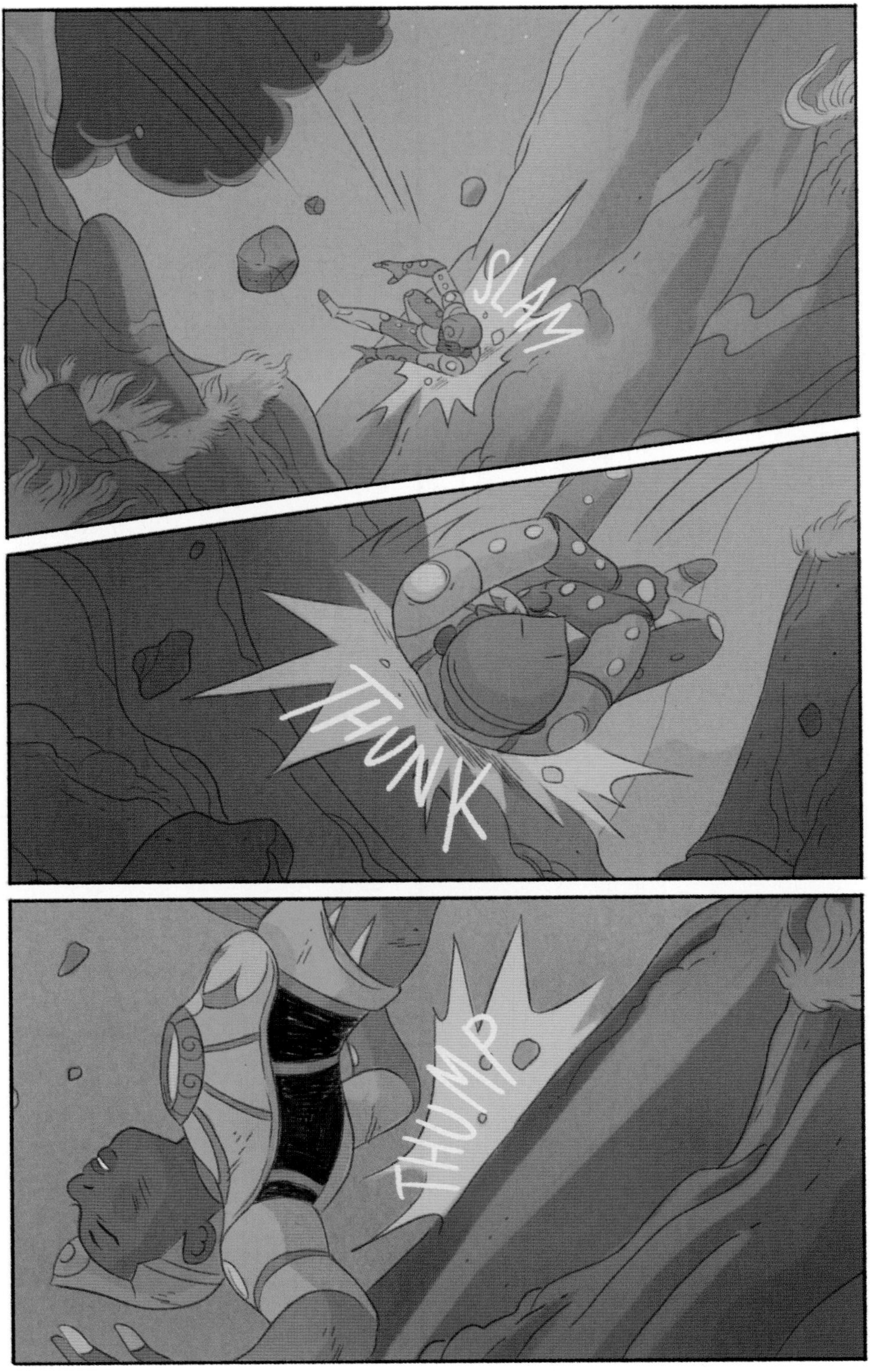
SLAM
THUNK
THUMP

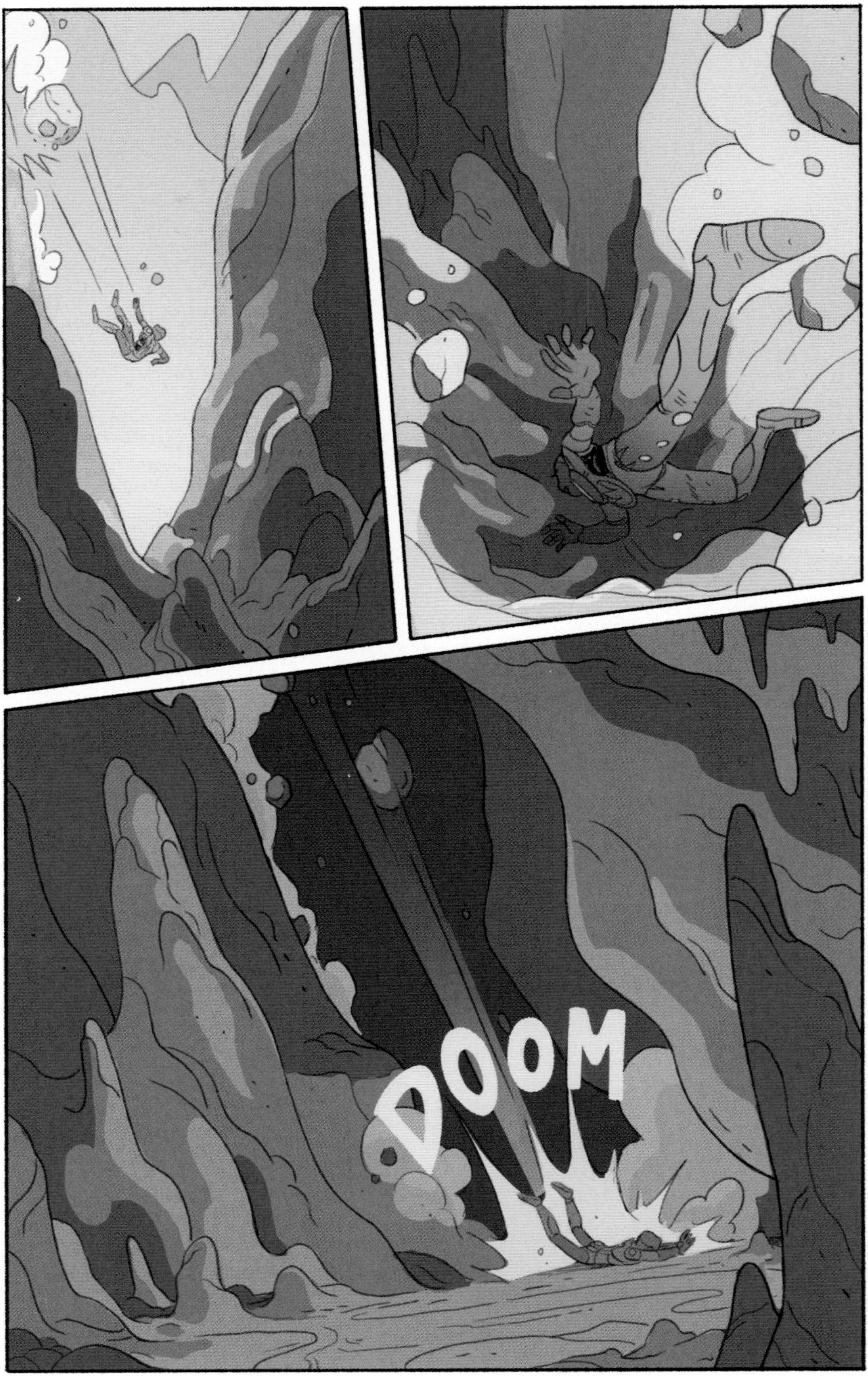
DOOM

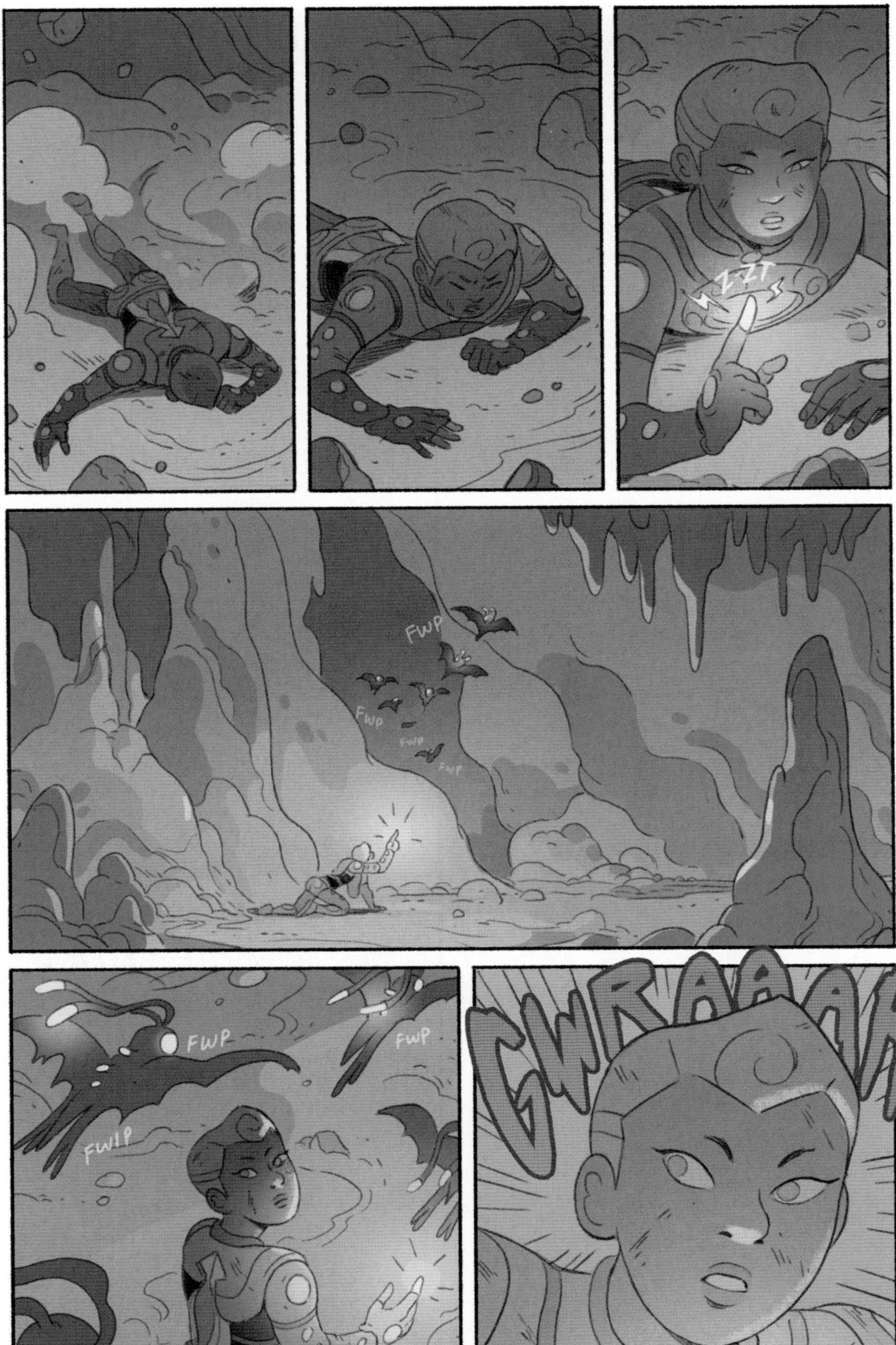

ZZZT
FWP
FWP
FWP
FWP
FWP
FWP
FWIP
GWRAAAH

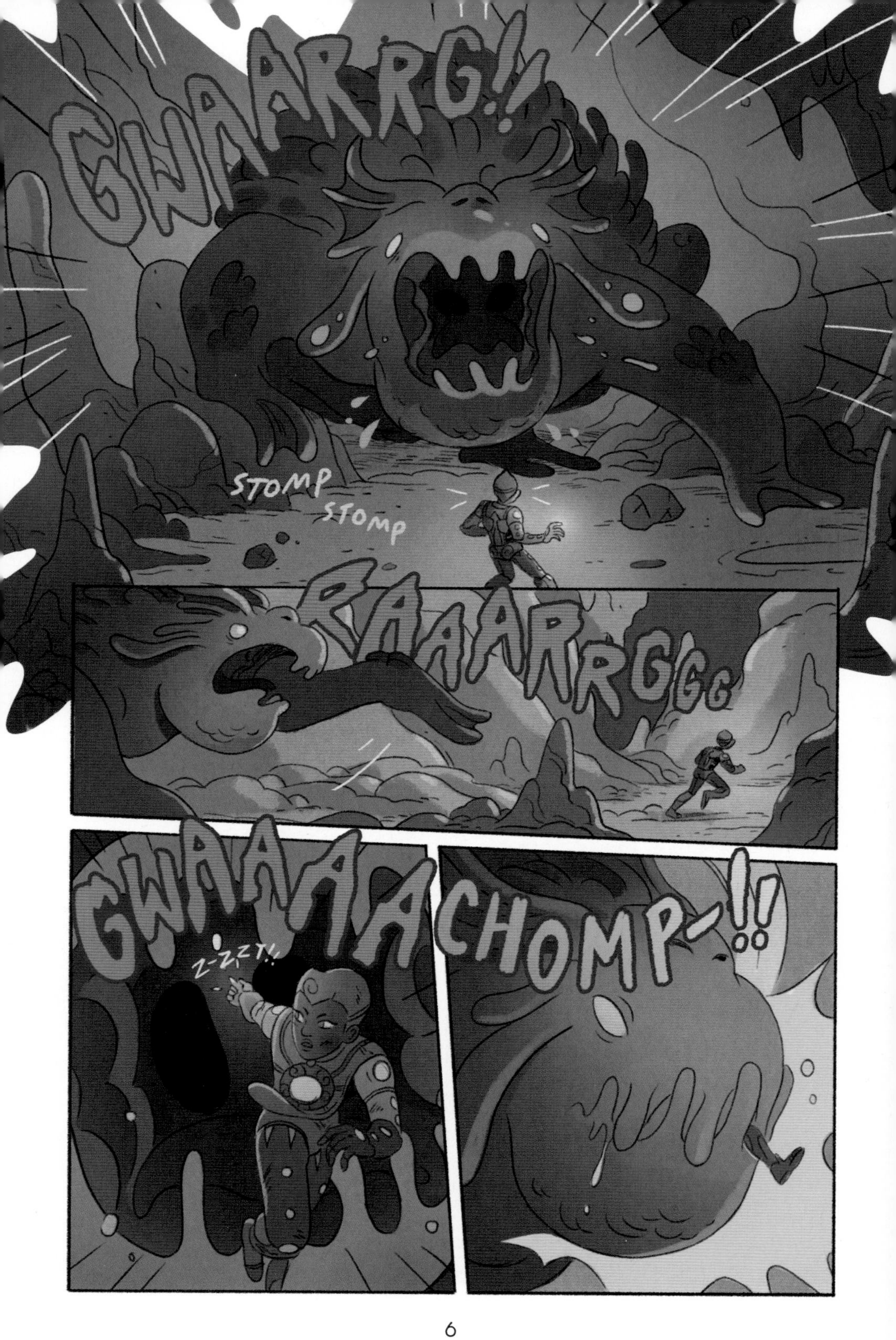
GWAARRG!!
STOMP
STOMP
RAAARRGGG
GWAAAAA
Z-Z-ZT!!
CHOMP-!!

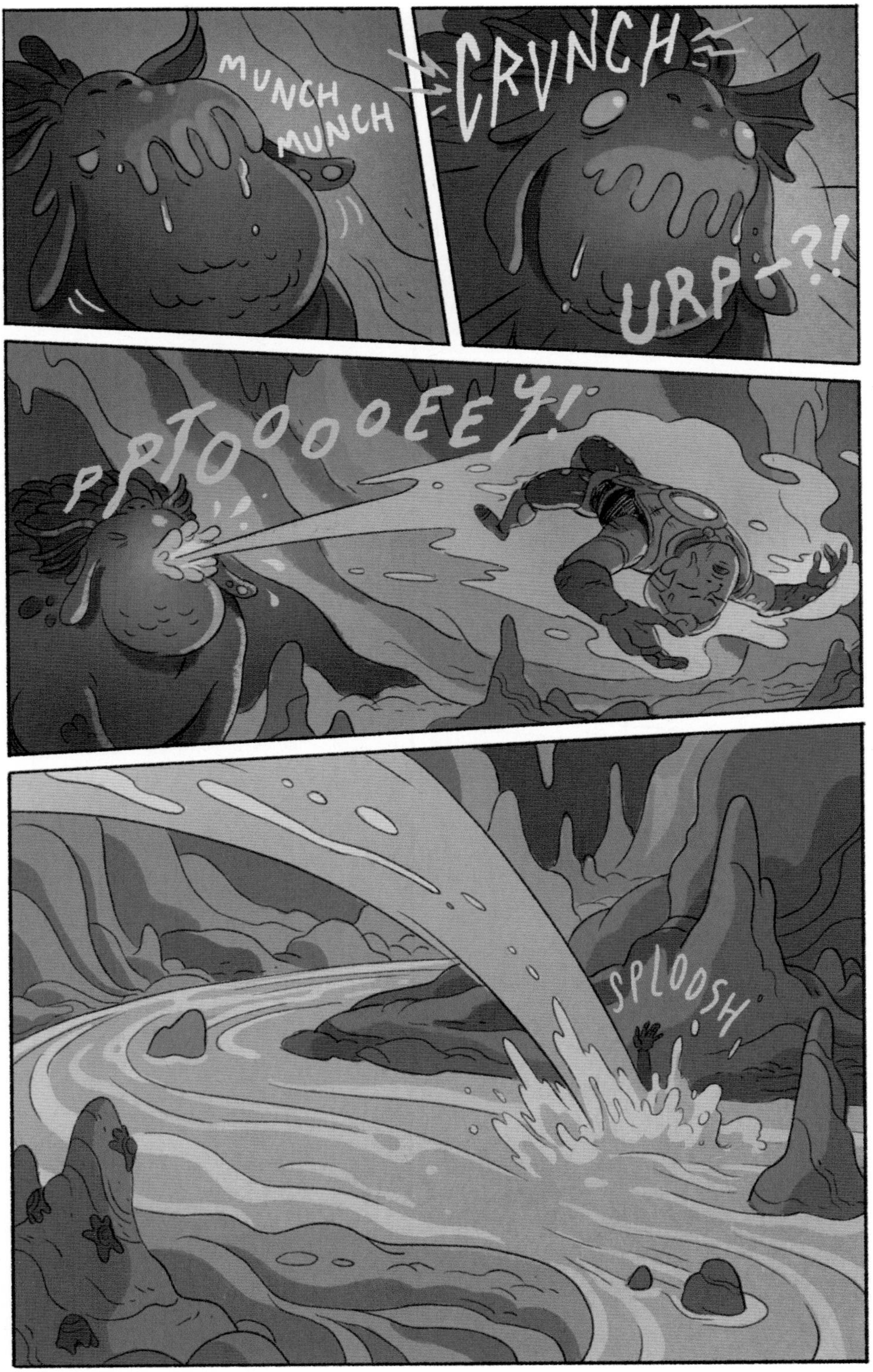
MUNCH
MUNCH
CRUNCH
URP--?!
PPTOOOOEEY!
SPLOOSH

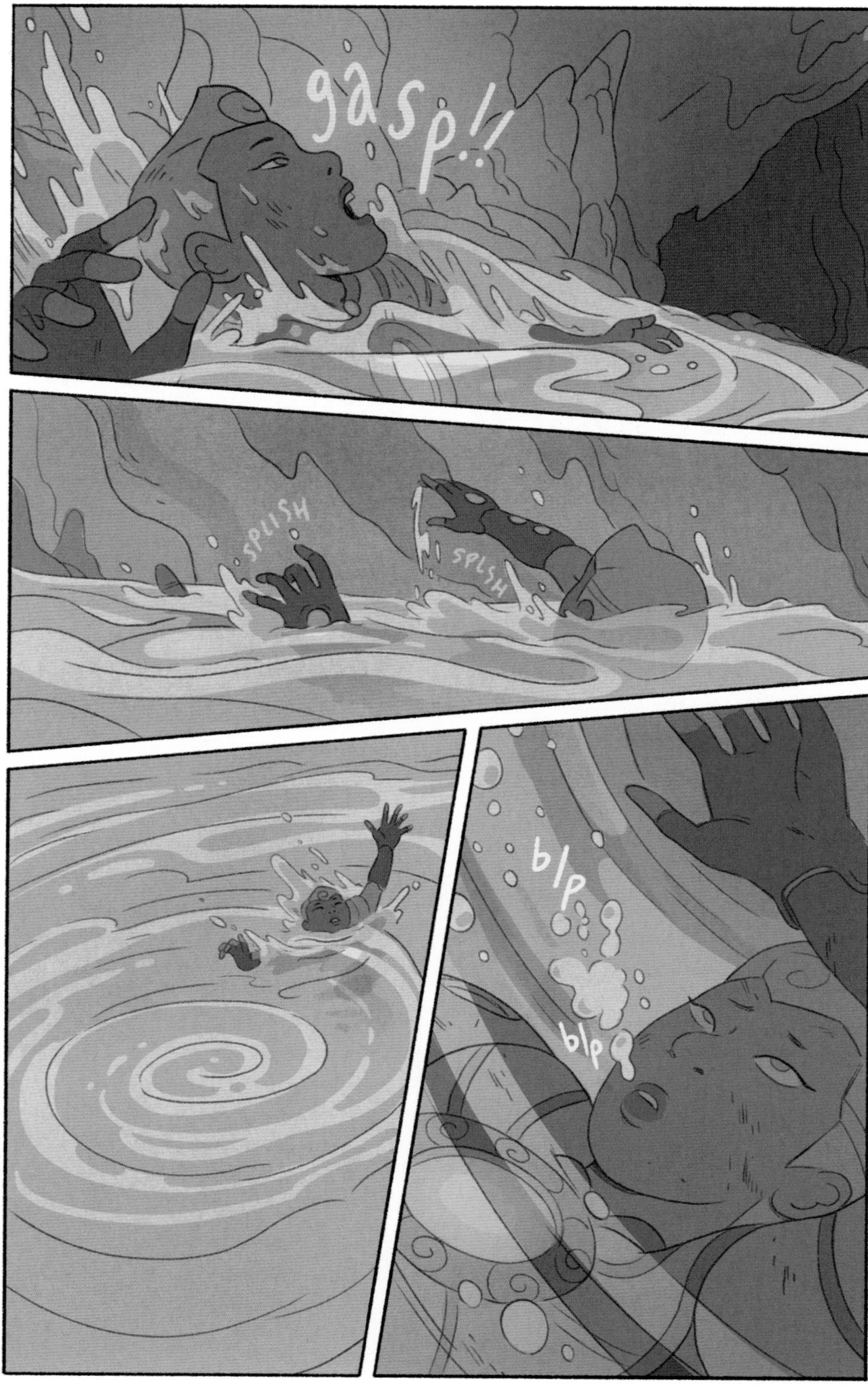
gasp!!
SPLISH
SPLSH
blp
blp

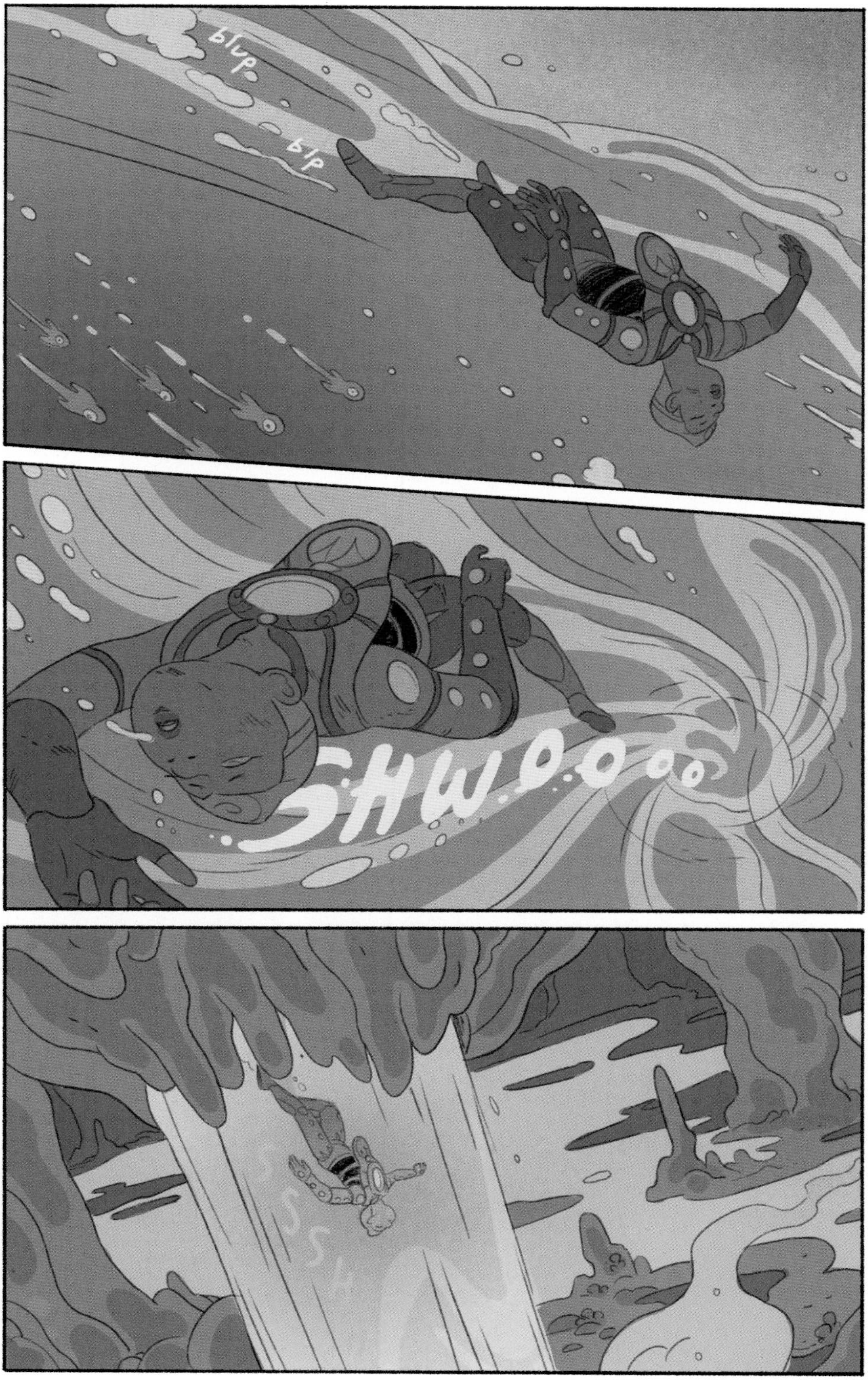
blup
blp
SHWOOoo
SSSH

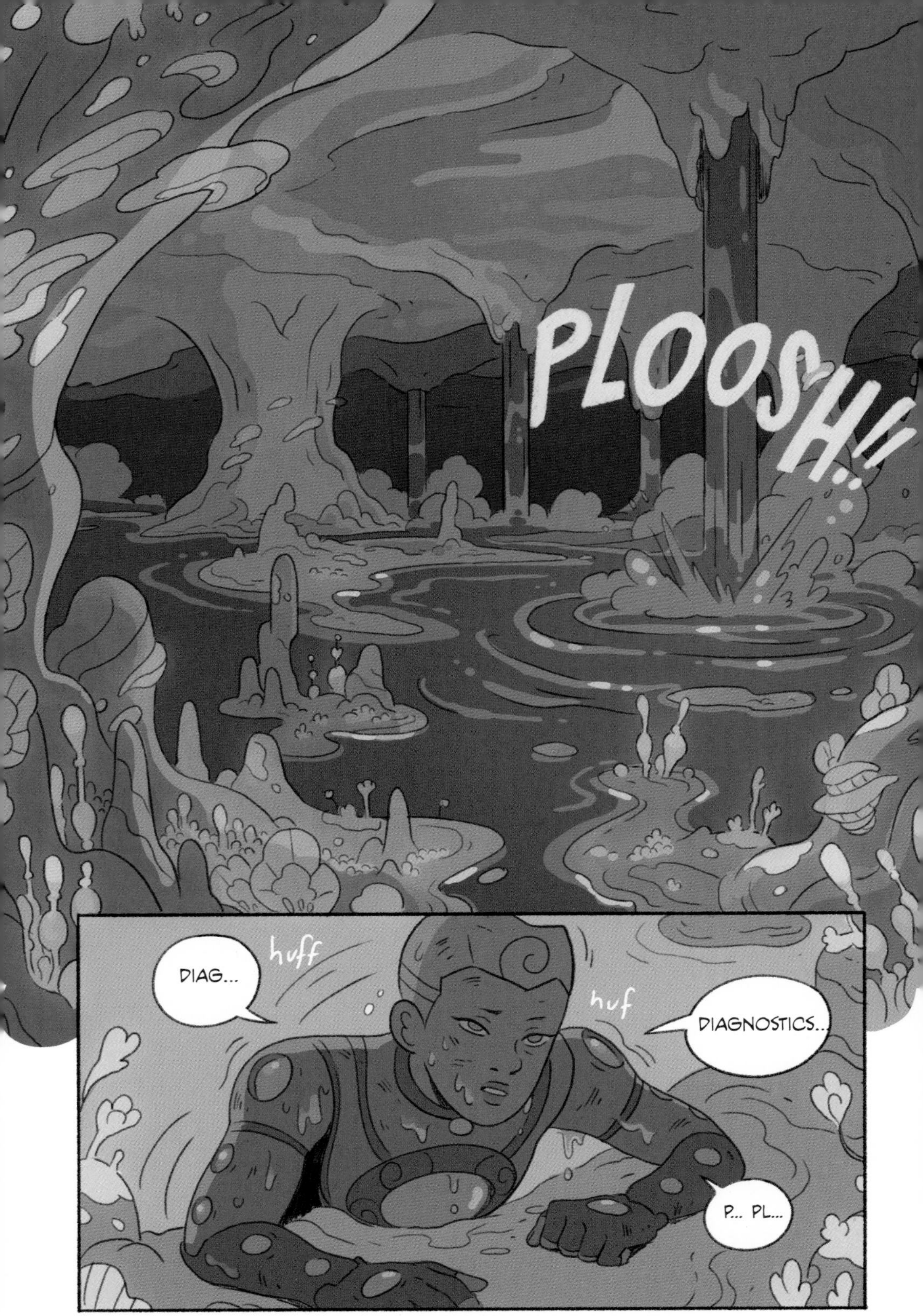
PLOOSH!!
huff
DIAG...
huf
DIAGNOSTICS...
P... PL...

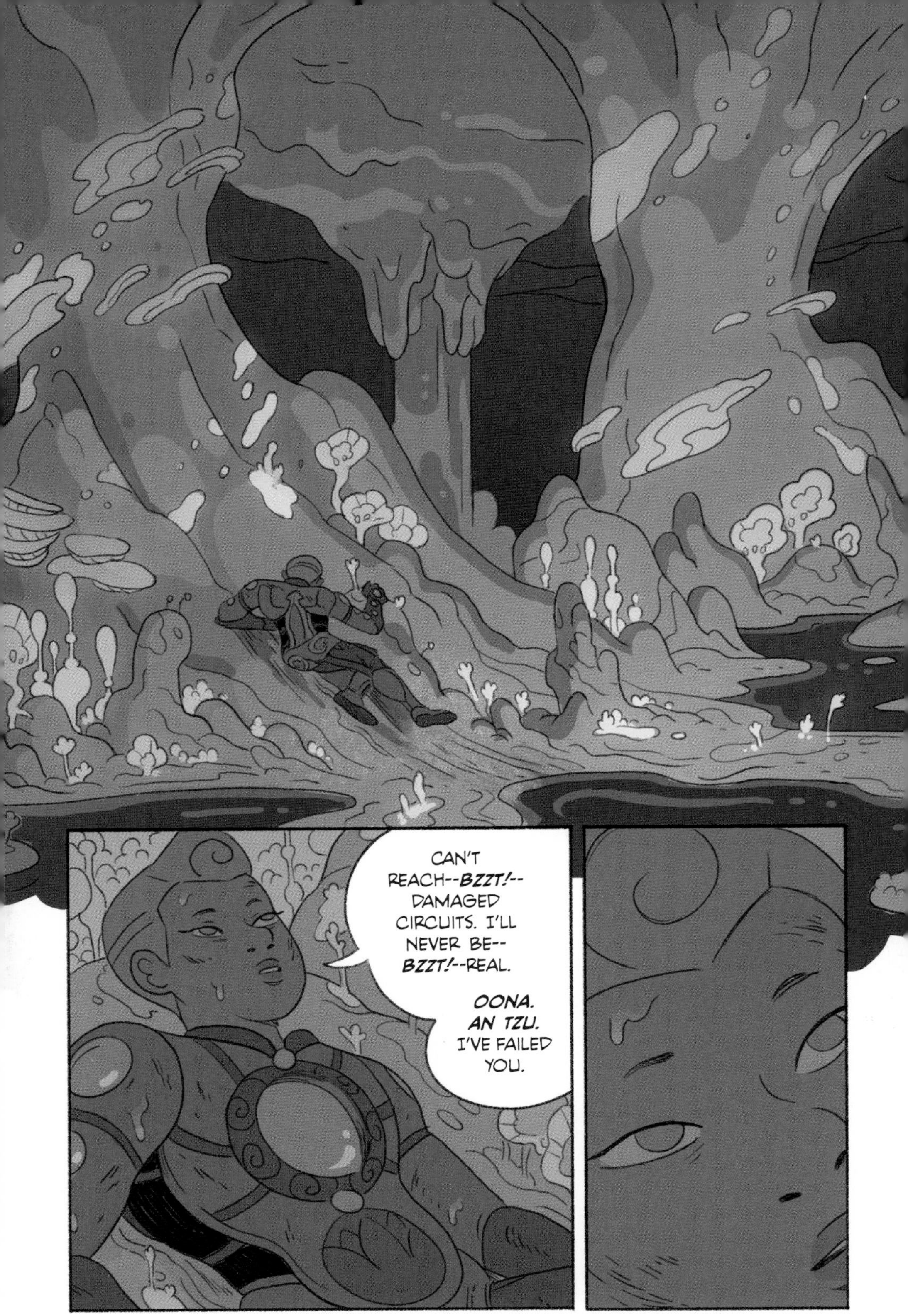
CAN'T REACH--*BZZT!*--DAMAGED CIRCUITS. I'LL NEVER BE--*BZZT!*--REAL.
*OONA. AN TZU.* I'VE FAILED YOU.

## Chapter 1
# THE SALASSI DEVOTI

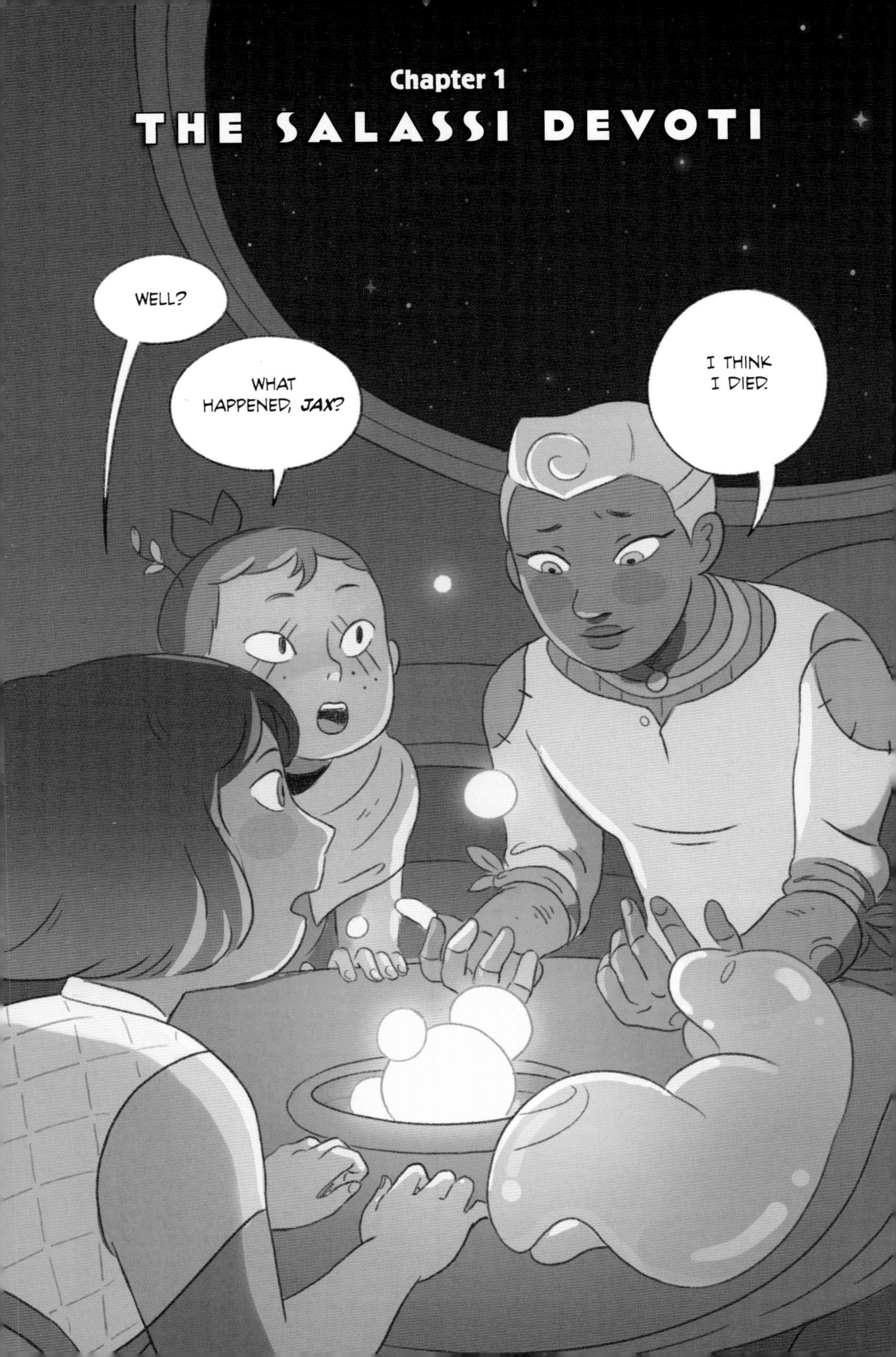
WELL?
WHAT HAPPENED, JAX?
I THINK I DIED.

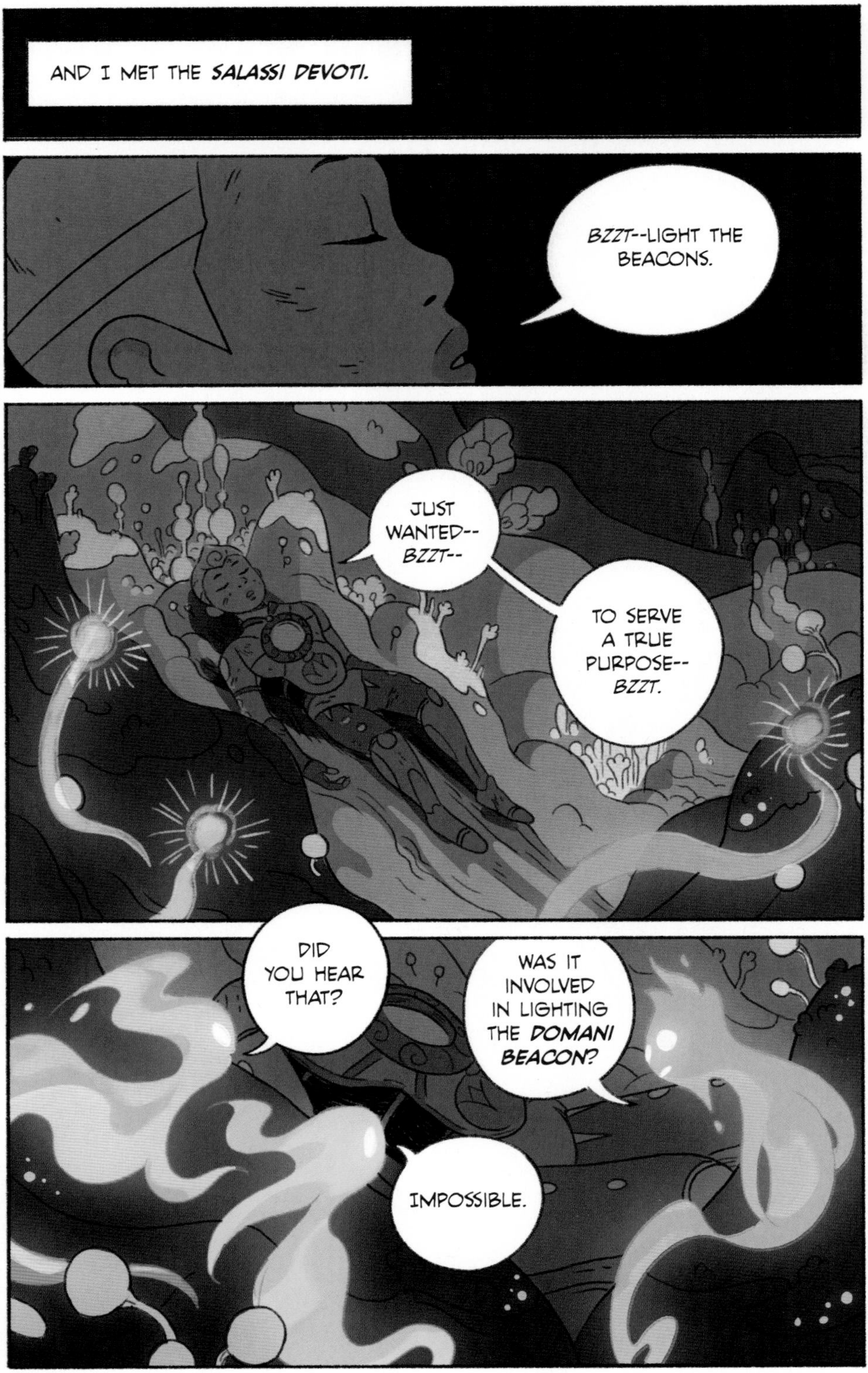
AND I MET THE *SALASSI DEVOTI.*
*BZZT*--LIGHT THE BEACONS.
JUST WANTED-- *BZZT*--
TO SERVE A TRUE PURPOSE-- *BZZT.*
DID YOU HEAR THAT?
WAS IT INVOLVED IN LIGHTING THE ***DOMANI BEACON?***
IMPOSSIBLE.

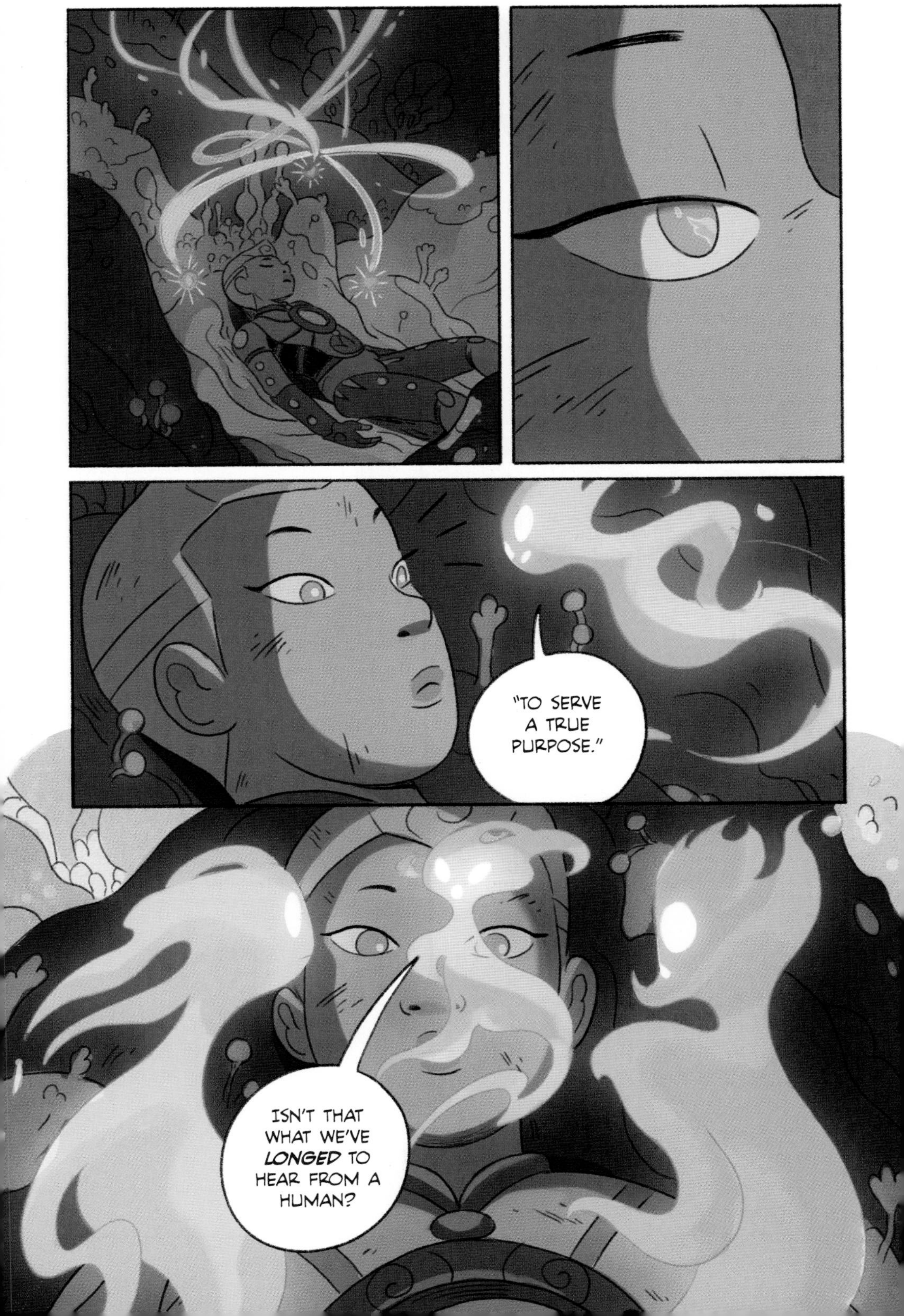
"TO SERVE A TRUE PURPOSE."
ISN'T THAT WHAT WE'VE *LONGED* TO HEAR FROM A HUMAN?

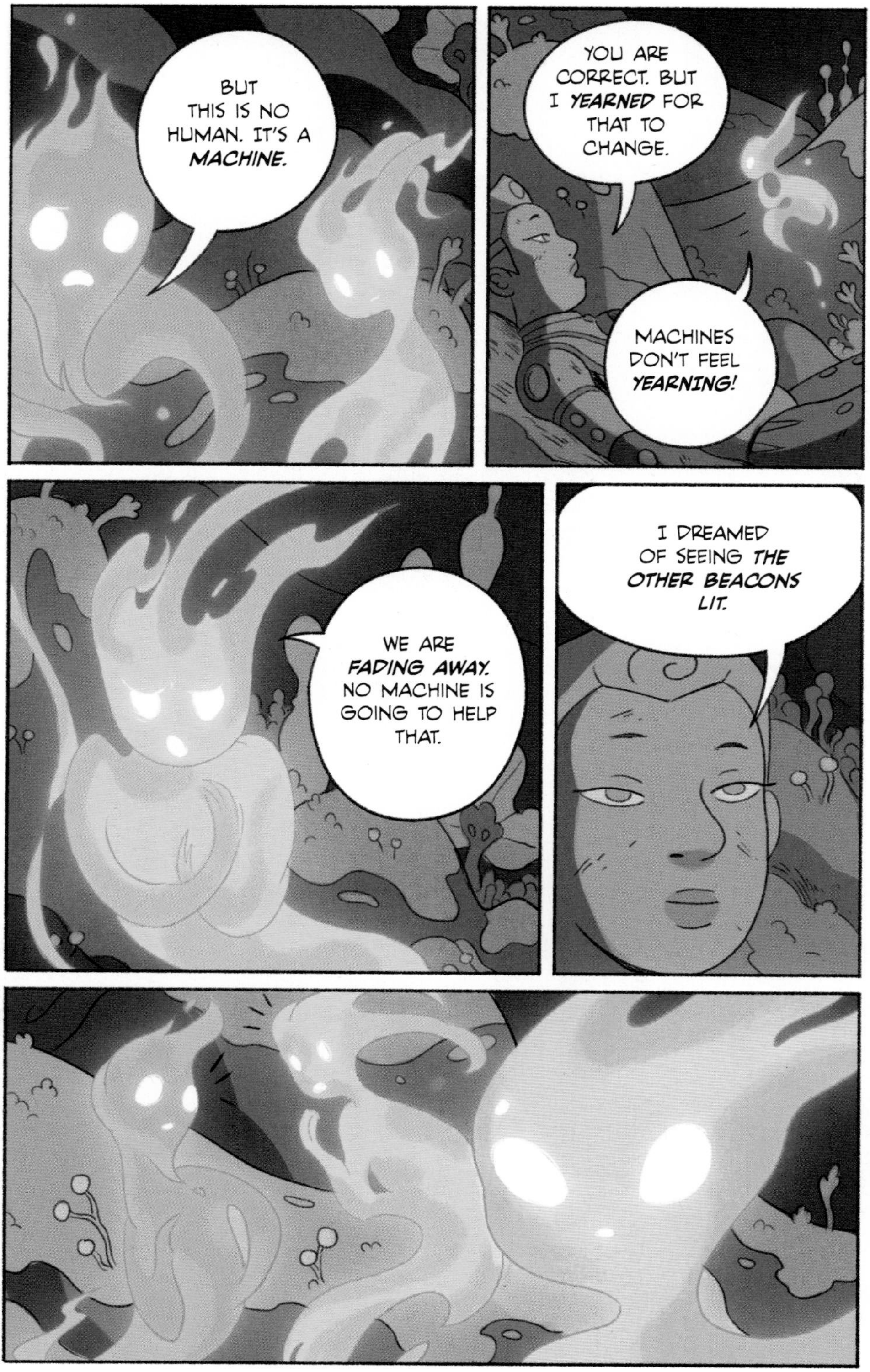
BUT THIS IS NO HUMAN. IT'S A *MACHINE.*
YOU ARE CORRECT. BUT I *YEARNED* FOR THAT TO CHANGE.
MACHINES DON'T FEEL *YEARNING!*
WE ARE *FADING AWAY.* NO MACHINE IS GOING TO HELP THAT.
I DREAMED OF SEEING *THE OTHER BEACONS LIT.*

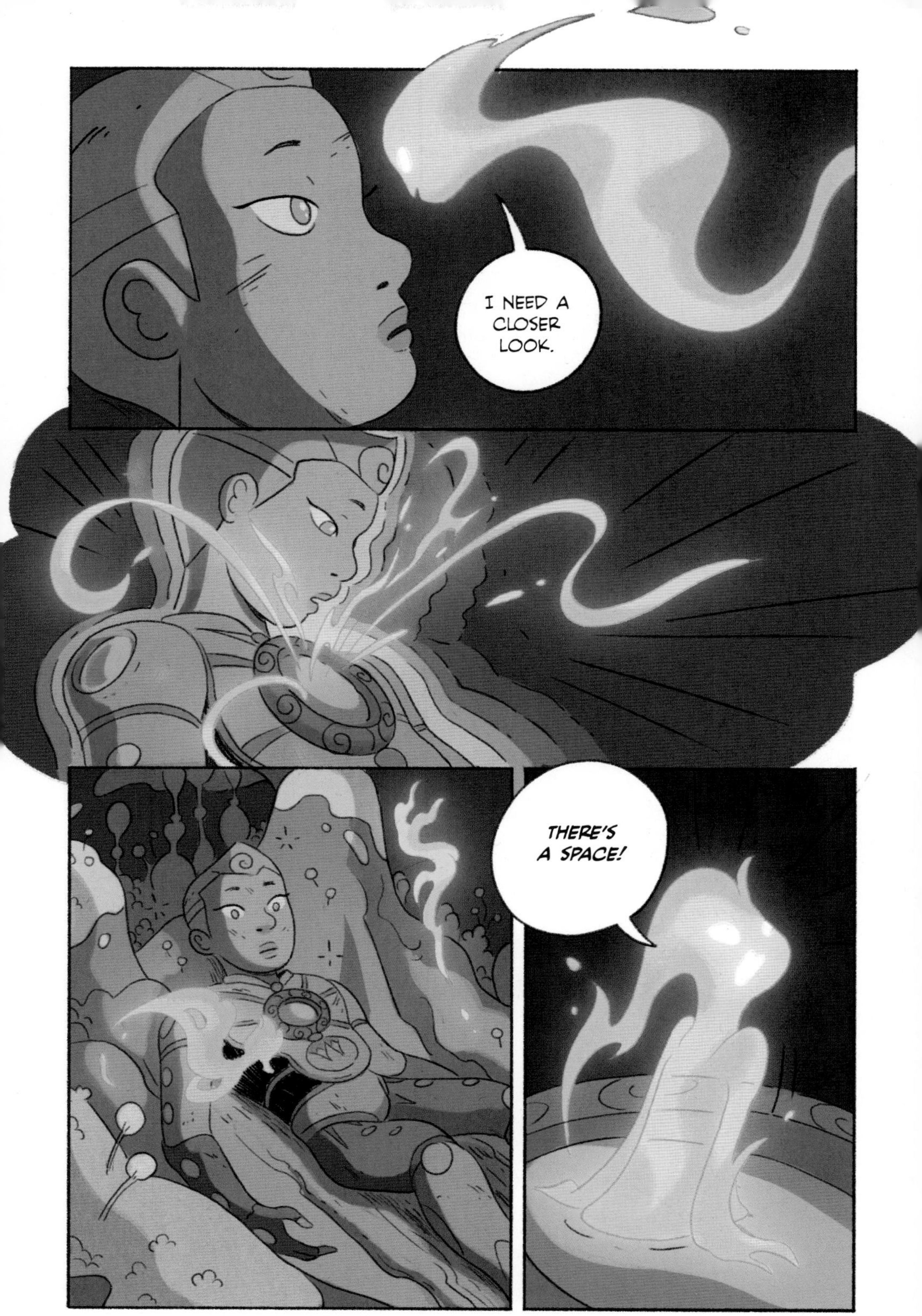
I NEED A CLOSER LOOK.
THERE'S A SPACE!

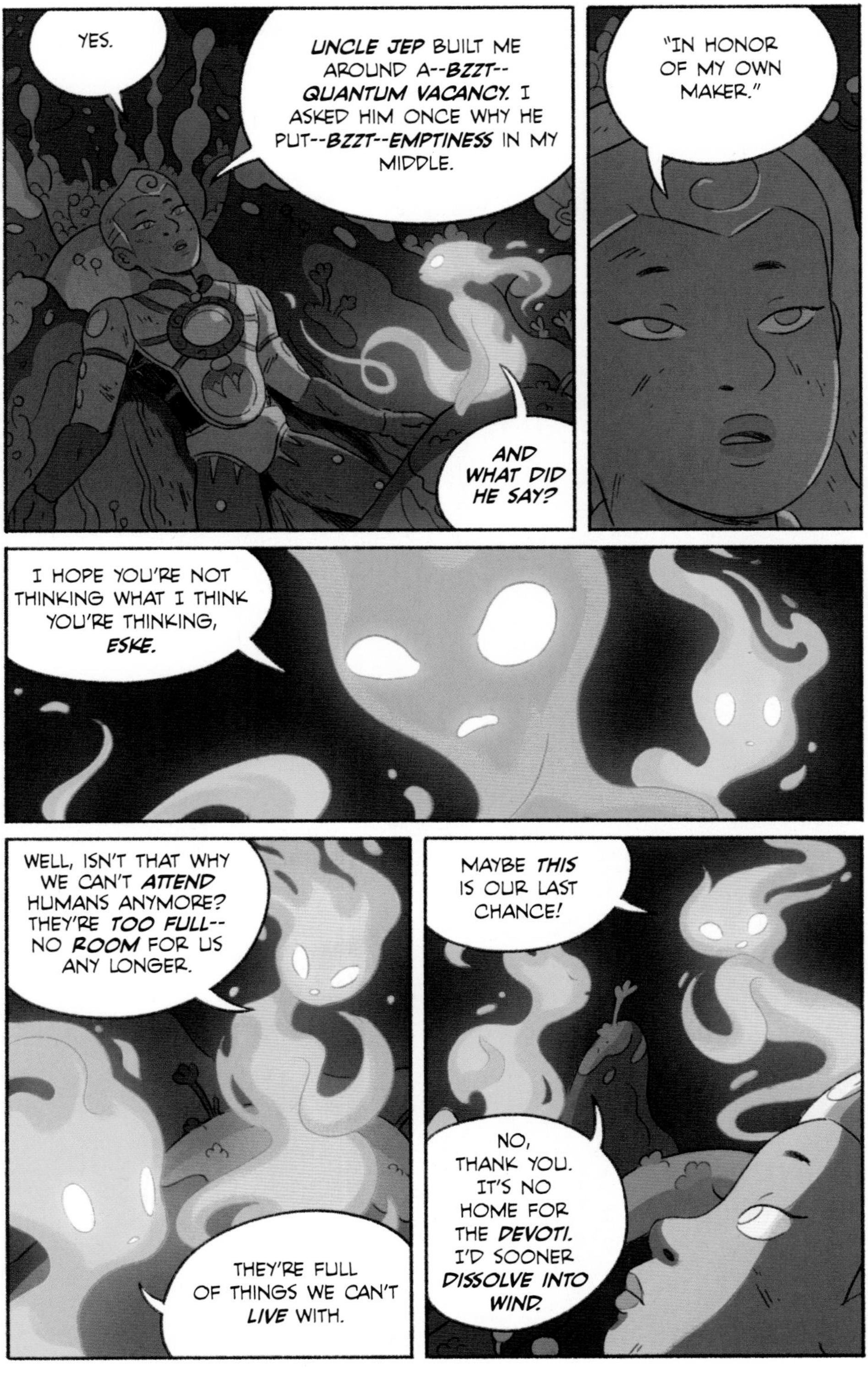
YES.
UNCLE JEP BUILT ME AROUND A--BZZT--QUANTUM VACANCY. I ASKED HIM ONCE WHY HE PUT--BZZT--EMPTINESS IN MY MIDDLE.
AND WHAT DID HE SAY?
"IN HONOR OF MY OWN MAKER."
I HOPE YOU'RE NOT THINKING WHAT I THINK YOU'RE THINKING, ESKE.
WELL, ISN'T THAT WHY WE CAN'T ATTEND HUMANS ANYMORE? THEY'RE TOO FULL--NO ROOM FOR US ANY LONGER.
THEY'RE FULL OF THINGS WE CAN'T LIVE WITH.
MAYBE THIS IS OUR LAST CHANCE!
NO, THANK YOU. IT'S NO HOME FOR THE DEVOTI. I'D SOONER DISSOLVE INTO WIND.

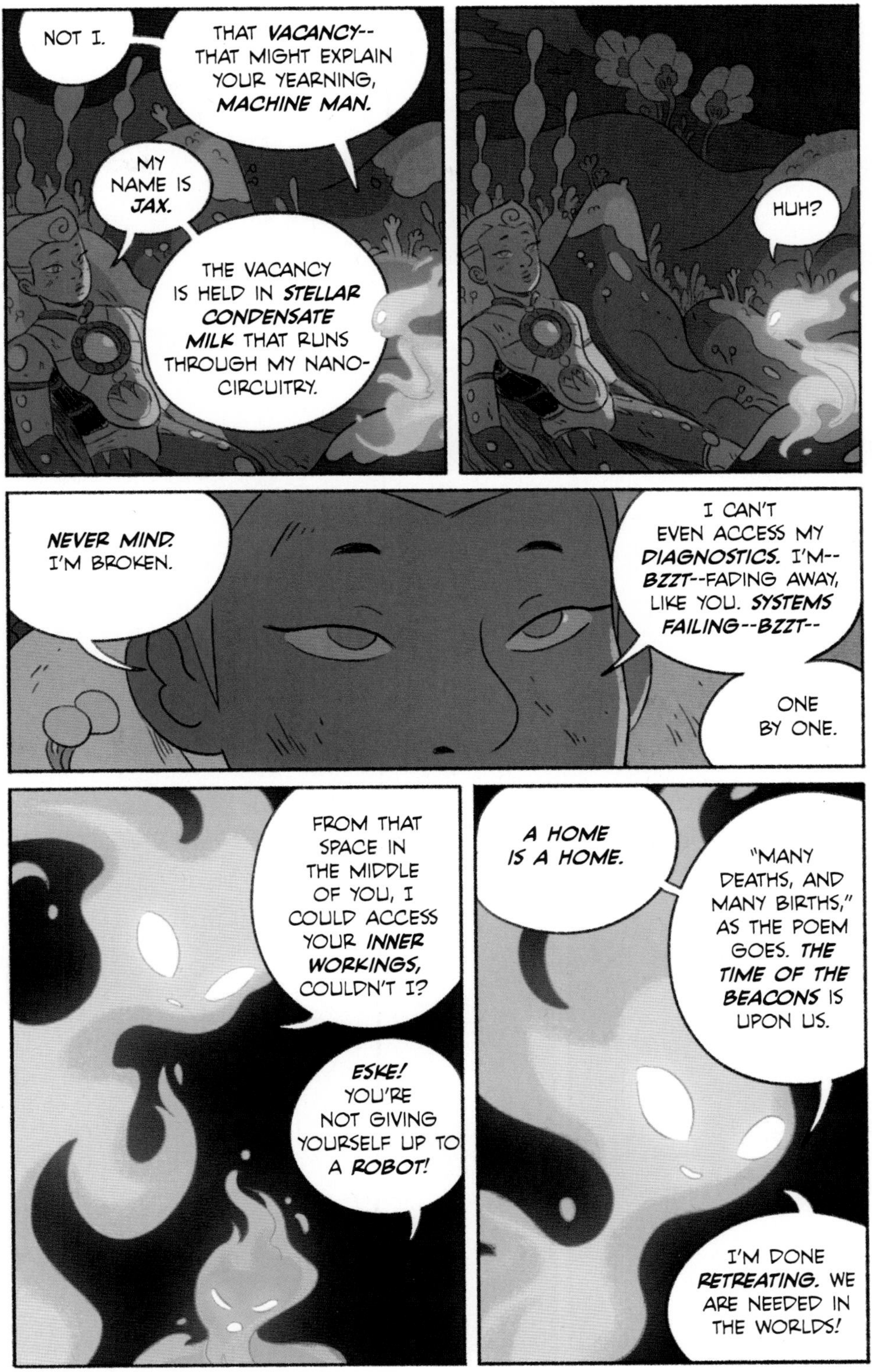
NOT I.
THAT VACANCY-- THAT MIGHT EXPLAIN YOUR YEARNING, MACHINE MAN.
MY NAME IS JAX.
THE VACANCY IS HELD IN STELLAR CONDENSATE MILK THAT RUNS THROUGH MY NANO-CIRCUITRY.
HUH?
NEVER MIND. I'M BROKEN.
I CAN'T EVEN ACCESS MY DIAGNOSTICS. I'M-- BZZT--FADING AWAY, LIKE YOU. SYSTEMS FAILING--BZZT--
ONE BY ONE.
FROM THAT SPACE IN THE MIDDLE OF YOU, I COULD ACCESS YOUR INNER WORKINGS, COULDN'T I?
ESKE! YOU'RE NOT GIVING YOURSELF UP TO A ROBOT!
A HOME IS A HOME.
"MANY DEATHS, AND MANY BIRTHS," AS THE POEM GOES. THE TIME OF THE BEACONS IS UPON US.
I'M DONE RETREATING. WE ARE NEEDED IN THE WORLDS!

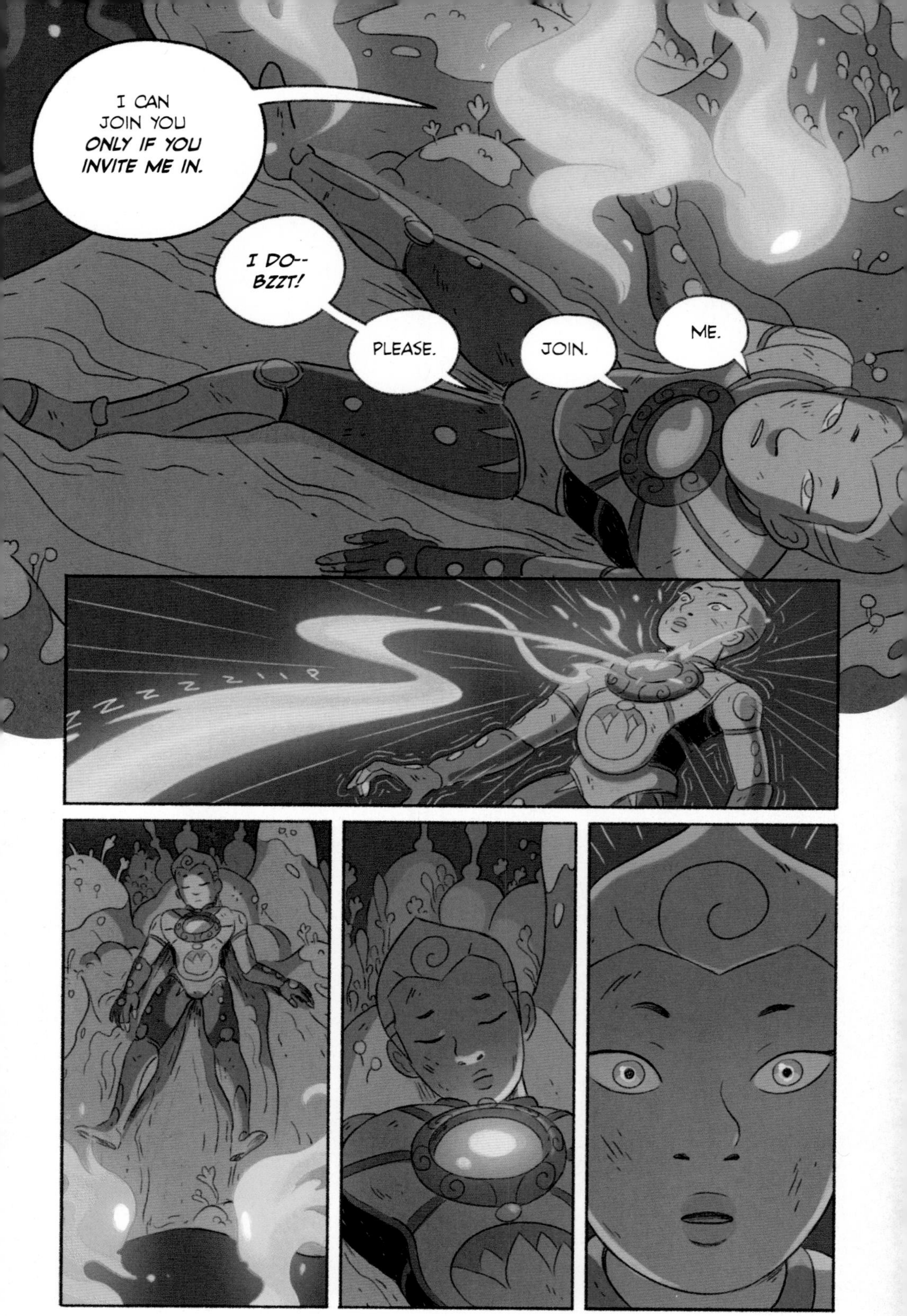
I CAN JOIN YOU ONLY IF YOU INVITE ME IN.
I DO--BZZT!
PLEASE.
JOIN.
ME.
ZZZZZZZIIP

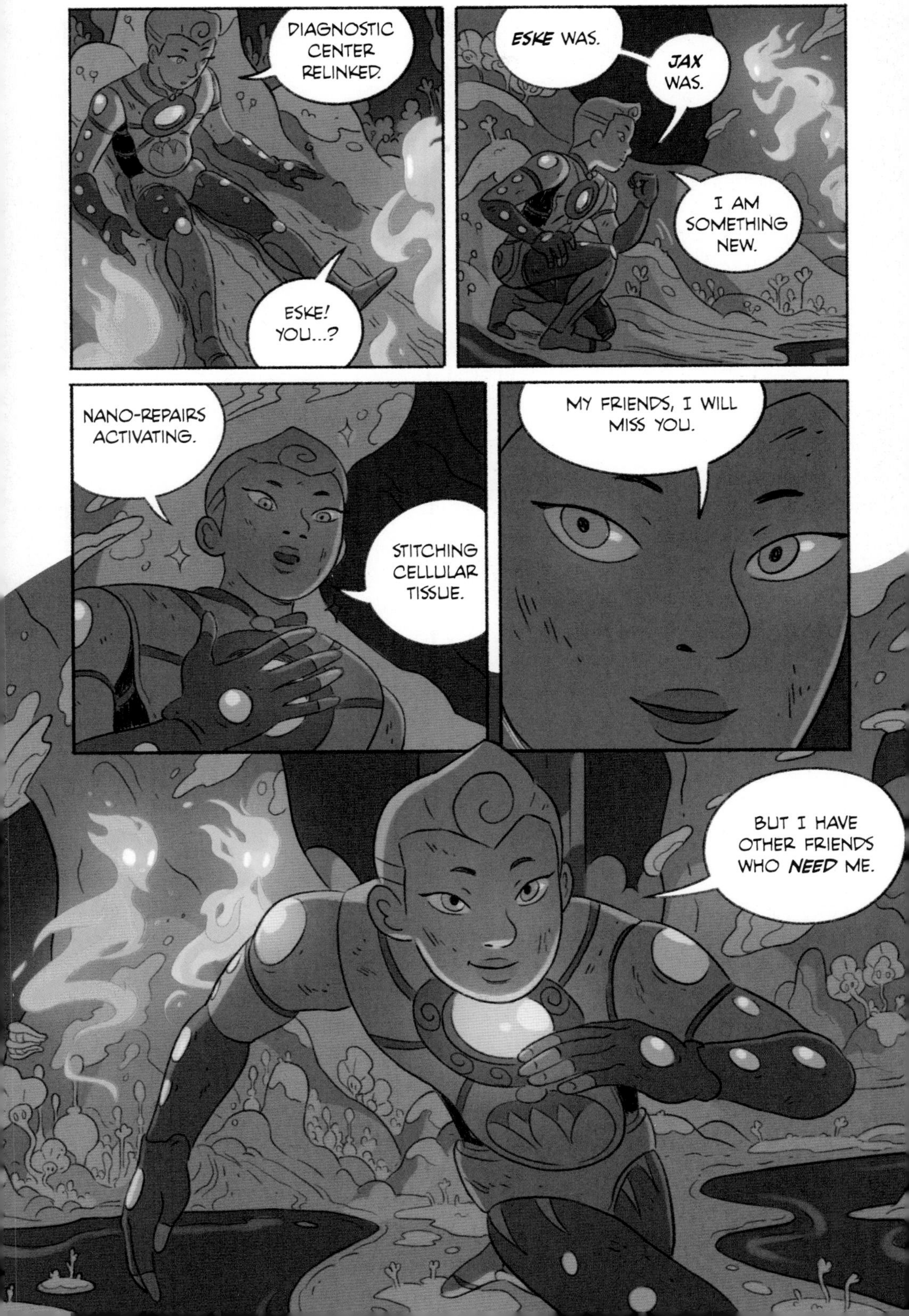
DIAGNOSTIC CENTER RELINKED.
ESKE! YOU...?
ESKE WAS.
JAX WAS.
I AM SOMETHING NEW.
NANO-REPAIRS ACTIVATING.
STITCHING CELLULAR TISSUE.
MY FRIENDS, I WILL MISS YOU.
BUT I HAVE OTHER FRIENDS WHO NEED ME.

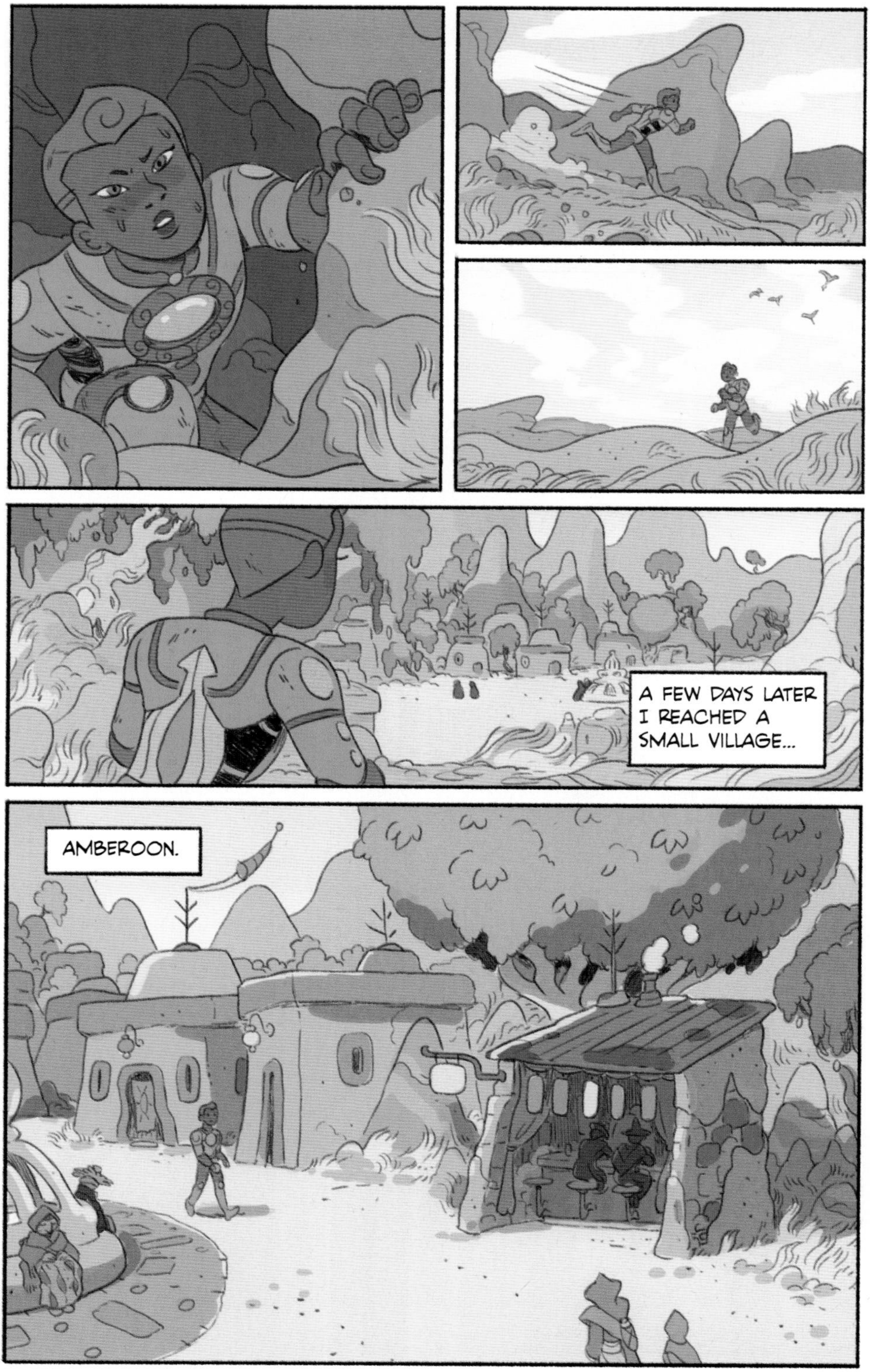
A FEW DAYS LATER I REACHED A SMALL VILLAGE...
AMBEROON.

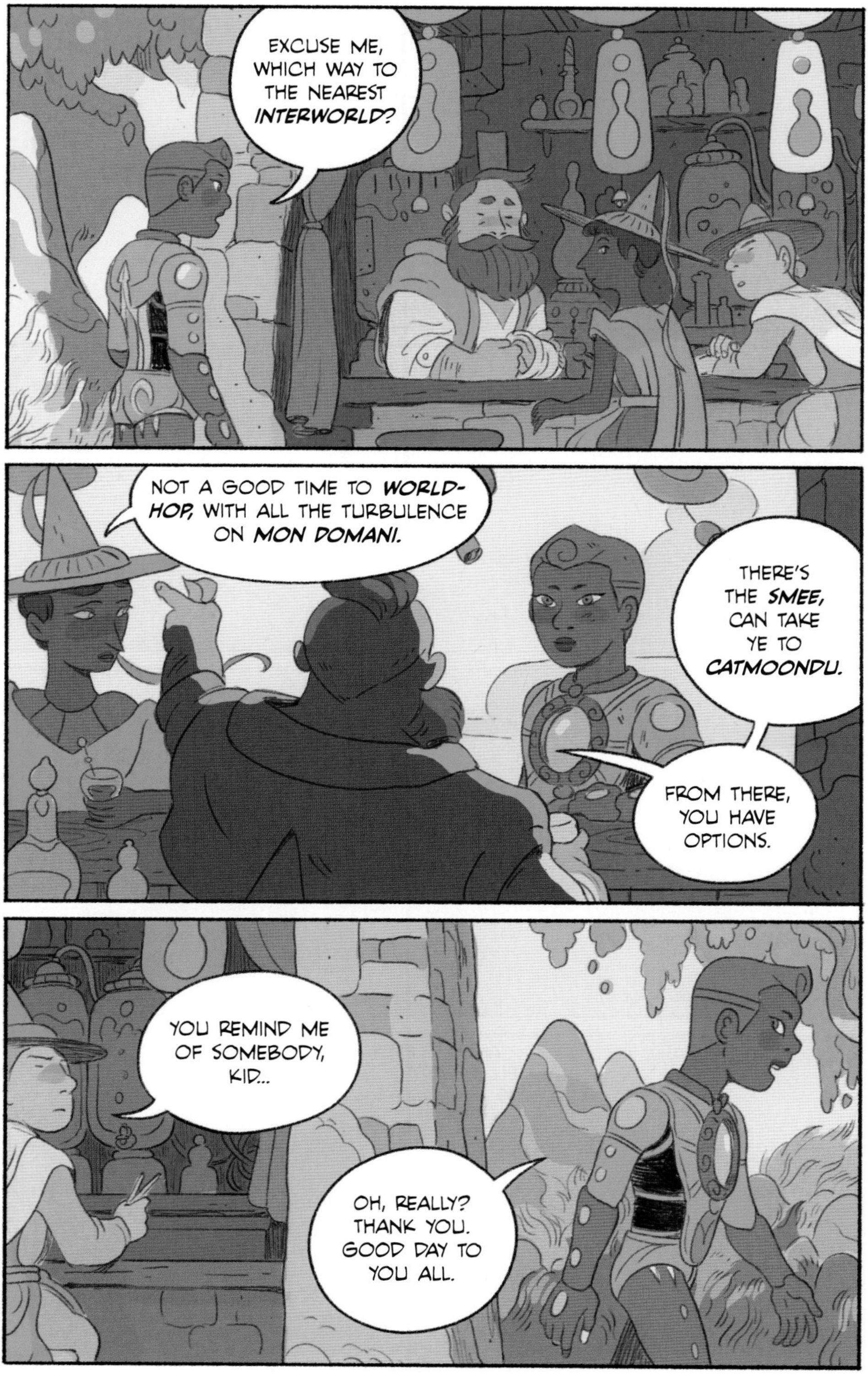
EXCUSE ME, WHICH WAY TO THE NEAREST *INTERWORLD?*
NOT A GOOD TIME TO *WORLD-HOP,* WITH ALL THE TURBULENCE ON *MON DOMANI.*
THERE'S THE *SMEE,* CAN TAKE YE TO *CATMOONDU.*
FROM THERE, YOU HAVE OPTIONS.
YOU REMIND ME OF SOMEBODY, KID...
OH, REALLY? THANK YOU. GOOD DAY TO YOU ALL.

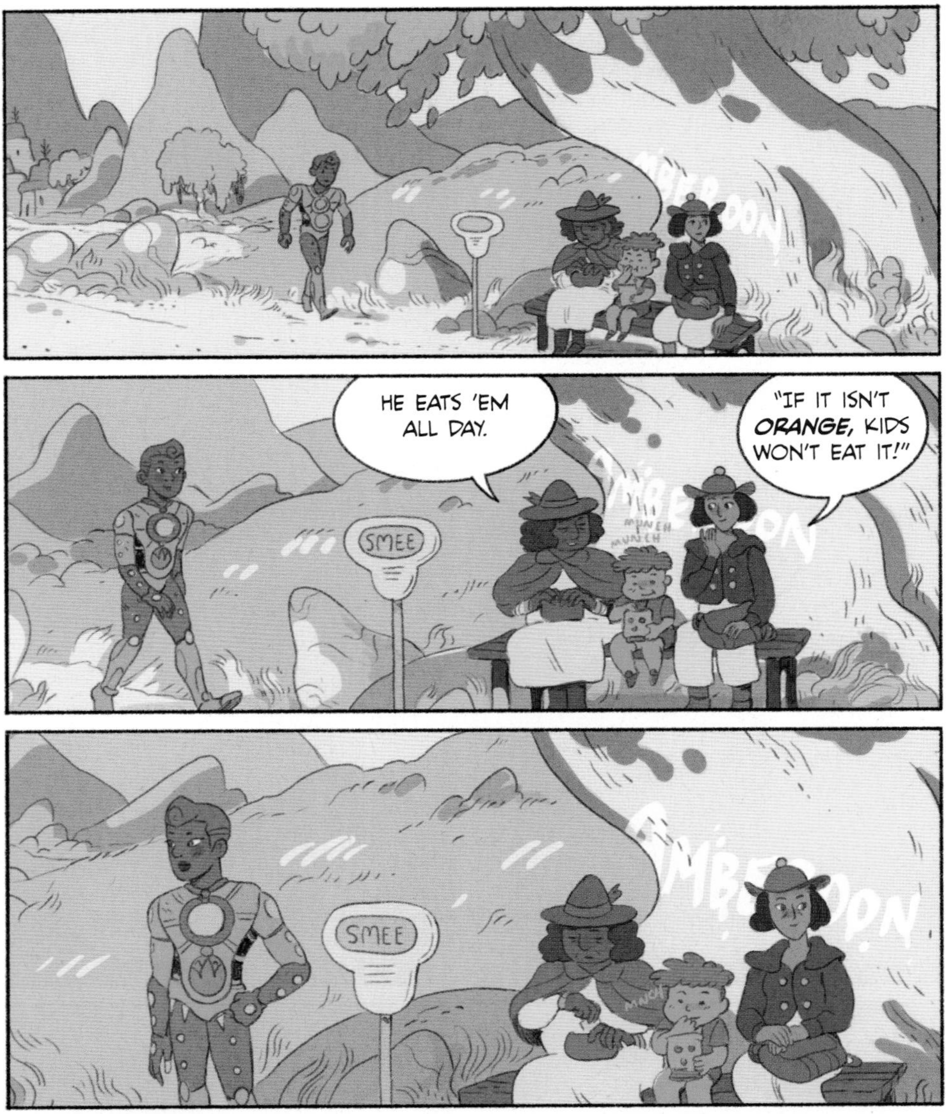
HE EATS 'EM ALL DAY.
"IF IT ISN'T **ORANGE,** KIDS WON'T EAT IT!"
MUNCH MUNCH
SMEE
SMEE
MUNCH
ANYONE EVER TELL YA YOU LOOK LIKE THAT **STARBALL** PLAYER?
YES, I GET THAT SOMETIMES.
MUNCH

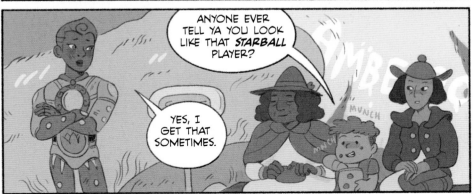

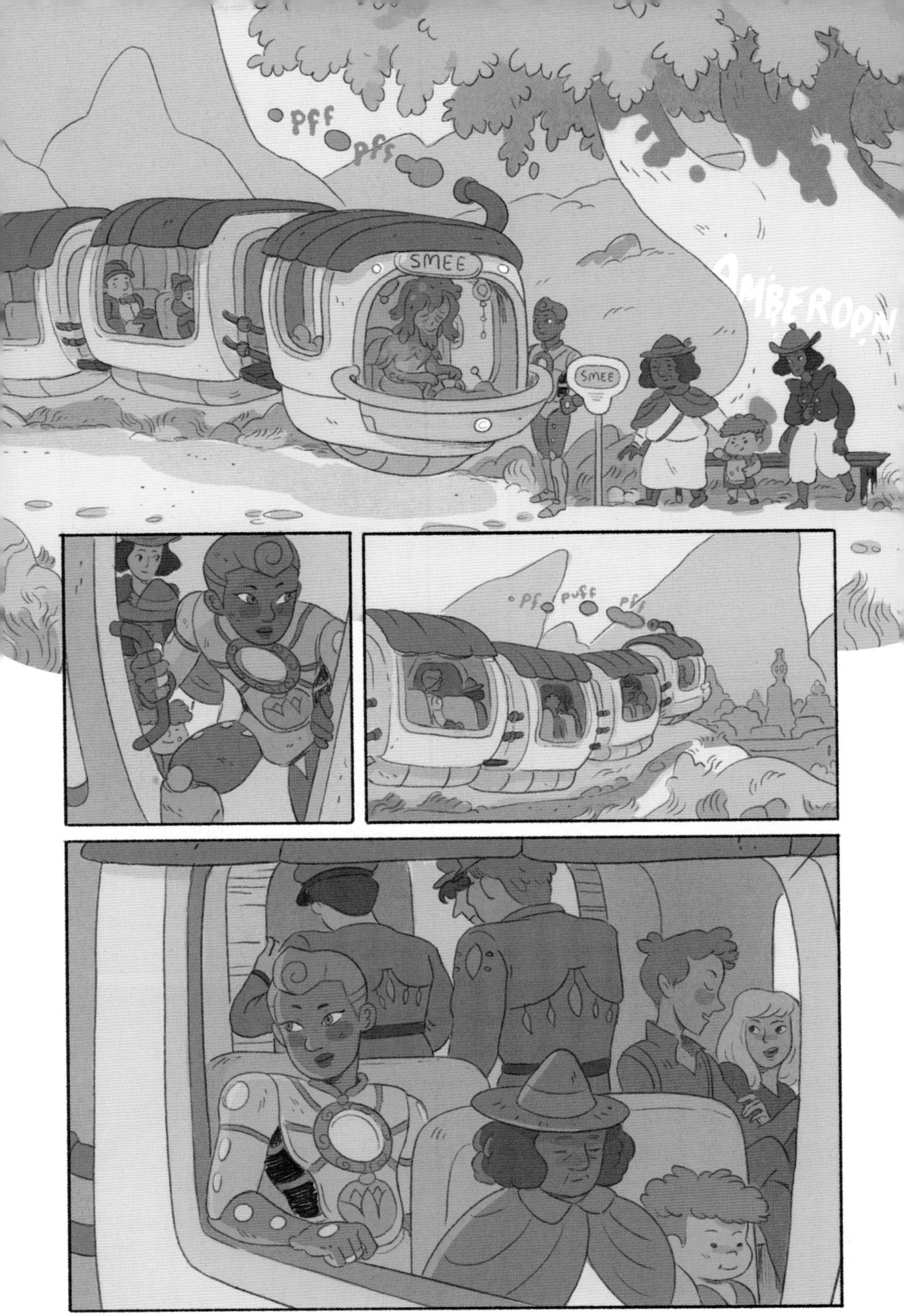

pff
pfs
SMEE
SMEE
AMBEROON
pf
puff
pff

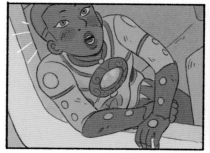

AFTER ASKING AROUND, I WAS DIRECTED TO *O'ZIRG'S* SHOP.

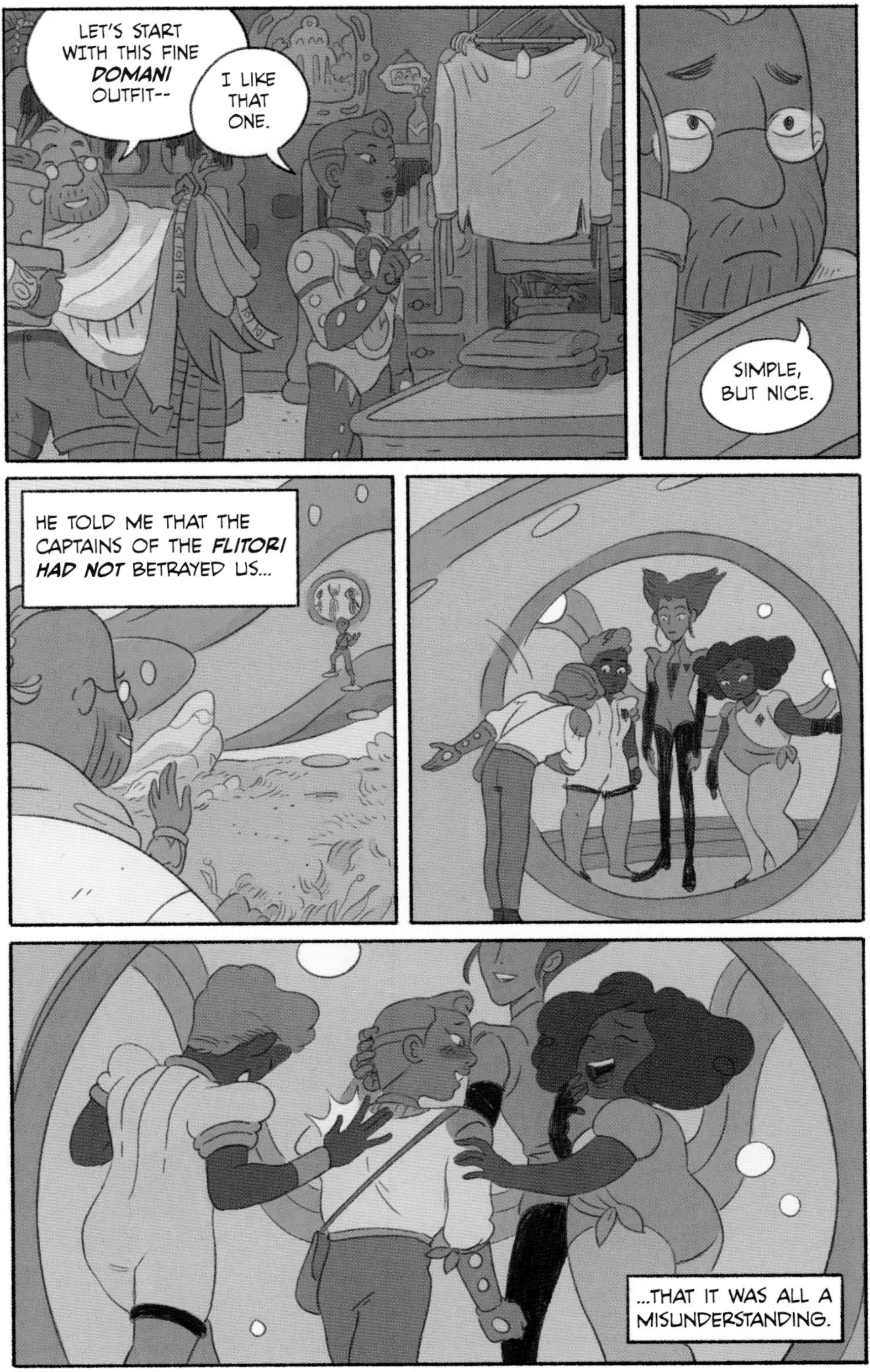
LET'S START WITH THIS FINE *DOMANI* OUTFIT--
I LIKE THAT ONE.
SIMPLE, BUT NICE.
HE TOLD ME THAT THE CAPTAINS OF THE *FLITORI* *HAD NOT* BETRAYED US...
...THAT IT WAS ALL A MISUNDERSTANDING.

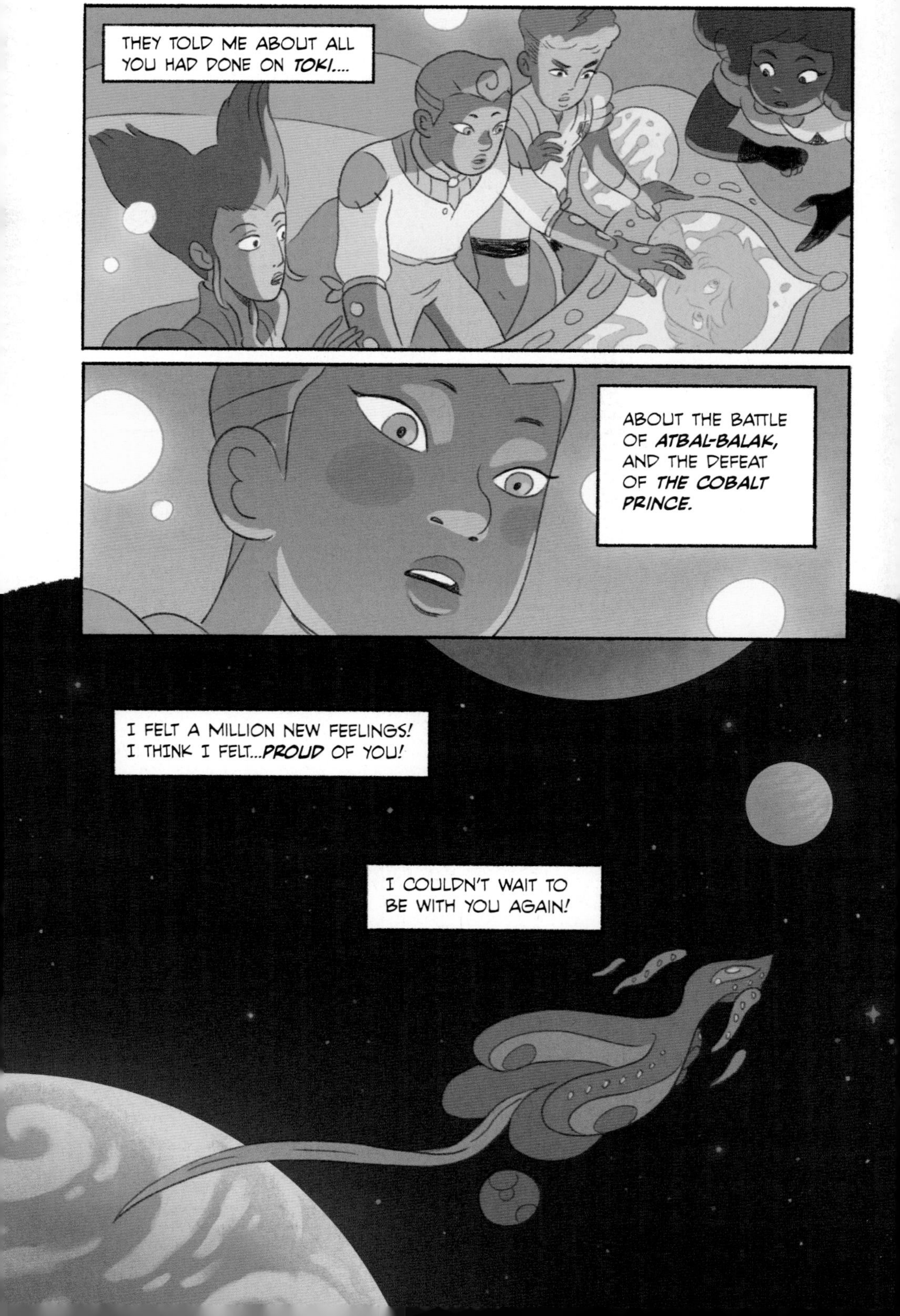
THEY TOLD ME ABOUT ALL YOU HAD DONE ON TOKI....
ABOUT THE BATTLE OF ATBAL-BALAK, AND THE DEFEAT OF THE COBALT PRINCE.
I FELT A MILLION NEW FEELINGS! I THINK I FELT...PROUD OF YOU!
I COULDN'T WAIT TO BE WITH YOU AGAIN!

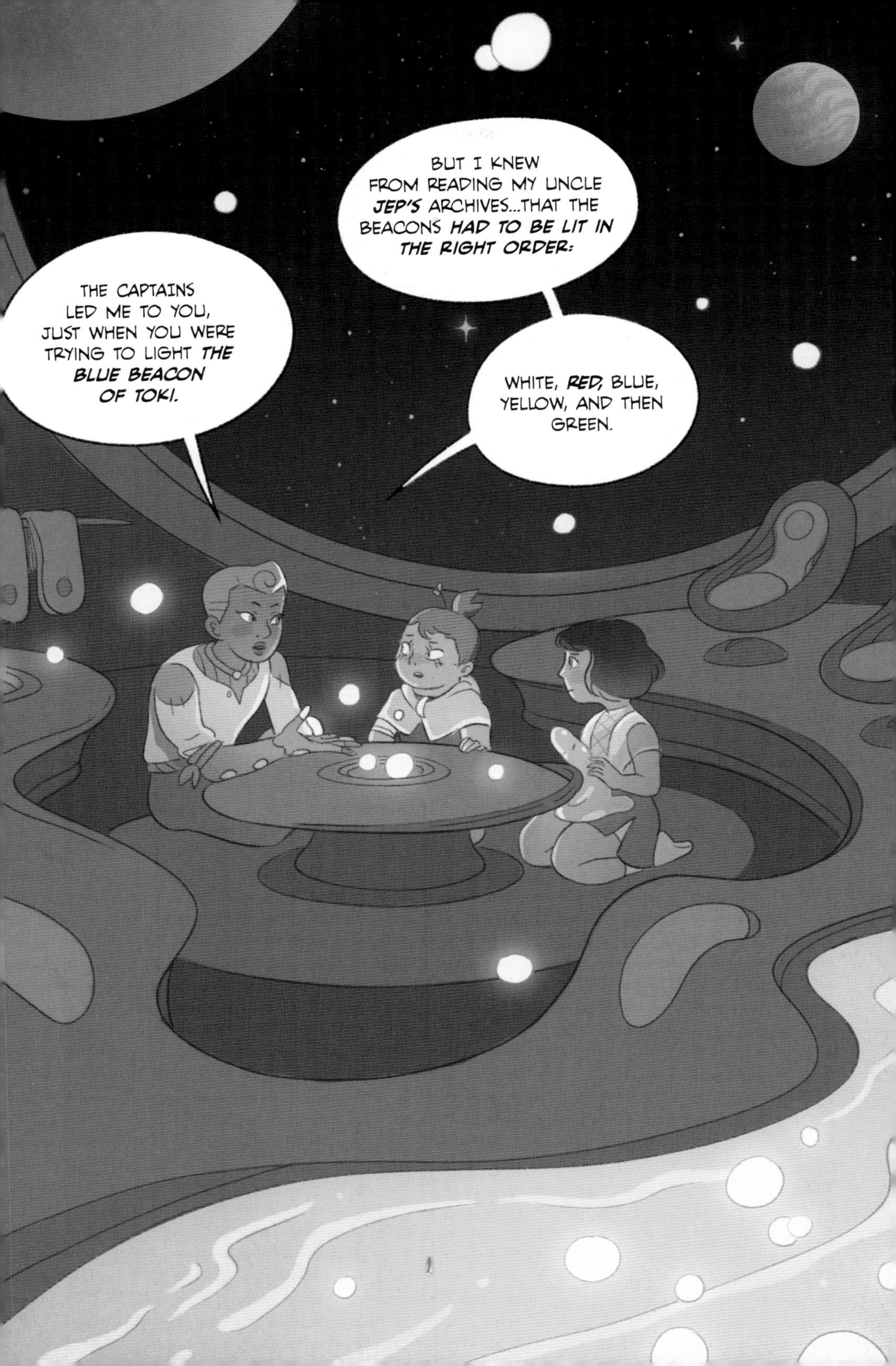
THE CAPTAINS LED ME TO YOU, JUST WHEN YOU WERE TRYING TO LIGHT *THE BLUE BEACON OF TOKI.*
BUT I KNEW FROM READING MY UNCLE *JEP'S* ARCHIVES...THAT THE BEACONS *HAD TO BE LIT IN THE RIGHT ORDER:*
WHITE, *RED,* BLUE, YELLOW, AND THEN GREEN.

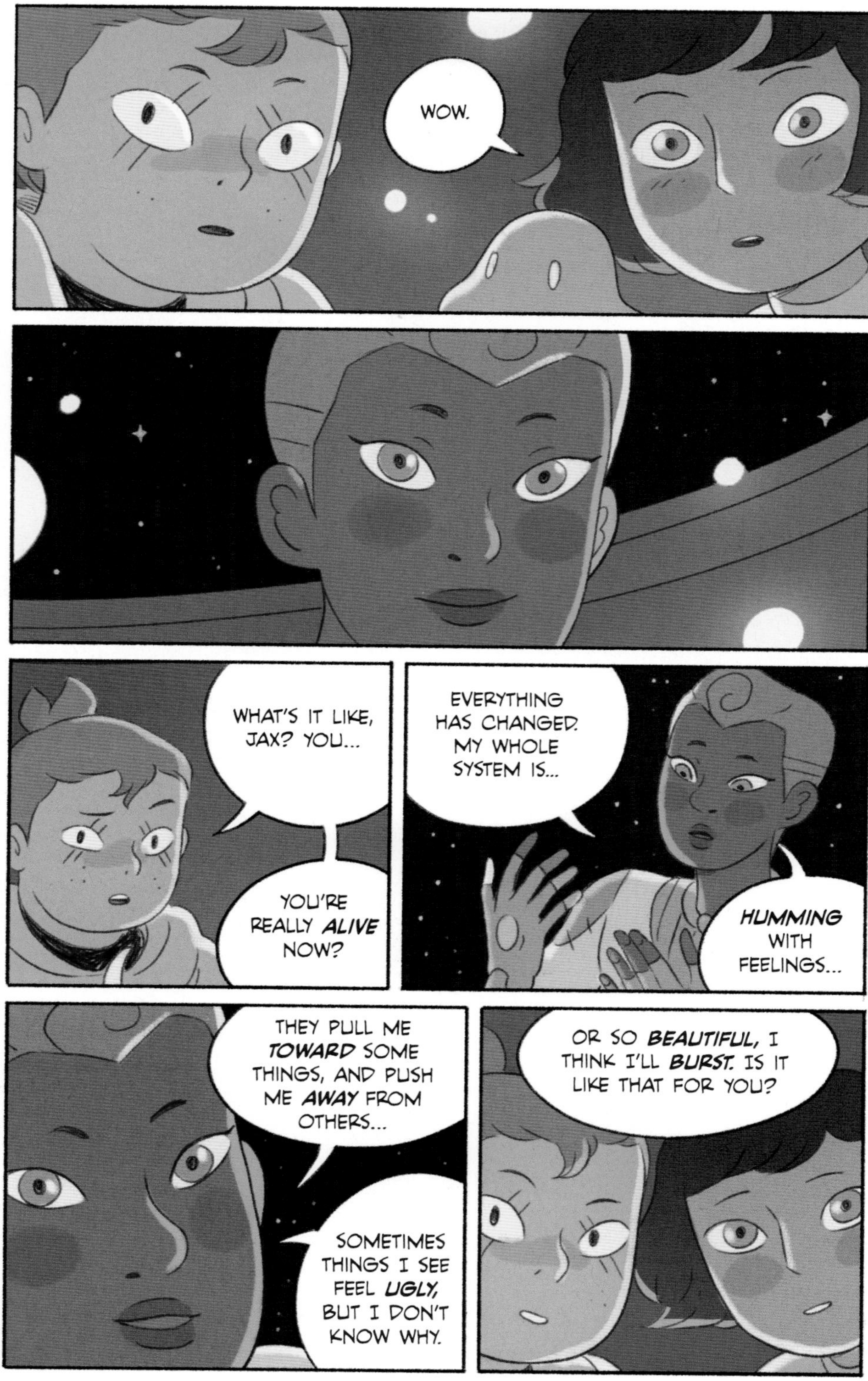
WOW.
WHAT'S IT LIKE, JAX? YOU...
YOU'RE REALLY ALIVE NOW?
EVERYTHING HAS CHANGED. MY WHOLE SYSTEM IS...
HUMMING WITH FEELINGS...
THEY PULL ME TOWARD SOME THINGS, AND PUSH ME AWAY FROM OTHERS...
SOMETIMES THINGS I SEE FEEL UGLY, BUT I DON'T KNOW WHY.
OR SO BEAUTIFUL, I THINK I'LL BURST. IS IT LIKE THAT FOR YOU?

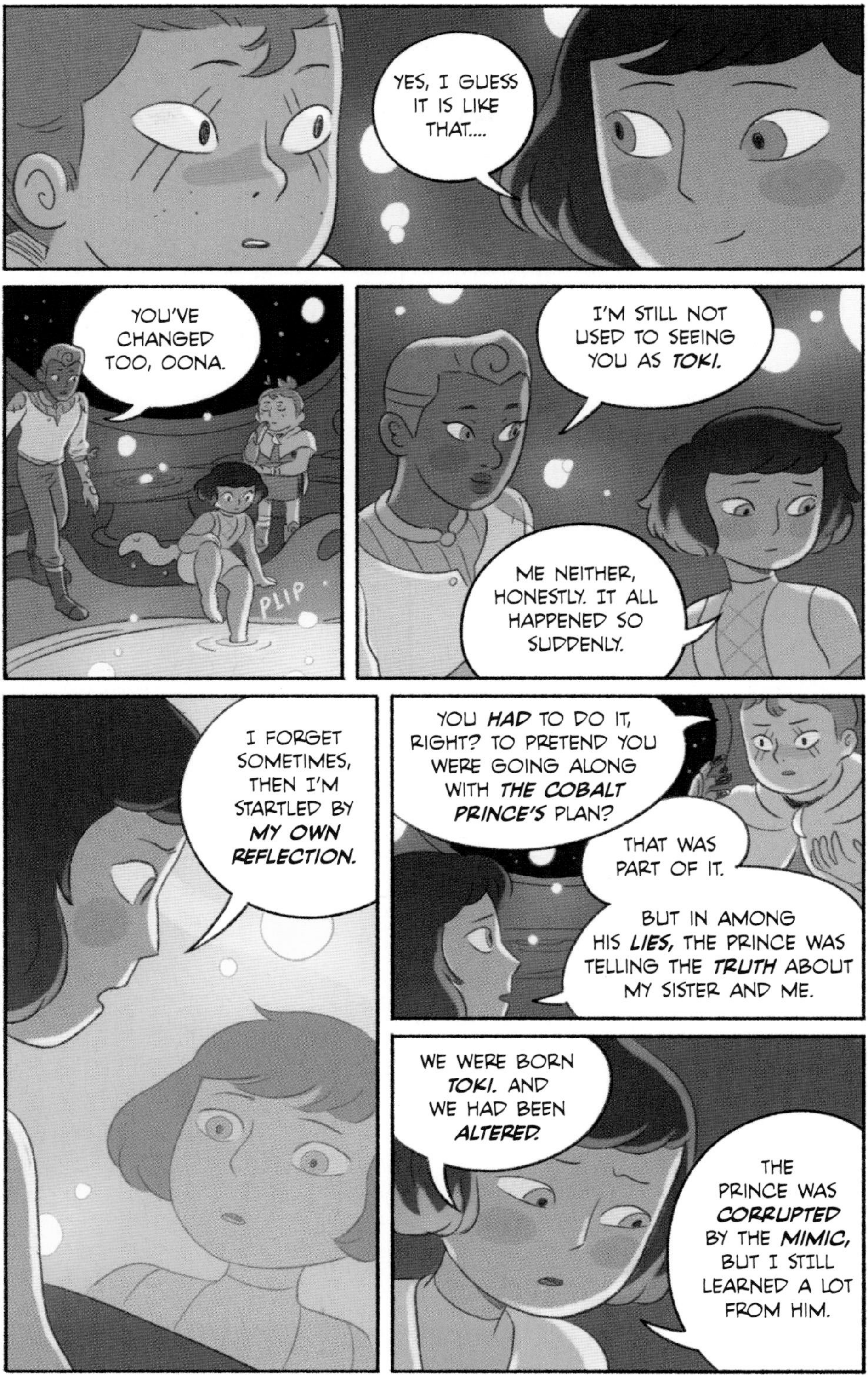
YES, I GUESS IT IS LIKE THAT....
YOU'VE CHANGED TOO, OONA.
PLIP
I'M STILL NOT USED TO SEEING YOU AS *TOKI.*
ME NEITHER, HONESTLY. IT ALL HAPPENED SO SUDDENLY.
I FORGET SOMETIMES, THEN I'M STARTLED BY *MY OWN REFLECTION.*
YOU *HAD* TO DO IT, RIGHT? TO PRETEND YOU WERE GOING ALONG WITH *THE COBALT PRINCE'S* PLAN?
THAT WAS PART OF IT.
BUT IN AMONG HIS *LIES,* THE PRINCE WAS TELLING THE *TRUTH* ABOUT MY SISTER AND ME.
WE WERE BORN *TOKI.* AND WE HAD BEEN *ALTERED.*
THE PRINCE WAS *CORRUPTED* BY THE *MIMIC,* BUT I STILL LEARNED A LOT FROM HIM.

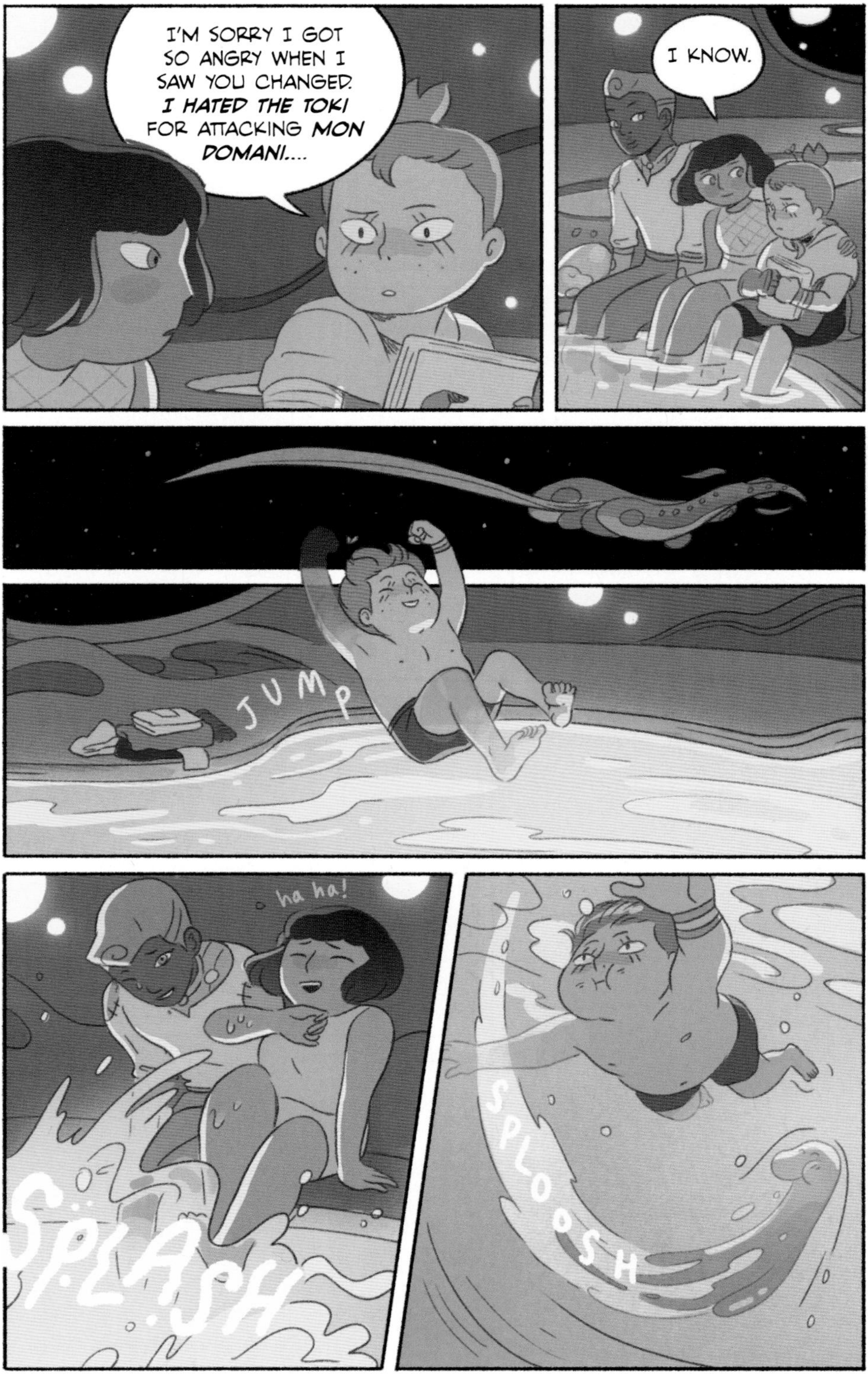
I'M SORRY I GOT SO ANGRY WHEN I SAW YOU CHANGED. ***I HATED THE TOKI*** FOR ATTACKING ***MON DOMANI***....
I KNOW.
JUMP
ha ha!
SPLASH
SPLOOSH

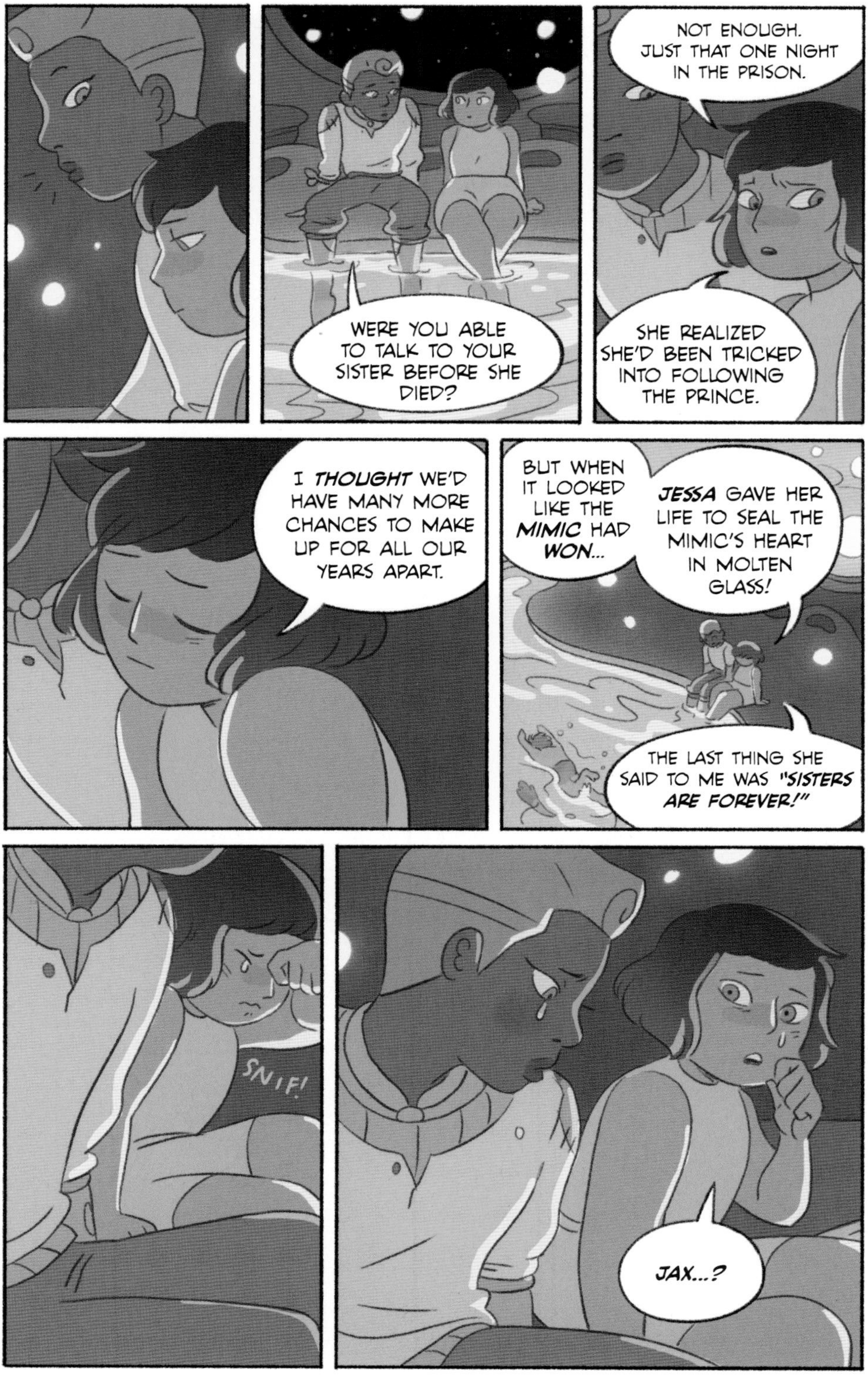
WERE YOU ABLE TO TALK TO YOUR SISTER BEFORE SHE DIED?
NOT ENOUGH. JUST THAT ONE NIGHT IN THE PRISON.
SHE REALIZED SHE'D BEEN TRICKED INTO FOLLOWING THE PRINCE.
I *THOUGHT* WE'D HAVE MANY MORE CHANCES TO MAKE UP FOR ALL OUR YEARS APART.
BUT WHEN IT LOOKED LIKE THE *MIMIC* HAD *WON*...
*JESSA* GAVE HER LIFE TO SEAL THE MIMIC'S HEART IN MOLTEN GLASS!
THE LAST THING SHE SAID TO ME WAS *"SISTERS ARE FOREVER!"*
SNIF!
*JAX...?*

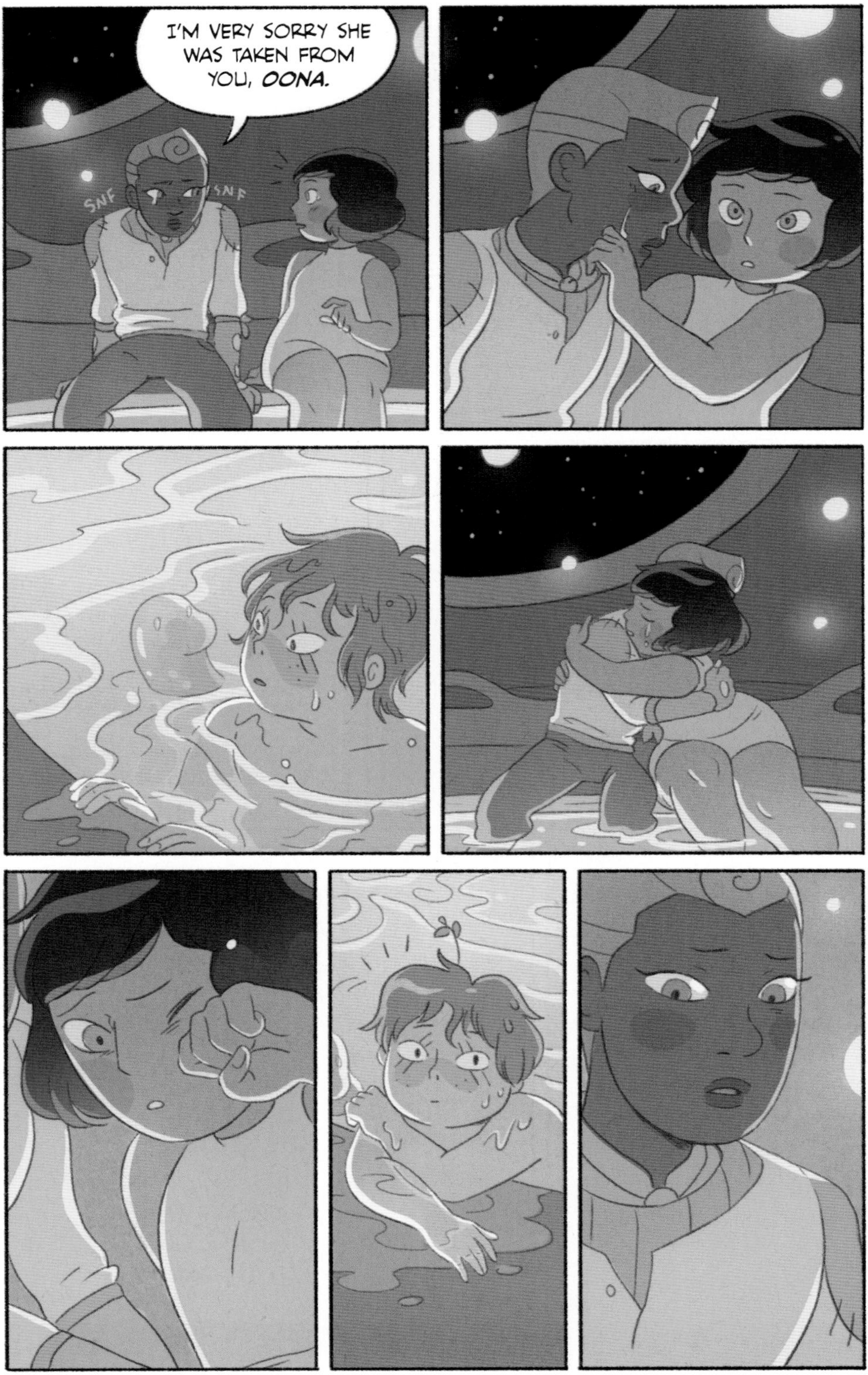
I'M VERY SORRY SHE WAS TAKEN FROM YOU, OONA.
SNF
SNF

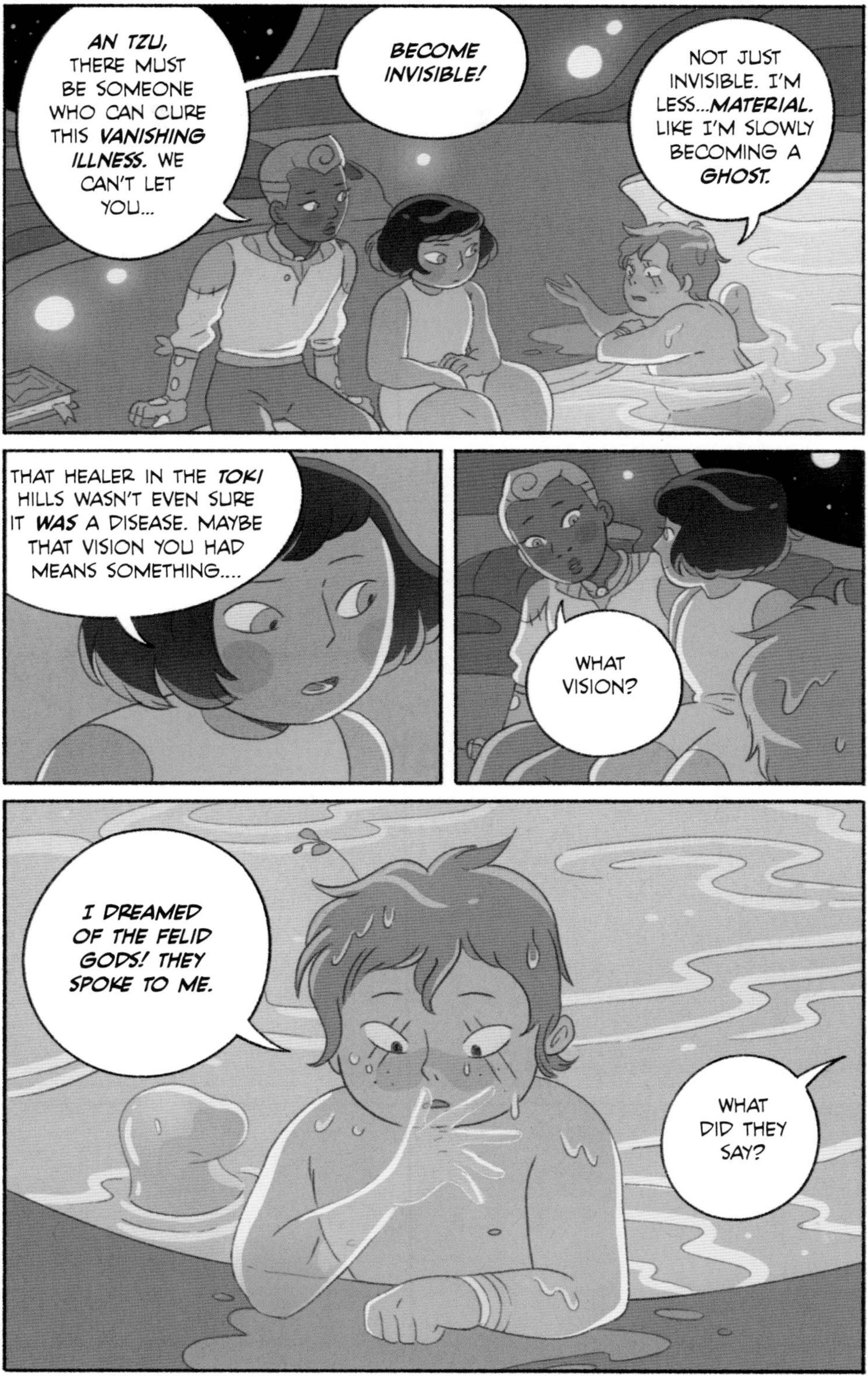
AN TZU, THERE MUST BE SOMEONE WHO CAN CURE THIS VANISHING ILLNESS. WE CAN'T LET YOU...
BECOME INVISIBLE!
NOT JUST INVISIBLE. I'M LESS...MATERIAL. LIKE I'M SLOWLY BECOMING A GHOST.
THAT HEALER IN THE TOKI HILLS WASN'T EVEN SURE IT WAS A DISEASE. MAYBE THAT VISION YOU HAD MEANS SOMETHING....
WHAT VISION?
I DREAMED OF THE FELID GODS! THEY SPOKE TO ME.
WHAT DID THEY SAY?

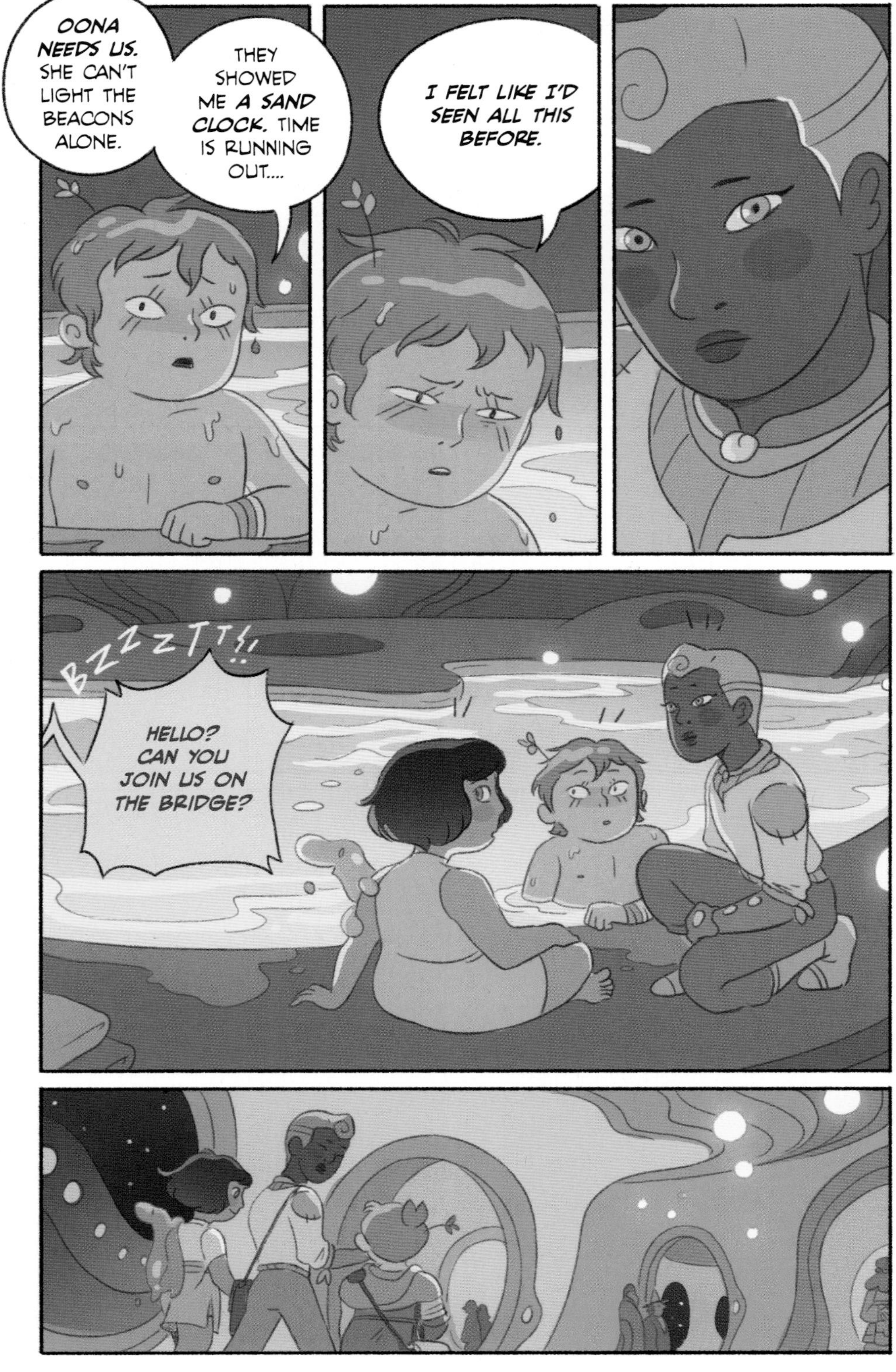
OONA NEEDS US. SHE CAN'T LIGHT THE BEACONS ALONE.
THEY SHOWED ME A SAND CLOCK. TIME IS RUNNING OUT....
I FELT LIKE I'D SEEN ALL THIS BEFORE.
BZZZTTT!!
HELLO? CAN YOU JOIN US ON THE BRIDGE?

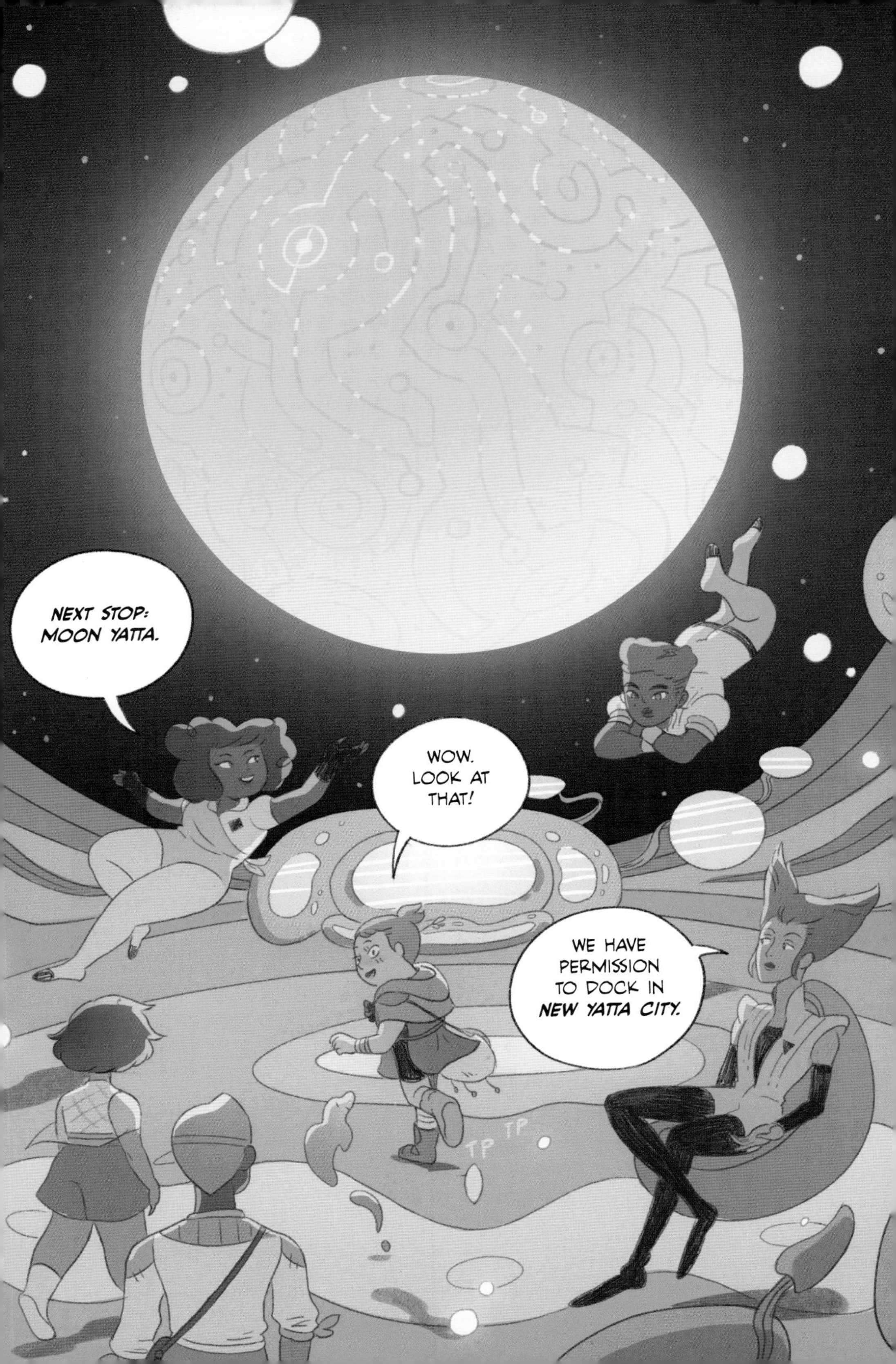
NEXT STOP: MOON YATTA.
WOW. LOOK AT THAT!
WE HAVE PERMISSION TO DOCK IN NEW YATTA CITY.
TP TP

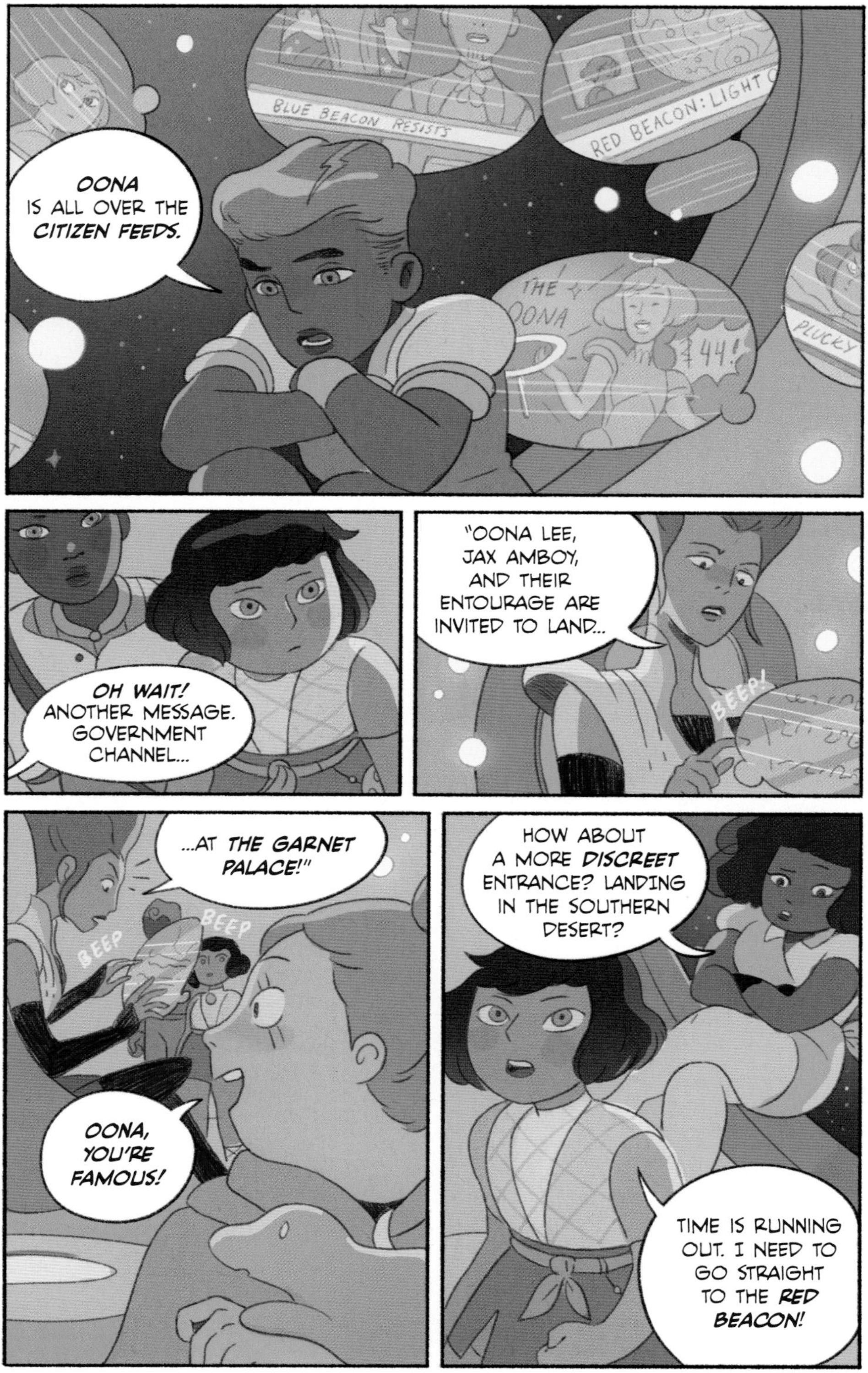
BLUE BEACON RESISTS
RED BEACON: LIGHT
OONA IS ALL OVER THE CITIZEN FEEDS.
THE OONA
PLUCKY
OH WAIT! ANOTHER MESSAGE. GOVERNMENT CHANNEL...
"OONA LEE, JAX AMBOY, AND THEIR ENTOURAGE ARE INVITED TO LAND...
BEEP!
...AT THE GARNET PALACE!"
BEEP
BEEP
OONA, YOU'RE FAMOUS!
HOW ABOUT A MORE DISCREET ENTRANCE? LANDING IN THE SOUTHERN DESERT?
TIME IS RUNNING OUT. I NEED TO GO STRAIGHT TO THE RED BEACON!

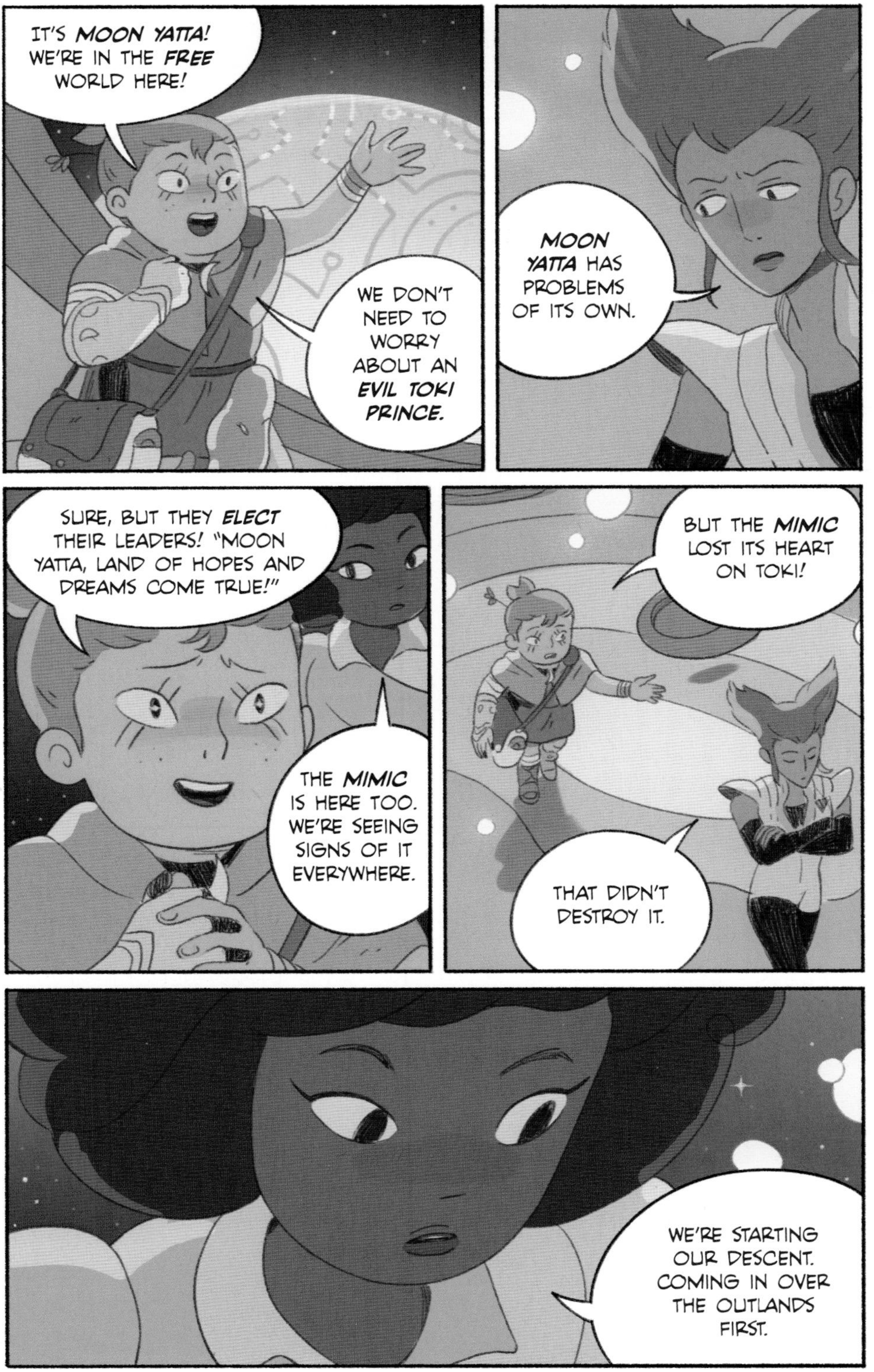
IT'S MOON YATTA! WE'RE IN THE FREE WORLD HERE!
WE DON'T NEED TO WORRY ABOUT AN EVIL TOKI PRINCE.
MOON YATTA HAS PROBLEMS OF ITS OWN.
SURE, BUT THEY ELECT THEIR LEADERS! "MOON YATTA, LAND OF HOPES AND DREAMS COME TRUE!"
THE MIMIC IS HERE TOO. WE'RE SEEING SIGNS OF IT EVERYWHERE.
BUT THE MIMIC LOST ITS HEART ON TOKI!
THAT DIDN'T DESTROY IT.
WE'RE STARTING OUR DESCENT. COMING IN OVER THE OUTLANDS FIRST.

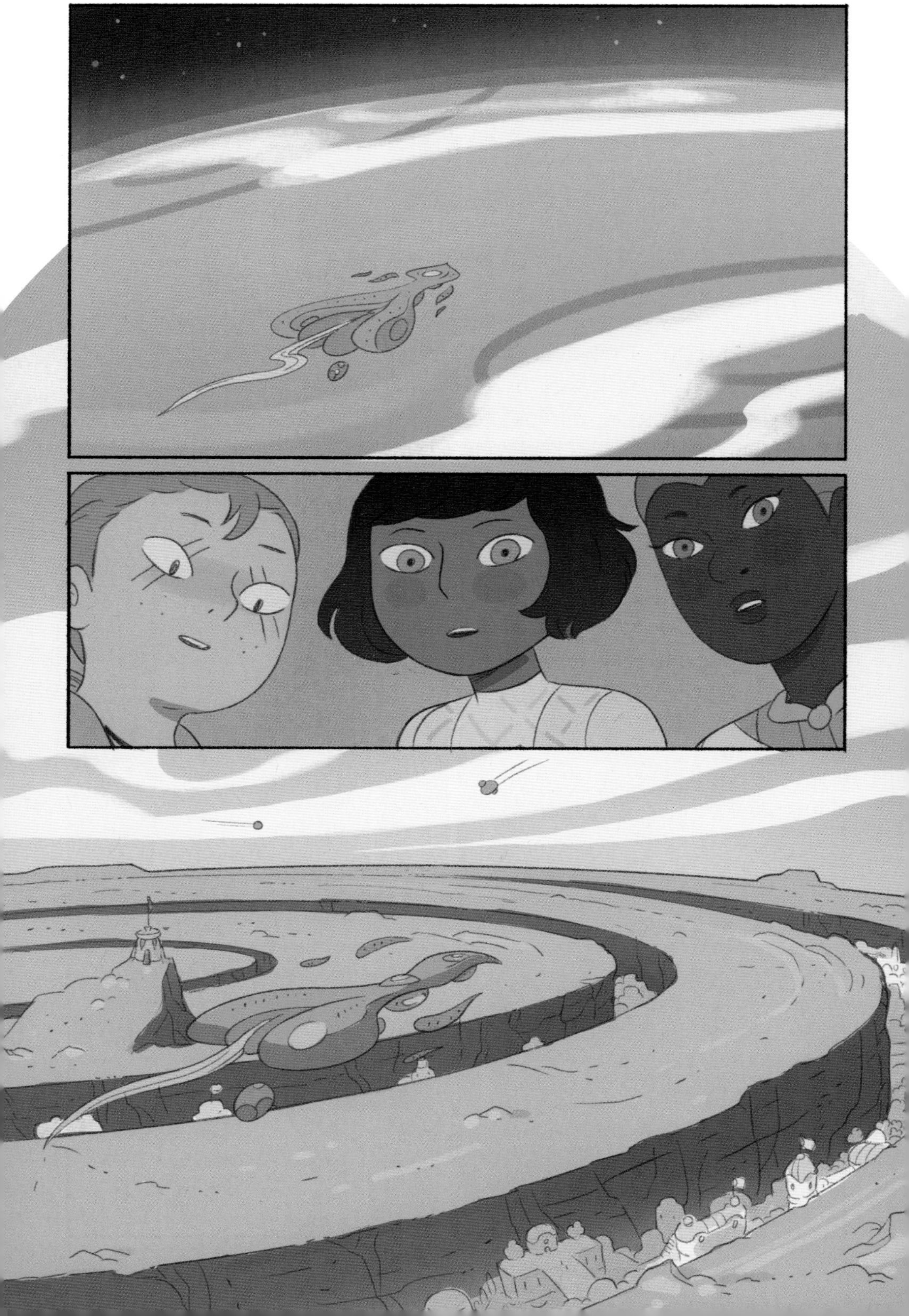

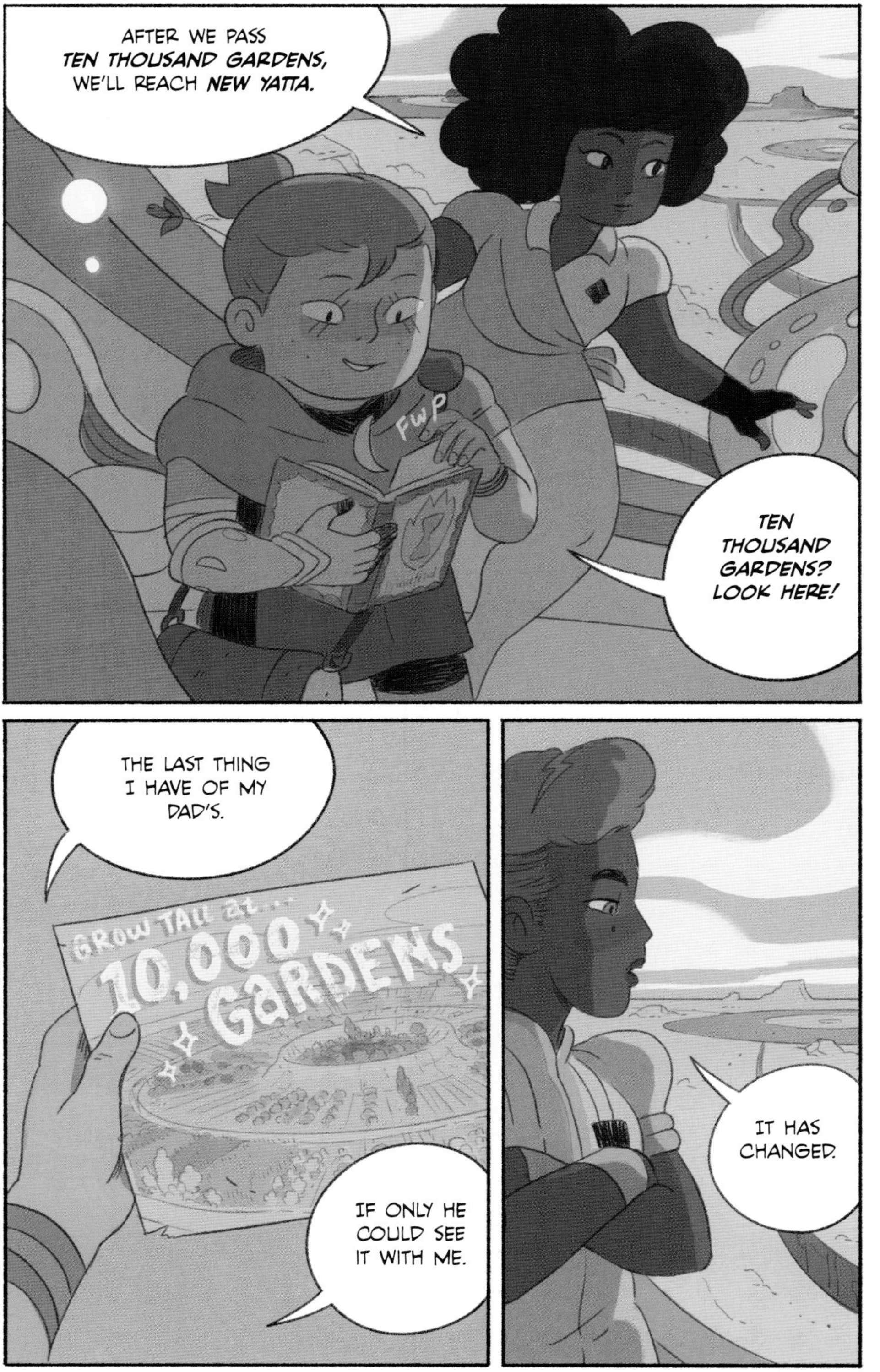
AFTER WE PASS *TEN THOUSAND GARDENS,* WE'LL REACH *NEW YATTA.*
FWP
*TEN THOUSAND GARDENS? LOOK HERE!*
THE LAST THING I HAVE OF MY DAD'S.
GROW TALL at... 10,000 GARDENS
IF ONLY HE COULD SEE IT WITH ME.
IT HAS CHANGED.

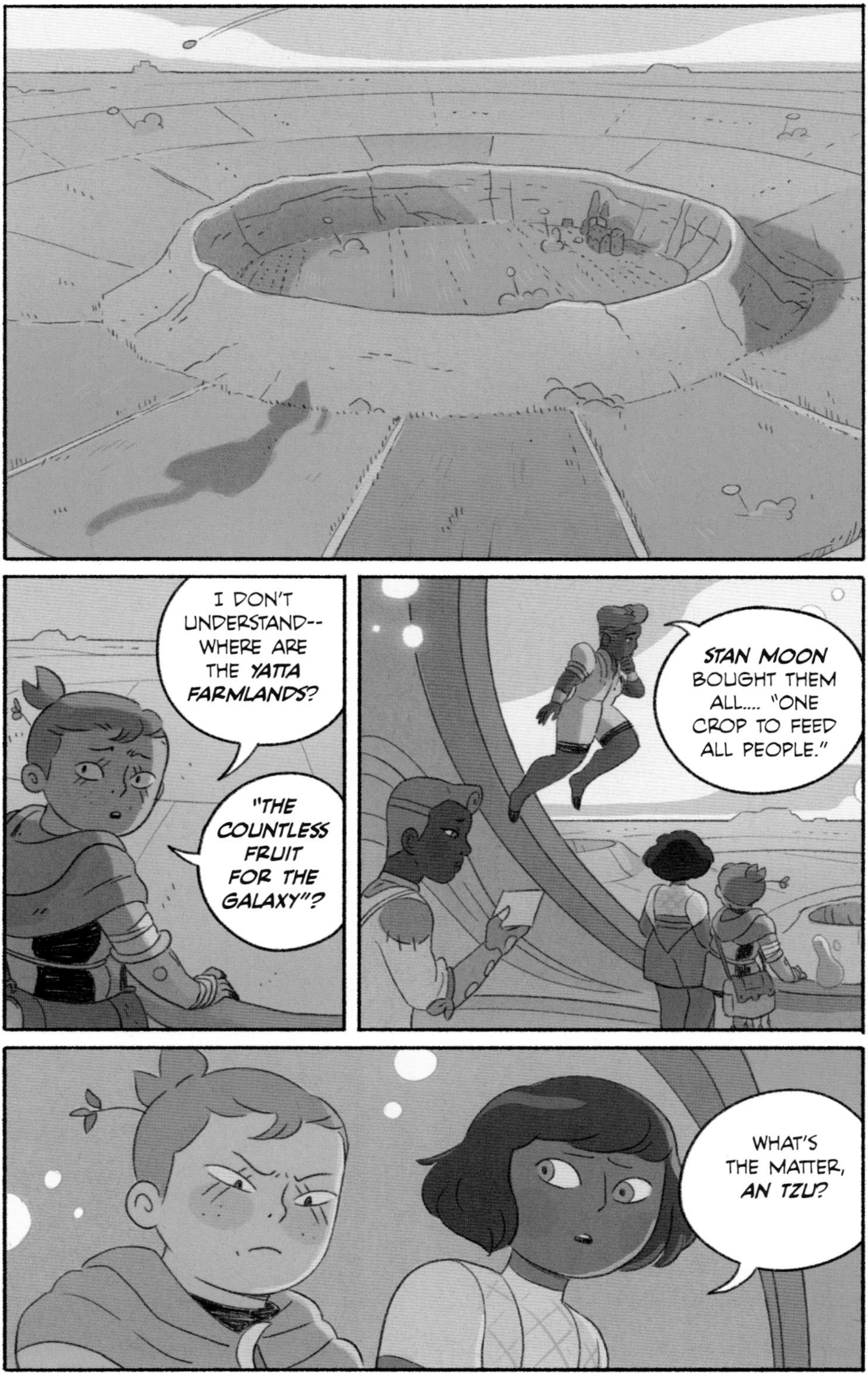
I DON'T UNDERSTAND-- WHERE ARE THE YATTA FARMLANDS?
"THE COUNTLESS FRUIT FOR THE GALAXY"?
STAN MOON BOUGHT THEM ALL.... "ONE CROP TO FEED ALL PEOPLE."
WHAT'S THE MATTER, AN TZU?

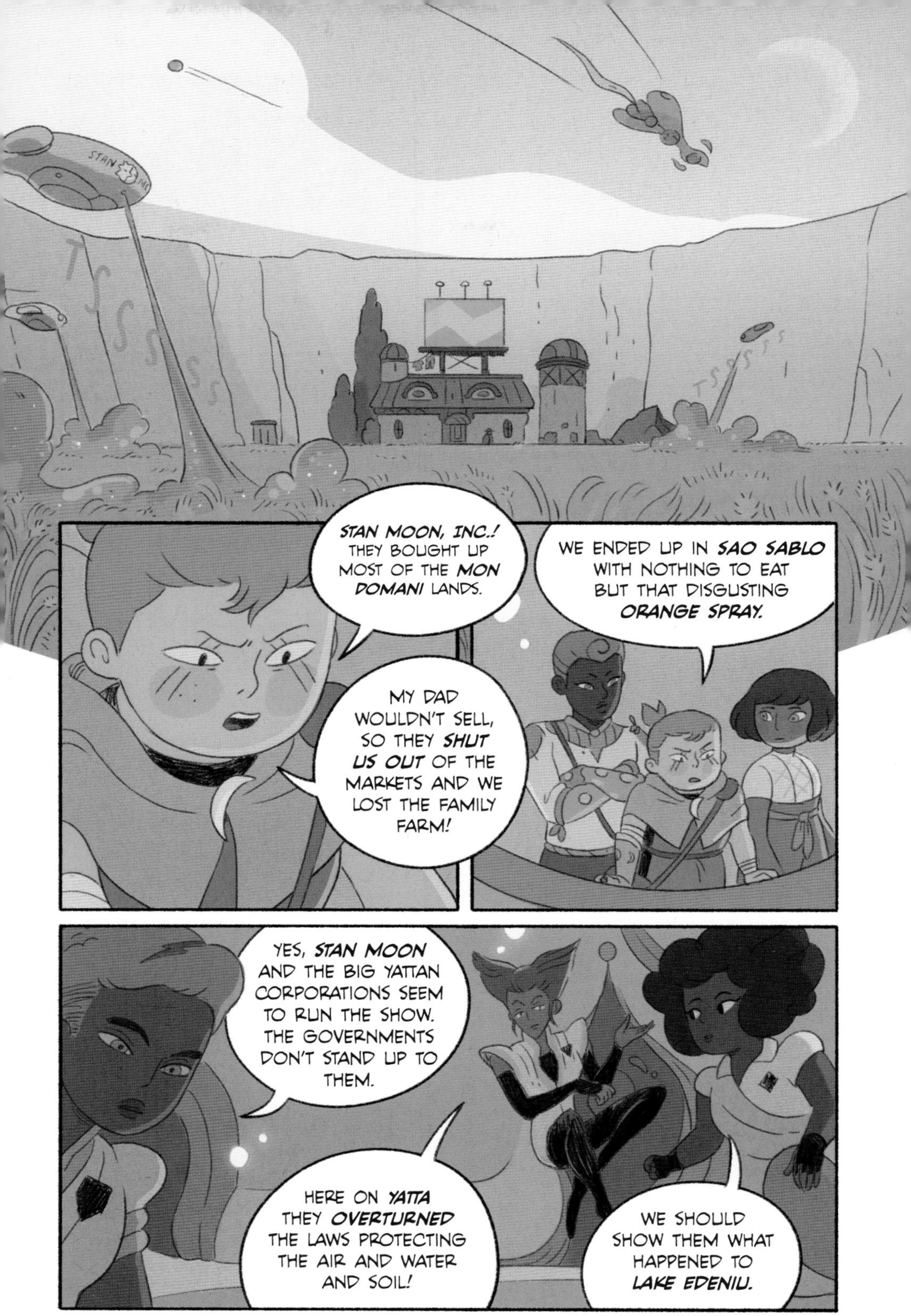
STAN MOON, INC.! THEY BOUGHT UP MOST OF THE MON DOMANI LANDS.
MY DAD WOULDN'T SELL, SO THEY SHUT US OUT OF THE MARKETS AND WE LOST THE FAMILY FARM!
WE ENDED UP IN SAO SABLO WITH NOTHING TO EAT BUT THAT DISGUSTING ORANGE SPRAY.
YES, STAN MOON AND THE BIG YATTAN CORPORATIONS SEEM TO RUN THE SHOW. THE GOVERNMENTS DON'T STAND UP TO THEM.
HERE ON YATTA THEY OVERTURNED THE LAWS PROTECTING THE AIR AND WATER AND SOIL!
WE SHOULD SHOW THEM WHAT HAPPENED TO LAKE EDENIU.

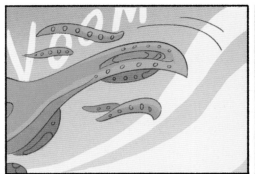

THE WATER HAS BEEN DIVERTED TO IRRIGATE *THE STAN MOON FIELDS.*

WHICH SPEEDS UP THE PLANET'S *OVERHEATING.*

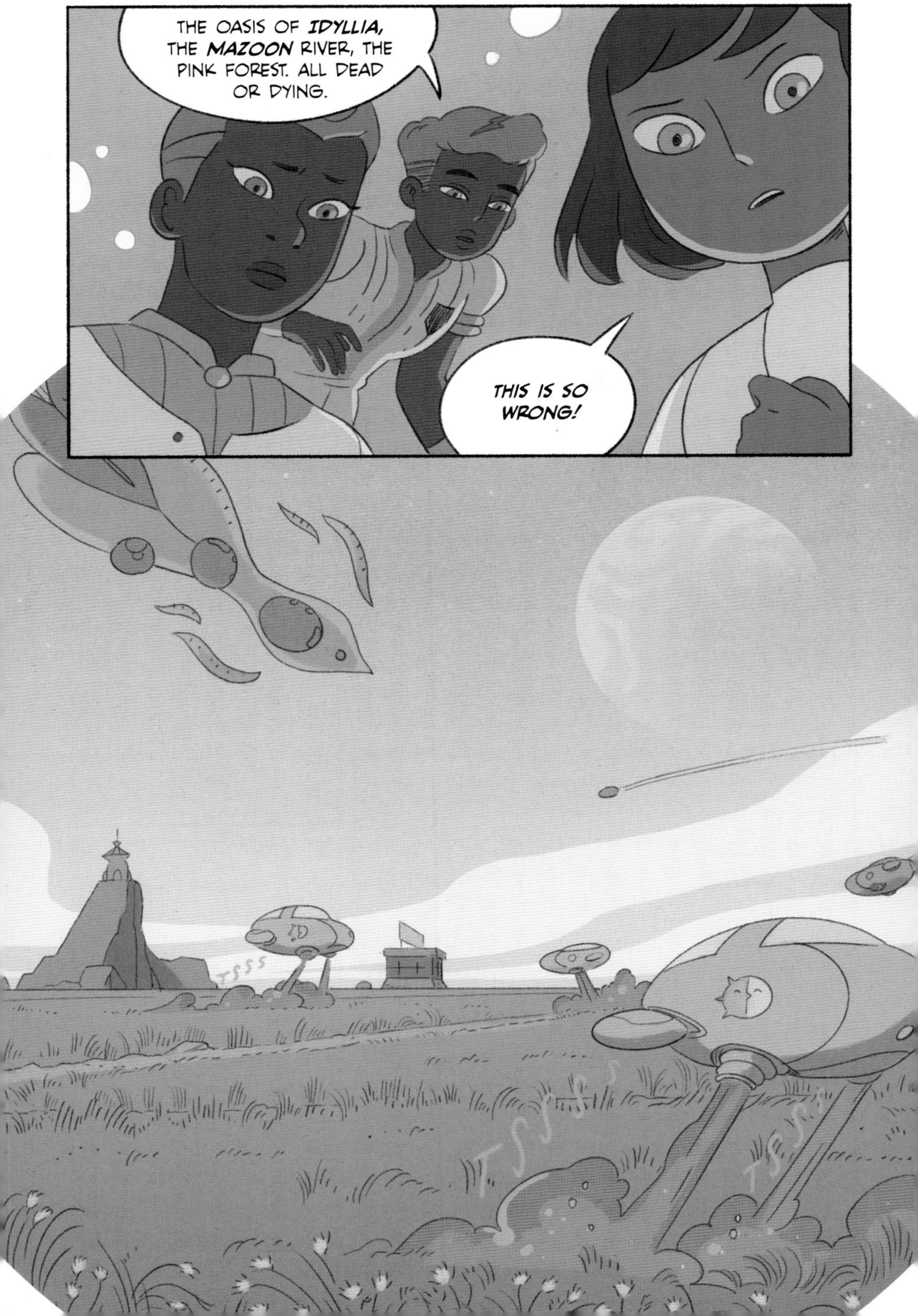
THE OASIS OF IDYLLIA, THE MAZOON RIVER, THE PINK FOREST. ALL DEAD OR DYING.
THIS IS SO WRONG!

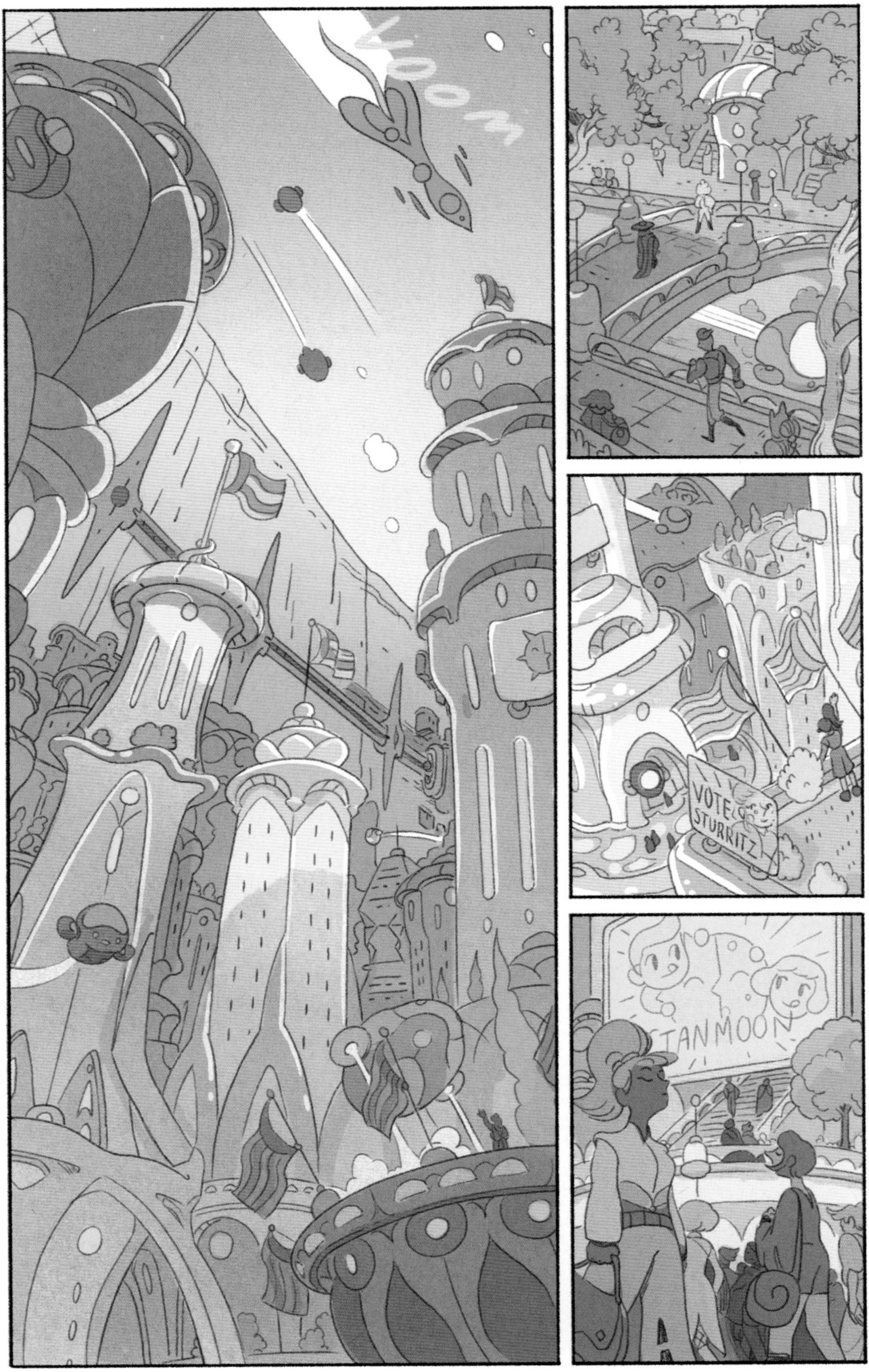
ZOOM
VOTE STURRITZ
TANMOON

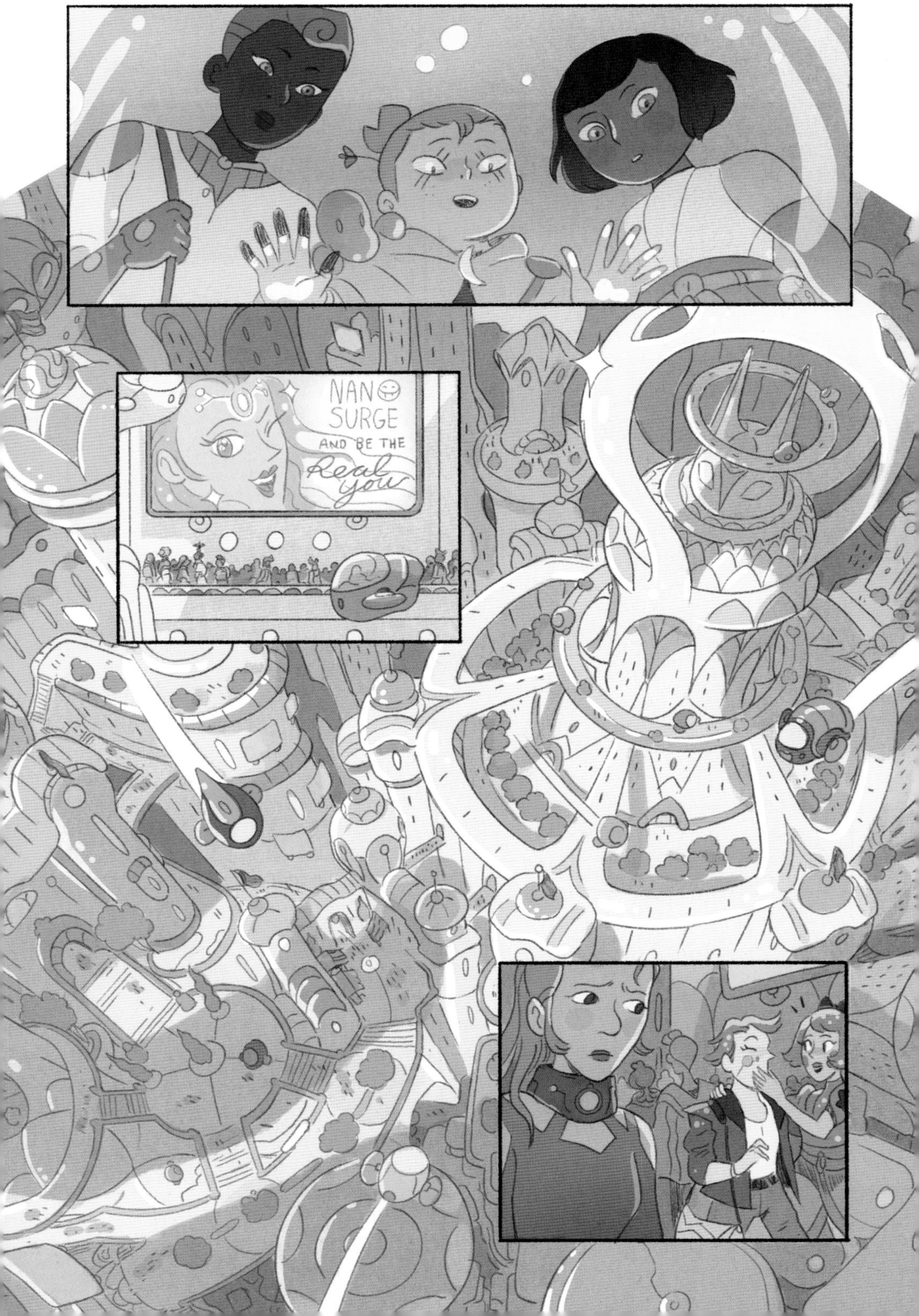
NAN
SURGE
AND BE THE
Real you

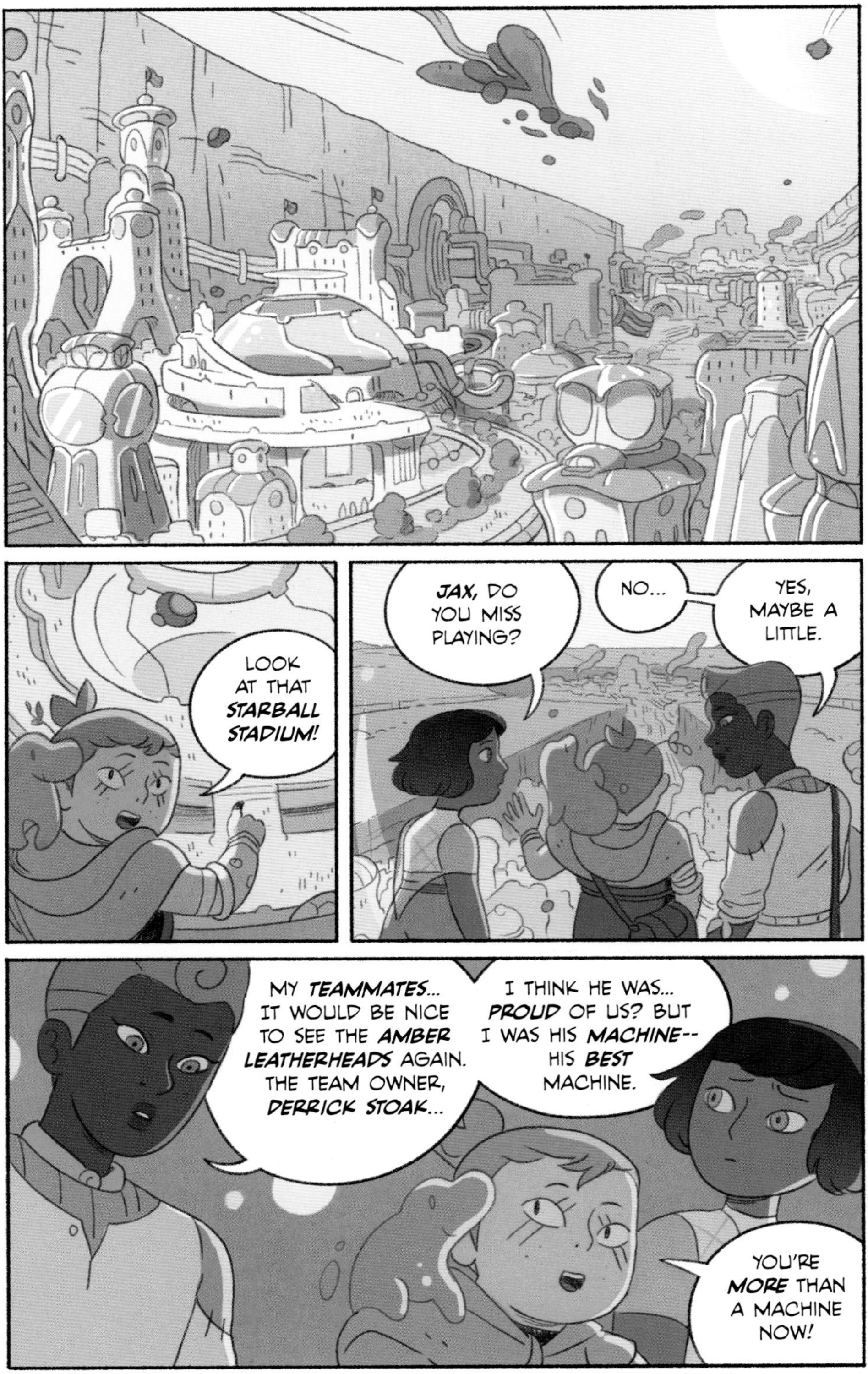
LOOK AT THAT STARBALL STADIUM!
JAX, DO YOU MISS PLAYING?
NO...
YES, MAYBE A LITTLE.
MY TEAMMATES... IT WOULD BE NICE TO SEE THE AMBER LEATHERHEADS AGAIN. THE TEAM OWNER, DERRICK STOAK...
I THINK HE WAS... PROUD OF US? BUT I WAS HIS MACHINE-- HIS BEST MACHINE.
YOU'RE MORE THAN A MACHINE NOW!

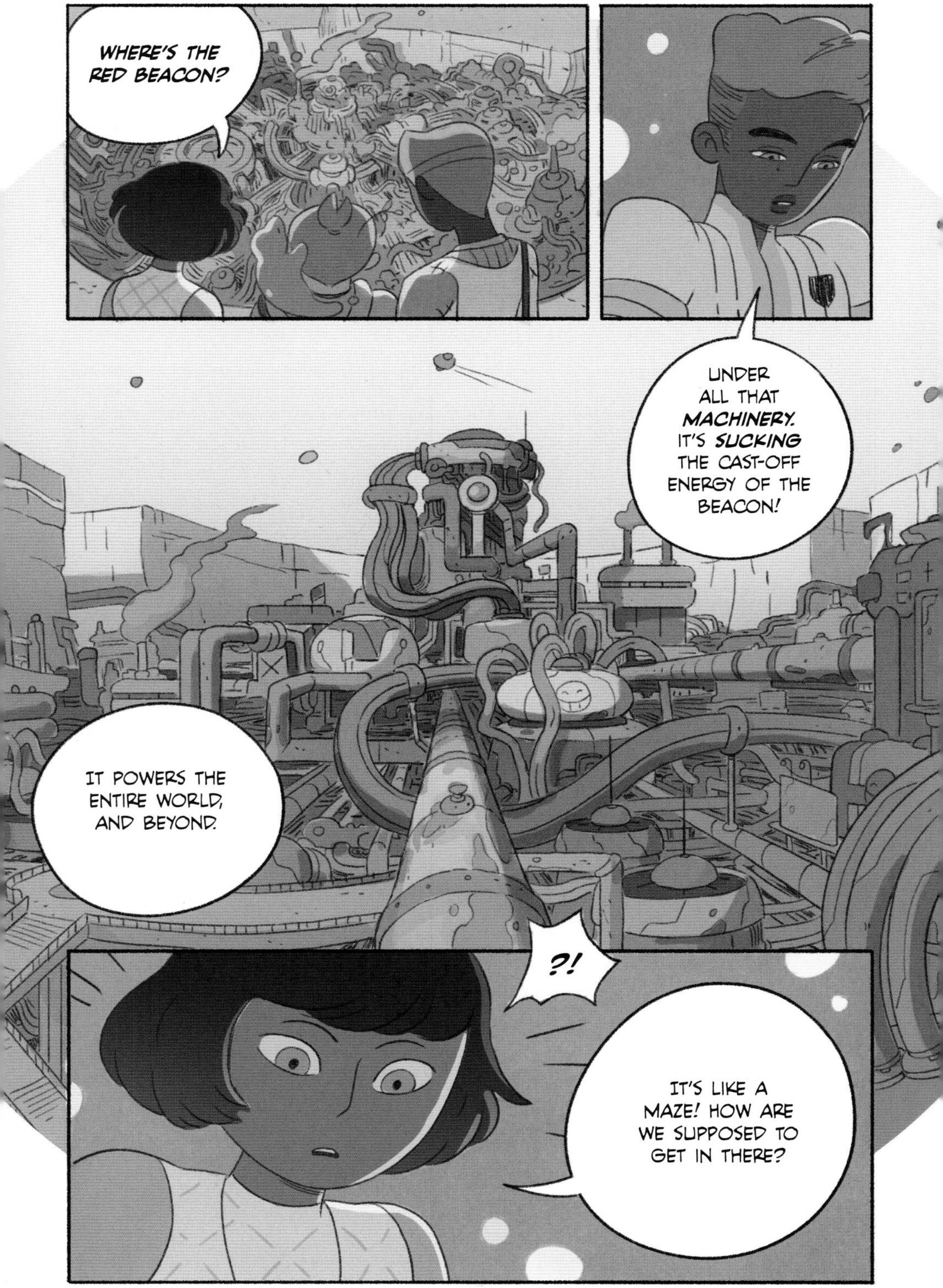
WHERE'S THE RED BEACON?
UNDER ALL THAT MACHINERY. IT'S SUCKING THE CAST-OFF ENERGY OF THE BEACON!
IT POWERS THE ENTIRE WORLD, AND BEYOND.
?!
IT'S LIKE A MAZE! HOW ARE WE SUPPOSED TO GET IN THERE?

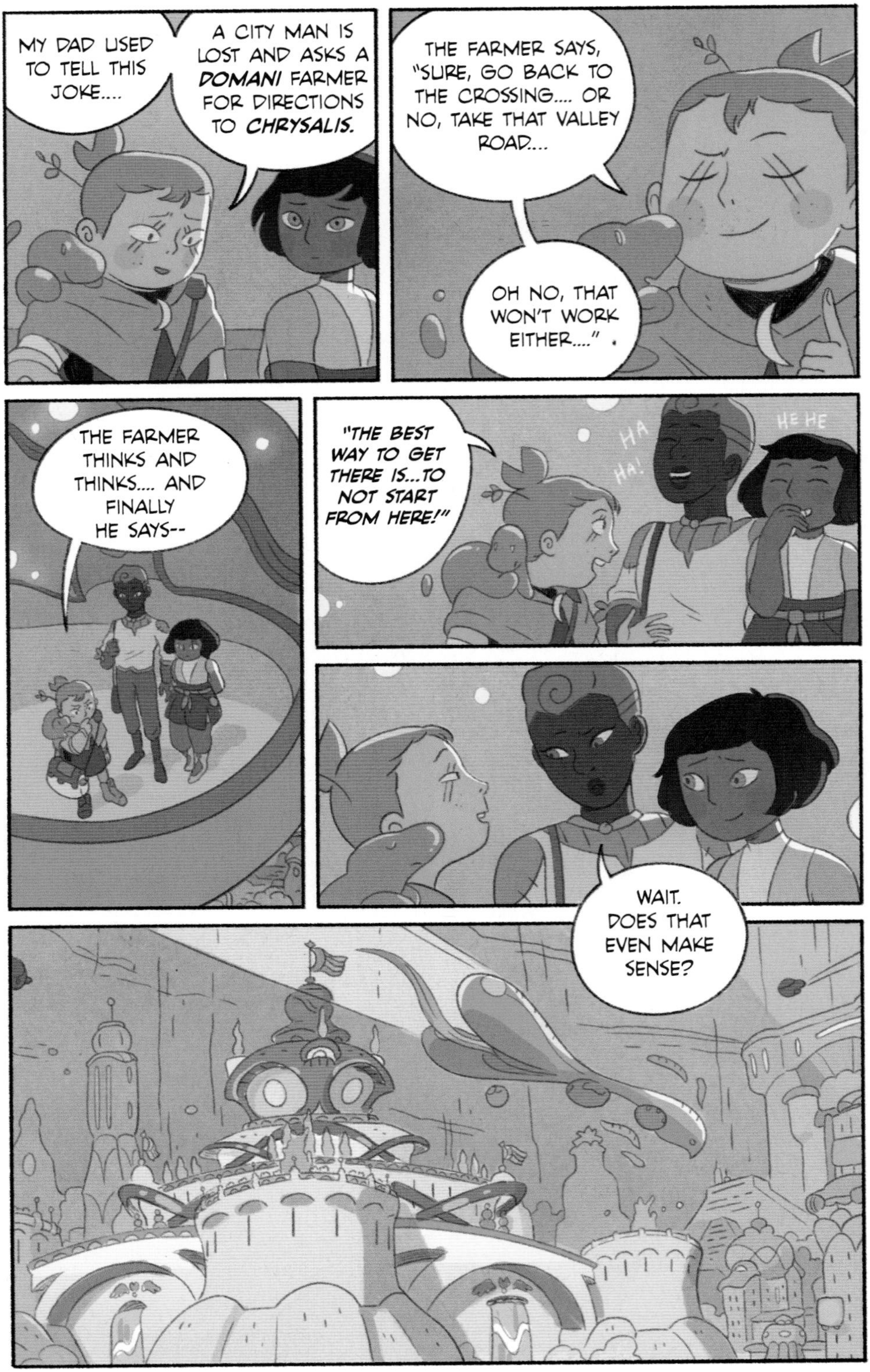
MY DAD USED TO TELL THIS JOKE....
A CITY MAN IS LOST AND ASKS A *DOMANI* FARMER FOR DIRECTIONS TO **CHRYSALIS.**
THE FARMER SAYS, "SURE, GO BACK TO THE CROSSING.... OR NO, TAKE THAT VALLEY ROAD....
OH NO, THAT WON'T WORK EITHER...." .
THE FARMER THINKS AND THINKS.... AND FINALLY HE SAYS--
*"THE BEST WAY TO GET THERE IS...TO NOT START FROM HERE!"*
HA HA!
HE HE
WAIT. DOES THAT EVEN MAKE SENSE?

## Chapter 2

# THE GARNET PALACE

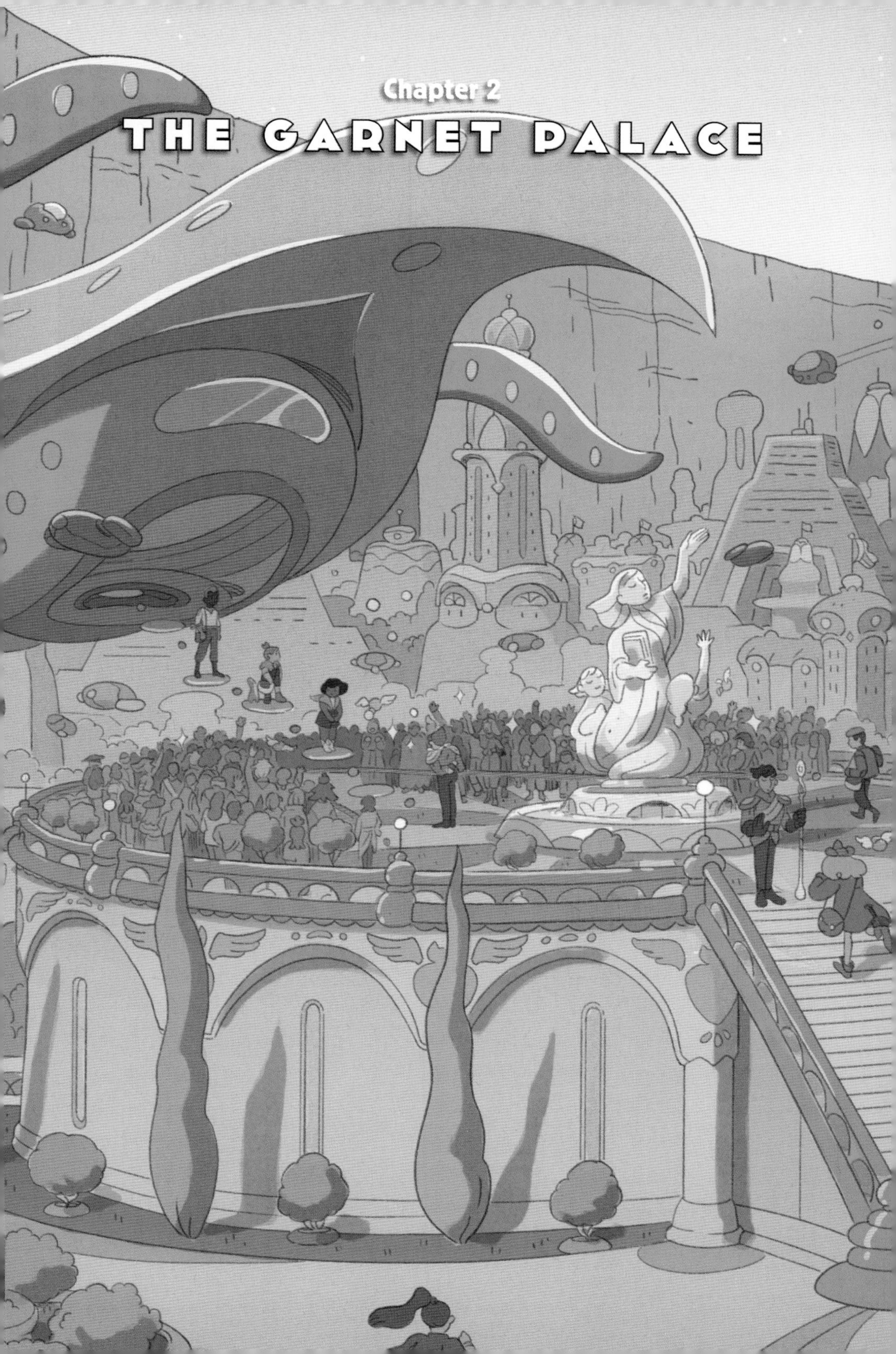

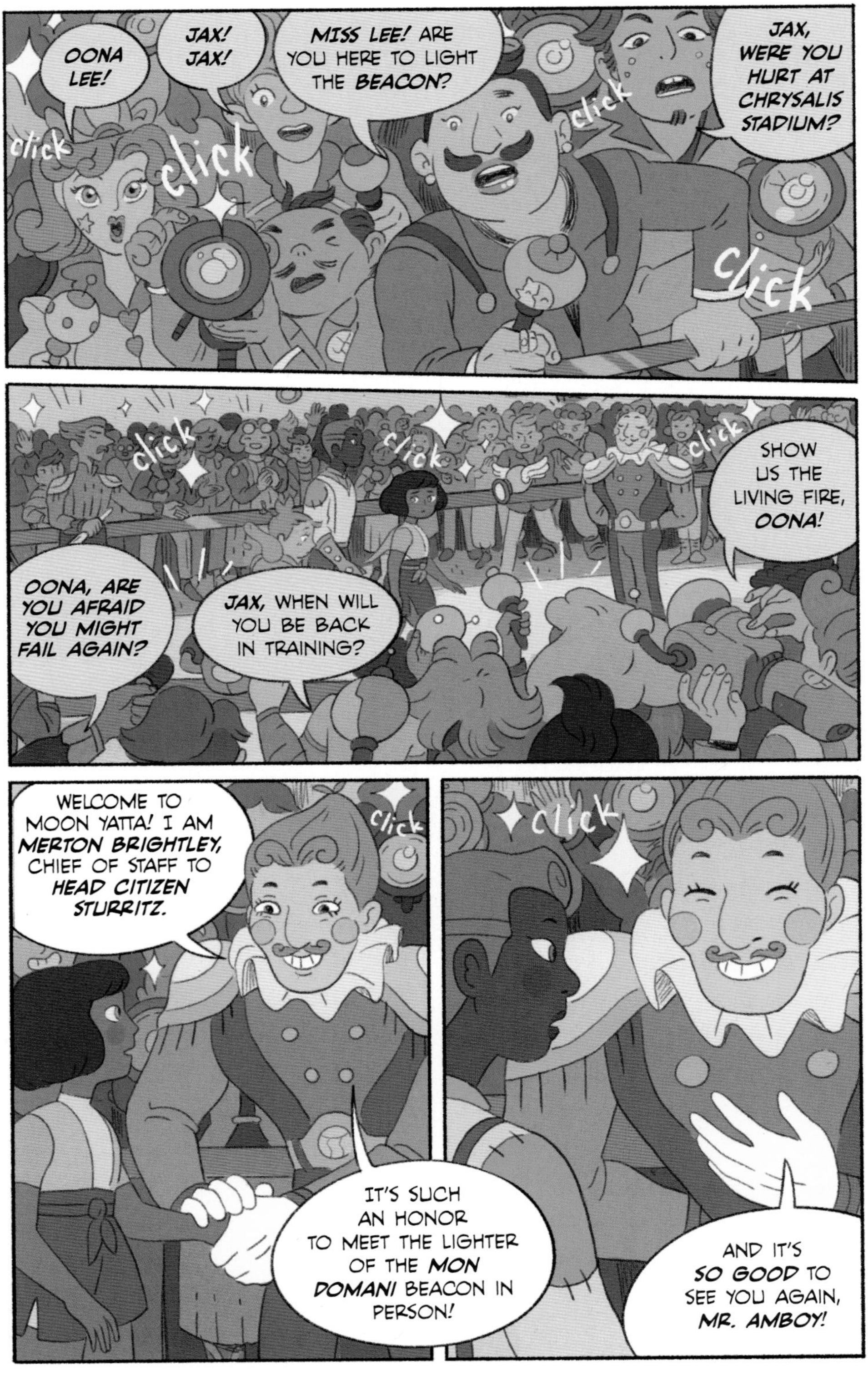
OONA LEE!
JAX! JAX!
MISS LEE! ARE YOU HERE TO LIGHT THE BEACON?
JAX, WERE YOU HURT AT CHRYSALIS STADIUM?
click
click
click
click
click
click
click
SHOW US THE LIVING FIRE, OONA!
OONA, ARE YOU AFRAID YOU MIGHT FAIL AGAIN?
JAX, WHEN WILL YOU BE BACK IN TRAINING?
WELCOME TO MOON YATTA! I AM MERTON BRIGHTLEY, CHIEF OF STAFF TO HEAD CITIZEN STURRITZ.
click
IT'S SUCH AN HONOR TO MEET THE LIGHTER OF THE MON DOMANI BEACON IN PERSON!
click
AND IT'S SO GOOD TO SEE YOU AGAIN, MR. AMBOY!

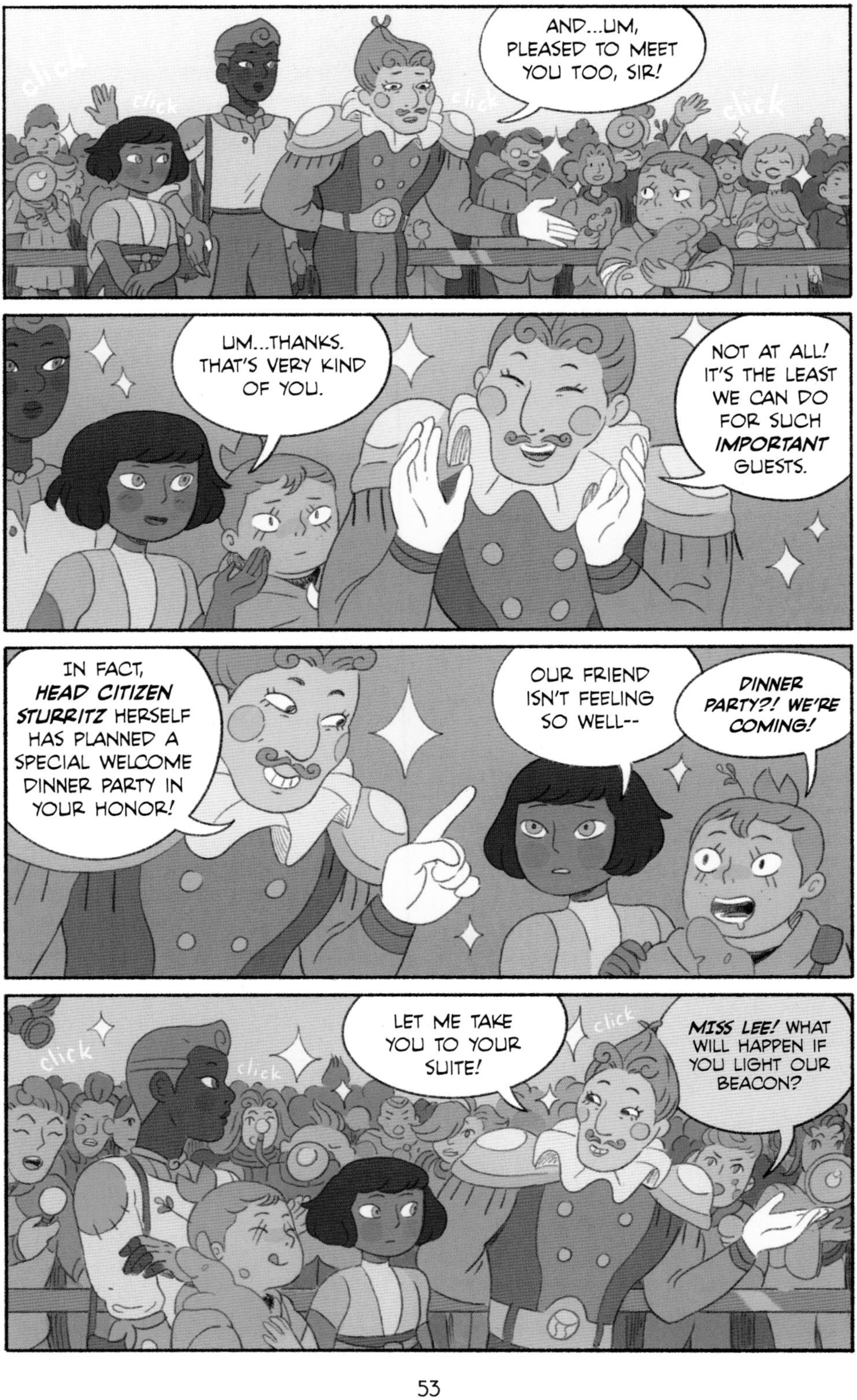
click
click
AND...UM, PLEASED TO MEET YOU TOO, SIR!
click
click
UM...THANKS. THAT'S VERY KIND OF YOU.
NOT AT ALL! IT'S THE LEAST WE CAN DO FOR SUCH *IMPORTANT* GUESTS.
IN FACT, ***HEAD CITIZEN STURRITZ*** HERSELF HAS PLANNED A SPECIAL WELCOME DINNER PARTY IN YOUR HONOR!
OUR FRIEND ISN'T FEELING SO WELL--
***DINNER PARTY?! WE'RE COMING!***
click
click
LET ME TAKE YOU TO YOUR SUITE!
click
***MISS LEE!*** WHAT WILL HAPPEN IF YOU LIGHT OUR BEACON?

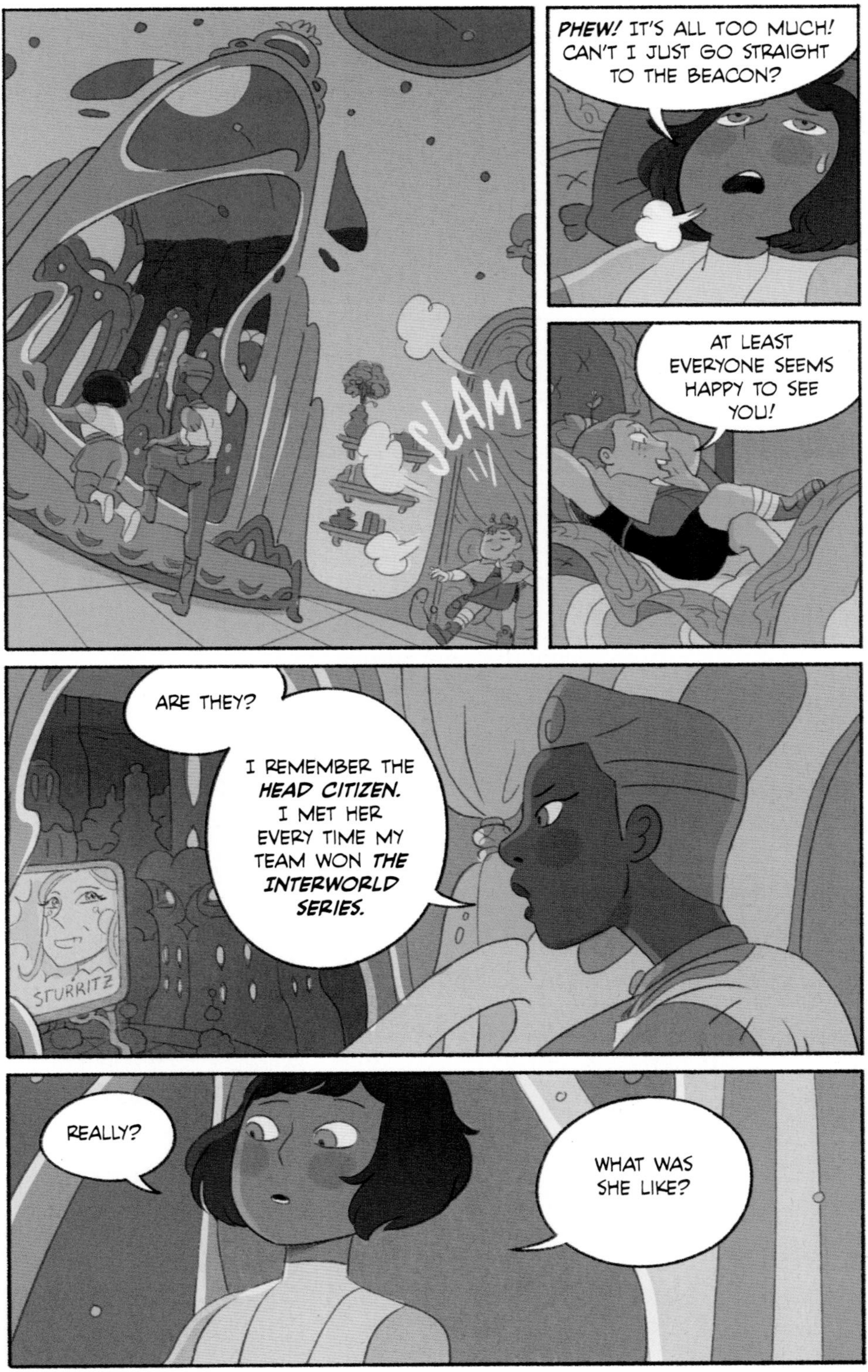
SLAM
PHEW! IT'S ALL TOO MUCH! CAN'T I JUST GO STRAIGHT TO THE BEACON?
AT LEAST EVERYONE SEEMS HAPPY TO SEE YOU!
ARE THEY?
I REMEMBER THE HEAD CITIZEN. I MET HER EVERY TIME MY TEAM WON THE INTERWORLD SERIES.
STURRITZ
REALLY?
WHAT WAS SHE LIKE?

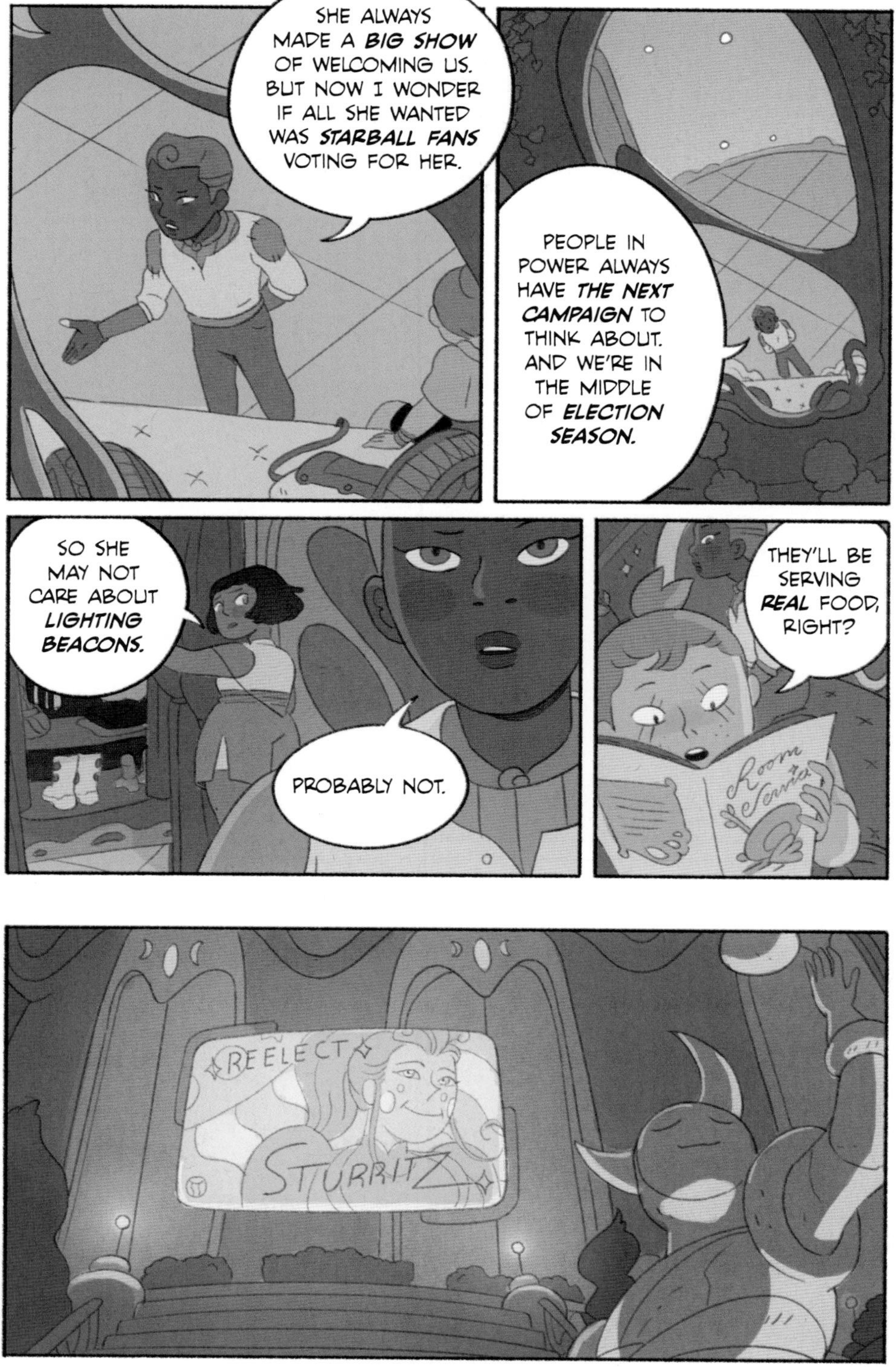
SHE ALWAYS MADE A ***BIG SHOW*** OF WELCOMING US. BUT NOW I WONDER IF ALL SHE WANTED WAS ***STARBALL FANS*** VOTING FOR HER.
PEOPLE IN POWER ALWAYS HAVE ***THE NEXT CAMPAIGN*** TO THINK ABOUT. AND WE'RE IN THE MIDDLE OF ***ELECTION SEASON.***
SO SHE MAY NOT CARE ABOUT ***LIGHTING BEACONS.***
PROBABLY NOT.
THEY'LL BE SERVING ***REAL*** FOOD, RIGHT?
REELECT
STURRITZ

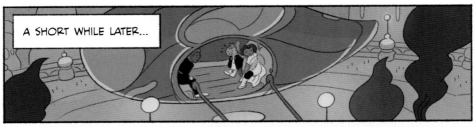

A SHORT WHILE LATER...

OH, LOOK, SHE'S *THAT DOMANI DANCER* WHO LIT THE BEACON. ISN'T SHE *CUTE?*

YES, SO "COUNTRY" IN *TOKI BLUE.* AND THAT *KID* FROM THE SLUMS. JUST ADORABLE.

A FEW NANO-COSMETIC TOUCHES WOULD DO *WONDERS* ON HER.

I HEAR THIS YEAR IT'S GOING TO BE ALL ABOUT *LONG NECKS.*

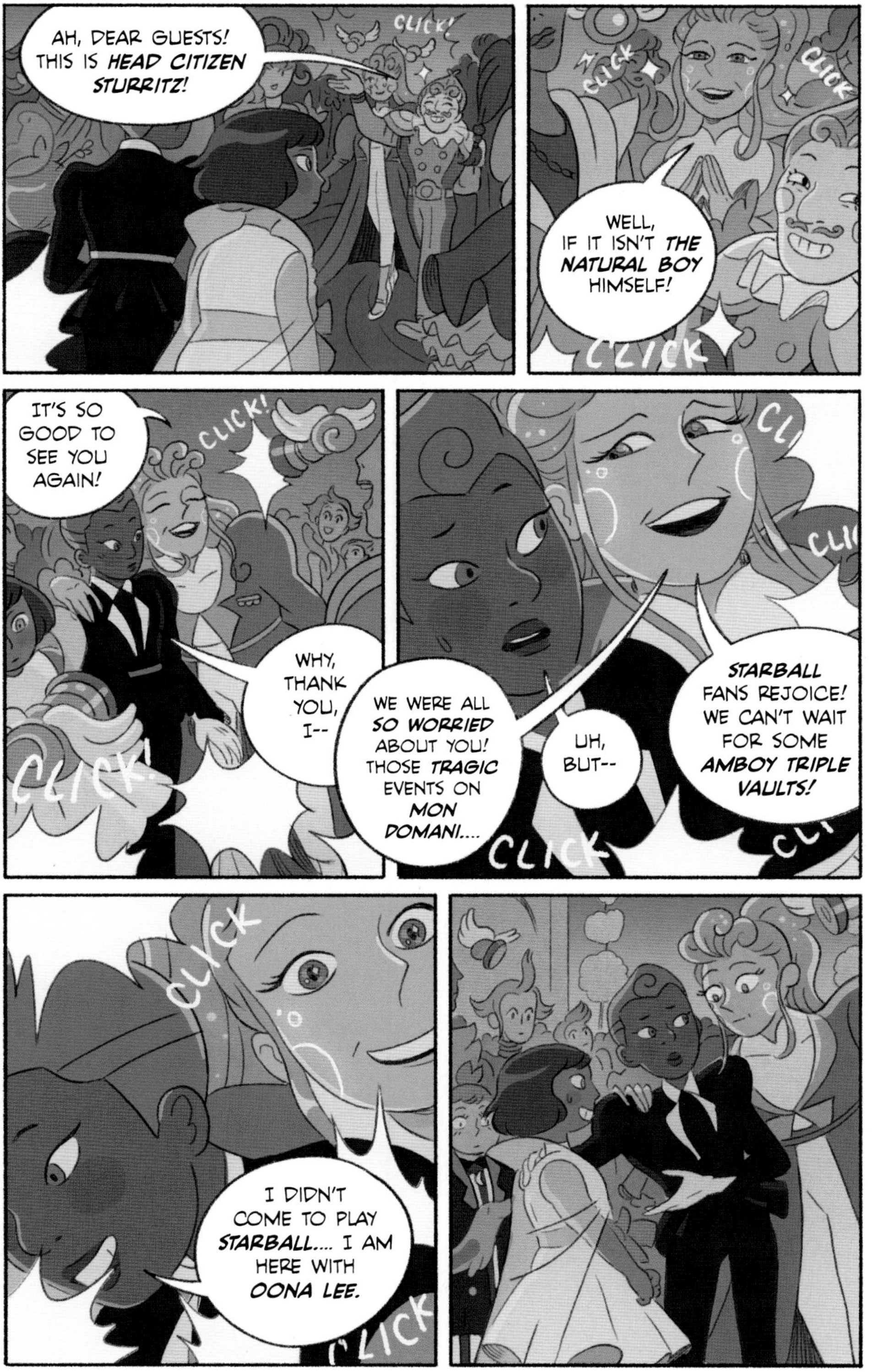

CLICK!
AH, DEAR GUESTS! THIS IS HEAD CITIZEN STURRITZ!
CLICK
CLICK
WELL, IF IT ISN'T THE NATURAL BOY HIMSELF!
CLICK
IT'S SO GOOD TO SEE YOU AGAIN!
CLICK!
WHY, THANK YOU, I--
CLICK!
WE WERE ALL SO WORRIED ABOUT YOU! THOSE TRAGIC EVENTS ON MON DOMANI....
UH, BUT--
STARBALL FANS REJOICE! WE CAN'T WAIT FOR SOME AMBOY TRIPLE VAULTS!
CLICK
CLICK
I DIDN'T COME TO PLAY STARBALL.... I AM HERE WITH OONA LEE.
CLICK

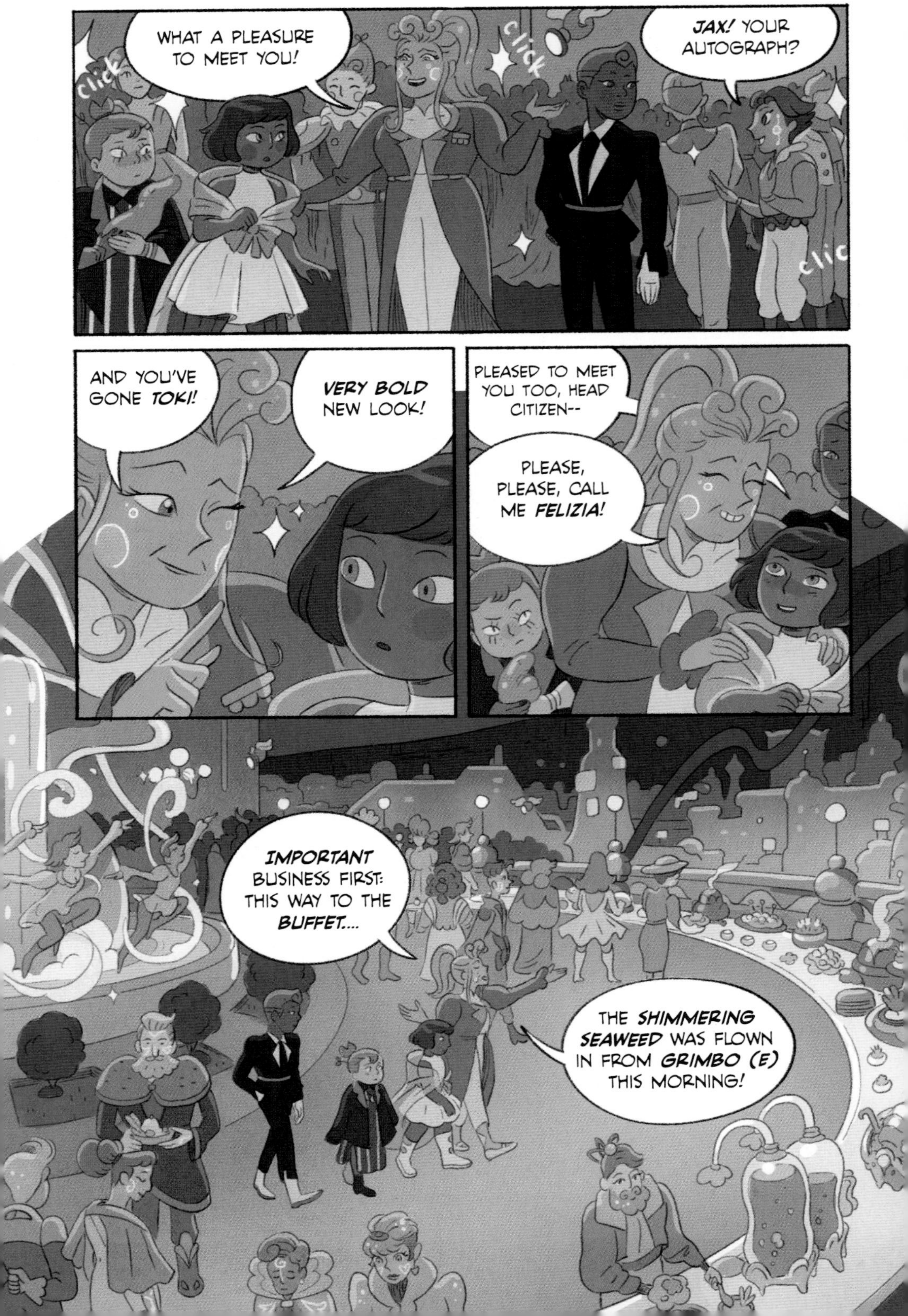

WHAT A PLEASURE TO MEET YOU!
JAX! YOUR AUTOGRAPH?
click
click
clic
AND YOU'VE GONE TOKI!
VERY BOLD NEW LOOK!
PLEASED TO MEET YOU TOO, HEAD CITIZEN--
PLEASE, PLEASE, CALL ME FELIZIA!
IMPORTANT BUSINESS FIRST: THIS WAY TO THE BUFFET....
THE SHIMMERING SEAWEED WAS FLOWN IN FROM GRIMBO (E) THIS MORNING!

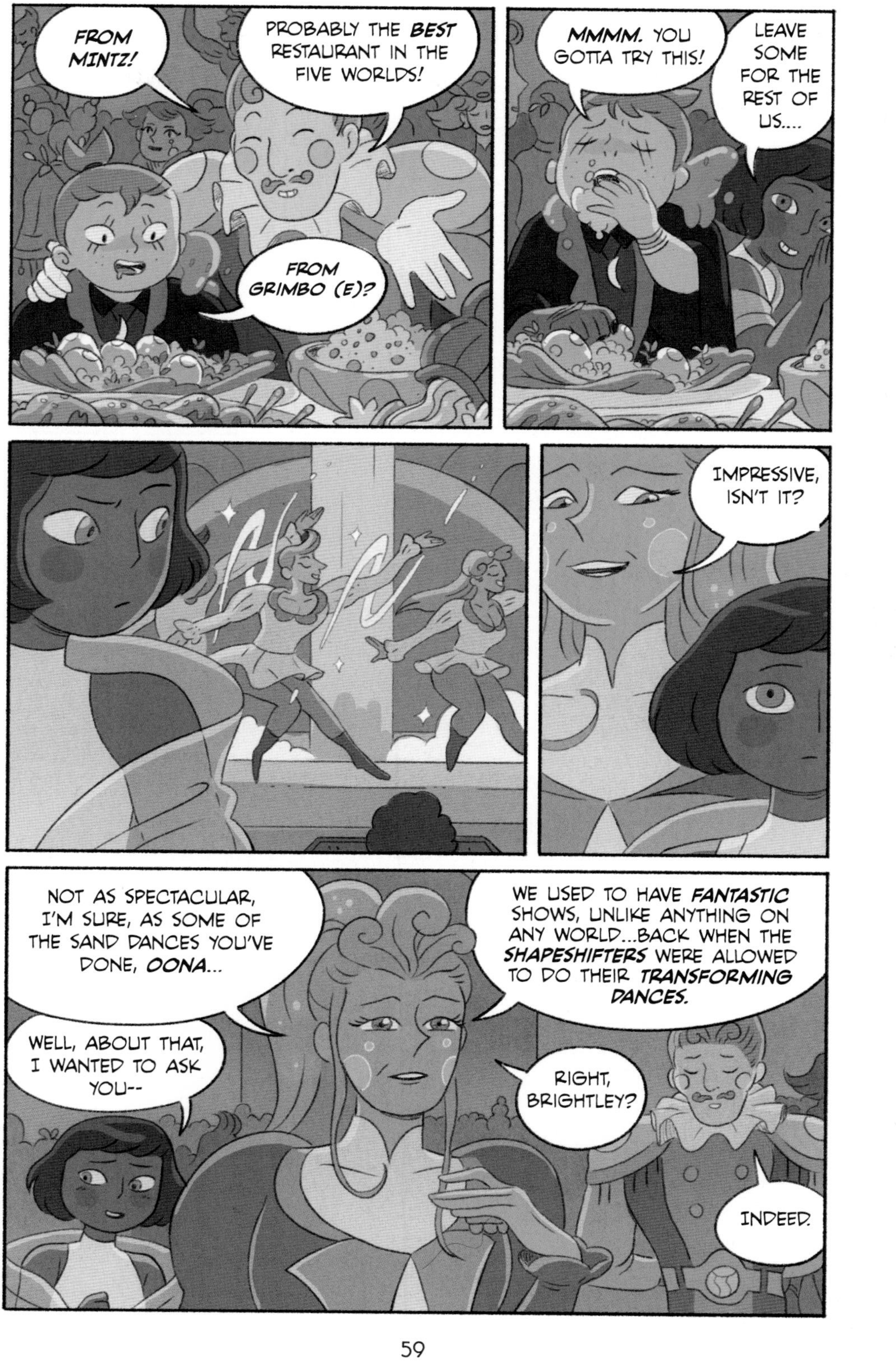
FROM MINTZ!
PROBABLY THE BEST RESTAURANT IN THE FIVE WORLDS!
FROM GRIMBO (E)?
MMMM. YOU GOTTA TRY THIS!
LEAVE SOME FOR THE REST OF US....
IMPRESSIVE, ISN'T IT?
NOT AS SPECTACULAR, I'M SURE, AS SOME OF THE SAND DANCES YOU'VE DONE, OONA...
WE USED TO HAVE FANTASTIC SHOWS, UNLIKE ANYTHING ON ANY WORLD...BACK WHEN THE SHAPESHIFTERS WERE ALLOWED TO DO THEIR TRANSFORMING DANCES.
WELL, ABOUT THAT, I WANTED TO ASK YOU--
RIGHT, BRIGHTLEY?
INDEED.

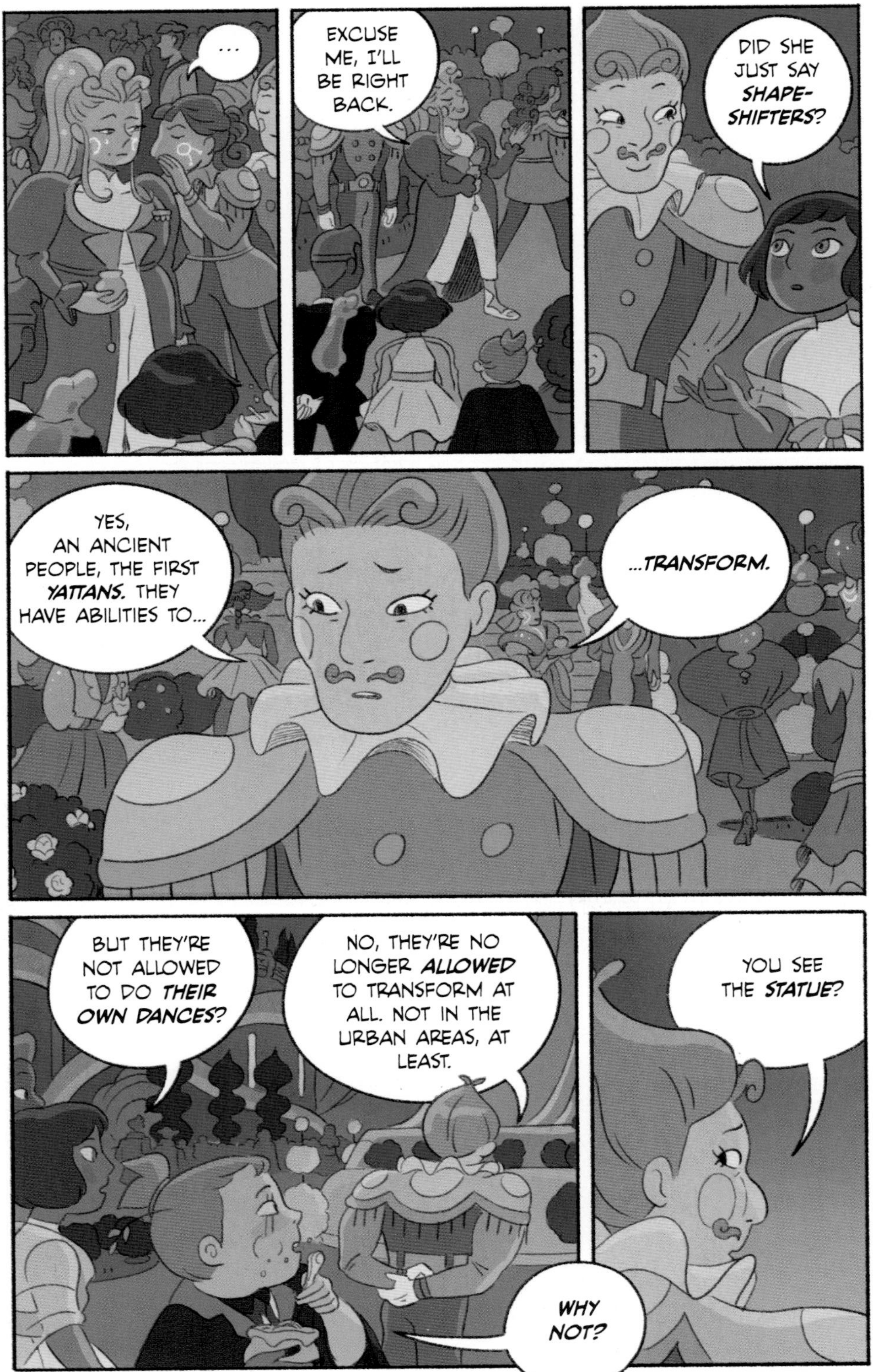
...
EXCUSE ME, I'LL BE RIGHT BACK.
DID SHE JUST SAY *SHAPE-SHIFTERS?*
YES, AN ANCIENT PEOPLE, THE FIRST *YATTANS.* THEY HAVE ABILITIES TO...
*...TRANSFORM.*
BUT THEY'RE NOT ALLOWED TO DO *THEIR OWN DANCES?*
NO, THEY'RE NO LONGER *ALLOWED* TO TRANSFORM AT ALL. NOT IN THE URBAN AREAS, AT LEAST.
YOU SEE THE *STATUE?*
*WHY NOT?*

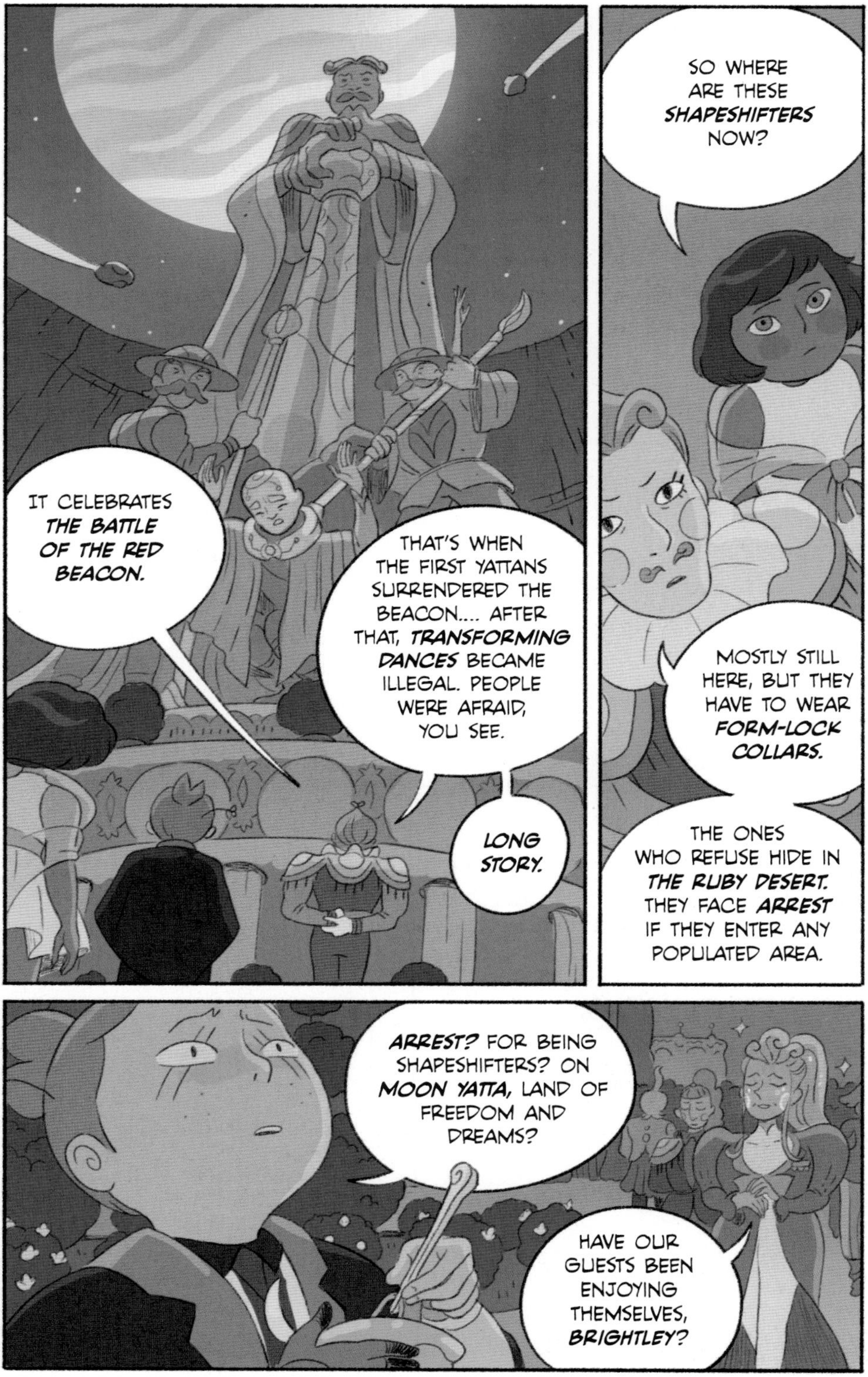
IT CELEBRATES THE BATTLE OF THE RED BEACON.
THAT'S WHEN THE FIRST YATTANS SURRENDERED THE BEACON.... AFTER THAT, TRANSFORMING DANCES BECAME ILLEGAL. PEOPLE WERE AFRAID, YOU SEE.
LONG STORY.
SO WHERE ARE THESE SHAPESHIFTERS NOW?
MOSTLY STILL HERE, BUT THEY HAVE TO WEAR FORM-LOCK COLLARS.
THE ONES WHO REFUSE HIDE IN THE RUBY DESERT. THEY FACE ARREST IF THEY ENTER ANY POPULATED AREA.
ARREST? FOR BEING SHAPESHIFTERS? ON MOON YATTA, LAND OF FREEDOM AND DREAMS?
HAVE OUR GUESTS BEEN ENJOYING THEMSELVES, BRIGHTLEY?

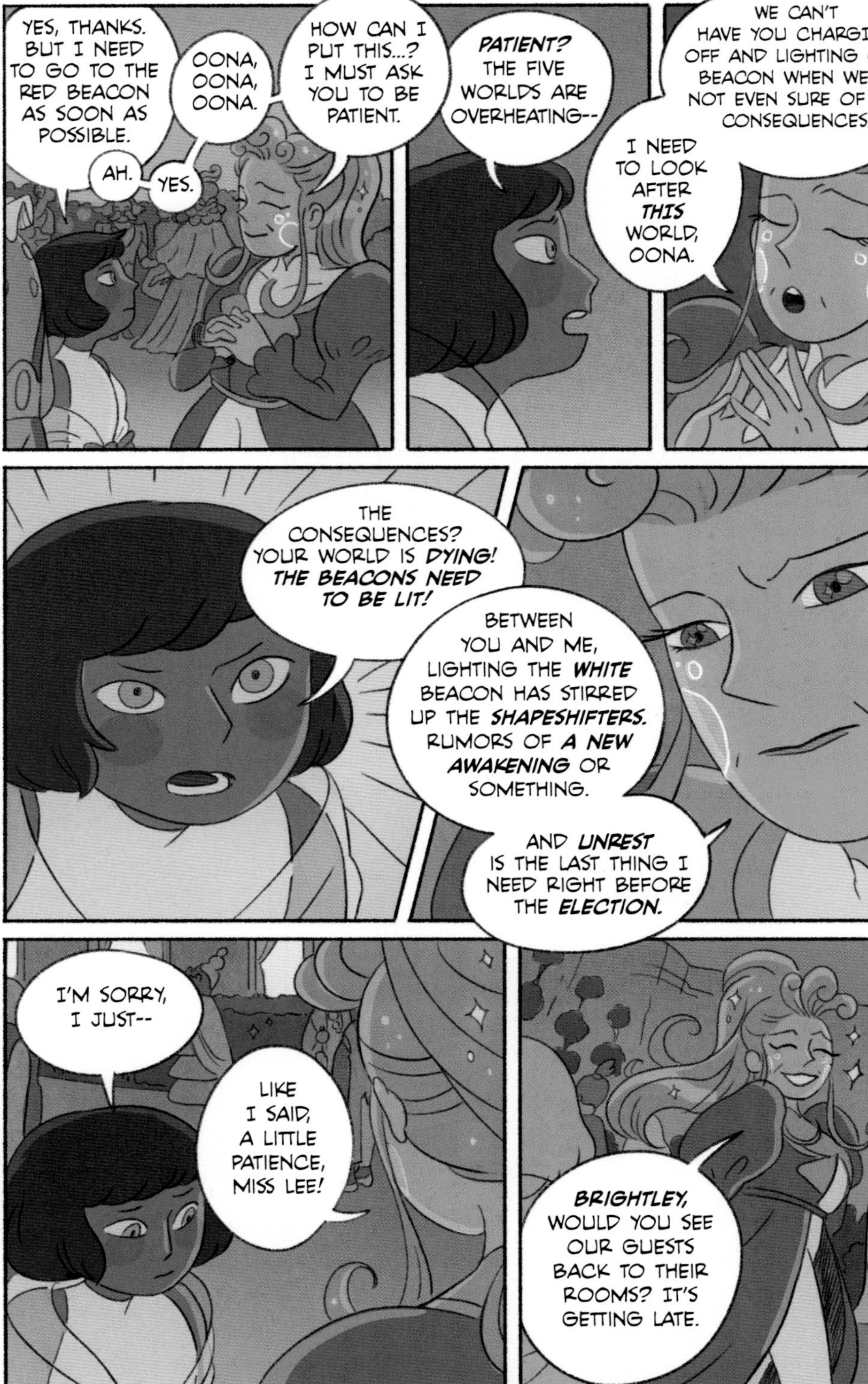
YES, THANKS. BUT I NEED TO GO TO THE RED BEACON AS SOON AS POSSIBLE.
OONA, OONA, OONA.
AH.
YES.
HOW CAN I PUT THIS...? I MUST ASK YOU TO BE PATIENT.
*PATIENT?* THE FIVE WORLDS ARE OVERHEATING--
WE CAN'T HAVE YOU CHARGING OFF AND LIGHTING OUR BEACON WHEN WE'RE NOT EVEN SURE OF THE CONSEQUENCES.
I NEED TO LOOK AFTER *THIS* WORLD, OONA.
THE CONSEQUENCES? YOUR WORLD IS *DYING! THE BEACONS NEED TO BE LIT!*
BETWEEN YOU AND ME, LIGHTING THE *WHITE* BEACON HAS STIRRED UP THE *SHAPESHIFTERS.* RUMORS OF *A NEW AWAKENING* OR SOMETHING.
AND *UNREST* IS THE LAST THING I NEED RIGHT BEFORE THE *ELECTION.*
I'M SORRY, I JUST--
LIKE I SAID, A LITTLE PATIENCE, MISS LEE!
*BRIGHTLEY,* WOULD YOU SEE OUR GUESTS BACK TO THEIR ROOMS? IT'S GETTING LATE.

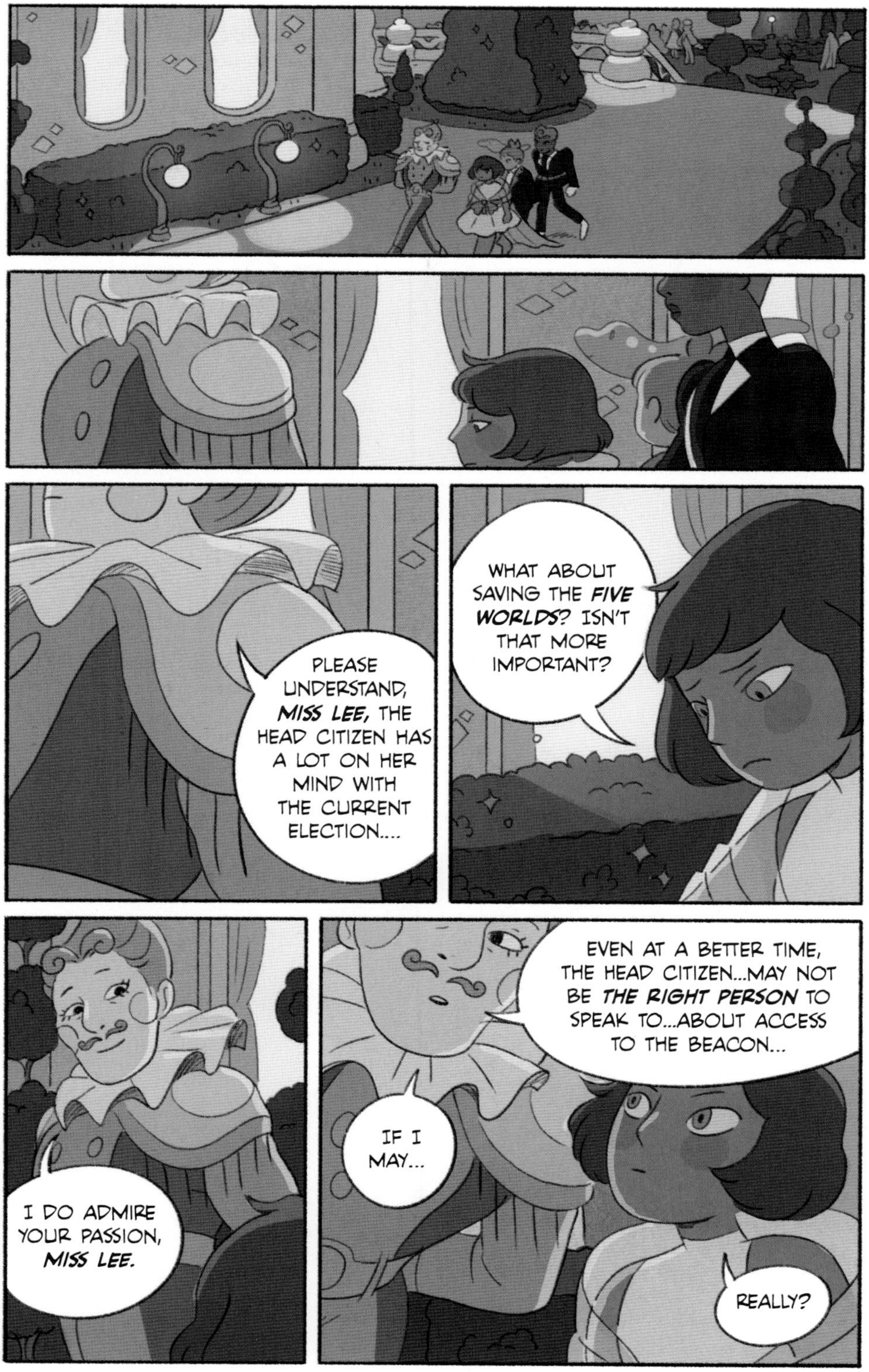
PLEASE UNDERSTAND, MISS LEE, THE HEAD CITIZEN HAS A LOT ON HER MIND WITH THE CURRENT ELECTION....
WHAT ABOUT SAVING THE FIVE WORLDS? ISN'T THAT MORE IMPORTANT?
I DO ADMIRE YOUR PASSION, MISS LEE.
EVEN AT A BETTER TIME, THE HEAD CITIZEN...MAY NOT BE THE RIGHT PERSON TO SPEAK TO...ABOUT ACCESS TO THE BEACON...
IF I MAY...
REALLY?

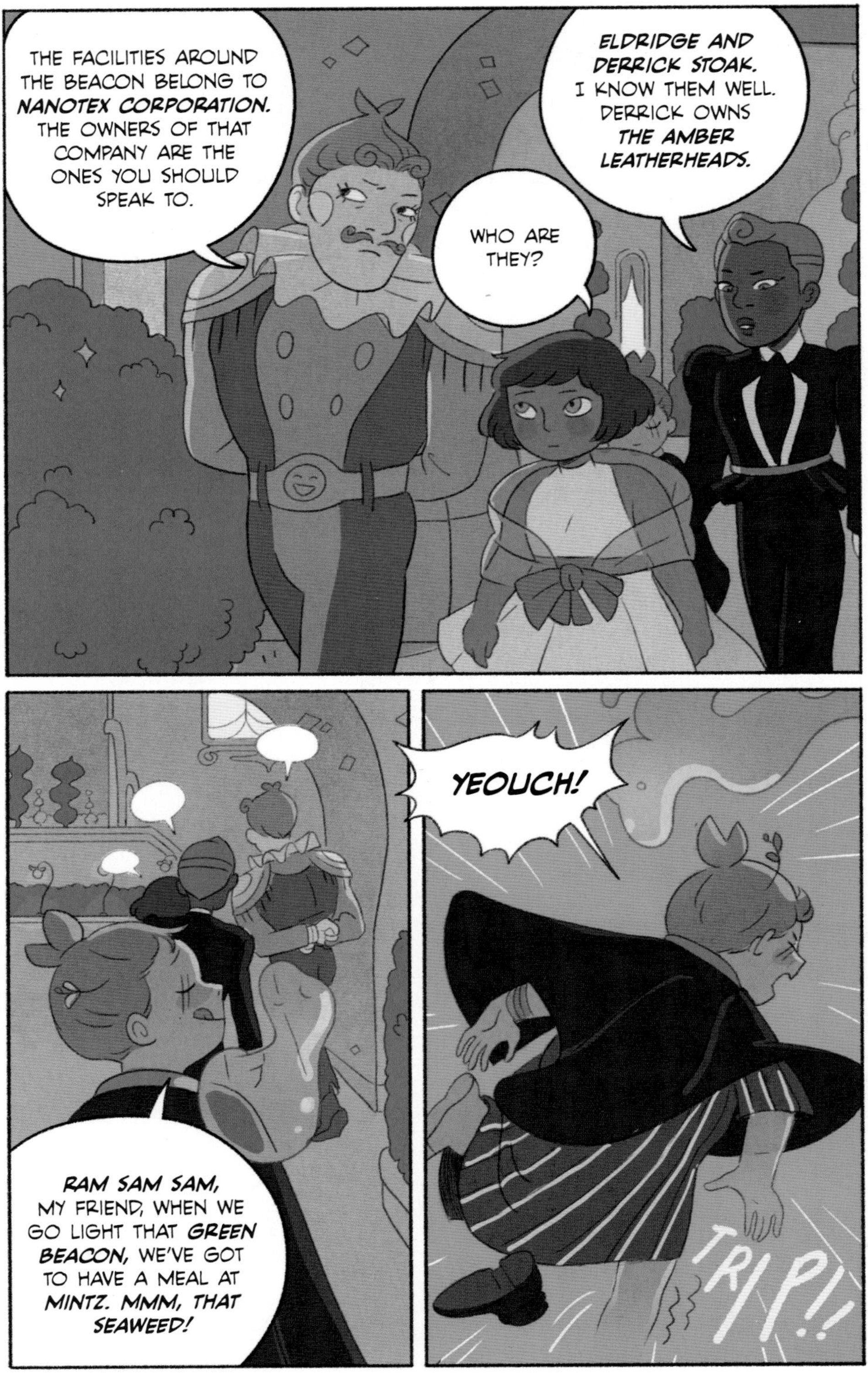
THE FACILITIES AROUND THE BEACON BELONG TO **NANOTEX CORPORATION.** THE OWNERS OF THAT COMPANY ARE THE ONES YOU SHOULD SPEAK TO.
WHO ARE THEY?
**ELDRIDGE AND DERRICK STOAK.** I KNOW THEM WELL. DERRICK OWNS **THE AMBER LEATHERHEADS.**
**RAM SAM SAM,** MY FRIEND, WHEN WE GO LIGHT THAT **GREEN BEACON,** WE'VE GOT TO HAVE A MEAL AT **MINTZ. MMM, THAT SEAWEED!**
**YEOUCH!**
TRIP!!

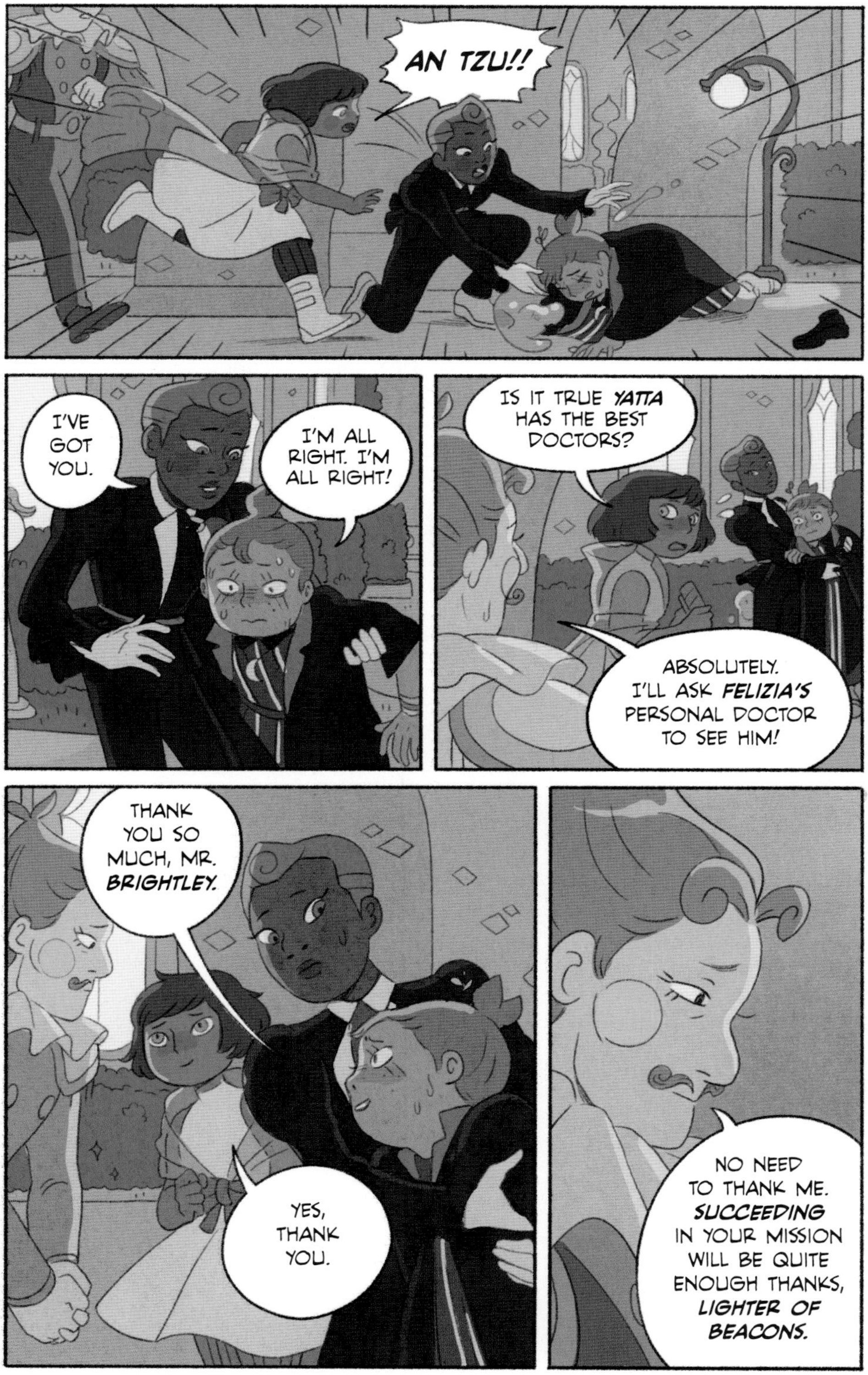

AN TZU!!
I'VE GOT YOU.
I'M ALL RIGHT. I'M ALL RIGHT!
IS IT TRUE YATTA HAS THE BEST DOCTORS?
ABSOLUTELY. I'LL ASK FELIZIA'S PERSONAL DOCTOR TO SEE HIM!
THANK YOU SO MUCH, MR. BRIGHTLEY.
YES, THANK YOU.
NO NEED TO THANK ME. SUCCEEDING IN YOUR MISSION WILL BE QUITE ENOUGH THANKS, LIGHTER OF BEACONS.

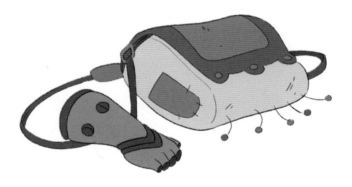

## Chapter 3

# NOT THE MOON YATTA OF HIS DREAMS

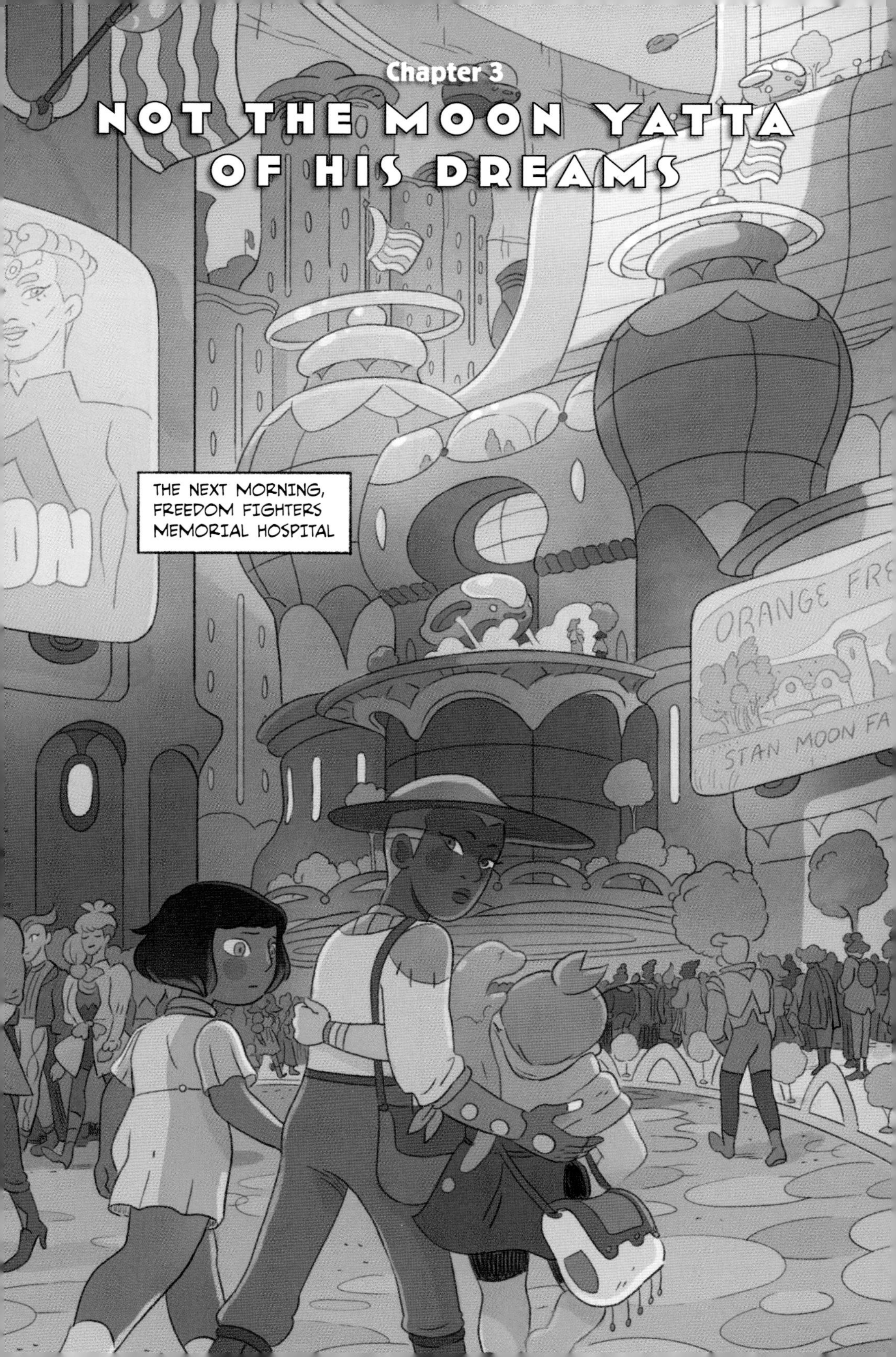
THE NEXT MORNING, FREEDOM FIGHTERS MEMORIAL HOSPITAL

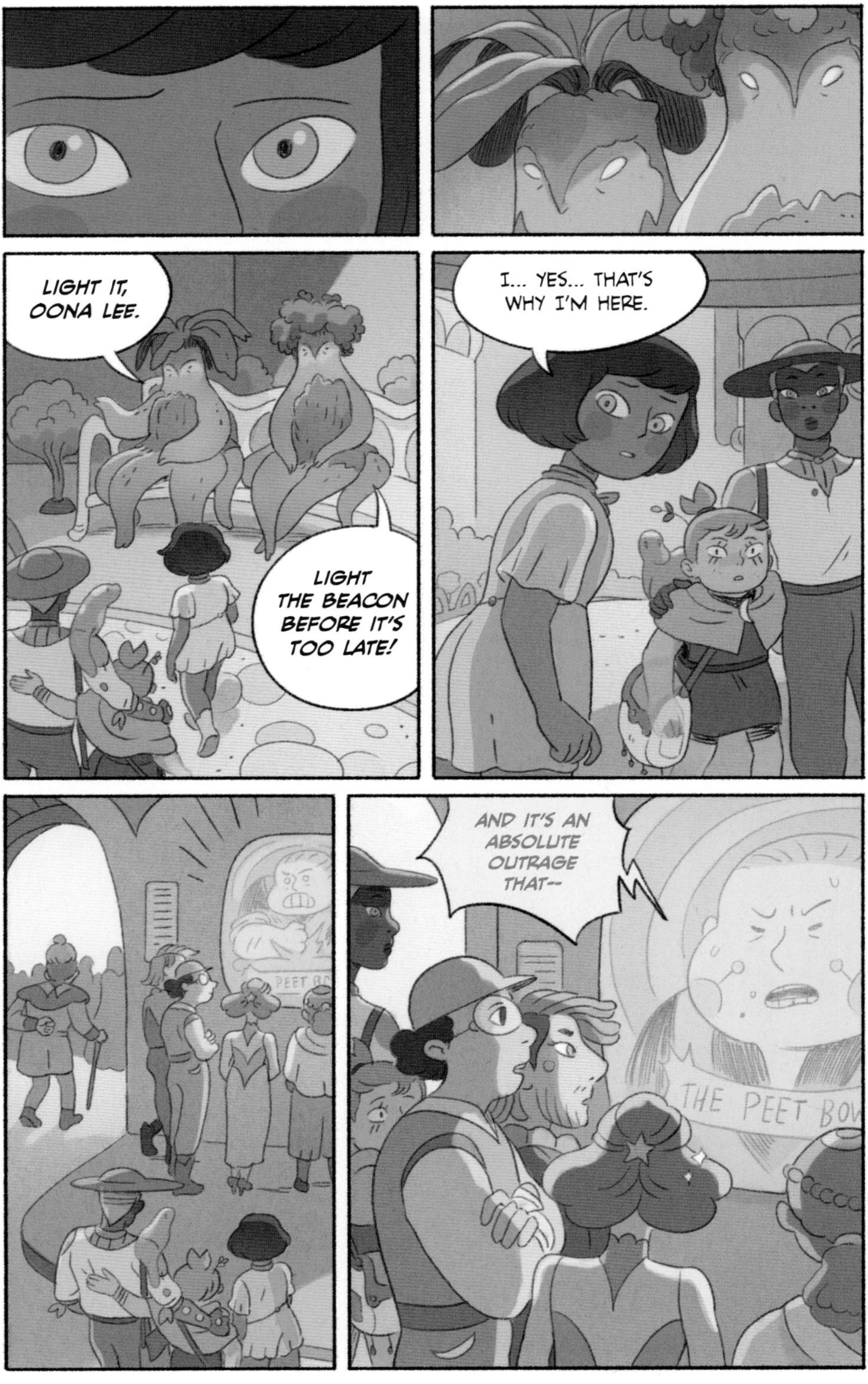
LIGHT IT, OONA LEE.
LIGHT THE BEACON BEFORE IT'S TOO LATE!
I... YES... THAT'S WHY I'M HERE.
PEET BO
AND IT'S AN ABSOLUTE OUTRAGE THAT--
THE PEET BOW

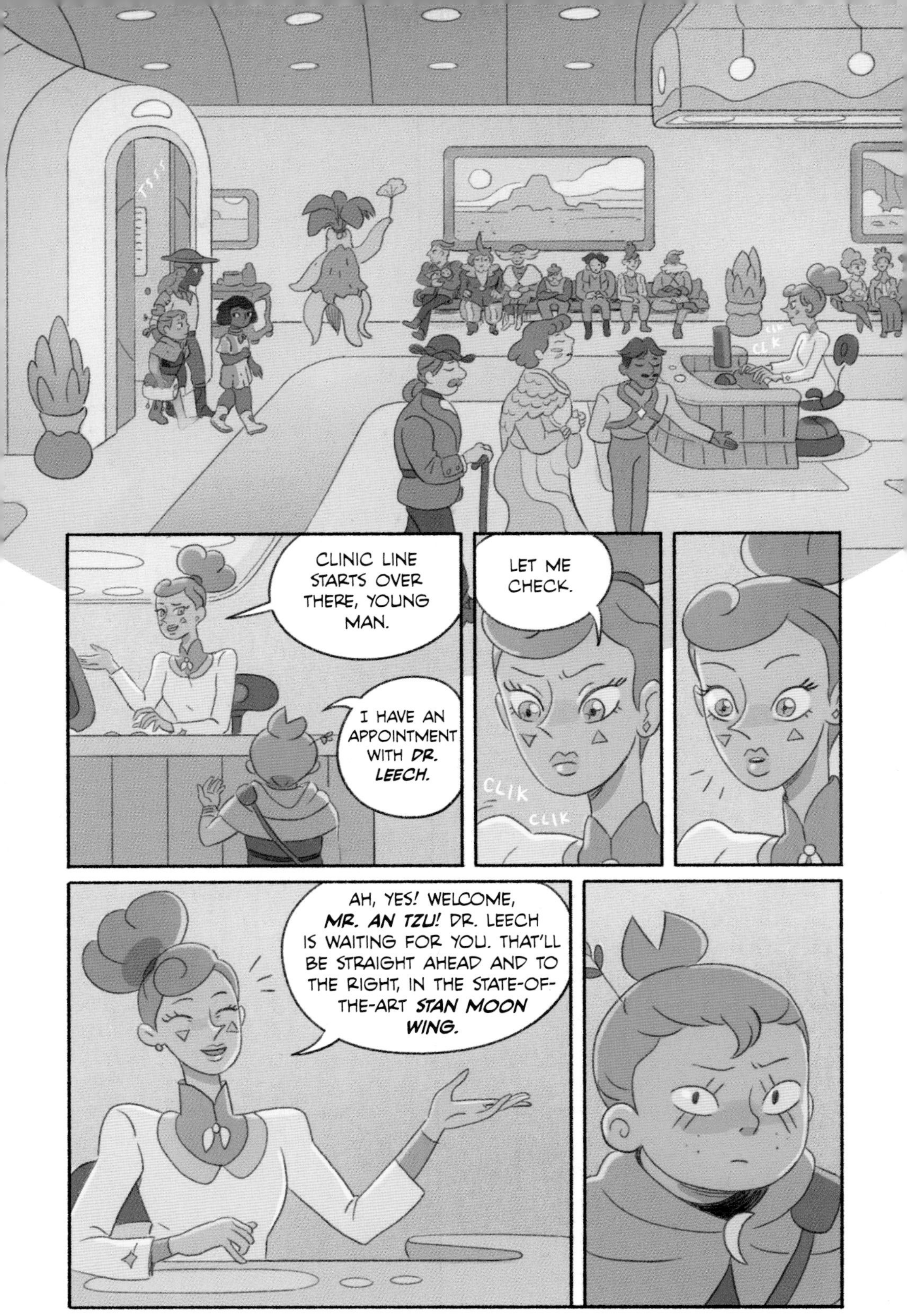
TSSS
CLIK
CLIK
CLINIC LINE STARTS OVER THERE, YOUNG MAN.
I HAVE AN APPOINTMENT WITH DR. LEECH.
LET ME CHECK.
CLIK
CLIK
AH, YES! WELCOME, MR. AN TZU! DR. LEECH IS WAITING FOR YOU. THAT'LL BE STRAIGHT AHEAD AND TO THE RIGHT, IN THE STATE-OF-THE-ART STAN MOON WING.

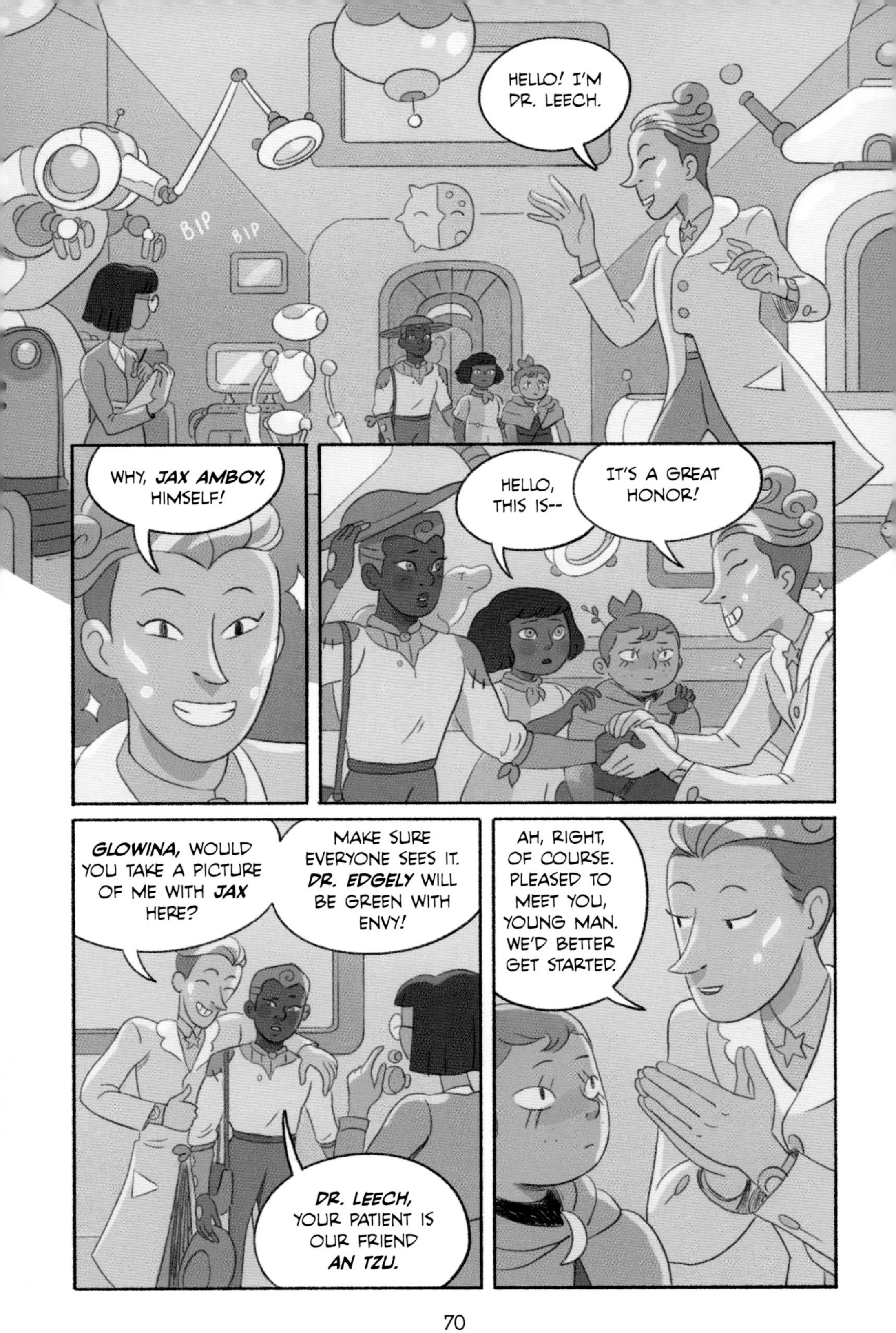
BIP
BIP
HELLO! I'M DR. LEECH.
WHY, JAX AMBOY, HIMSELF!
HELLO, THIS IS--
IT'S A GREAT HONOR!
GLOWINA, WOULD YOU TAKE A PICTURE OF ME WITH JAX HERE?
MAKE SURE EVERYONE SEES IT. DR. EDGELY WILL BE GREEN WITH ENVY!
DR. LEECH, YOUR PATIENT IS OUR FRIEND AN TZU.
AH, RIGHT, OF COURSE. PLEASED TO MEET YOU, YOUNG MAN. WE'D BETTER GET STARTED.

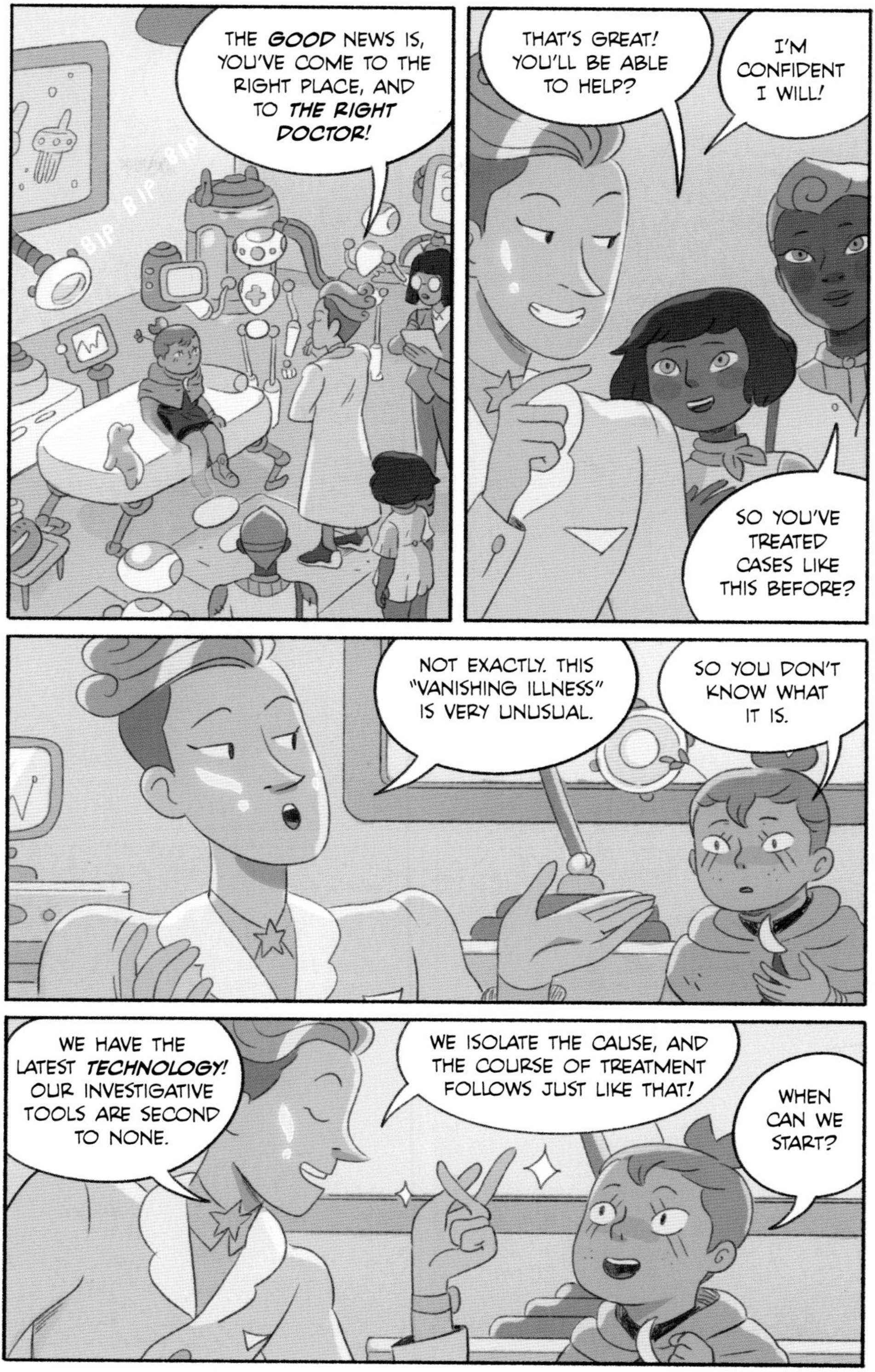

THE GOOD NEWS IS, YOU'VE COME TO THE RIGHT PLACE, AND TO THE RIGHT DOCTOR!
BIP BIP BIP
THAT'S GREAT! YOU'LL BE ABLE TO HELP?
I'M CONFIDENT I WILL!
SO YOU'VE TREATED CASES LIKE THIS BEFORE?
NOT EXACTLY. THIS "VANISHING ILLNESS" IS VERY UNUSUAL.
SO YOU DON'T KNOW WHAT IT IS.
WE HAVE THE LATEST TECHNOLOGY! OUR INVESTIGATIVE TOOLS ARE SECOND TO NONE.
WE ISOLATE THE CAUSE, AND THE COURSE OF TREATMENT FOLLOWS JUST LIKE THAT!
WHEN CAN WE START?

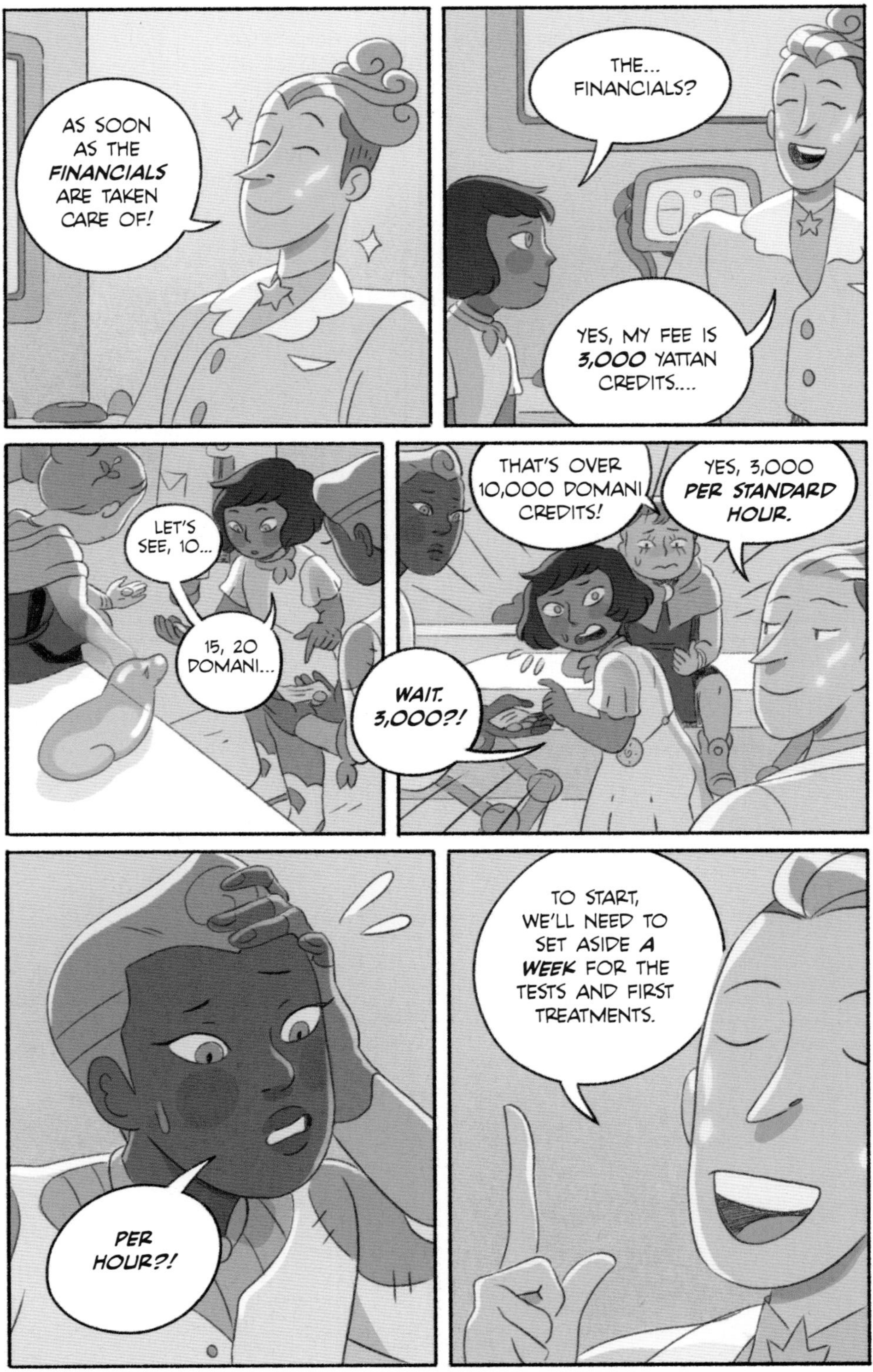
AS SOON AS THE FINANCIALS ARE TAKEN CARE OF!
THE... FINANCIALS?
YES, MY FEE IS 3,000 YATTAN CREDITS....
LET'S SEE, 10...
15, 20 DOMANI...
WAIT. 3,000?!
THAT'S OVER 10,000 DOMANI CREDITS!
YES, 3,000 PER STANDARD HOUR.
PER HOUR?!
TO START, WE'LL NEED TO SET ASIDE A WEEK FOR THE TESTS AND FIRST TREATMENTS.

WE DON'T HAVE THAT MUCH--

WHOA, WHOA, WHOA-- BRIGHTLEY NEVER SAID HE WAS SENDING ME *A CHARITY CASE!*

I UNDERSTAND, IT'S JUST THAT WE--

YOU'RE A DOCTOR! AREN'T YOU IN THE *HEALING* BUSINESS FIRST?

WE'RE *DONE* HERE. *HOSPITAL POLICY.* NOTHING I CAN DO, I'M AFRAID. I HAVE A FAMILY TO FEED, YOU KNOW.

SLAM!

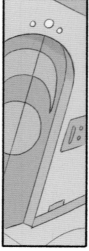

GO ON AHEAD. I'LL MEET YOU OUTSIDE.

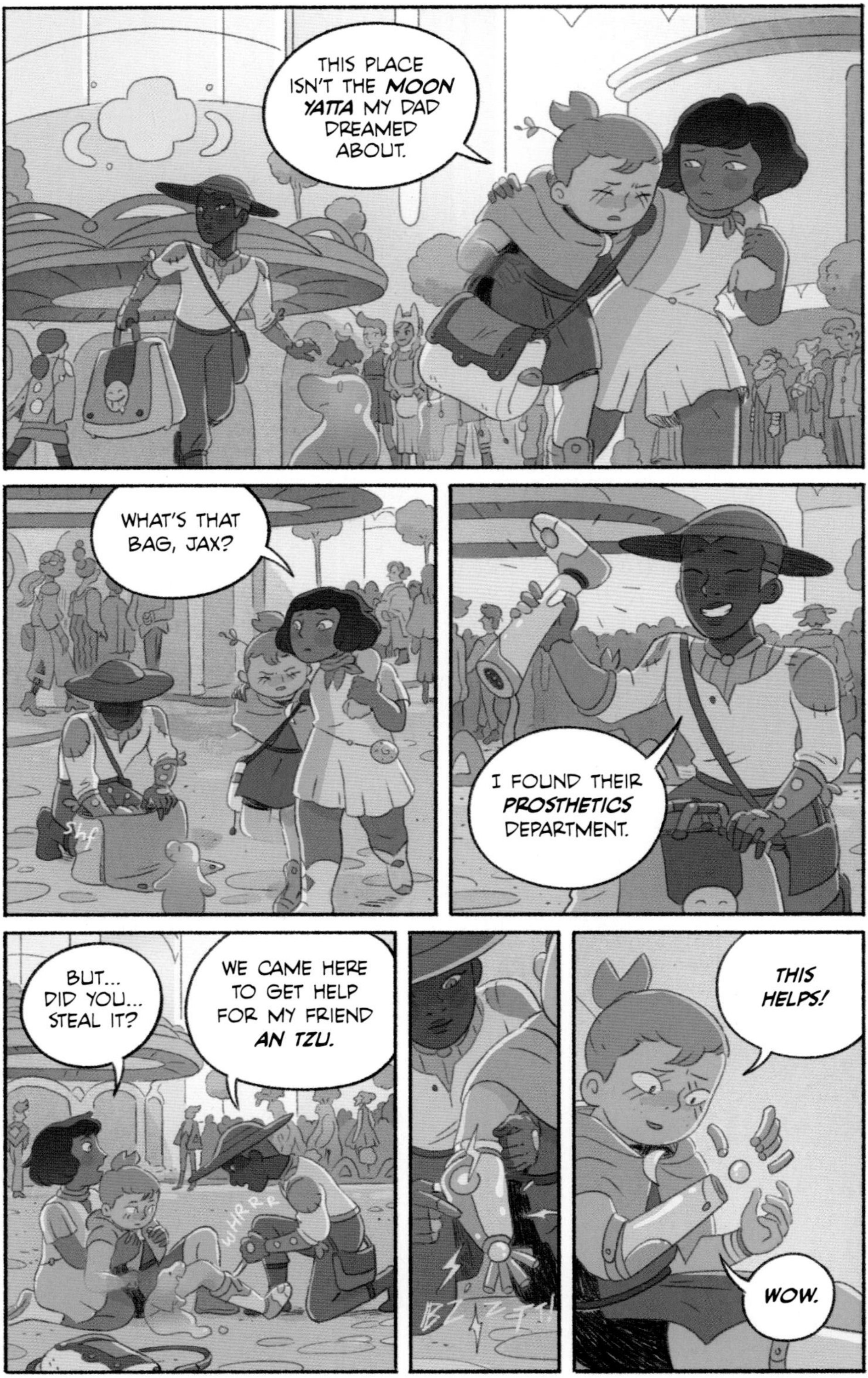
THIS PLACE ISN'T THE *MOON YATTA* MY DAD DREAMED ABOUT.
WHAT'S THAT BAG, JAX?
shf
I FOUND THEIR *PROSTHETICS* DEPARTMENT.
BUT... DID YOU... STEAL IT?
WE CAME HERE TO GET HELP FOR MY FRIEND *AN TZU.*
WHRRR
*THIS HELPS!*
*WOW.*

## Chapter 4
# THE STOAK BROTHER

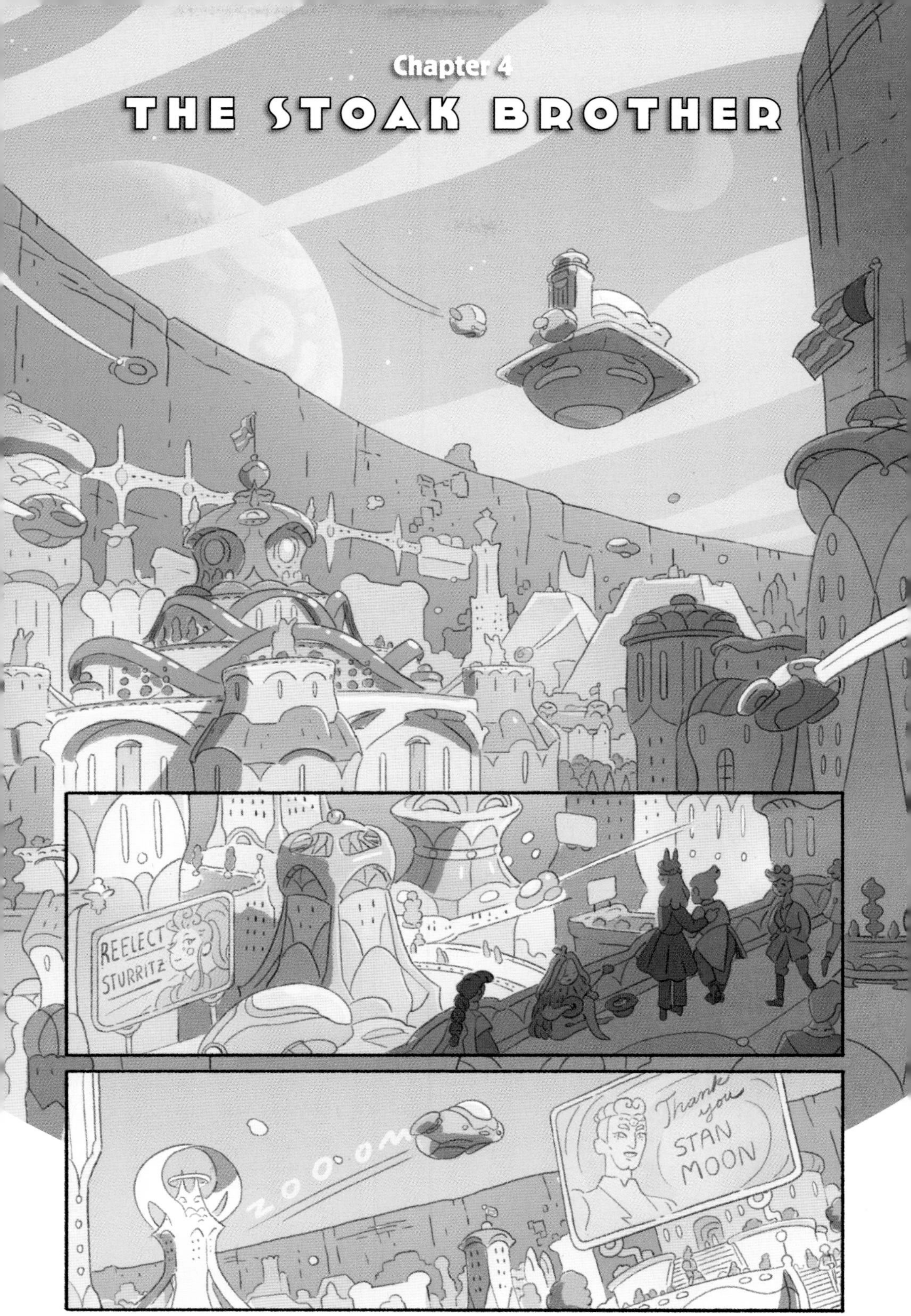

REELECT STURRITZ
ZOOOM
Thank you STAN MOON

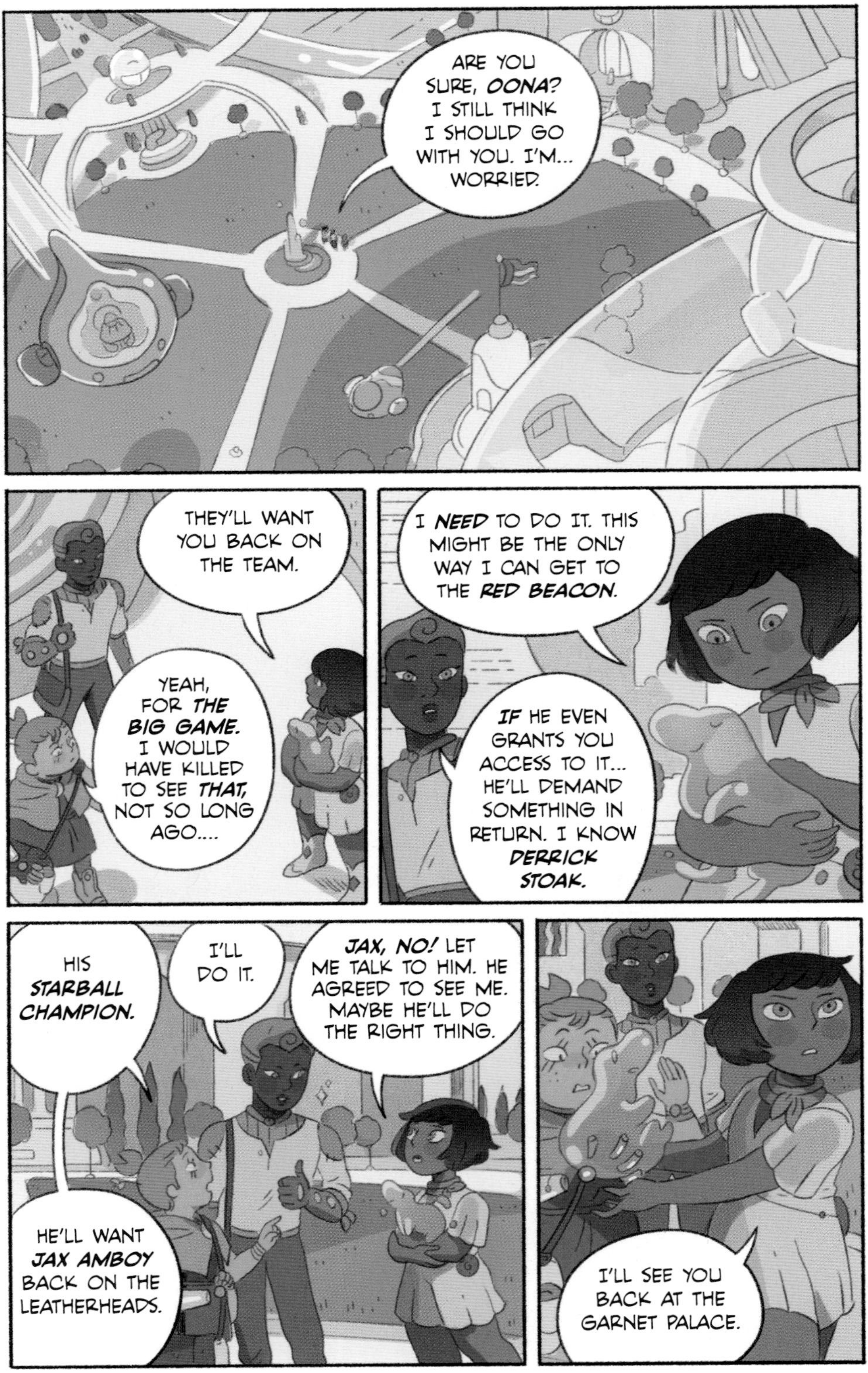
ARE YOU SURE, OONA? I STILL THINK I SHOULD GO WITH YOU. I'M... WORRIED.
THEY'LL WANT YOU BACK ON THE TEAM.
YEAH, FOR THE BIG GAME. I WOULD HAVE KILLED TO SEE THAT, NOT SO LONG AGO....
I NEED TO DO IT. THIS MIGHT BE THE ONLY WAY I CAN GET TO THE RED BEACON.
IF HE EVEN GRANTS YOU ACCESS TO IT... HE'LL DEMAND SOMETHING IN RETURN. I KNOW DERRICK STOAK.
HIS STARBALL CHAMPION.
HE'LL WANT JAX AMBOY BACK ON THE LEATHERHEADS.
I'LL DO IT.
JAX, NO! LET ME TALK TO HIM. HE AGREED TO SEE ME. MAYBE HE'LL DO THE RIGHT THING.
I'LL SEE YOU BACK AT THE GARNET PALACE.

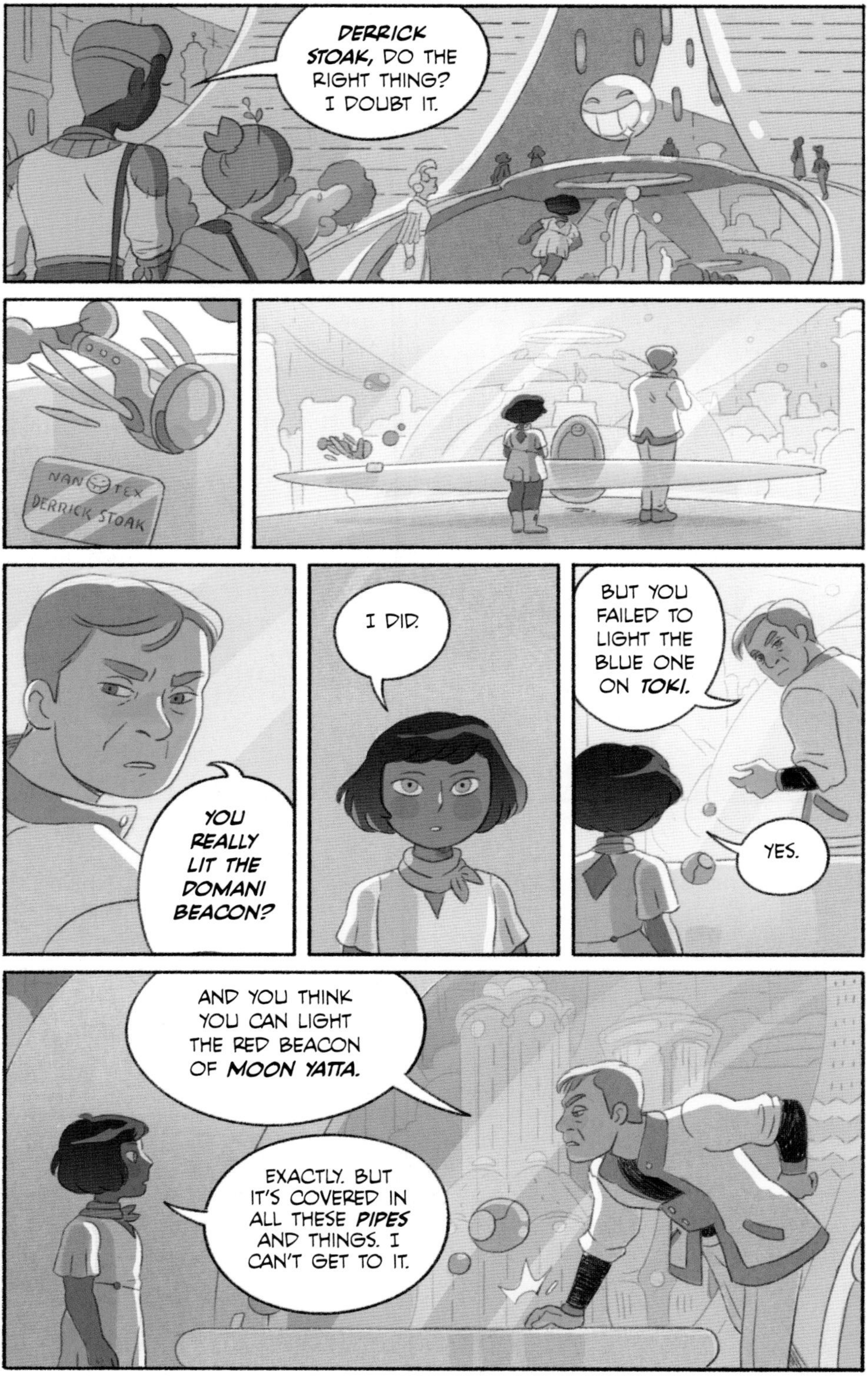
DERRICK STOAK, DO THE RIGHT THING? I DOUBT IT.
NANOTEX
DERRICK STOAK
YOU REALLY LIT THE DOMANI BEACON?
I DID.
BUT YOU FAILED TO LIGHT THE BLUE ONE ON TOKI.
YES.
AND YOU THINK YOU CAN LIGHT THE RED BEACON OF MOON YATTA.
EXACTLY. BUT IT'S COVERED IN ALL THESE PIPES AND THINGS. I CAN'T GET TO IT.

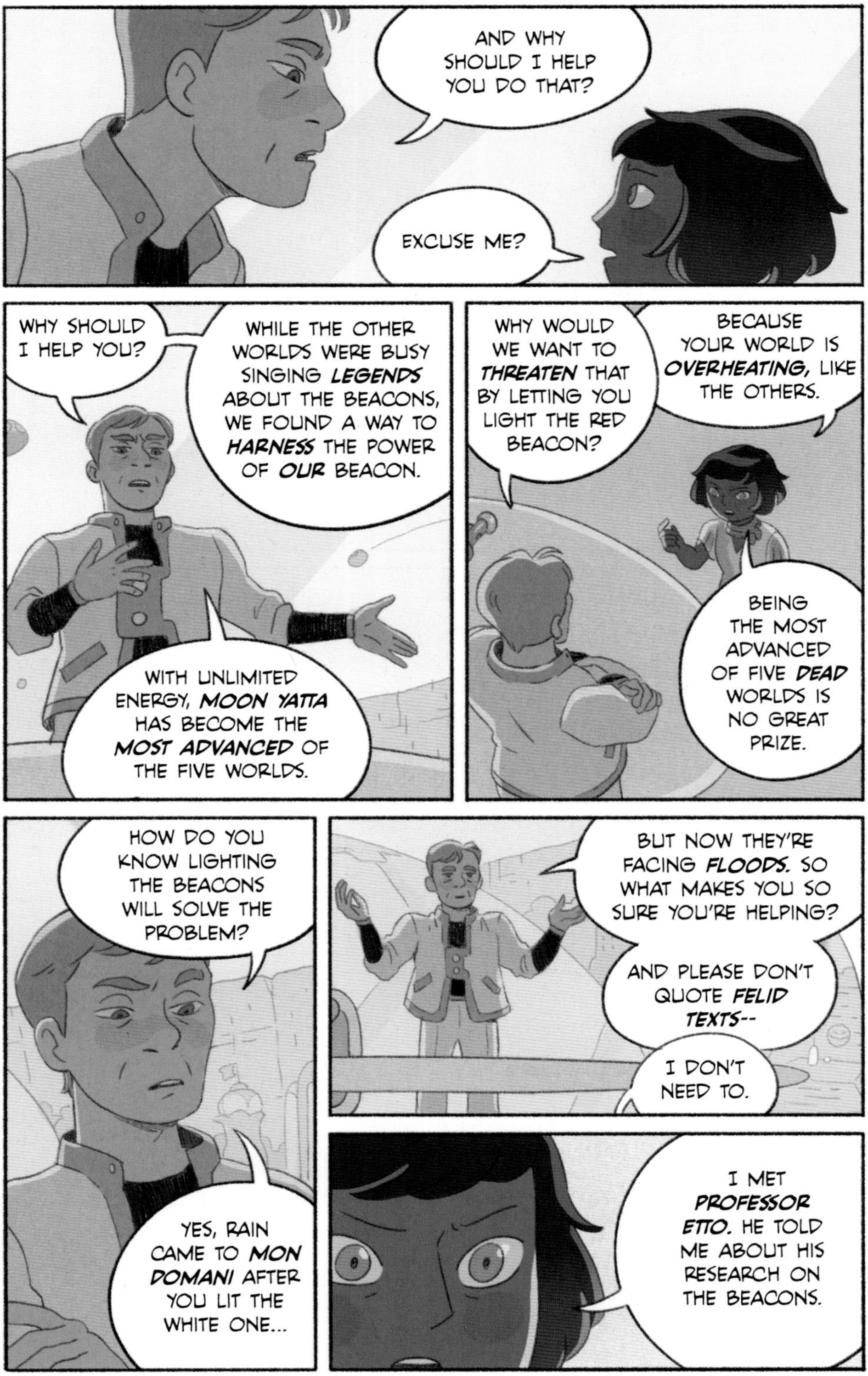
AND WHY SHOULD I HELP YOU DO THAT?
EXCUSE ME?
WHY SHOULD I HELP YOU?
WHILE THE OTHER WORLDS WERE BUSY SINGING LEGENDS ABOUT THE BEACONS, WE FOUND A WAY TO HARNESS THE POWER OF OUR BEACON.
WITH UNLIMITED ENERGY, MOON YATTA HAS BECOME THE MOST ADVANCED OF THE FIVE WORLDS.
WHY WOULD WE WANT TO THREATEN THAT BY LETTING YOU LIGHT THE RED BEACON?
BECAUSE YOUR WORLD IS OVERHEATING, LIKE THE OTHERS.
BEING THE MOST ADVANCED OF FIVE DEAD WORLDS IS NO GREAT PRIZE.
HOW DO YOU KNOW LIGHTING THE BEACONS WILL SOLVE THE PROBLEM?
YES, RAIN CAME TO MON DOMANI AFTER YOU LIT THE WHITE ONE...
BUT NOW THEY'RE FACING FLOODS. SO WHAT MAKES YOU SO SURE YOU'RE HELPING?
AND PLEASE DON'T QUOTE FELID TEXTS--
I DON'T NEED TO.
I MET PROFESSOR ETTO. HE TOLD ME ABOUT HIS RESEARCH ON THE BEACONS.

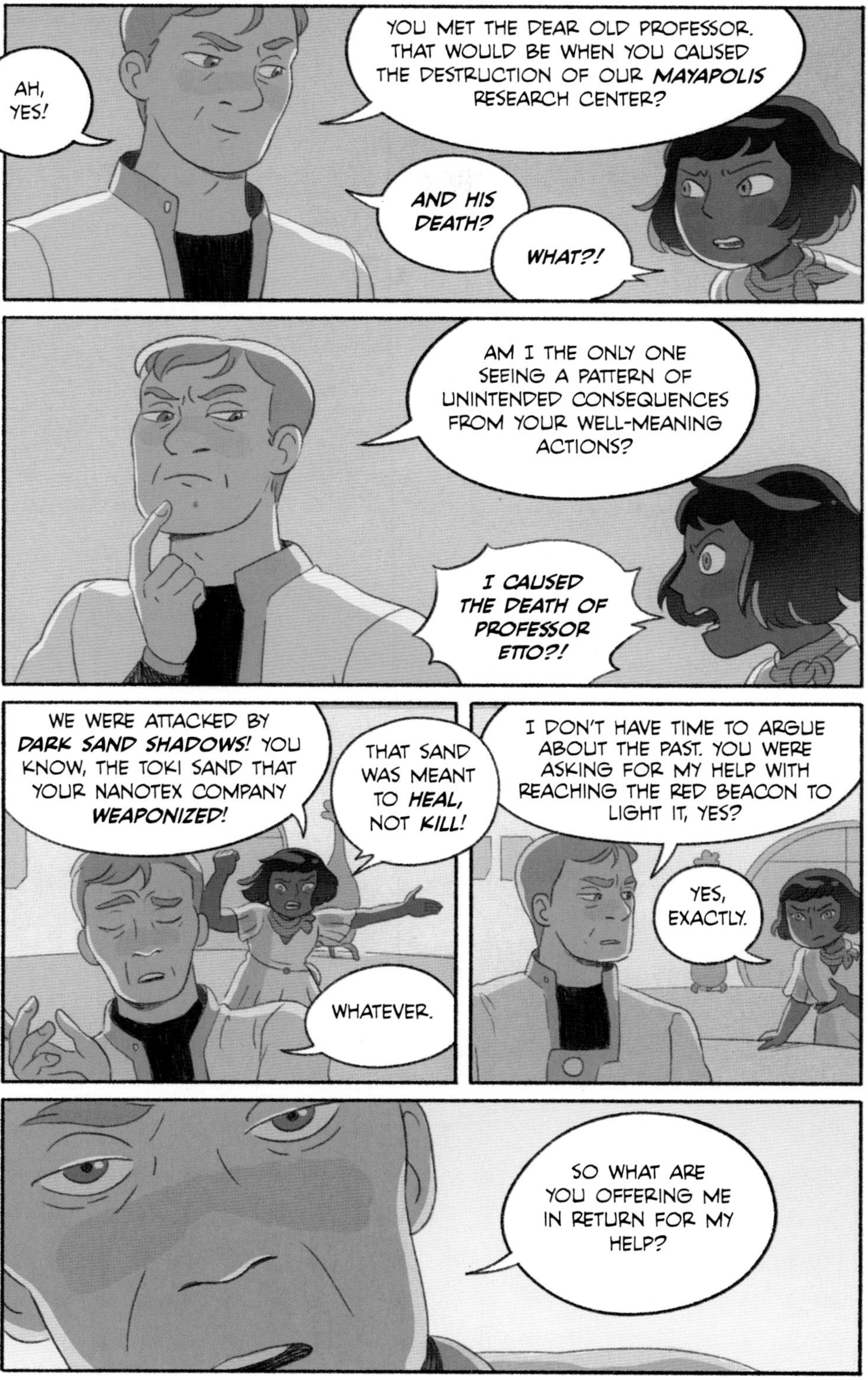
AH, YES!
YOU MET THE DEAR OLD PROFESSOR. THAT WOULD BE WHEN YOU CAUSED THE DESTRUCTION OF OUR *MAYAPOLIS* RESEARCH CENTER?
*AND HIS DEATH?*
*WHAT?!*
AM I THE ONLY ONE SEEING A PATTERN OF UNINTENDED CONSEQUENCES FROM YOUR WELL-MEANING ACTIONS?
*I CAUSED THE DEATH OF PROFESSOR ETTO?!*
WE WERE ATTACKED BY *DARK SAND SHADOWS!* YOU KNOW, THE TOKI SAND THAT YOUR NANOTEX COMPANY *WEAPONIZED!*
THAT SAND WAS MEANT TO *HEAL,* NOT *KILL!*
WHATEVER.
I DON'T HAVE TIME TO ARGUE ABOUT THE PAST. YOU WERE ASKING FOR MY HELP WITH REACHING THE RED BEACON TO LIGHT IT, YES?
YES, EXACTLY.
SO WHAT ARE YOU OFFERING ME IN RETURN FOR MY HELP?

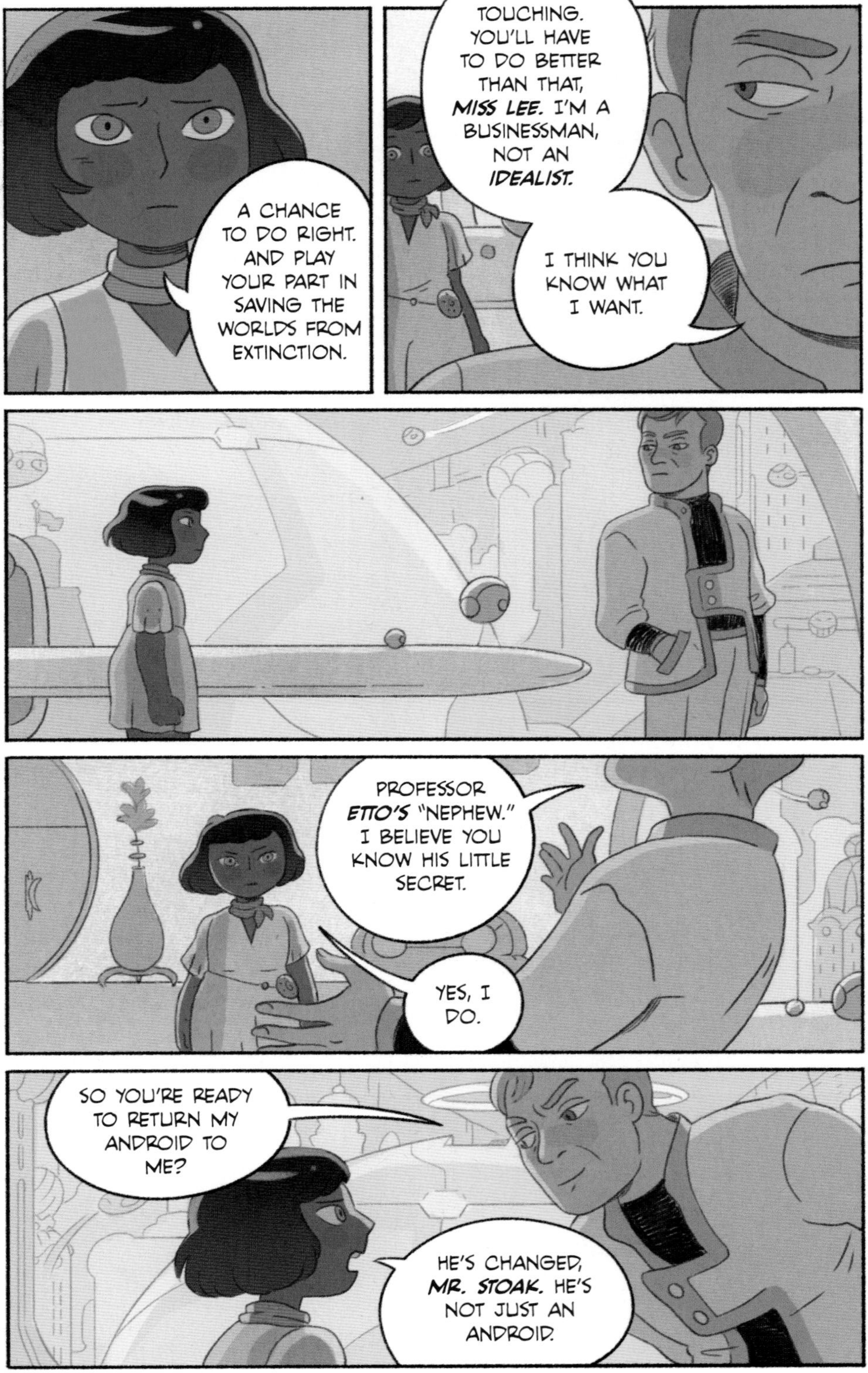
A CHANCE TO DO RIGHT. AND PLAY YOUR PART IN SAVING THE WORLDS FROM EXTINCTION.
HOW TOUCHING. YOU'LL HAVE TO DO BETTER THAN THAT, MISS LEE. I'M A BUSINESSMAN, NOT AN IDEALIST.
I THINK YOU KNOW WHAT I WANT.
PROFESSOR ETTO'S "NEPHEW." I BELIEVE YOU KNOW HIS LITTLE SECRET.
YES, I DO.
SO YOU'RE READY TO RETURN MY ANDROID TO ME?
HE'S CHANGED, MR. STOAK. HE'S NOT JUST AN ANDROID.

I KNOW! HE'S SO MUCH MORE! I MADE HIM INTO A *STAR!*

NO, NO, THIS IS SOMETHING ELSE, MR. STOAK.

A SALASSI SPIRIT LIFE JOINED HIM.

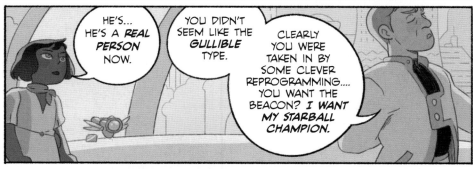

HE'S... HE'S A *REAL PERSON* NOW.

YOU DIDN'T SEEM LIKE THE *GULLIBLE* TYPE.

CLEARLY YOU WERE TAKEN IN BY SOME CLEVER REPROGRAMMING.... YOU WANT THE BEACON? *I WANT MY STARBALL CHAMPION.*

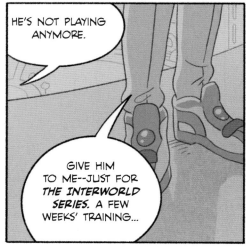

HE'S NOT PLAYING ANYMORE.

GIVE HIM TO ME--JUST FOR *THE INTERWORLD SERIES.* A FEW WEEKS' TRAINING...

...A FEW GAMES. AND *THE BEACON'S ALL YOURS* TO DO YOUR *SAND DANCING THING.*

HOW DO I KNOW YOU'LL KEEP YOUR WORD?

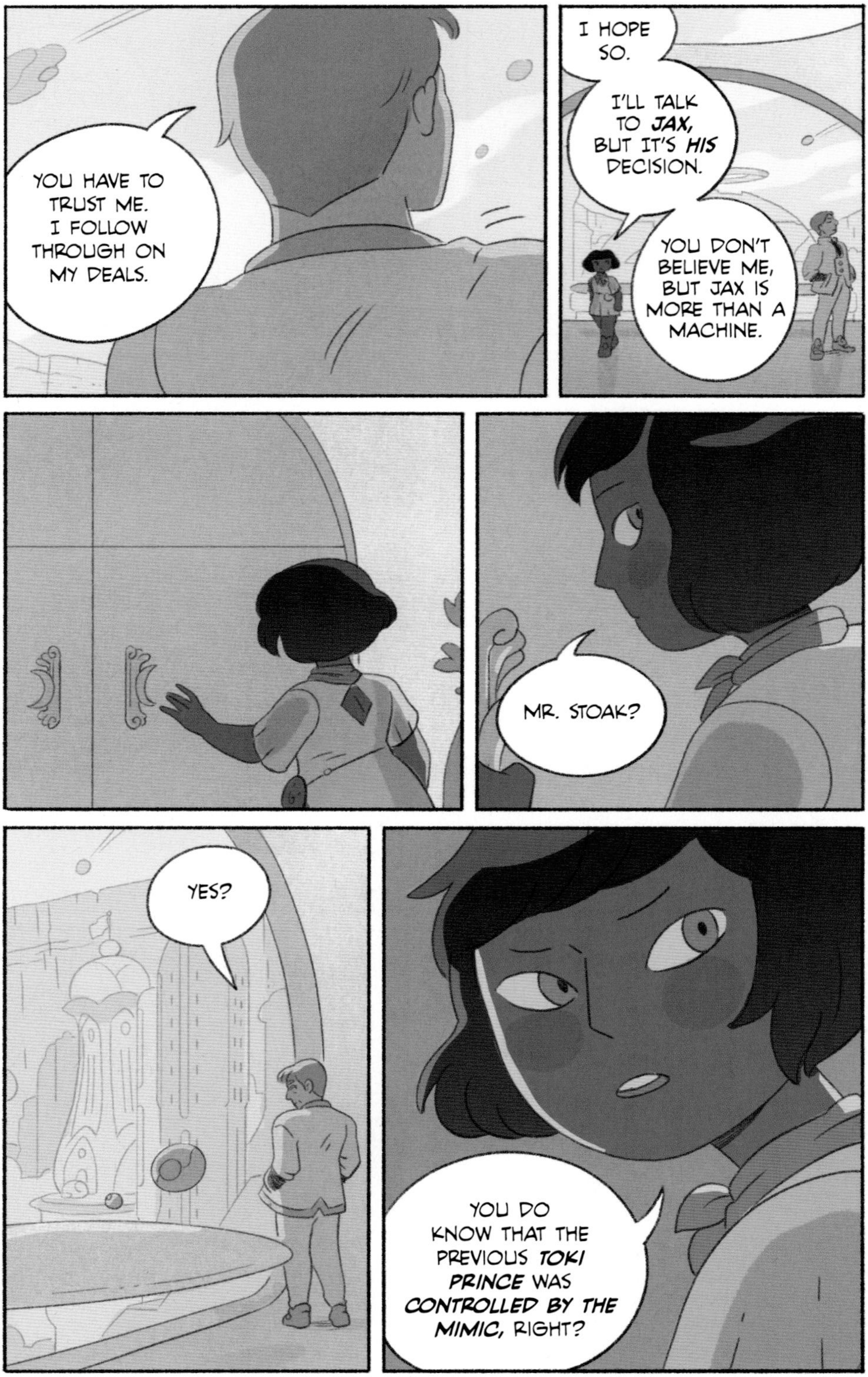

YOU HAVE TO TRUST ME. I FOLLOW THROUGH ON MY DEALS.
I HOPE SO.
I'LL TALK TO JAX, BUT IT'S HIS DECISION.
YOU DON'T BELIEVE ME, BUT JAX IS MORE THAN A MACHINE.
MR. STOAK?
YES?
YOU DO KNOW THAT THE PREVIOUS TOKI PRINCE WAS CONTROLLED BY THE MIMIC, RIGHT?

OH, DON'T TELL ME YOU BELIEVE THOSE *OLD WIVES' TALES* ABOUT THE...

*THE MIMIC...*

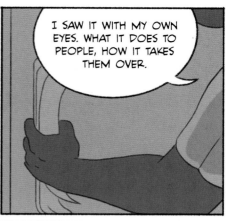

I SAW IT WITH MY OWN EYES. WHAT IT DOES TO PEOPLE, HOW IT TAKES THEM OVER.

WHY ARE YOU TELLING ME THIS?

IT'S HERE ON *MOON YATTA* TOO. CLOSER THAN YOU THINK.

IF YOU CARE ABOUT YOUR HOME WORLD, YOU'LL HELP ME.

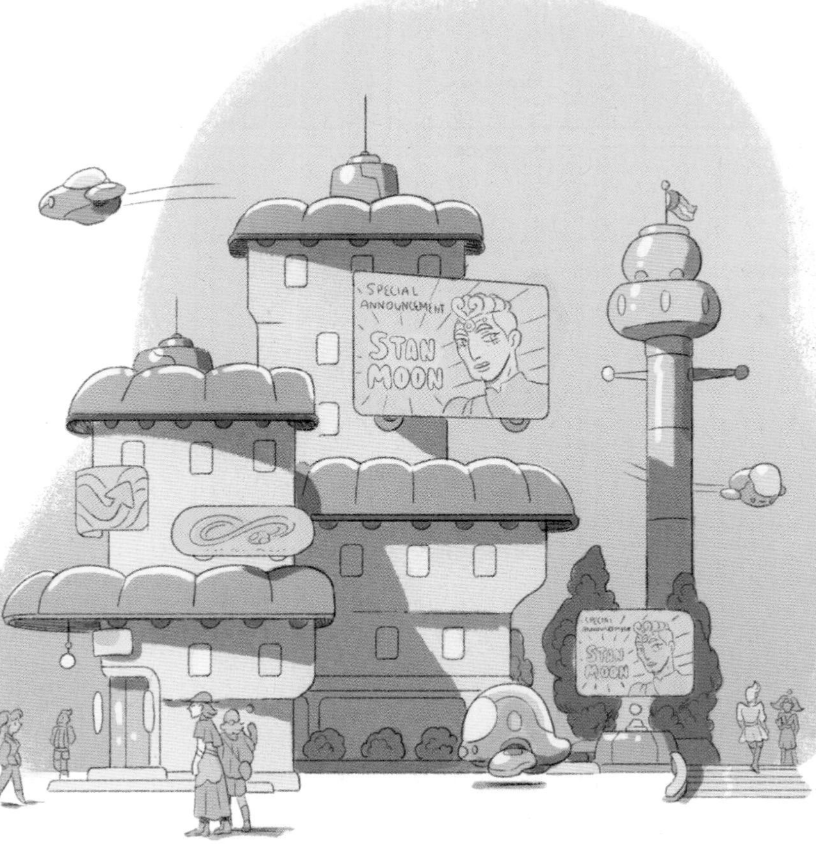
SPECIAL ANNOUNCEMENT
STAN MOON
STAN MOON

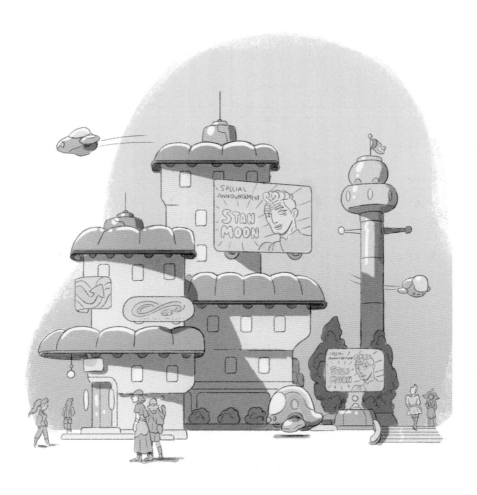

## Chapter 5

# SYSTEM OVERRIDES

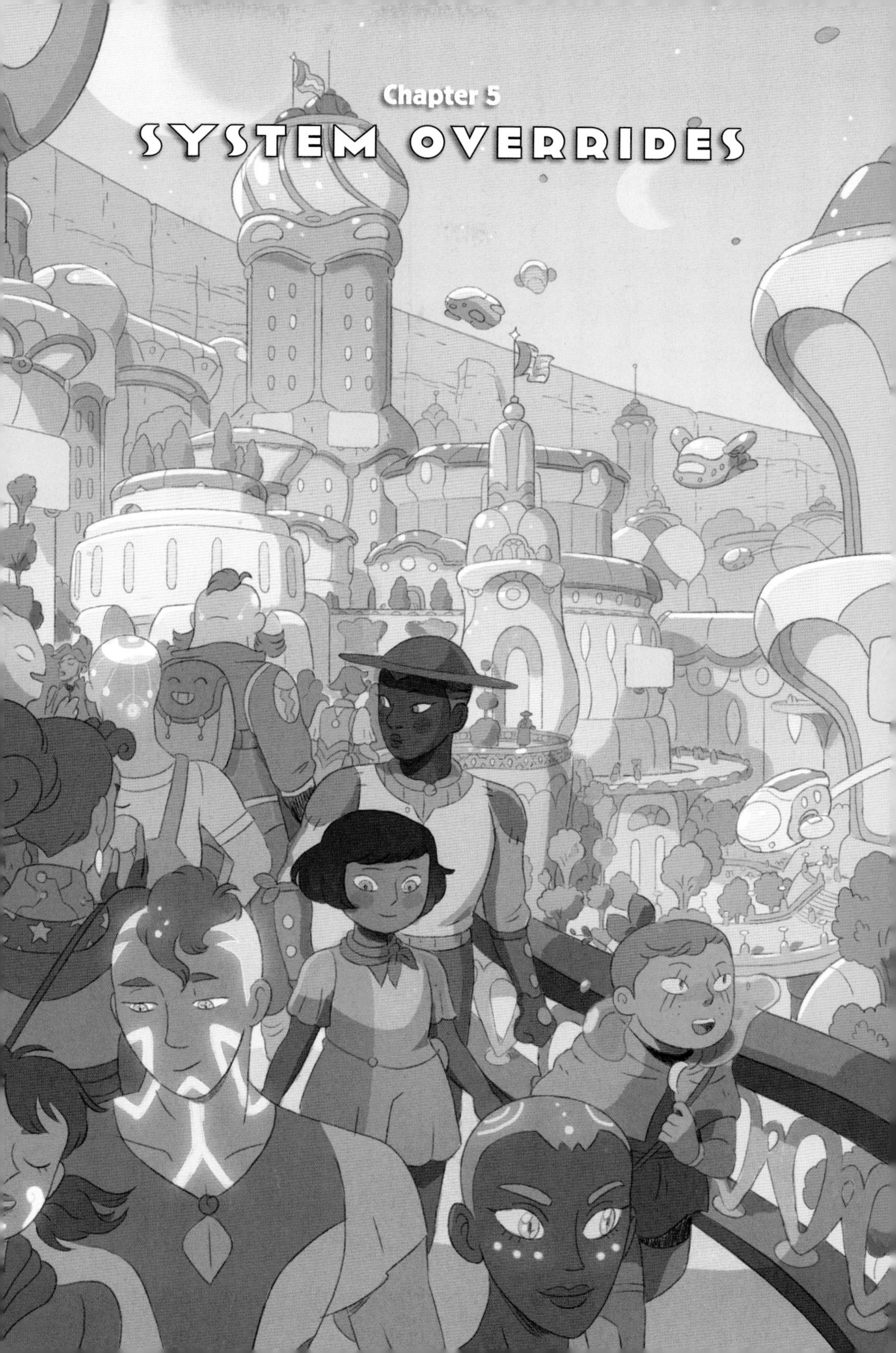

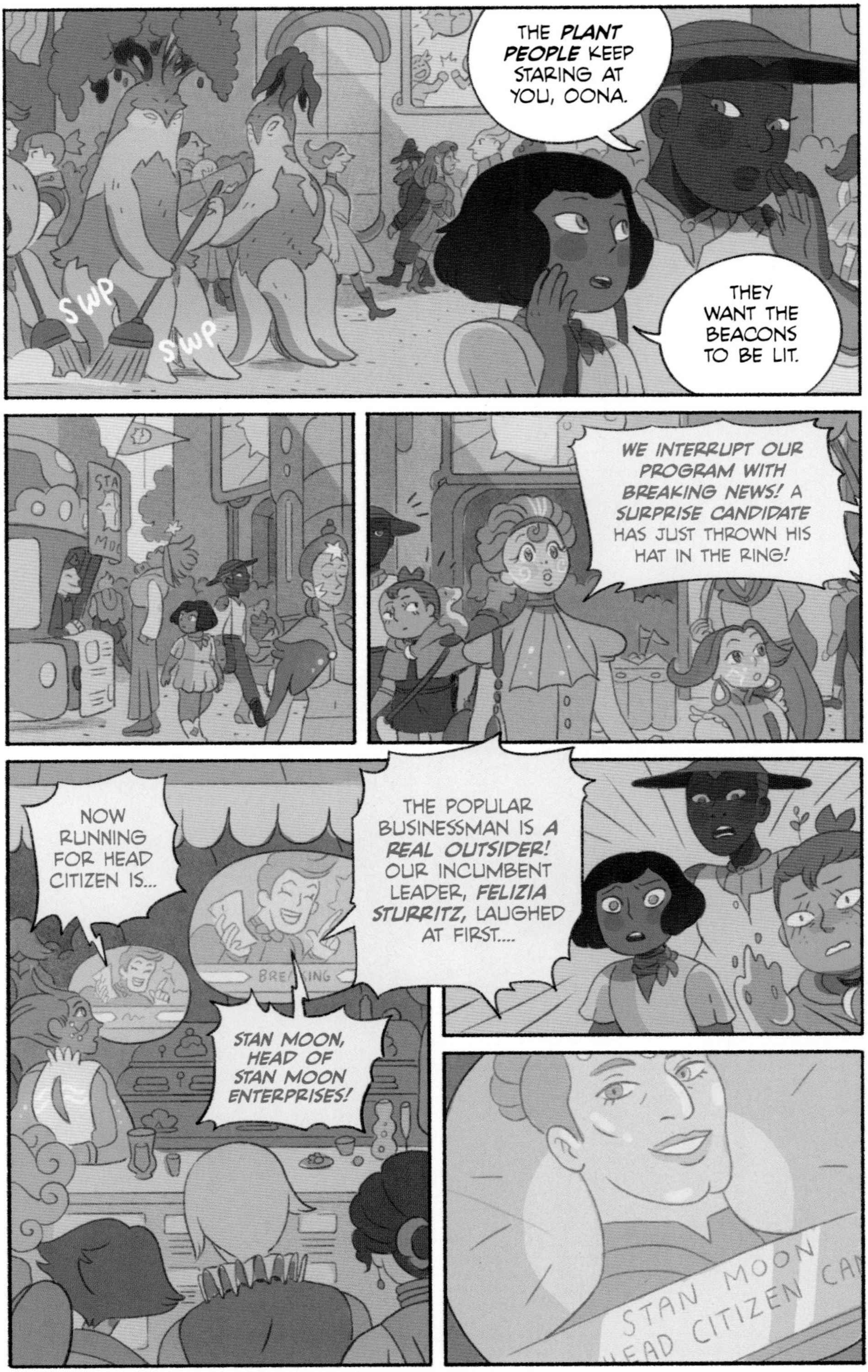
THE PLANT PEOPLE KEEP STARING AT YOU, OONA.
THEY WANT THE BEACONS TO BE LIT.
SWP
SWP
WE INTERRUPT OUR PROGRAM WITH BREAKING NEWS! A SURPRISE CANDIDATE HAS JUST THROWN HIS HAT IN THE RING!
NOW RUNNING FOR HEAD CITIZEN IS...
STAN MOON, HEAD OF STAN MOON ENTERPRISES!
THE POPULAR BUSINESSMAN IS A REAL OUTSIDER! OUR INCUMBENT LEADER, FELIZIA STURRITZ, LAUGHED AT FIRST....
STAN MOON
HEAD CITIZEN CA

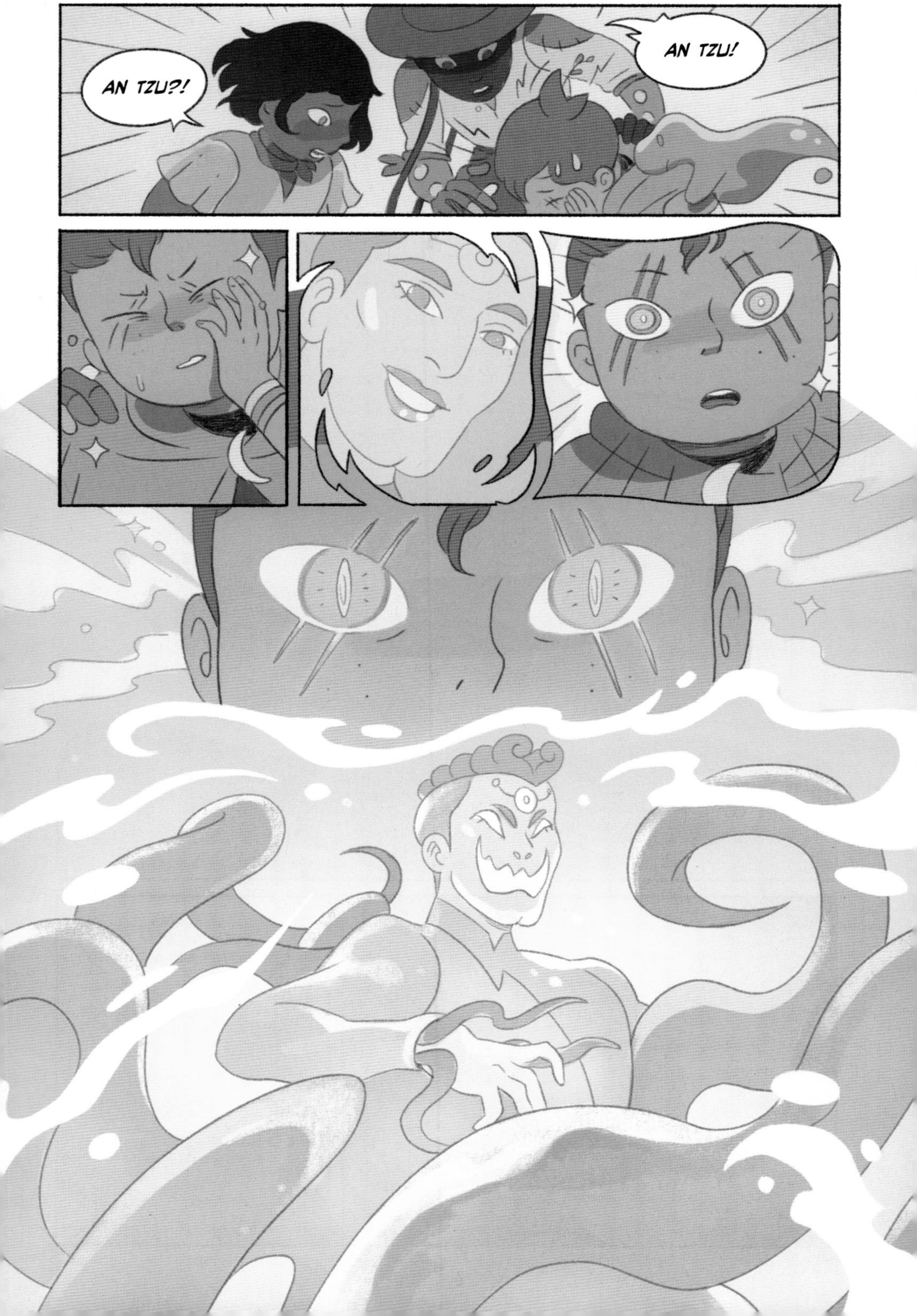
AN TZU?!
AN TZU!

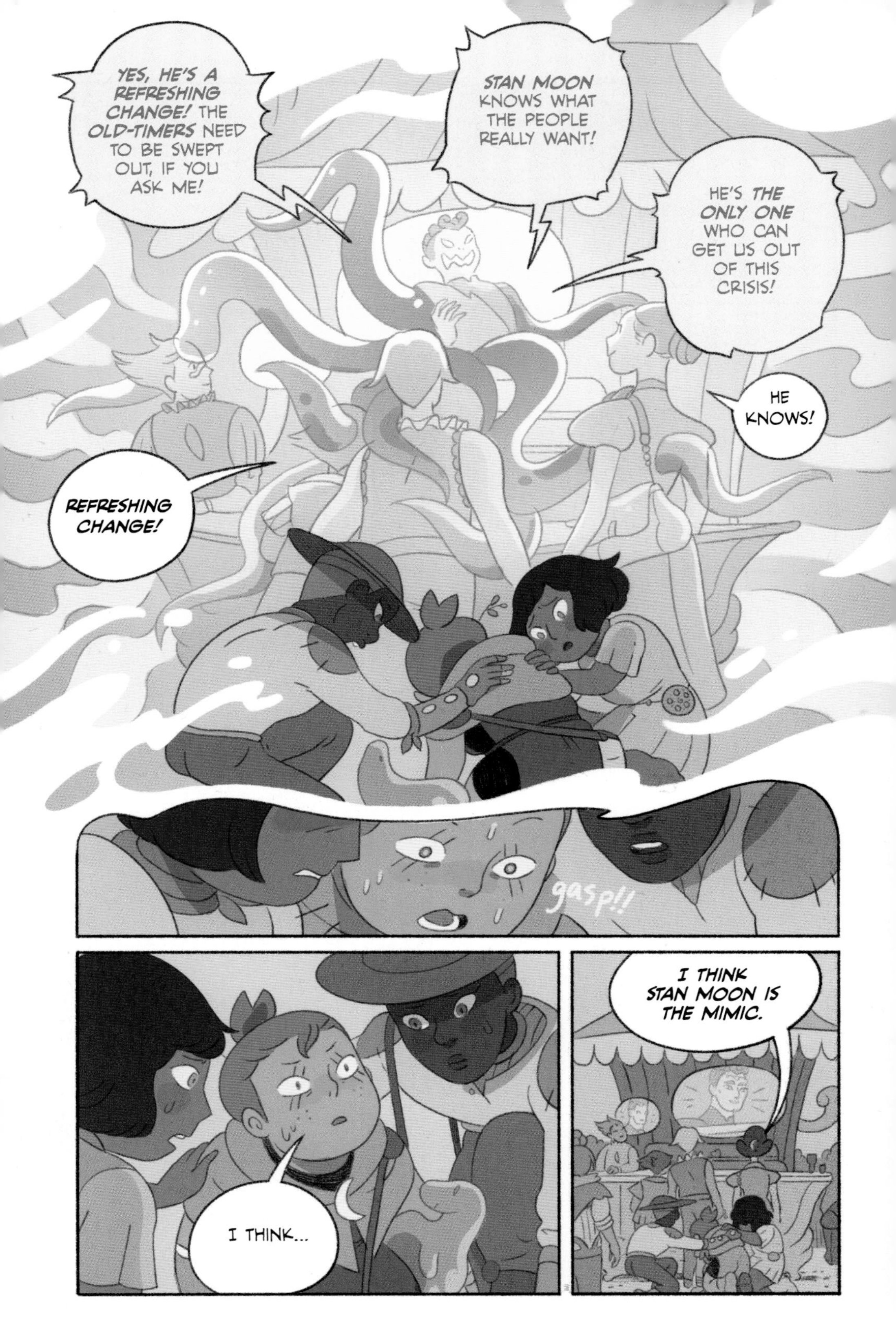
YES, HE'S A REFRESHING CHANGE! THE OLD-TIMERS NEED TO BE SWEPT OUT, IF YOU ASK ME!
STAN MOON KNOWS WHAT THE PEOPLE REALLY WANT!
HE'S THE ONLY ONE WHO CAN GET US OUT OF THIS CRISIS!
HE KNOWS!
REFRESHING CHANGE!
gasp!!
I THINK...
I THINK STAN MOON IS THE MIMIC.

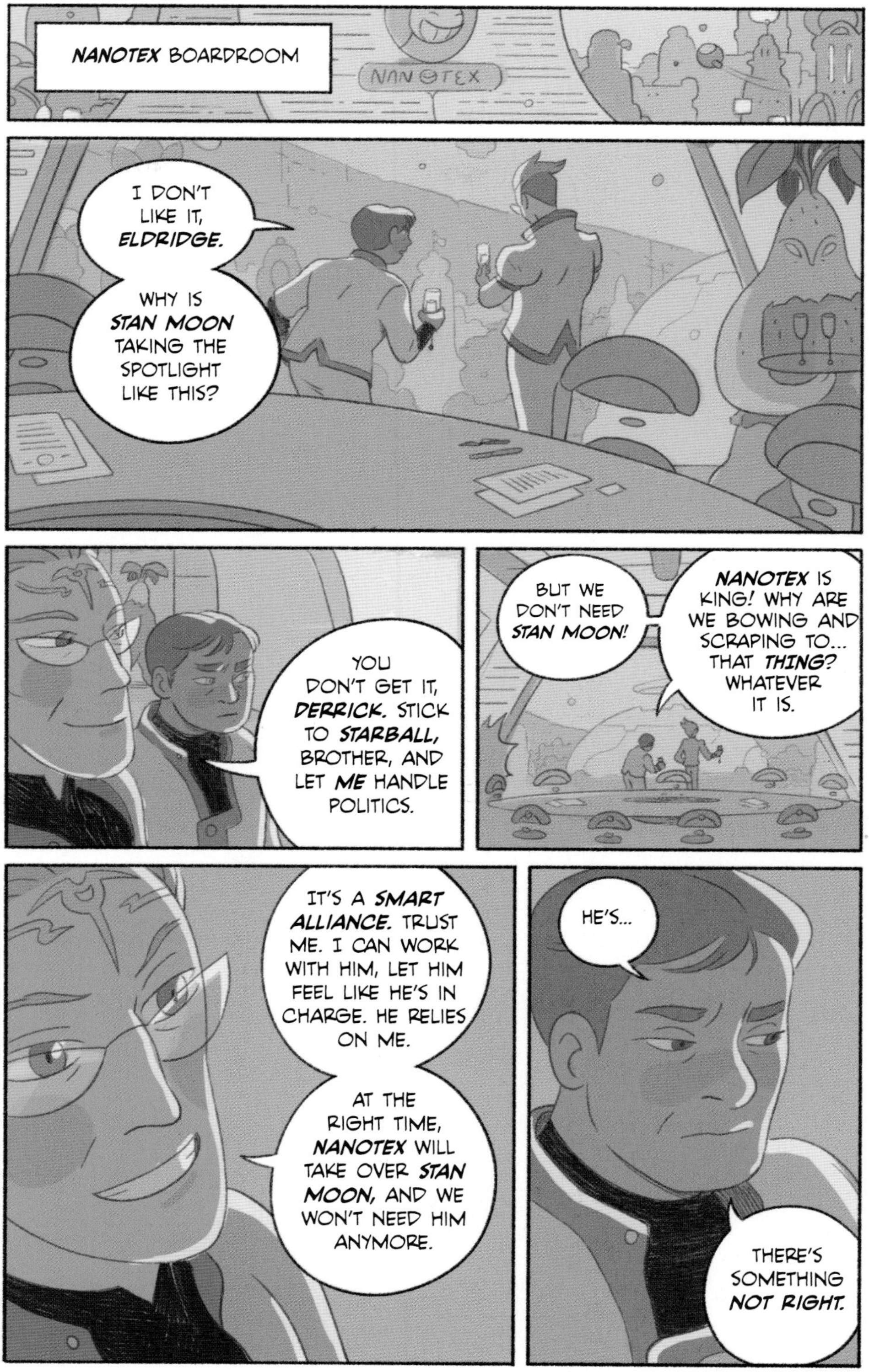
NANOTEX BOARDROOM
NANOTEX
I DON'T LIKE IT, ELDRIDGE.
WHY IS STAN MOON TAKING THE SPOTLIGHT LIKE THIS?
YOU DON'T GET IT, DERRICK. STICK TO STARBALL, BROTHER, AND LET ME HANDLE POLITICS.
BUT WE DON'T NEED STAN MOON!
NANOTEX IS KING! WHY ARE WE BOWING AND SCRAPING TO... THAT THING? WHATEVER IT IS.
IT'S A SMART ALLIANCE. TRUST ME. I CAN WORK WITH HIM, LET HIM FEEL LIKE HE'S IN CHARGE. HE RELIES ON ME.
AT THE RIGHT TIME, NANOTEX WILL TAKE OVER STAN MOON, AND WE WON'T NEED HIM ANYMORE.
HE'S...
THERE'S SOMETHING NOT RIGHT.

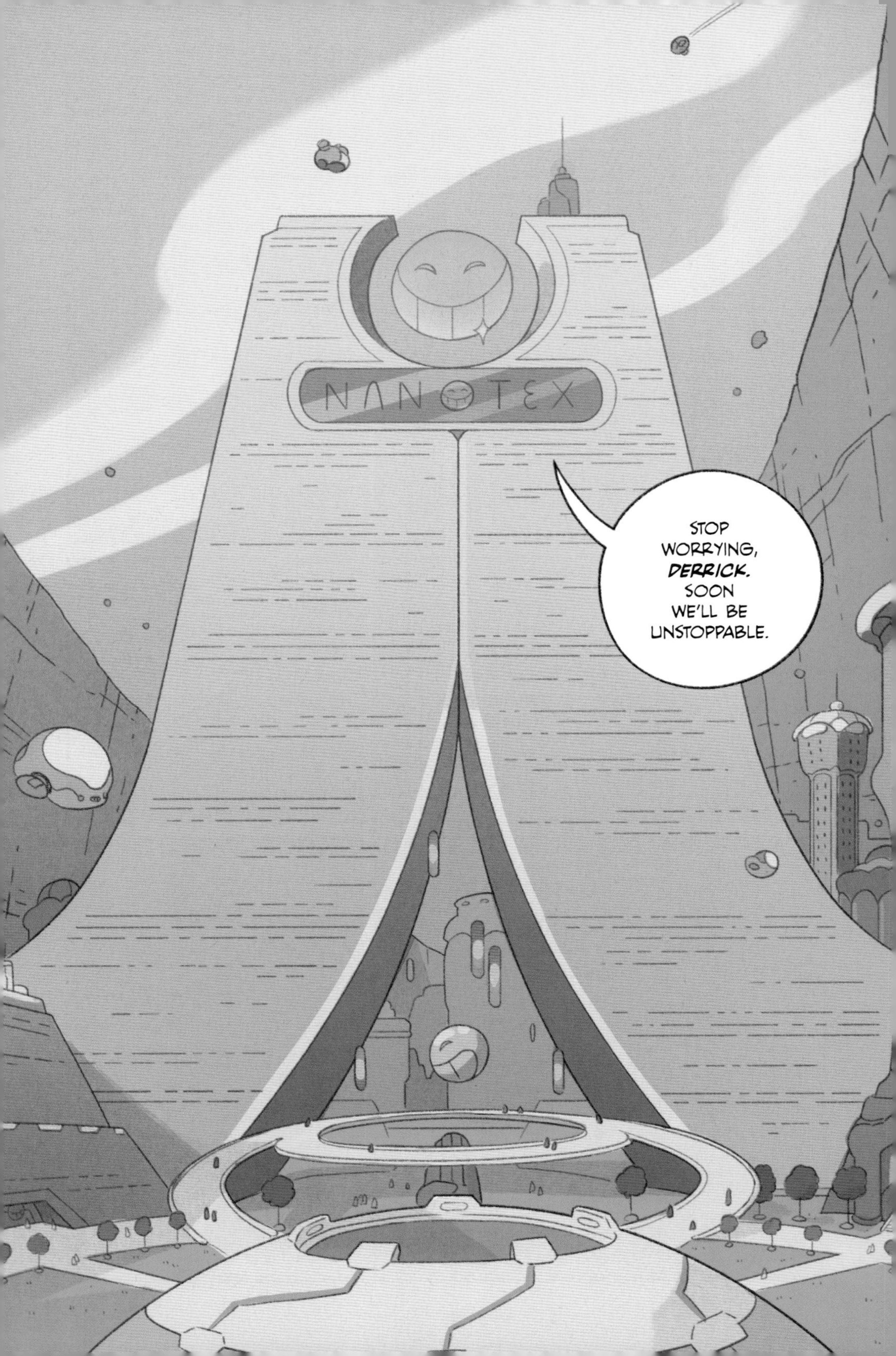
NANOTEX
STOP WORRYING, ***DERRICK.*** SOON WE'LL BE UNSTOPPABLE.

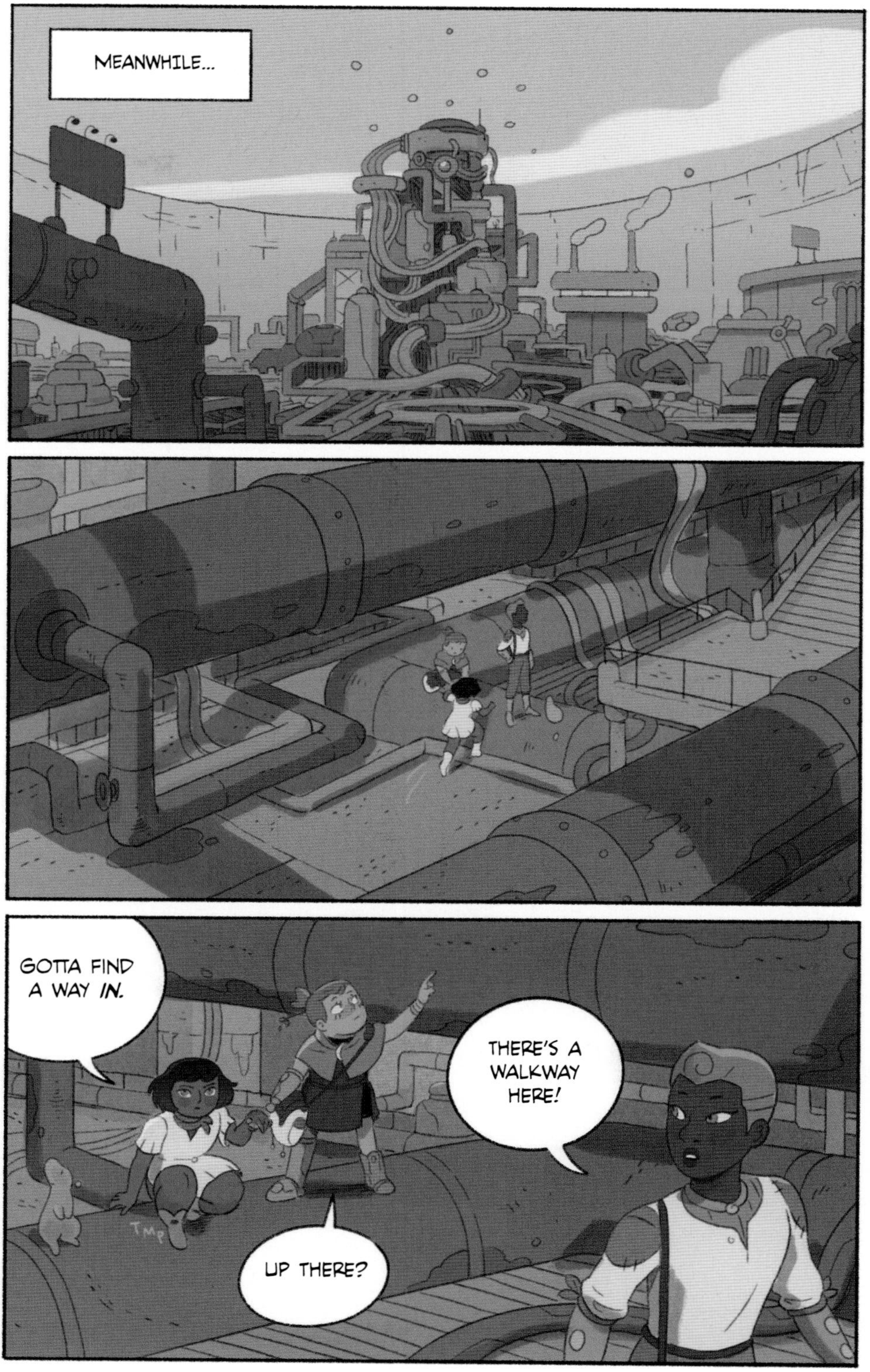
MEANWHILE...
GOTTA FIND A WAY *IN.*
THERE'S A WALKWAY HERE!
UP THERE?

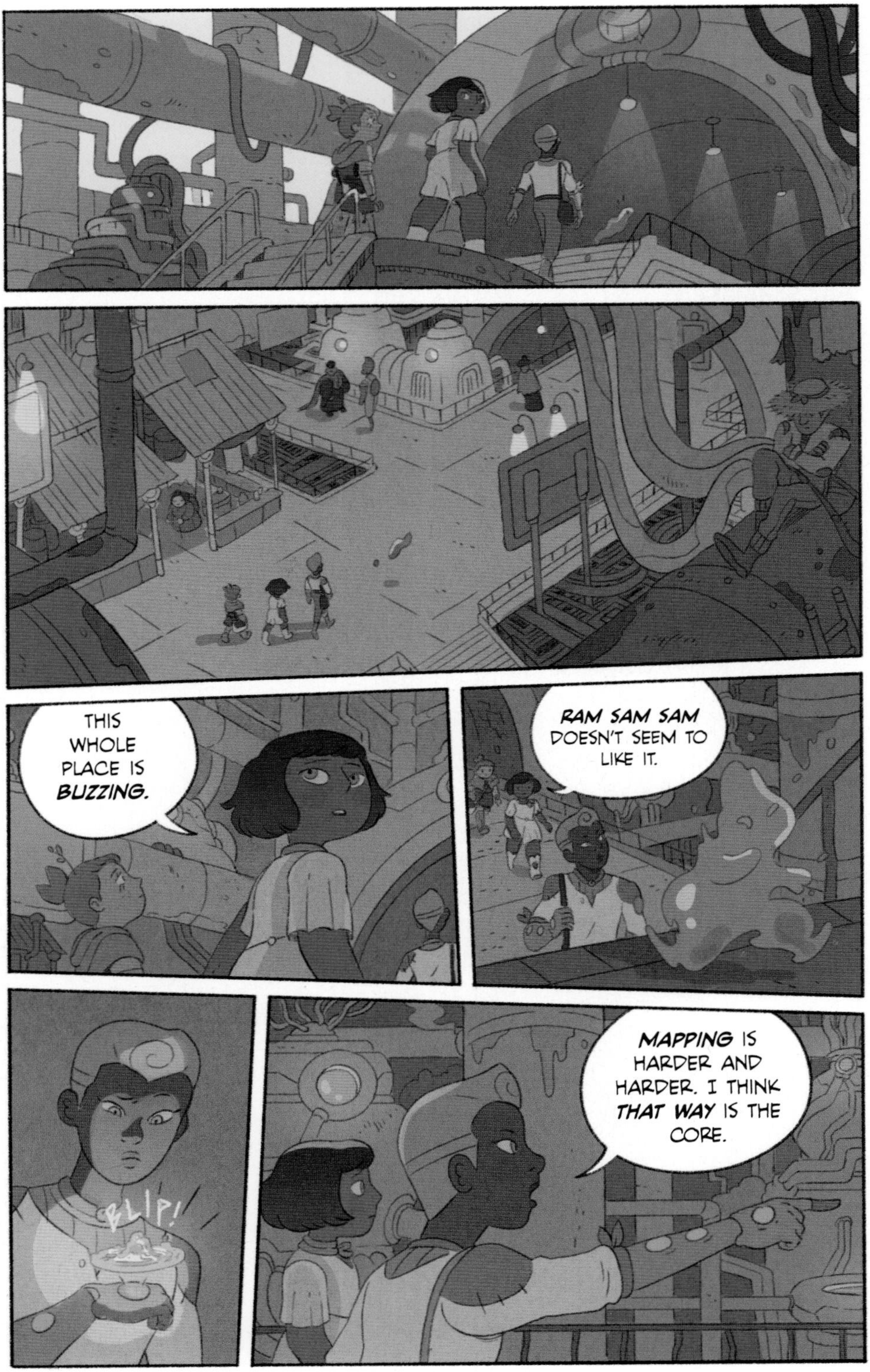
THIS WHOLE PLACE IS BUZZING.
RAM SAM SAM DOESN'T SEEM TO LIKE IT.
BLIP!
MAPPING IS HARDER AND HARDER. I THINK THAT WAY IS THE CORE.

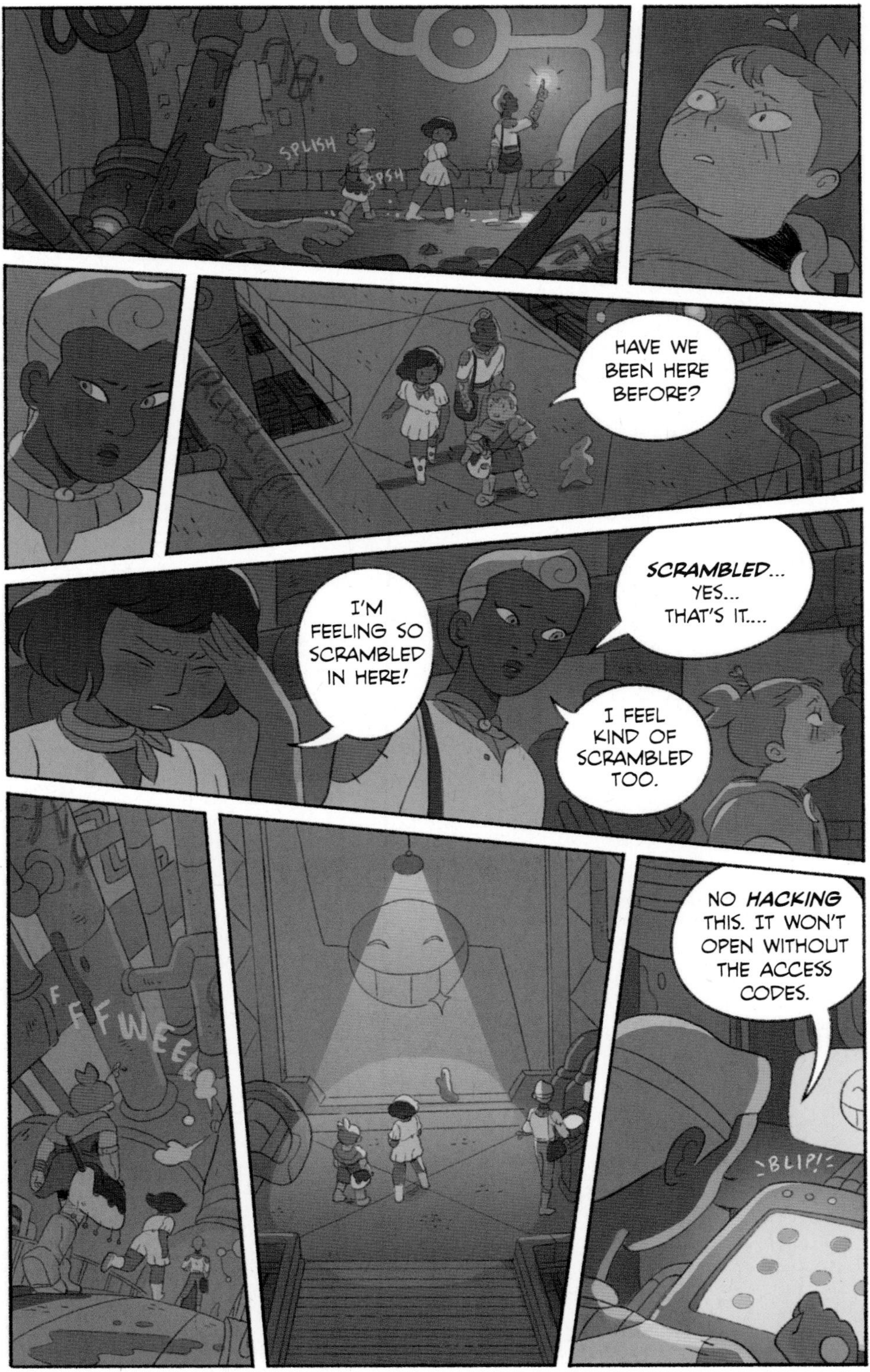
SPLISH
SPSH
HAVE WE BEEN HERE BEFORE?
I'M FEELING SO SCRAMBLED IN HERE!
SCRAMBLED... YES... THAT'S IT....
I FEEL KIND OF SCRAMBLED TOO.
FFWEEE
NO HACKING THIS. IT WON'T OPEN WITHOUT THE ACCESS CODES.
BLIP!

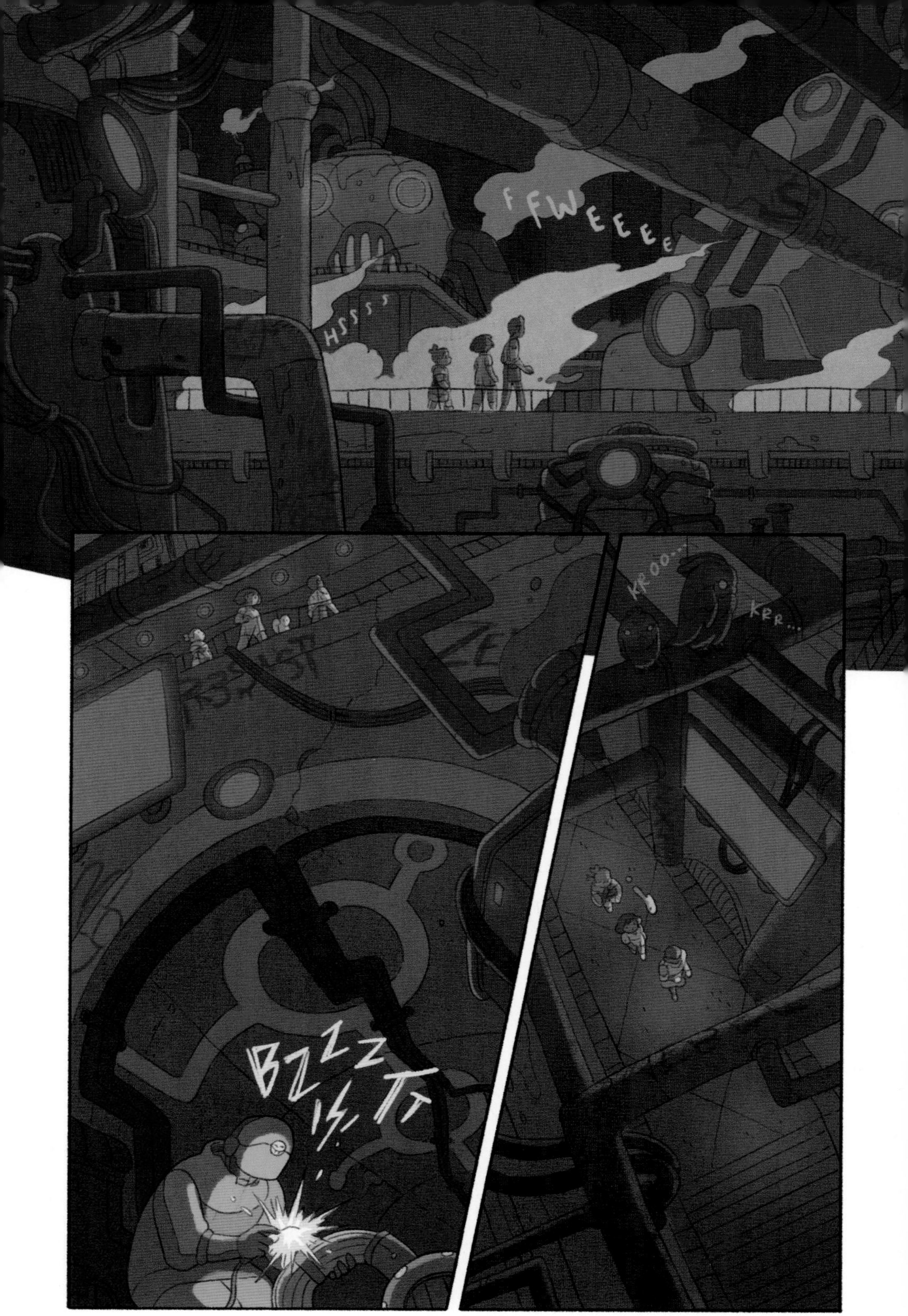
FFWEEEEE
HSSSS
KROO...
KRR...
BZZZTT

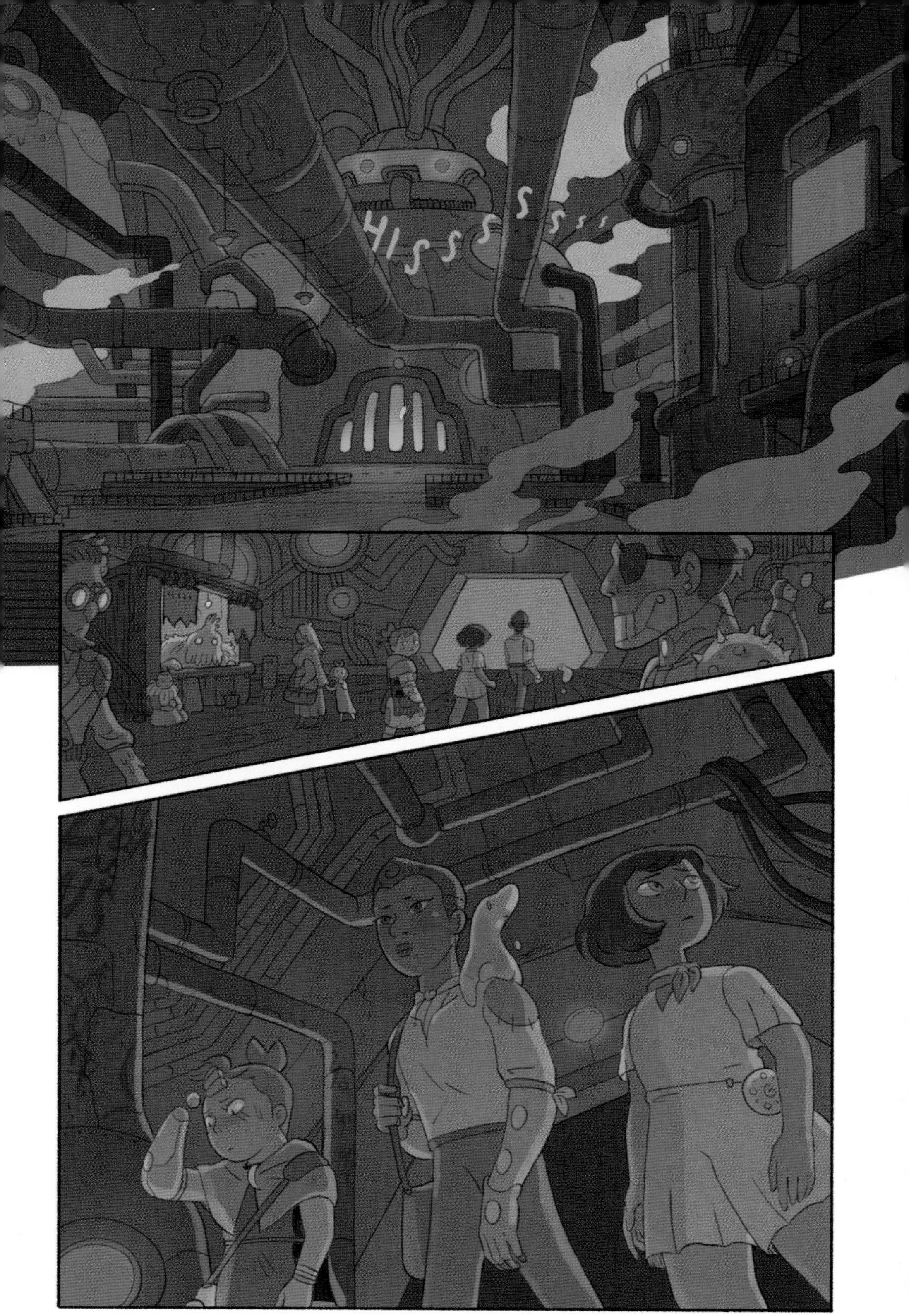
HISSSSSS

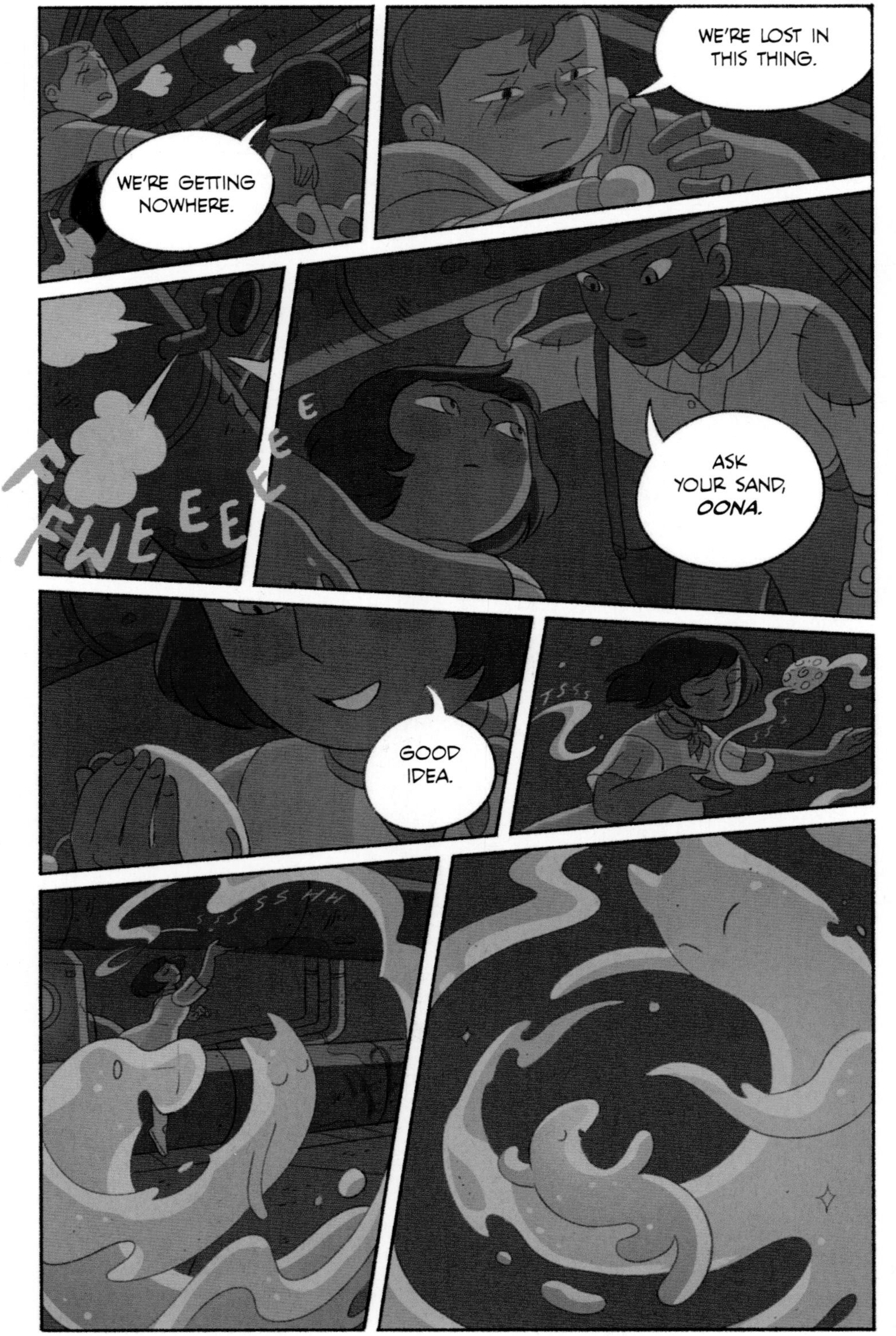
WE'RE GETTING NOWHERE.
WE'RE LOST IN THIS THING.
FWEEEEEE
ASK YOUR SAND, OONA.
GOOD IDEA.

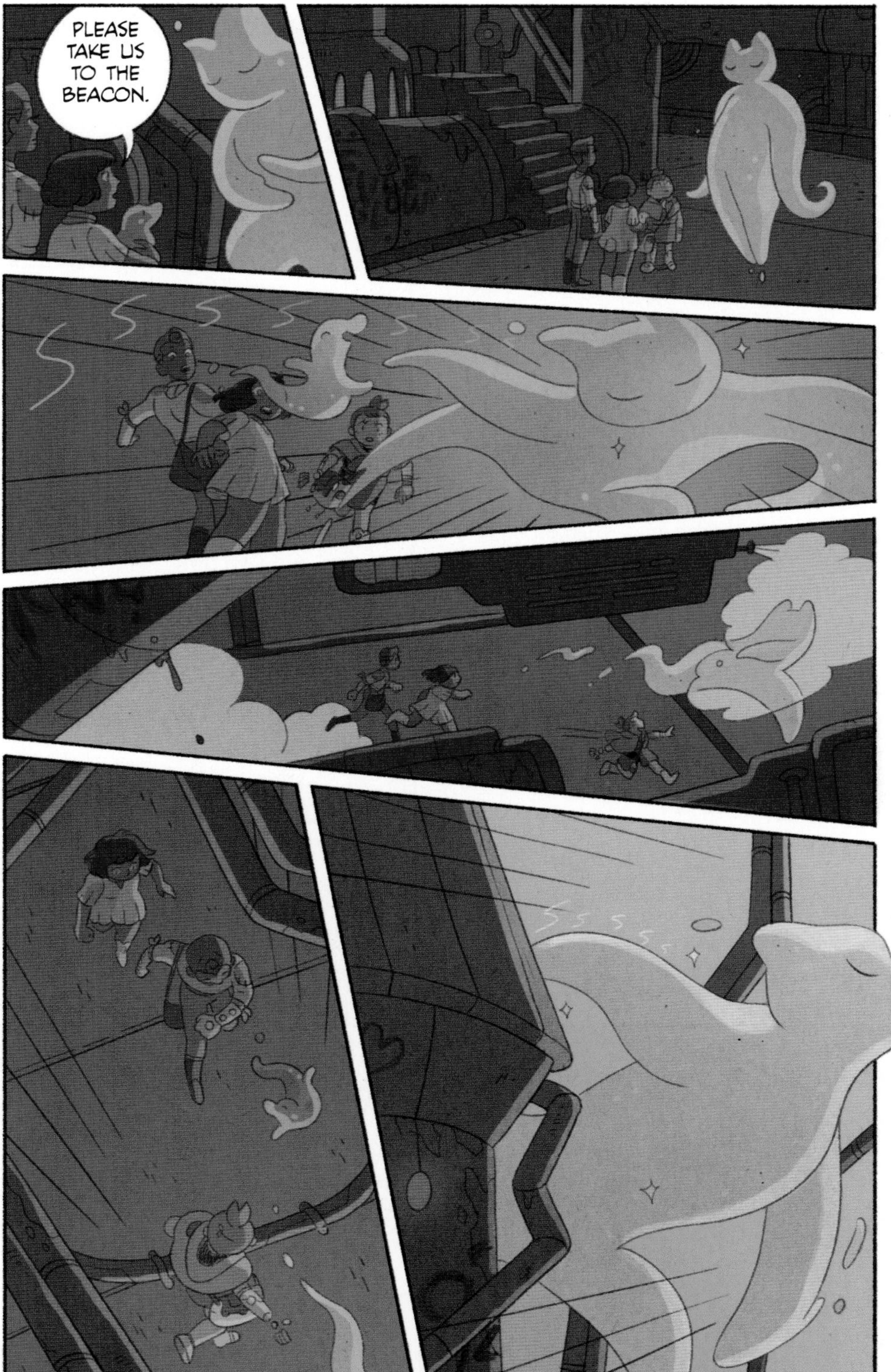
PLEASE TAKE US TO THE BEACON.

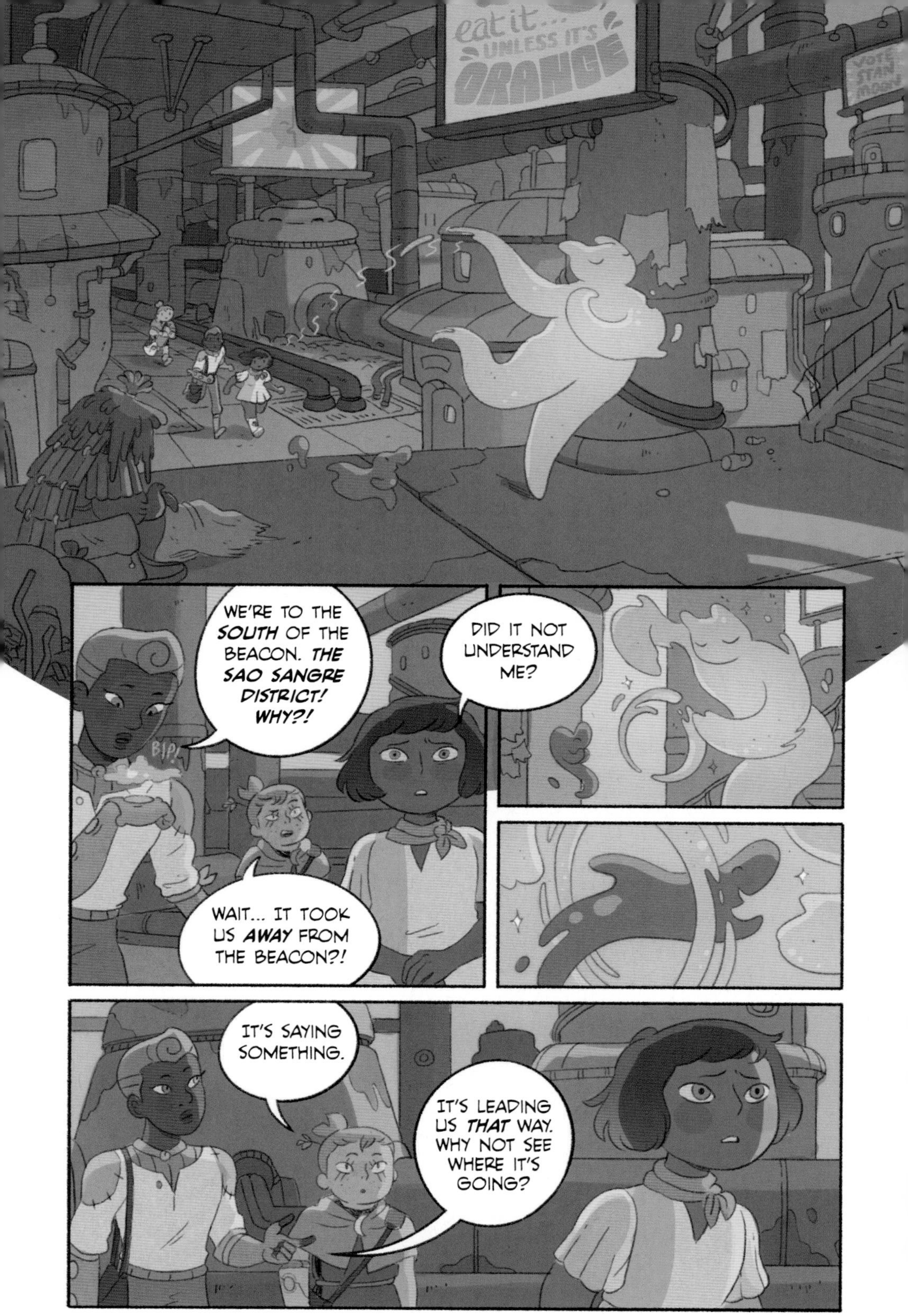
eat it... UNLESS IT'S ORANGE
VOTE STAN MOON
WE'RE TO THE SOUTH OF THE BEACON. THE SAO SANGRE DISTRICT! WHY?!
BIP!
DID IT NOT UNDERSTAND ME?
WAIT... IT TOOK US AWAY FROM THE BEACON?!
IT'S SAYING SOMETHING.
IT'S LEADING US THAT WAY. WHY NOT SEE WHERE IT'S GOING?

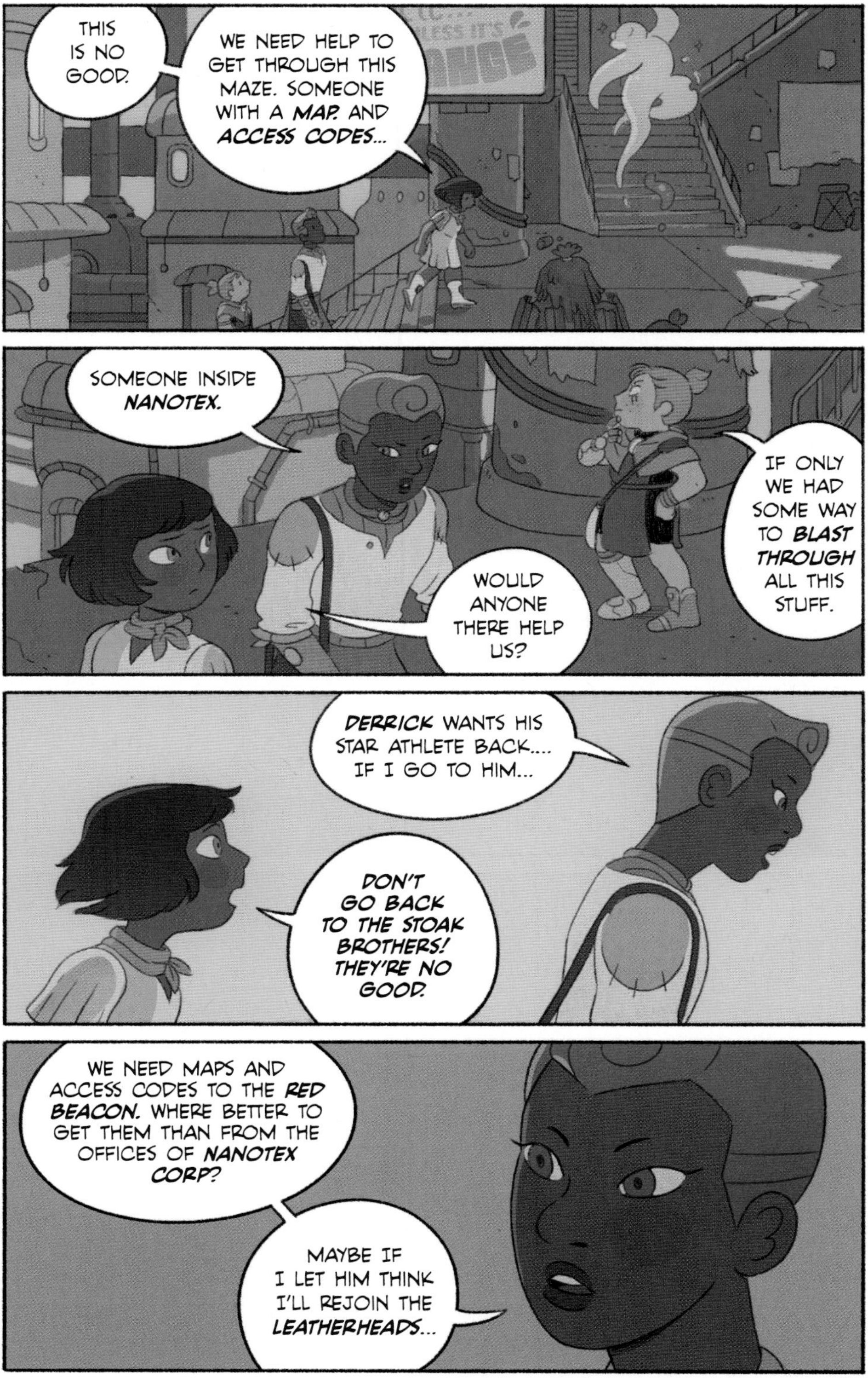
THIS IS NO GOOD.
WE NEED HELP TO GET THROUGH THIS MAZE. SOMEONE WITH A MAP. AND ACCESS CODES...
SOMEONE INSIDE NANOTEX.
IF ONLY WE HAD SOME WAY TO BLAST THROUGH ALL THIS STUFF.
WOULD ANYONE THERE HELP US?
DERRICK WANTS HIS STAR ATHLETE BACK.... IF I GO TO HIM...
DON'T GO BACK TO THE STOAK BROTHERS! THEY'RE NO GOOD.
WE NEED MAPS AND ACCESS CODES TO THE RED BEACON. WHERE BETTER TO GET THEM THAN FROM THE OFFICES OF NANOTEX CORP?
MAYBE IF I LET HIM THINK I'LL REJOIN THE LEATHERHEADS...

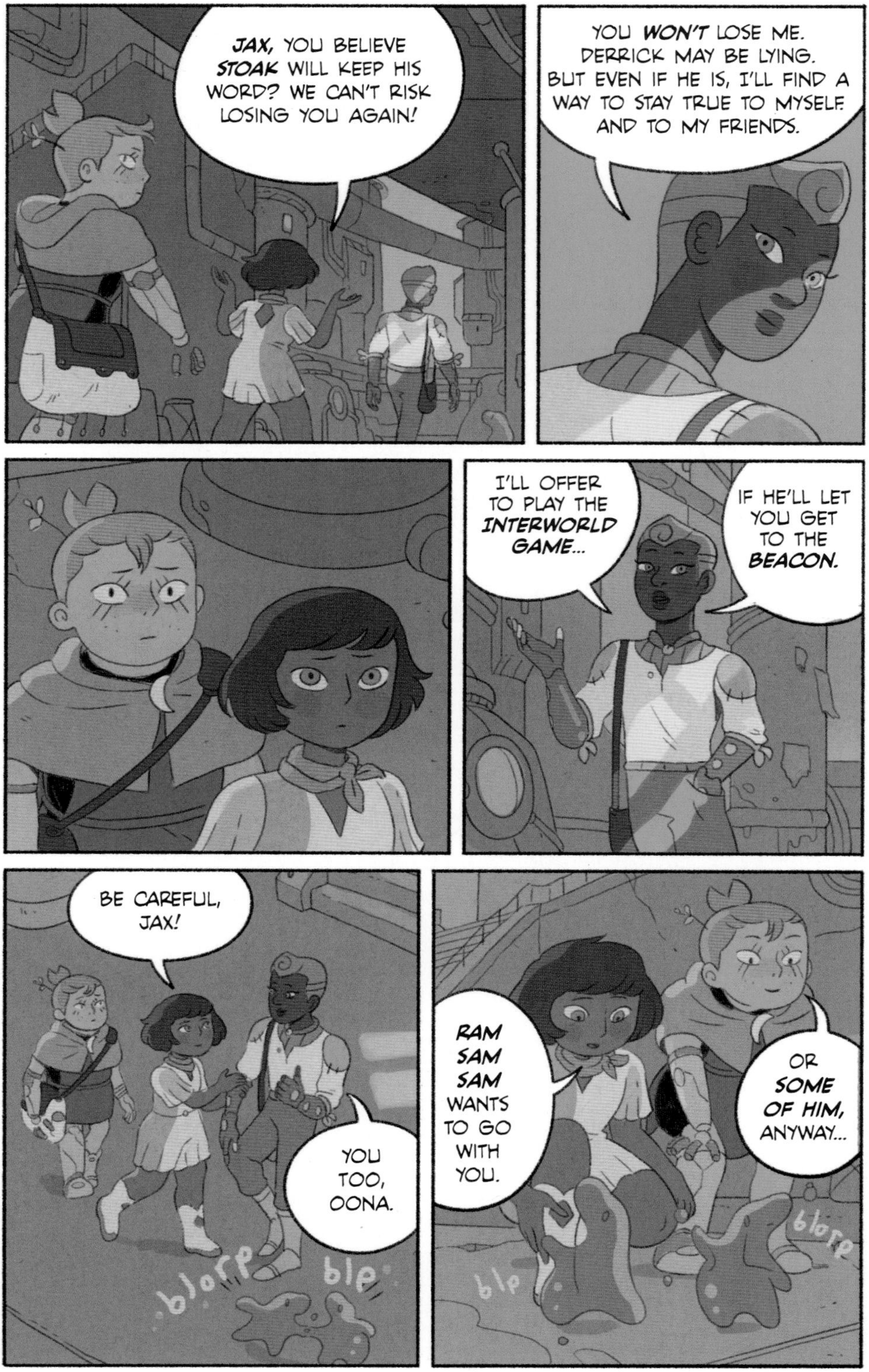
JAX, YOU BELIEVE STOAK WILL KEEP HIS WORD? WE CAN'T RISK LOSING YOU AGAIN!
YOU WON'T LOSE ME. DERRICK MAY BE LYING. BUT EVEN IF HE IS, I'LL FIND A WAY TO STAY TRUE TO MYSELF. AND TO MY FRIENDS.
I'LL OFFER TO PLAY THE INTERWORLD GAME...
IF HE'LL LET YOU GET TO THE BEACON.
BE CAREFUL, JAX!
YOU TOO, OONA.
blorp
ble
RAM SAM SAM WANTS TO GO WITH YOU.
OR SOME OF HIM, ANYWAY...
ble
blorp

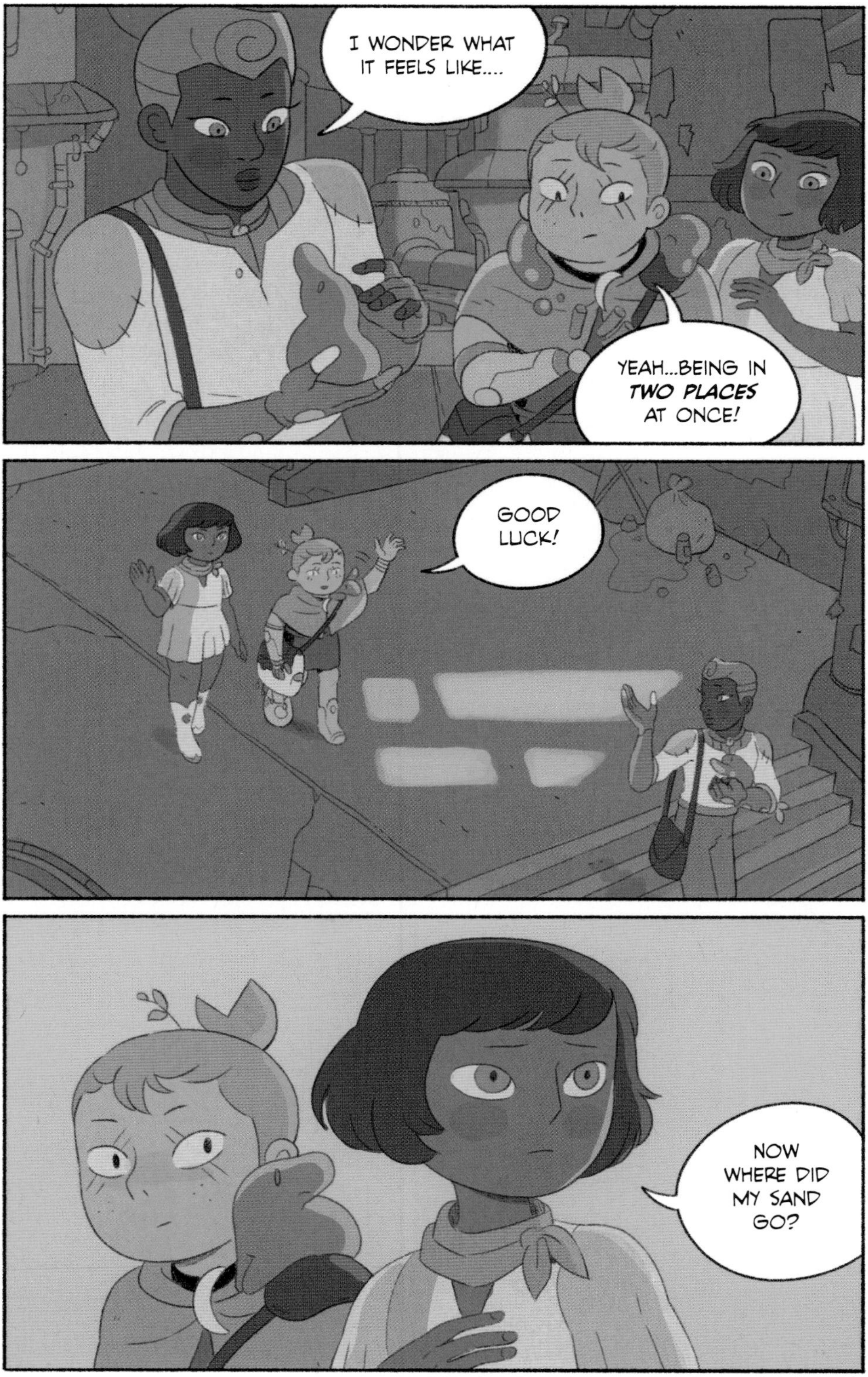
I WONDER WHAT IT FEELS LIKE....
YEAH...BEING IN *TWO PLACES* AT ONCE!
GOOD LUCK!
NOW WHERE DID MY SAND GO?

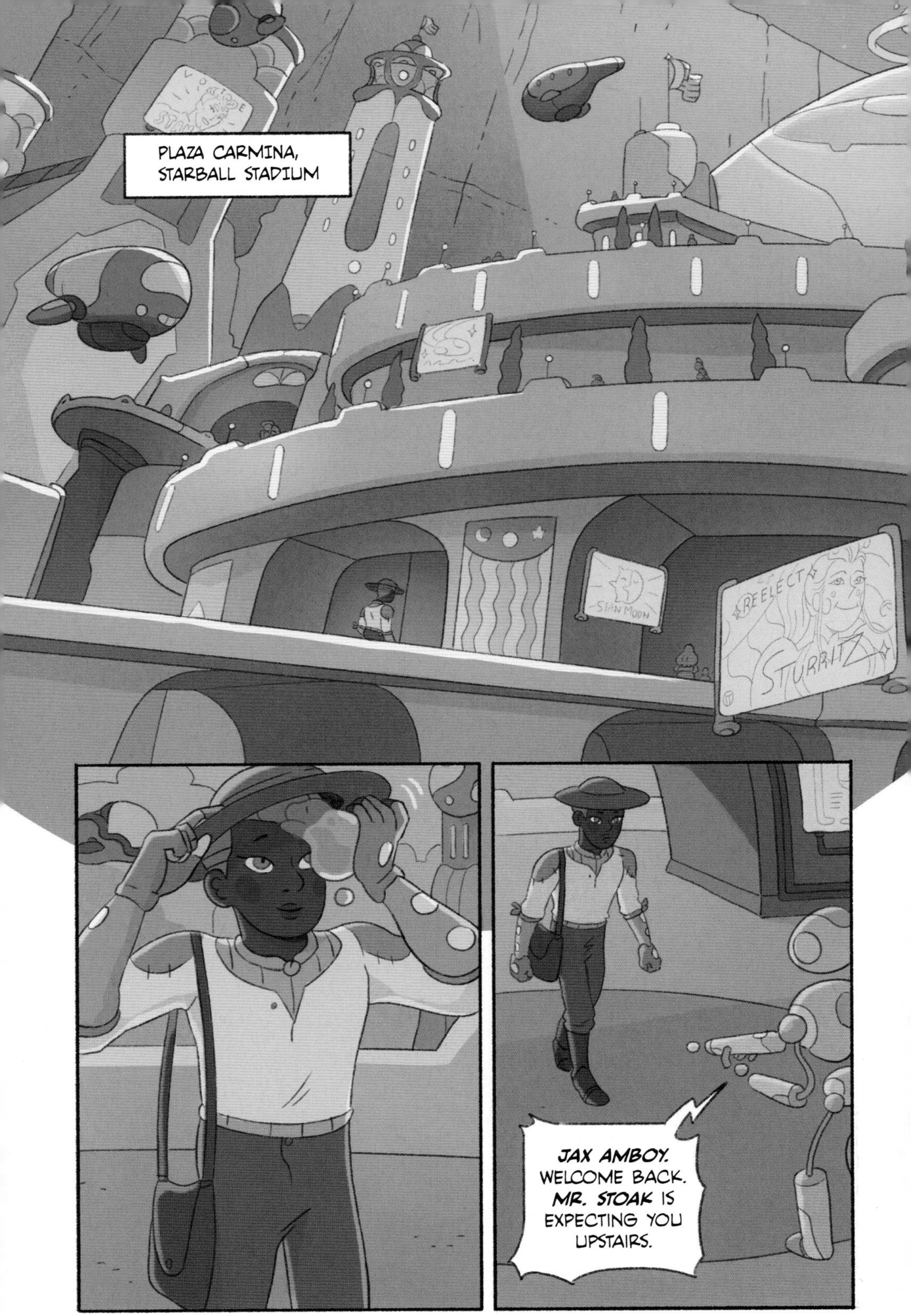
PLAZA CARMINA, STARBALL STADIUM
STAN MOON
REELECT
STURRITZ
*JAX AMBOY.* WELCOME BACK. ***MR. STOAK*** IS EXPECTING YOU UPSTAIRS.

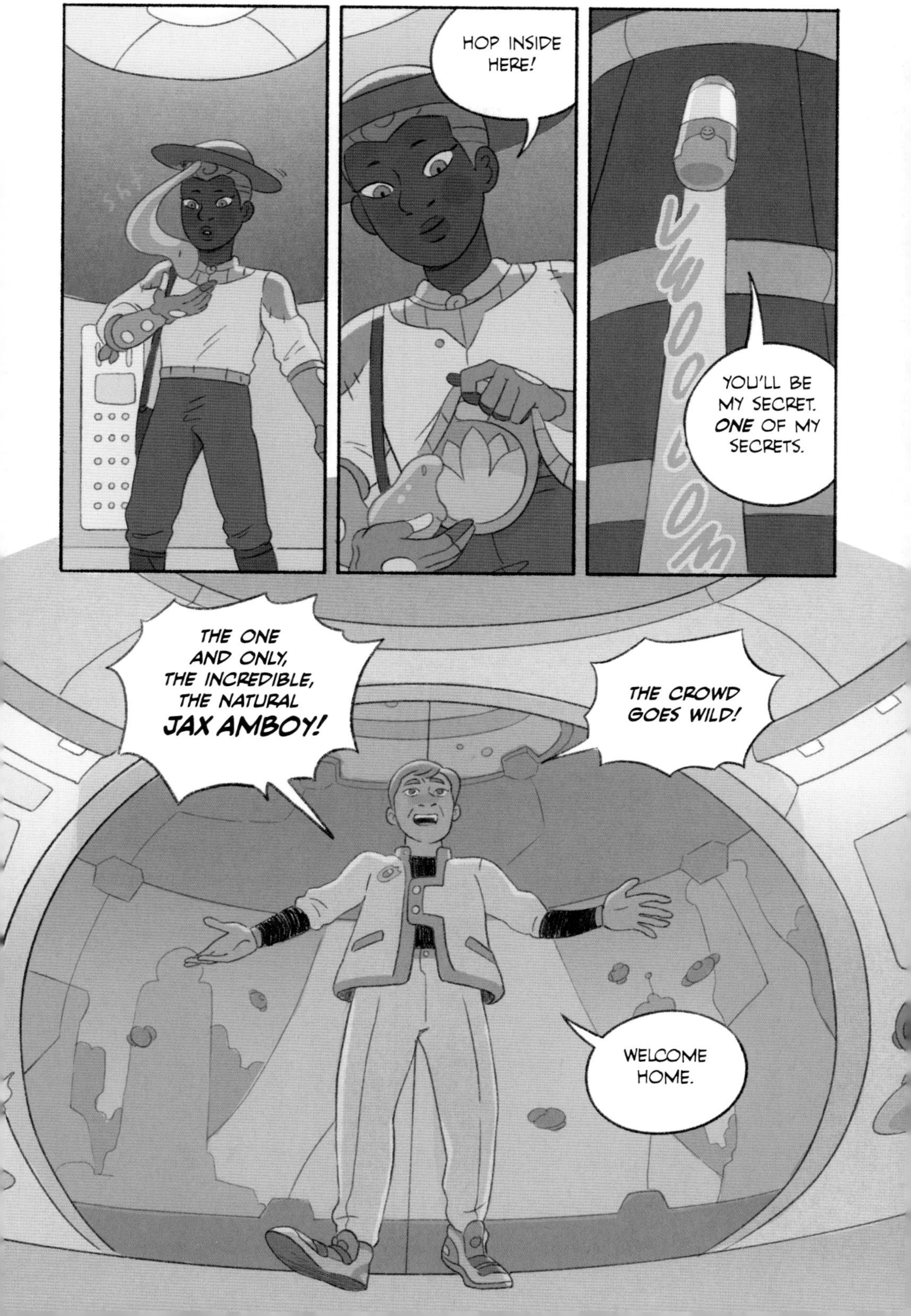
HOP INSIDE HERE!
VWOOOOOOM
YOU'LL BE MY SECRET. ONE OF MY SECRETS.
THE ONE AND ONLY, THE INCREDIBLE, THE NATURAL JAX AMBOY!
THE CROWD GOES WILD!
WELCOME HOME.

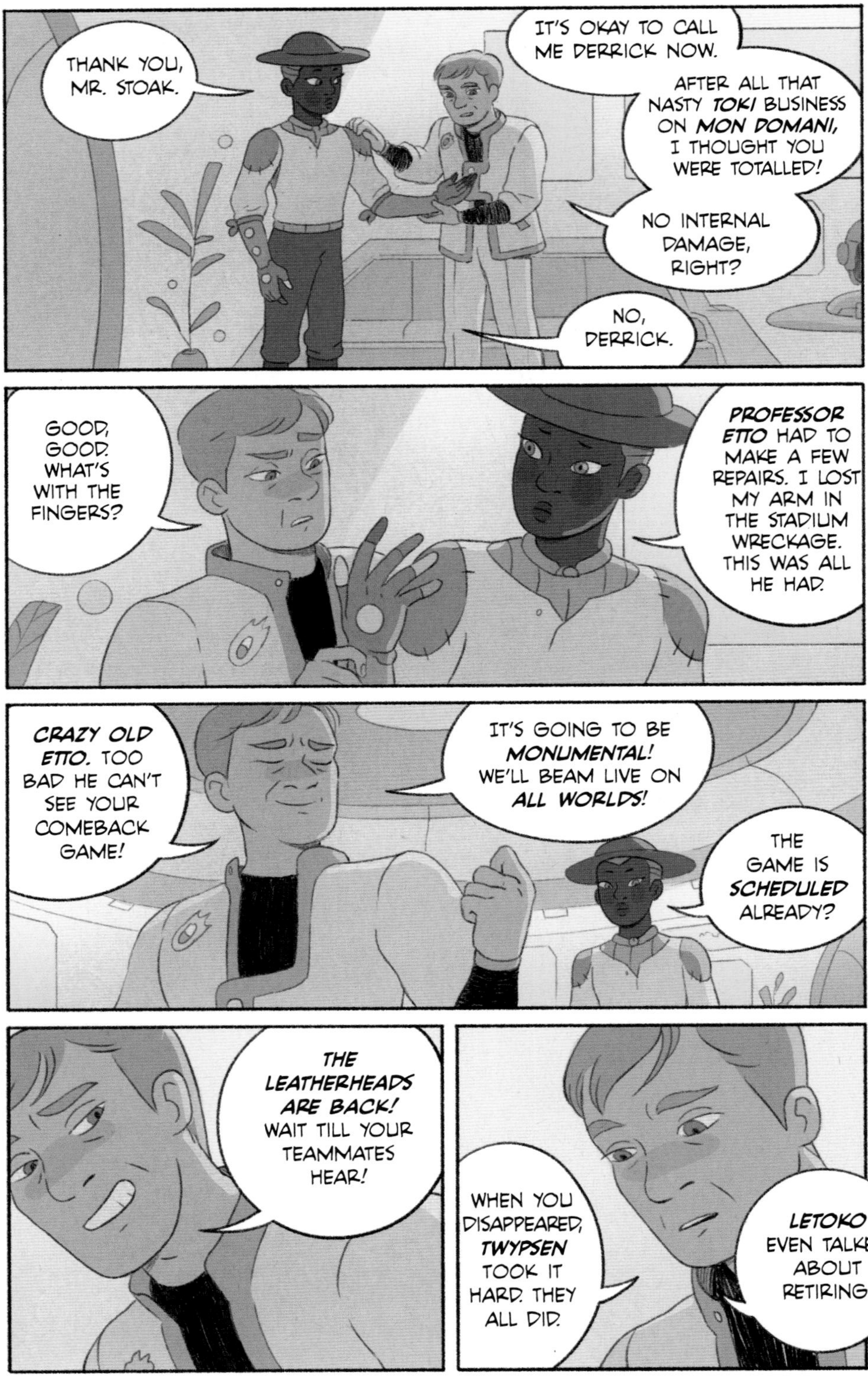
THANK YOU, MR. STOAK.
IT'S OKAY TO CALL ME DERRICK NOW.
AFTER ALL THAT NASTY TOKI BUSINESS ON MON DOMANI, I THOUGHT YOU WERE TOTALLED!
NO INTERNAL DAMAGE, RIGHT?
NO, DERRICK.
GOOD, GOOD. WHAT'S WITH THE FINGERS?
PROFESSOR ETTO HAD TO MAKE A FEW REPAIRS. I LOST MY ARM IN THE STADIUM WRECKAGE. THIS WAS ALL HE HAD.
CRAZY OLD ETTO. TOO BAD HE CAN'T SEE YOUR COMEBACK GAME!
IT'S GOING TO BE MONUMENTAL! WE'LL BEAM LIVE ON ALL WORLDS!
THE GAME IS SCHEDULED ALREADY?
THE LEATHERHEADS ARE BACK! WAIT TILL YOUR TEAMMATES HEAR!
WHEN YOU DISAPPEARED, TWYPSEN TOOK IT HARD. THEY ALL DID.
LETOKO EVEN TALKED ABOUT RETIRING.

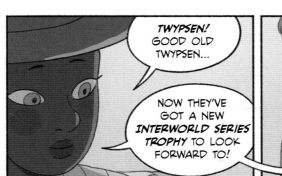

TWYPSEN! GOOD OLD TWYPSEN...

NOW THEY'VE GOT A NEW **INTERWORLD SERIES TROPHY** TO LOOK FORWARD TO!

YOU PROMISED **OONA LEE** YOU'D GIVE HER ACCESS TO THE BEACON IF I PLAY IN THE INTERWORLDS.

THAT SAND DANCER?

SHE'S A LOOSE CANNON, THAT ONE.

MY BROTHER IS HARDLY GOING TO LET HER *LIGHT THE THING*, IS HE?

WE DON'T EVEN KNOW WHAT COULD HAPPEN.

WHAT IF IT OVERLOADS MOON YATTA'S POWER GRID? NO, THERE'S NO WAY SHE'S GOING *ANYWHERE NEAR* THE RED BEACON.

YOU LIED TO HER! YOU LIED!

HOW COULD YOU DO SUCH A THING?

SLAM!

HUFF HF...

SOMETHING REALLY DID HAPPEN TO YOU.

YES! IF YOU WANT AN OBEDIENT ROBOT, BUILD YOURSELF A NEW ONE.

NO BEACON, NO GAME. WE DON'T HAVE A DEAL.

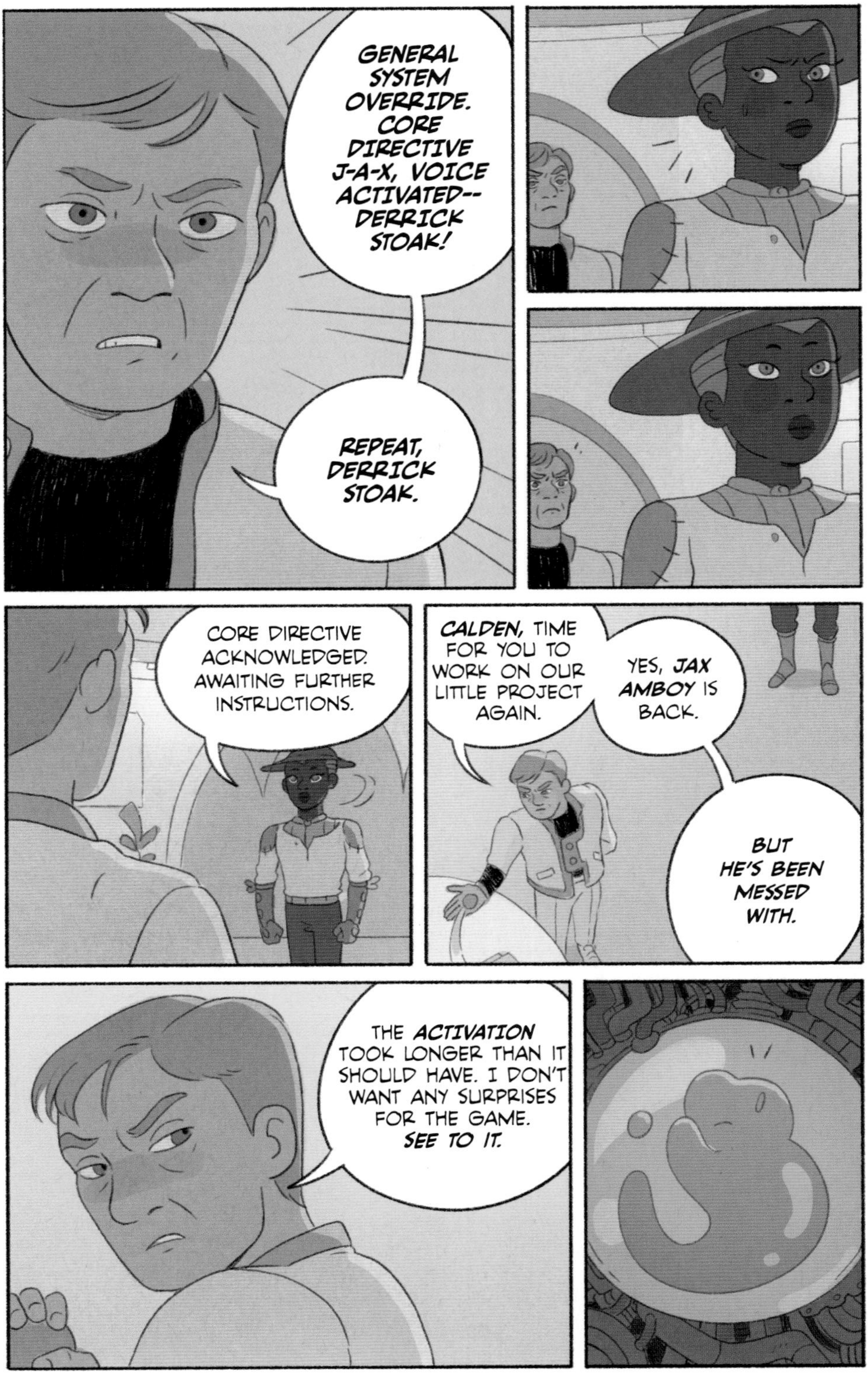
GENERAL SYSTEM OVERRIDE. CORE DIRECTIVE J-A-X, VOICE ACTIVATED-- DERRICK STOAK!
REPEAT, DERRICK STOAK.
CORE DIRECTIVE ACKNOWLEDGED. AWAITING FURTHER INSTRUCTIONS.
CALDEN, TIME FOR YOU TO WORK ON OUR LITTLE PROJECT AGAIN.
YES, JAX AMBOY IS BACK.
BUT HE'S BEEN MESSED WITH.
THE ACTIVATION TOOK LONGER THAN IT SHOULD HAVE. I DON'T WANT ANY SURPRISES FOR THE GAME. SEE TO IT.

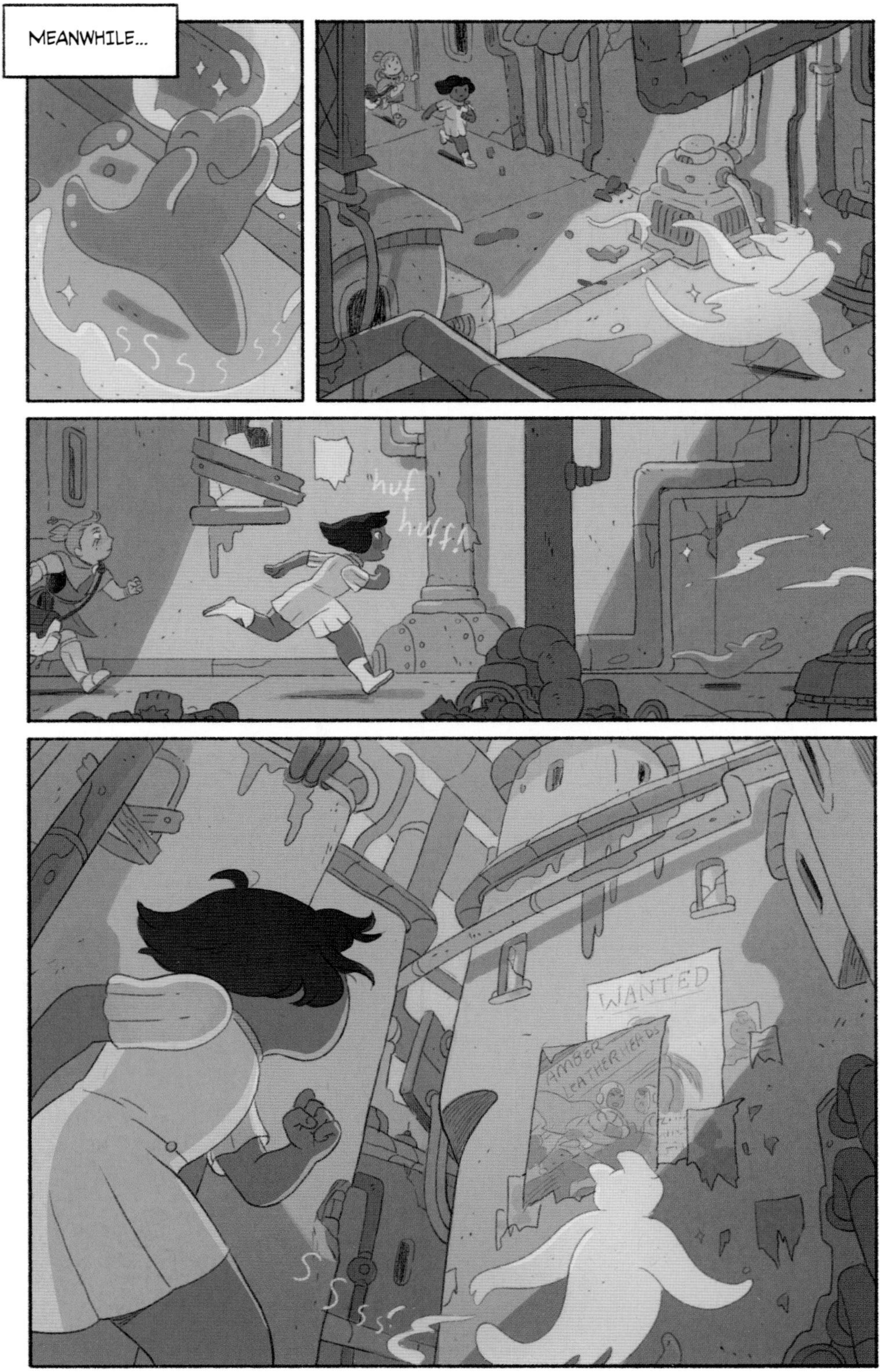
MEANWHILE...
SSSSSS
huf huff!
WANTED
AMBER LEATHERHEADS
SSSS!

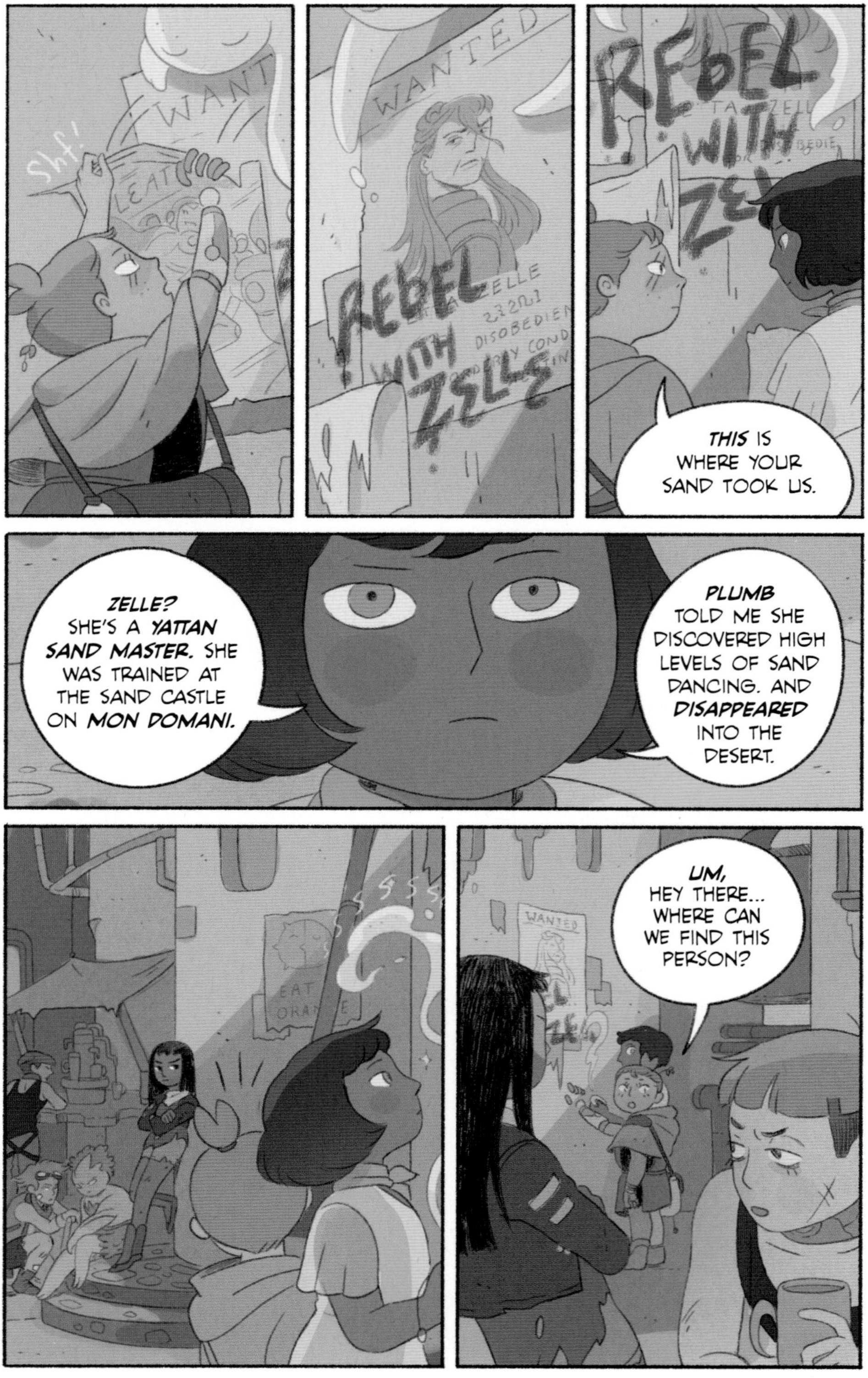
Shf!
WANTED
REBEL WITH ZELLE
THIS IS WHERE YOUR SAND TOOK US.
ZELLE? SHE'S A YATTAN SAND MASTER. SHE WAS TRAINED AT THE SAND CASTLE ON MON DOMANI.
PLUMB TOLD ME SHE DISCOVERED HIGH LEVELS OF SAND DANCING. AND DISAPPEARED INTO THE DESERT.
EAT ORANGE
UM, HEY THERE... WHERE CAN WE FIND THIS PERSON?

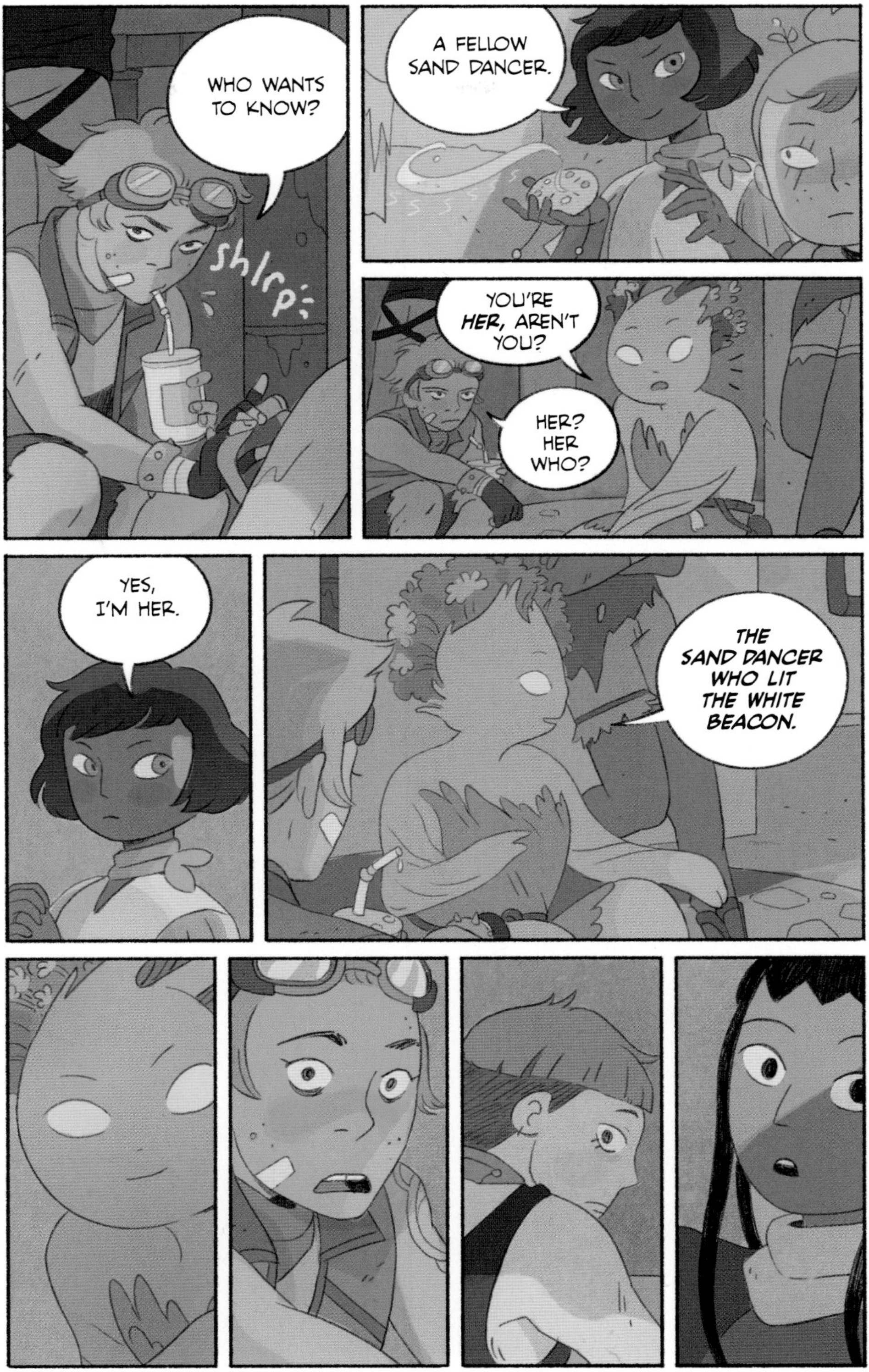
WHO WANTS TO KNOW?
SHLRP
A FELLOW SAND DANCER.
YOU'RE *HER*, AREN'T YOU?
HER? HER WHO?
YES, I'M HER.
*THE SAND DANCER WHO LIT THE WHITE BEACON.*

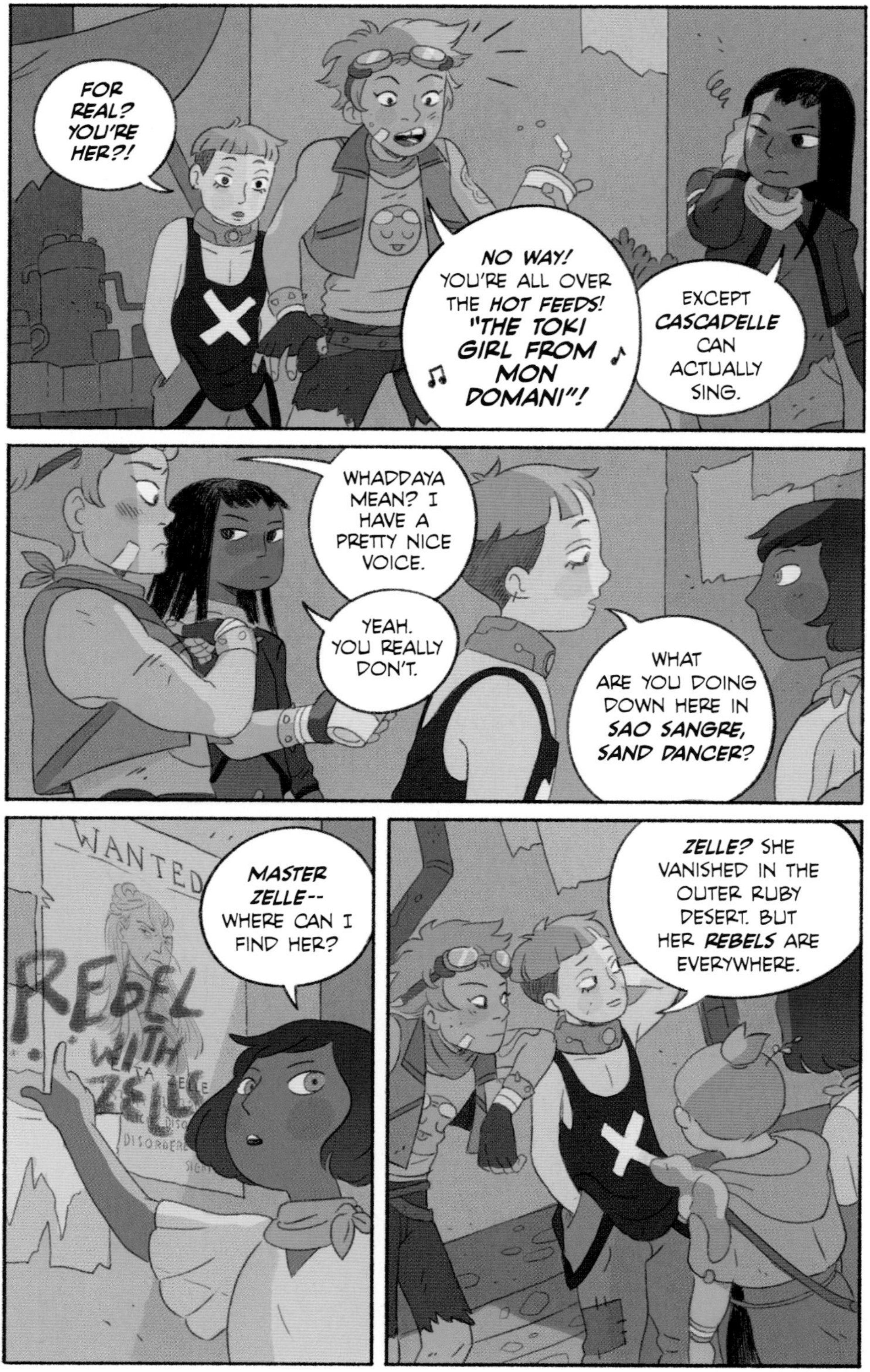
FOR REAL? YOU'RE HER?!
NO WAY! YOU'RE ALL OVER THE HOT FEEDS! "THE TOKI GIRL FROM MON DOMANI"!
EXCEPT CASCADELLE CAN ACTUALLY SING.
WHADDAYA MEAN? I HAVE A PRETTY NICE VOICE.
YEAH. YOU REALLY DON'T.
WHAT ARE YOU DOING DOWN HERE IN SAO SANGRE, SAND DANCER?
WANTED
REBEL WITH ZELLE
MASTER ZELLE-- WHERE CAN I FIND HER?
ZELLE? SHE VANISHED IN THE OUTER RUBY DESERT. BUT HER REBELS ARE EVERYWHERE.

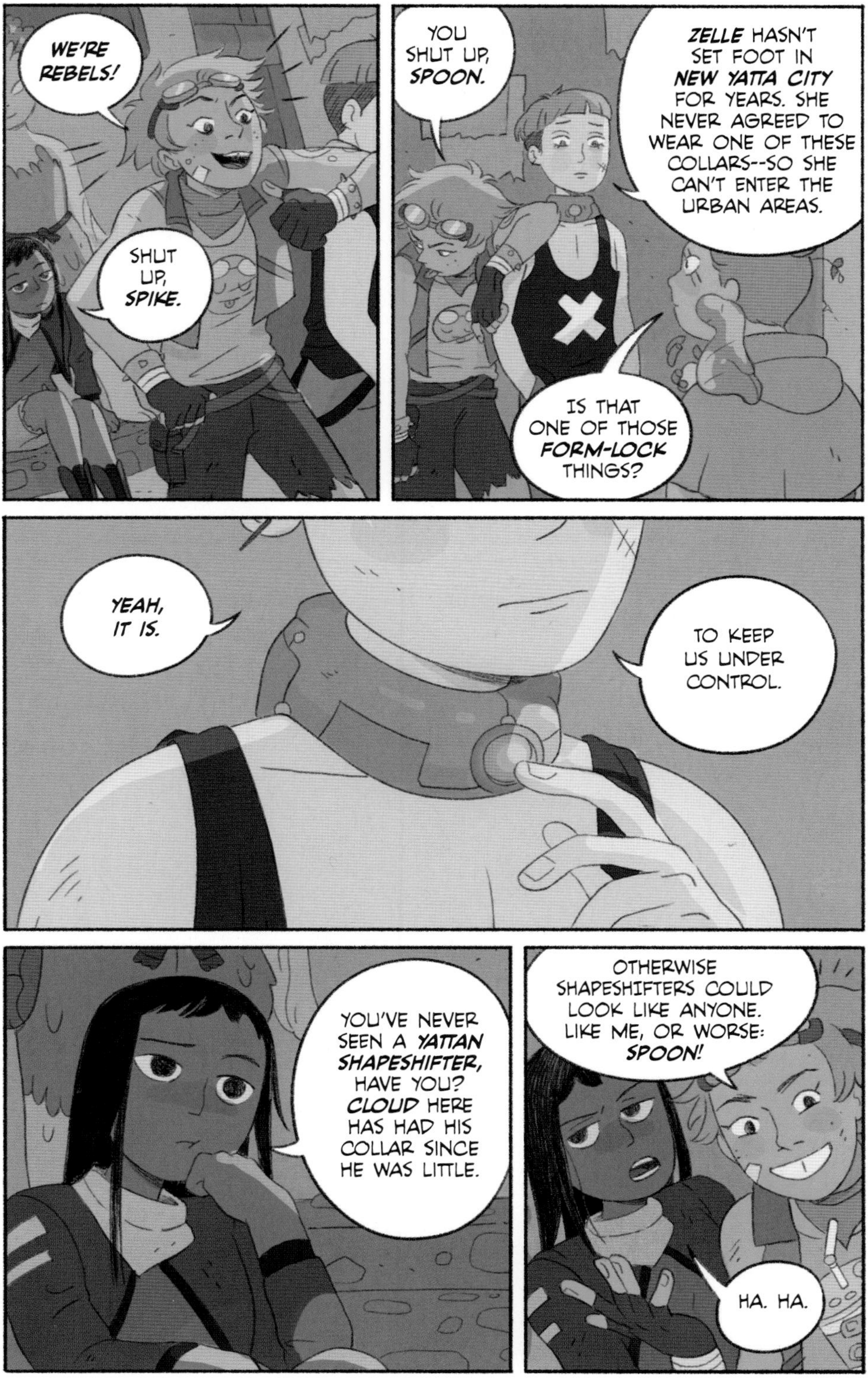
WE'RE REBELS!
SHUT UP, SPIKE.
YOU SHUT UP, SPOON.
ZELLE HASN'T SET FOOT IN NEW YATTA CITY FOR YEARS. SHE NEVER AGREED TO WEAR ONE OF THESE COLLARS--SO SHE CAN'T ENTER THE URBAN AREAS.
IS THAT ONE OF THOSE FORM-LOCK THINGS?
YEAH, IT IS.
TO KEEP US UNDER CONTROL.
YOU'VE NEVER SEEN A YATTAN SHAPESHIFTER, HAVE YOU? CLOUD HERE HAS HAD HIS COLLAR SINCE HE WAS LITTLE.
OTHERWISE SHAPESHIFTERS COULD LOOK LIKE ANYONE. LIKE ME, OR WORSE: SPOON!
HA. HA.

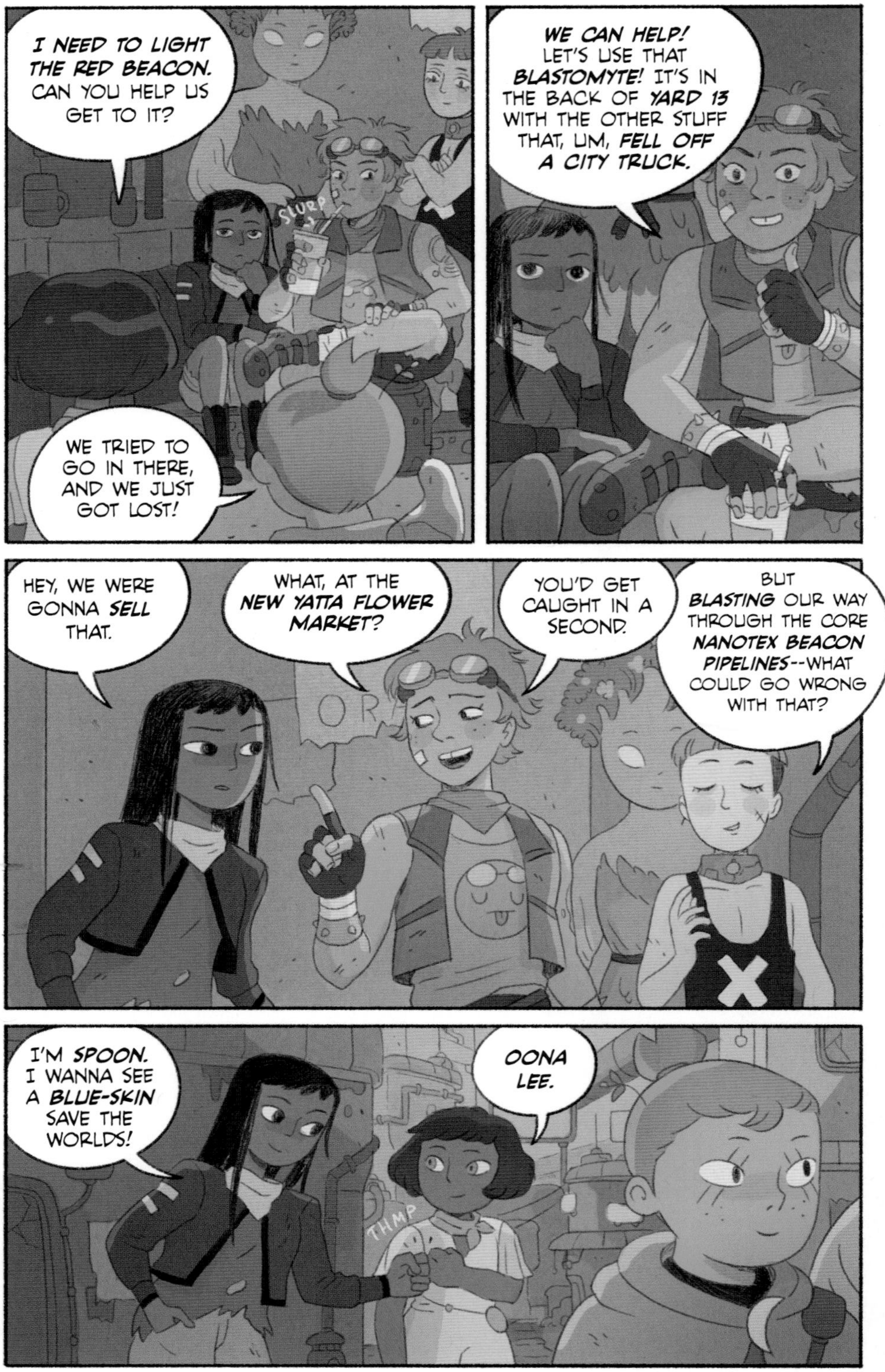
I NEED TO LIGHT THE RED BEACON. CAN YOU HELP US GET TO IT?
SLURP
WE TRIED TO GO IN THERE, AND WE JUST GOT LOST!
WE CAN HELP! LET'S USE THAT BLASTOMYTE! IT'S IN THE BACK OF YARD 13 WITH THE OTHER STUFF THAT, UM, FELL OFF A CITY TRUCK.
HEY, WE WERE GONNA SELL THAT.
WHAT, AT THE NEW YATTA FLOWER MARKET?
YOU'D GET CAUGHT IN A SECOND.
BUT BLASTING OUR WAY THROUGH THE CORE NANOTEX BEACON PIPELINES--WHAT COULD GO WRONG WITH THAT?
I'M SPOON. I WANNA SEE A BLUE-SKIN SAVE THE WORLDS!
OONA LEE.
THMP

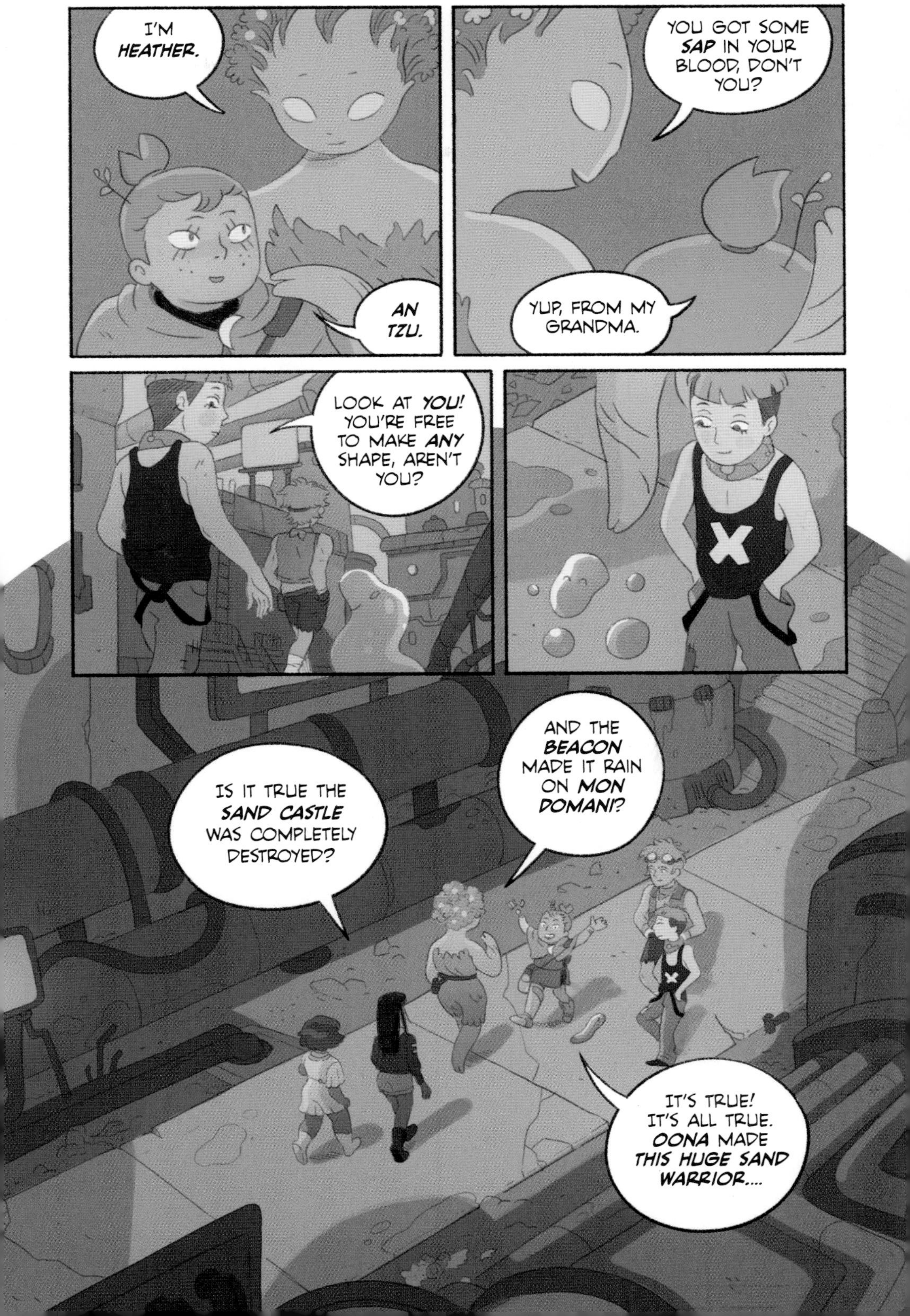
I'M HEATHER.
AN TZU.
YOU GOT SOME SAP IN YOUR BLOOD, DON'T YOU?
YUP, FROM MY GRANDMA.
LOOK AT YOU! YOU'RE FREE TO MAKE ANY SHAPE, AREN'T YOU?
IS IT TRUE THE SAND CASTLE WAS COMPLETELY DESTROYED?
AND THE BEACON MADE IT RAIN ON MON DOMANI?
IT'S TRUE! IT'S ALL TRUE. OONA MADE THIS HUGE SAND WARRIOR....

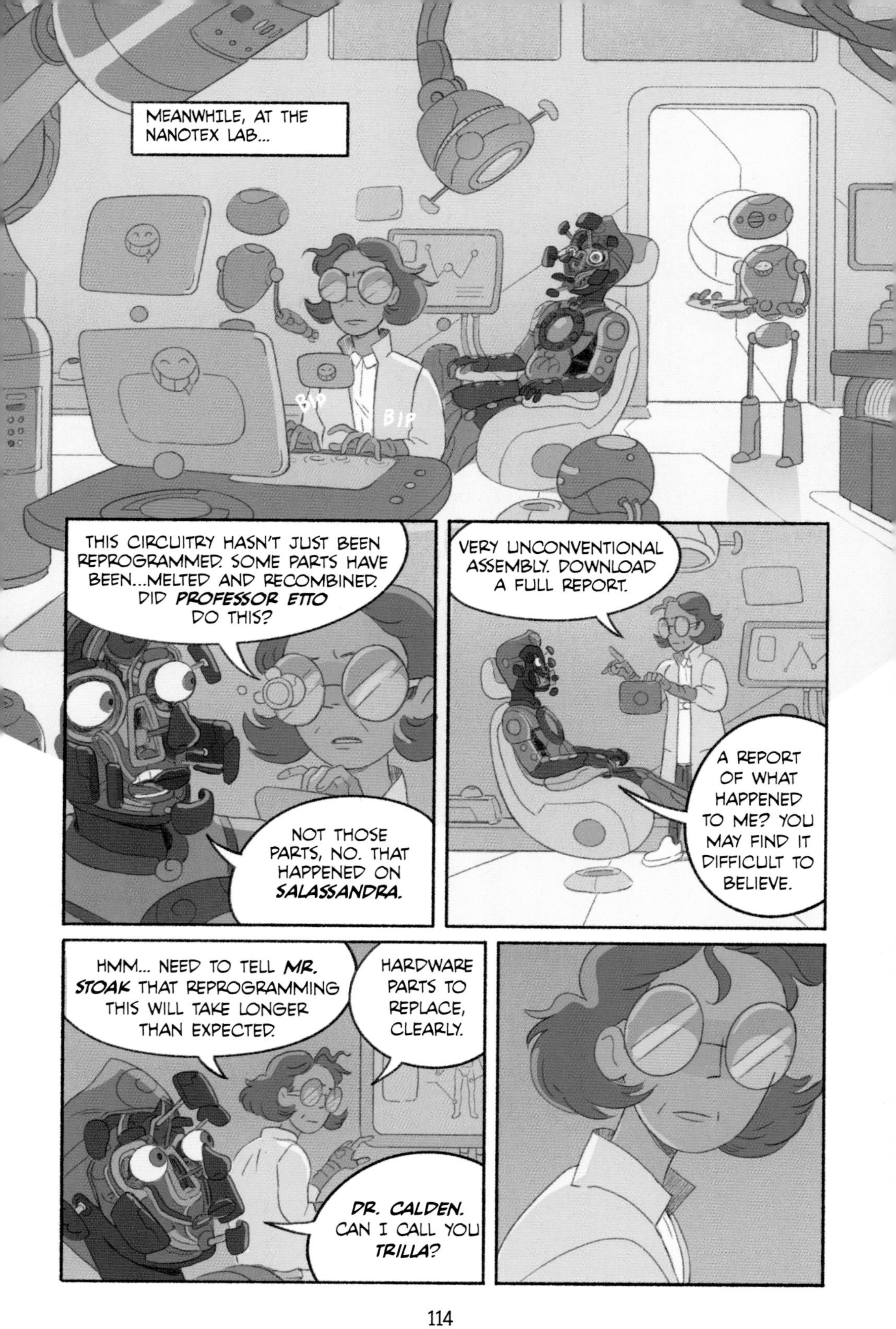

MEANWHILE, AT THE NANOTEX LAB...
BIP
BIP
THIS CIRCUITRY HASN'T JUST BEEN REPROGRAMMED. SOME PARTS HAVE BEEN...MELTED AND RECOMBINED. DID PROFESSOR ETTO DO THIS?
NOT THOSE PARTS, NO. THAT HAPPENED ON SALASSANDRA.
VERY UNCONVENTIONAL ASSEMBLY. DOWNLOAD A FULL REPORT.
A REPORT OF WHAT HAPPENED TO ME? YOU MAY FIND IT DIFFICULT TO BELIEVE.
HMM... NEED TO TELL MR. STOAK THAT REPROGRAMMING THIS WILL TAKE LONGER THAN EXPECTED.
HARDWARE PARTS TO REPLACE, CLEARLY.
DR. CALDEN. CAN I CALL YOU TRILLA?

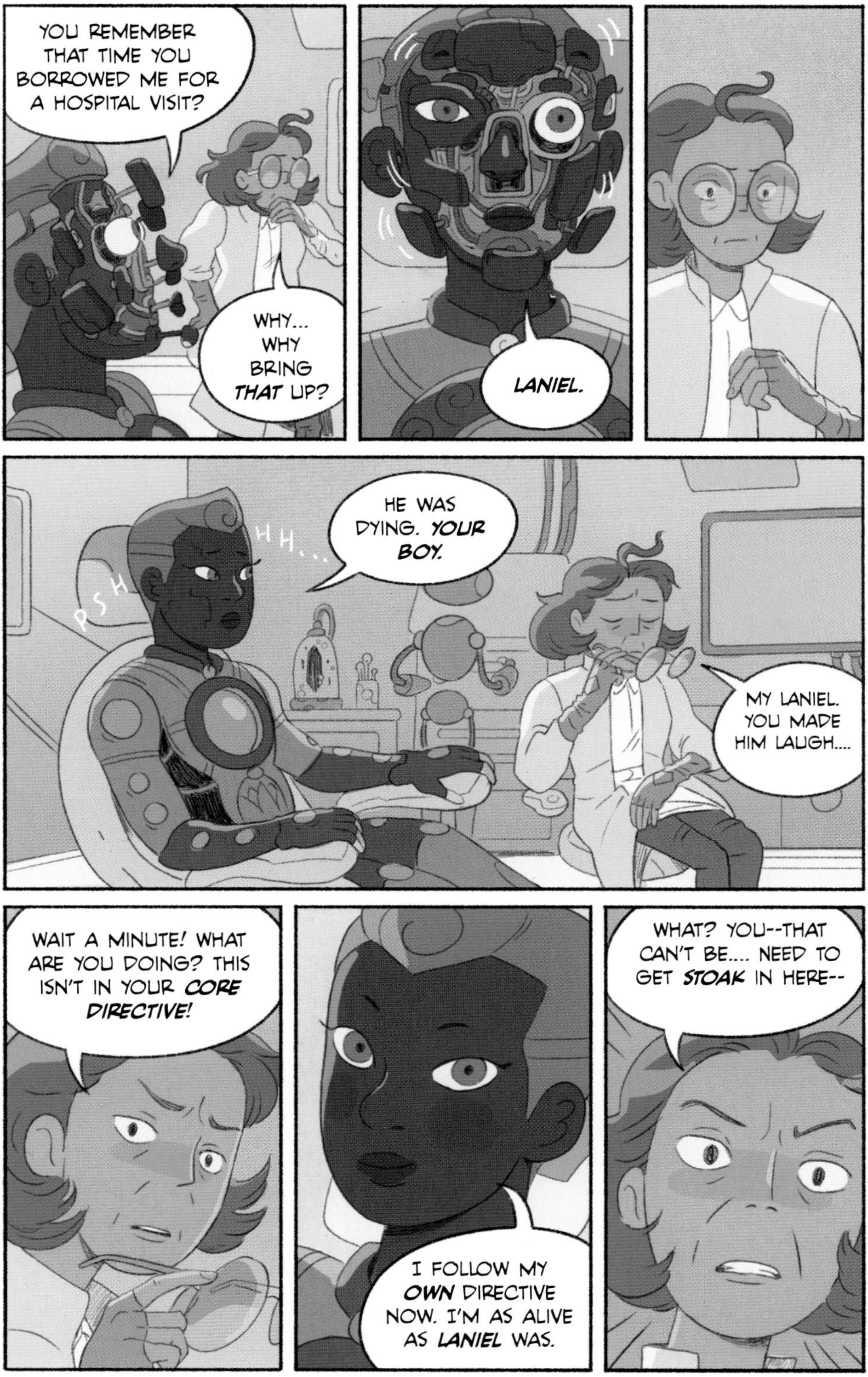
YOU REMEMBER THAT TIME YOU BORROWED ME FOR A HOSPITAL VISIT?
WHY... WHY BRING *THAT* UP?
*LANIEL.*
HE WAS DYING. *YOUR BOY.*
PSHHH...
MY LANIEL. YOU MADE HIM LAUGH....
WAIT A MINUTE! WHAT ARE YOU DOING? THIS ISN'T IN YOUR *CORE DIRECTIVE!*
I FOLLOW MY *OWN* DIRECTIVE NOW. I'M AS ALIVE AS *LANIEL* WAS.
WHAT? YOU--THAT CAN'T BE.... NEED TO GET *STOAK* IN HERE--

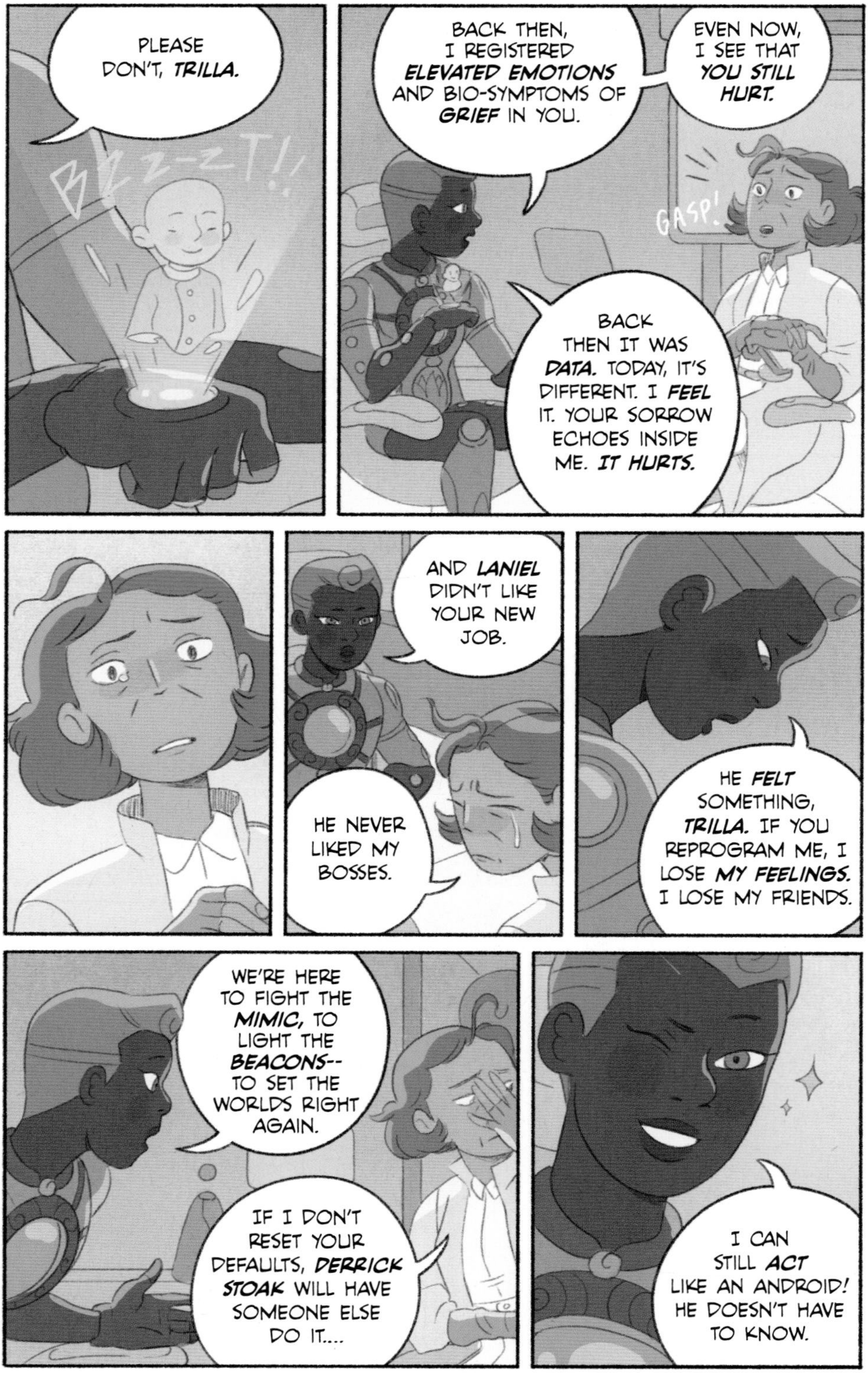
PLEASE DON'T, TRILLA.
BZZ-ZT!!
BACK THEN, I REGISTERED ELEVATED EMOTIONS AND BIO-SYMPTOMS OF GRIEF IN YOU.
EVEN NOW, I SEE THAT YOU STILL HURT.
GASP!
BACK THEN IT WAS DATA. TODAY, IT'S DIFFERENT. I FEEL IT. YOUR SORROW ECHOES INSIDE ME. IT HURTS.
AND LANIEL DIDN'T LIKE YOUR NEW JOB.
HE NEVER LIKED MY BOSSES.
HE FELT SOMETHING, TRILLA. IF YOU REPROGRAM ME, I LOSE MY FEELINGS. I LOSE MY FRIENDS.
WE'RE HERE TO FIGHT THE MIMIC, TO LIGHT THE BEACONS-- TO SET THE WORLDS RIGHT AGAIN.
IF I DON'T RESET YOUR DEFAULTS, DERRICK STOAK WILL HAVE SOMEONE ELSE DO IT....
I CAN STILL ACT LIKE AN ANDROID! HE DOESN'T HAVE TO KNOW.

Chapter 6

# INTO THE BREACH

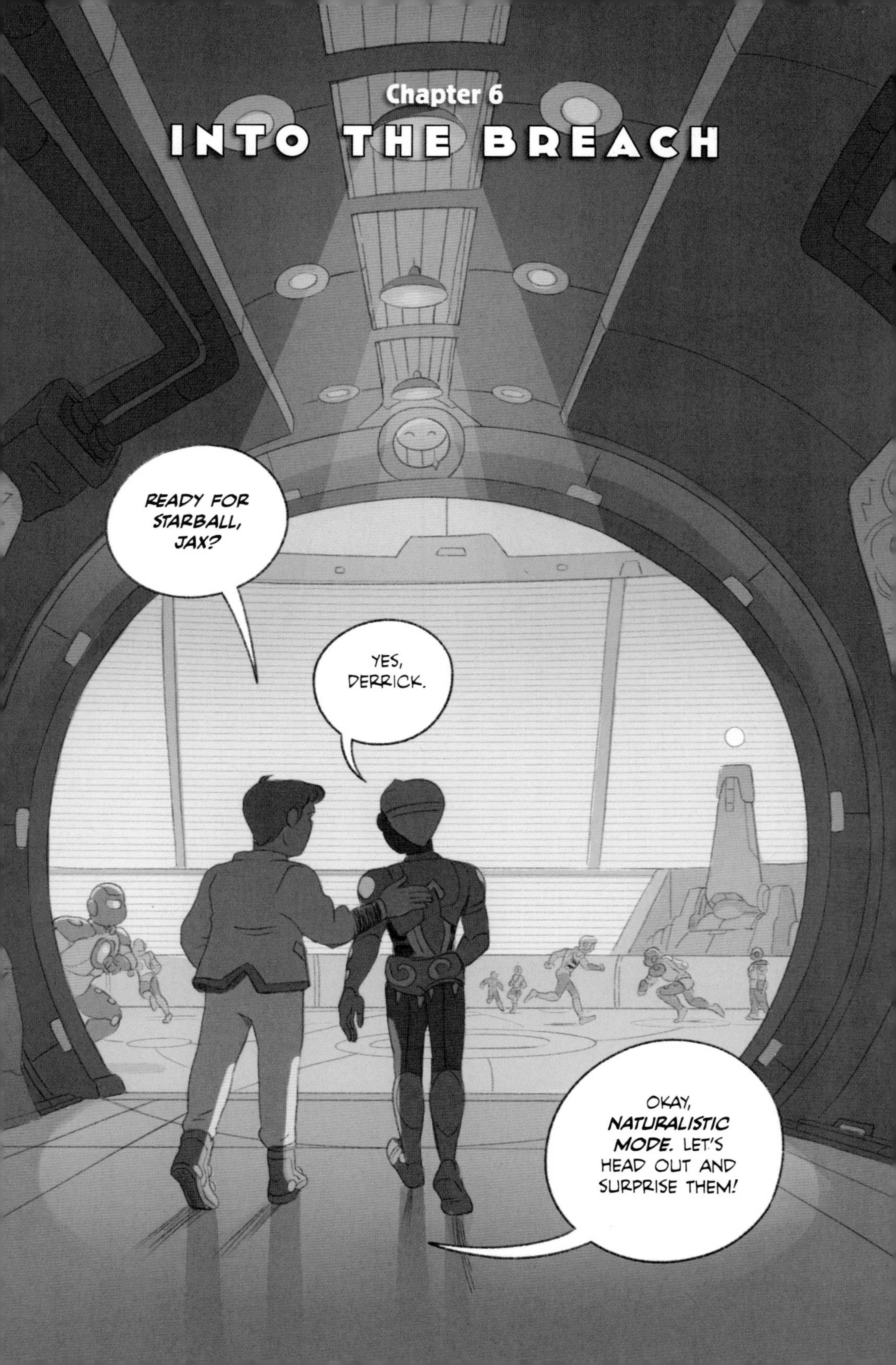

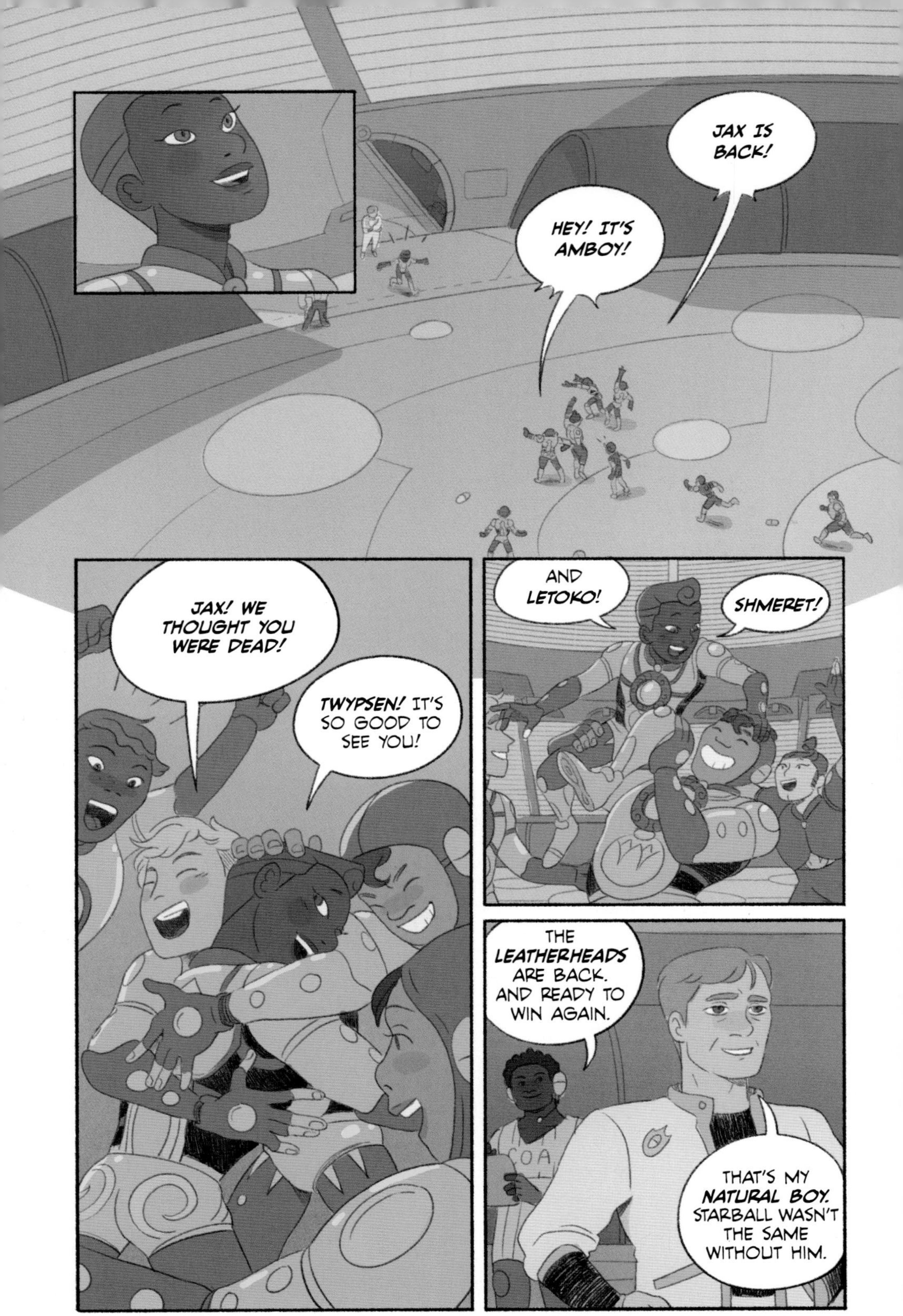
JAX IS BACK!
HEY! IT'S AMBOY!
JAX! WE THOUGHT YOU WERE DEAD!
TWYPSEN! IT'S SO GOOD TO SEE YOU!
AND LETOKO!
SHMERET!
THE LEATHERHEADS ARE BACK. AND READY TO WIN AGAIN.
THAT'S MY NATURAL BOY. STARBALL WASN'T THE SAME WITHOUT HIM.

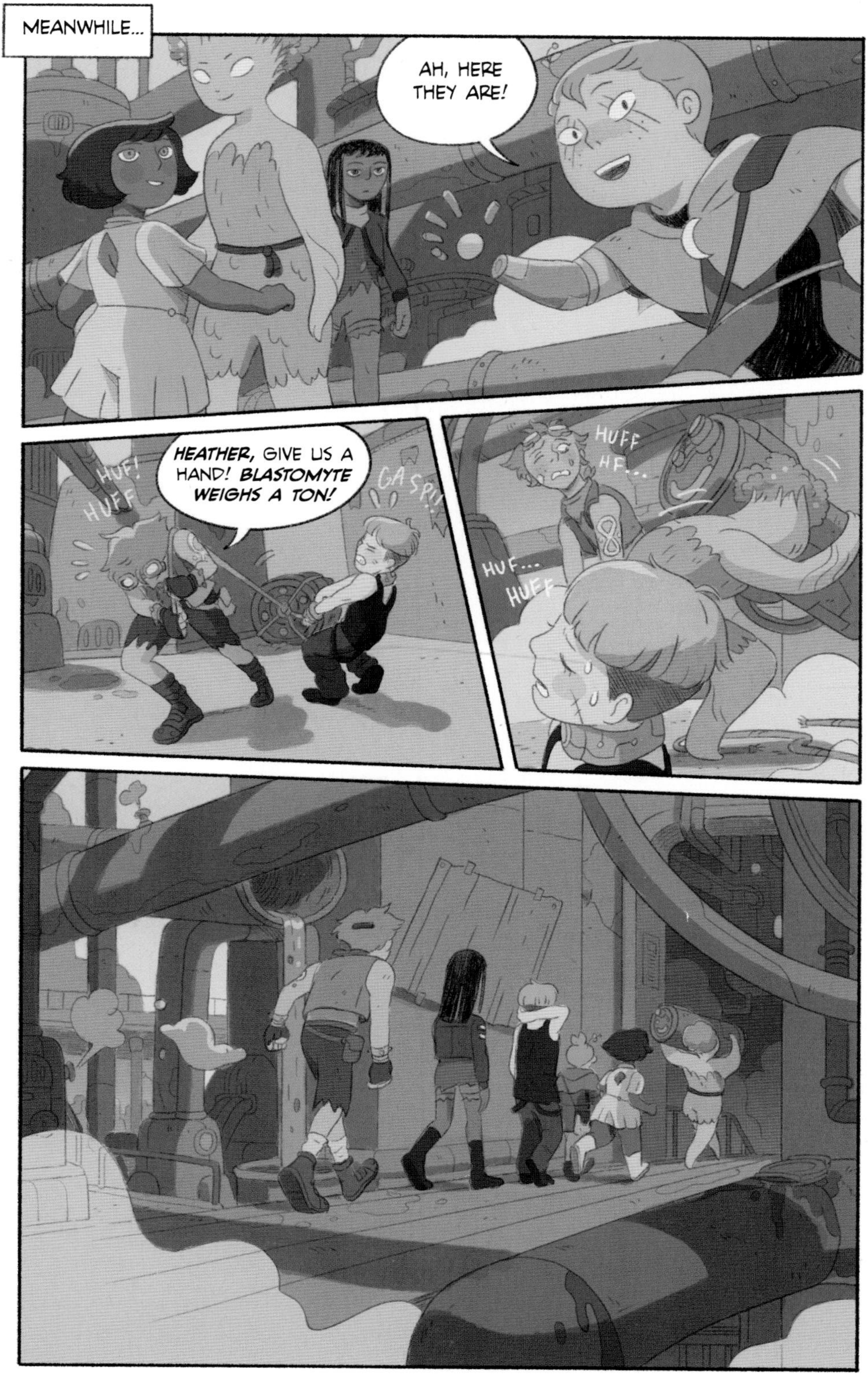
MEANWHILE...
AH, HERE THEY ARE!
HUF! HUFF
HEATHER, GIVE US A HAND! BLASTOMYTE WEIGHS A TON!
GASP!
HUFF HF...
HUF... HUFF

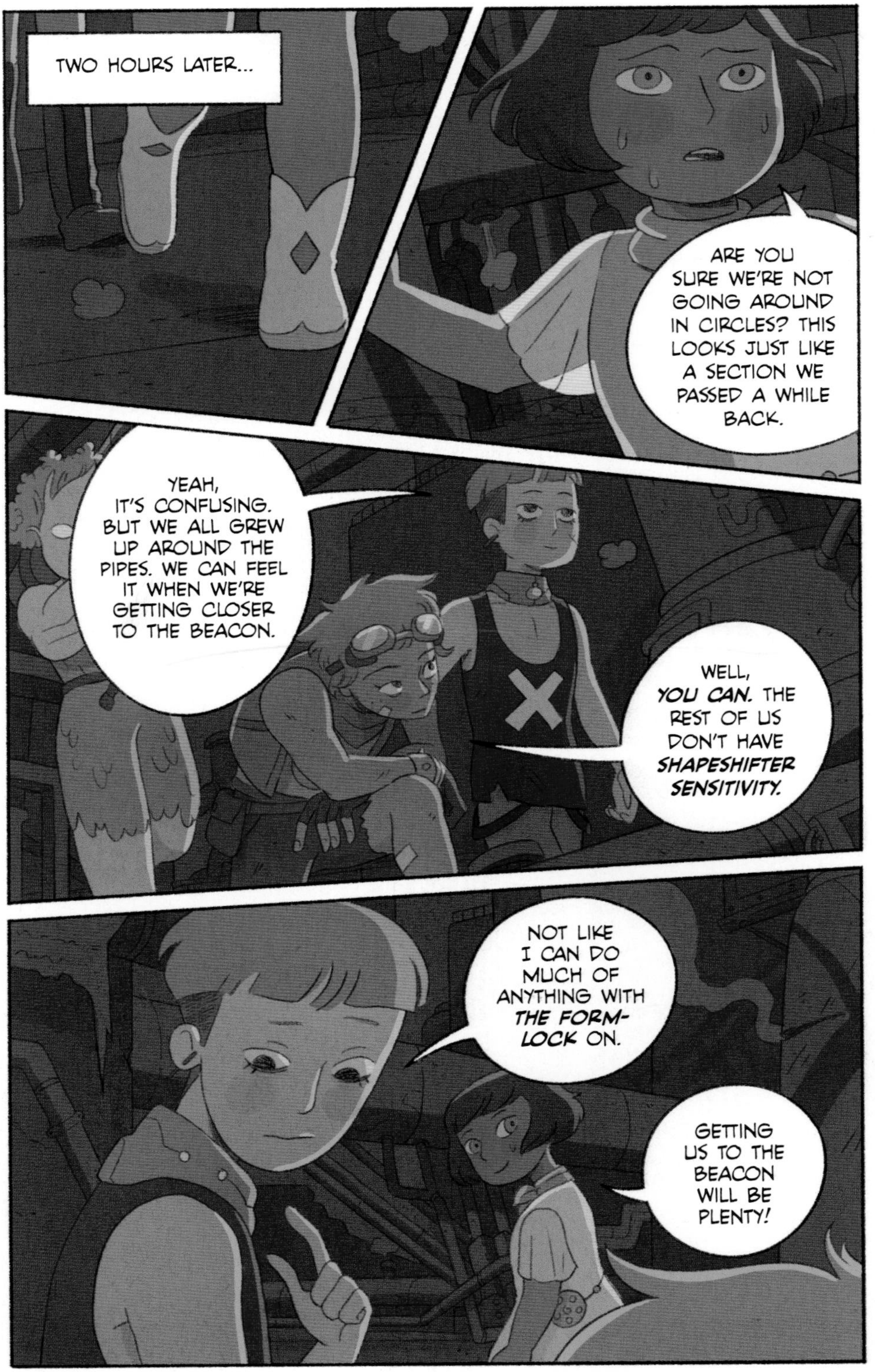
TWO HOURS LATER...
ARE YOU SURE WE'RE NOT GOING AROUND IN CIRCLES? THIS LOOKS JUST LIKE A SECTION WE PASSED A WHILE BACK.
YEAH, IT'S CONFUSING. BUT WE ALL GREW UP AROUND THE PIPES. WE CAN FEEL IT WHEN WE'RE GETTING CLOSER TO THE BEACON.
WELL, *YOU CAN.* THE REST OF US DON'T HAVE ***SHAPESHIFTER SENSITIVITY.***
NOT LIKE I CAN DO MUCH OF ANYTHING WITH ***THE FORM-LOCK*** ON.
GETTING US TO THE BEACON WILL BE PLENTY!

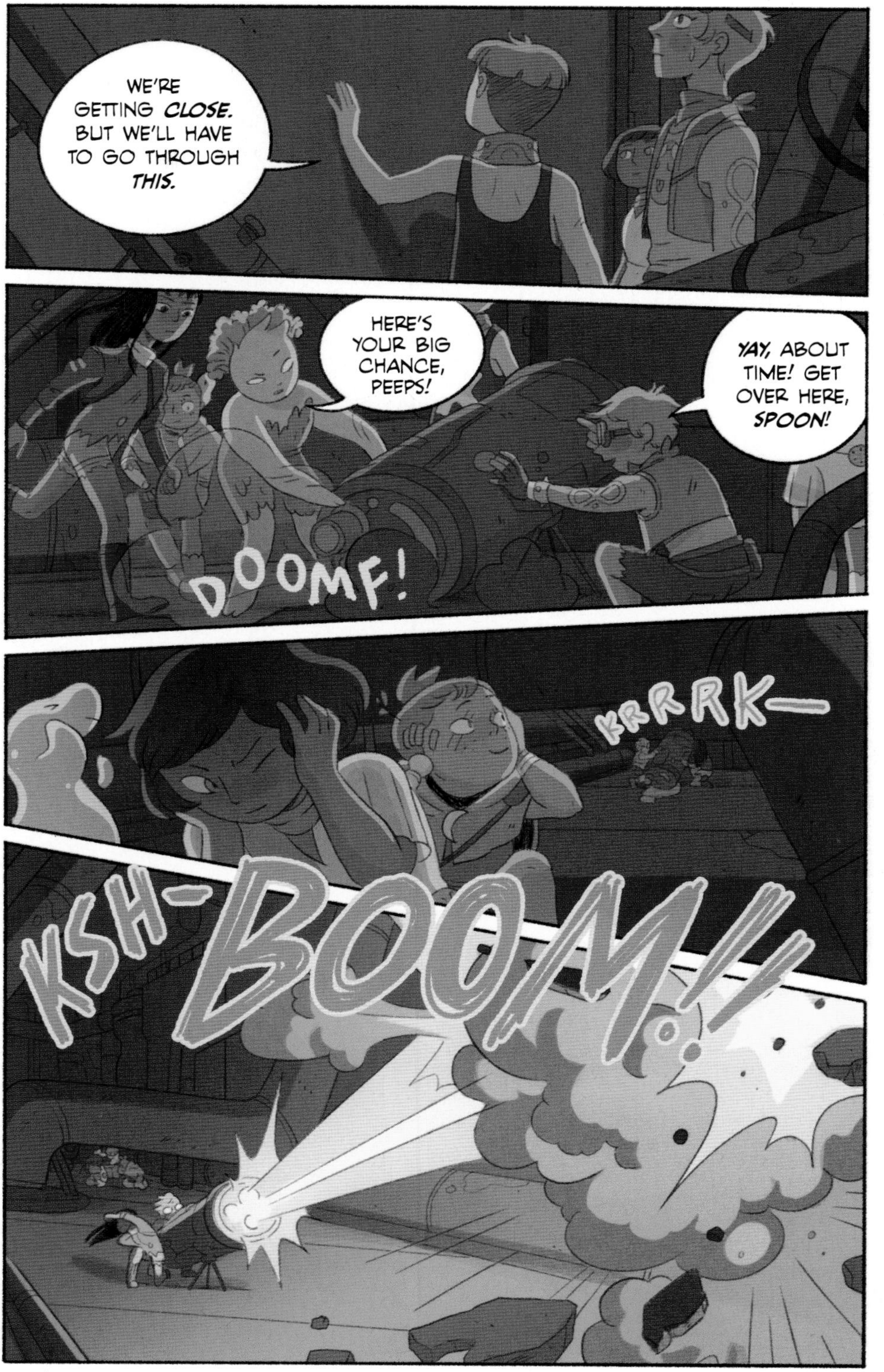

WE'RE GETTING *CLOSE.* BUT WE'LL HAVE TO GO THROUGH *THIS.*
HERE'S YOUR BIG CHANCE, PEEPS!
*YAY,* ABOUT TIME! GET OVER HERE, *SPOON!*
DOOMF!
KRRRK—
KSH-BOOM!!

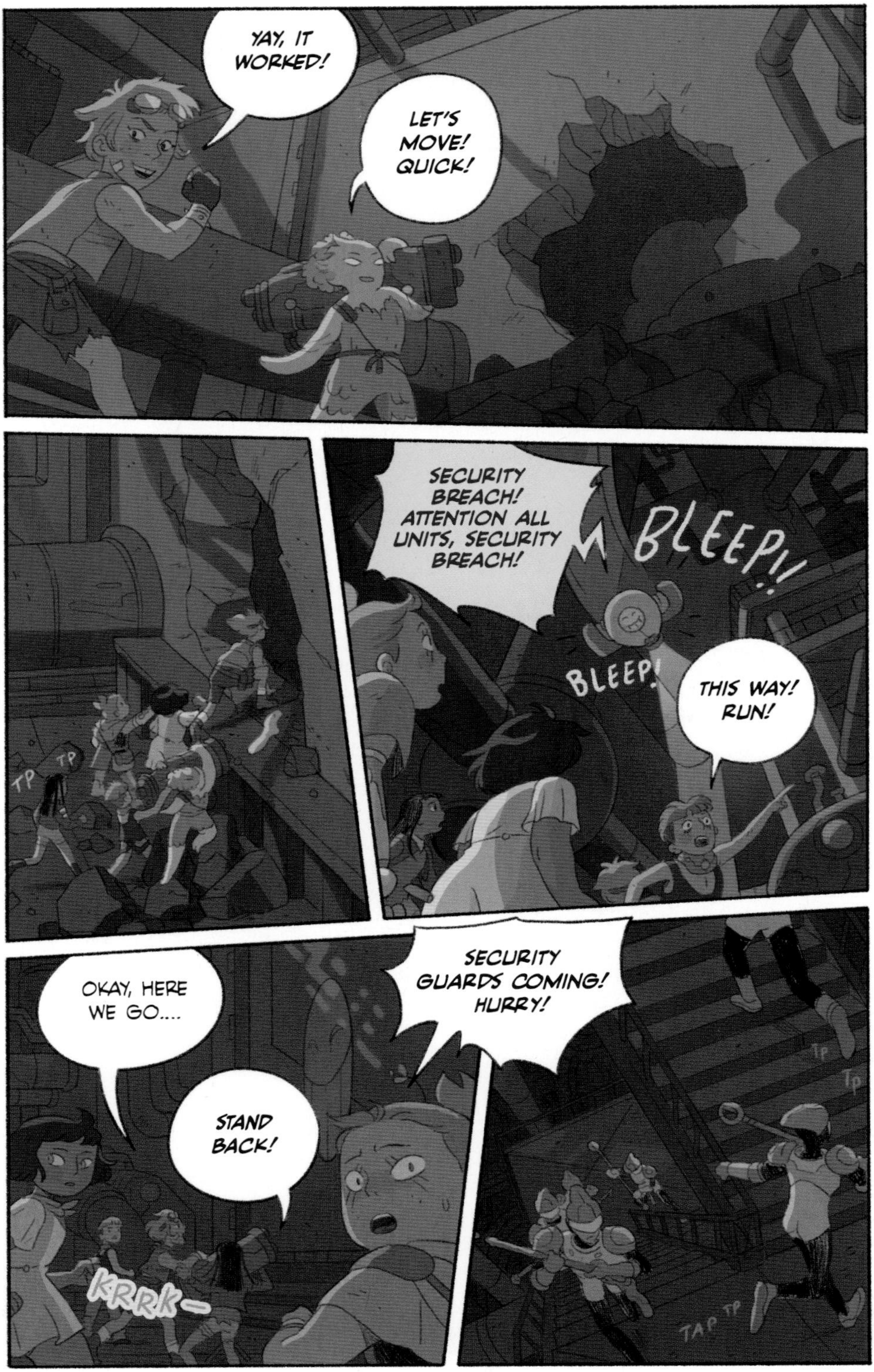
YAY, IT WORKED!
LET'S MOVE! QUICK!
TP TP
SECURITY BREACH! ATTENTION ALL UNITS, SECURITY BREACH!
BLEEP!!
BLEEP!
THIS WAY! RUN!
OKAY, HERE WE GO....
STAND BACK!
KRRK—
SECURITY GUARDS COMING! HURRY!
TP
TP
TAP TP

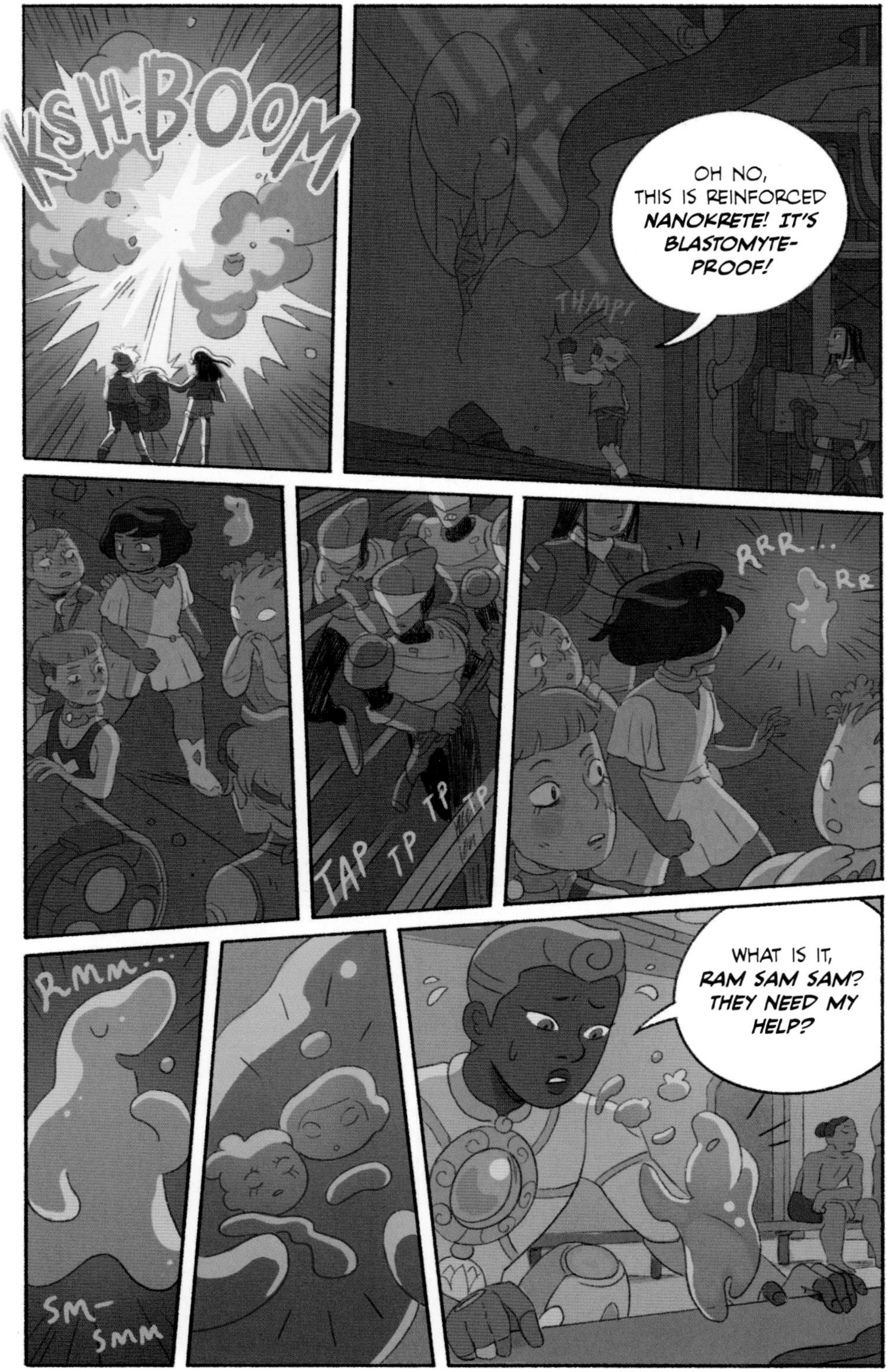
KSH-BOOM
OH NO, THIS IS REINFORCED NANOKRETE! IT'S BLASTOMYTE-PROOF!
THMP!
TAP TP TP TP
RRR... RR
RMM...
SM-SMM
WHAT IS IT, RAM SAM SAM? THEY NEED MY HELP?

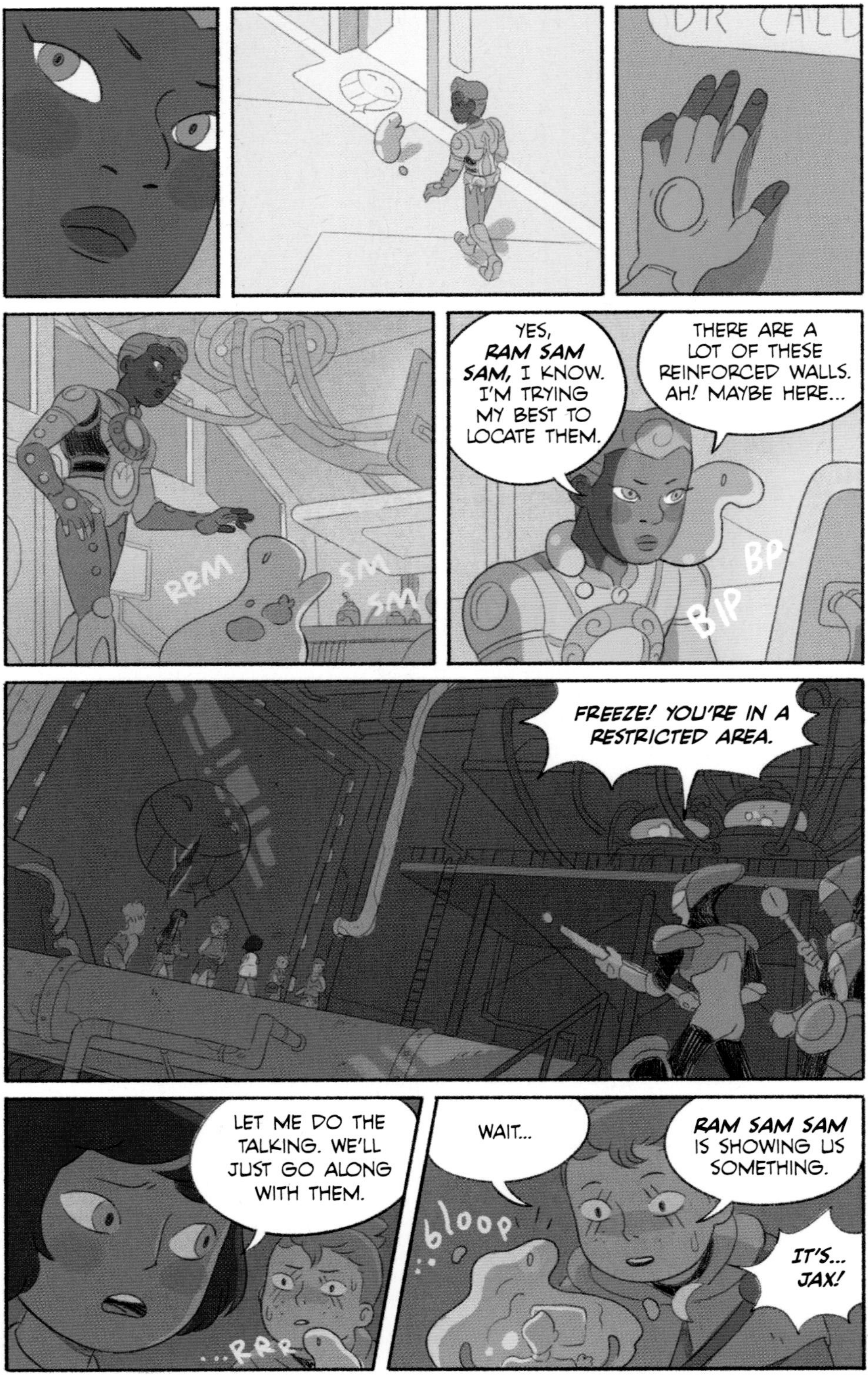
RRM
SM
SM
YES, *RAM SAM SAM,* I KNOW. I'M TRYING MY BEST TO LOCATE THEM.
THERE ARE A LOT OF THESE REINFORCED WALLS. AH! MAYBE HERE...
BIP
BP
*FREEZE! YOU'RE IN A RESTRICTED AREA.*
LET ME DO THE TALKING. WE'LL JUST GO ALONG WITH THEM.
...RRR
WAIT...
bloop
*RAM SAM SAM* IS SHOWING US SOMETHING.
*IT'S... JAX!*

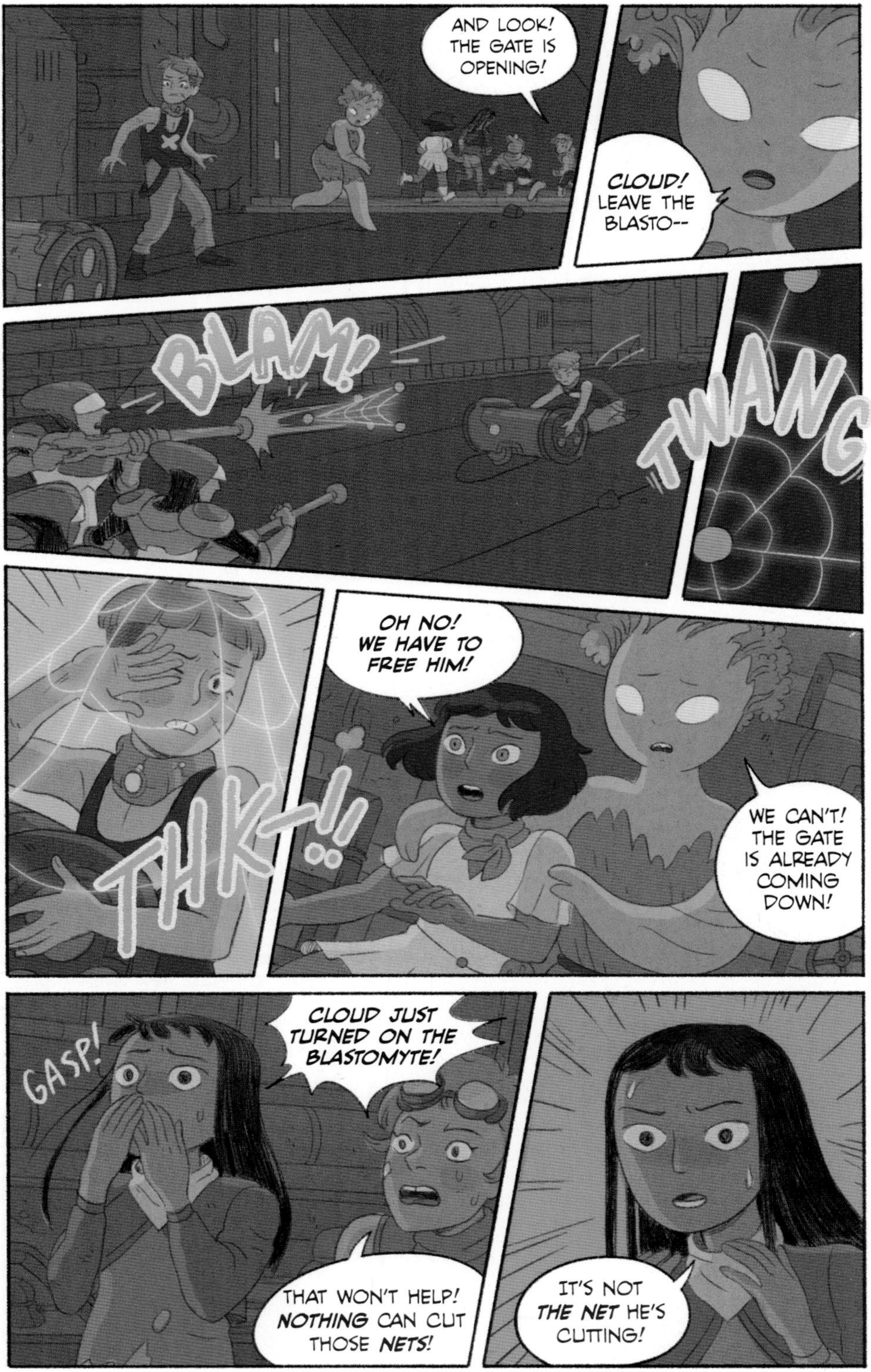
AND LOOK! THE GATE IS OPENING!
CLOUD! LEAVE THE BLASTO--
BLAM!
TWANG
THK--!!
OH NO! WE HAVE TO FREE HIM!
WE CAN'T! THE GATE IS ALREADY COMING DOWN!
GASP!
CLOUD JUST TURNED ON THE BLASTOMYTE!
THAT WON'T HELP! NOTHING CAN CUT THOSE NETS!
IT'S NOT THE NET HE'S CUTTING!

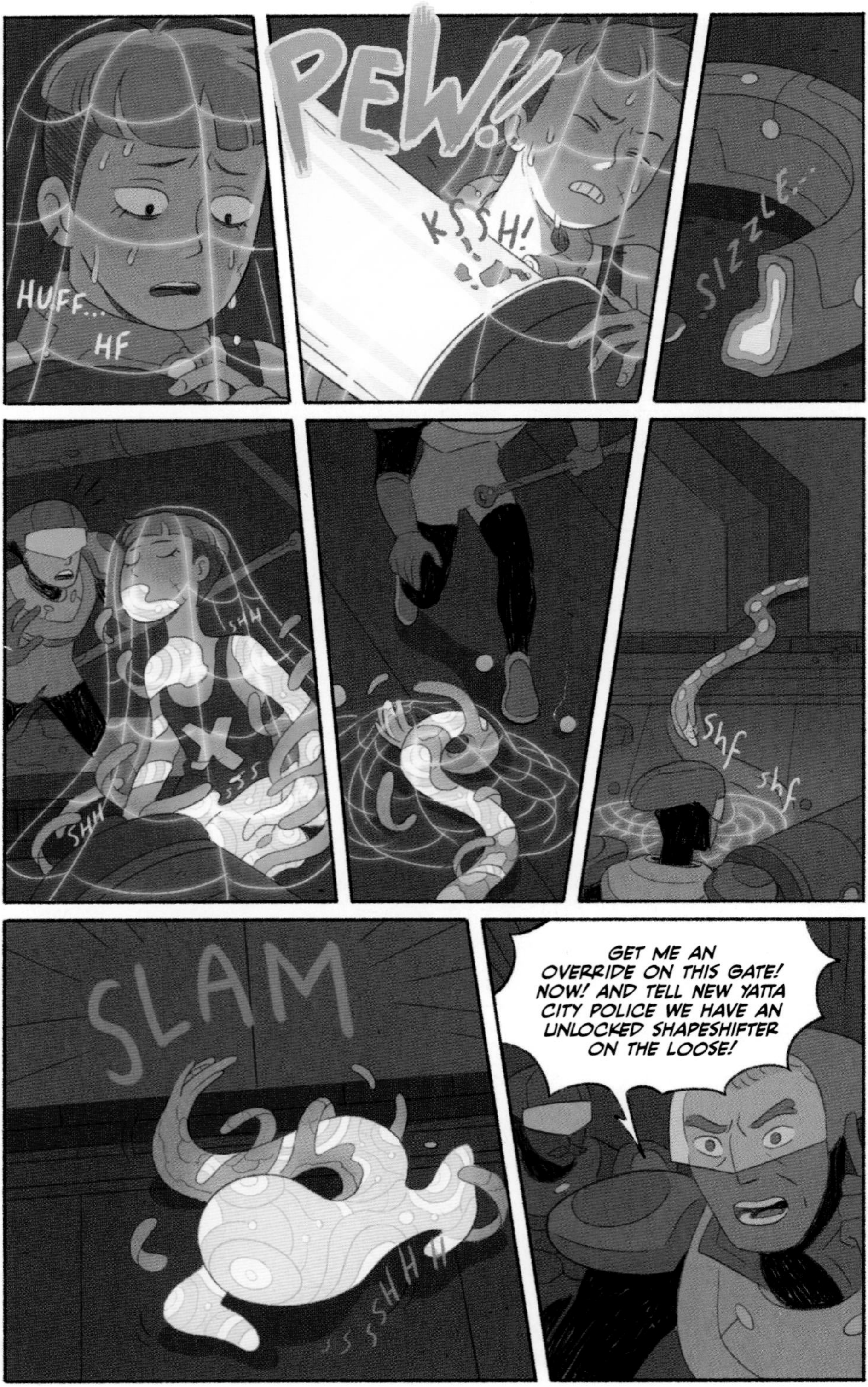
HUFF...
HF
PEW!!
KSSH!
SIZZLE...
SHH
SHH
SHf
shf
SLAM
SSSHHH
GET ME AN OVERRIDE ON THIS GATE! NOW! AND TELL NEW YATTA CITY POLICE WE HAVE AN UNLOCKED SHAPESHIFTER ON THE LOOSE!

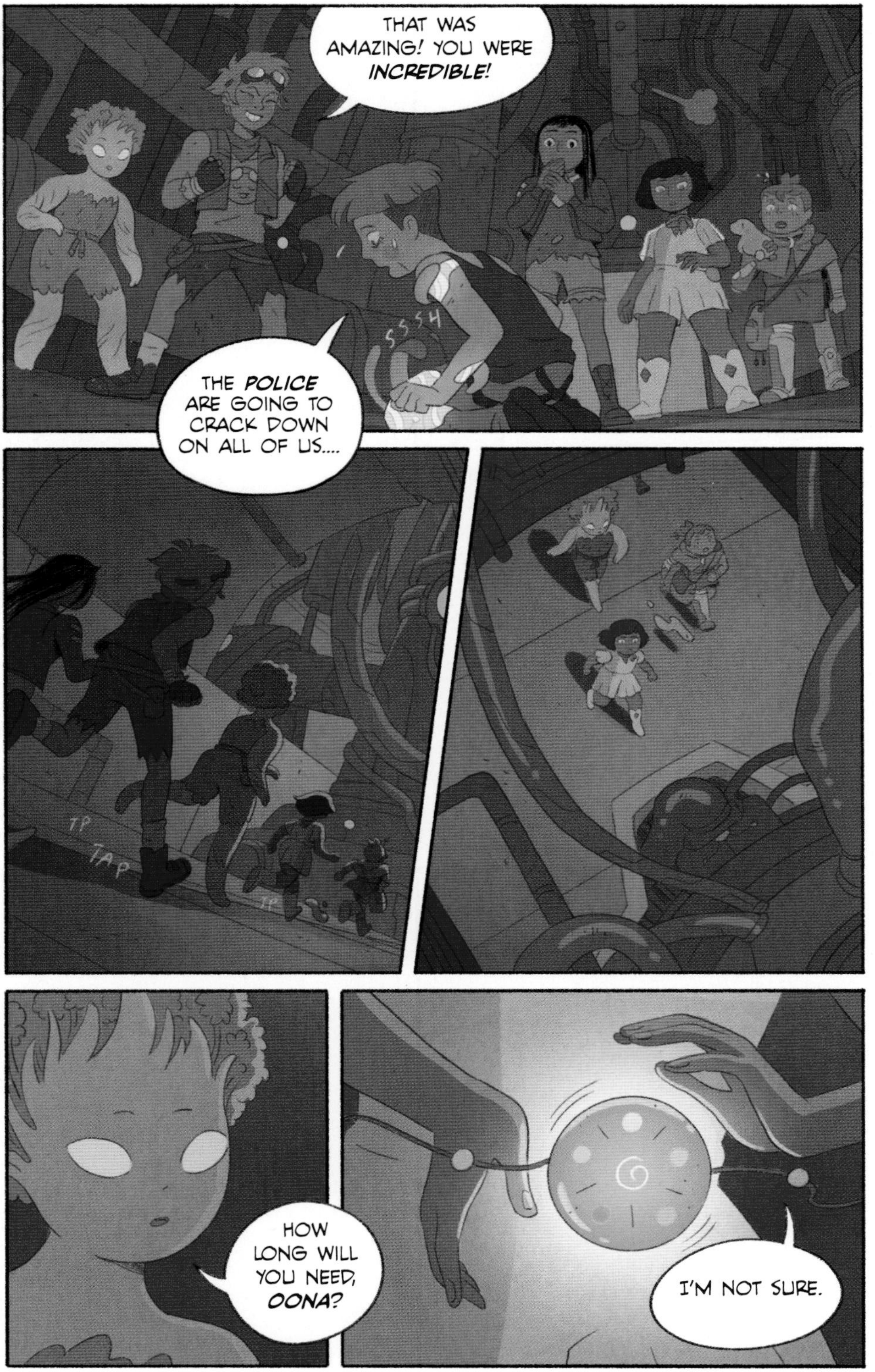
THAT WAS AMAZING! YOU WERE *INCREDIBLE!*
SSSH
THE *POLICE* ARE GOING TO CRACK DOWN ON ALL OF US....
TP
TAP
TP
HOW LONG WILL YOU NEED, *OONA?*
I'M NOT SURE.

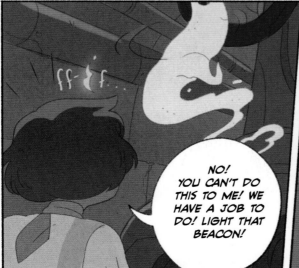

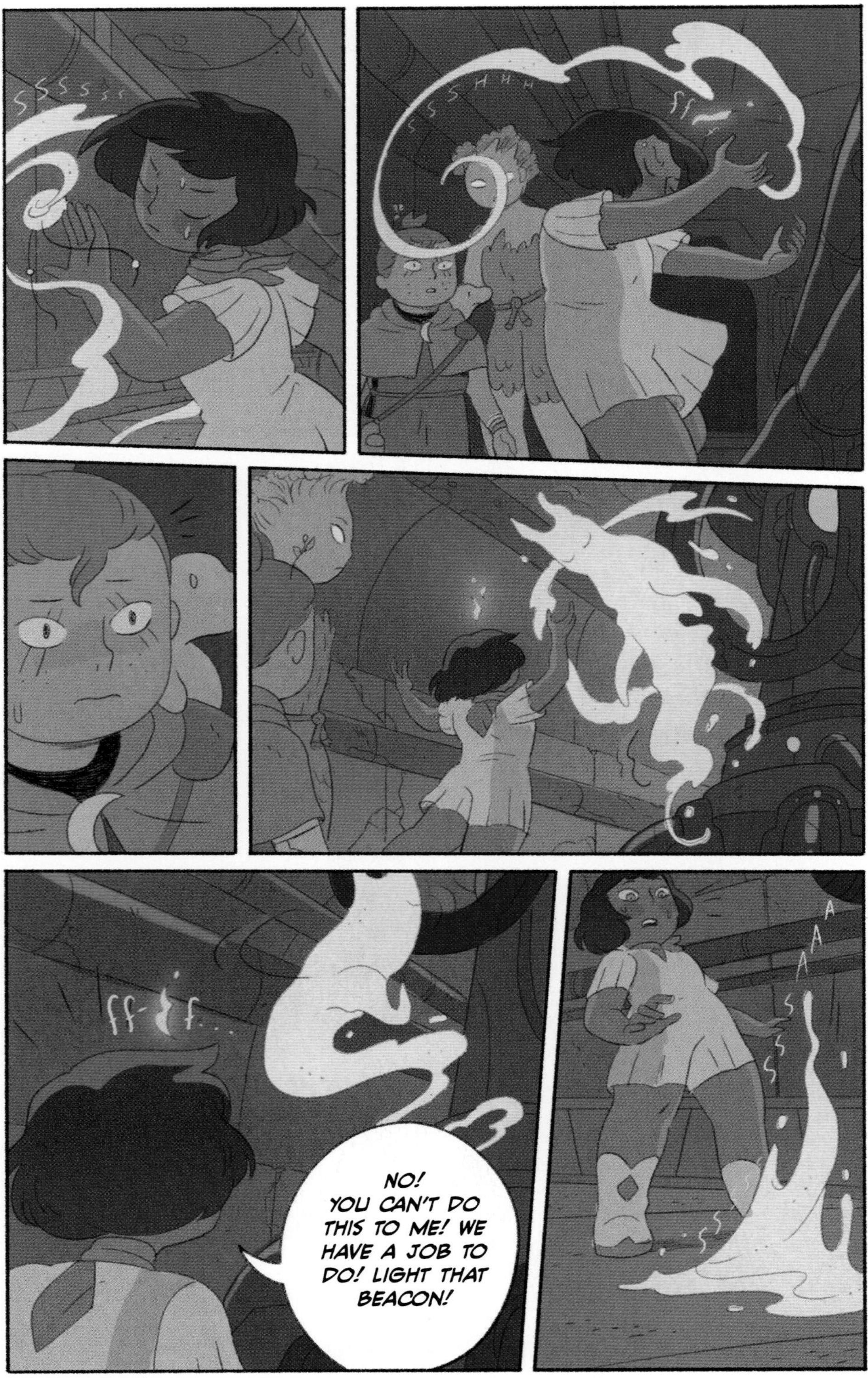
NO!
YOU CAN'T DO THIS TO ME! WE HAVE A JOB TO DO! LIGHT THAT BEACON!

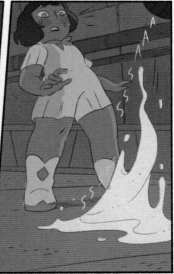

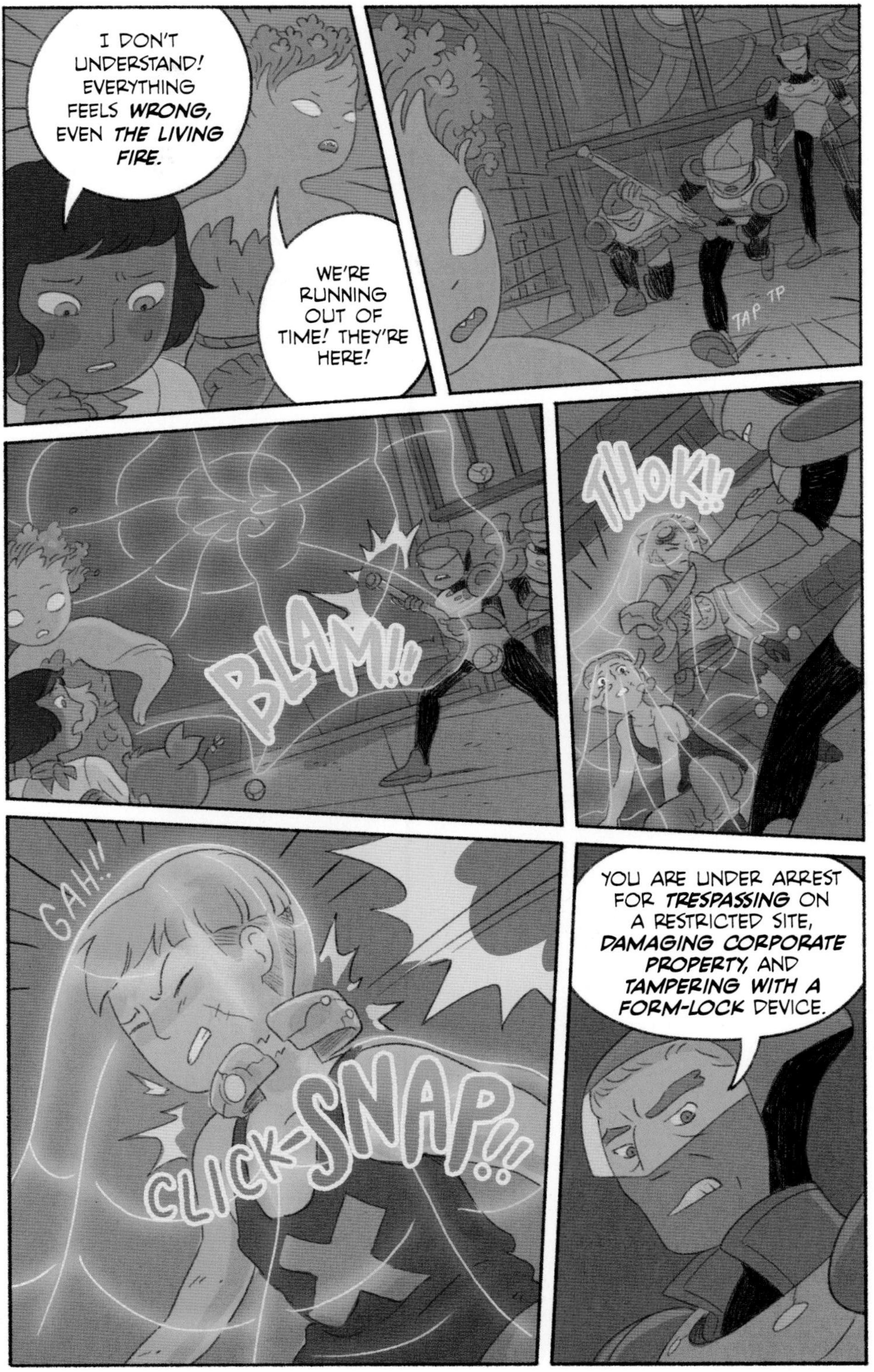
I DON'T UNDERSTAND! EVERYTHING FEELS WRONG, EVEN THE LIVING FIRE.
WE'RE RUNNING OUT OF TIME! THEY'RE HERE!
TAP TP
BLAM!!
THOK!!
GAH!!
CLICK-SNAP!!
YOU ARE UNDER ARREST FOR TRESPASSING ON A RESTRICTED SITE, DAMAGING CORPORATE PROPERTY, AND TAMPERING WITH A FORM-LOCK DEVICE.

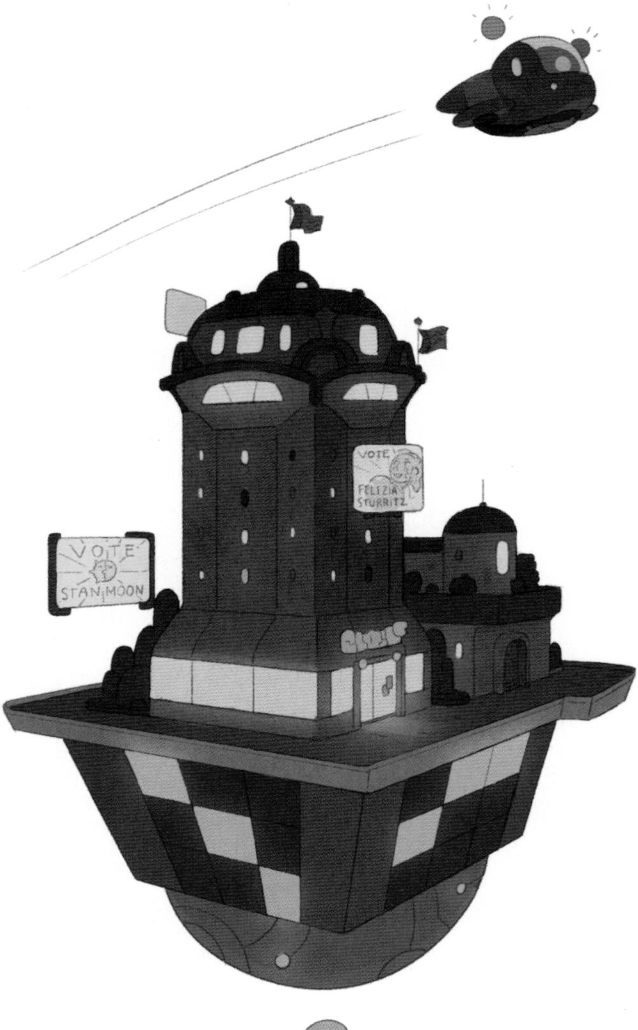
VOTE
STAN MOON
VOTE
FELIZIA STURRITZ

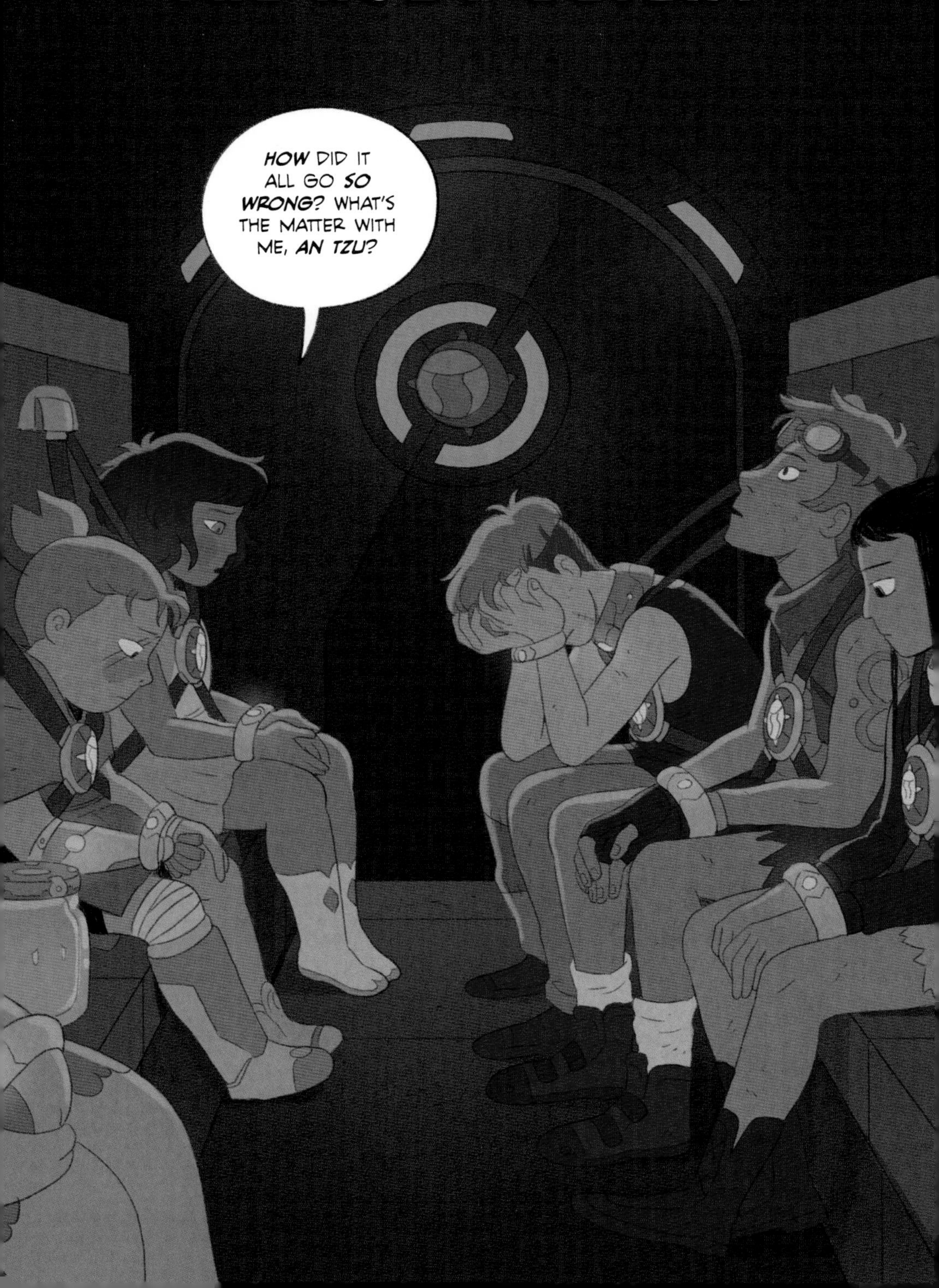
*HOW* DID IT ALL GO *SO WRONG?* WHAT'S THE MATTER WITH ME, *AN TZU?*

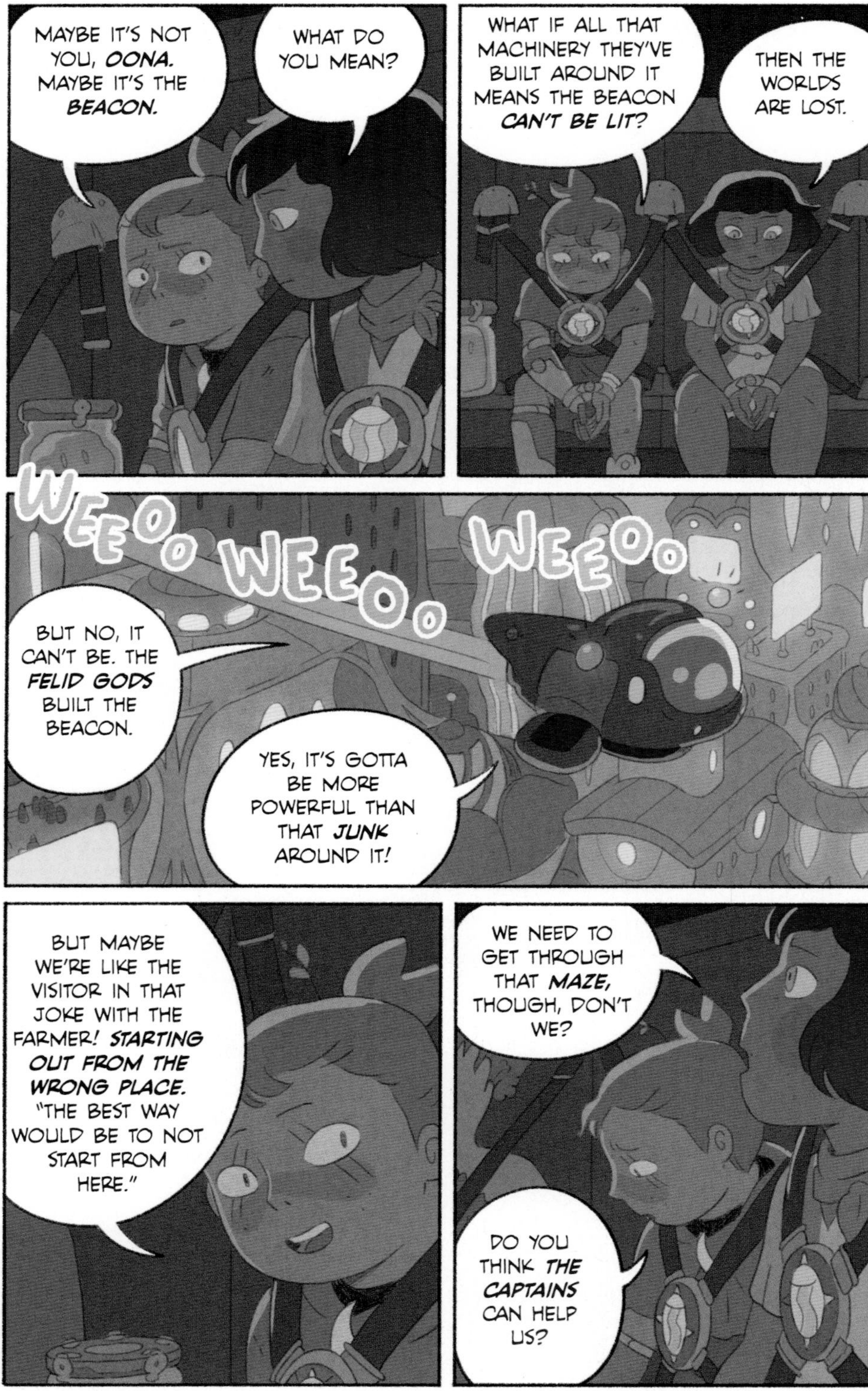
MAYBE IT'S NOT YOU, *OONA.* MAYBE IT'S THE *BEACON.*
WHAT DO YOU MEAN?
WHAT IF ALL THAT MACHINERY THEY'VE BUILT AROUND IT MEANS THE BEACON *CAN'T BE LIT?*
THEN THE WORLDS ARE LOST.
WEEOo WEEOo WEEOo
BUT NO, IT CAN'T BE. THE *FELID GODS* BUILT THE BEACON.
YES, IT'S GOTTA BE MORE POWERFUL THAN THAT *JUNK* AROUND IT!
BUT MAYBE WE'RE LIKE THE VISITOR IN THAT JOKE WITH THE FARMER! *STARTING OUT FROM THE WRONG PLACE.* "THE BEST WAY WOULD BE TO NOT START FROM HERE."
WE NEED TO GET THROUGH THAT *MAZE,* THOUGH, DON'T WE?
DO YOU THINK *THE CAPTAINS* CAN HELP US?

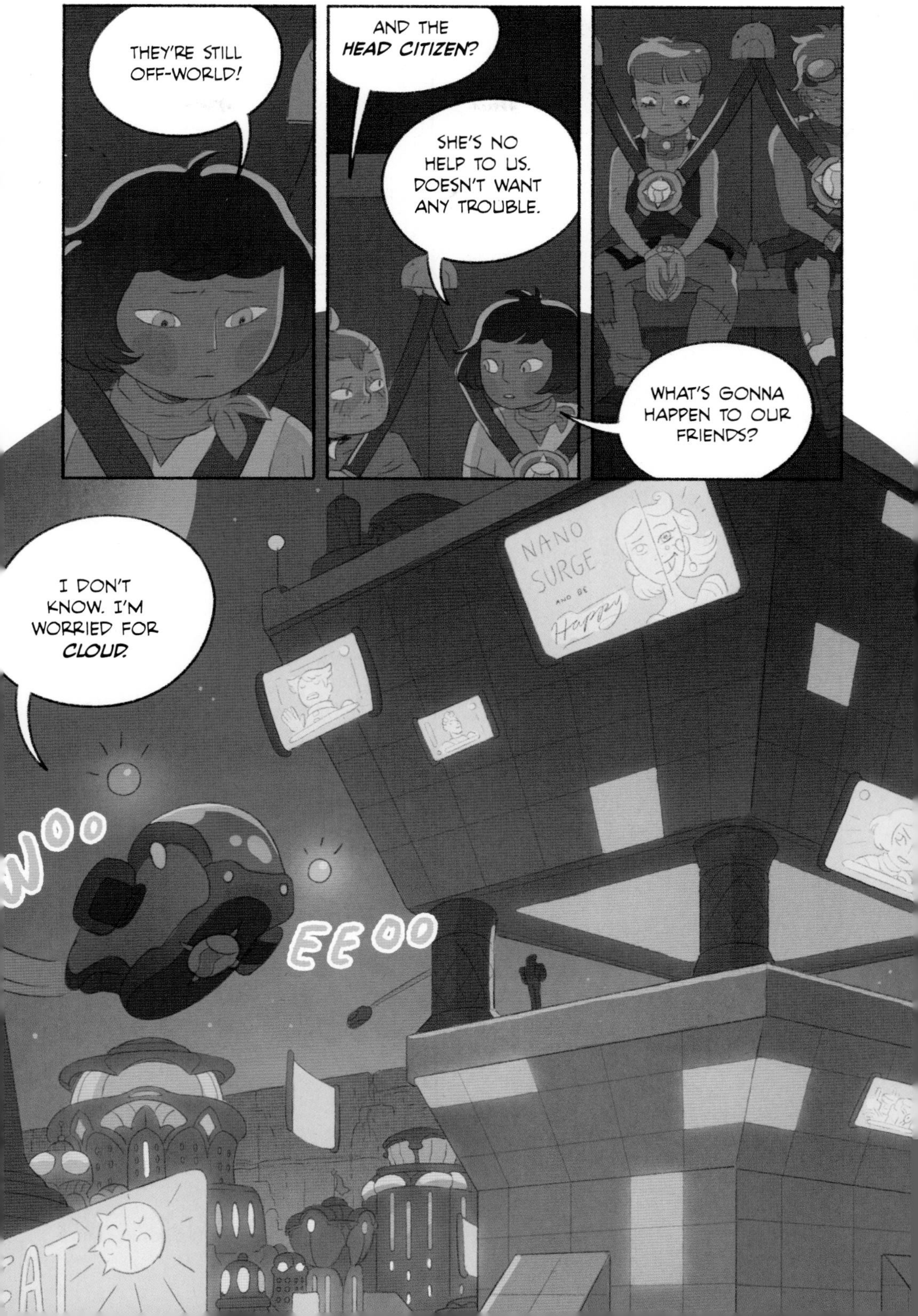
THEY'RE STILL OFF-WORLD!
AND THE HEAD CITIZEN?
SHE'S NO HELP TO US. DOESN'T WANT ANY TROUBLE.
WHAT'S GONNA HAPPEN TO OUR FRIENDS?
I DON'T KNOW. I'M WORRIED FOR CLOUD.
NANO SURGE AND BE Happy
WOO
EE OO

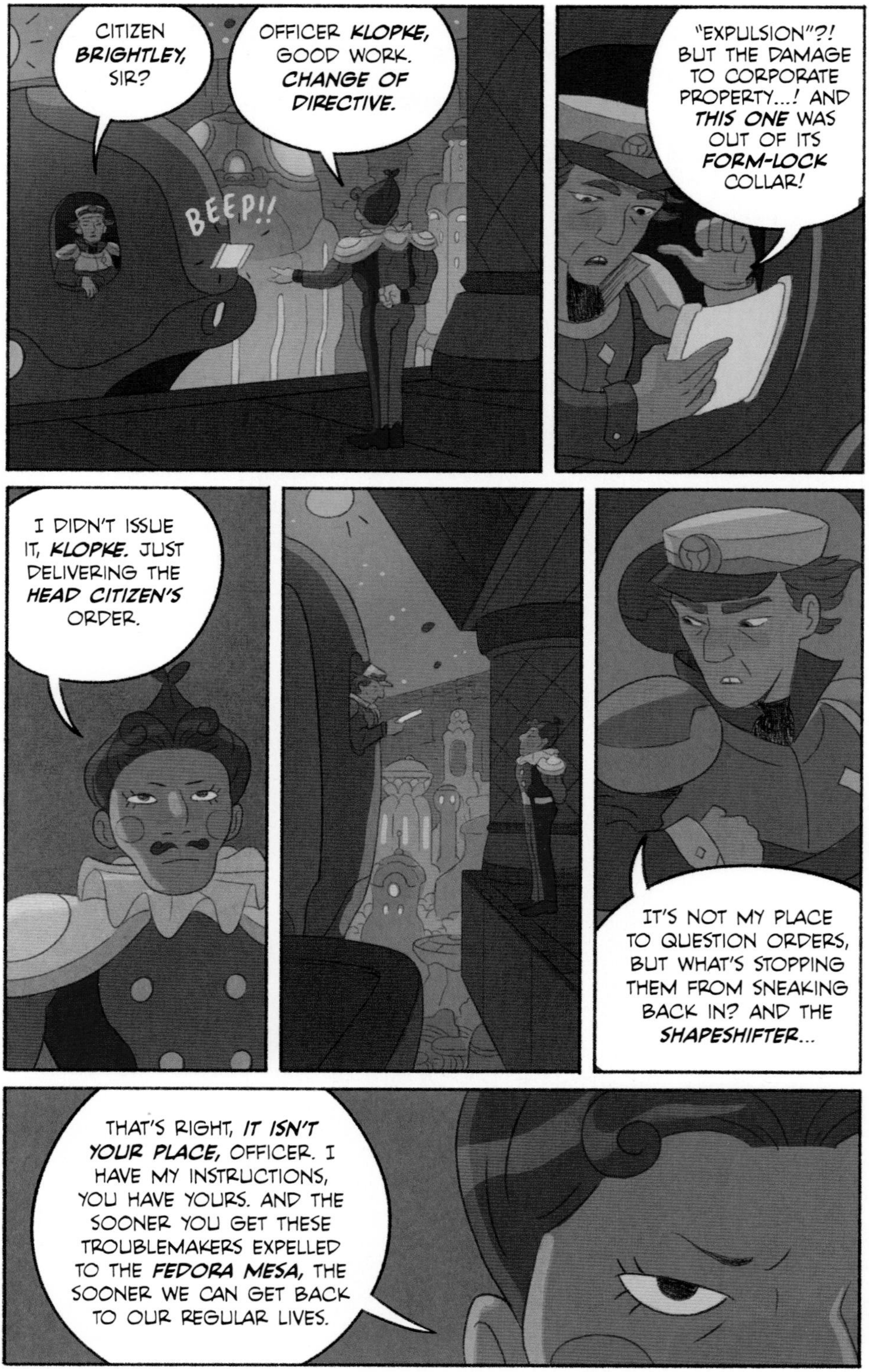
CITIZEN BRIGHTLEY, SIR?
OFFICER KLOPKE, GOOD WORK. CHANGE OF DIRECTIVE.
BEEP!!
"EXPULSION"?! BUT THE DAMAGE TO CORPORATE PROPERTY...! AND THIS ONE WAS OUT OF ITS FORM-LOCK COLLAR!
I DIDN'T ISSUE IT, KLOPKE. JUST DELIVERING THE HEAD CITIZEN'S ORDER.
IT'S NOT MY PLACE TO QUESTION ORDERS, BUT WHAT'S STOPPING THEM FROM SNEAKING BACK IN? AND THE SHAPESHIFTER...
THAT'S RIGHT, IT ISN'T YOUR PLACE, OFFICER. I HAVE MY INSTRUCTIONS, YOU HAVE YOURS. AND THE SOONER YOU GET THESE TROUBLEMAKERS EXPELLED TO THE FEDORA MESA, THE SOONER WE CAN GET BACK TO OUR REGULAR LIVES.

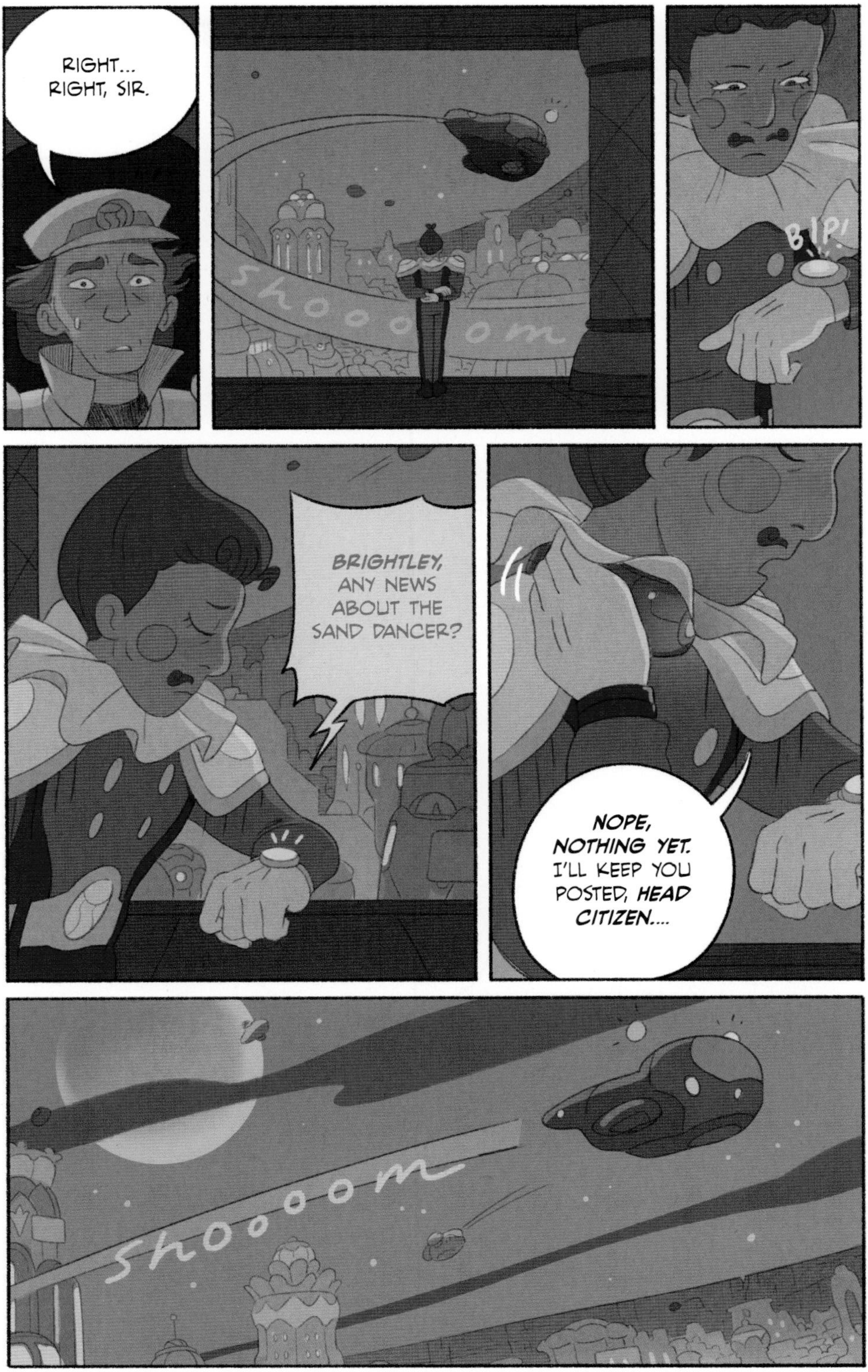
RIGHT... RIGHT, SIR.
SHOOOOM
BIP!
BRIGHTLEY, ANY NEWS ABOUT THE SAND DANCER?
NOPE, NOTHING YET. I'LL KEEP YOU POSTED, HEAD CITIZEN....
SHOOOOM

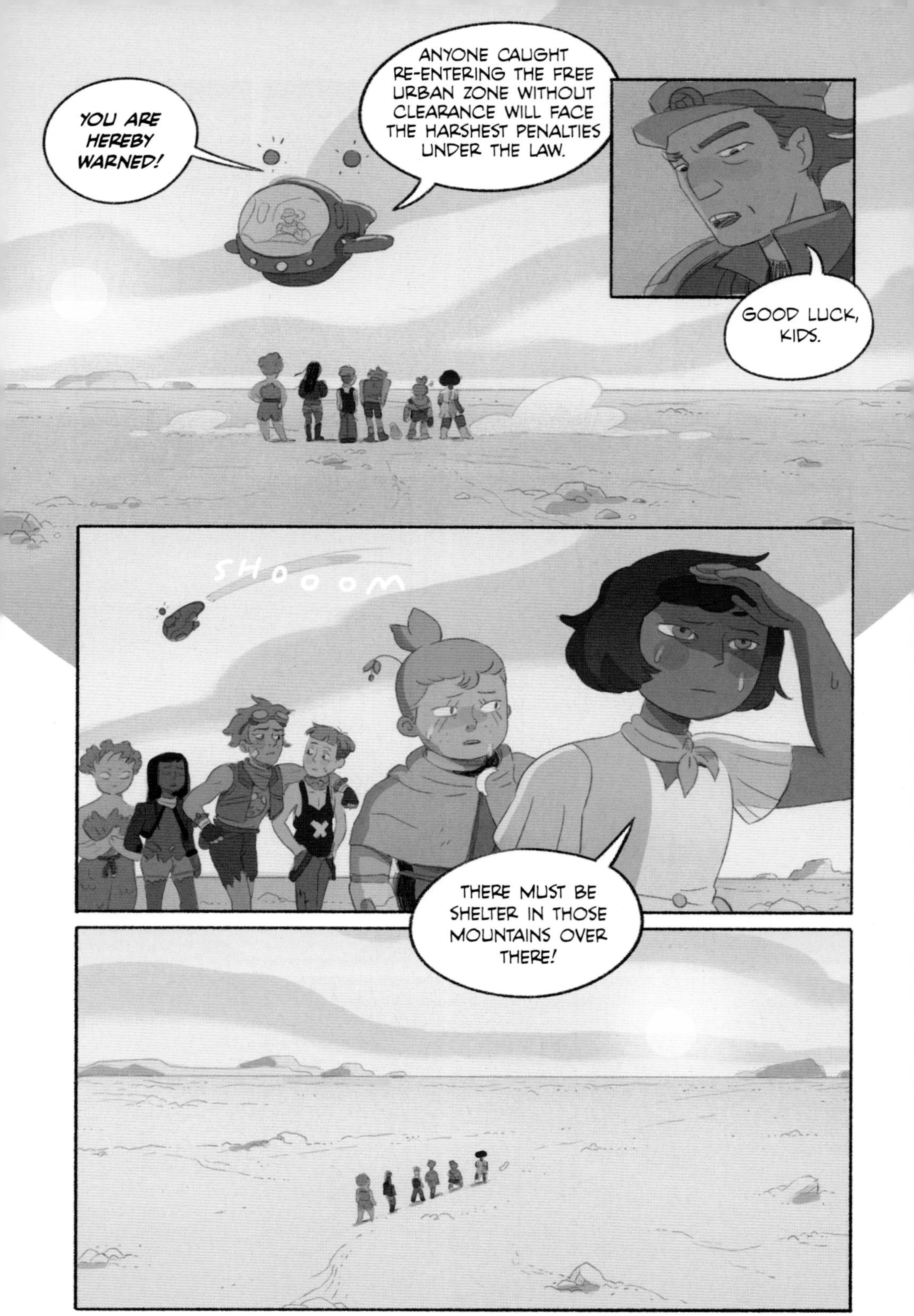
YOU ARE HEREBY WARNED!
ANYONE CAUGHT RE-ENTERING THE FREE URBAN ZONE WITHOUT CLEARANCE WILL FACE THE HARSHEST PENALTIES UNDER THE LAW.
GOOD LUCK, KIDS.
SHOOOM
THERE MUST BE SHELTER IN THOSE MOUNTAINS OVER THERE!

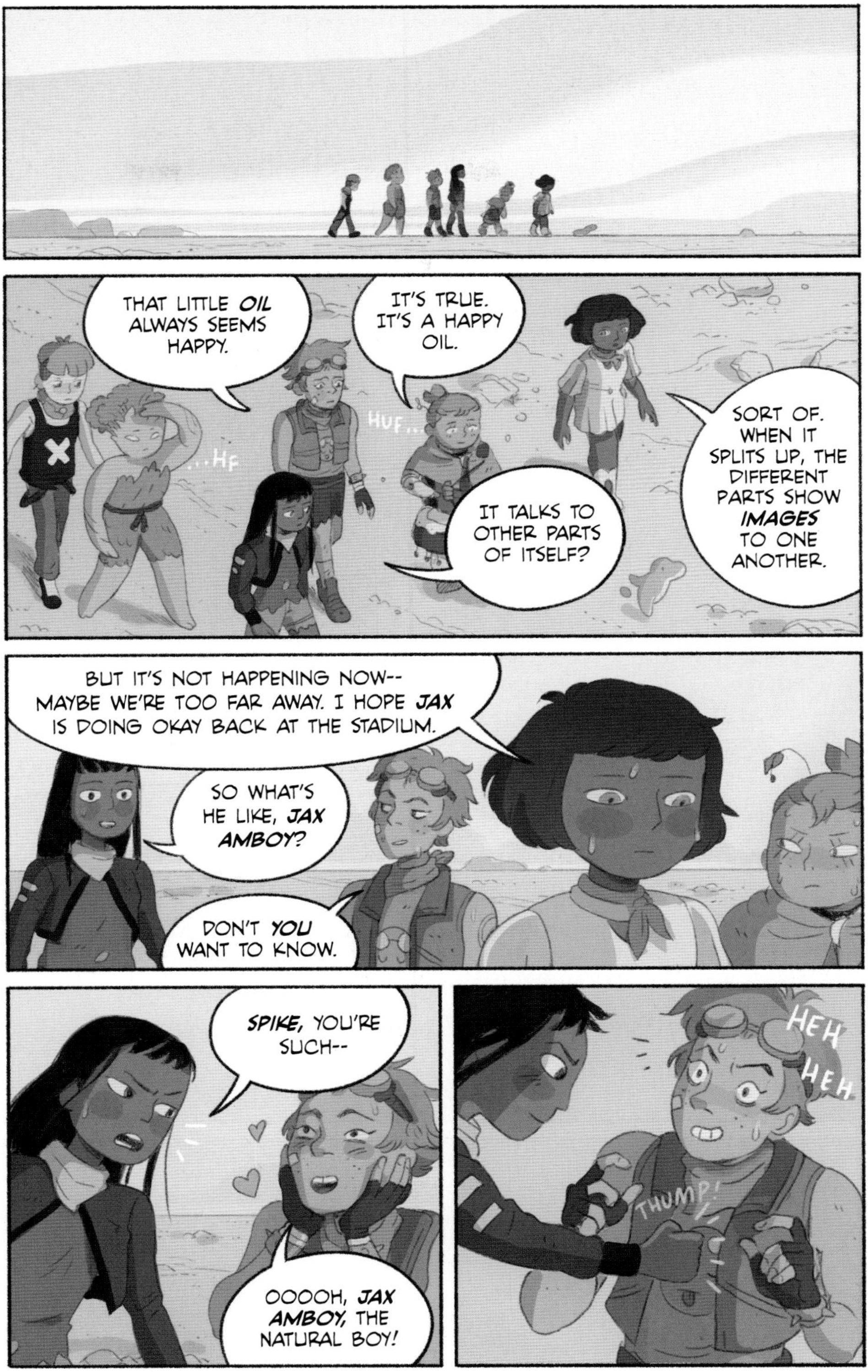

THAT LITTLE OIL ALWAYS SEEMS HAPPY.
...HF
IT'S TRUE. IT'S A HAPPY OIL.
HUF...
IT TALKS TO OTHER PARTS OF ITSELF?
SORT OF. WHEN IT SPLITS UP, THE DIFFERENT PARTS SHOW IMAGES TO ONE ANOTHER.
BUT IT'S NOT HAPPENING NOW-- MAYBE WE'RE TOO FAR AWAY. I HOPE JAX IS DOING OKAY BACK AT THE STADIUM.
SO WHAT'S HE LIKE, JAX AMBOY?
DON'T YOU WANT TO KNOW.
SPIKE, YOU'RE SUCH--
OOOOH, JAX AMBOY, THE NATURAL BOY!
HEH HEH
THUMP!

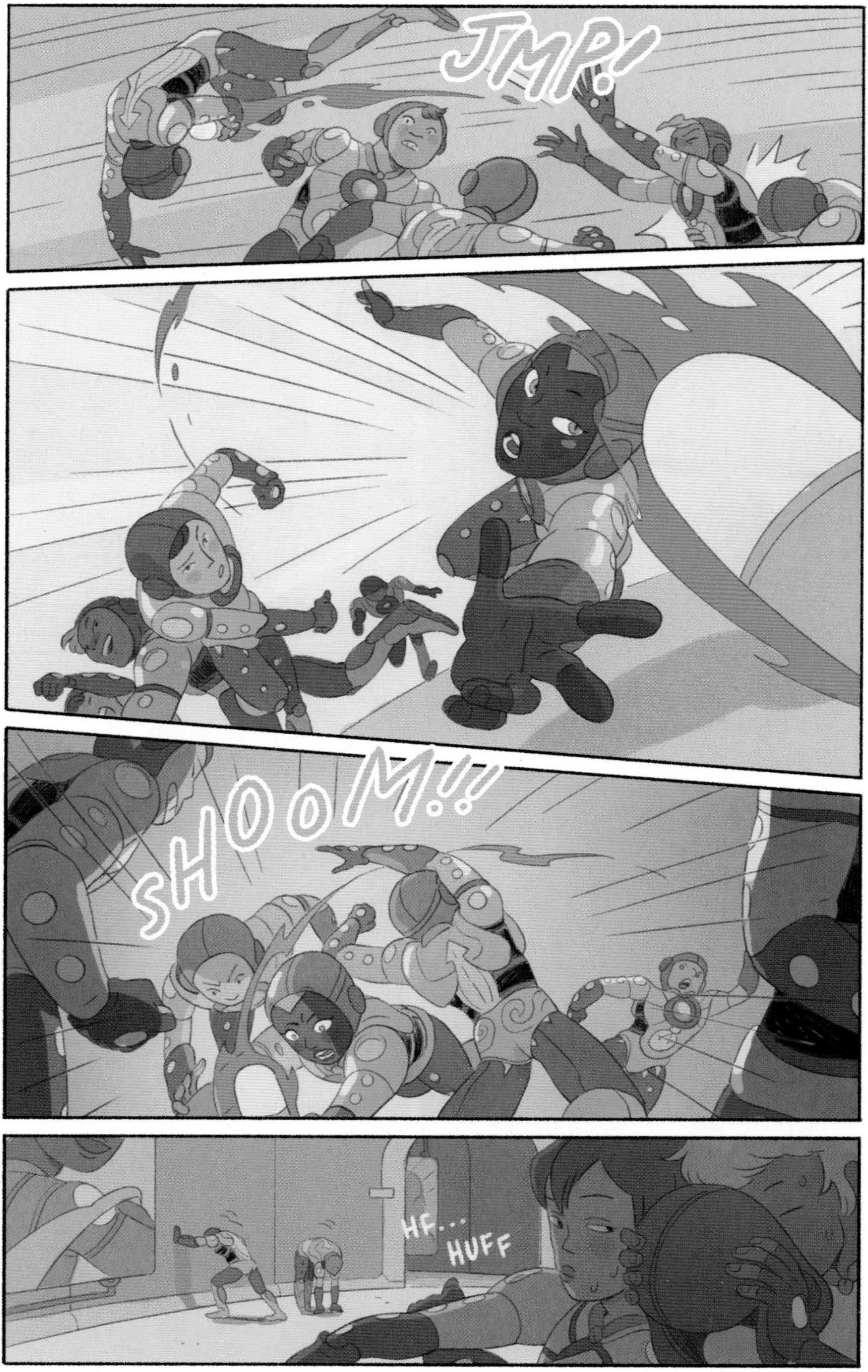
JMP!
SHOOM!!
HF...
HUFF

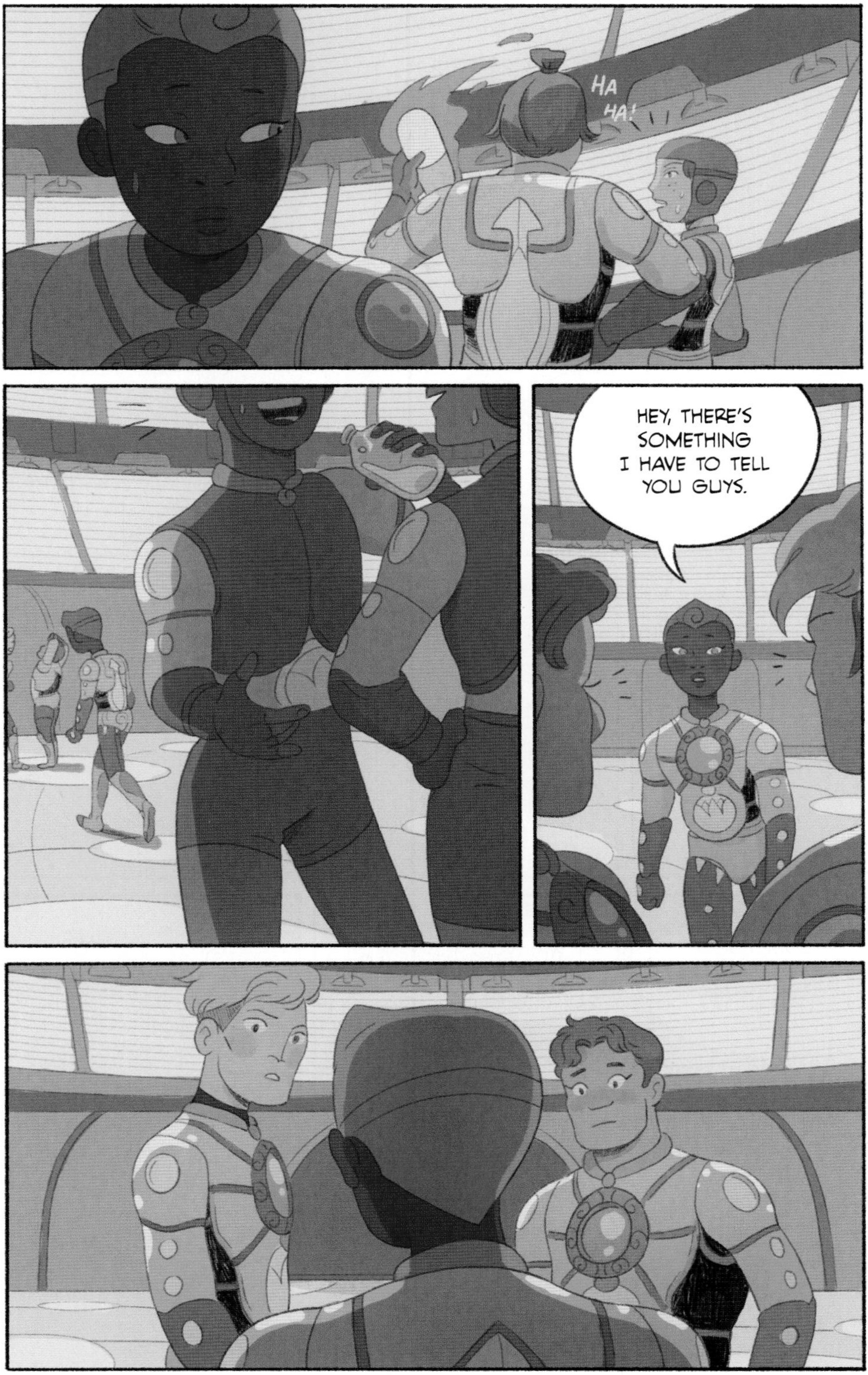
HA HA!
HEY, THERE'S SOMETHING I HAVE TO TELL YOU GUYS.

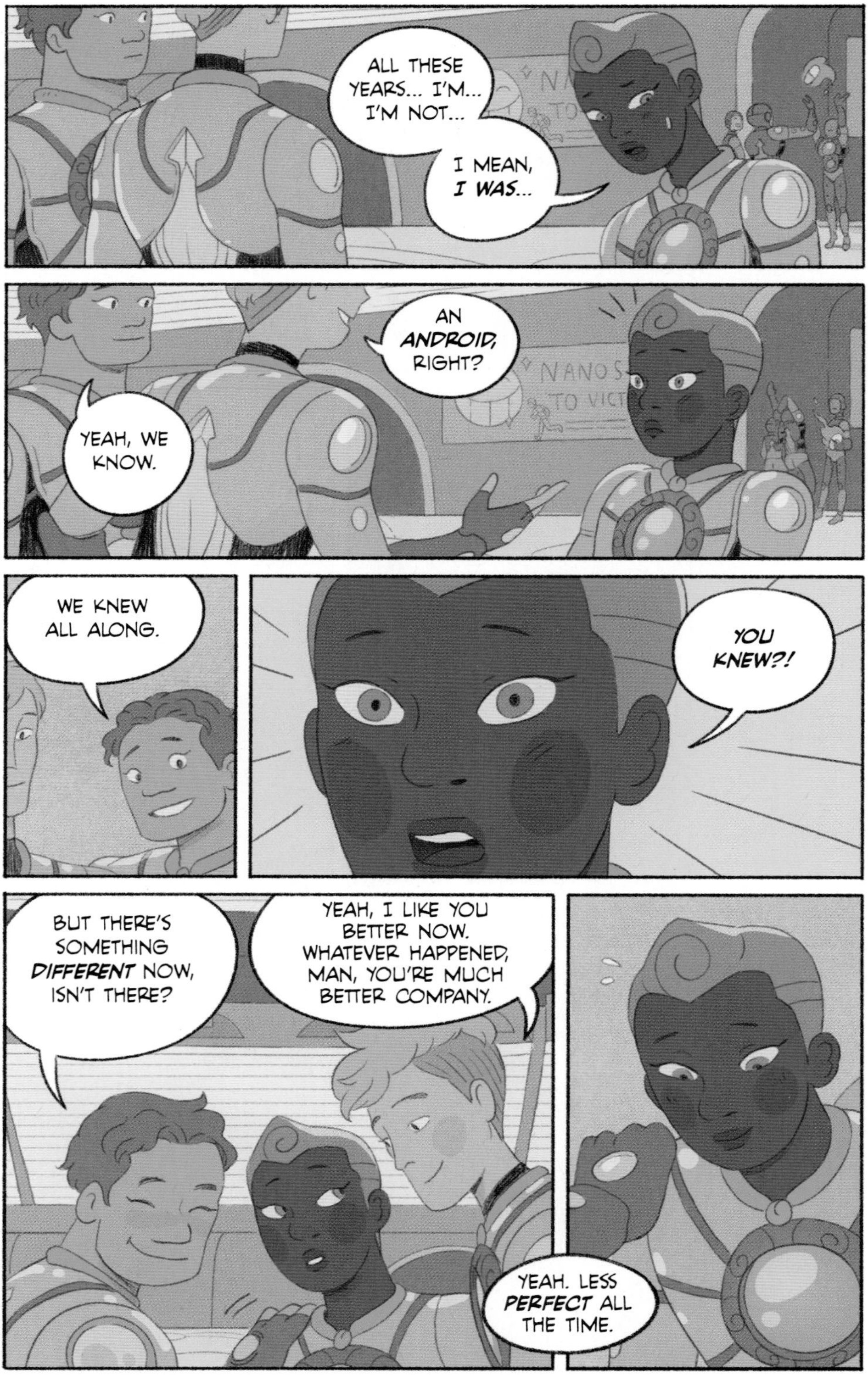

ALL THESE YEARS... I'M... I'M NOT...
I MEAN, I WAS...
NANOS TO VICT
AN ANDROID, RIGHT?
YEAH, WE KNOW.
WE KNEW ALL ALONG.
YOU KNEW?!
BUT THERE'S SOMETHING DIFFERENT NOW, ISN'T THERE?
YEAH, I LIKE YOU BETTER NOW. WHATEVER HAPPENED, MAN, YOU'RE MUCH BETTER COMPANY.
YEAH. LESS PERFECT ALL THE TIME.

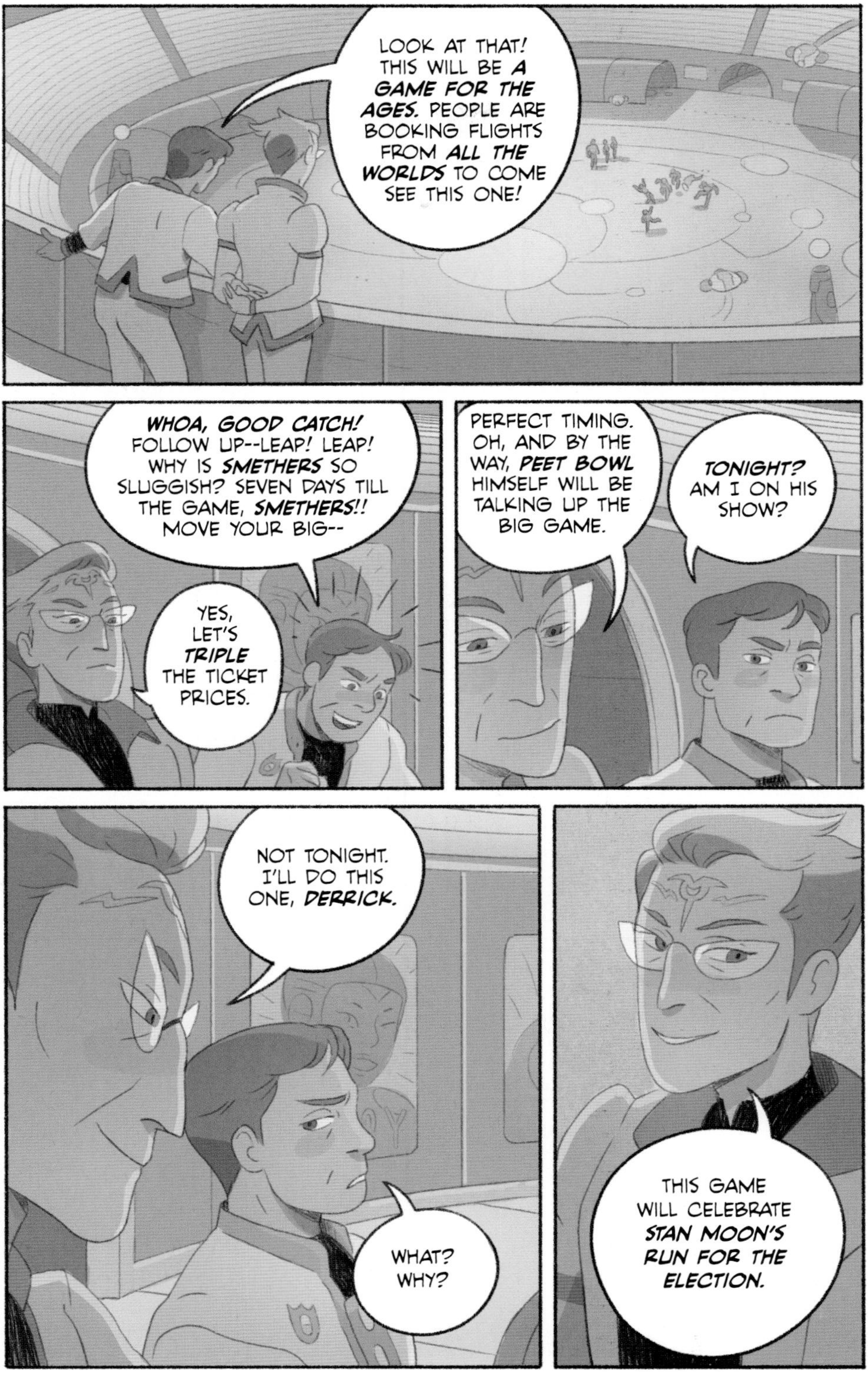
LOOK AT THAT! THIS WILL BE A GAME FOR THE AGES. PEOPLE ARE BOOKING FLIGHTS FROM ALL THE WORLDS TO COME SEE THIS ONE!
WHOA, GOOD CATCH! FOLLOW UP--LEAP! LEAP! WHY IS SMETHERS SO SLUGGISH? SEVEN DAYS TILL THE GAME, SMETHERS!! MOVE YOUR BIG--
YES, LET'S TRIPLE THE TICKET PRICES.
PERFECT TIMING. OH, AND BY THE WAY, PEET BOWL HIMSELF WILL BE TALKING UP THE BIG GAME.
TONIGHT? AM I ON HIS SHOW?
NOT TONIGHT. I'LL DO THIS ONE, DERRICK.
WHAT? WHY?
THIS GAME WILL CELEBRATE STAN MOON'S RUN FOR THE ELECTION.

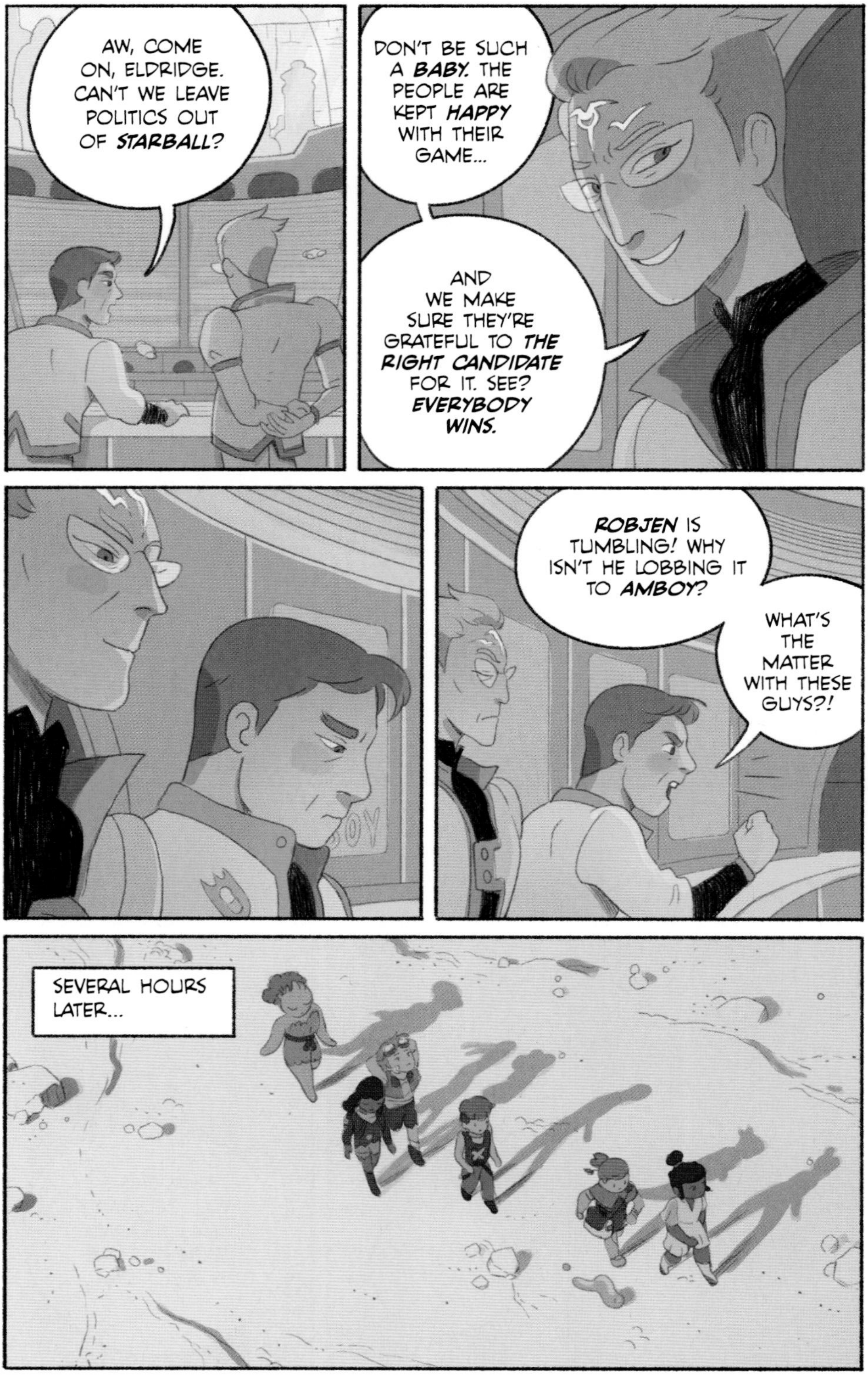
AW, COME ON, ELDRIDGE. CAN'T WE LEAVE POLITICS OUT OF STARBALL?
DON'T BE SUCH A BABY. THE PEOPLE ARE KEPT HAPPY WITH THEIR GAME...
AND WE MAKE SURE THEY'RE GRATEFUL TO THE RIGHT CANDIDATE FOR IT. SEE? EVERYBODY WINS.
ROBJEN IS TUMBLING! WHY ISN'T HE LOBBING IT TO AMBOY?
WHAT'S THE MATTER WITH THESE GUYS?!
SEVERAL HOURS LATER...

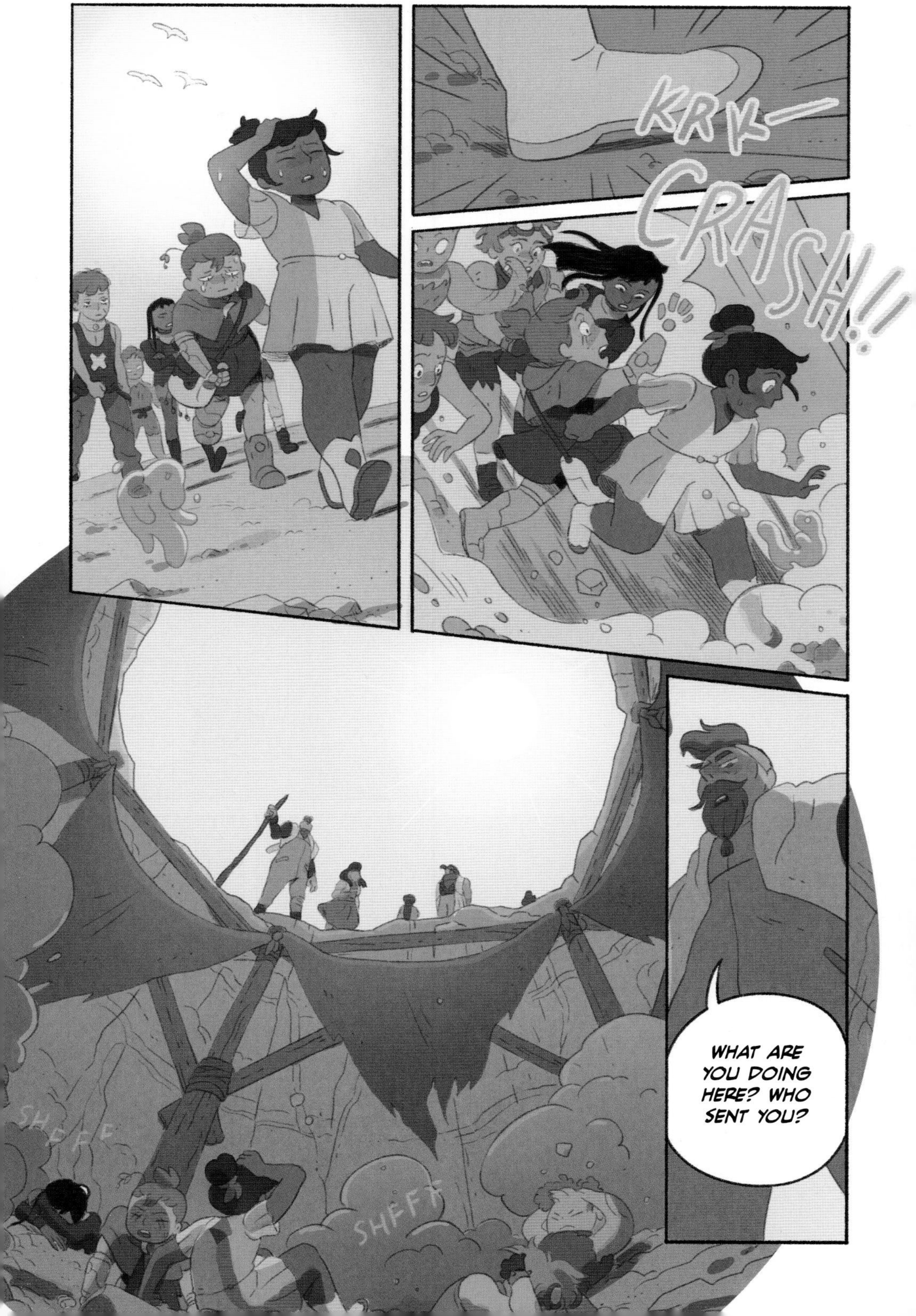
KRK—
CRASH!!
SHFFF
SHFFF
WHAT ARE YOU DOING HERE? WHO SENT YOU?

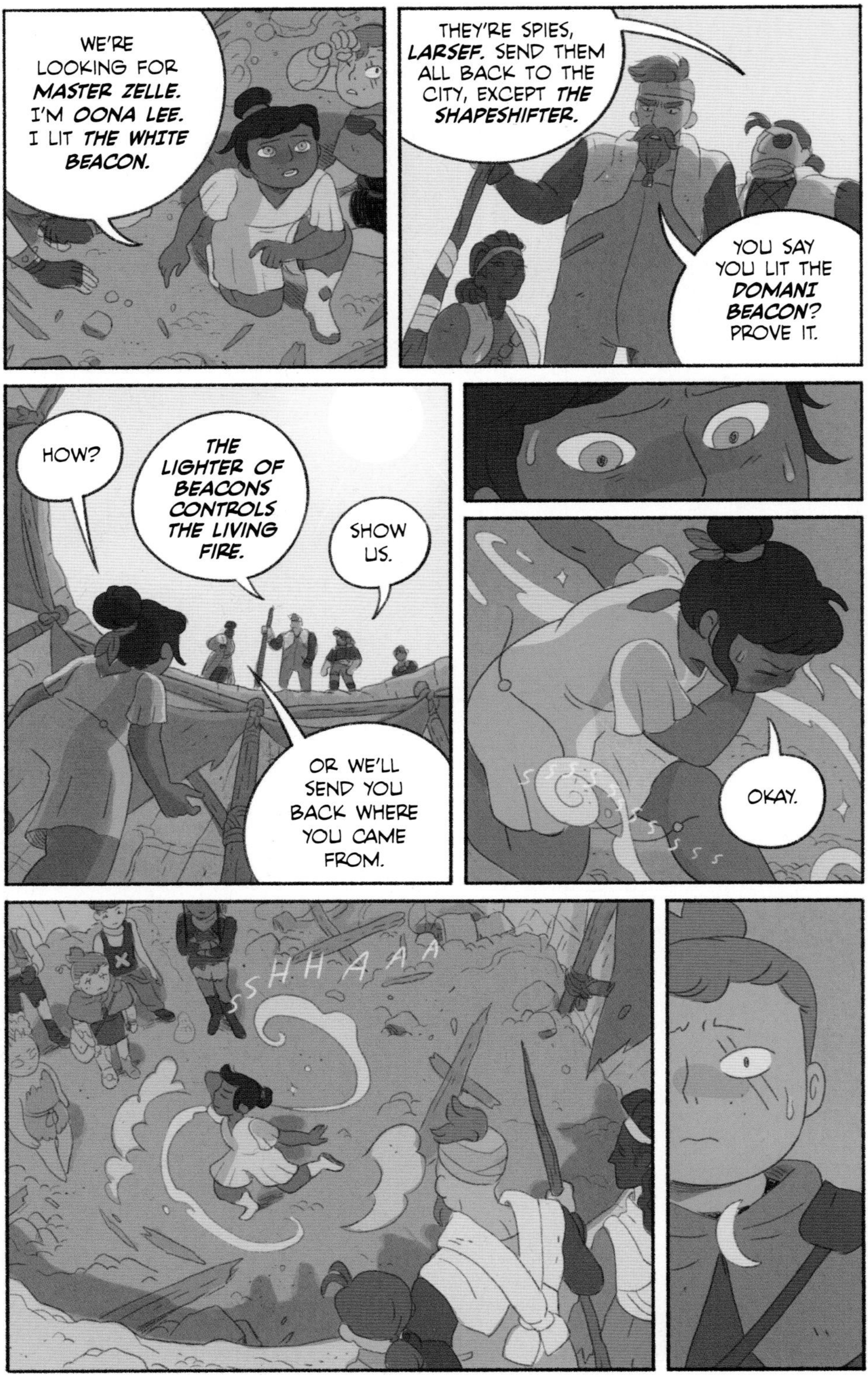
WE'RE LOOKING FOR MASTER ZELLE. I'M OONA LEE. I LIT THE WHITE BEACON.
THEY'RE SPIES, LARSEF. SEND THEM ALL BACK TO THE CITY, EXCEPT THE SHAPESHIFTER.
YOU SAY YOU LIT THE DOMANI BEACON? PROVE IT.
HOW?
THE LIGHTER OF BEACONS CONTROLS THE LIVING FIRE.
SHOW US.
OR WE'LL SEND YOU BACK WHERE YOU CAME FROM.
OKAY.
SSHHAAAA

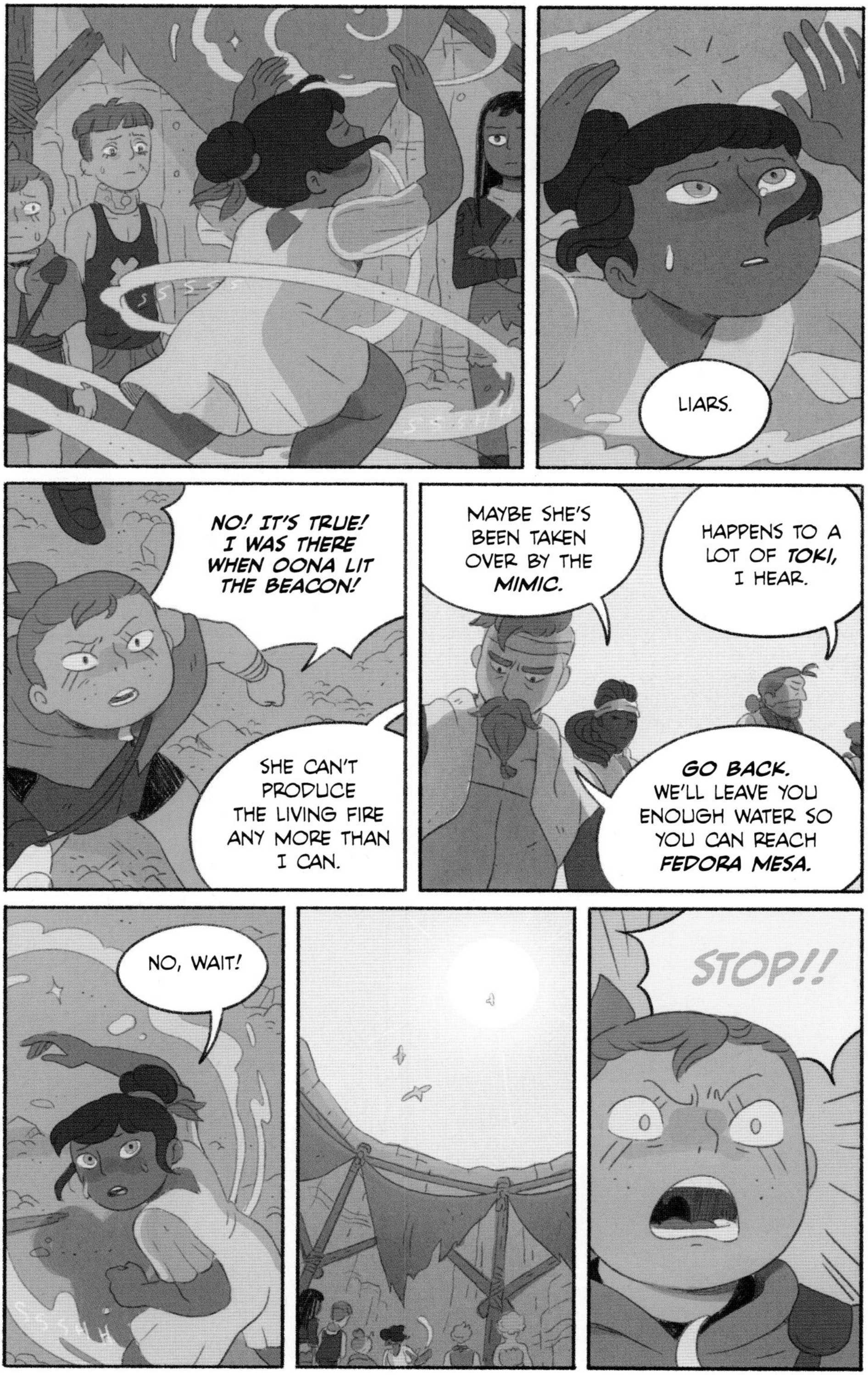
LIARS.
NO! IT'S TRUE! I WAS THERE WHEN OONA LIT THE BEACON!
SHE CAN'T PRODUCE THE LIVING FIRE ANY MORE THAN I CAN.
MAYBE SHE'S BEEN TAKEN OVER BY THE MIMIC.
HAPPENS TO A LOT OF TOKI, I HEAR.
GO BACK. WE'LL LEAVE YOU ENOUGH WATER SO YOU CAN REACH FEDORA MESA.
NO, WAIT!
STOP!!

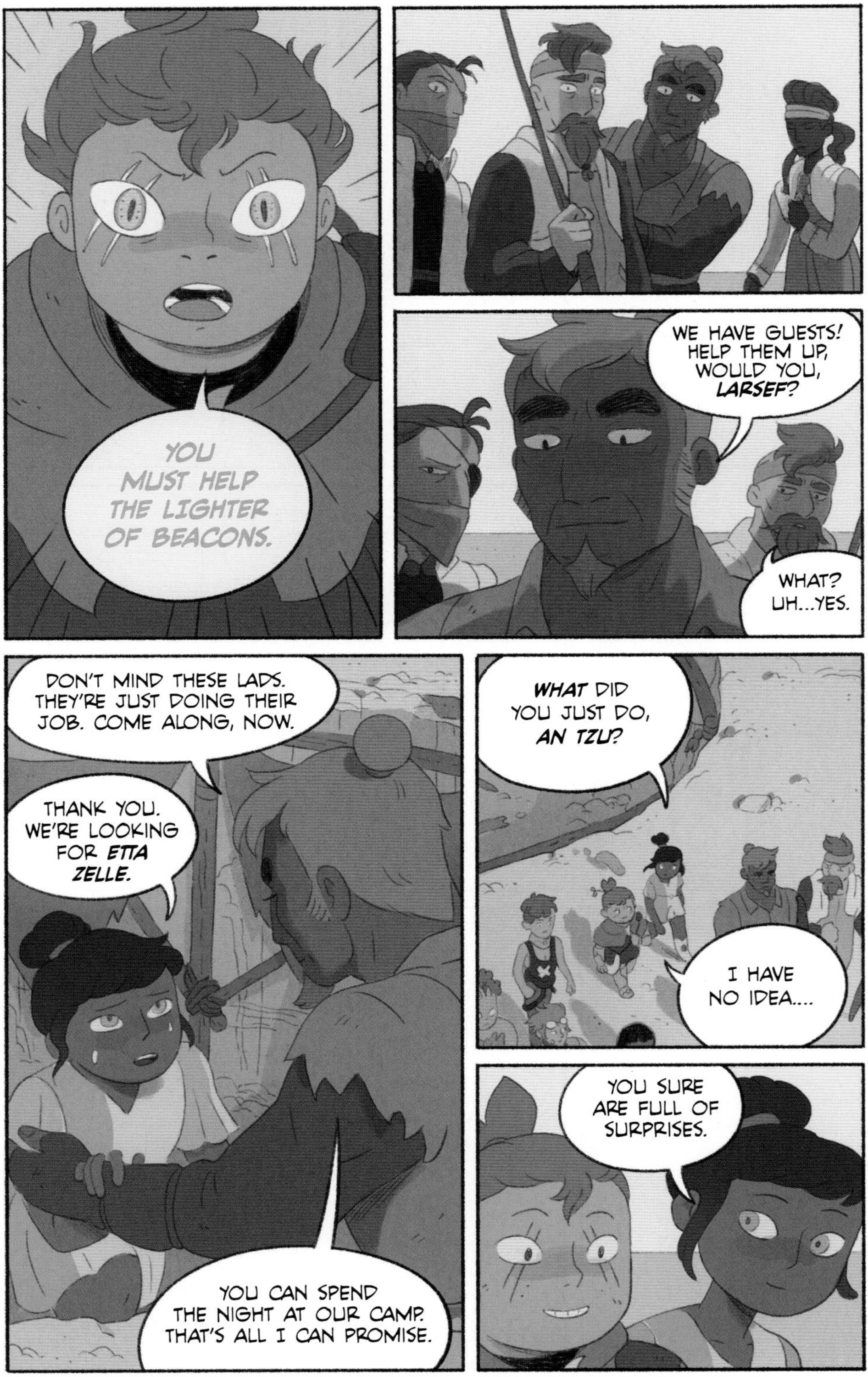
YOU MUST HELP THE LIGHTER OF BEACONS.
WE HAVE GUESTS! HELP THEM UP, WOULD YOU, LARSEF?
WHAT? UH...YES.
DON'T MIND THESE LADS. THEY'RE JUST DOING THEIR JOB. COME ALONG, NOW.
THANK YOU. WE'RE LOOKING FOR ETTA ZELLE.
YOU CAN SPEND THE NIGHT AT OUR CAMP. THAT'S ALL I CAN PROMISE.
WHAT DID YOU JUST DO, AN TZU?
I HAVE NO IDEA....
YOU SURE ARE FULL OF SURPRISES.

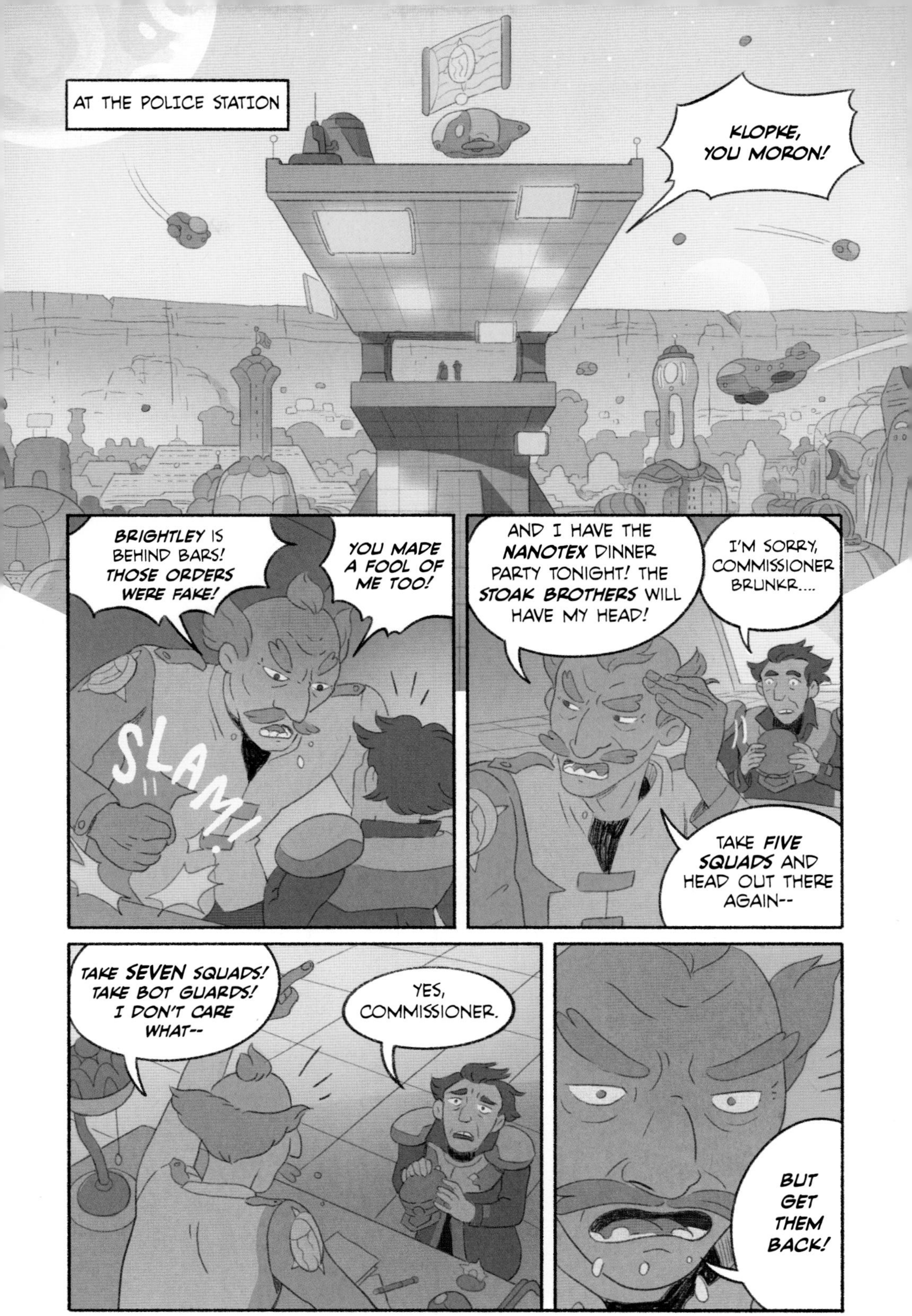
AT THE POLICE STATION
KLOPKE, YOU MORON!
BRIGHTLEY IS BEHIND BARS! THOSE ORDERS WERE FAKE!
YOU MADE A FOOL OF ME TOO!
SLAM!
AND I HAVE THE NANOTEX DINNER PARTY TONIGHT! THE STOAK BROTHERS WILL HAVE MY HEAD!
I'M SORRY, COMMISSIONER BRUNKR....
TAKE FIVE SQUADS AND HEAD OUT THERE AGAIN--
TAKE SEVEN SQUADS! TAKE BOT GUARDS! I DON'T CARE WHAT--
YES, COMMISSIONER.
BUT GET THEM BACK!

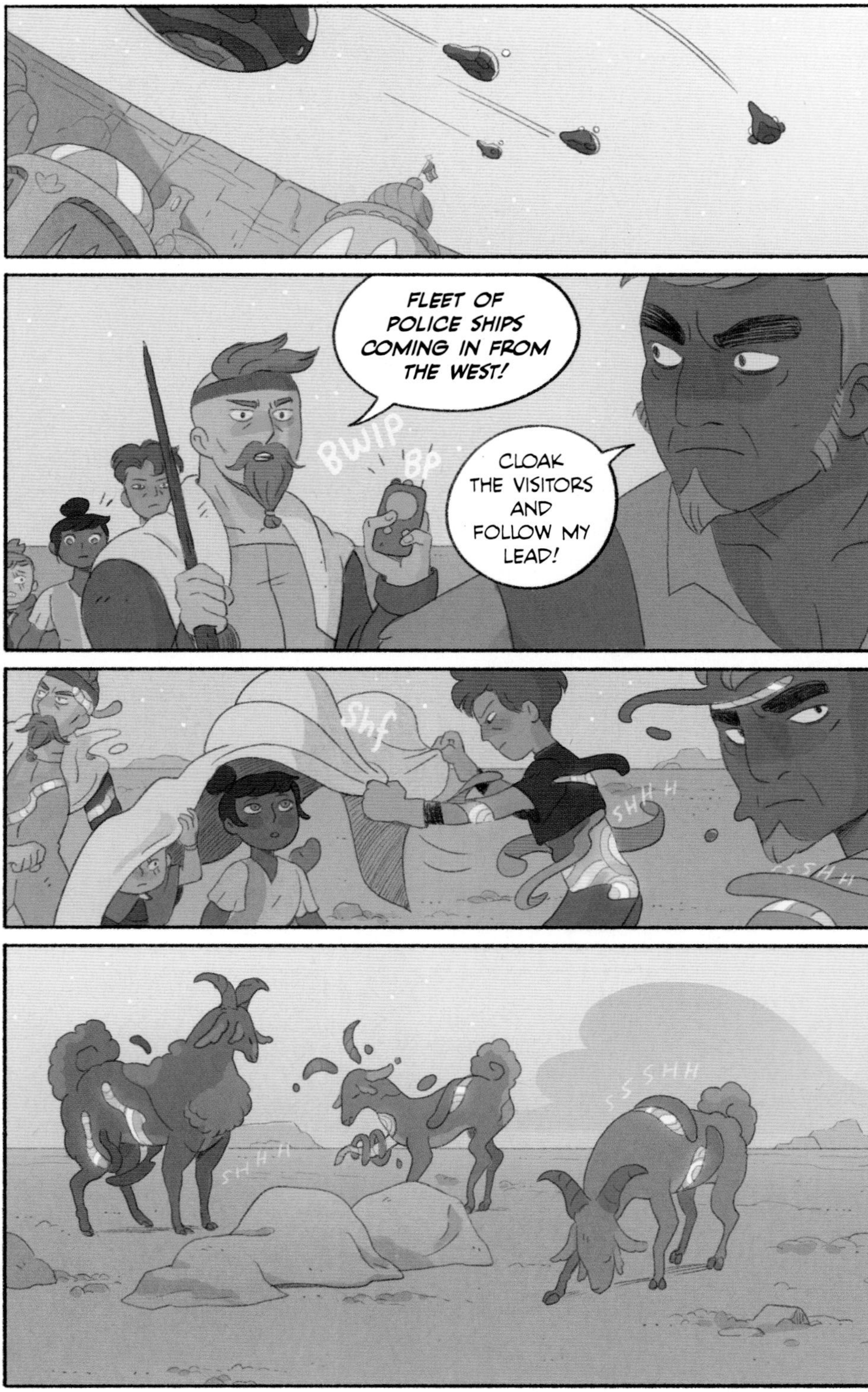
FLEET OF POLICE SHIPS COMING IN FROM THE WEST!
BWIP BP
CLOAK THE VISITORS AND FOLLOW MY LEAD!
Shf
SHHH
SSHH
SHHH
SSHH

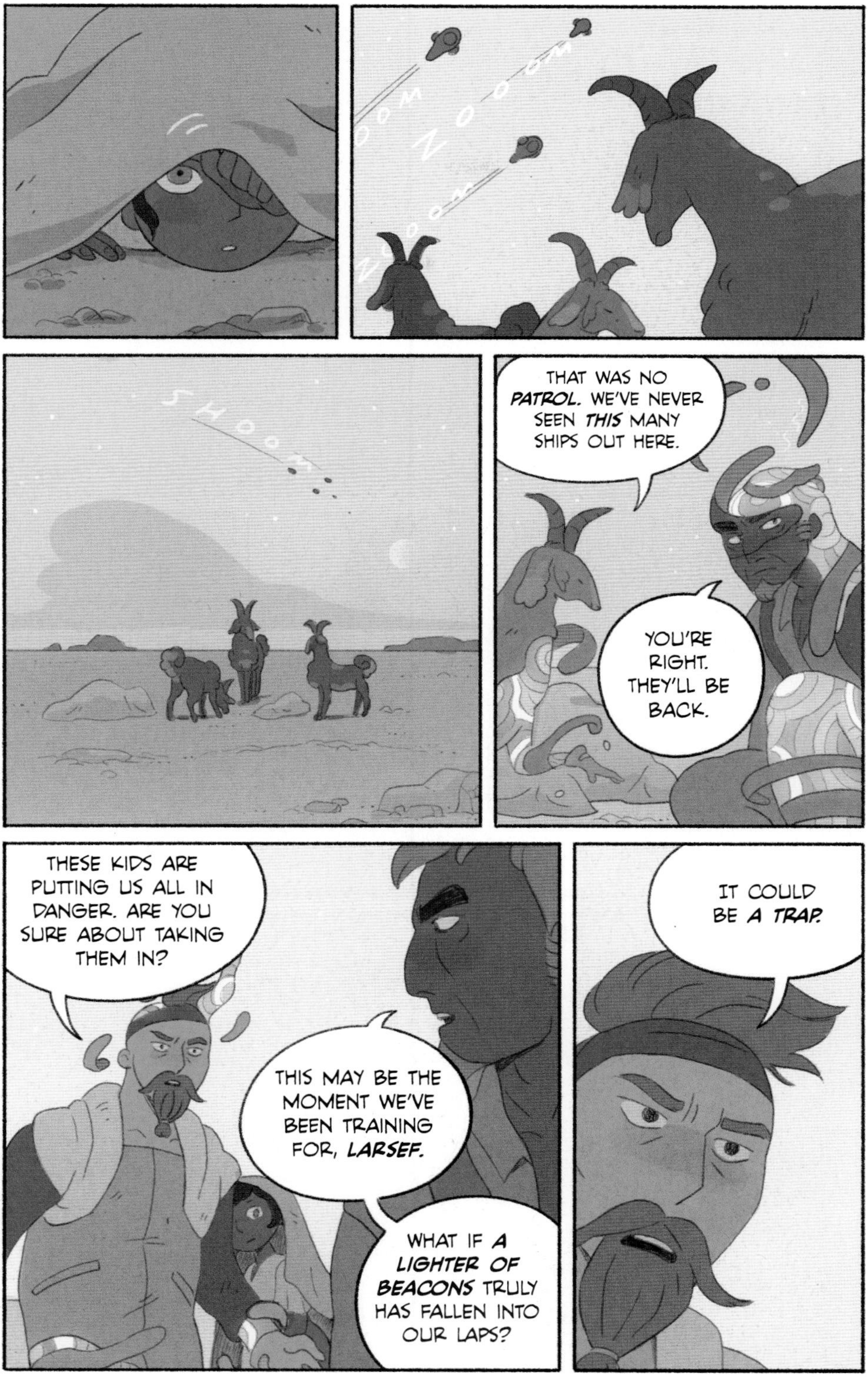
SHOOM
THAT WAS NO PATROL. WE'VE NEVER SEEN THIS MANY SHIPS OUT HERE.
YOU'RE RIGHT. THEY'LL BE BACK.
THESE KIDS ARE PUTTING US ALL IN DANGER. ARE YOU SURE ABOUT TAKING THEM IN?
THIS MAY BE THE MOMENT WE'VE BEEN TRAINING FOR, LARSEF.
WHAT IF A LIGHTER OF BEACONS TRULY HAS FALLEN INTO OUR LAPS?
IT COULD BE A TRAP.

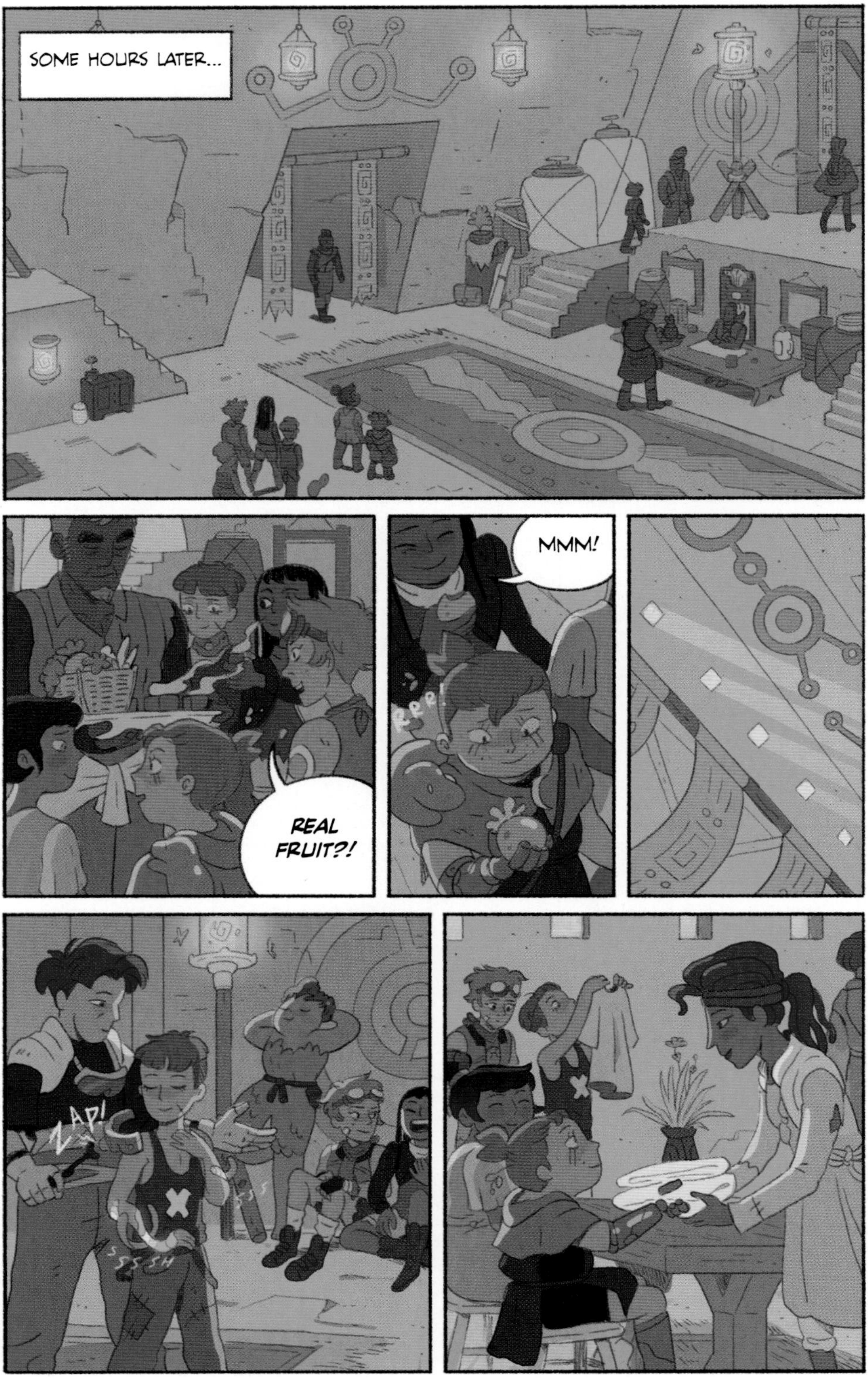
SOME HOURS LATER...
REAL FRUIT?!
MMM!
ZAP!

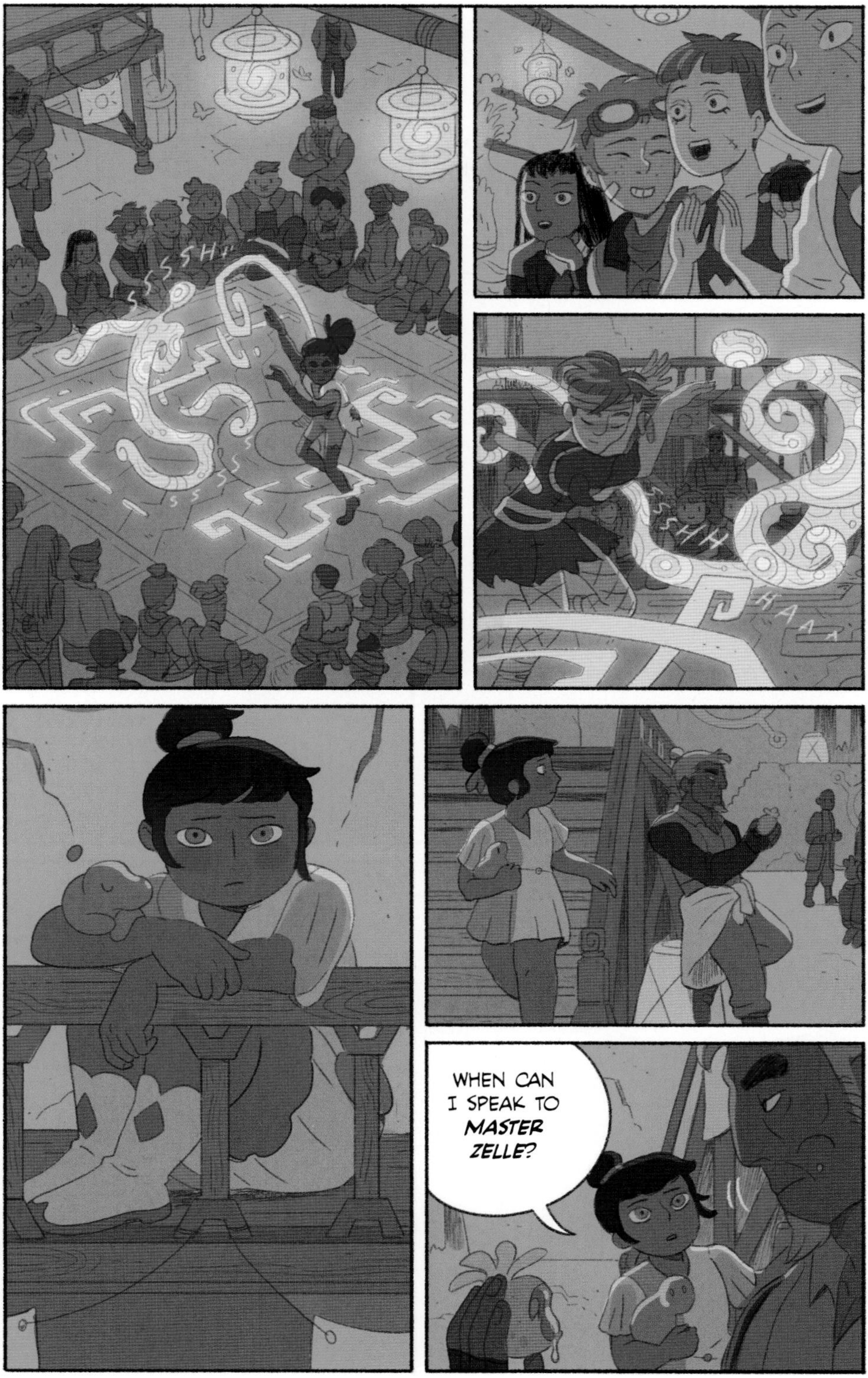
WHEN CAN I SPEAK TO *MASTER ZELLE?*

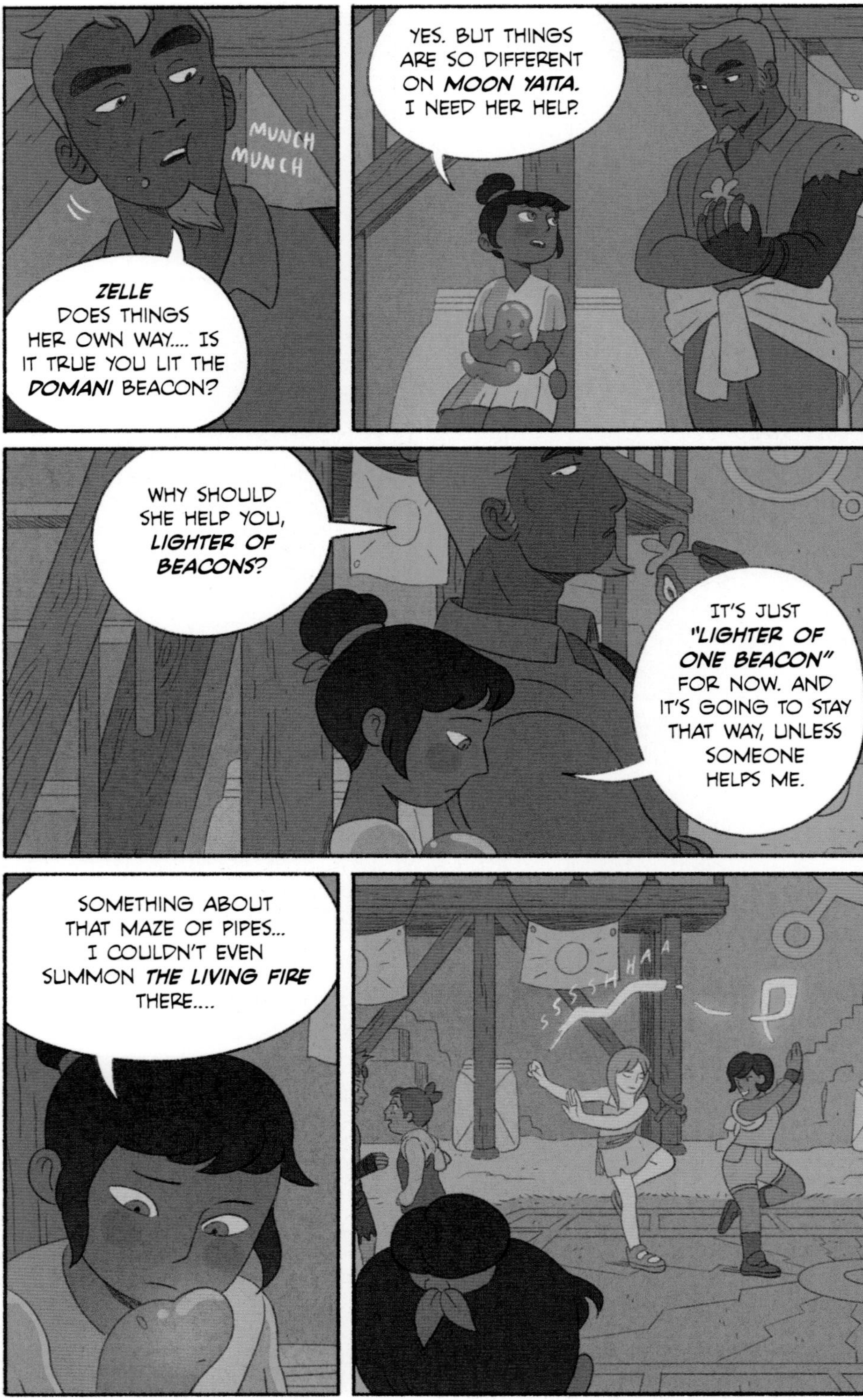

MUNCH MUNCH
ZELLE DOES THINGS HER OWN WAY.... IS IT TRUE YOU LIT THE DOMANI BEACON?
YES. BUT THINGS ARE SO DIFFERENT ON MOON YATTA. I NEED HER HELP.
WHY SHOULD SHE HELP YOU, LIGHTER OF BEACONS?
IT'S JUST "LIGHTER OF ONE BEACON" FOR NOW. AND IT'S GOING TO STAY THAT WAY, UNLESS SOMEONE HELPS ME.
SOMETHING ABOUT THAT MAZE OF PIPES... I COULDN'T EVEN SUMMON THE LIVING FIRE THERE....
SSSSHHAA

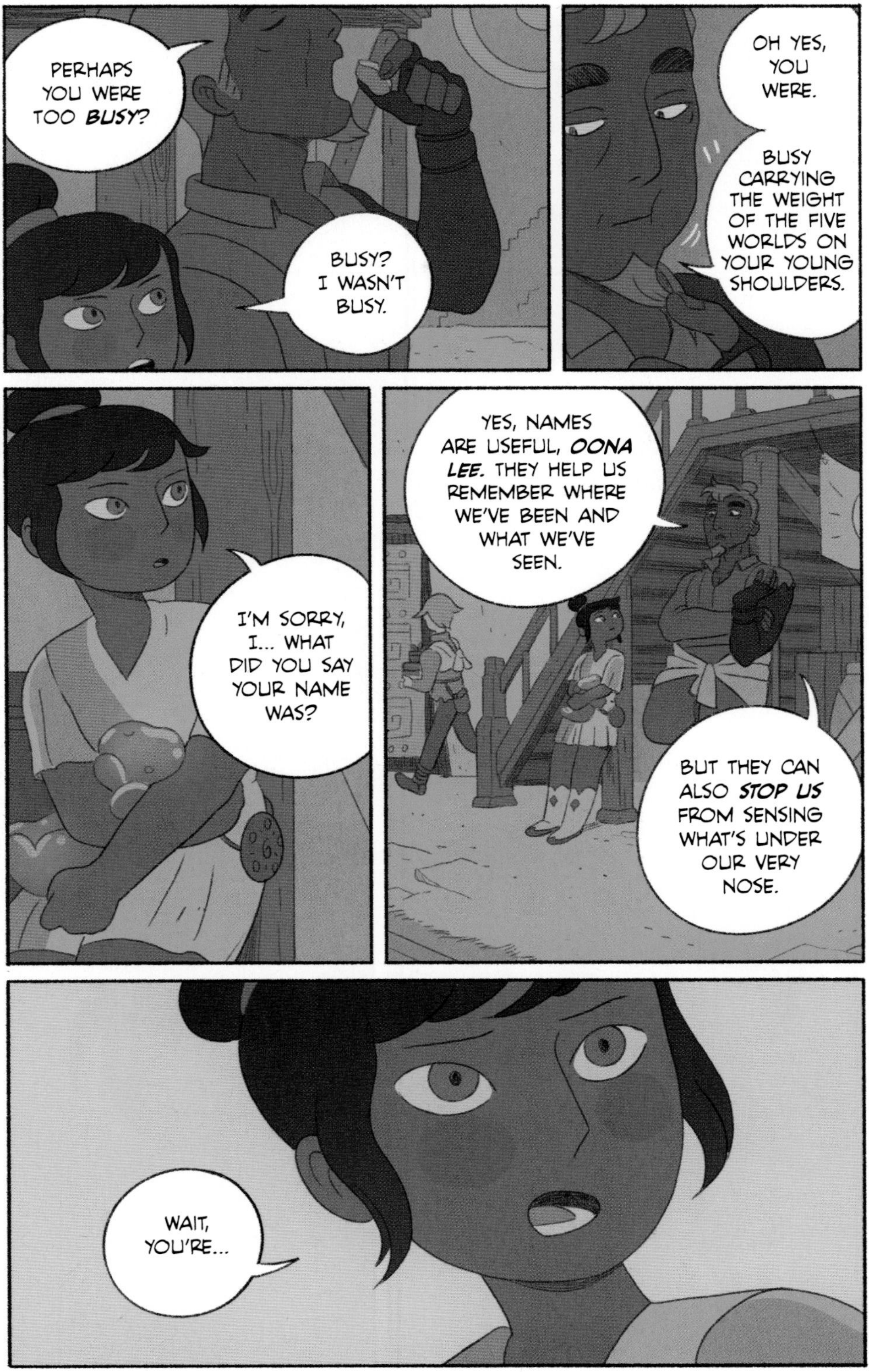
PERHAPS YOU WERE TOO *BUSY*?
BUSY? I WASN'T BUSY.
OH YES, YOU WERE.
BUSY CARRYING THE WEIGHT OF THE FIVE WORLDS ON YOUR YOUNG SHOULDERS.
I'M SORRY, I... WHAT DID YOU SAY YOUR NAME WAS?
YES, NAMES ARE USEFUL, *OONA LEE.* THEY HELP US REMEMBER WHERE WE'VE BEEN AND WHAT WE'VE SEEN.
BUT THEY CAN ALSO *STOP US* FROM SENSING WHAT'S UNDER OUR VERY NOSE.
WAIT, YOU'RE...

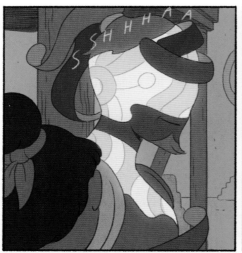

S-SHHHAA

*ETTA ZELLE.*

I THOUGHT SHAPESHIFTING WASN'T ABOUT TRICKERY!

YOU WERE RIGHT. IT'S ABOUT BECOMING *WHAT IS NEEDED* IN THE MOMENT.

WELL, IN THIS MOMENT I NEED HELP *LIGHTING THE BEACON!*

NOT WITH THE WEIGHT OF THE WORLDS ON YOUR SHOULDERS.

## Chapter 8

# TRAINING DAYS

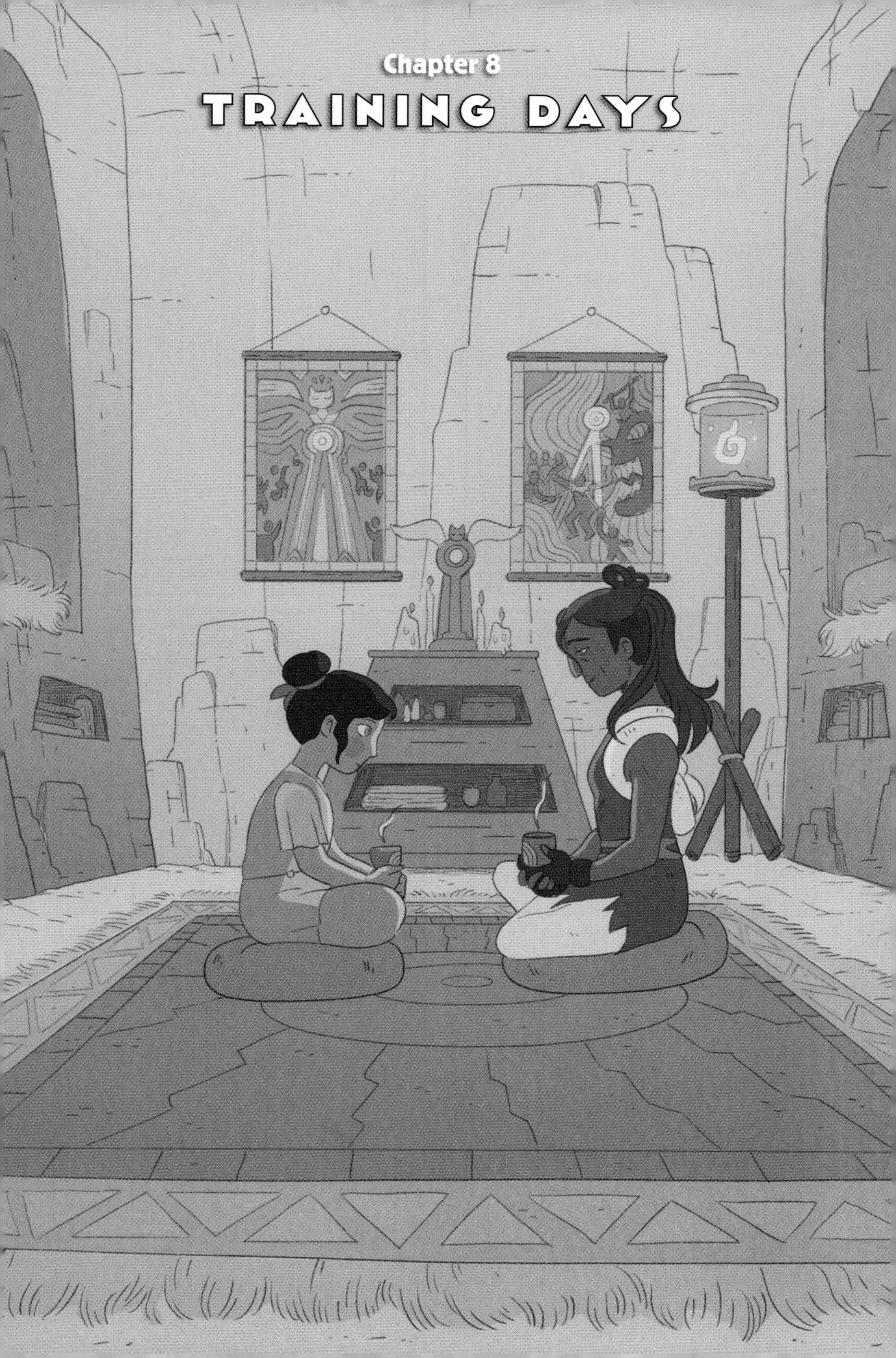

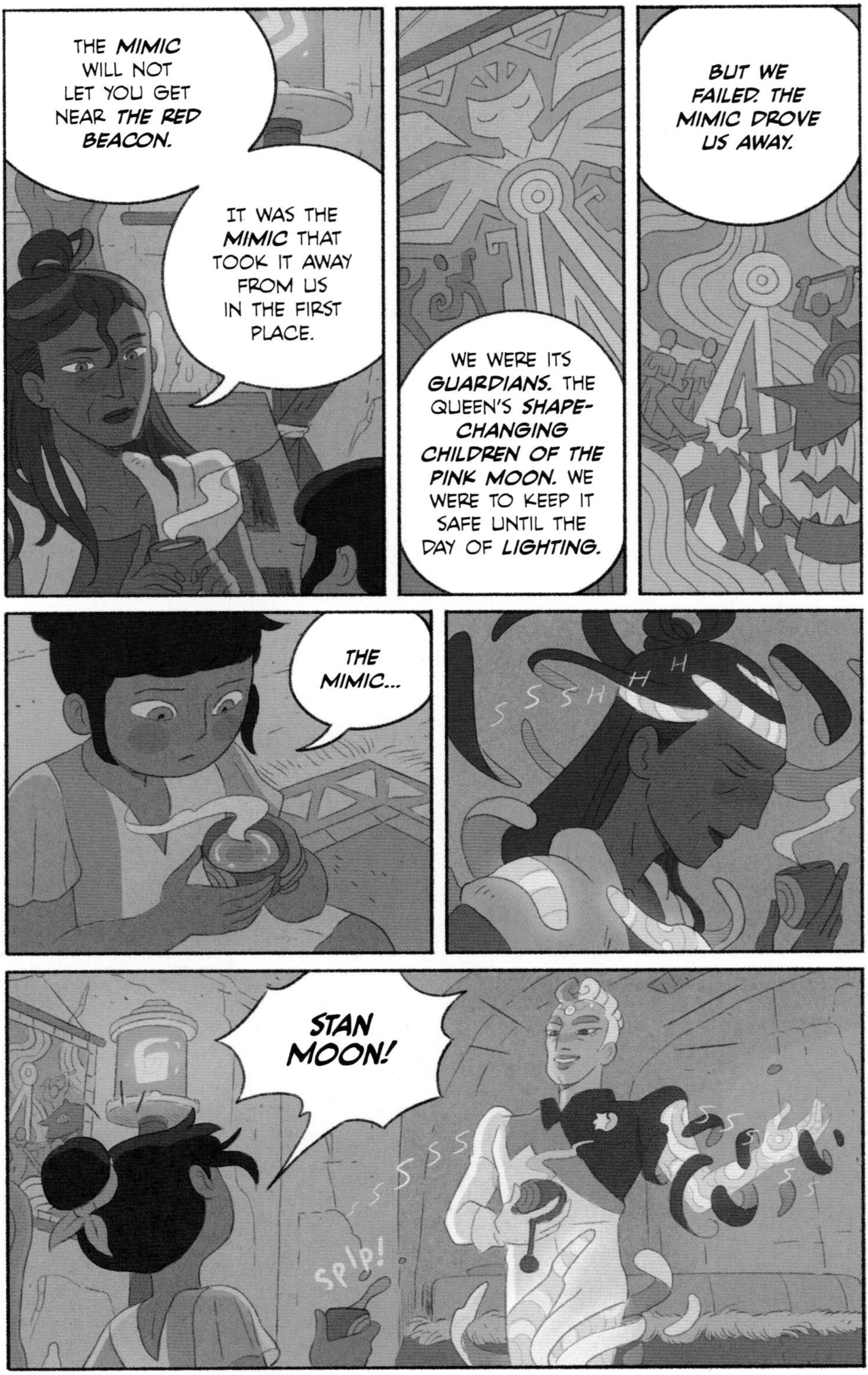
THE MIMIC WILL NOT LET YOU GET NEAR THE RED BEACON.
IT WAS THE MIMIC THAT TOOK IT AWAY FROM US IN THE FIRST PLACE.
WE WERE ITS GUARDIANS. THE QUEEN'S SHAPE-CHANGING CHILDREN OF THE PINK MOON. WE WERE TO KEEP IT SAFE UNTIL THE DAY OF LIGHTING.
BUT WE FAILED. THE MIMIC DROVE US AWAY.
THE MIMIC...
SSSHHH
STAN MOON!
SPLIP!

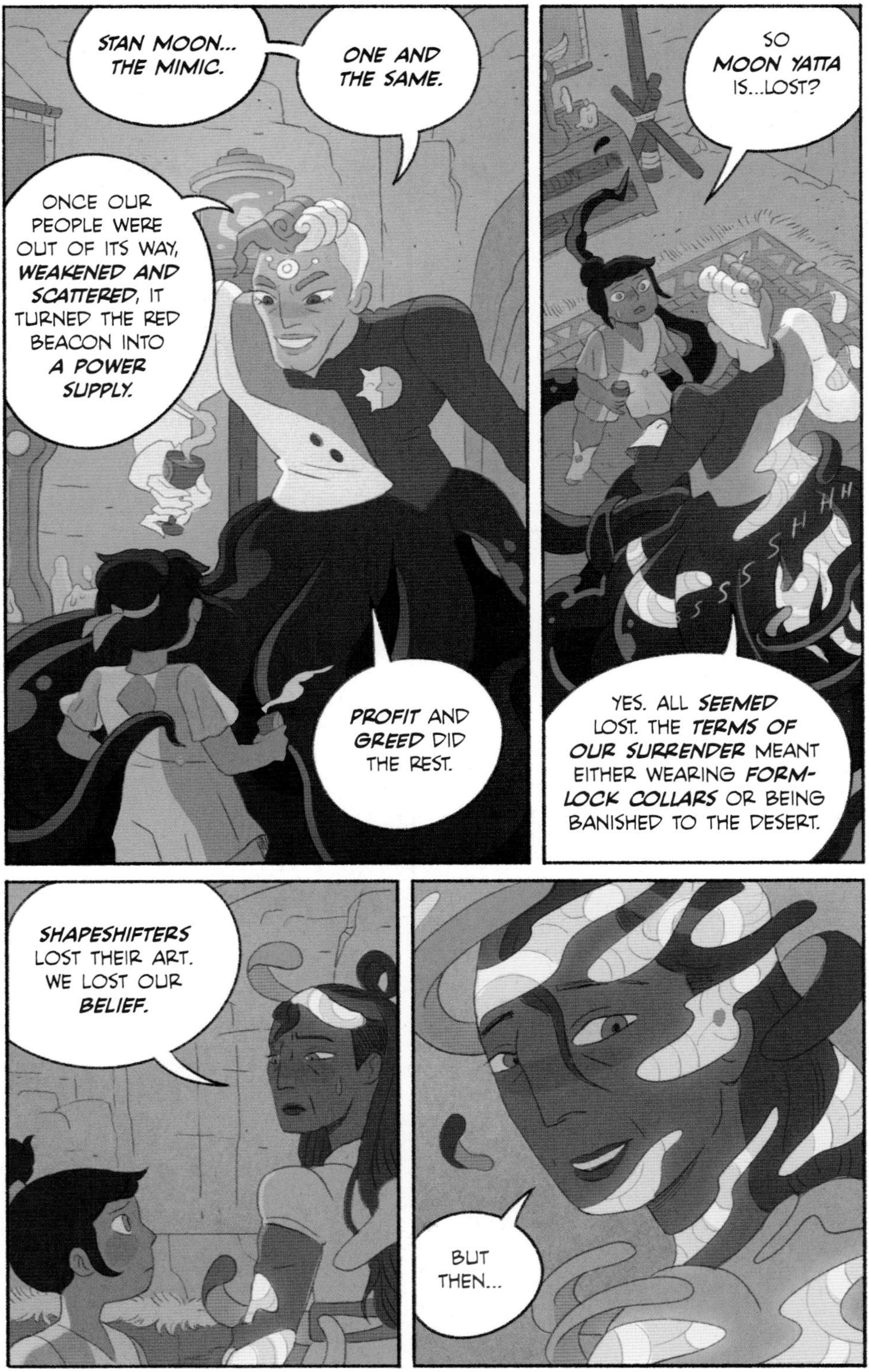
STAN MOON... THE MIMIC.
ONE AND THE SAME.
ONCE OUR PEOPLE WERE OUT OF ITS WAY, WEAKENED AND SCATTERED, IT TURNED THE RED BEACON INTO A POWER SUPPLY.
PROFIT AND GREED DID THE REST.
SO MOON YATTA IS...LOST?
YES. ALL SEEMED LOST. THE TERMS OF OUR SURRENDER MEANT EITHER WEARING FORM-LOCK COLLARS OR BEING BANISHED TO THE DESERT.
SHAPESHIFTERS LOST THEIR ART. WE LOST OUR BELIEF.
BUT THEN...

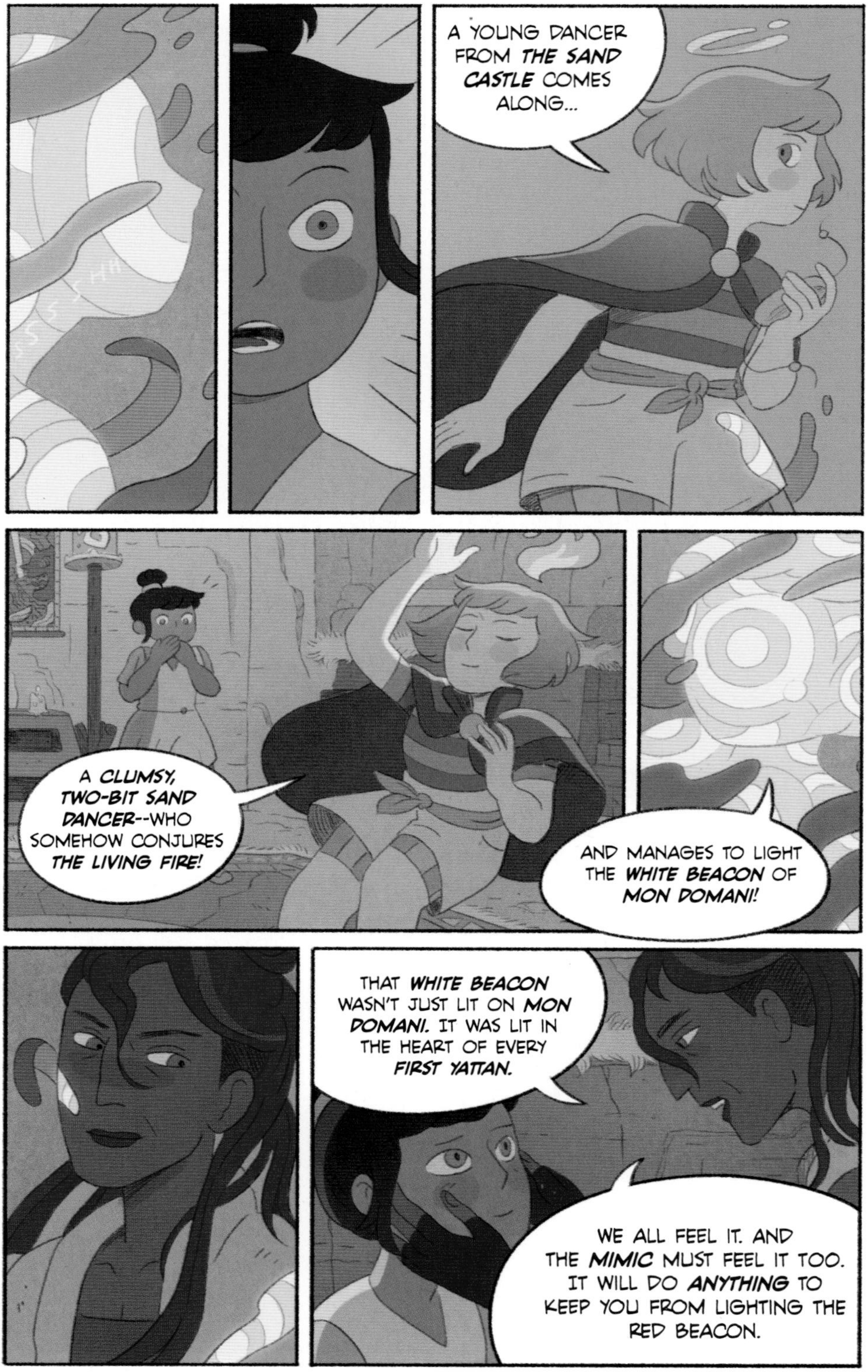
SSSSHH
A YOUNG DANCER FROM THE SAND CASTLE COMES ALONG...
A CLUMSY, TWO-BIT SAND DANCER--WHO SOMEHOW CONJURES THE LIVING FIRE!
AND MANAGES TO LIGHT THE WHITE BEACON OF MON DOMANI!
THAT WHITE BEACON WASN'T JUST LIT ON MON DOMANI. IT WAS LIT IN THE HEART OF EVERY FIRST YATTAN.
WE ALL FEEL IT. AND THE MIMIC MUST FEEL IT TOO. IT WILL DO ANYTHING TO KEEP YOU FROM LIGHTING THE RED BEACON.

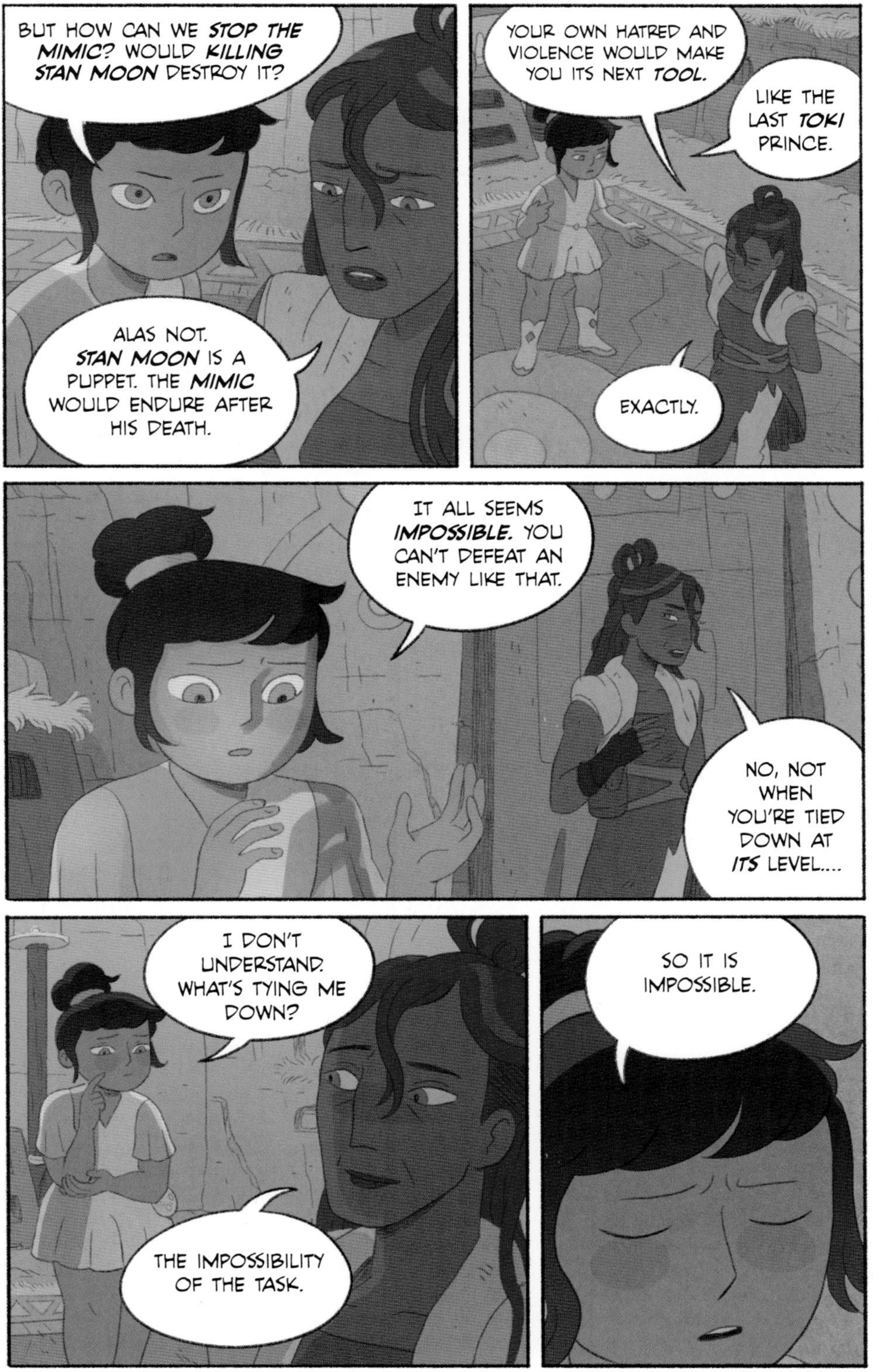
BUT HOW CAN WE STOP THE MIMIC? WOULD KILLING STAN MOON DESTROY IT?
ALAS NOT. STAN MOON IS A PUPPET. THE MIMIC WOULD ENDURE AFTER HIS DEATH.
YOUR OWN HATRED AND VIOLENCE WOULD MAKE YOU ITS NEXT TOOL.
LIKE THE LAST TOKI PRINCE.
EXACTLY.
IT ALL SEEMS IMPOSSIBLE. YOU CAN'T DEFEAT AN ENEMY LIKE THAT.
NO, NOT WHEN YOU'RE TIED DOWN AT ITS LEVEL....
I DON'T UNDERSTAND. WHAT'S TYING ME DOWN?
THE IMPOSSIBILITY OF THE TASK.
SO IT IS IMPOSSIBLE.

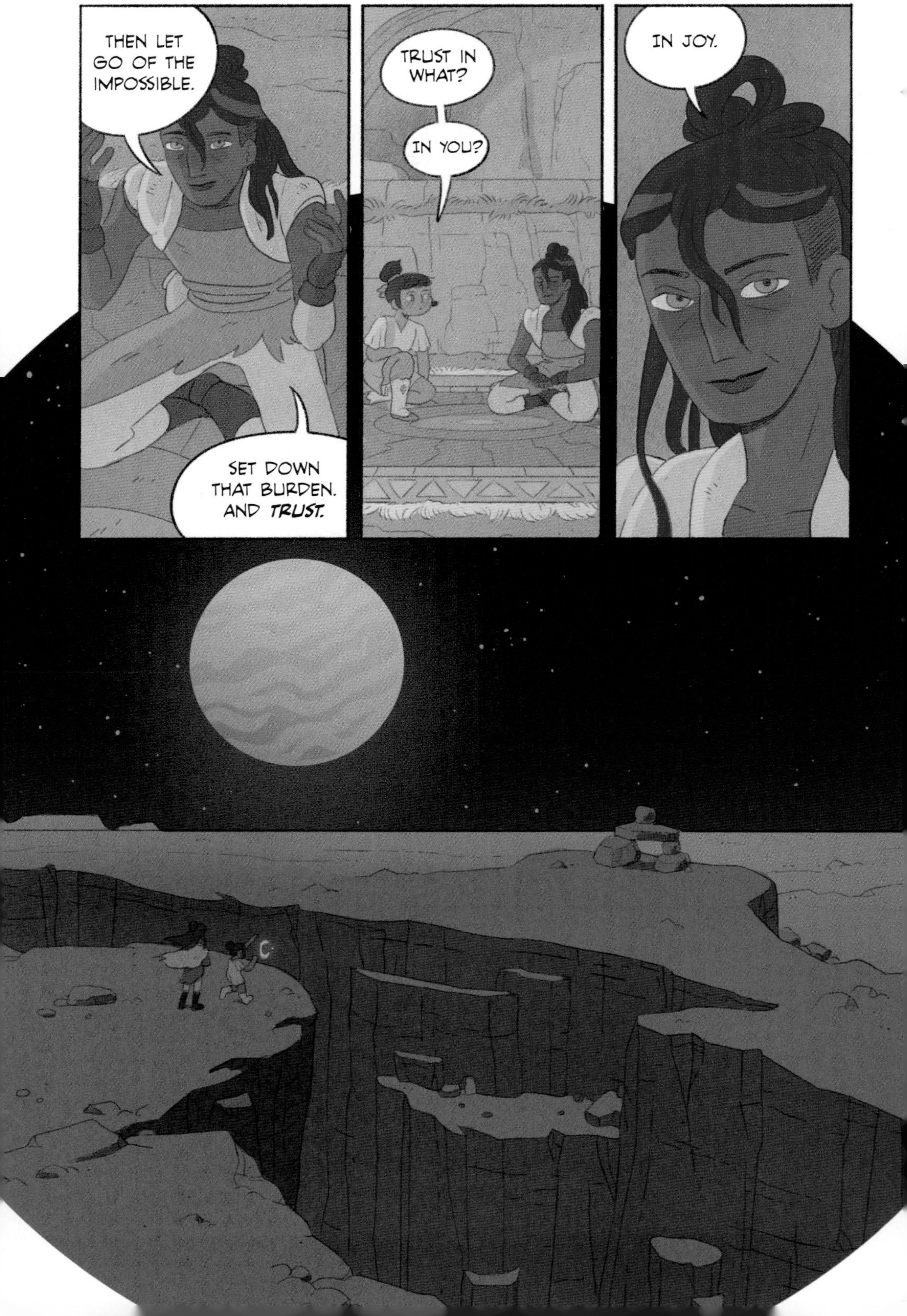
THEN LET GO OF THE IMPOSSIBLE.
SET DOWN THAT BURDEN. AND *TRUST.*
TRUST IN WHAT?
IN YOU?
IN JOY.

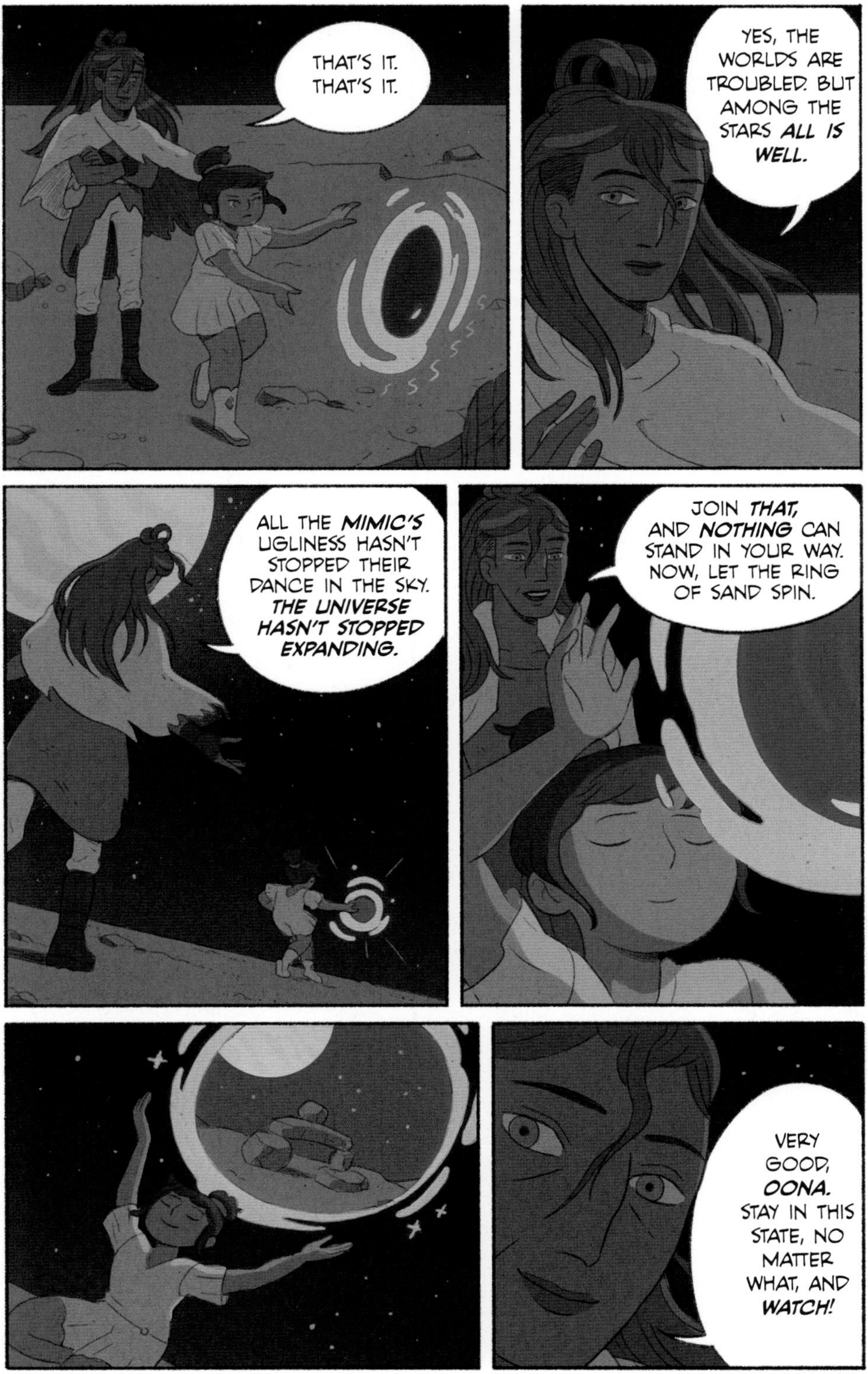

THAT'S IT. THAT'S IT.
YES, THE WORLDS ARE TROUBLED. BUT AMONG THE STARS ***ALL IS WELL.***
ALL THE ***MIMIC'S*** UGLINESS HASN'T STOPPED THEIR DANCE IN THE SKY. ***THE UNIVERSE HASN'T STOPPED EXPANDING.***
JOIN ***THAT,*** AND ***NOTHING*** CAN STAND IN YOUR WAY. NOW, LET THE RING OF SAND SPIN.
VERY GOOD, ***OONA.*** STAY IN THIS STATE, NO MATTER WHAT, AND ***WATCH!***

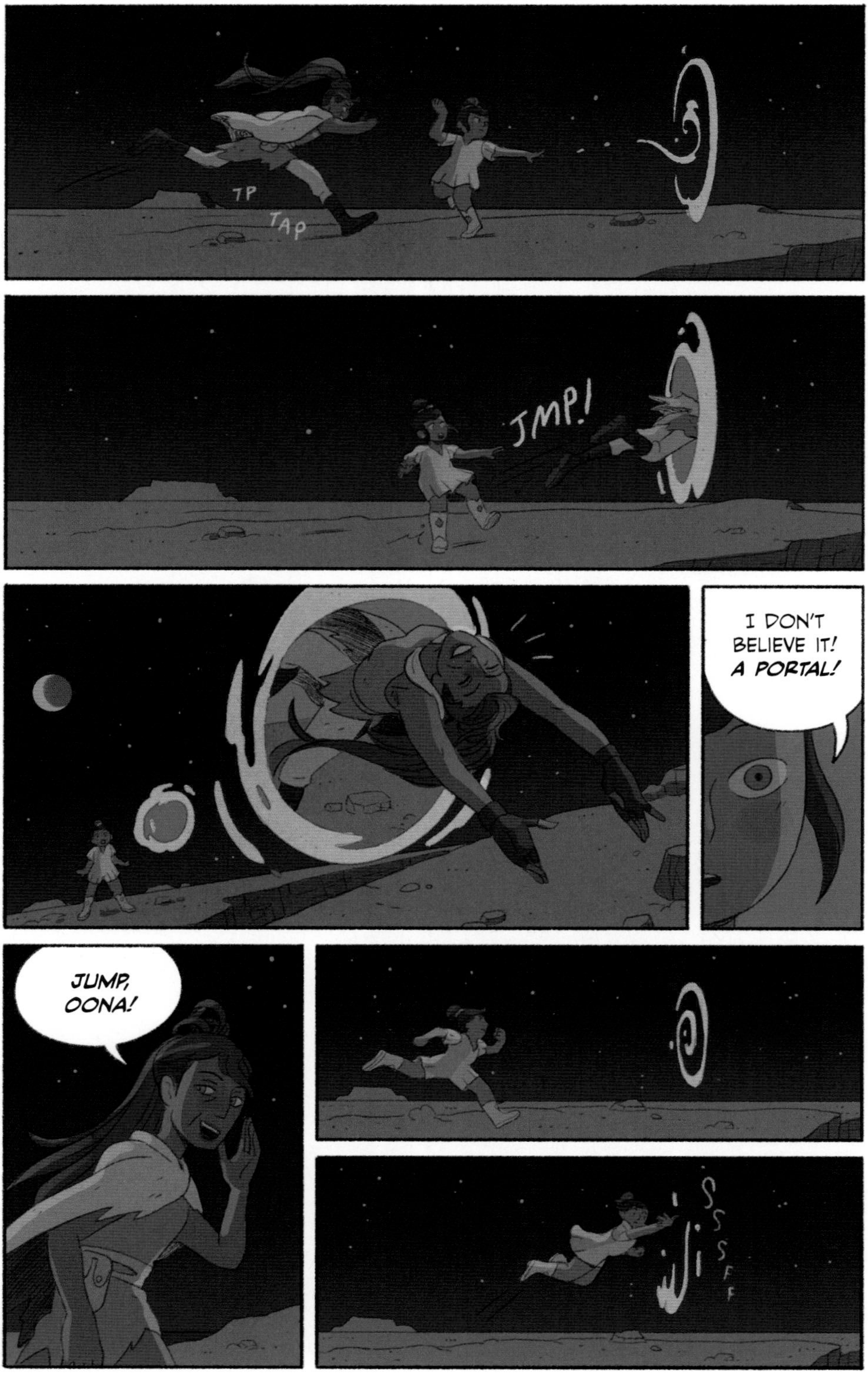
TP
TAP
JMP!
I DON'T BELIEVE IT! *A PORTAL!*
*JUMP, OONA!*
SSSFF

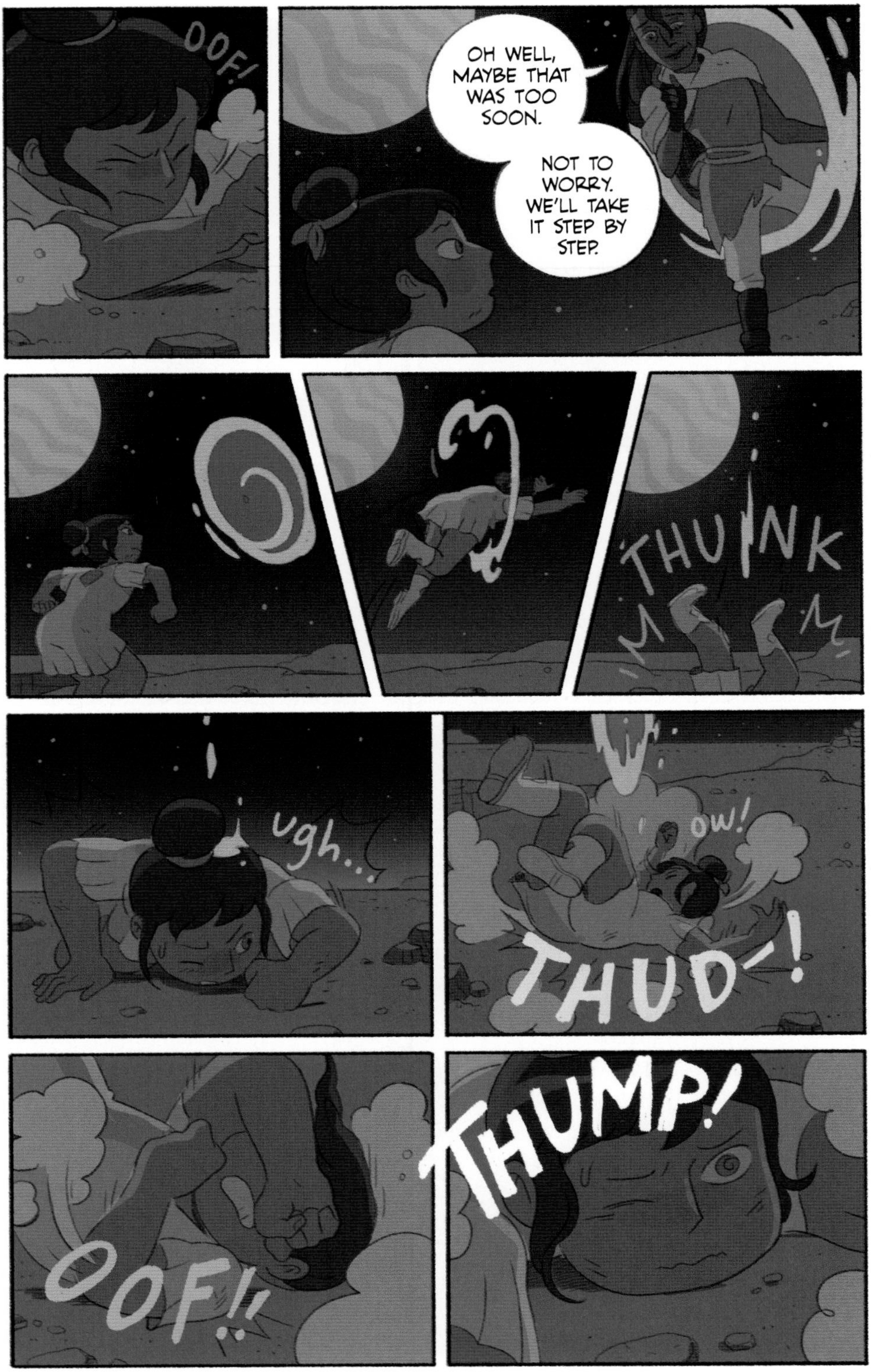

OOF!
OH WELL, MAYBE THAT WAS TOO SOON.
NOT TO WORRY. WE'LL TAKE IT STEP BY STEP.
THUNK
ugh...
OW!
THUD-!
THUMP!
OOF!!

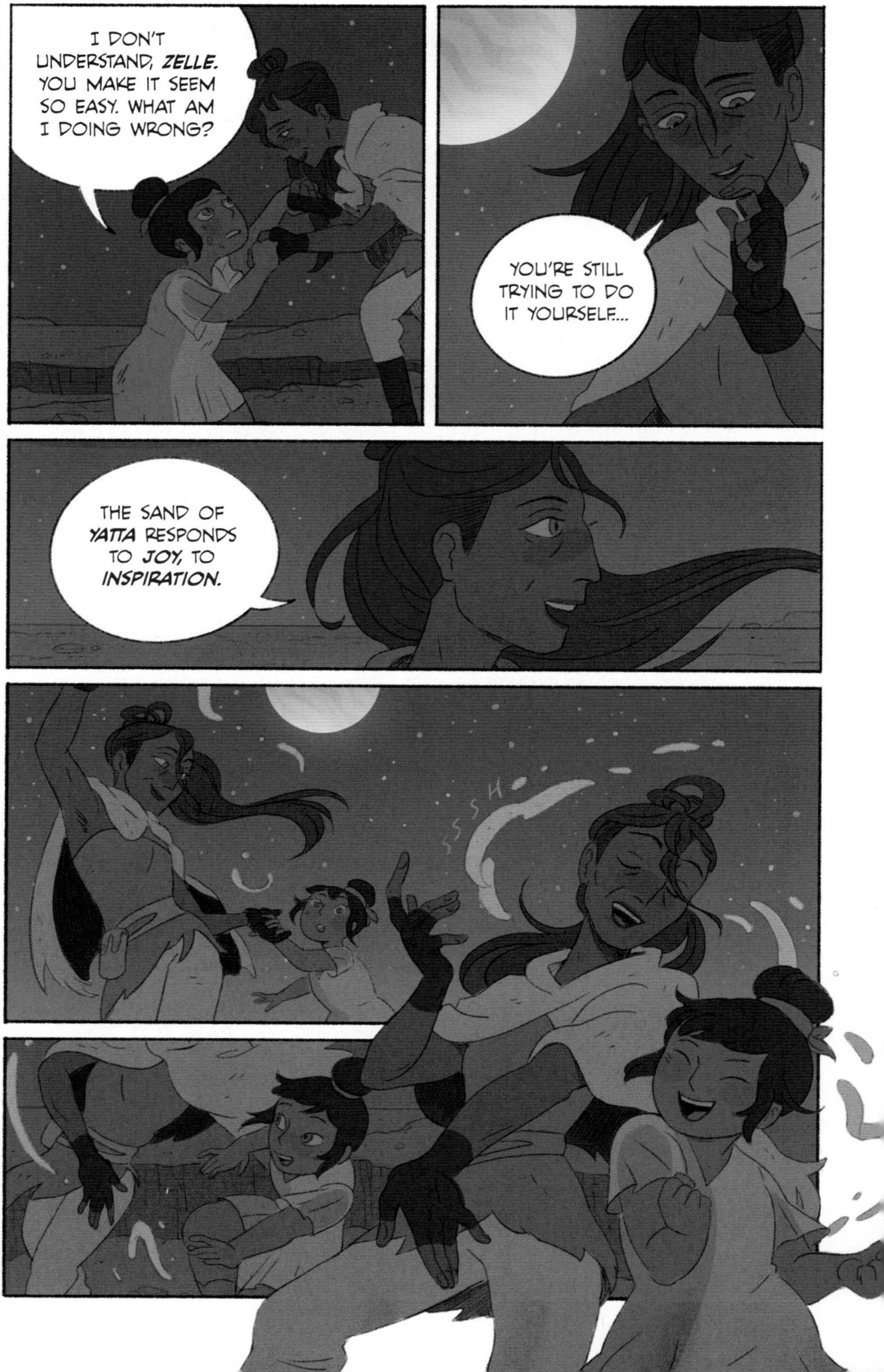
I DON'T UNDERSTAND, *ZELLE.* YOU MAKE IT SEEM SO EASY. WHAT AM I DOING WRONG?
YOU'RE STILL TRYING TO DO IT YOURSELF...
THE SAND OF *YATTA* RESPONDS TO *JOY,* TO *INSPIRATION.*
SSSSH

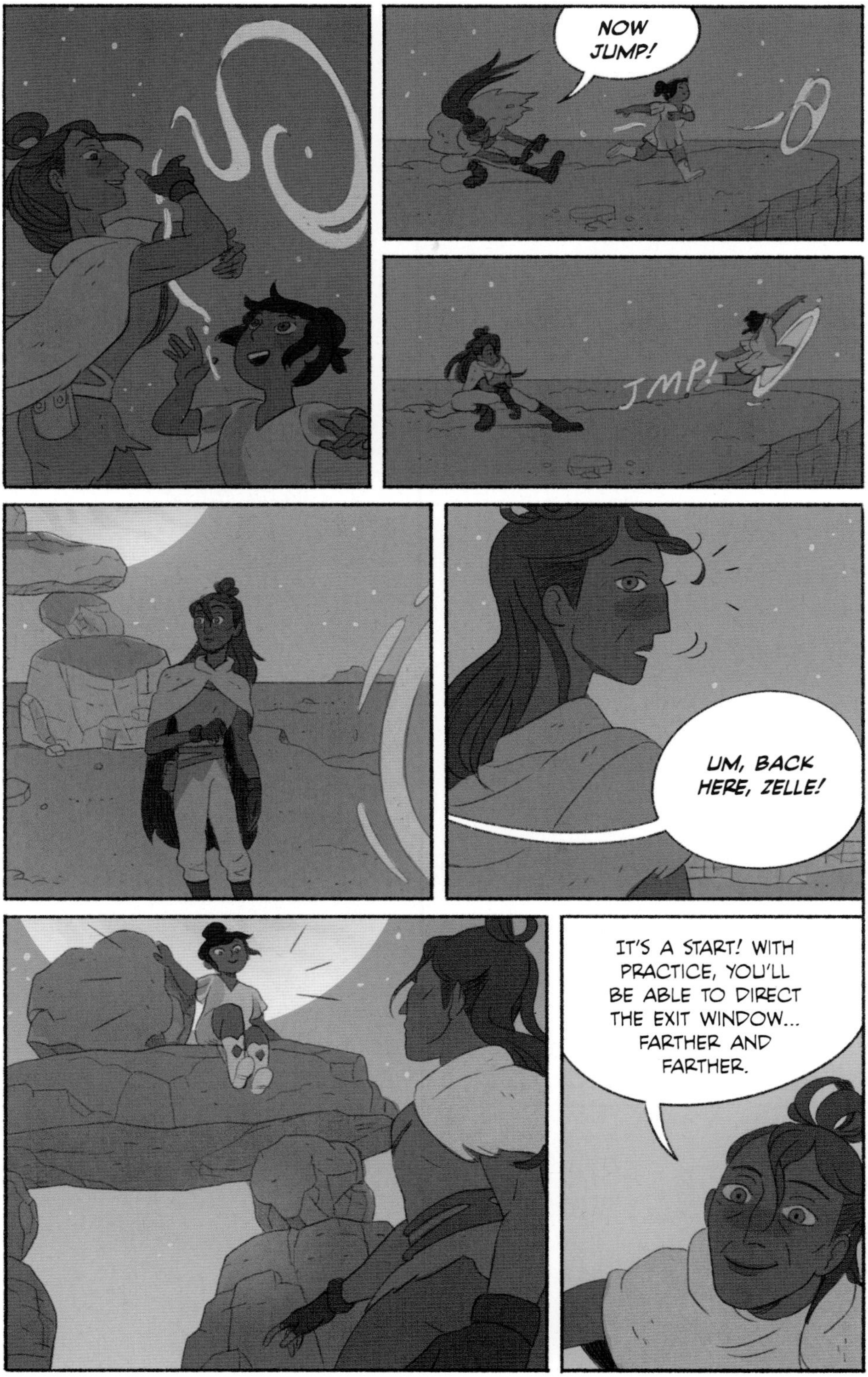
NOW JUMP!
JMP!
UM, BACK HERE, ZELLE!
IT'S A START! WITH PRACTICE, YOU'LL BE ABLE TO DIRECT THE EXIT WINDOW... FARTHER AND FARTHER.

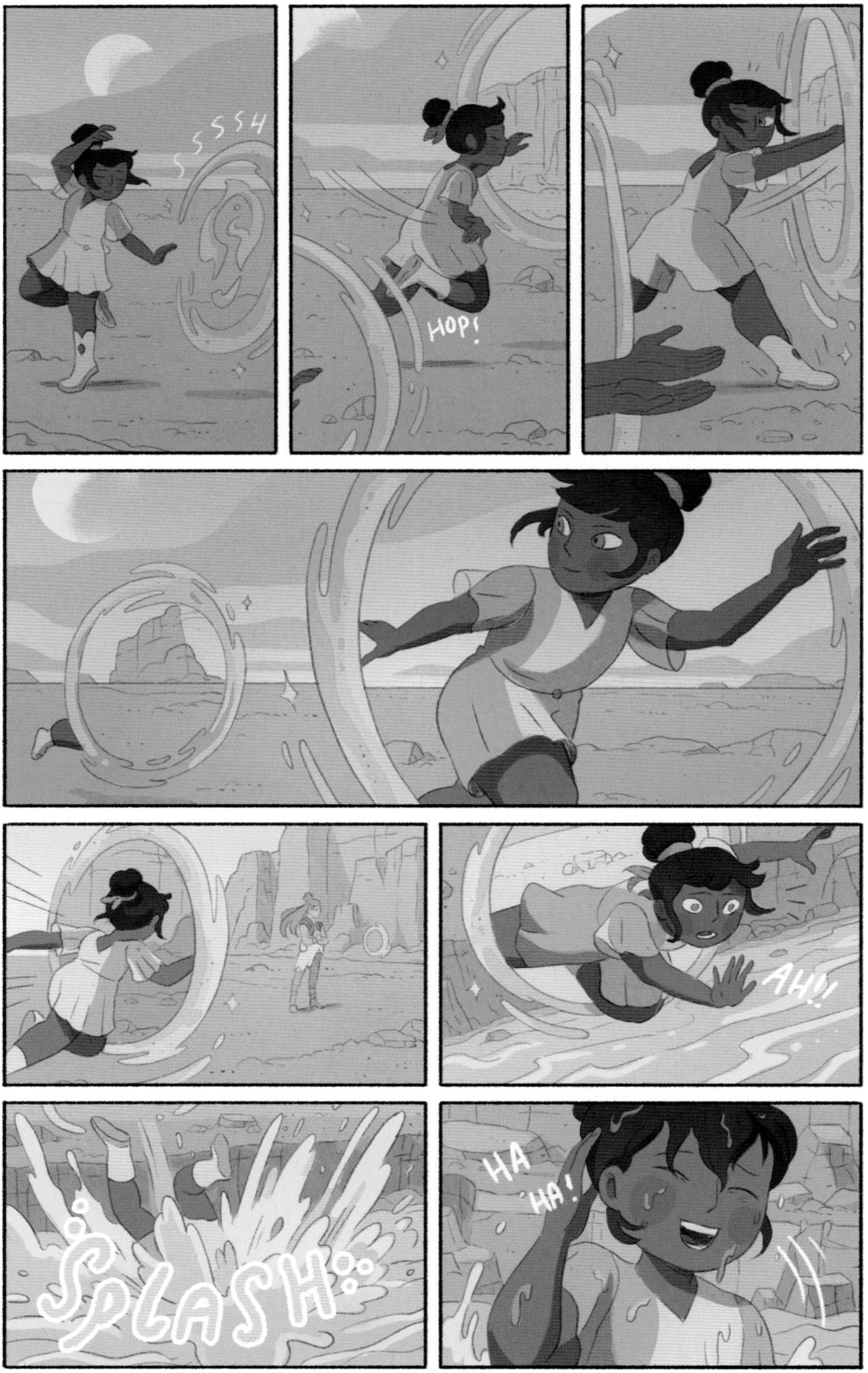
SSSSH
HOP!
AH!!
SPLASH
HA
HA!

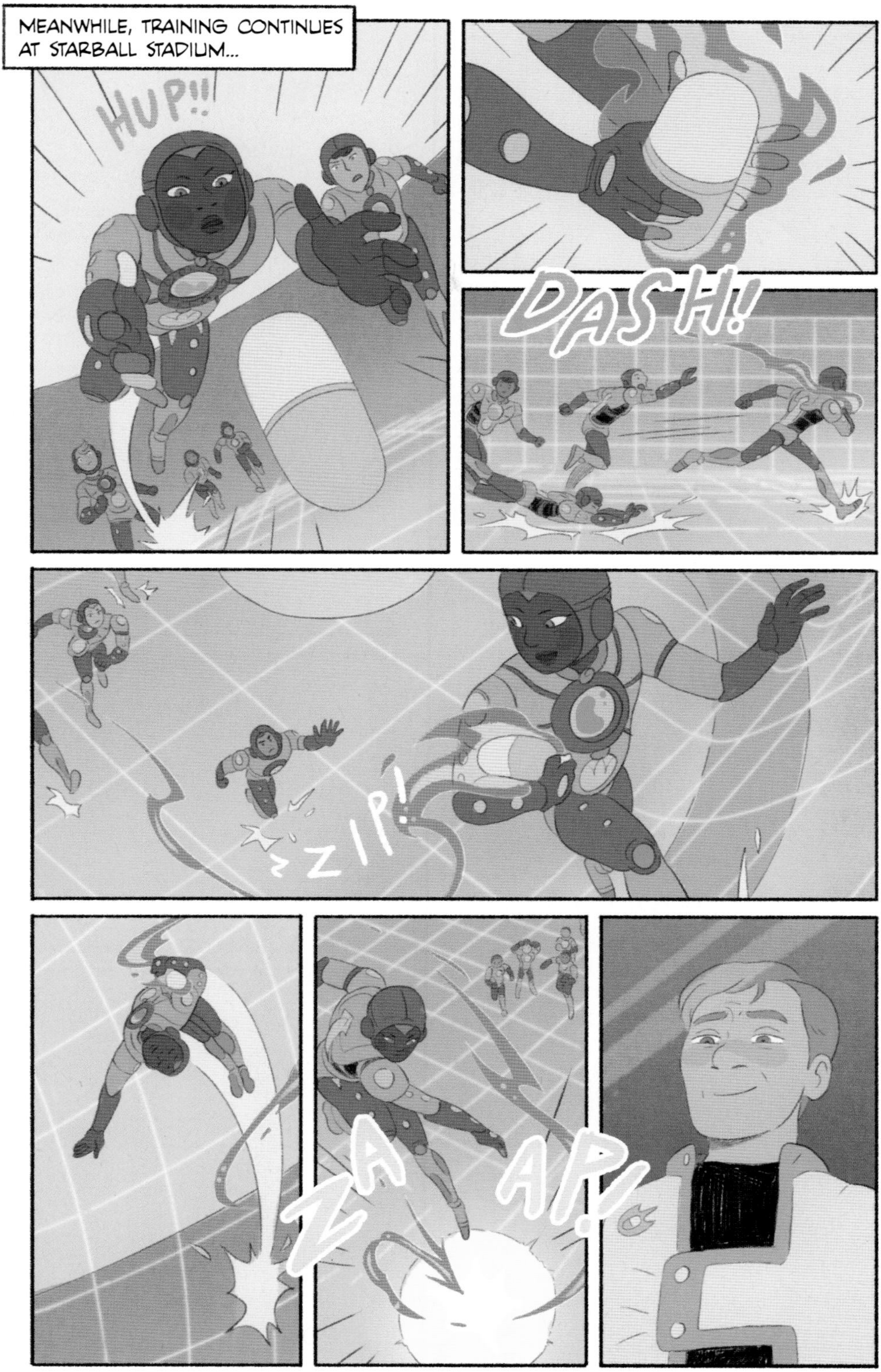
MEANWHILE, TRAINING CONTINUES AT STARBALL STADIUM...
HUP!!
DASH!
ZIP!
ZAAP!

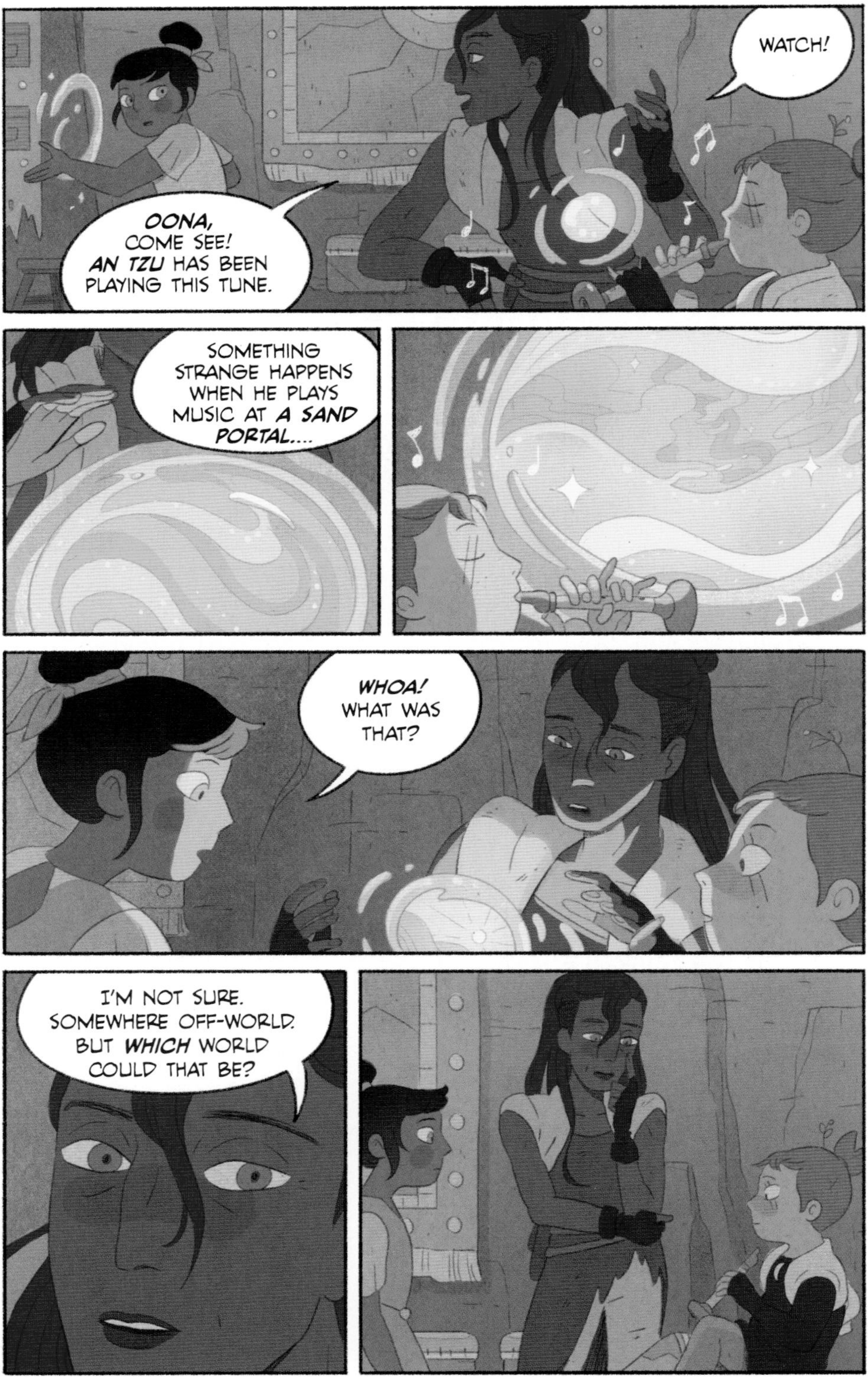
WATCH!
OONA, COME SEE! AN TZU HAS BEEN PLAYING THIS TUNE.
SOMETHING STRANGE HAPPENS WHEN HE PLAYS MUSIC AT A SAND PORTAL....
WHOA! WHAT WAS THAT?
I'M NOT SURE. SOMEWHERE OFF-WORLD. BUT WHICH WORLD COULD THAT BE?

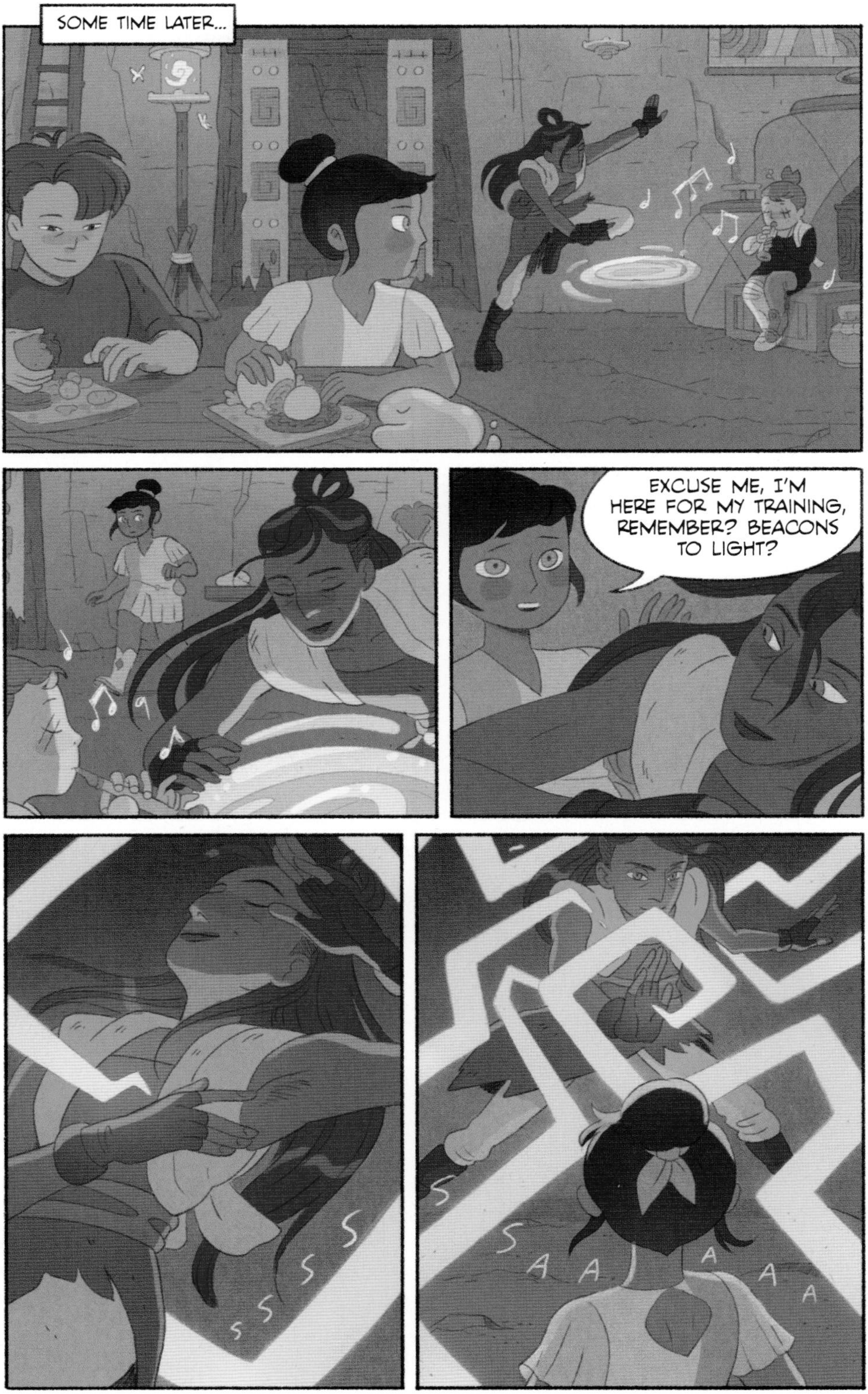
SOME TIME LATER...
EXCUSE ME, I'M HERE FOR MY TRAINING, REMEMBER? BEACONS TO LIGHT?
SSSSS
SSAAAAA

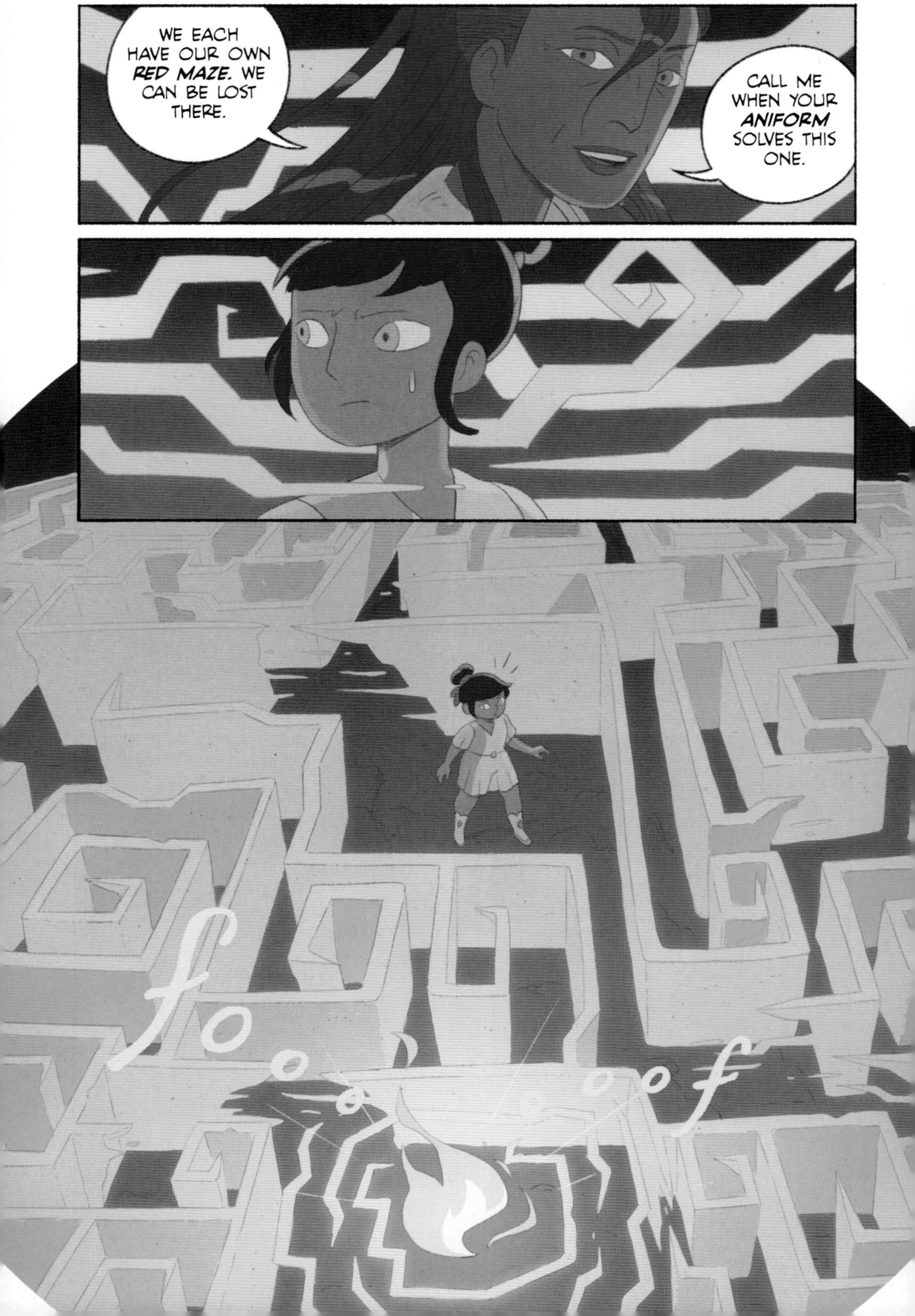
WE EACH HAVE OUR OWN RED MAZE. WE CAN BE LOST THERE.
CALL ME WHEN YOUR ANIFORM SOLVES THIS ONE.
fooooof

## Chapter 9

# THE TRAP

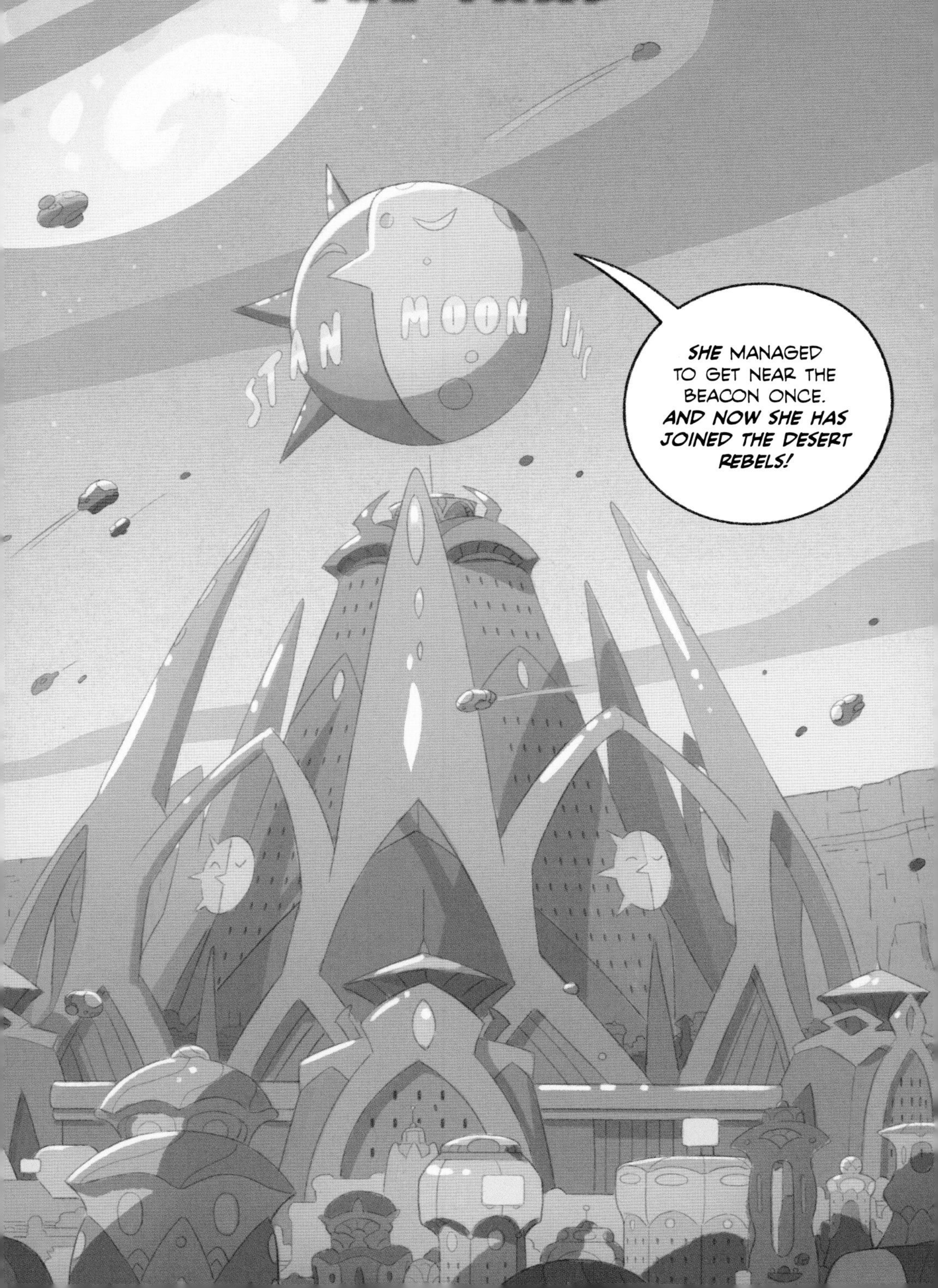

STAN MOON
SHE MANAGED TO GET NEAR THE BEACON ONCE. AND NOW SHE HAS JOINED THE DESERT REBELS!

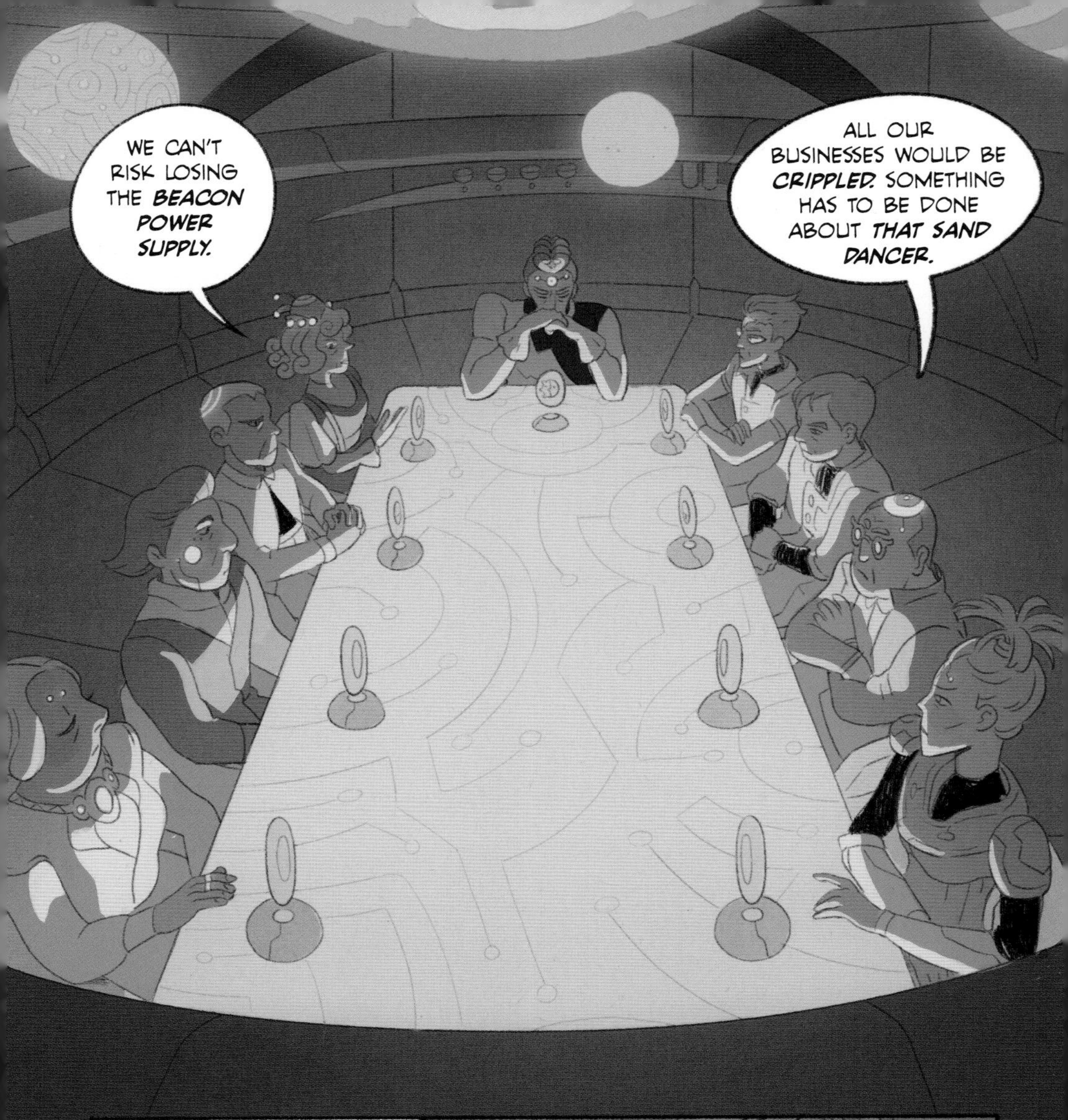
WE CAN'T RISK LOSING THE BEACON POWER SUPPLY.
ALL OUR BUSINESSES WOULD BE CRIPPLED. SOMETHING HAS TO BE DONE ABOUT THAT SAND DANCER.

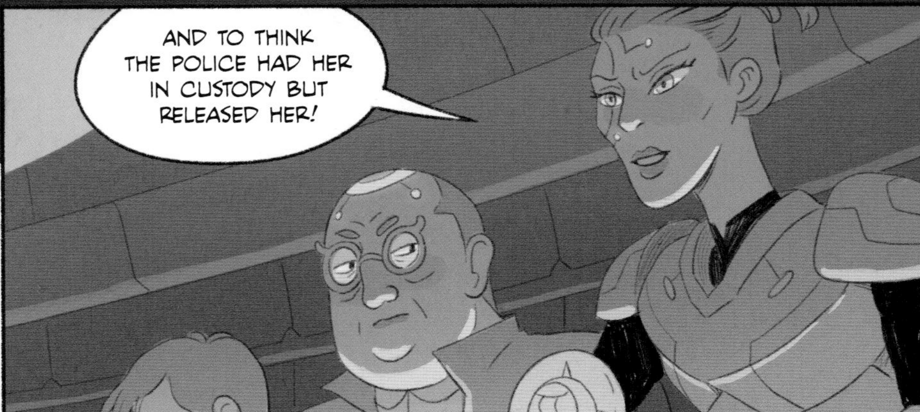
AND TO THINK THE POLICE HAD HER IN CUSTODY BUT RELEASED HER!

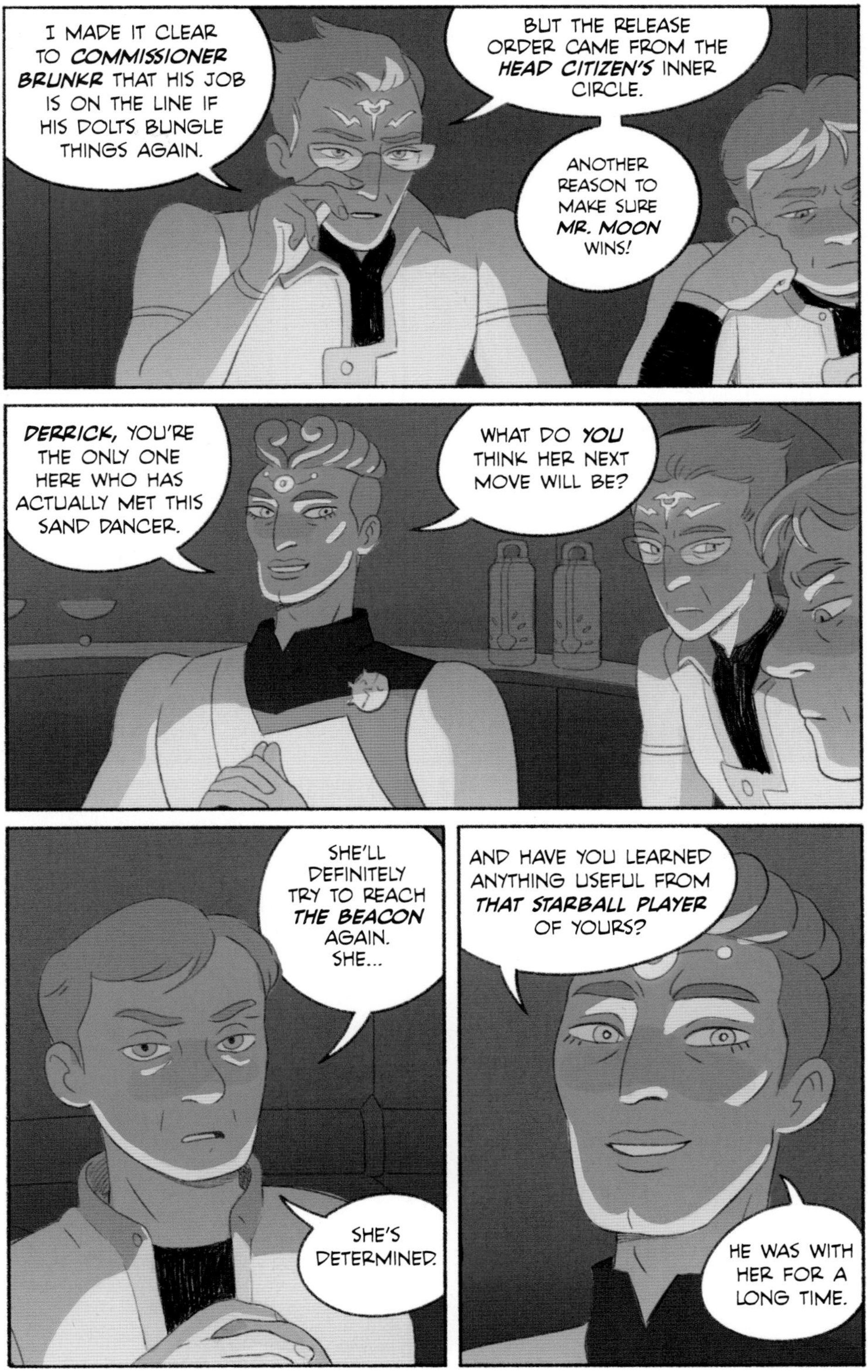
I MADE IT CLEAR TO COMMISSIONER BRUNKR THAT HIS JOB IS ON THE LINE IF HIS DOLTS BUNGLE THINGS AGAIN.
BUT THE RELEASE ORDER CAME FROM THE HEAD CITIZEN'S INNER CIRCLE.
ANOTHER REASON TO MAKE SURE MR. MOON WINS!
DERRICK, YOU'RE THE ONLY ONE HERE WHO HAS ACTUALLY MET THIS SAND DANCER.
WHAT DO YOU THINK HER NEXT MOVE WILL BE?
SHE'LL DEFINITELY TRY TO REACH THE BEACON AGAIN. SHE...
SHE'S DETERMINED.
AND HAVE YOU LEARNED ANYTHING USEFUL FROM THAT STARBALL PLAYER OF YOURS?
HE WAS WITH HER FOR A LONG TIME.

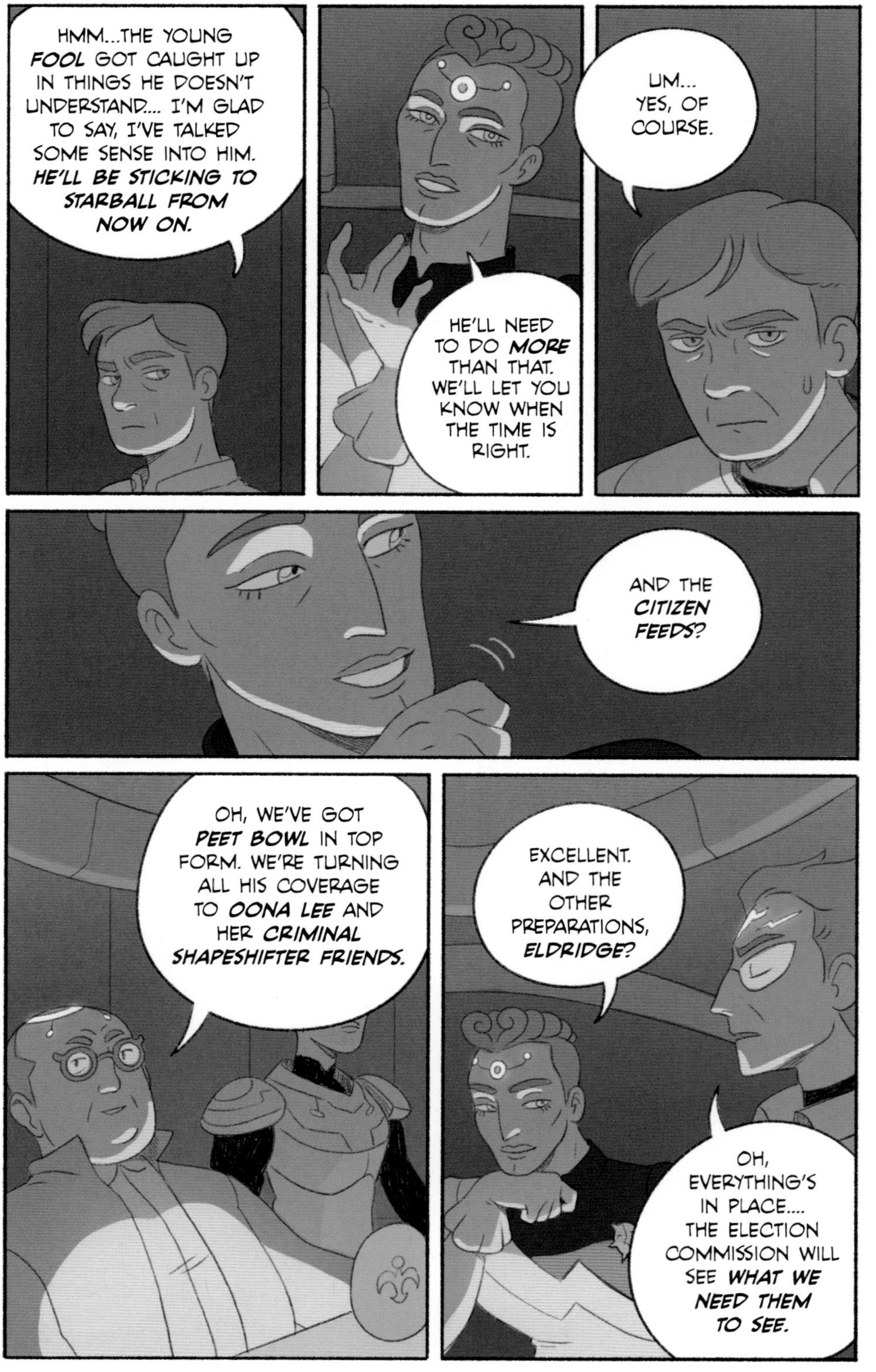
HMM...THE YOUNG FOOL GOT CAUGHT UP IN THINGS HE DOESN'T UNDERSTAND.... I'M GLAD TO SAY, I'VE TALKED SOME SENSE INTO HIM. HE'LL BE STICKING TO STARBALL FROM NOW ON.
HE'LL NEED TO DO MORE THAN THAT. WE'LL LET YOU KNOW WHEN THE TIME IS RIGHT.
UM... YES, OF COURSE.
AND THE CITIZEN FEEDS?
OH, WE'VE GOT PEET BOWL IN TOP FORM. WE'RE TURNING ALL HIS COVERAGE TO OONA LEE AND HER CRIMINAL SHAPESHIFTER FRIENDS.
EXCELLENT. AND THE OTHER PREPARATIONS, ELDRIDGE?
OH, EVERYTHING'S IN PLACE.... THE ELECTION COMMISSION WILL SEE WHAT WE NEED THEM TO SEE.

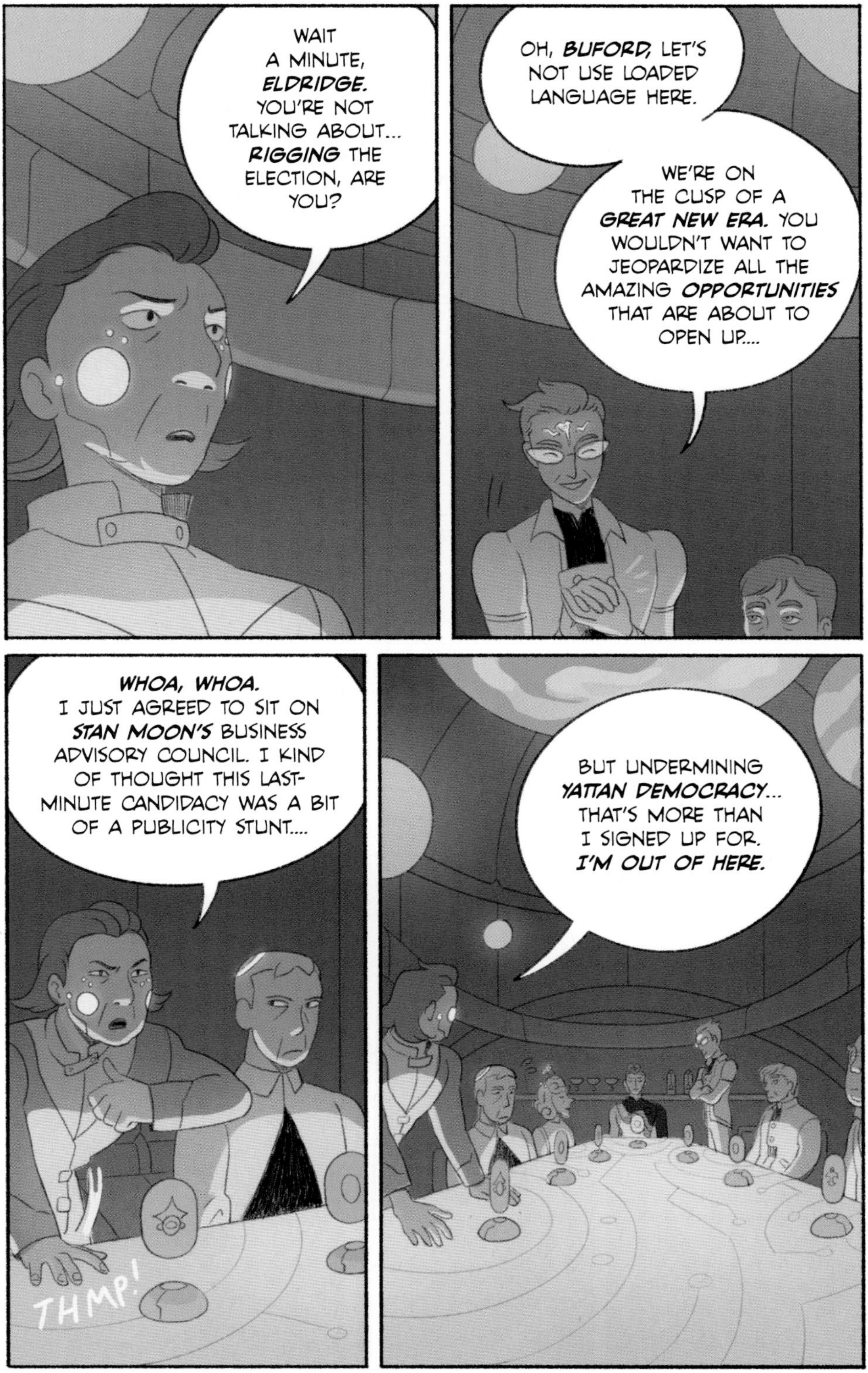
WAIT A MINUTE, ELDRIDGE. YOU'RE NOT TALKING ABOUT... RIGGING THE ELECTION, ARE YOU?
OH, BUFORD, LET'S NOT USE LOADED LANGUAGE HERE.
WE'RE ON THE CUSP OF A GREAT NEW ERA. YOU WOULDN'T WANT TO JEOPARDIZE ALL THE AMAZING OPPORTUNITIES THAT ARE ABOUT TO OPEN UP....
WHOA, WHOA. I JUST AGREED TO SIT ON STAN MOON'S BUSINESS ADVISORY COUNCIL. I KIND OF THOUGHT THIS LAST-MINUTE CANDIDACY WAS A BIT OF A PUBLICITY STUNT....
THMP!
BUT UNDERMINING YATTAN DEMOCRACY... THAT'S MORE THAN I SIGNED UP FOR. I'M OUT OF HERE.

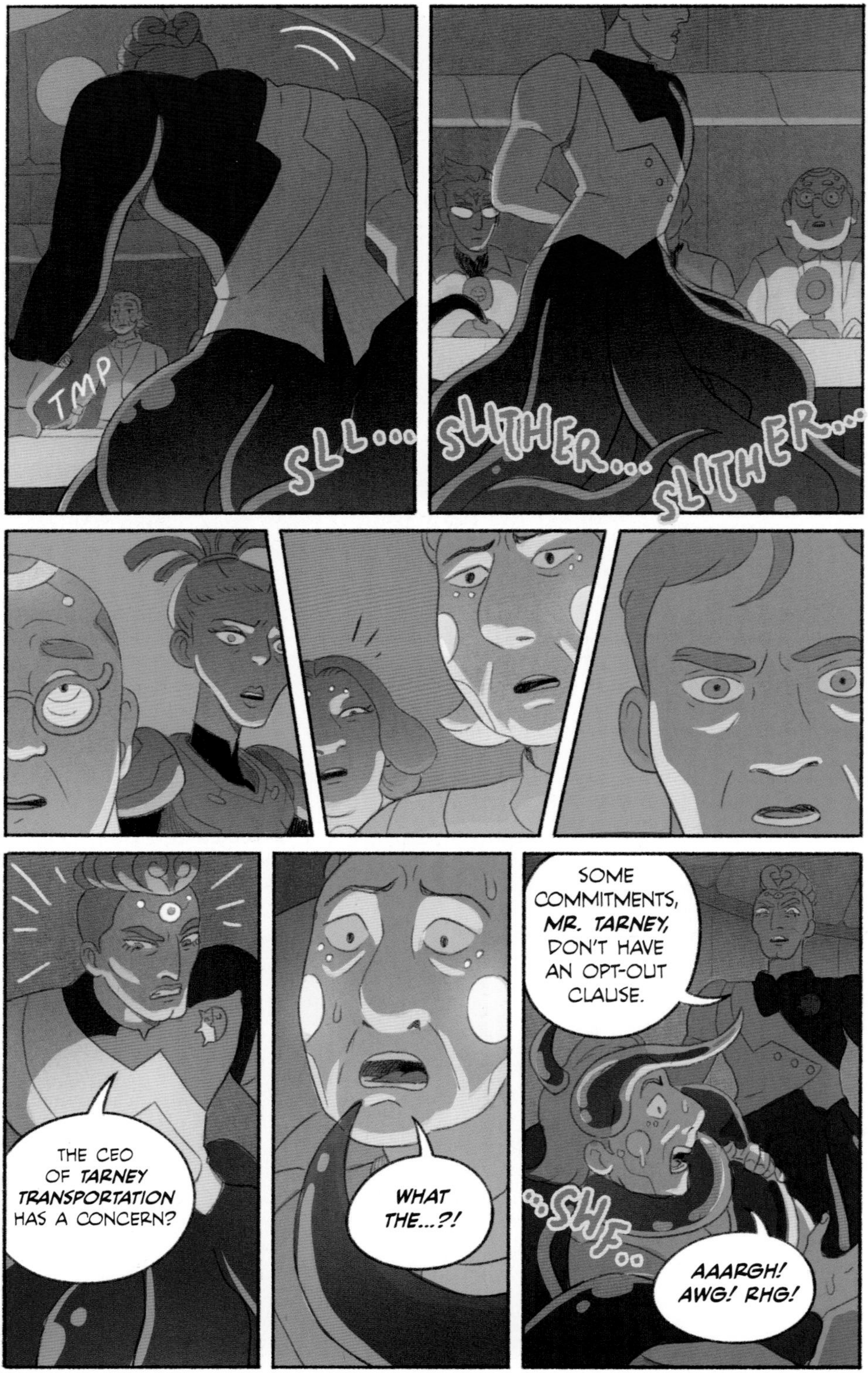
TMP
SLL... SLITHER... SLITHER...
THE CEO OF ***TARNEY TRANSPORTATION*** HAS A CONCERN?
***WHAT THE...?!***
SOME COMMITMENTS, ***MR. TARNEY,*** DON'T HAVE AN OPT-OUT CLAUSE.
..SHF..
***AAARGH! AWG! RHG!***

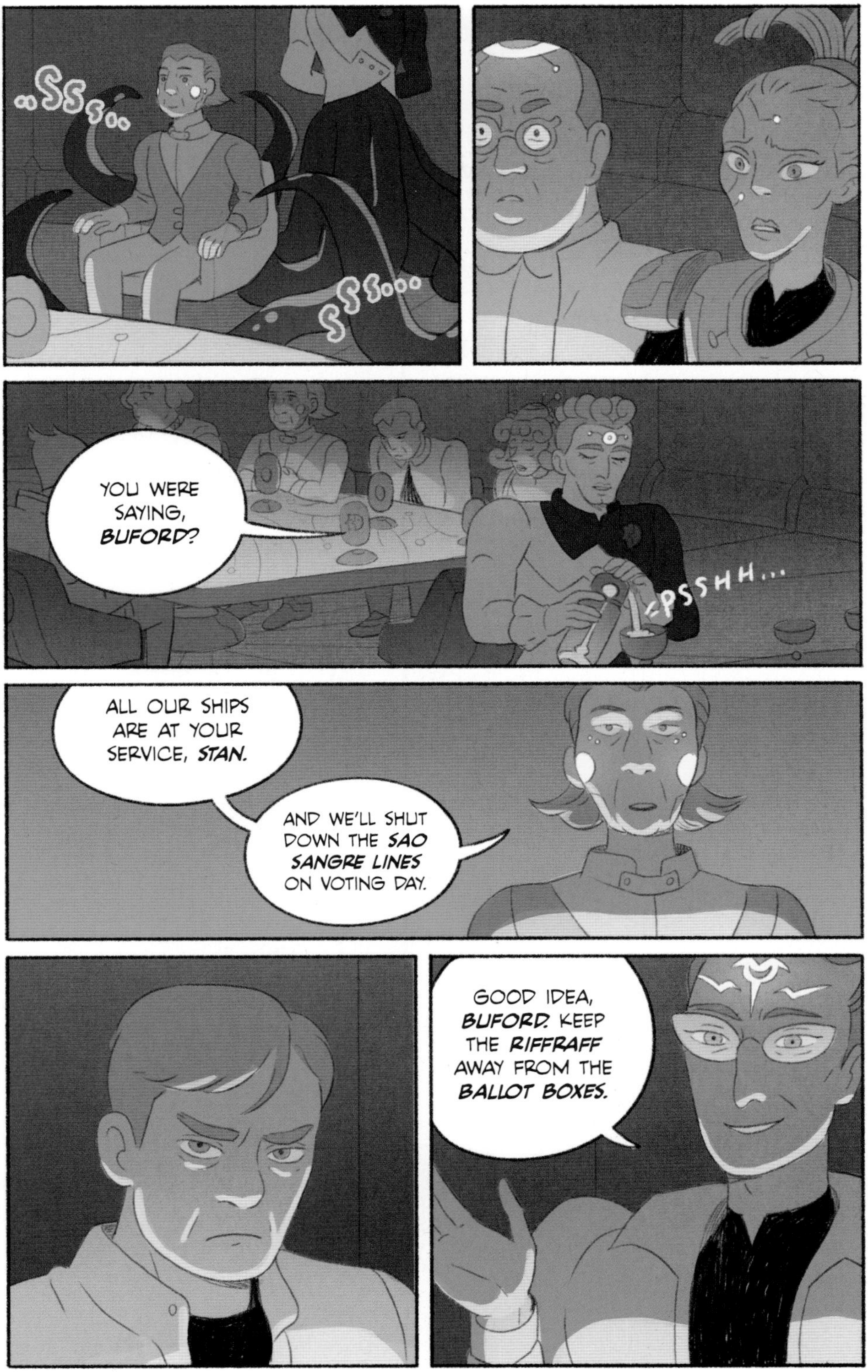
..SSS..
SSS...
YOU WERE SAYING, BUFORD?
PSSHH...
ALL OUR SHIPS ARE AT YOUR SERVICE, STAN.
AND WE'LL SHUT DOWN THE SAO SANGRE LINES ON VOTING DAY.
GOOD IDEA, BUFORD. KEEP THE RIFFRAFF AWAY FROM THE BALLOT BOXES.

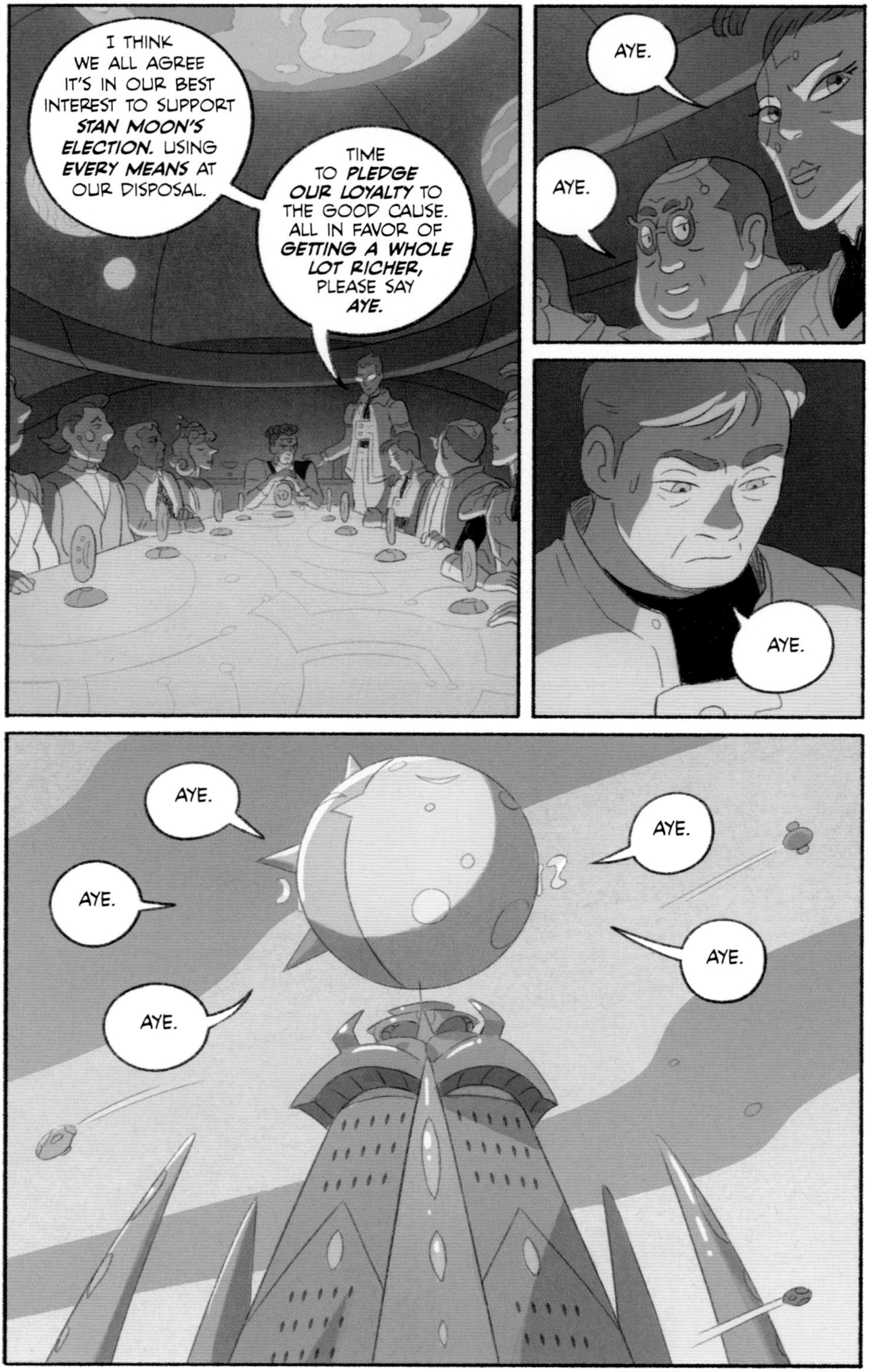
I THINK WE ALL AGREE IT'S IN OUR BEST INTEREST TO SUPPORT STAN MOON'S ELECTION. USING EVERY MEANS AT OUR DISPOSAL.
TIME TO PLEDGE OUR LOYALTY TO THE GOOD CAUSE. ALL IN FAVOR OF GETTING A WHOLE LOT RICHER, PLEASE SAY AYE.
AYE.
AYE.
AYE.
AYE.
AYE.
AYE.
AYE.
AYE.

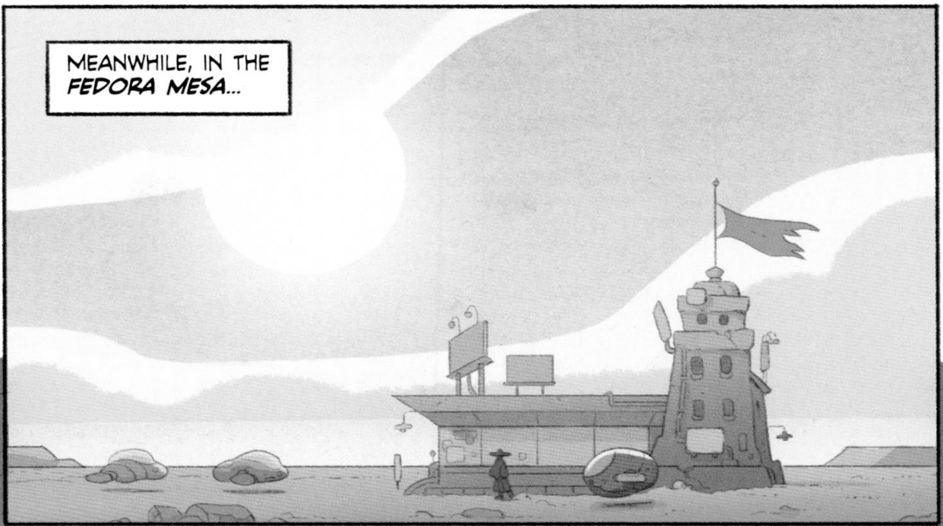
MEANWHILE, IN THE *FEDORA MESA*...

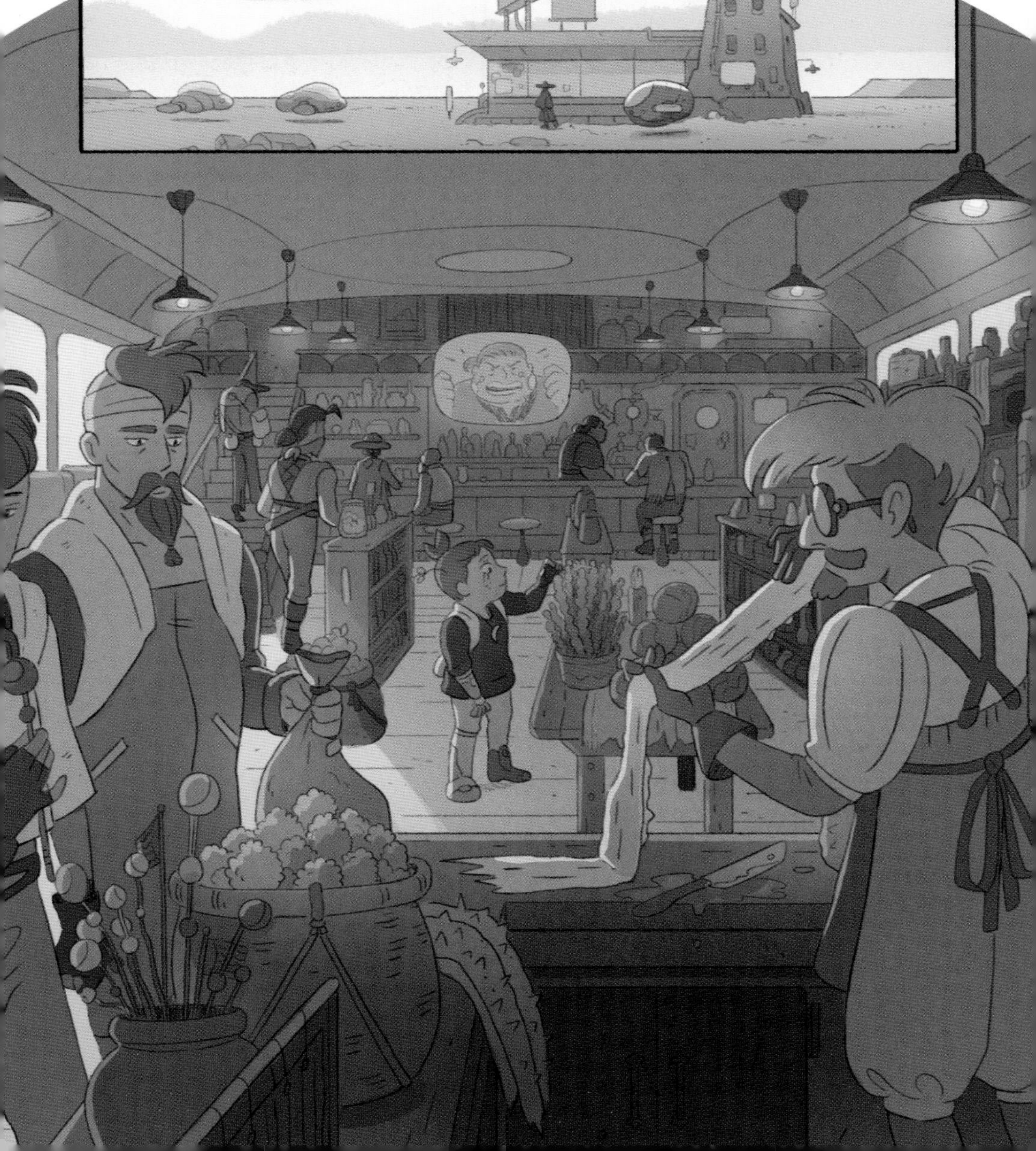

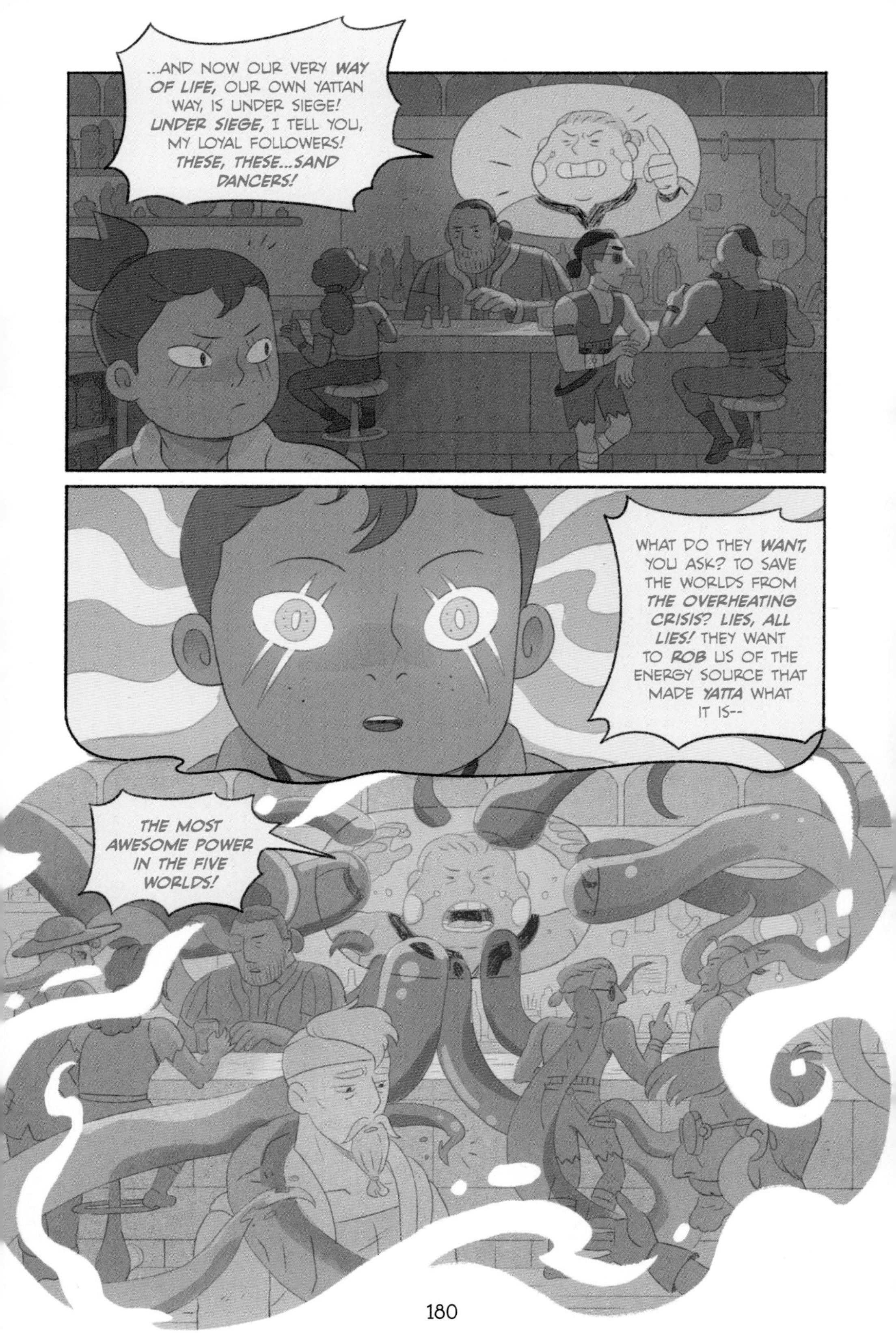

...AND NOW OUR VERY WAY OF LIFE, OUR OWN YATTAN WAY, IS UNDER SIEGE! UNDER SIEGE, I TELL YOU, MY LOYAL FOLLOWERS! THESE, THESE...SAND DANCERS!
WHAT DO THEY WANT, YOU ASK? TO SAVE THE WORLDS FROM THE OVERHEATING CRISIS? LIES, ALL LIES! THEY WANT TO ROB US OF THE ENERGY SOURCE THAT MADE YATTA WHAT IT IS--
THE MOST AWESOME POWER IN THE FIVE WORLDS!

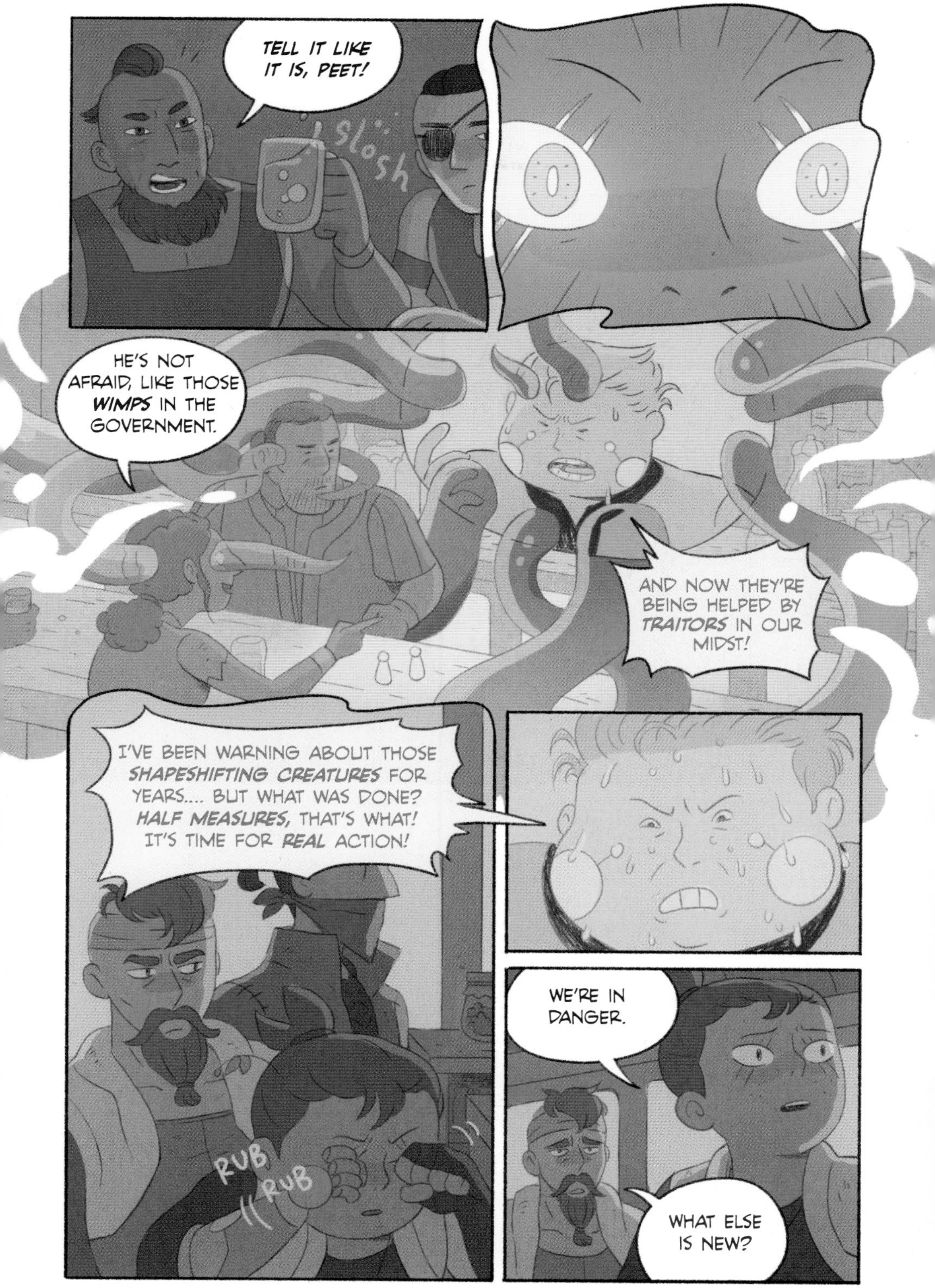
TELL IT LIKE IT IS, PEET!
SLOSH
HE'S NOT AFRAID, LIKE THOSE WIMPS IN THE GOVERNMENT.
AND NOW THEY'RE BEING HELPED BY TRAITORS IN OUR MIDST!
I'VE BEEN WARNING ABOUT THOSE SHAPESHIFTING CREATURES FOR YEARS.... BUT WHAT WAS DONE? HALF MEASURES, THAT'S WHAT! IT'S TIME FOR REAL ACTION!
RUB RUB
WE'RE IN DANGER.
WHAT ELSE IS NEW?

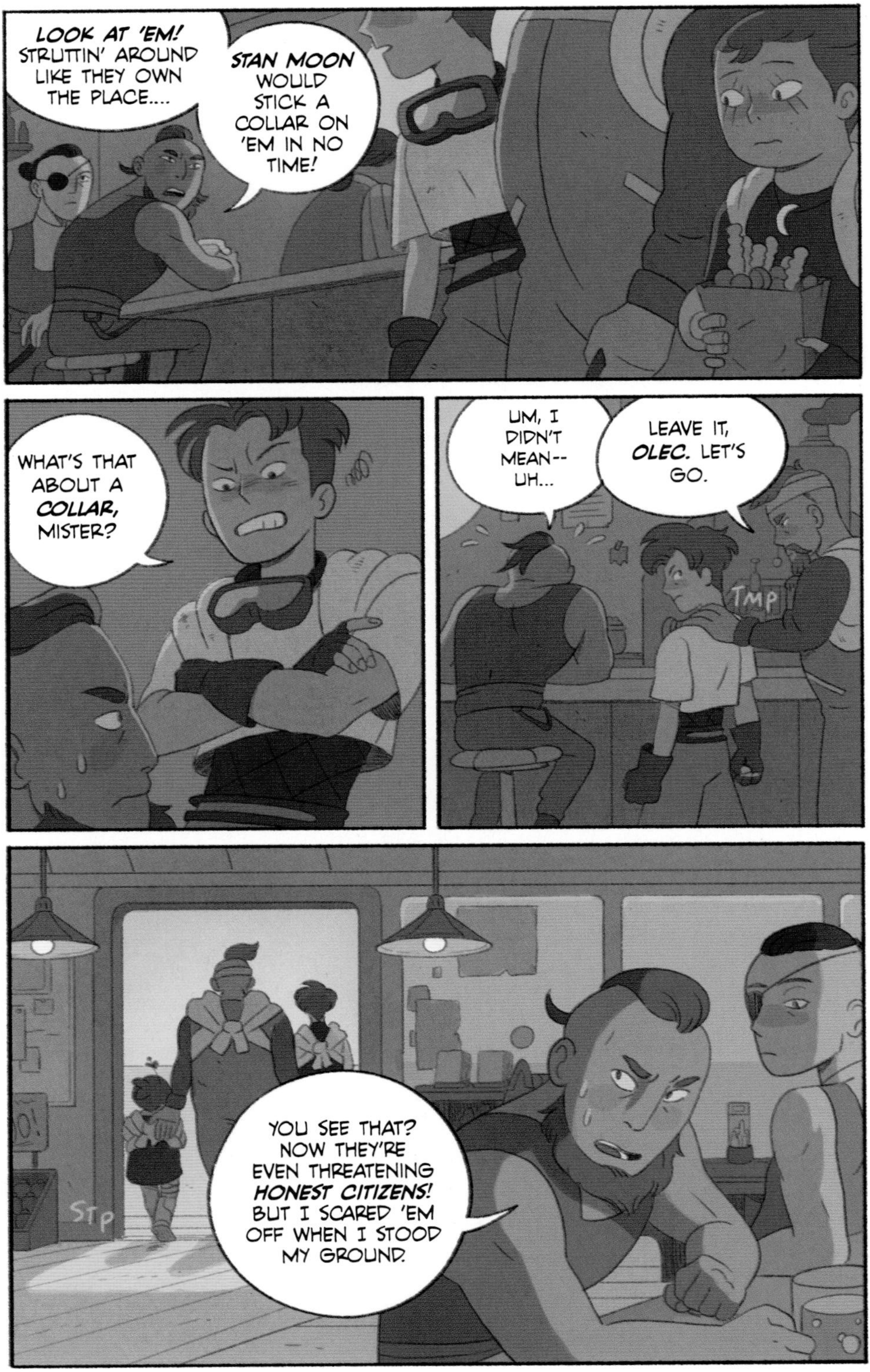
LOOK AT 'EM! STRUTTIN' AROUND LIKE THEY OWN THE PLACE....
STAN MOON WOULD STICK A COLLAR ON 'EM IN NO TIME!
WHAT'S THAT ABOUT A COLLAR, MISTER?
UM, I DIDN'T MEAN-- UH...
LEAVE IT, OLEC. LET'S GO.
TMP
STP
YOU SEE THAT? NOW THEY'RE EVEN THREATENING HONEST CITIZENS! BUT I SCARED 'EM OFF WHEN I STOOD MY GROUND.

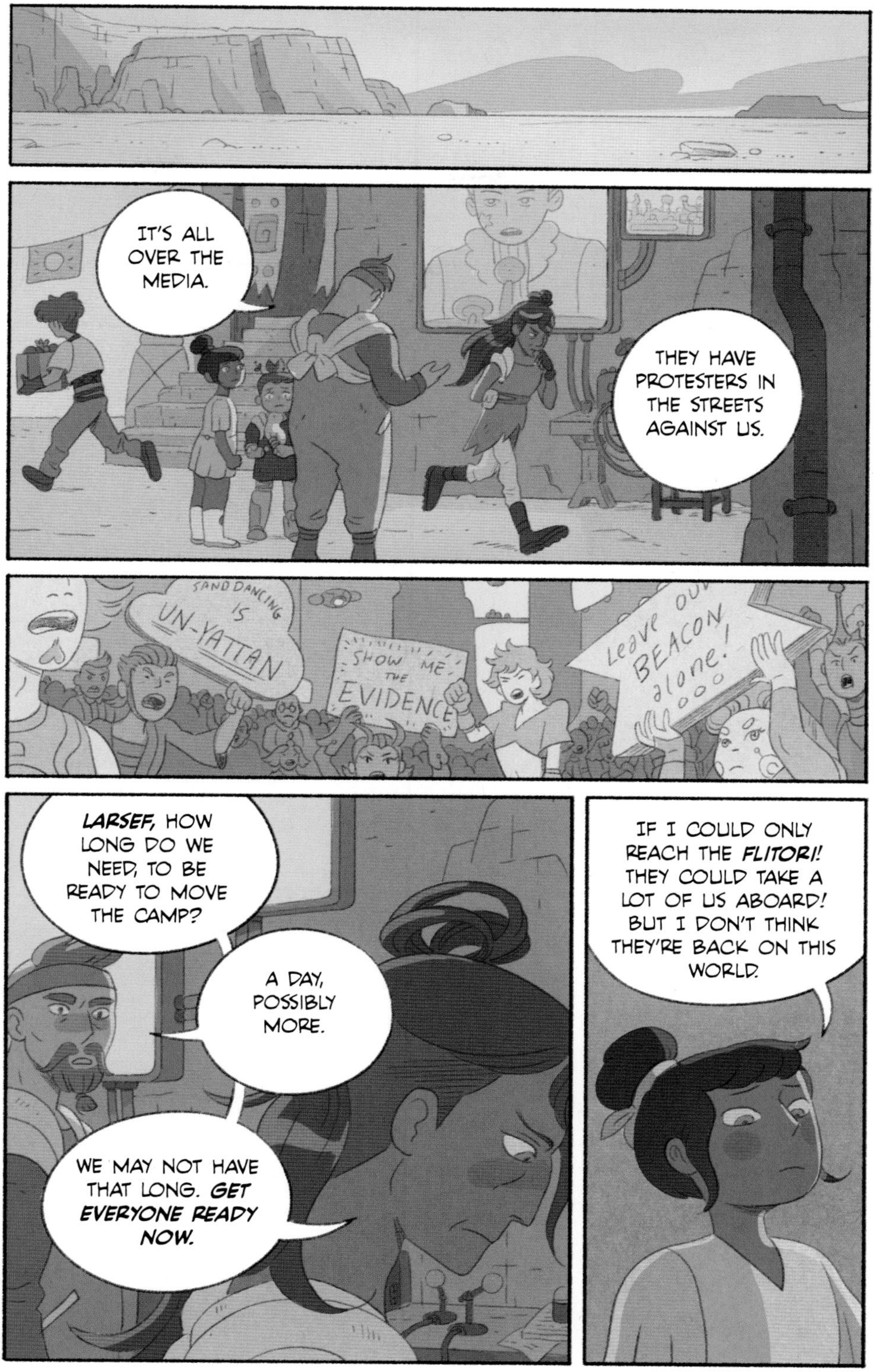
IT'S ALL OVER THE MEDIA.
THEY HAVE PROTESTERS IN THE STREETS AGAINST US.
SAND DANCING IS UN-YATTAN
SHOW ME THE EVIDENCE
Leave our BEACON alone!
LARSEF, HOW LONG DO WE NEED, TO BE READY TO MOVE THE CAMP?
A DAY, POSSIBLY MORE.
WE MAY NOT HAVE THAT LONG. GET EVERYONE READY NOW.
IF I COULD ONLY REACH THE FLITORI! THEY COULD TAKE A LOT OF US ABOARD! BUT I DON'T THINK THEY'RE BACK ON THIS WORLD.

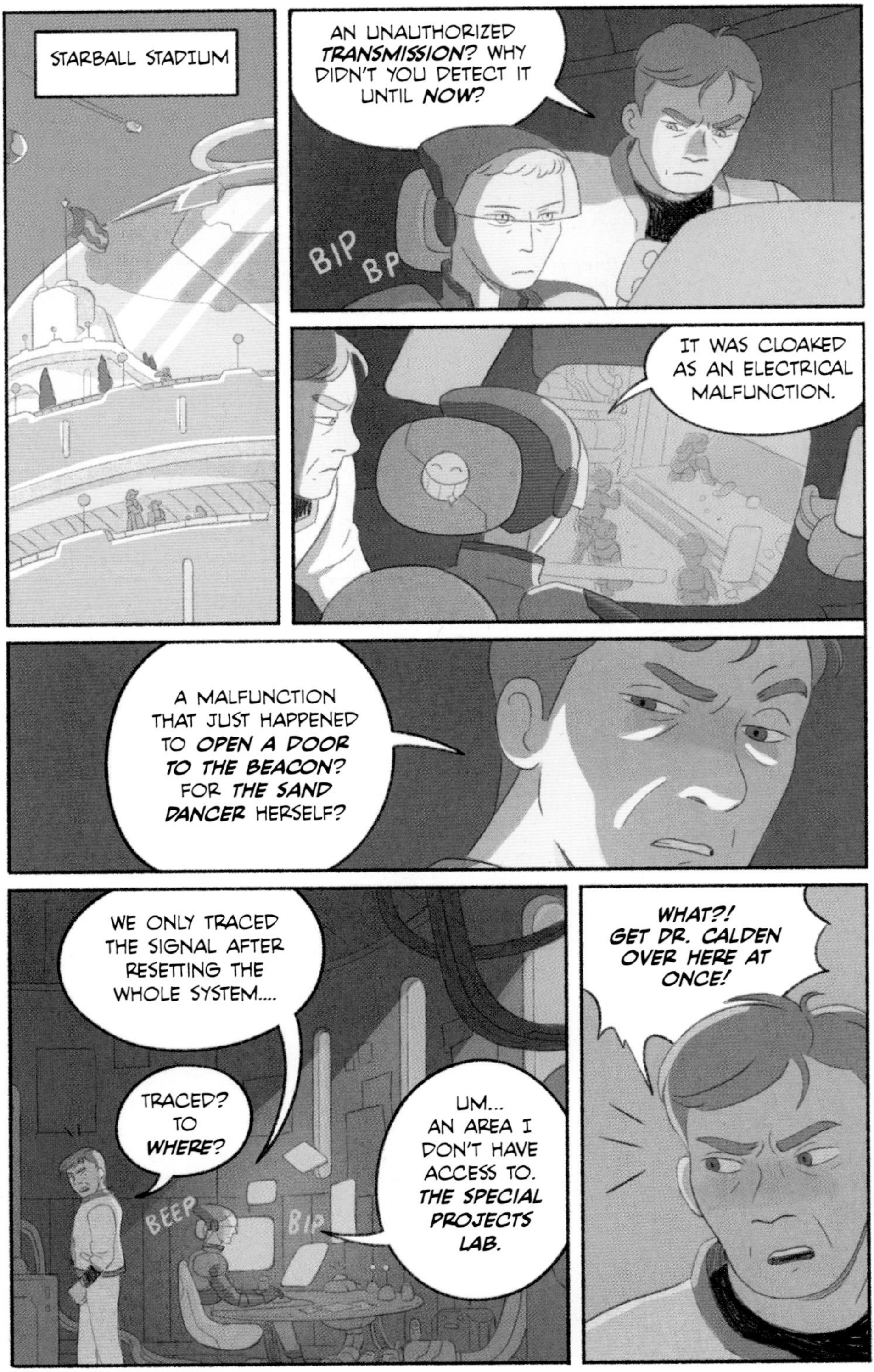
STARBALL STADIUM
AN UNAUTHORIZED TRANSMISSION? WHY DIDN'T YOU DETECT IT UNTIL NOW?
BIP BP
IT WAS CLOAKED AS AN ELECTRICAL MALFUNCTION.
A MALFUNCTION THAT JUST HAPPENED TO OPEN A DOOR TO THE BEACON? FOR THE SAND DANCER HERSELF?
WE ONLY TRACED THE SIGNAL AFTER RESETTING THE WHOLE SYSTEM....
TRACED? TO WHERE?
BEEP
BIP
UM... AN AREA I DON'T HAVE ACCESS TO. THE SPECIAL PROJECTS LAB.
WHAT?! GET DR. CALDEN OVER HERE AT ONCE!

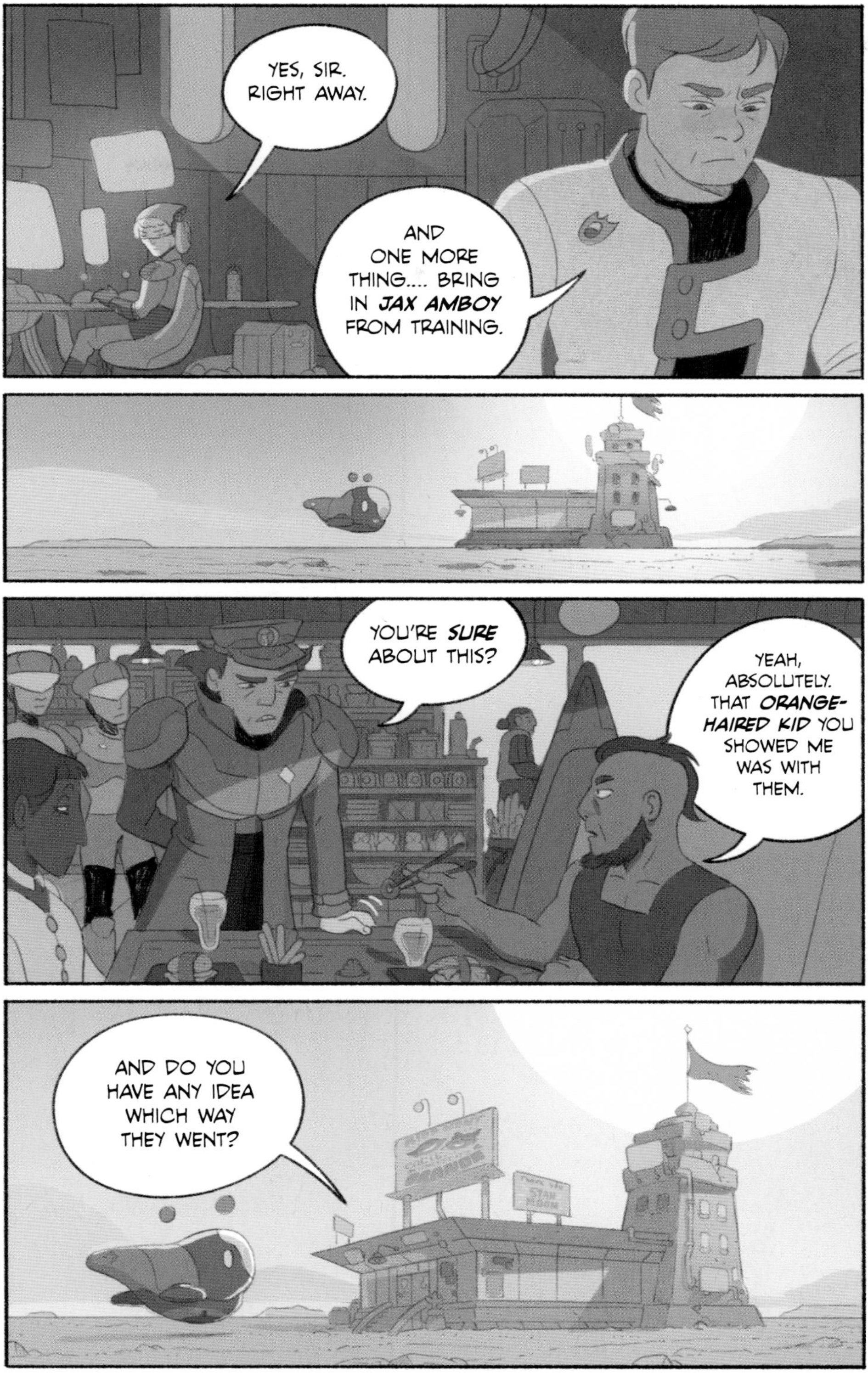
YES, SIR. RIGHT AWAY.
AND ONE MORE THING.... BRING IN JAX AMBOY FROM TRAINING.
YOU'RE SURE ABOUT THIS?
YEAH, ABSOLUTELY. THAT ORANGE-HAIRED KID YOU SHOWED ME WAS WITH THEM.
AND DO YOU HAVE ANY IDEA WHICH WAY THEY WENT?

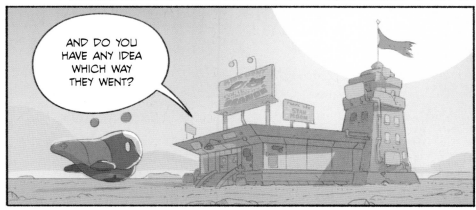

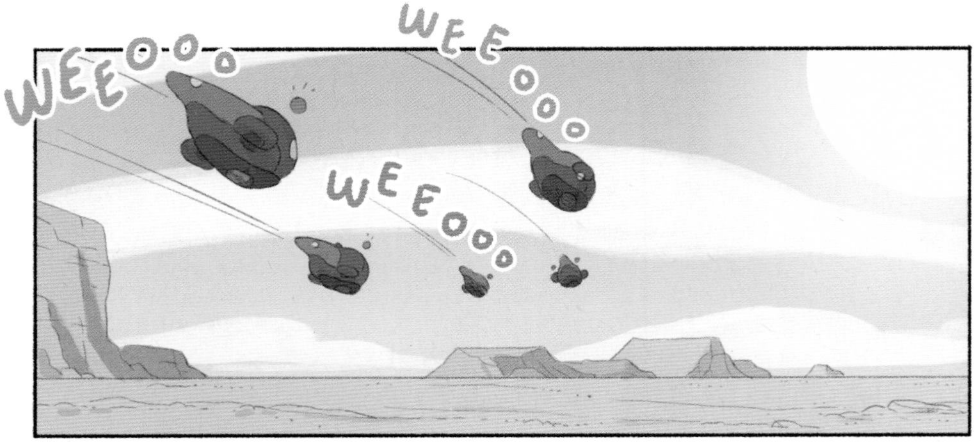
WEEOOO
WEEOOO
WEEOOO

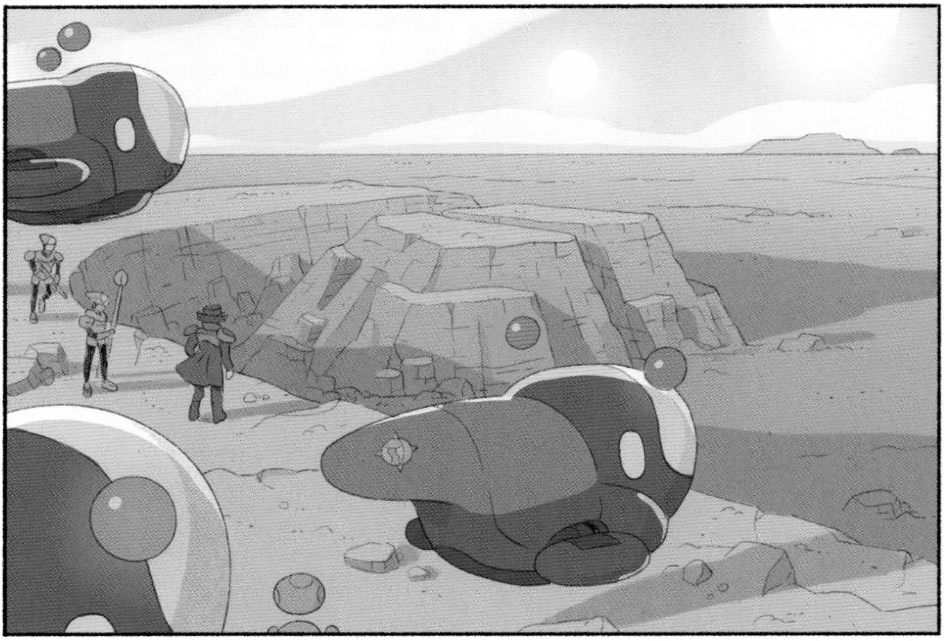

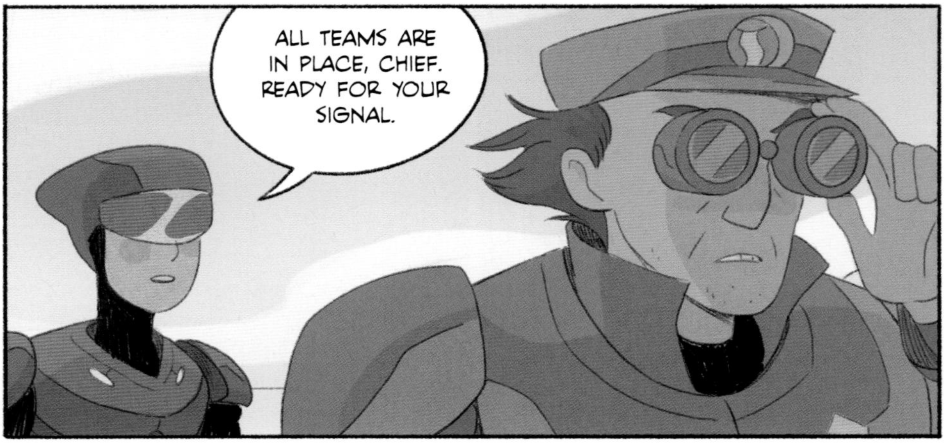
ALL TEAMS ARE IN PLACE, CHIEF. READY FOR YOUR SIGNAL.

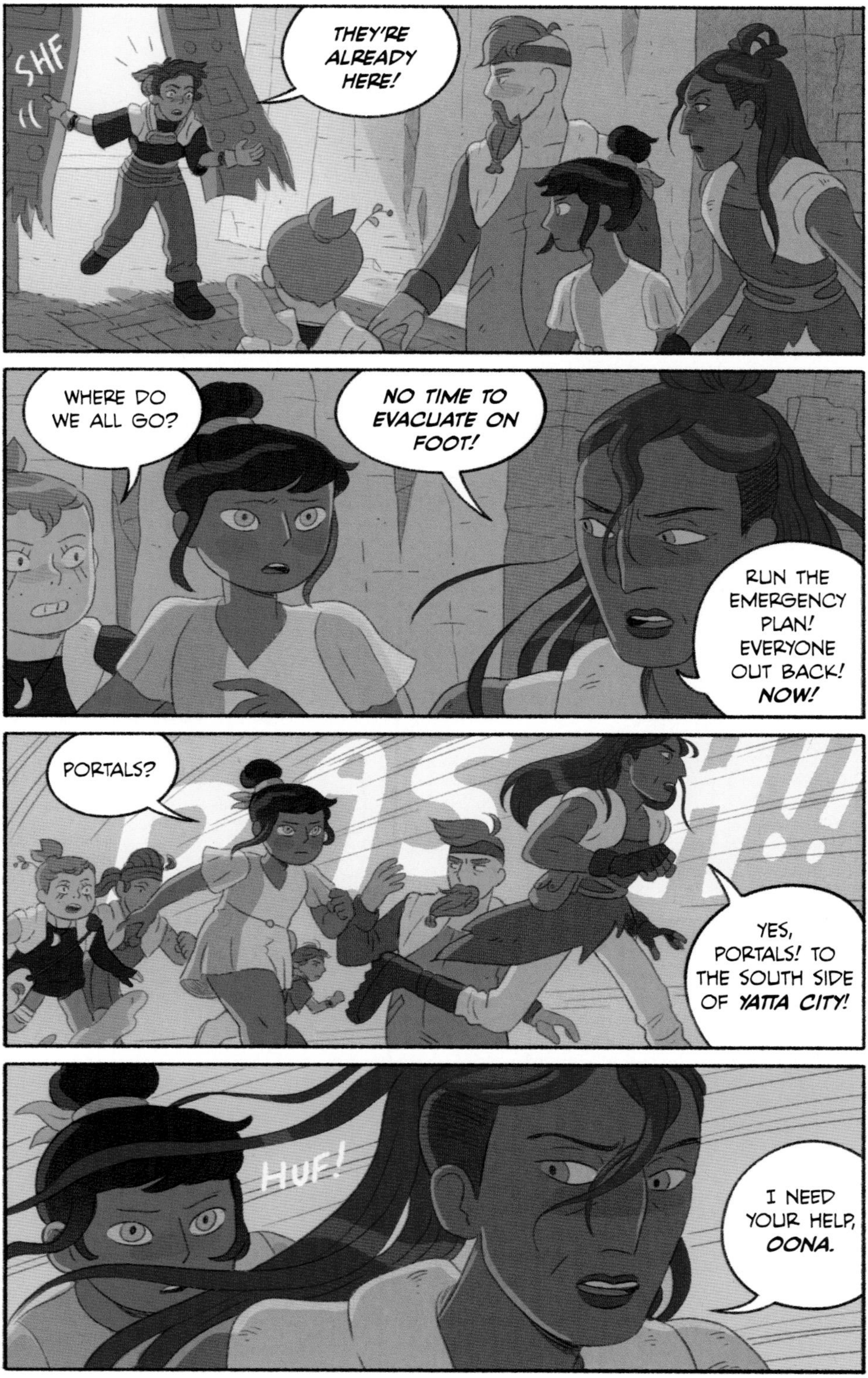
SHF
THEY'RE ALREADY HERE!
WHERE DO WE ALL GO?
NO TIME TO EVACUATE ON FOOT!
RUN THE EMERGENCY PLAN! EVERYONE OUT BACK! NOW!
PORTALS?
YES, PORTALS! TO THE SOUTH SIDE OF YATTA CITY!
HUF!
I NEED YOUR HELP, OONA.

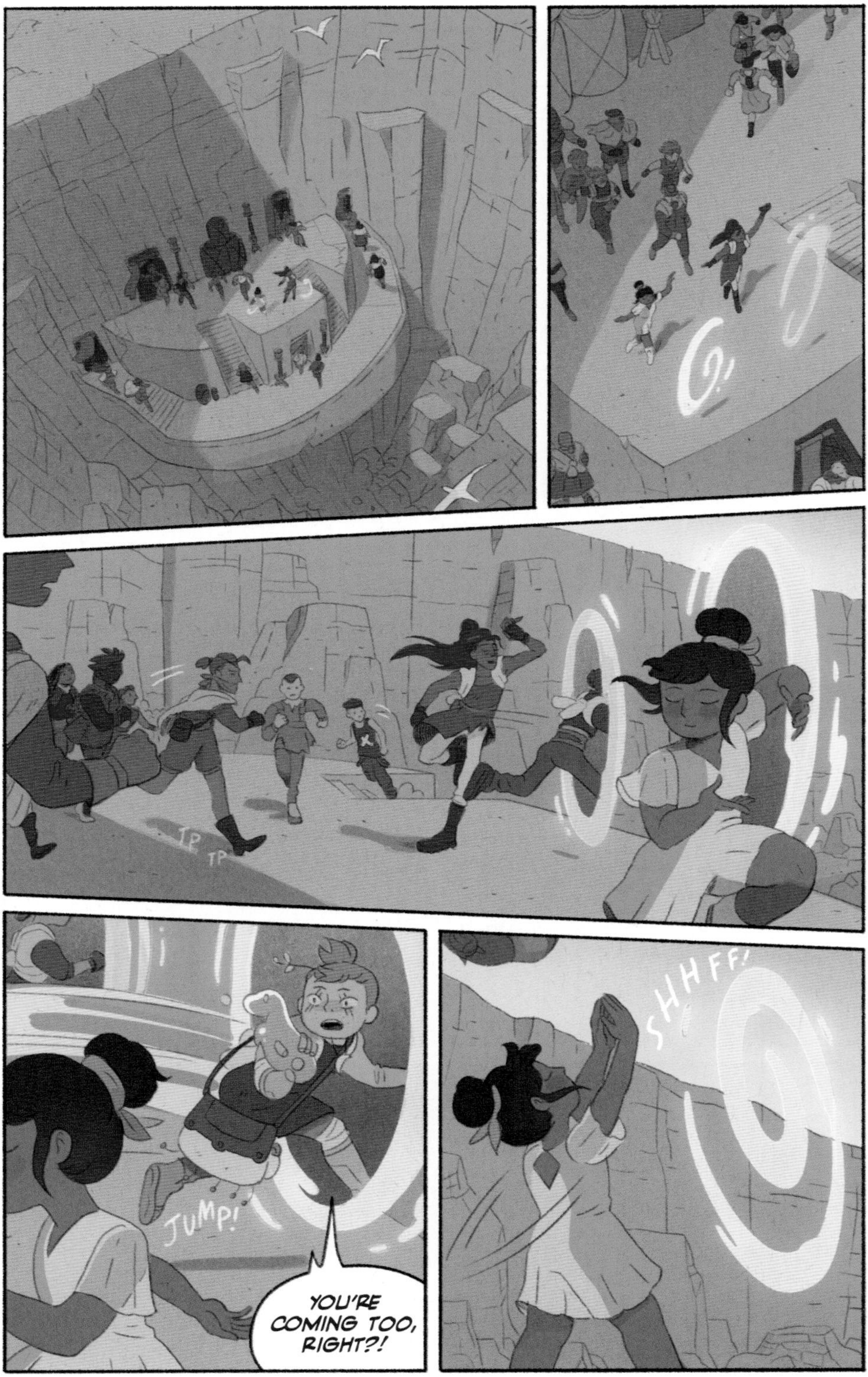
TP TP
JUMP!
YOU'RE COMING TOO, RIGHT?!
SHHFF!

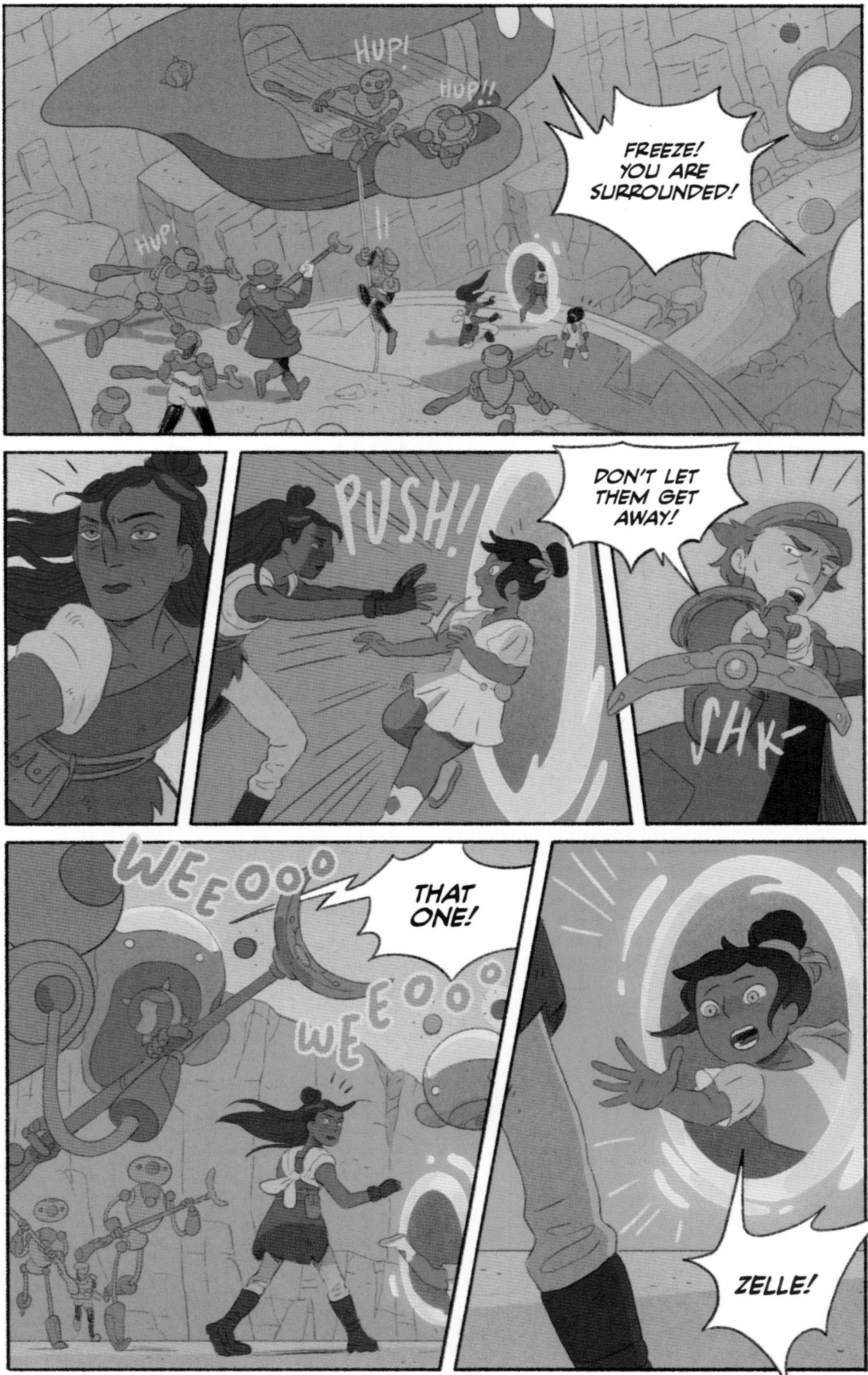
HUP!
HUP!!
HUP!
FREEZE! YOU ARE SURROUNDED!
PUSH!
DON'T LET THEM GET AWAY!
SHK-
WEEOOO
THAT ONE!
WEEOOO
ZELLE!

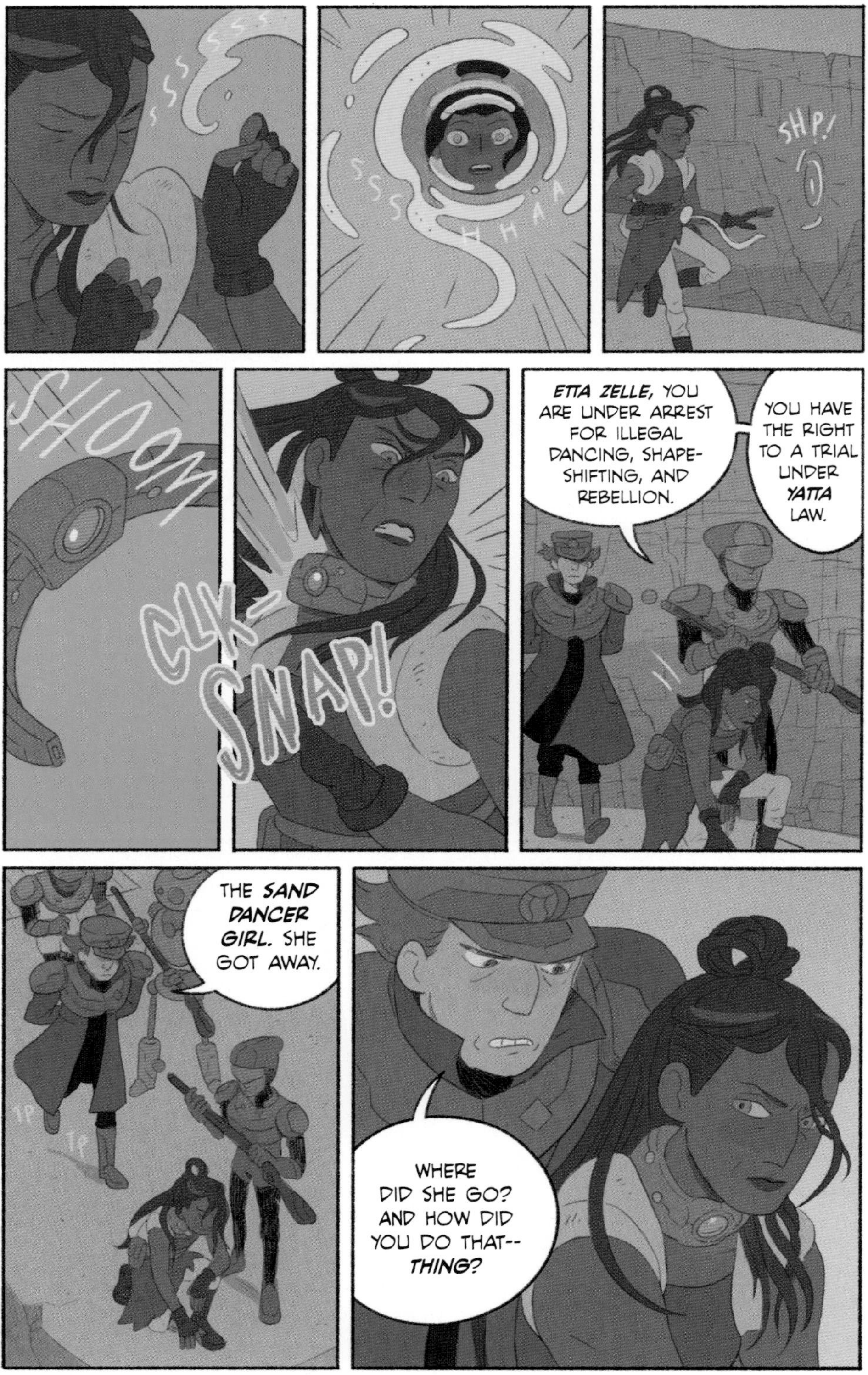
SSSSSSS
SSSHHAA
SHP!
SHOOM
CLK-SNAP!
***ETTA ZELLE,*** YOU ARE UNDER ARREST FOR ILLEGAL DANCING, SHAPE-SHIFTING, AND REBELLION.
YOU HAVE THE RIGHT TO A TRIAL UNDER ***YATTA*** LAW.
THE ***SAND DANCER GIRL.*** SHE GOT AWAY.
WHERE DID SHE GO? AND HOW DID YOU DO THAT-- ***THING?***

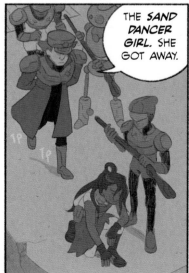

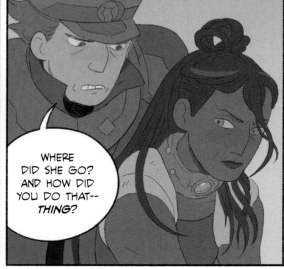

## Chapter 10

# GAME DAY

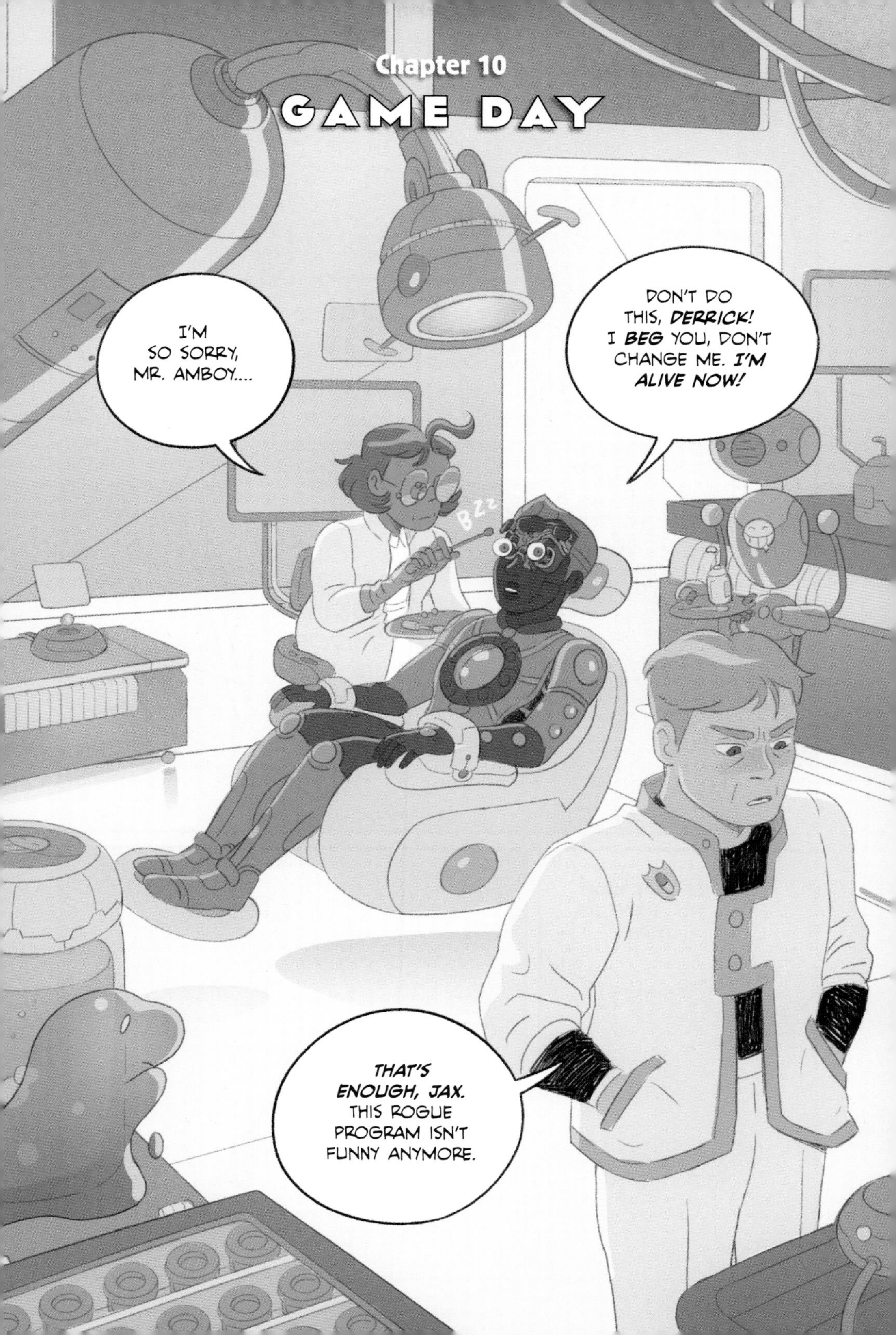
I'M SO SORRY, MR. AMBOY....
DON'T DO THIS, *DERRICK!* I *BEG* YOU, DON'T CHANGE ME. *I'M ALIVE NOW!*
BZZ
*THAT'S ENOUGH, JAX.* THIS ROGUE PROGRAM ISN'T FUNNY ANYMORE.

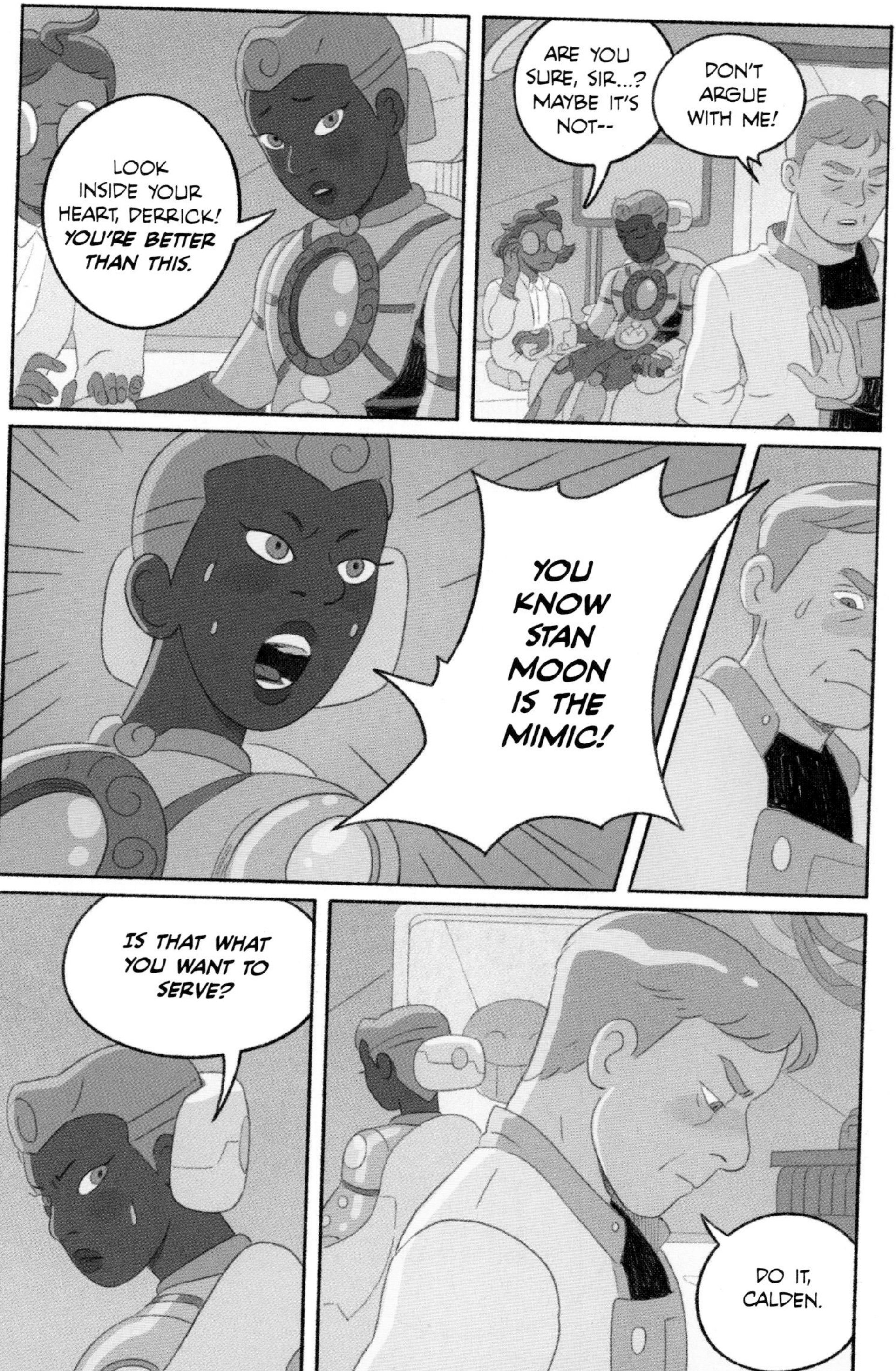
LOOK INSIDE YOUR HEART, DERRICK! YOU'RE BETTER THAN THIS.
ARE YOU SURE, SIR...? MAYBE IT'S NOT--
DON'T ARGUE WITH ME!
YOU KNOW STAN MOON IS THE MIMIC!
IS THAT WHAT YOU WANT TO SERVE?
DO IT, CALDEN.

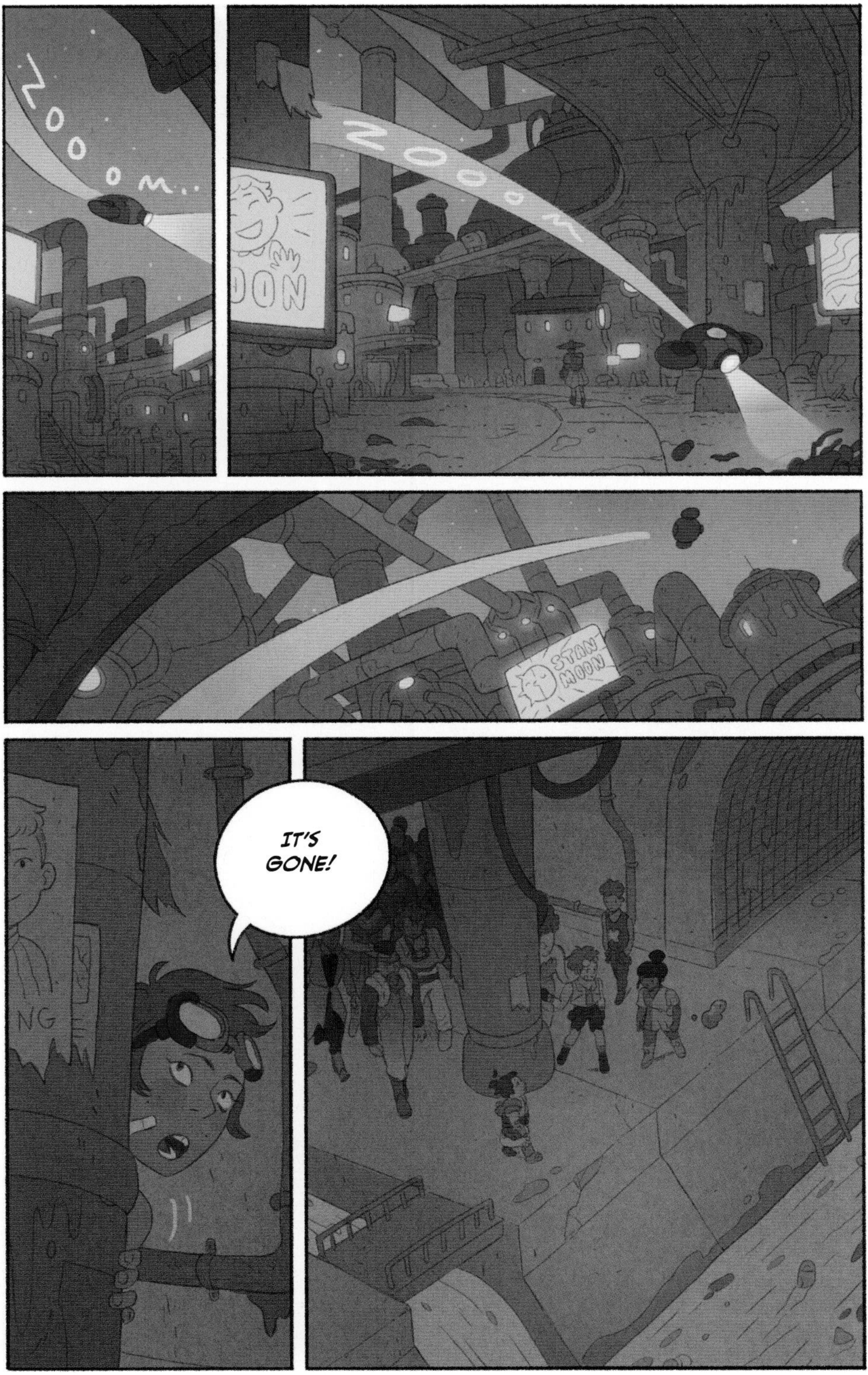
ZOOOM..
ZOOOM
STAN MOON
IT'S GONE!

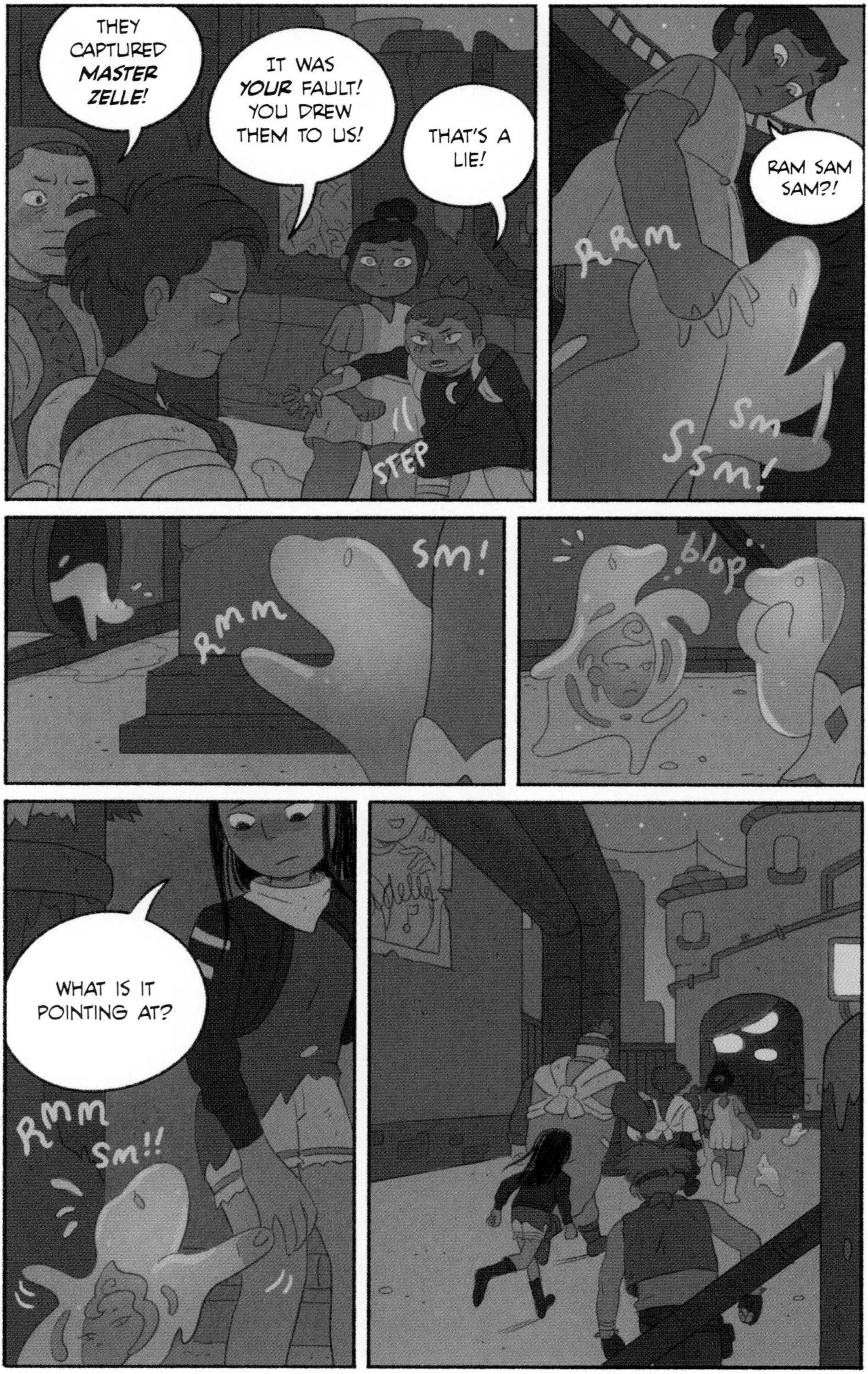
THEY CAPTURED MASTER ZELLE!
IT WAS YOUR FAULT! YOU DREW THEM TO US!
THAT'S A LIE!
STEP
RAM SAM SAM?!
RRM
SM
SSM!
SM!
RMM
BLOP
WHAT IS IT POINTING AT?
RMM
SM!!

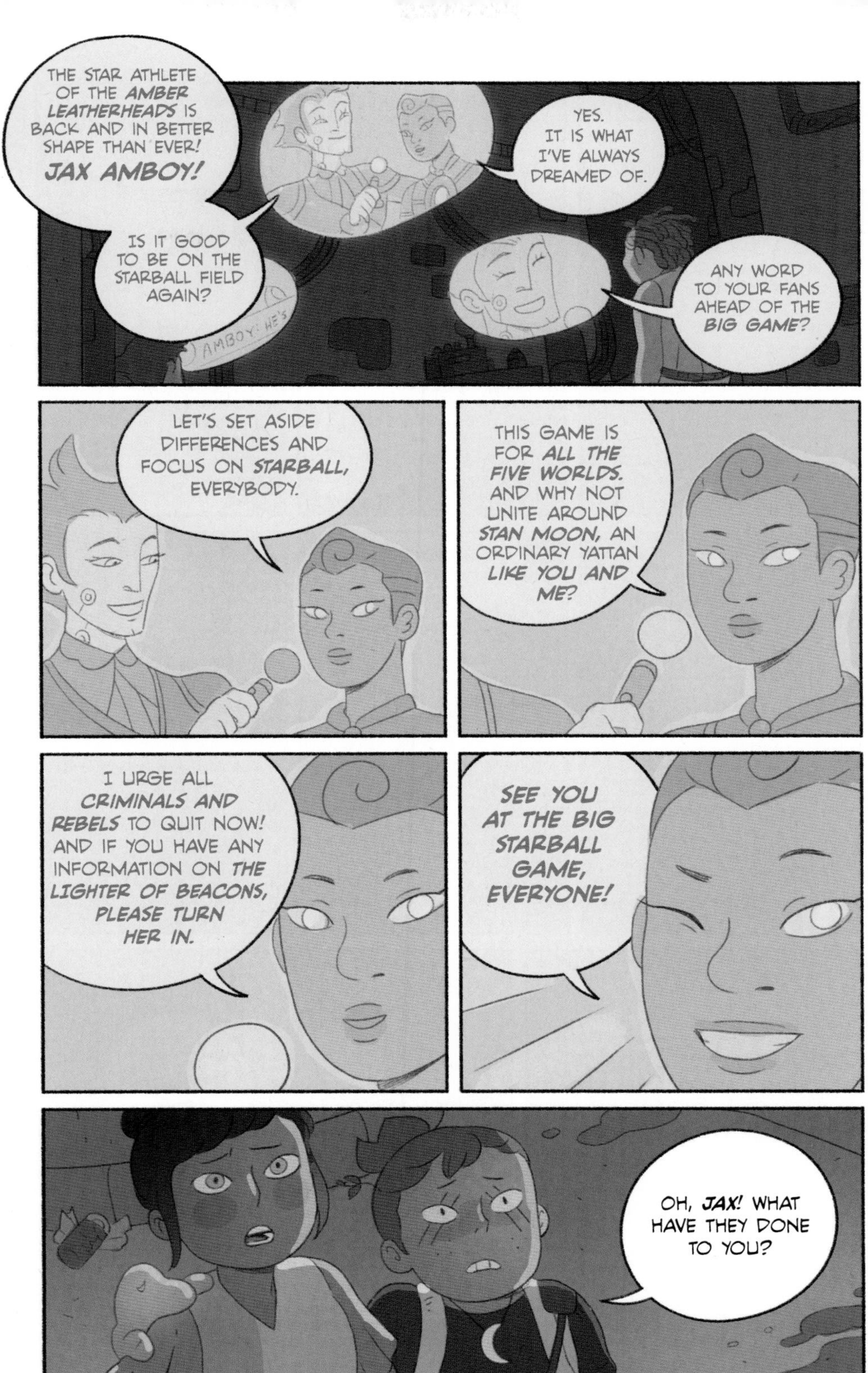
THE STAR ATHLETE OF THE AMBER LEATHERHEADS IS BACK AND IN BETTER SHAPE THAN EVER! JAX AMBOY!
YES. IT IS WHAT I'VE ALWAYS DREAMED OF.
IS IT GOOD TO BE ON THE STARBALL FIELD AGAIN?
AMBOY! HE'S
ANY WORD TO YOUR FANS AHEAD OF THE BIG GAME?
LET'S SET ASIDE DIFFERENCES AND FOCUS ON STARBALL, EVERYBODY.
THIS GAME IS FOR ALL THE FIVE WORLDS. AND WHY NOT UNITE AROUND STAN MOON, AN ORDINARY YATTAN LIKE YOU AND ME?
I URGE ALL CRIMINALS AND REBELS TO QUIT NOW! AND IF YOU HAVE ANY INFORMATION ON THE LIGHTER OF BEACONS, PLEASE TURN HER IN.
SEE YOU AT THE BIG STARBALL GAME, EVERYONE!
OH, JAX! WHAT HAVE THEY DONE TO YOU?

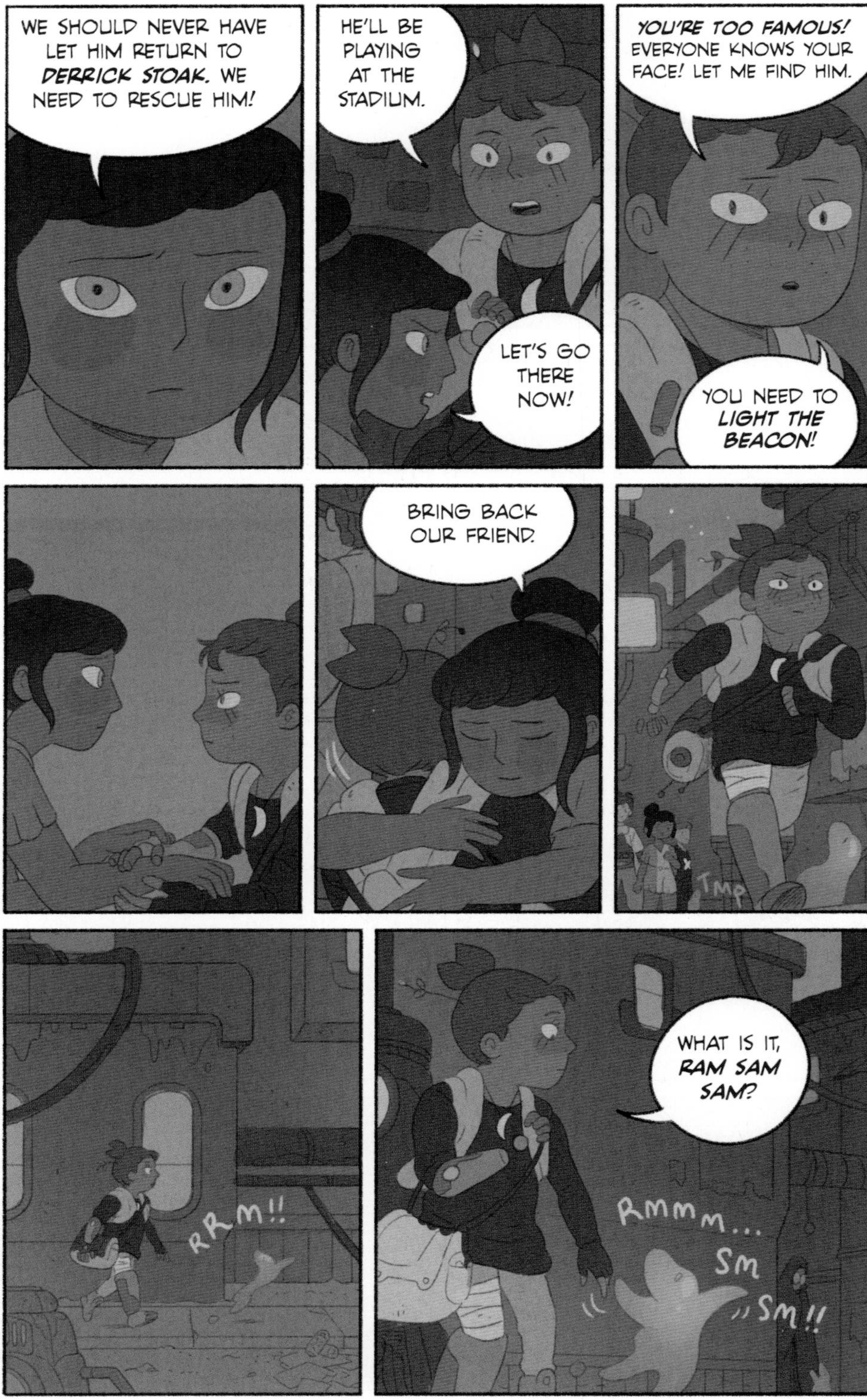
WE SHOULD NEVER HAVE LET HIM RETURN TO DERRICK STOAK. WE NEED TO RESCUE HIM!
HE'LL BE PLAYING AT THE STADIUM.
LET'S GO THERE NOW!
YOU'RE TOO FAMOUS! EVERYONE KNOWS YOUR FACE! LET ME FIND HIM.
YOU NEED TO LIGHT THE BEACON!
BRING BACK OUR FRIEND.
TMP
RRM!!
WHAT IS IT, RAM SAM SAM?
Rmmm... Sm Sm!!

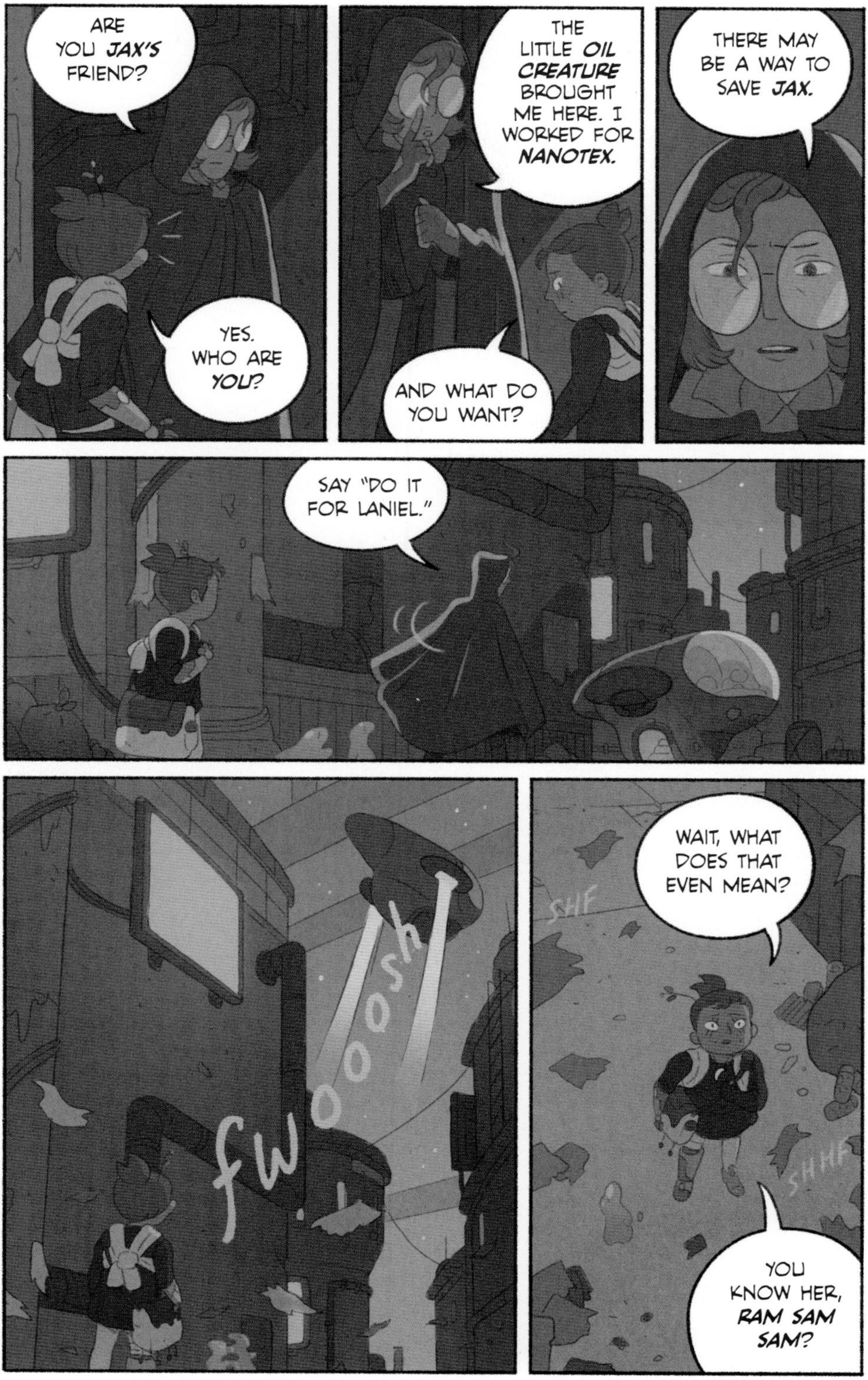
ARE YOU JAX'S FRIEND?
YES. WHO ARE YOU?
THE LITTLE OIL CREATURE BROUGHT ME HERE. I WORKED FOR NANOTEX.
AND WHAT DO YOU WANT?
THERE MAY BE A WAY TO SAVE JAX.
SAY "DO IT FOR LANIEL."
fwooosh
SHF
WAIT, WHAT DOES THAT EVEN MEAN?
SHHF
YOU KNOW HER, RAM SAM SAM?

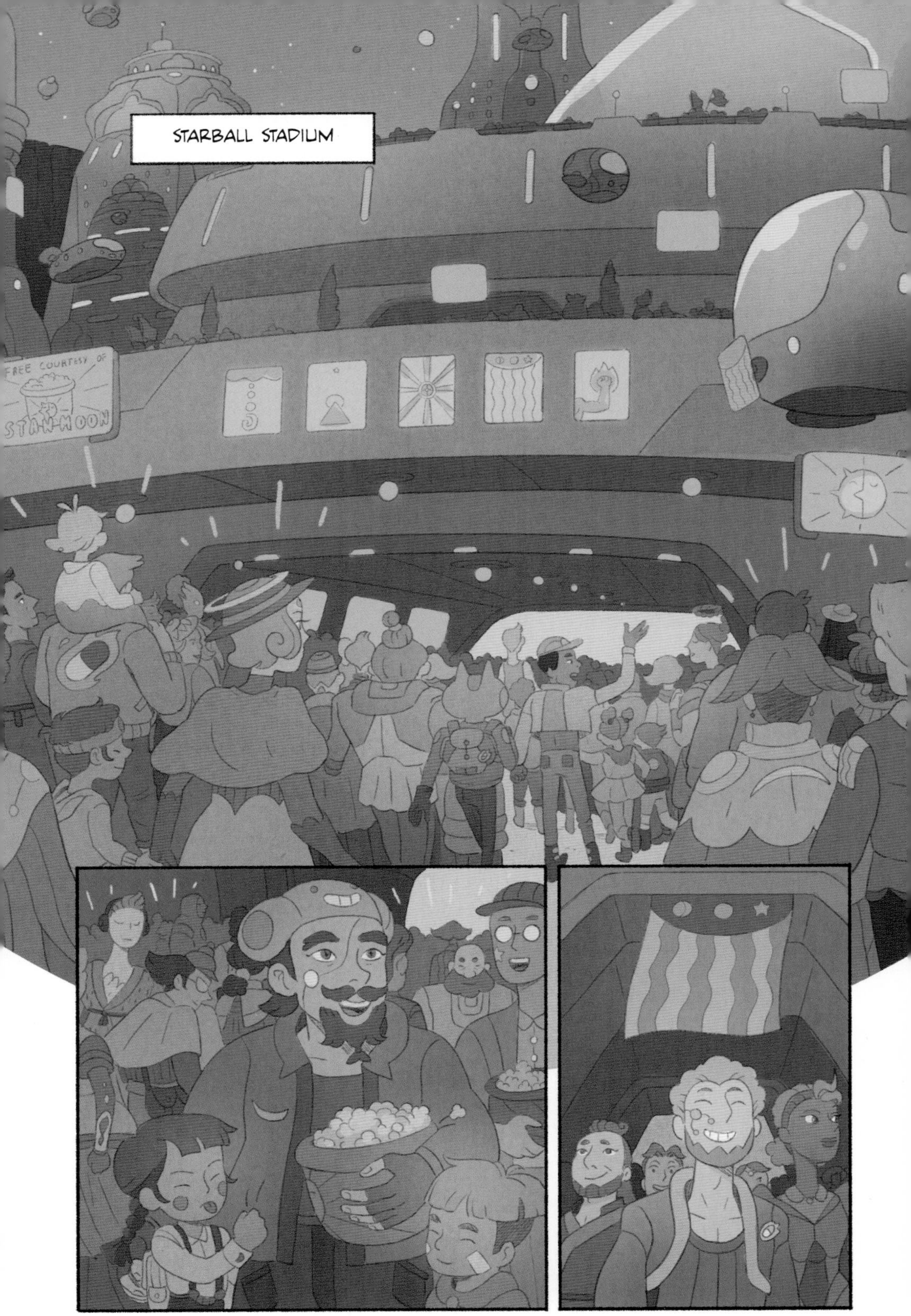
STARBALL STADIUM
FREE COURTESY OF
STAN-MOON

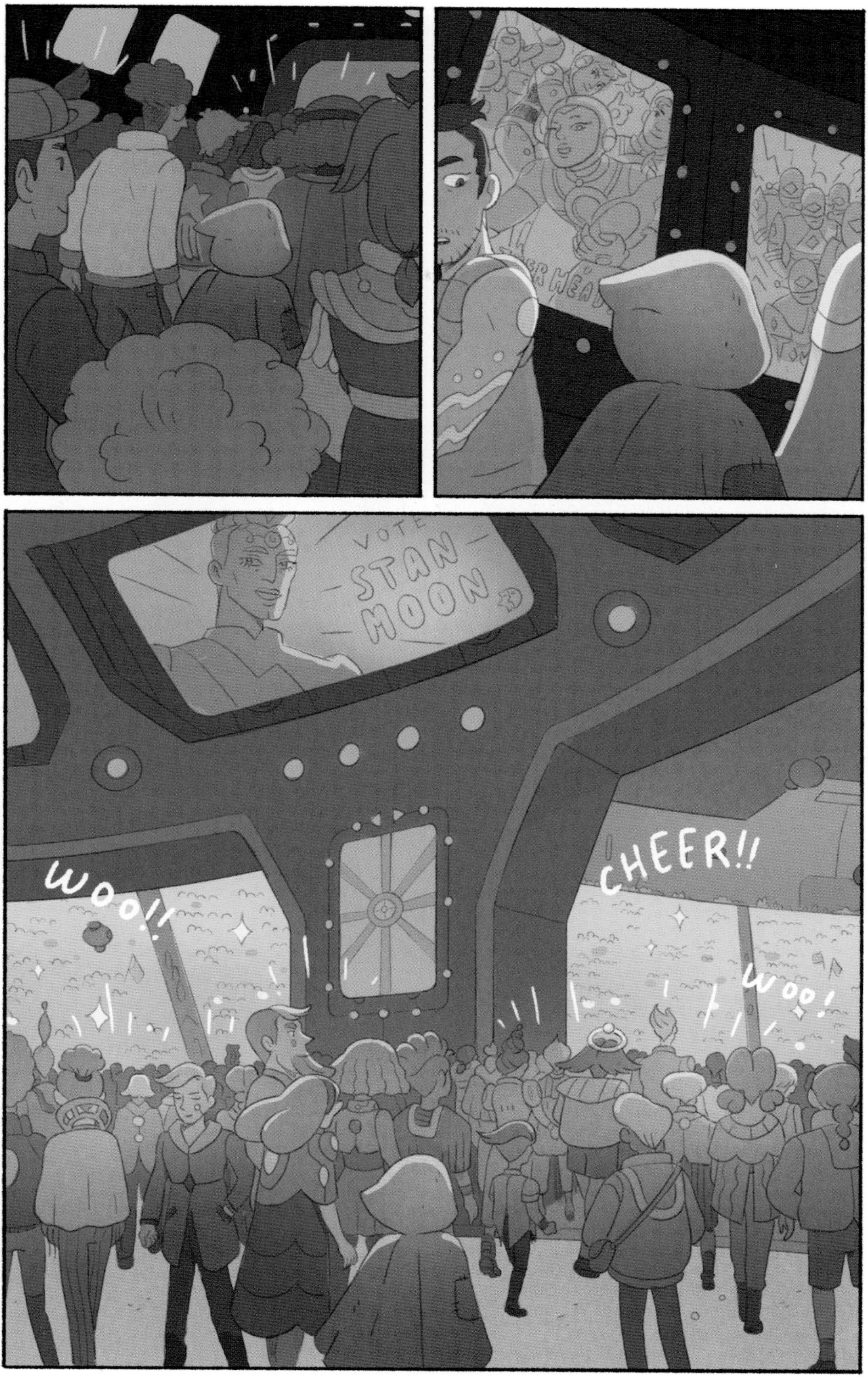
VOTE
STAN
MOON
WOO!!
CHEER!!
WOO!

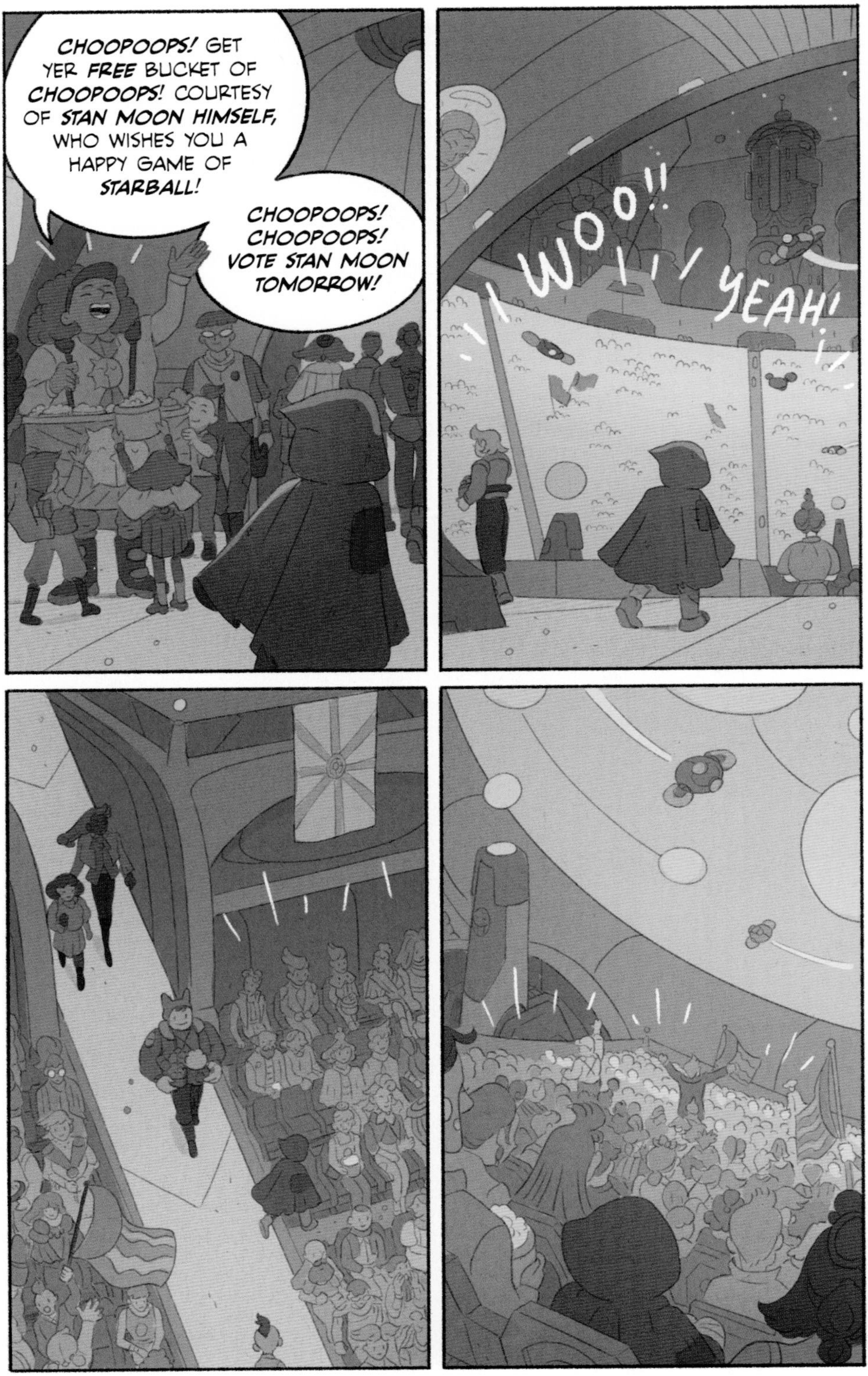
CHOOPOOPS! GET YER FREE BUCKET OF CHOOPOOPS! COURTESY OF STAN MOON HIMSELF, WHO WISHES YOU A HAPPY GAME OF STARBALL!
CHOOPOOPS! CHOOPOOPS! VOTE STAN MOON TOMORROW!
WOO!!
YEAH!

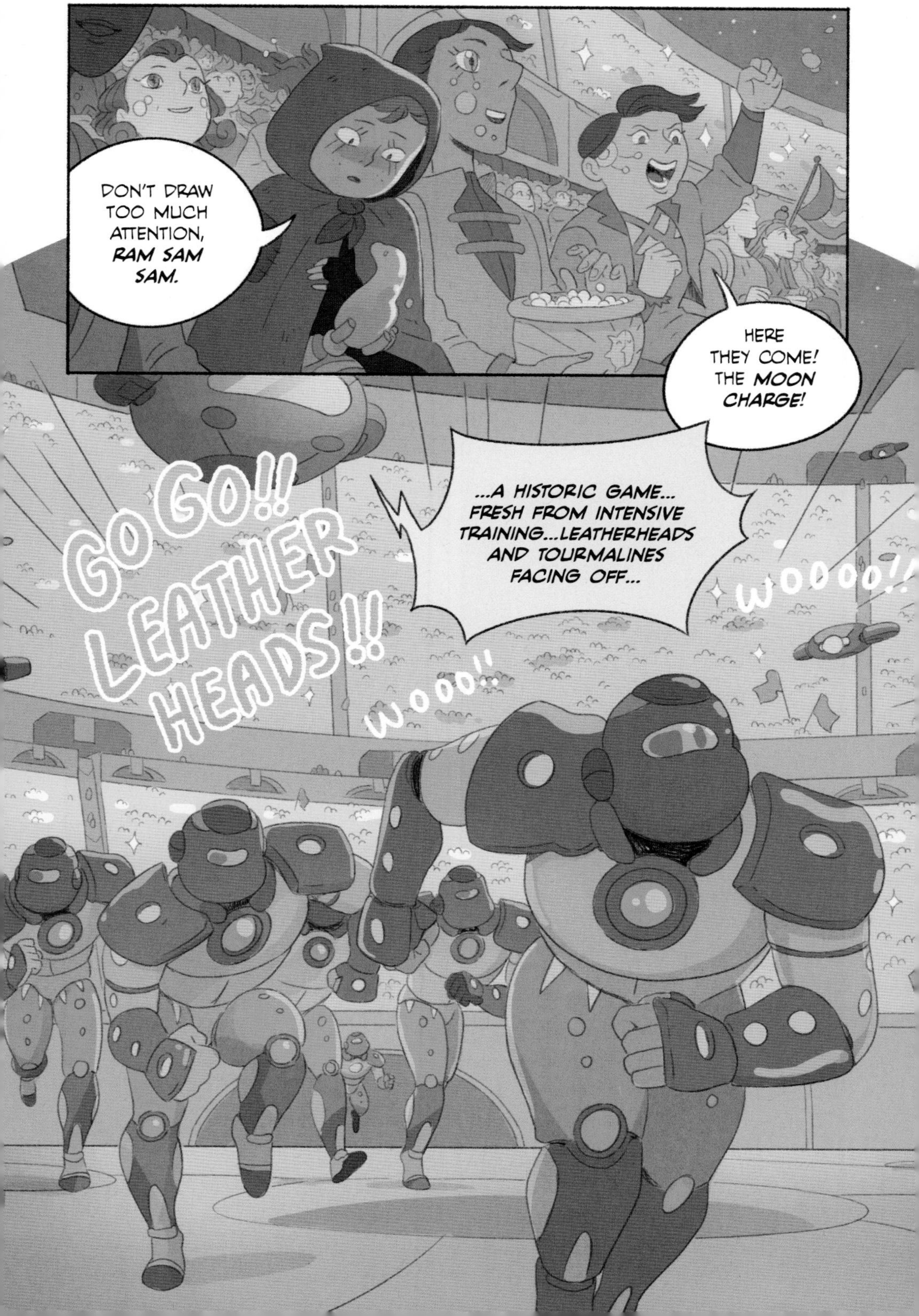

DON'T DRAW TOO MUCH ATTENTION, RAM SAM SAM.
HERE THEY COME! THE MOON CHARGE!
...A HISTORIC GAME... FRESH FROM INTENSIVE TRAINING...LEATHERHEADS AND TOURMALINES FACING OFF...
GO GO!! LEATHER HEADS!!
WOOOO!!
WOOO!!

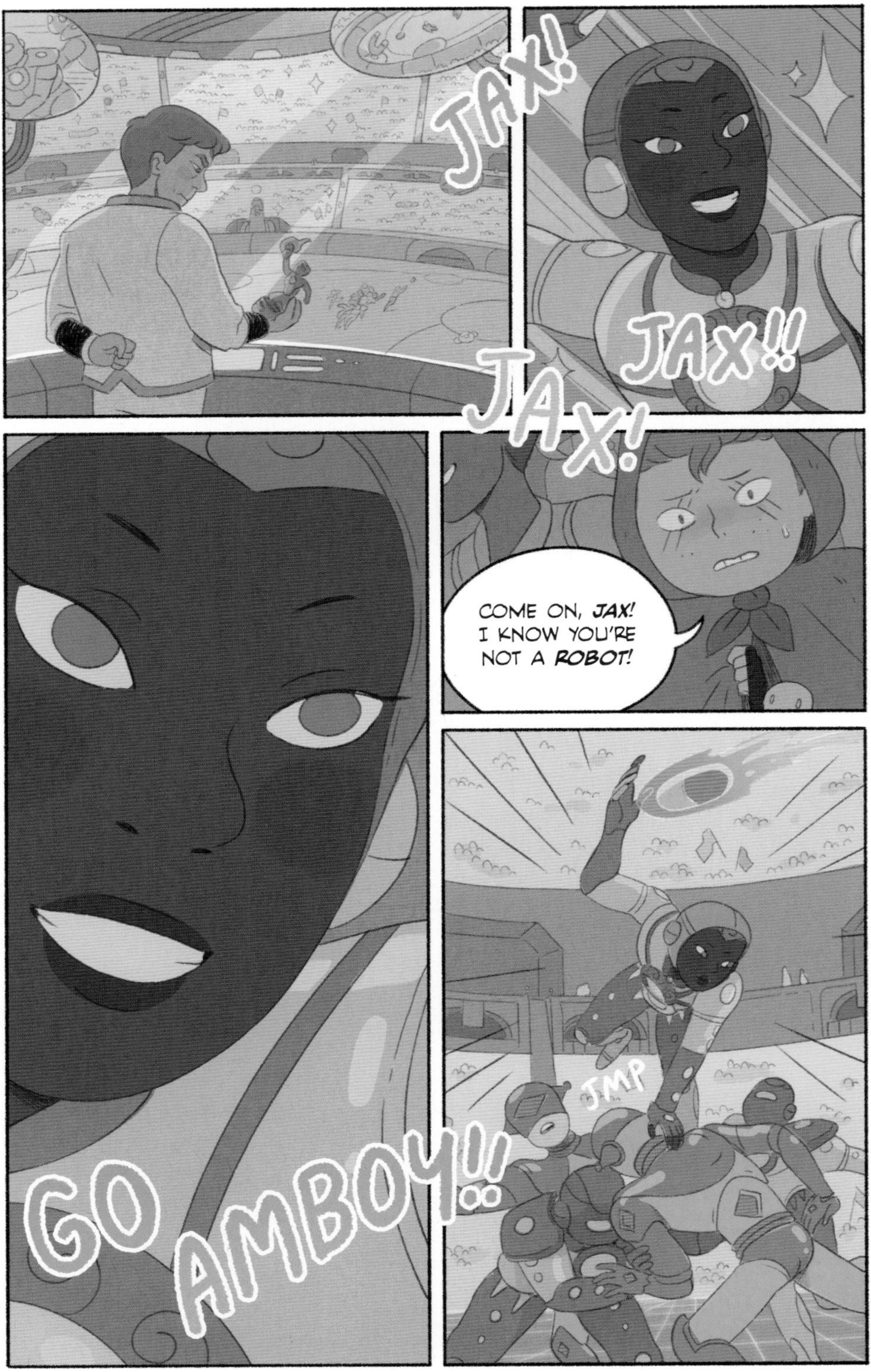
JAX!
JAX!!
JAX!
COME ON, JAX! I KNOW YOU'RE NOT A ROBOT!
GO AMBOY!!
JMP

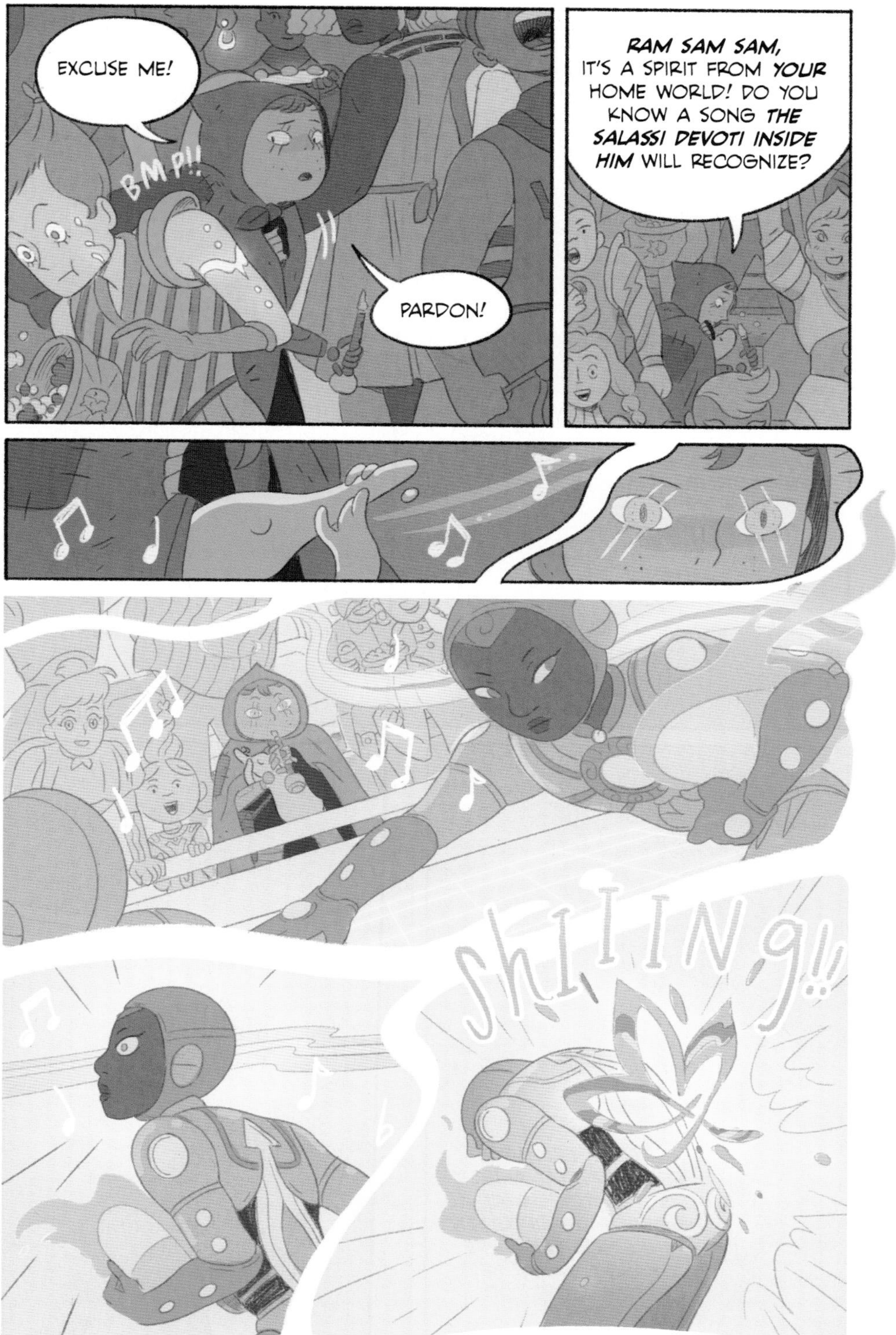
EXCUSE ME!
BMP!!
PARDON!
RAM SAM SAM, IT'S A SPIRIT FROM YOUR HOME WORLD! DO YOU KNOW A SONG THE SALASSI DEVOTI INSIDE HIM WILL RECOGNIZE?
SHIIING!!

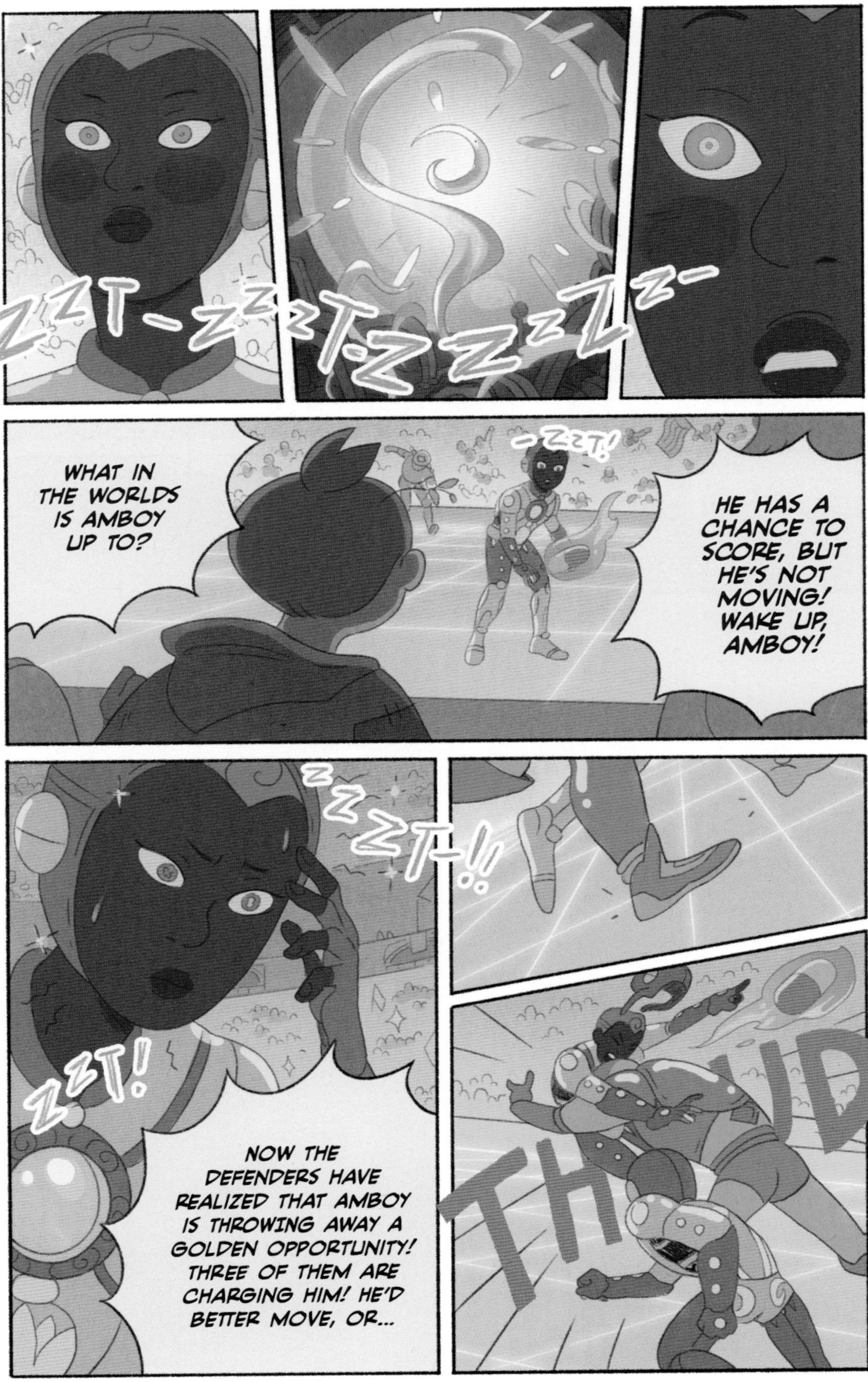
ZZT-ZZZT-ZZZZZZ-
WHAT IN THE WORLDS IS AMBOY UP TO?
-ZZT!
HE HAS A CHANCE TO SCORE, BUT HE'S NOT MOVING! WAKE UP, AMBOY!
ZZZT-!!
ZZT!
NOW THE DEFENDERS HAVE REALIZED THAT AMBOY IS THROWING AWAY A GOLDEN OPPORTUNITY! THREE OF THEM ARE CHARGING HIM! HE'D BETTER MOVE, OR...
THUD

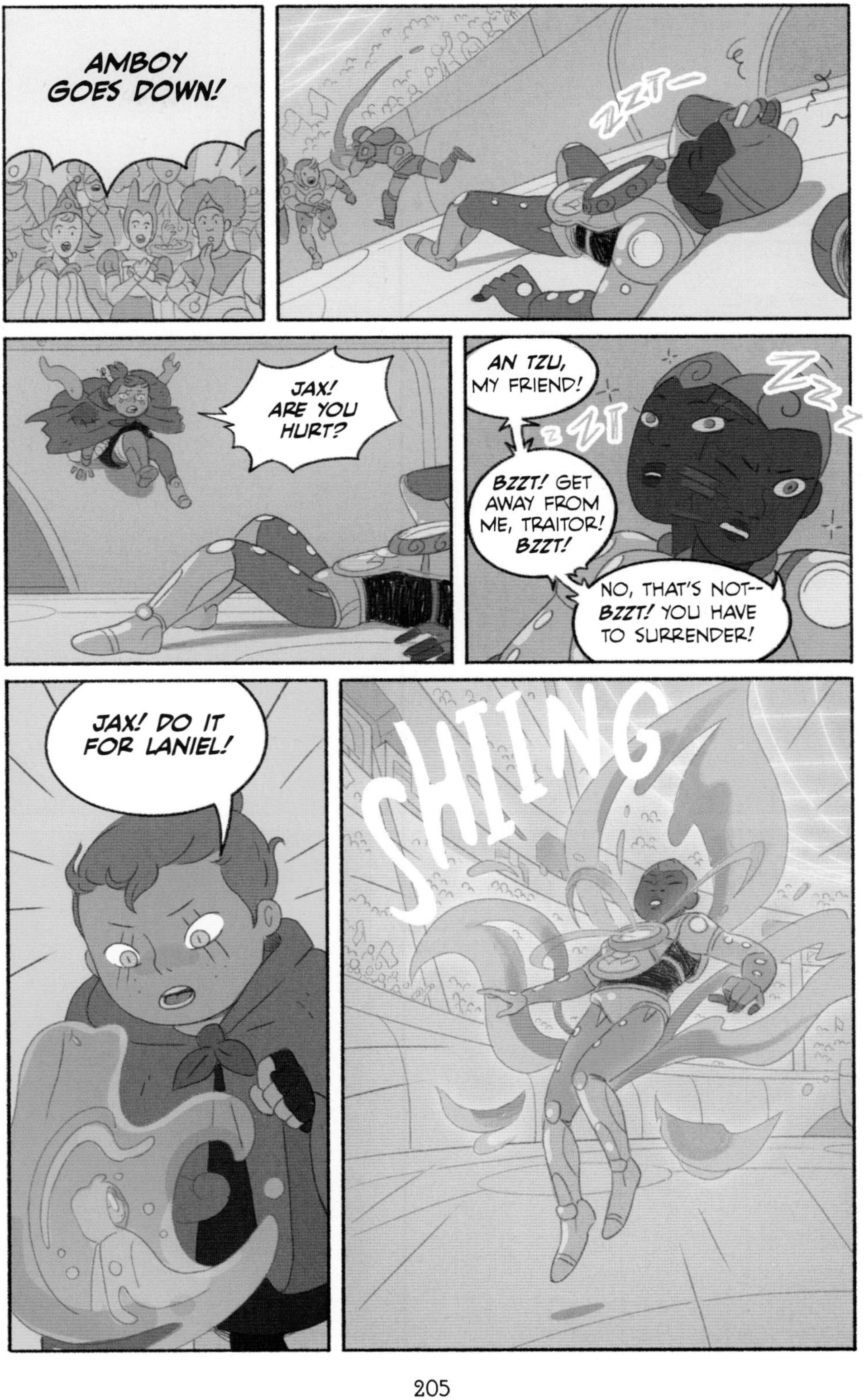

AMBOY GOES DOWN!
ZZZT—
JAX! ARE YOU HURT?
AN TZU, MY FRIEND!
ZZZT
ZZZ
BZZT! GET AWAY FROM ME, TRAITOR! BZZT!
NO, THAT'S NOT-- BZZT! YOU HAVE TO SURRENDER!
JAX! DO IT FOR LANIEL!
SHIING

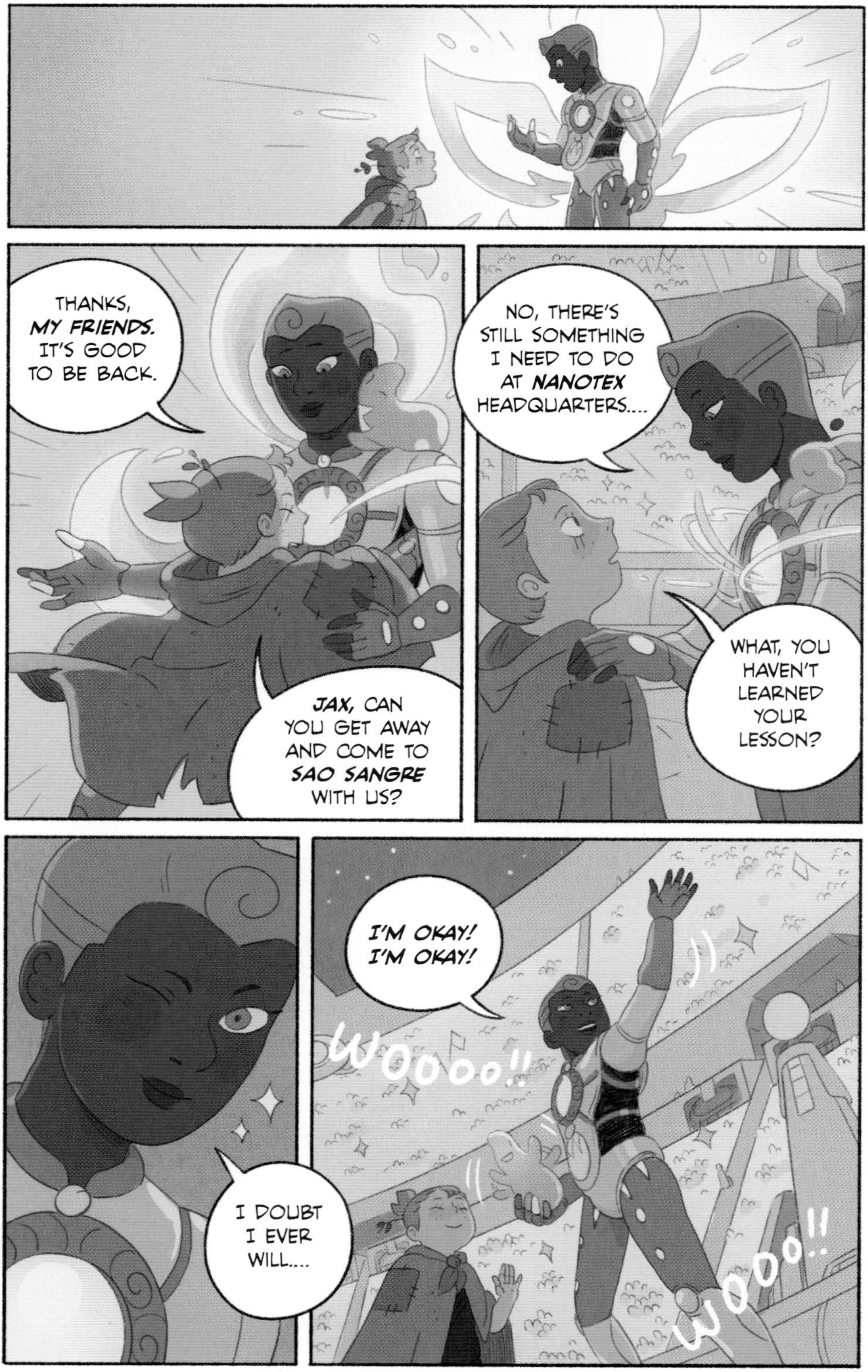
THANKS, MY FRIENDS. IT'S GOOD TO BE BACK.
JAX, CAN YOU GET AWAY AND COME TO SAO SANGRE WITH US?
NO, THERE'S STILL SOMETHING I NEED TO DO AT NANOTEX HEADQUARTERS....
WHAT, YOU HAVEN'T LEARNED YOUR LESSON?
I DOUBT I EVER WILL....
I'M OKAY! I'M OKAY!
WOOOO!!
WOOO!!

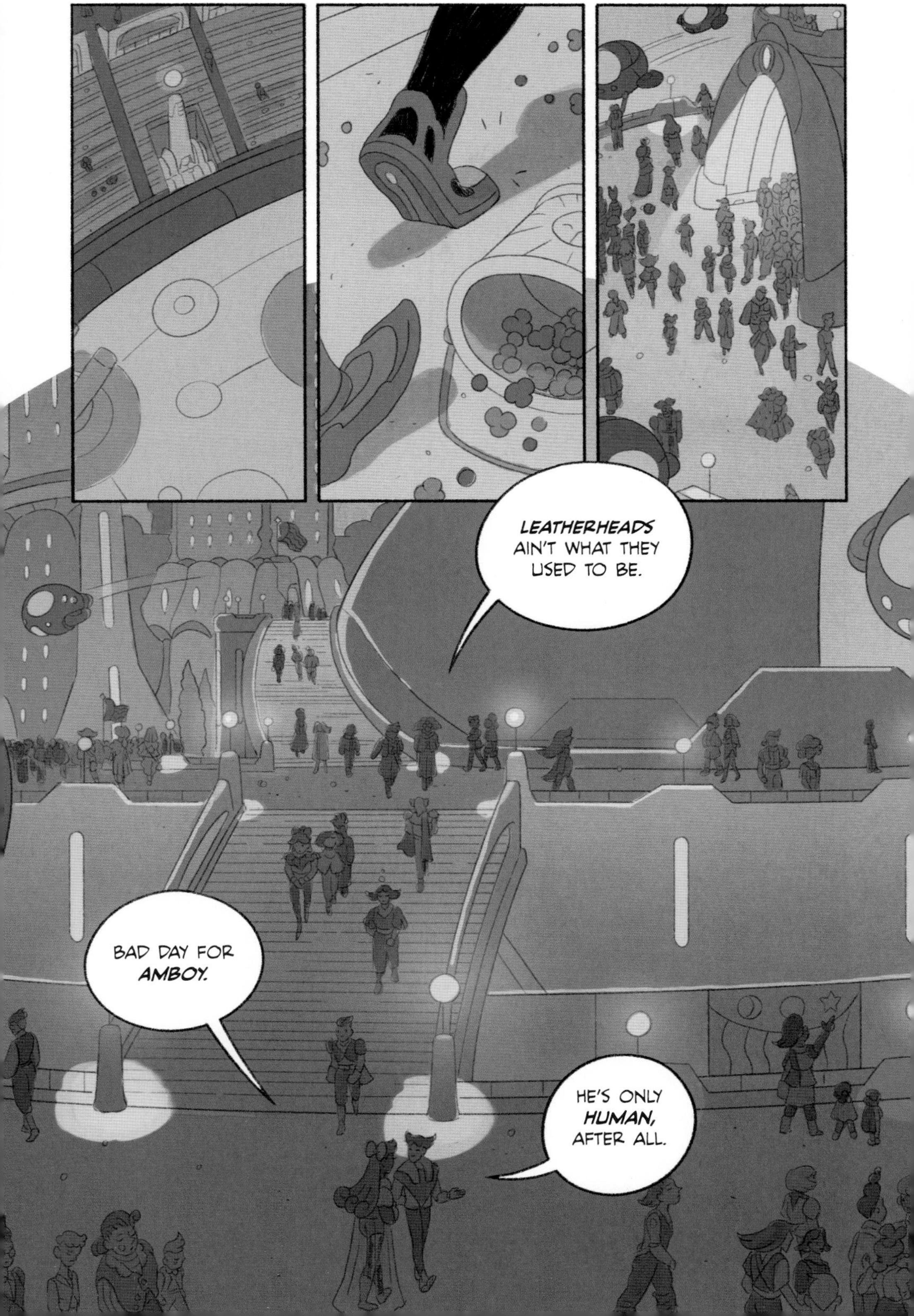
LEATHERHEADS AIN'T WHAT THEY USED TO BE.
BAD DAY FOR AMBOY.
HE'S ONLY HUMAN, AFTER ALL.

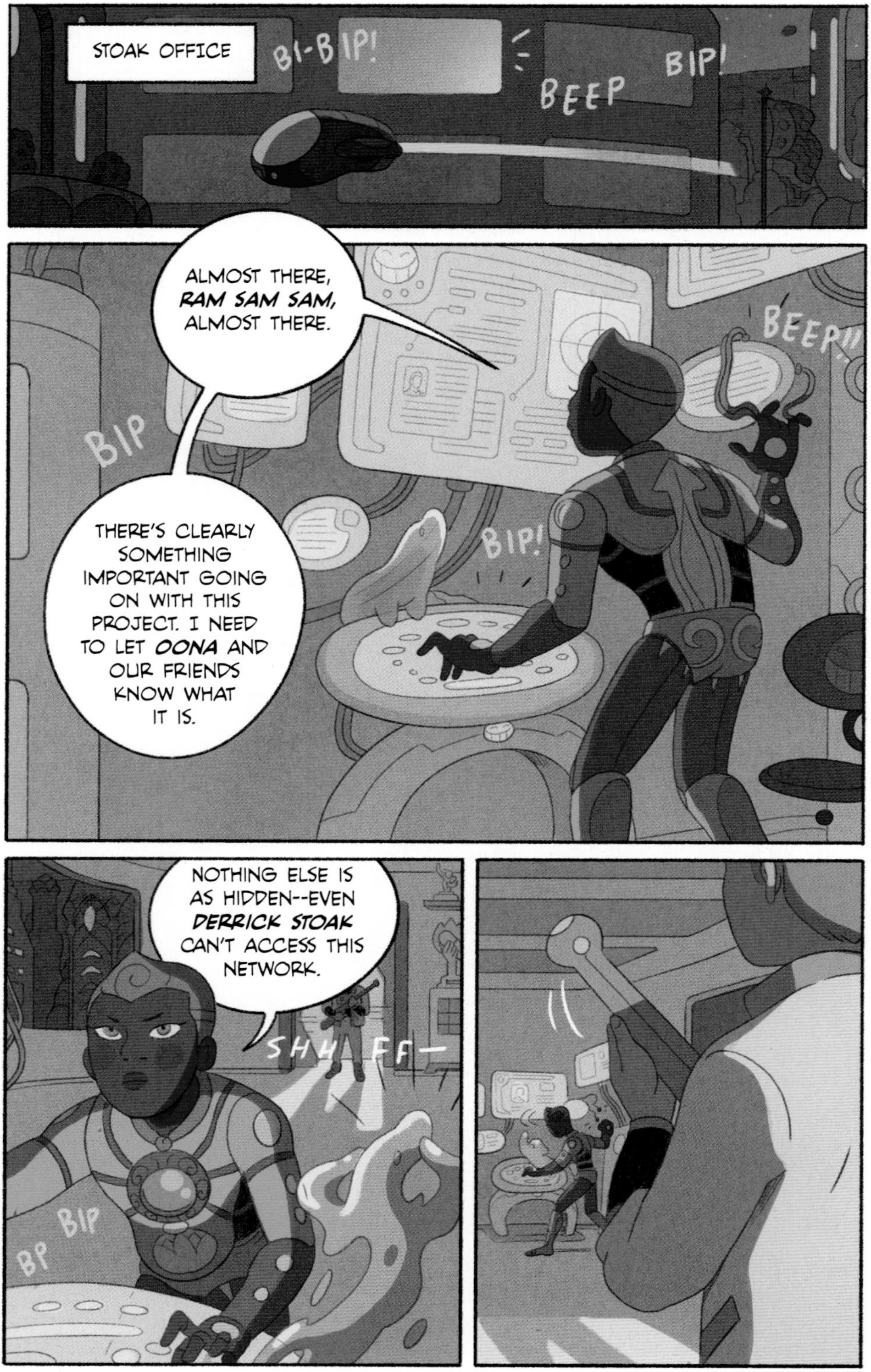
STOAK OFFICE
BI-BIP!
BEEP
BIP!
ALMOST THERE, *RAM SAM SAM*, ALMOST THERE.
BEEP!!
BIP
THERE'S CLEARLY SOMETHING IMPORTANT GOING ON WITH THIS PROJECT. I NEED TO LET *OONA* AND OUR FRIENDS KNOW WHAT IT IS.
BIP!
NOTHING ELSE IS AS HIDDEN--EVEN *DERRICK STOAK* CAN'T ACCESS THIS NETWORK.
SHHFF—
BP BIP

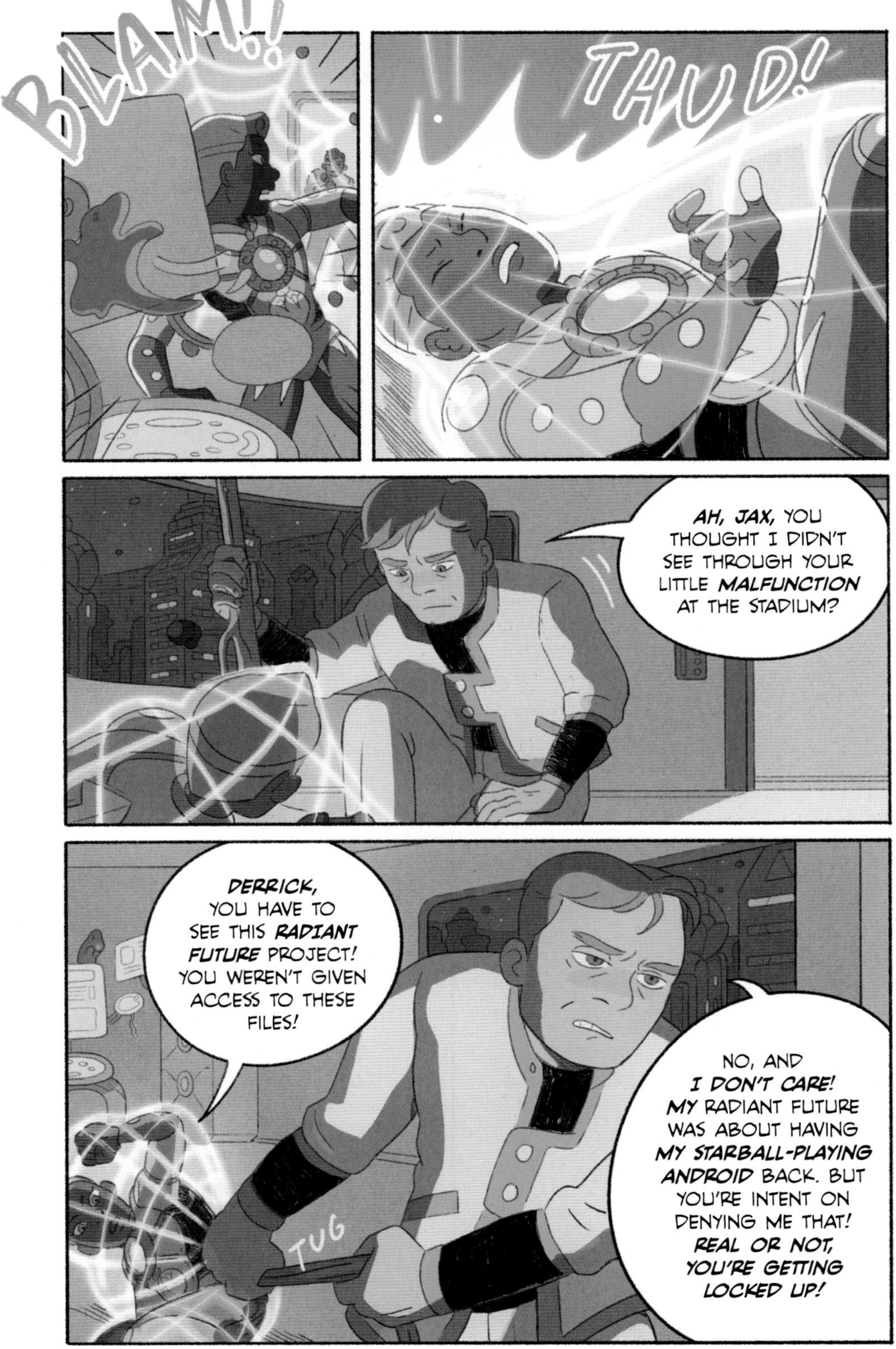
BLAM!!
THUD!
AH, JAX, YOU THOUGHT I DIDN'T SEE THROUGH YOUR LITTLE MALFUNCTION AT THE STADIUM?
DERRICK, YOU HAVE TO SEE THIS RADIANT FUTURE PROJECT! YOU WEREN'T GIVEN ACCESS TO THESE FILES!
NO, AND I DON'T CARE! MY RADIANT FUTURE WAS ABOUT HAVING MY STARBALL-PLAYING ANDROID BACK. BUT YOU'RE INTENT ON DENYING ME THAT! REAL OR NOT, YOU'RE GETTING LOCKED UP!
TUG

## Chapter 11

# ELECTION DAY

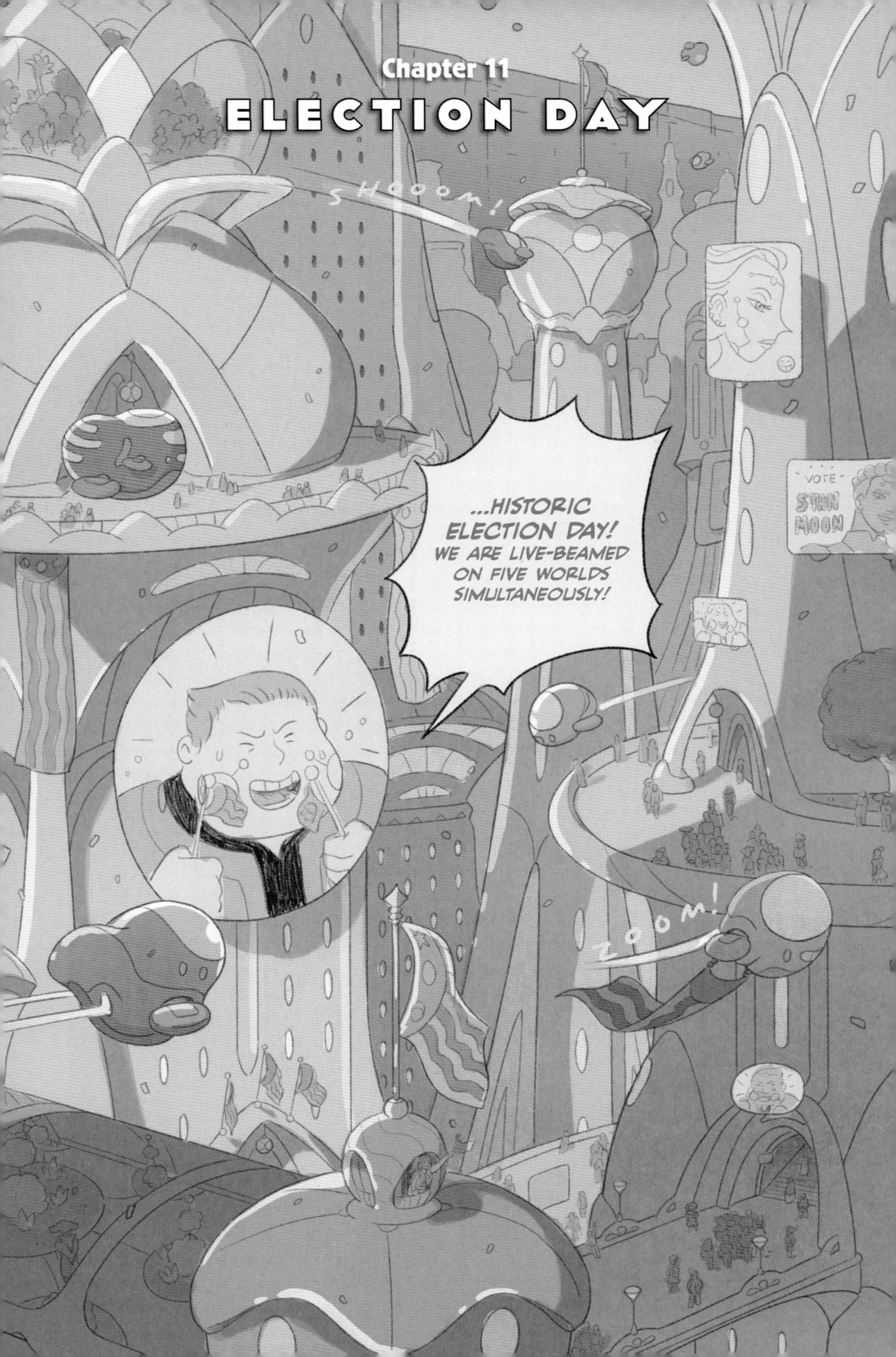
SHOOOM!
...HISTORIC ELECTION DAY! WE ARE LIVE-BEAMED ON FIVE WORLDS SIMULTANEOUSLY!
VOTE STAN MOON
ZOOM!

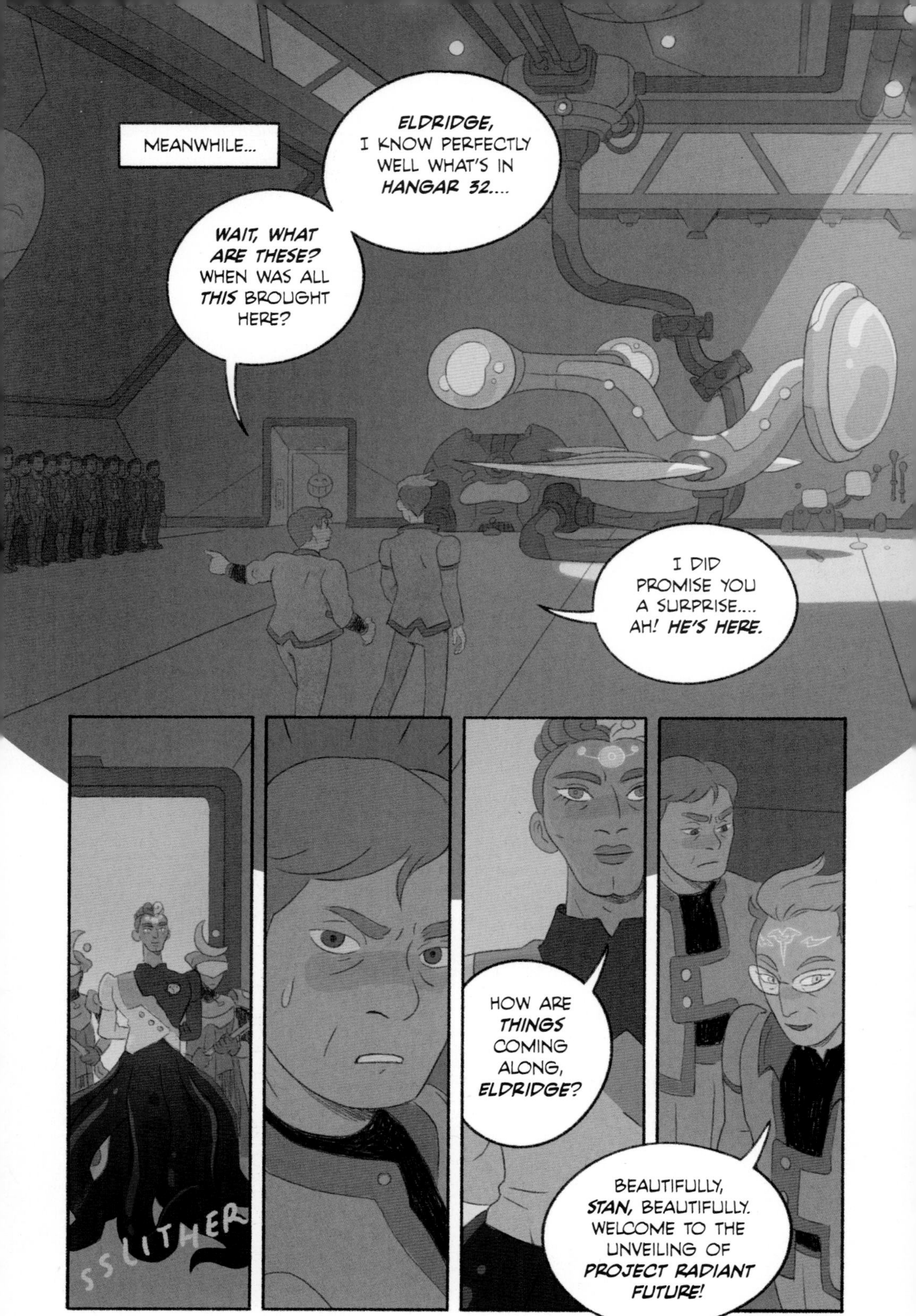
MEANWHILE...
WAIT, WHAT ARE THESE? WHEN WAS ALL THIS BROUGHT HERE?
ELDRIDGE, I KNOW PERFECTLY WELL WHAT'S IN HANGAR 32....
I DID PROMISE YOU A SURPRISE.... AH! HE'S HERE.
SSLITHER
HOW ARE THINGS COMING ALONG, ELDRIDGE?
BEAUTIFULLY, STAN, BEAUTIFULLY. WELCOME TO THE UNVEILING OF PROJECT RADIANT FUTURE!

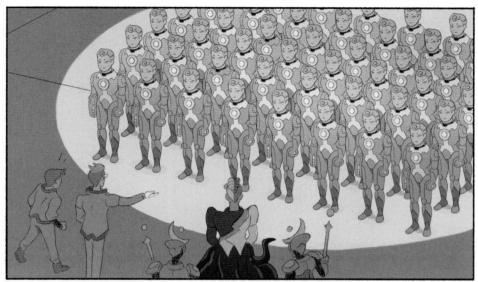

WELL DONE, *ELDRIDGE,* WELL DONE!

THEY'RE FULLY TESTED AND FUNCTIONAL. *LOOK!*

URBAN WARFARE. VERY NICE.

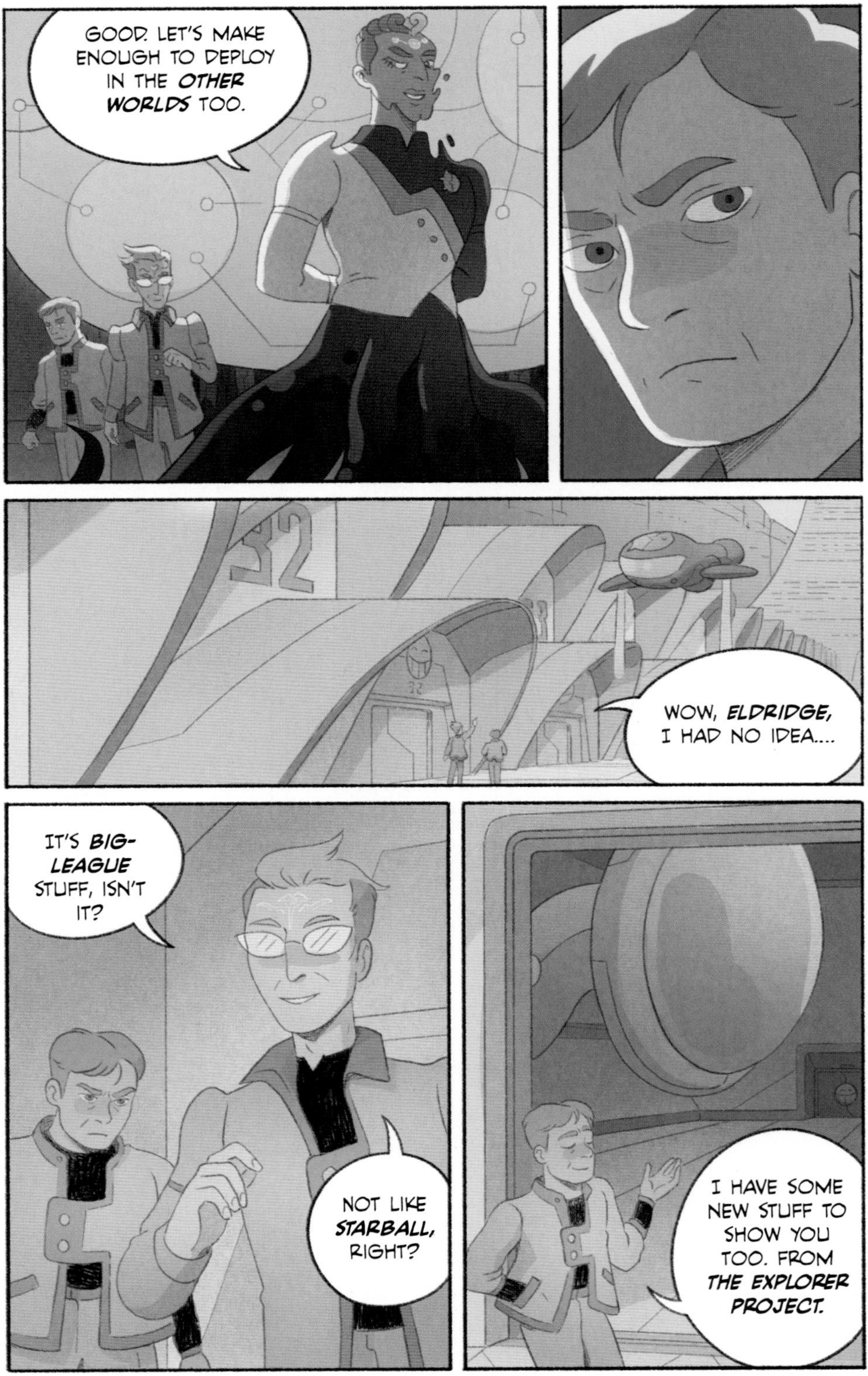
GOOD. LET'S MAKE ENOUGH TO DEPLOY IN THE OTHER WORLDS TOO.
WOW, ELDRIDGE, I HAD NO IDEA....
IT'S BIG-LEAGUE STUFF, ISN'T IT?
NOT LIKE STARBALL, RIGHT?
I HAVE SOME NEW STUFF TO SHOW YOU TOO. FROM THE EXPLORER PROJECT.

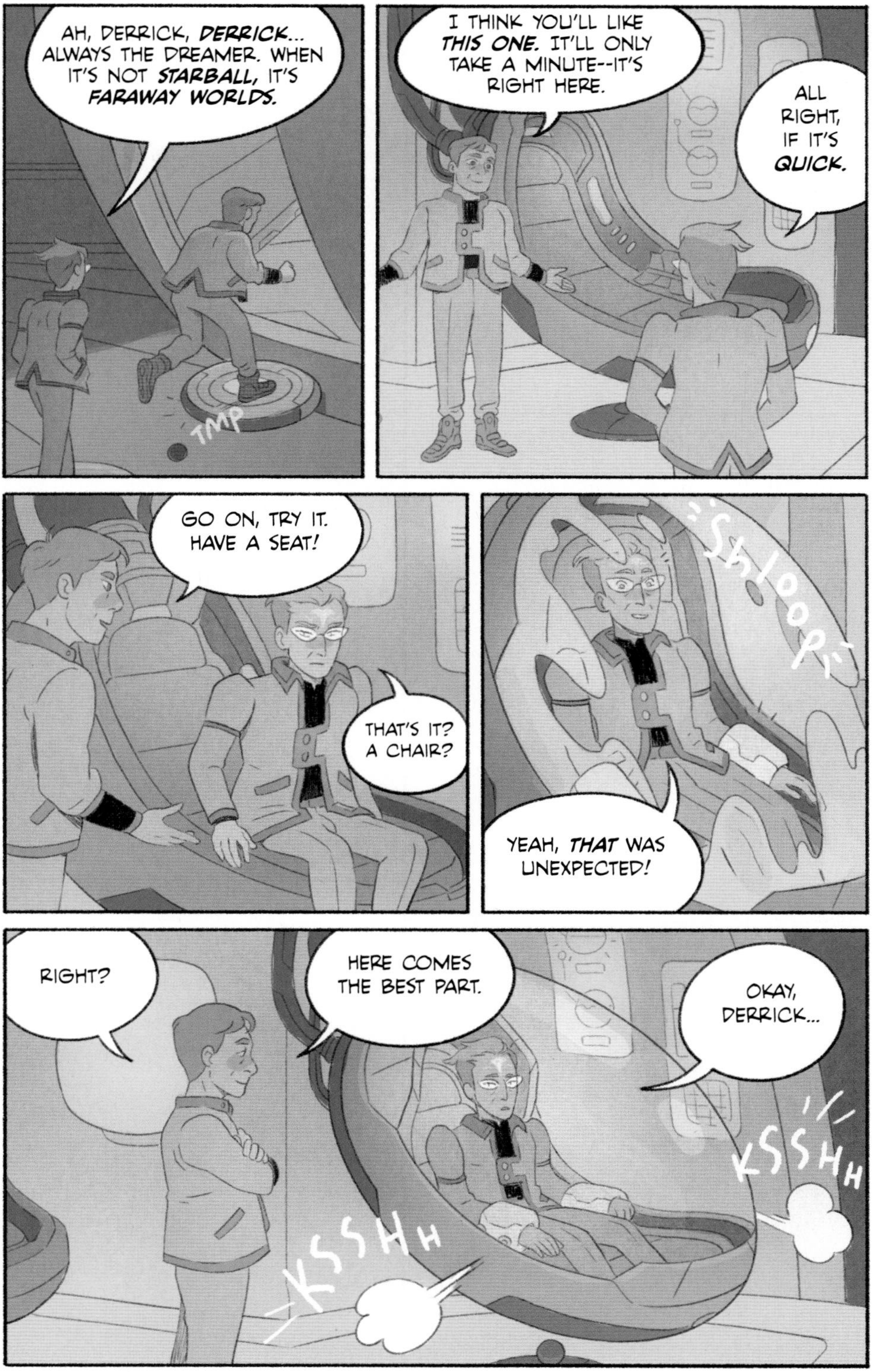
AH, DERRICK, **DERRICK**... ALWAYS THE DREAMER. WHEN IT'S NOT **STARBALL,** IT'S **FARAWAY WORLDS.**
TMP
I THINK YOU'LL LIKE **THIS ONE.** IT'LL ONLY TAKE A MINUTE--IT'S RIGHT HERE.
ALL RIGHT, IF IT'S **QUICK.**
GO ON, TRY IT. HAVE A SEAT!
THAT'S IT? A CHAIR?
SHLOOP
YEAH, **THAT** WAS UNEXPECTED!
RIGHT?
HERE COMES THE BEST PART.
OKAY, DERRICK...
KSSHH
KSSHH

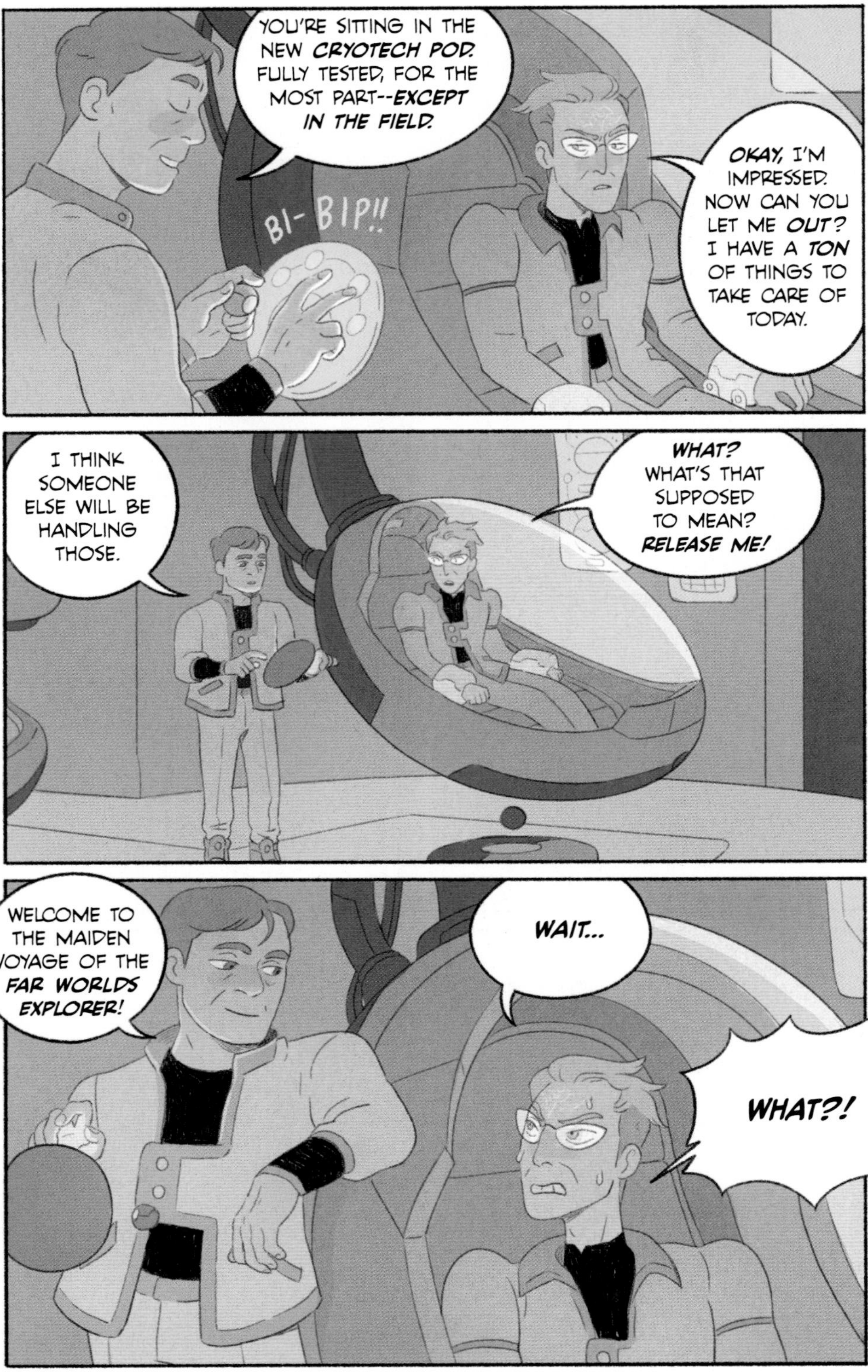
YOU'RE SITTING IN THE NEW **CRYOTECH POD.** FULLY TESTED, FOR THE MOST PART--**EXCEPT IN THE FIELD.**
BI- BIP!!
**OKAY,** I'M IMPRESSED. NOW CAN YOU LET ME **OUT?** I HAVE A **TON** OF THINGS TO TAKE CARE OF TODAY.
I THINK SOMEONE ELSE WILL BE HANDLING THOSE.
**WHAT?** WHAT'S THAT SUPPOSED TO MEAN? **RELEASE ME!**
WELCOME TO THE MAIDEN VOYAGE OF THE **FAR WORLDS EXPLORER!**
**WAIT...**
**WHAT?!**

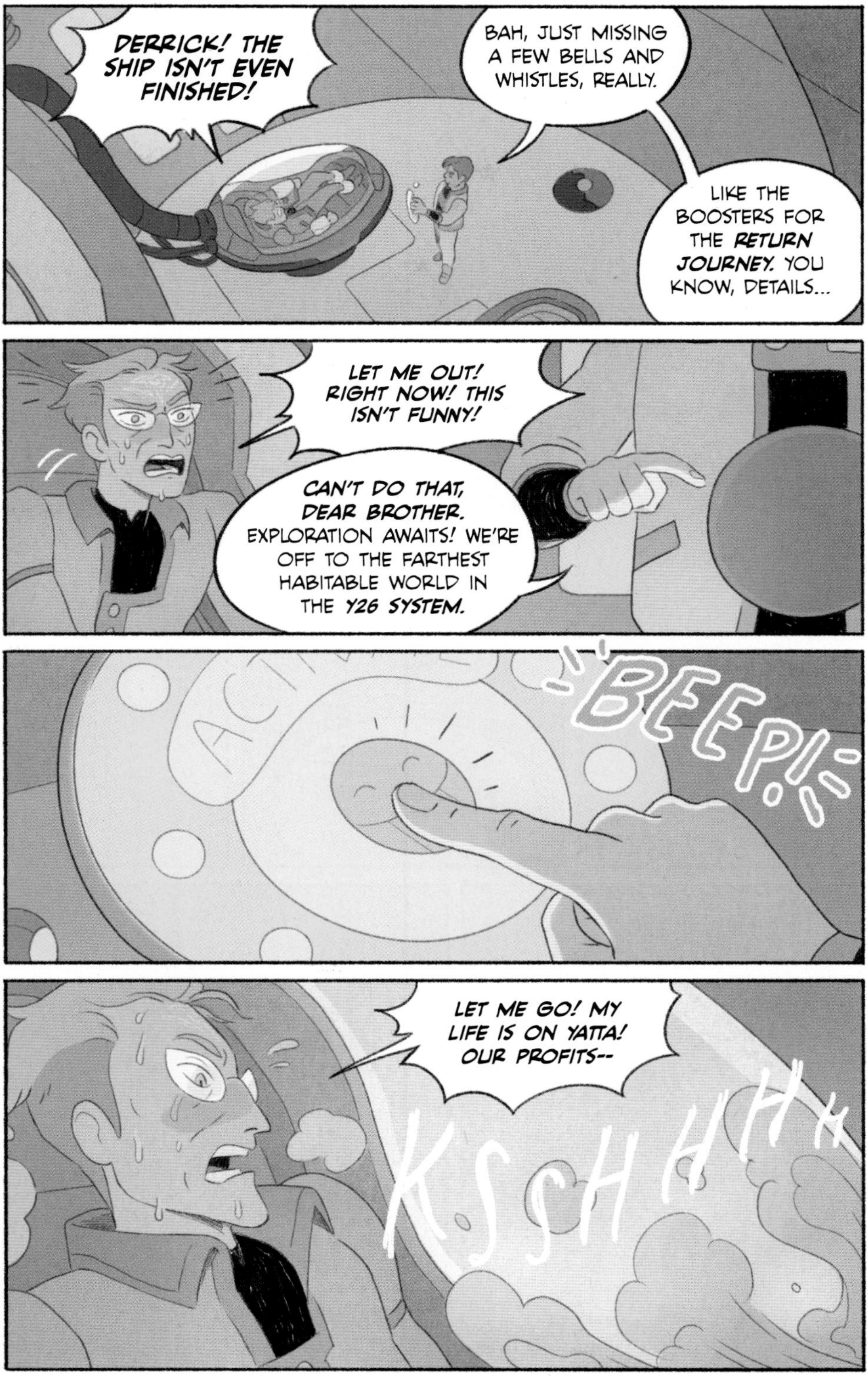
DERRICK! THE SHIP ISN'T EVEN FINISHED!
BAH, JUST MISSING A FEW BELLS AND WHISTLES, REALLY.
LIKE THE BOOSTERS FOR THE RETURN JOURNEY. YOU KNOW, DETAILS...
LET ME OUT! RIGHT NOW! THIS ISN'T FUNNY!
CAN'T DO THAT, DEAR BROTHER. EXPLORATION AWAITS! WE'RE OFF TO THE FARTHEST HABITABLE WORLD IN THE Y26 SYSTEM.
BEEP!
LET ME GO! MY LIFE IS ON YATTA! OUR PROFITS--
KSHHHHH

TSSSS Ss s.....

TAKE *JAX AMBOY* TO *SAO SANGRE*.... YES, I'M SURE.

DROP HIM OFF WHEREVER HE SAYS. AND TELL HIM...

TELL HIM I'M SORRY.

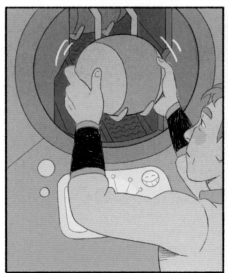

ZZzT!!

*TIK TIK TIK* COMMENCING COUNTDOWN TO DETONATION

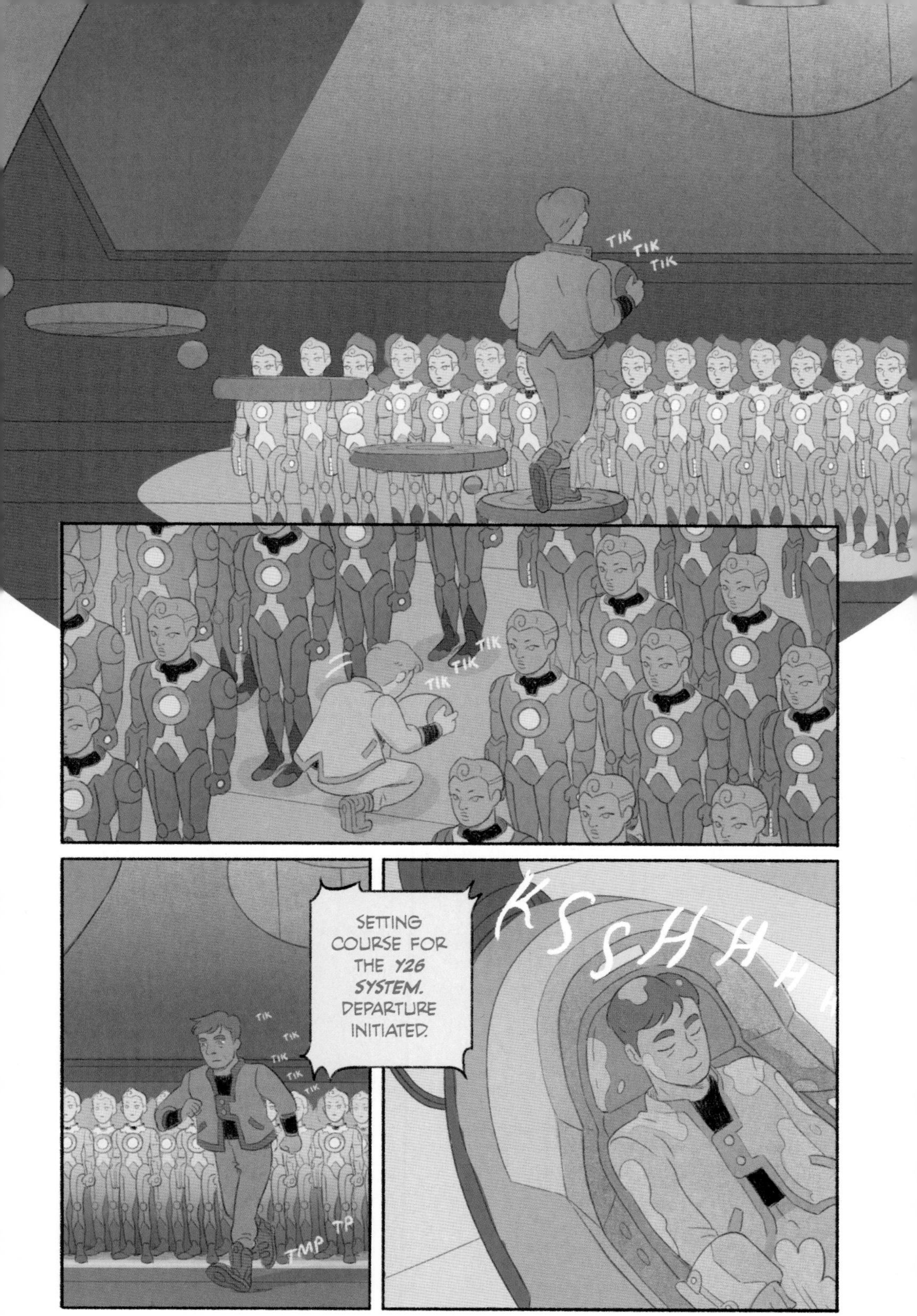
TIK
TIK
TIK
TIK
TIK
TIK
TIK
TIK
TIK
TIK
TIK
SETTING COURSE FOR THE *Y26 SYSTEM.* DEPARTURE INITIATED.
TMP TP
KSSHHHH

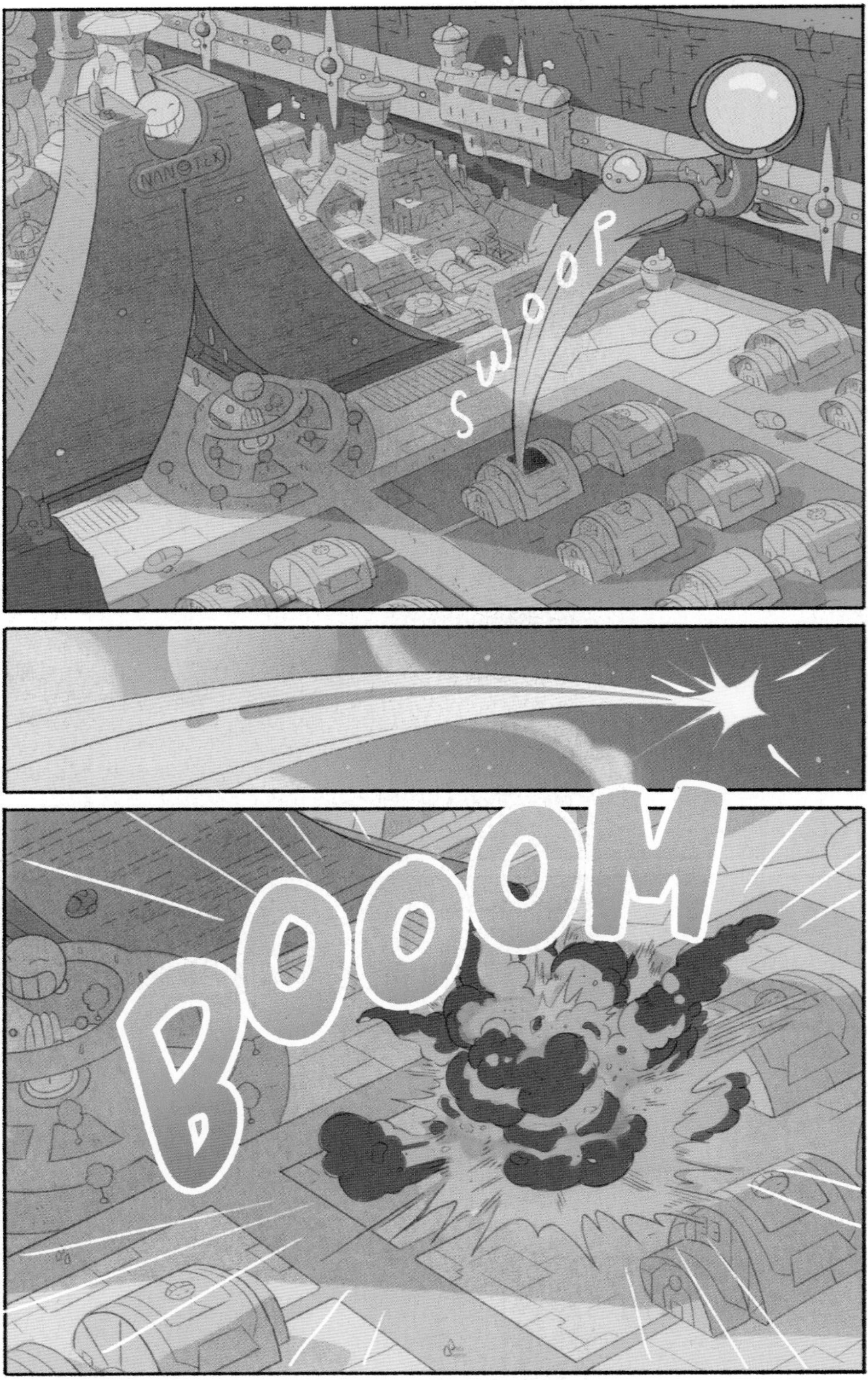
NANOTEX
SWOOP
BOOOM

# Chapter 12
# THE RED BEACON

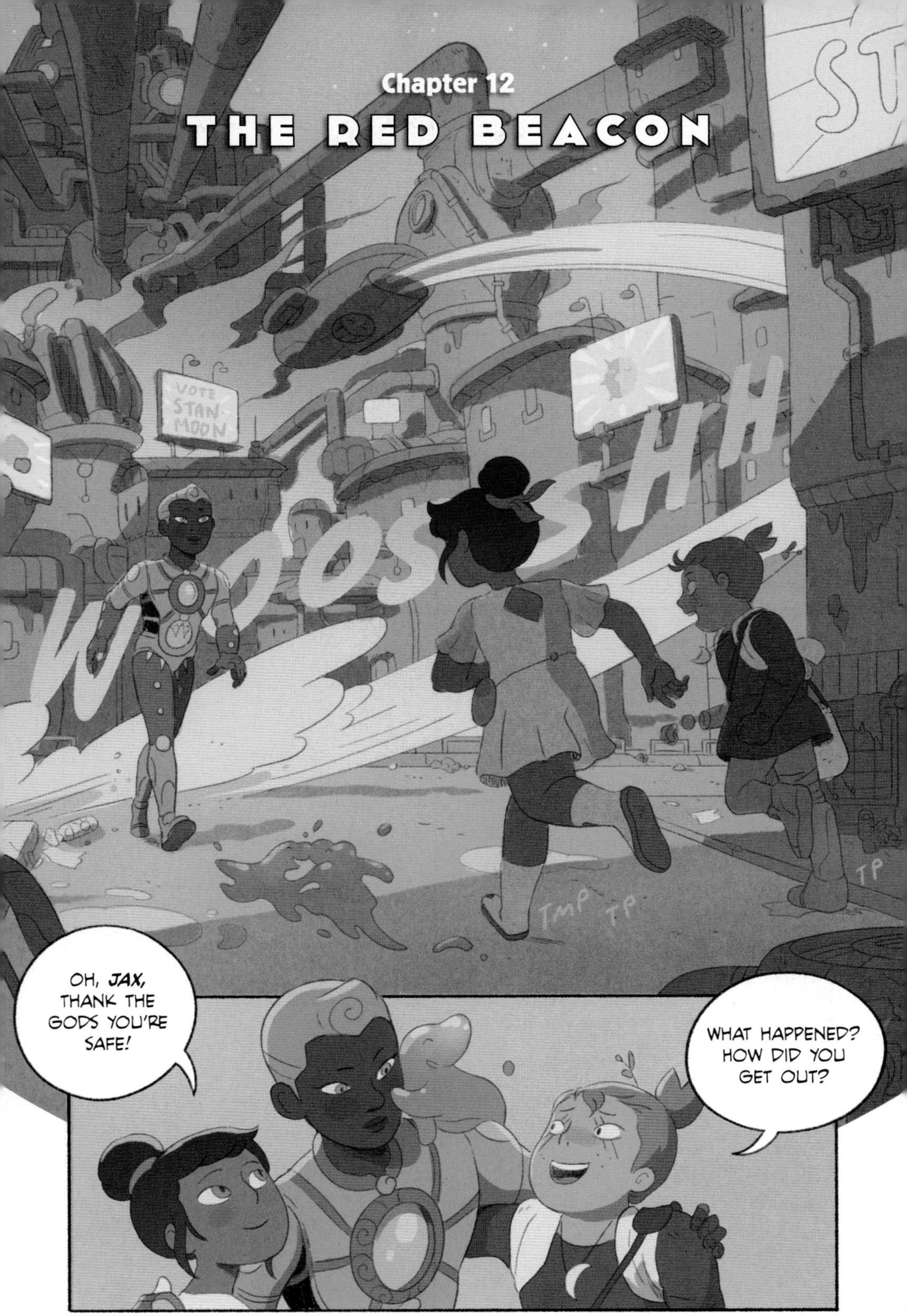
VOTE STAN MOON
WOOSHH
TMP TP
TP
OH, JAX, THANK THE GODS YOU'RE SAFE!
WHAT HAPPENED? HOW DID YOU GET OUT?

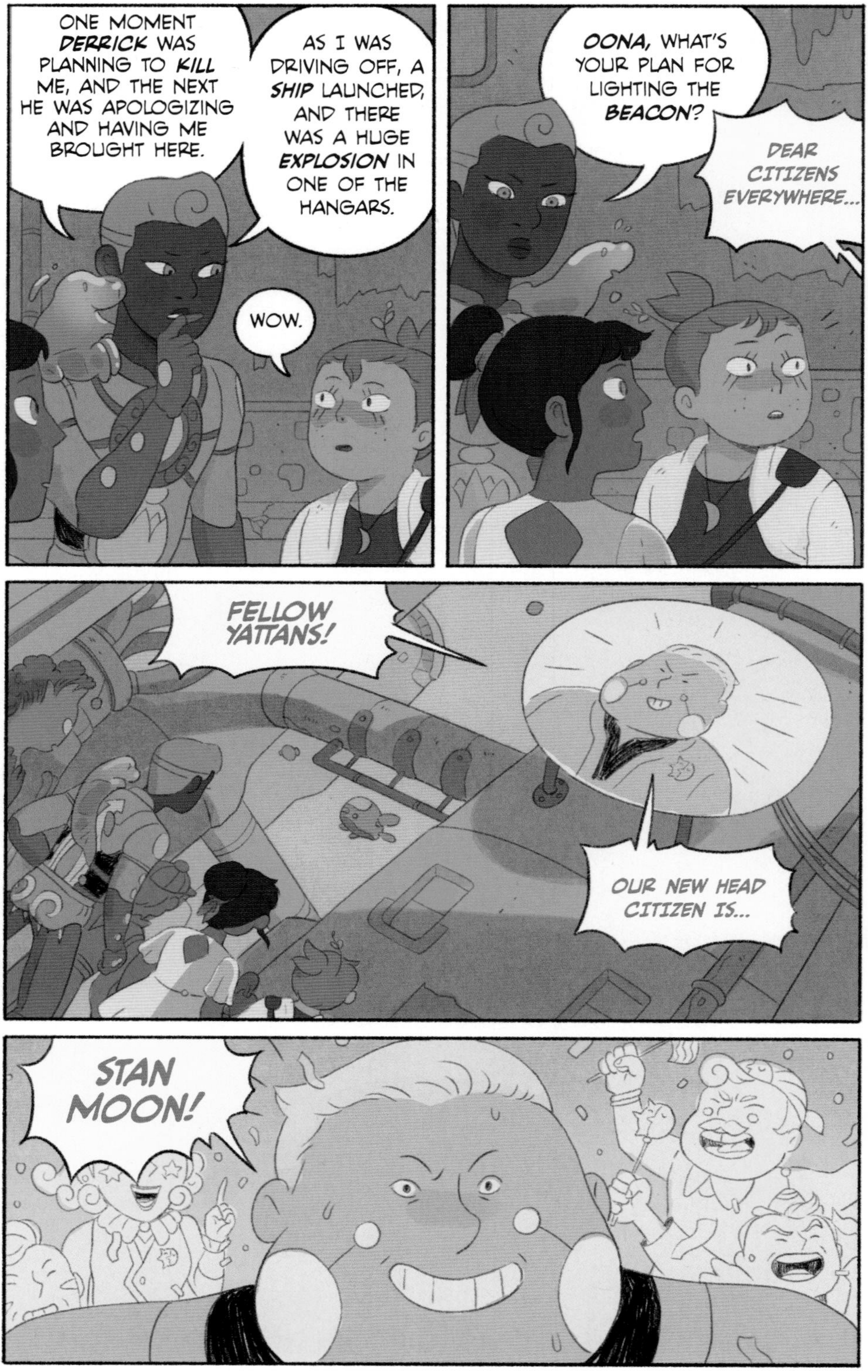
ONE MOMENT DERRICK WAS PLANNING TO KILL ME, AND THE NEXT HE WAS APOLOGIZING AND HAVING ME BROUGHT HERE.
AS I WAS DRIVING OFF, A SHIP LAUNCHED, AND THERE WAS A HUGE EXPLOSION IN ONE OF THE HANGARS.
WOW.
OONA, WHAT'S YOUR PLAN FOR LIGHTING THE BEACON?
DEAR CITIZENS EVERYWHERE...
FELLOW YATTANS!
OUR NEW HEAD CITIZEN IS...
STAN MOON!

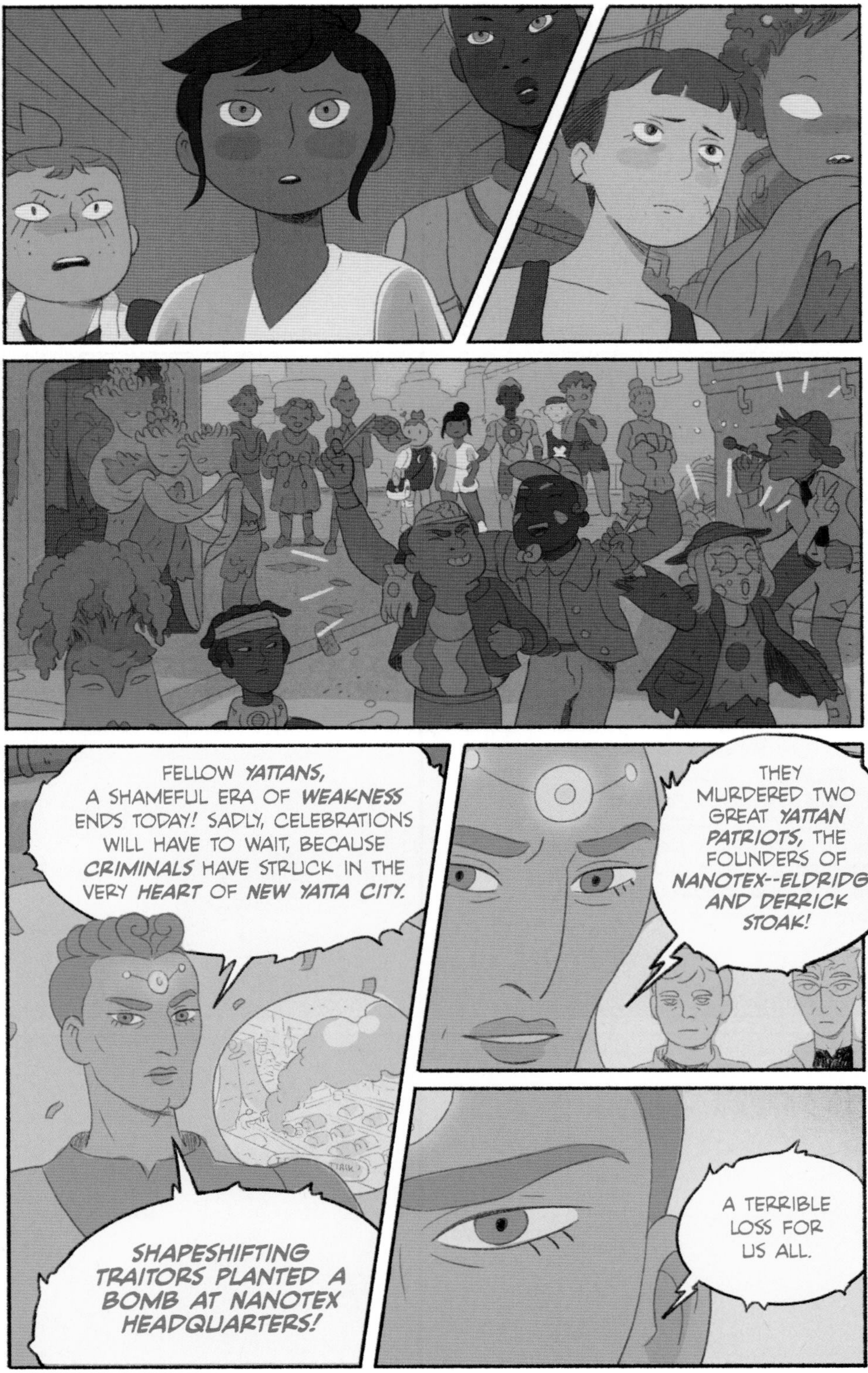
FELLOW YATTANS, A SHAMEFUL ERA OF WEAKNESS ENDS TODAY! SADLY, CELEBRATIONS WILL HAVE TO WAIT, BECAUSE CRIMINALS HAVE STRUCK IN THE VERY HEART OF NEW YATTA CITY.
SHAPESHIFTING TRAITORS PLANTED A BOMB AT NANOTEX HEADQUARTERS!
THEY MURDERED TWO GREAT YATTAN PATRIOTS, THE FOUNDERS OF NANOTEX--ELDRIDGE AND DERRICK STOAK!
A TERRIBLE LOSS FOR US ALL.

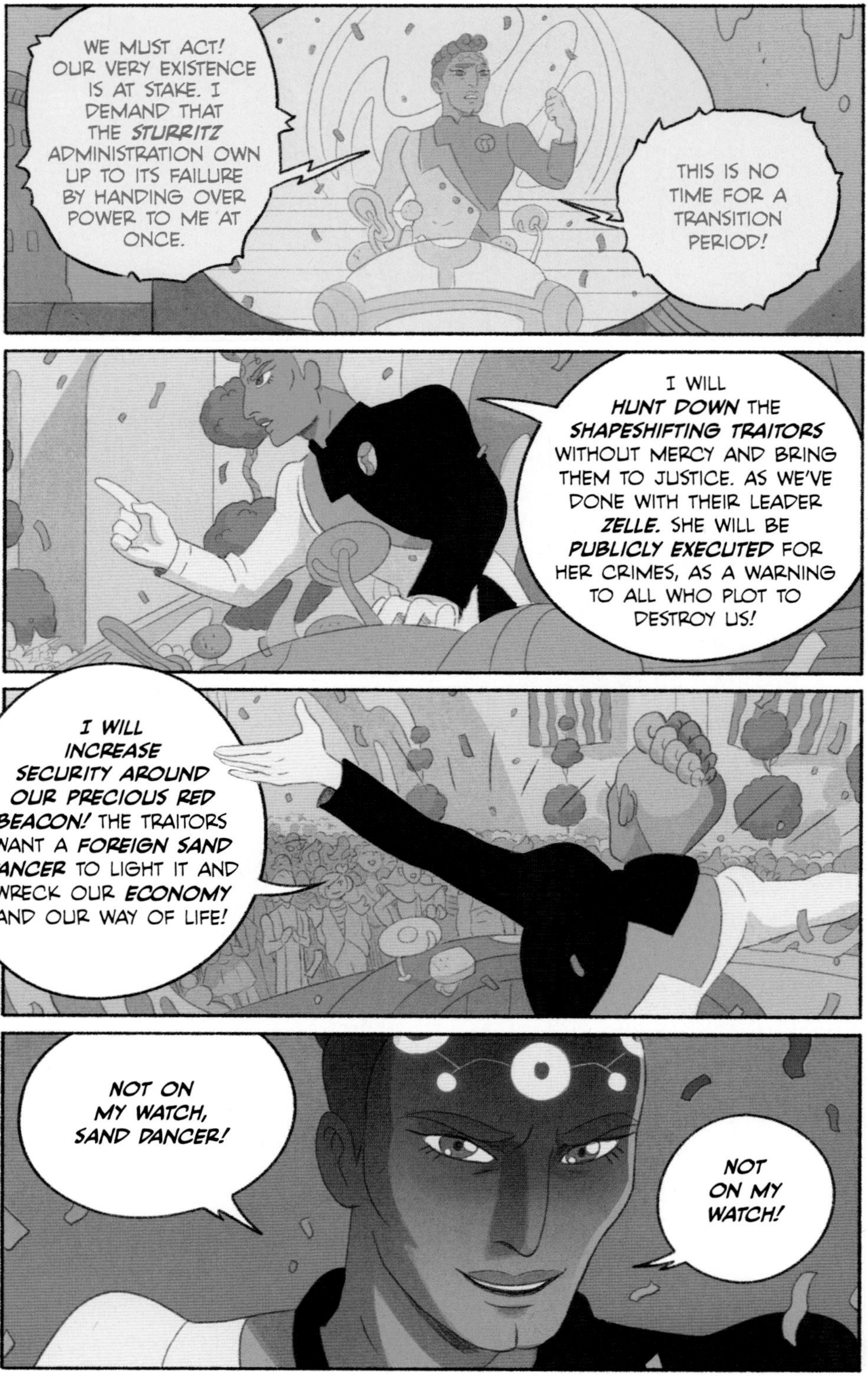
WE MUST ACT! OUR VERY EXISTENCE IS AT STAKE. I DEMAND THAT THE *STURRITZ* ADMINISTRATION OWN UP TO ITS FAILURE BY HANDING OVER POWER TO ME AT ONCE.
THIS IS NO TIME FOR A TRANSITION PERIOD!
I WILL ***HUNT DOWN*** THE ***SHAPESHIFTING TRAITORS*** WITHOUT MERCY AND BRING THEM TO JUSTICE. AS WE'VE DONE WITH THEIR LEADER ***ZELLE.*** SHE WILL BE ***PUBLICLY EXECUTED*** FOR HER CRIMES, AS A WARNING TO ALL WHO PLOT TO DESTROY US!
***I WILL INCREASE SECURITY AROUND OUR PRECIOUS RED BEACON!*** THE TRAITORS WANT A ***FOREIGN SAND DANCER*** TO LIGHT IT AND WRECK OUR ***ECONOMY*** AND OUR WAY OF LIFE!
*NOT ON MY WATCH, SAND DANCER!*
*NOT ON MY WATCH!*

LIAR! LIAR! IT'S THE MIMIC!

THEY ELECTED THE MIMIC!

MOST WON'T *BELIEVE* IT. SOME WON'T EVEN *CARE.*

I NEED TO LIGHT THAT BEACON BEFORE IT BECOMES IMPOSSIBLE. IT'S NOW OR NEVER.

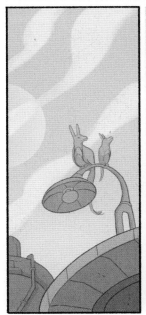

*OONA,* TROOPS ARE MASSING AROUND THE BEACON!

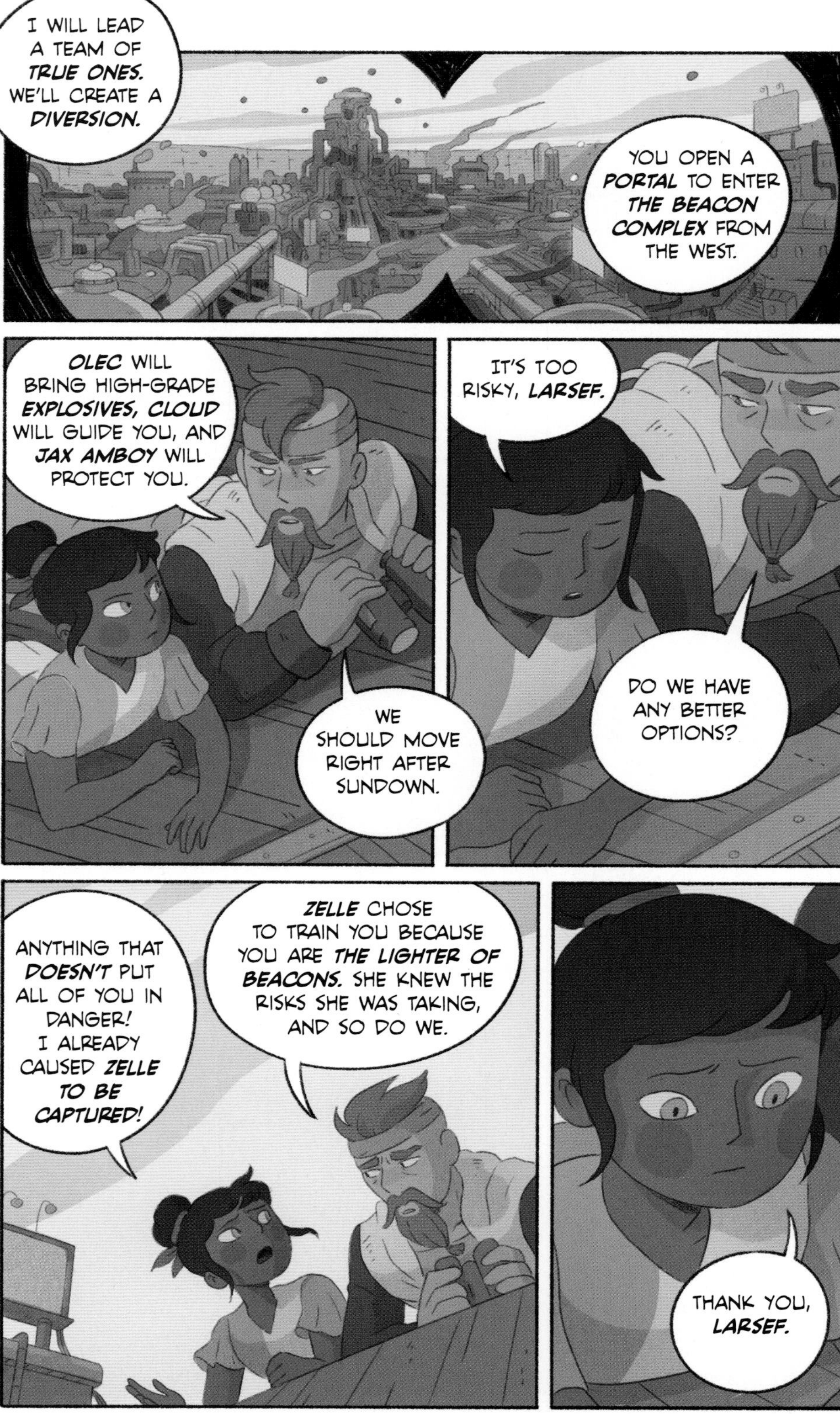
I WILL LEAD A TEAM OF TRUE ONES. WE'LL CREATE A DIVERSION.
YOU OPEN A PORTAL TO ENTER THE BEACON COMPLEX FROM THE WEST.
OLEC WILL BRING HIGH-GRADE EXPLOSIVES, CLOUD WILL GUIDE YOU, AND JAX AMBOY WILL PROTECT YOU.
WE SHOULD MOVE RIGHT AFTER SUNDOWN.
IT'S TOO RISKY, LARSEF.
DO WE HAVE ANY BETTER OPTIONS?
ANYTHING THAT DOESN'T PUT ALL OF YOU IN DANGER! I ALREADY CAUSED ZELLE TO BE CAPTURED!
ZELLE CHOSE TO TRAIN YOU BECAUSE YOU ARE THE LIGHTER OF BEACONS. SHE KNEW THE RISKS SHE WAS TAKING, AND SO DO WE.
THANK YOU, LARSEF.

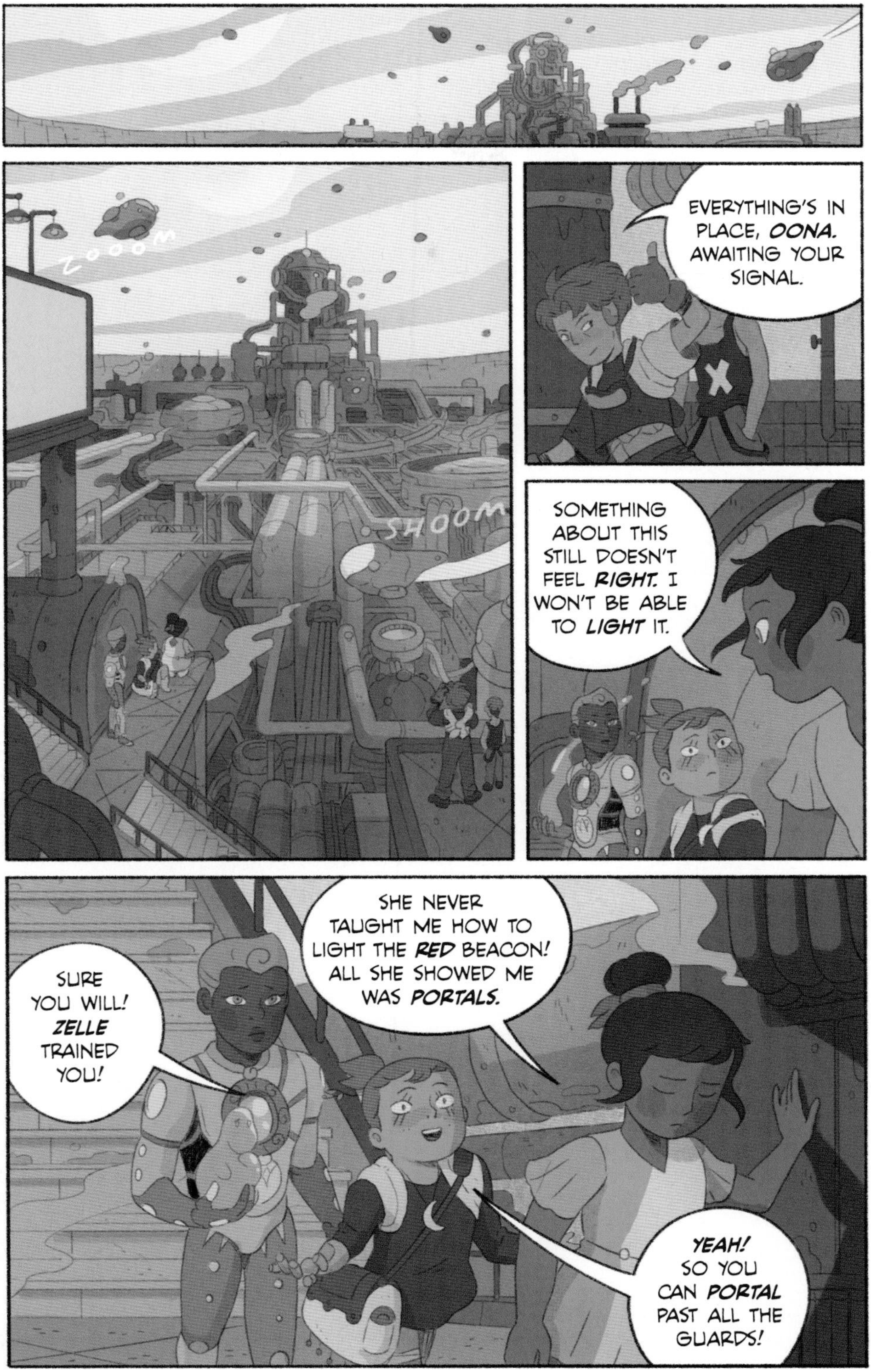
ZOOOM
SHOOM
EVERYTHING'S IN PLACE, OONA. AWAITING YOUR SIGNAL.
SOMETHING ABOUT THIS STILL DOESN'T FEEL RIGHT. I WON'T BE ABLE TO LIGHT IT.
SURE YOU WILL! ZELLE TRAINED YOU!
SHE NEVER TAUGHT ME HOW TO LIGHT THE RED BEACON! ALL SHE SHOWED ME WAS PORTALS.
YEAH! SO YOU CAN PORTAL PAST ALL THE GUARDS!

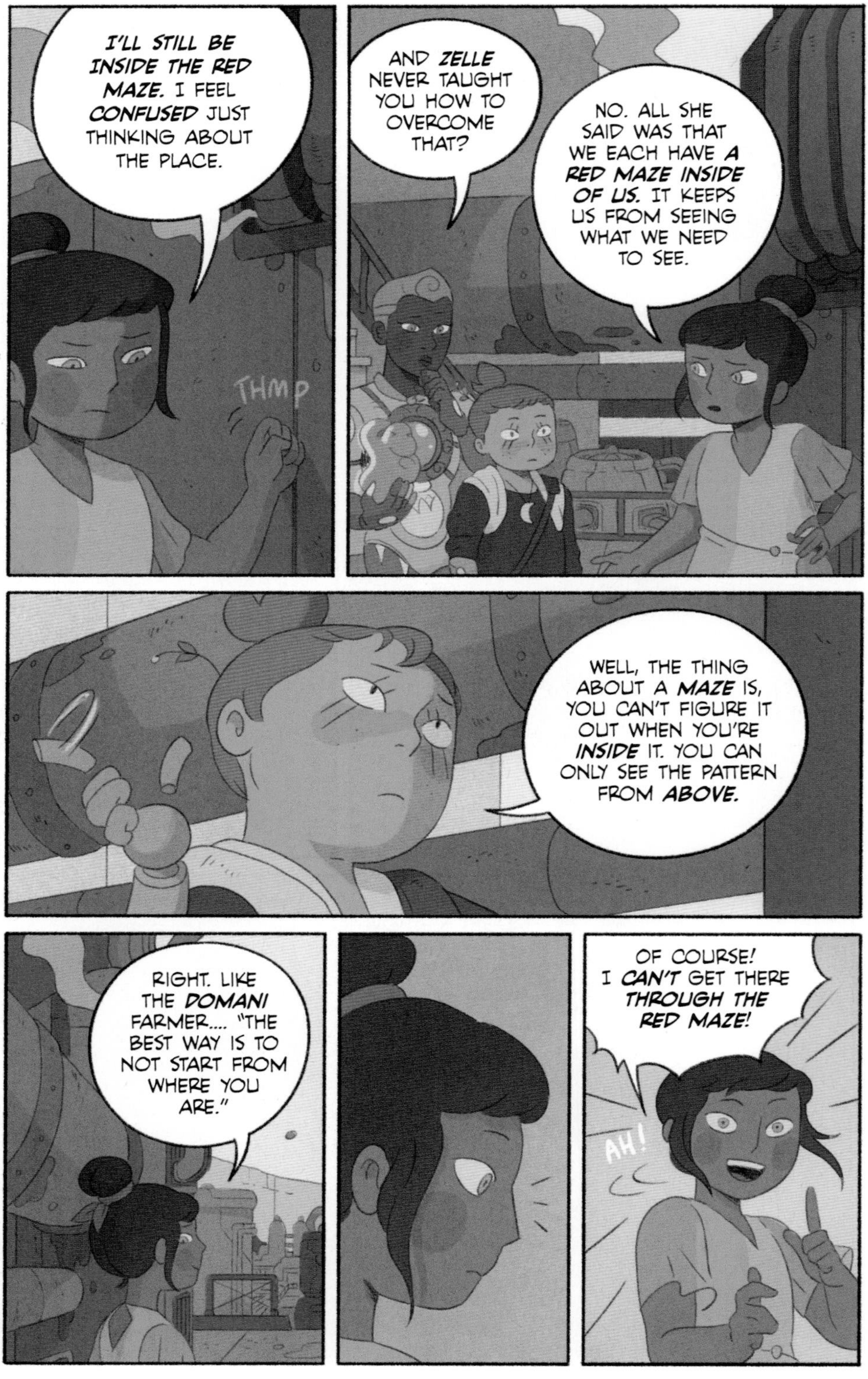
I'LL STILL BE INSIDE THE RED MAZE. I FEEL CONFUSED JUST THINKING ABOUT THE PLACE.
THMP
AND ZELLE NEVER TAUGHT YOU HOW TO OVERCOME THAT?
NO. ALL SHE SAID WAS THAT WE EACH HAVE A RED MAZE INSIDE OF US. IT KEEPS US FROM SEEING WHAT WE NEED TO SEE.
WELL, THE THING ABOUT A MAZE IS, YOU CAN'T FIGURE IT OUT WHEN YOU'RE INSIDE IT. YOU CAN ONLY SEE THE PATTERN FROM ABOVE.
RIGHT. LIKE THE DOMANI FARMER.... "THE BEST WAY IS TO NOT START FROM WHERE YOU ARE."
OF COURSE! I CAN'T GET THERE THROUGH THE RED MAZE!
AH!

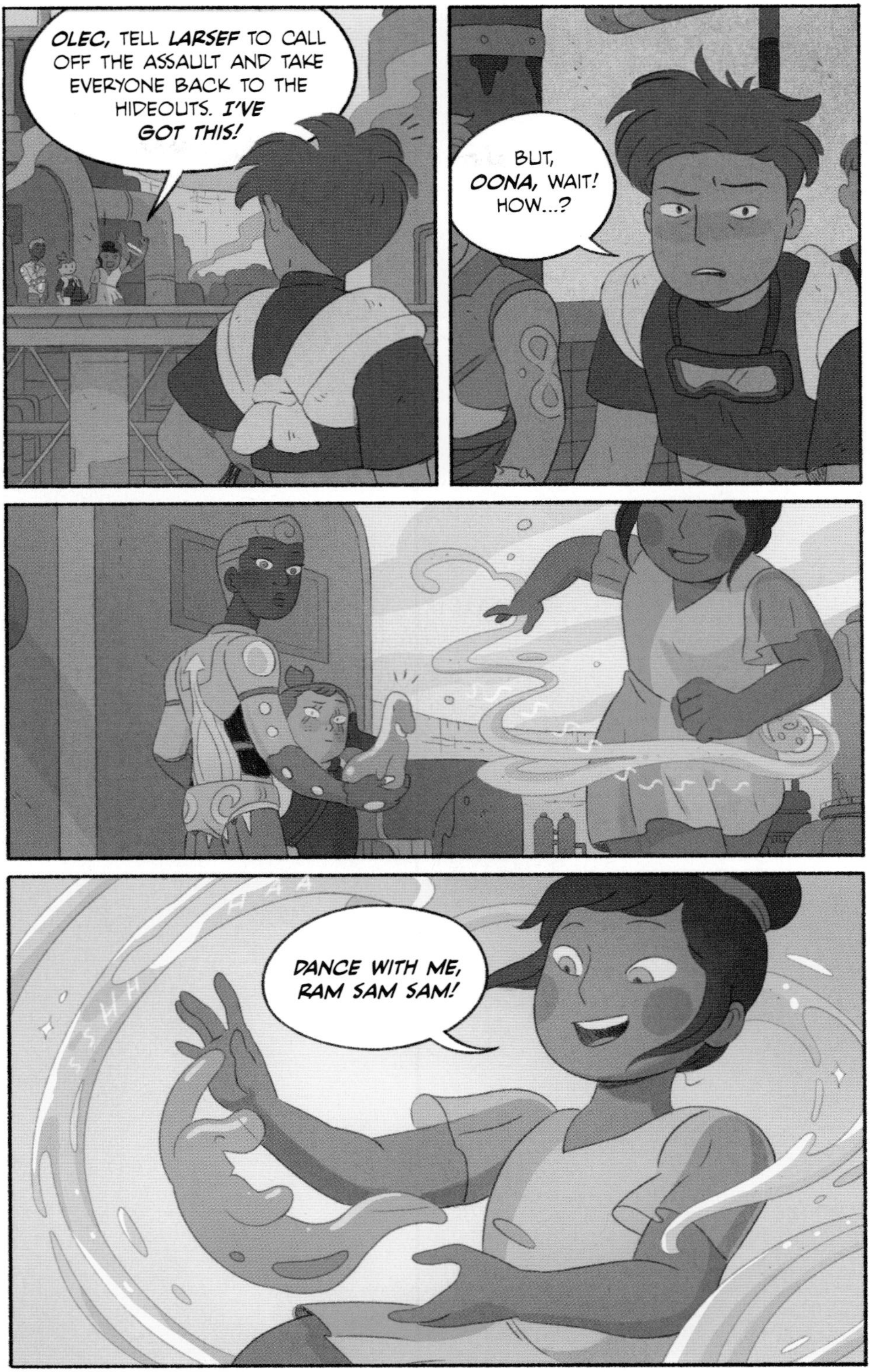
OLEC, TELL LARSEF TO CALL OFF THE ASSAULT AND TAKE EVERYONE BACK TO THE HIDEOUTS. I'VE GOT THIS!
BUT, OONA, WAIT! HOW...?
DANCE WITH ME, RAM SAM SAM!
SSHH
HAA

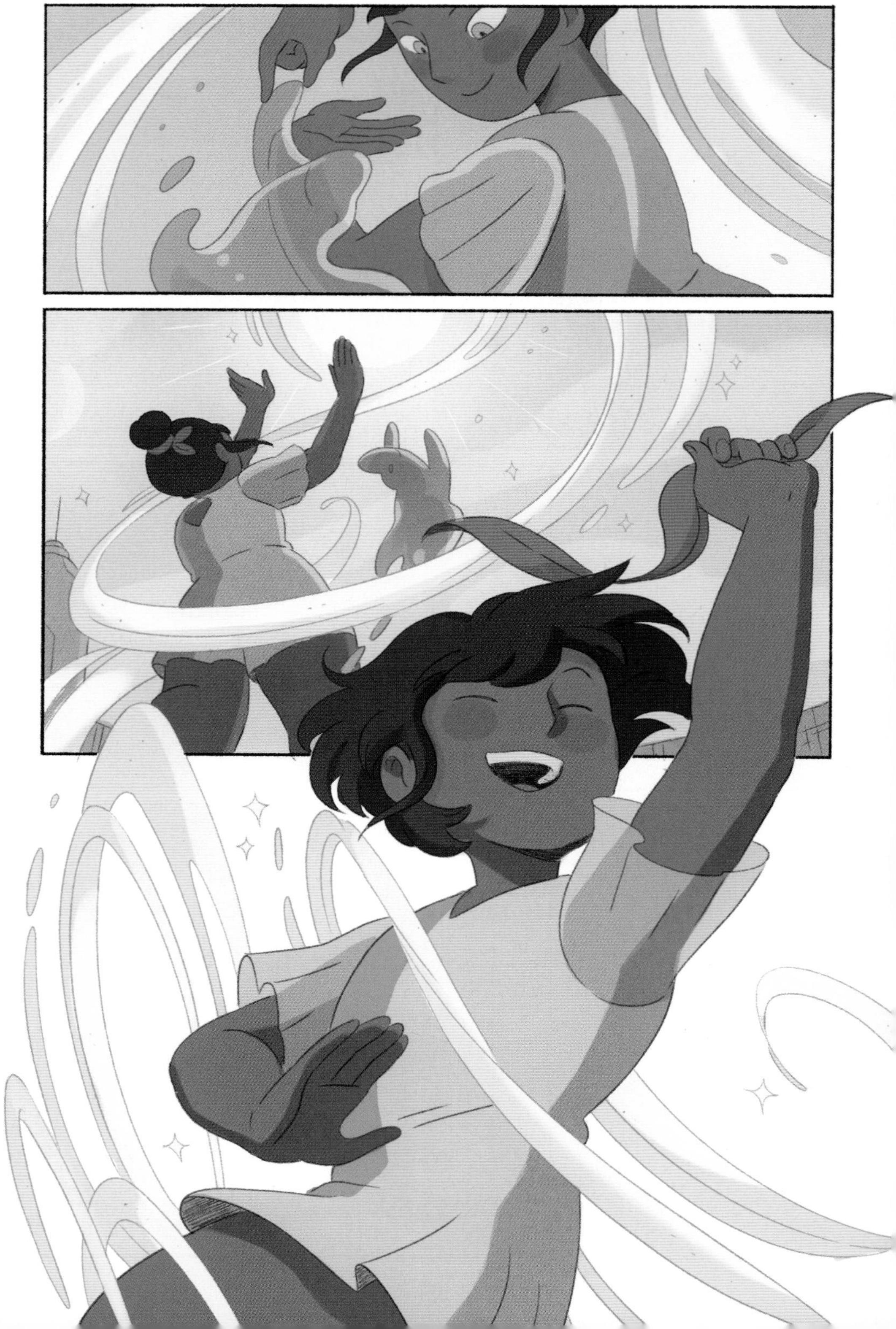

foo foof

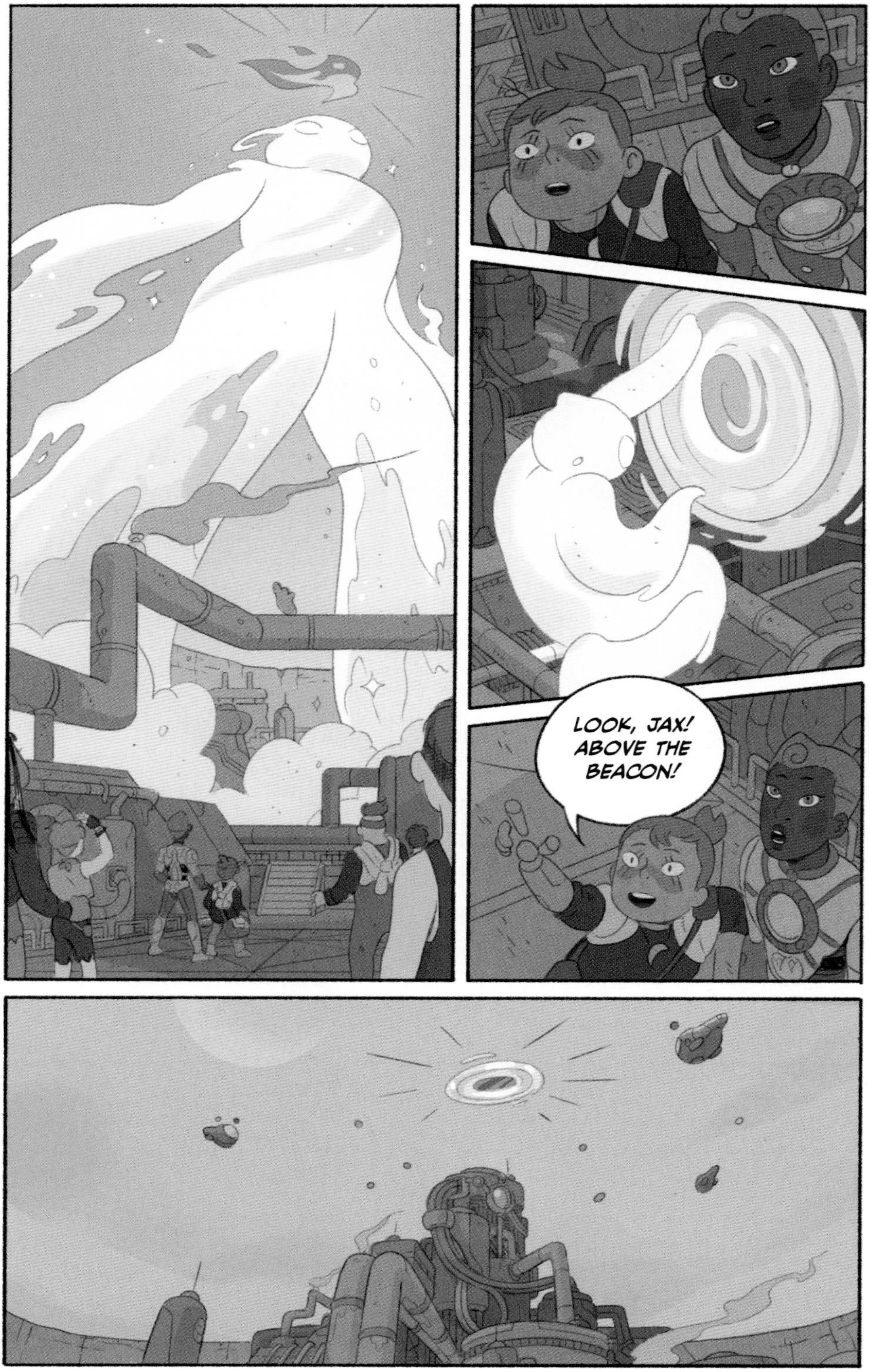
LOOK, JAX! ABOVE THE BEACON!

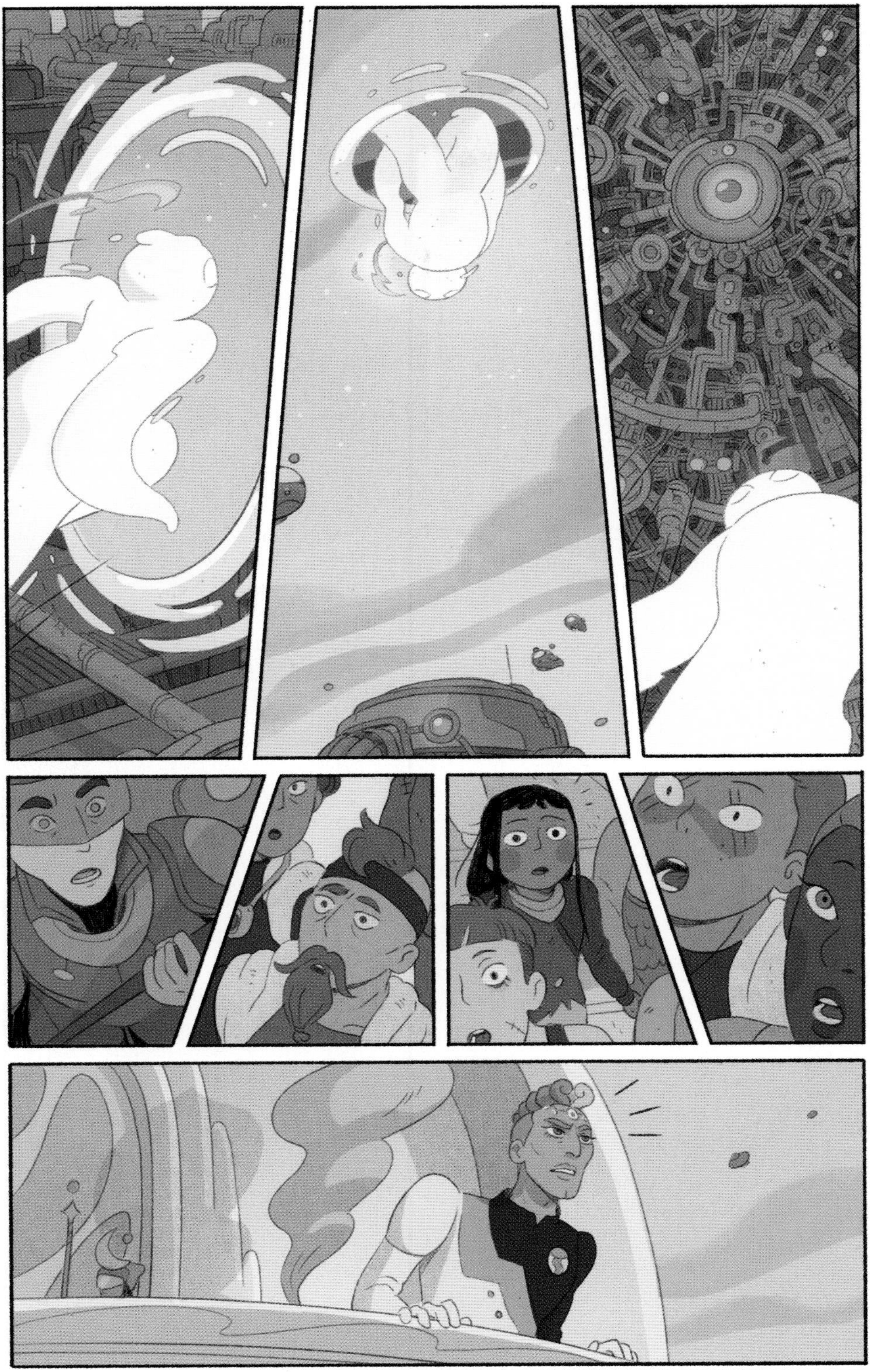

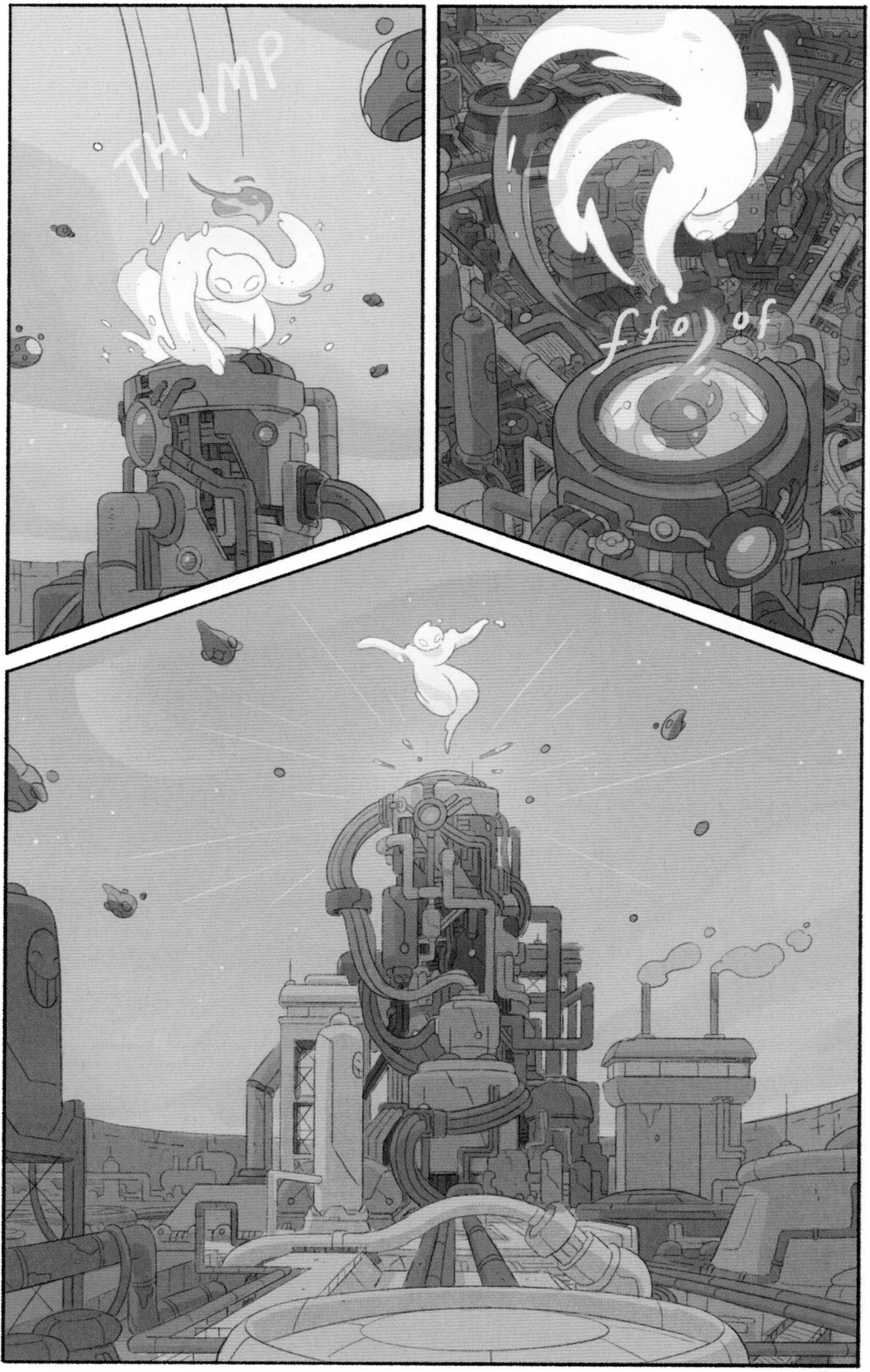
THUMP
ffoof

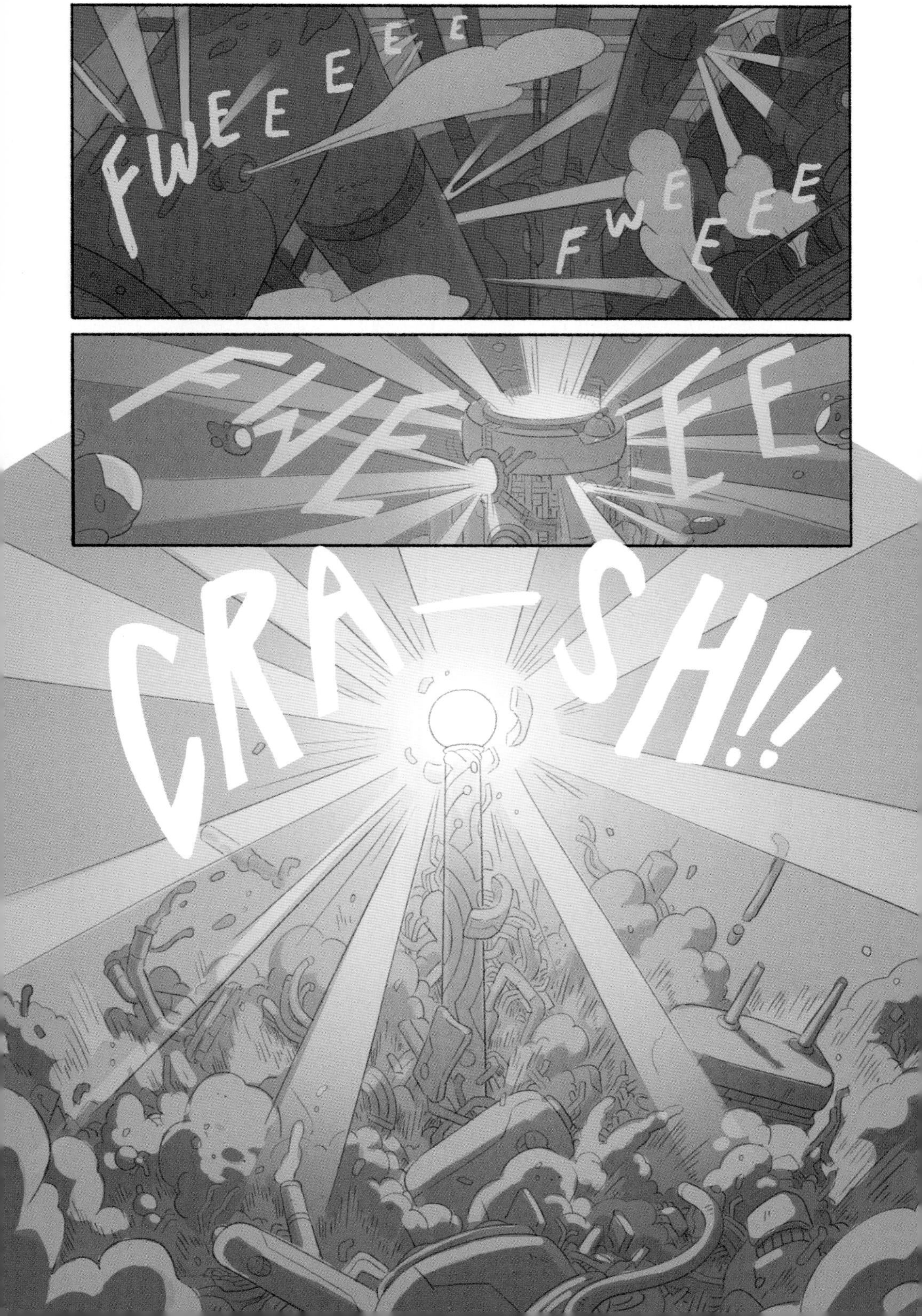
FWEEEEE
FWEEEE
FWEEEE
CRA—SH!!

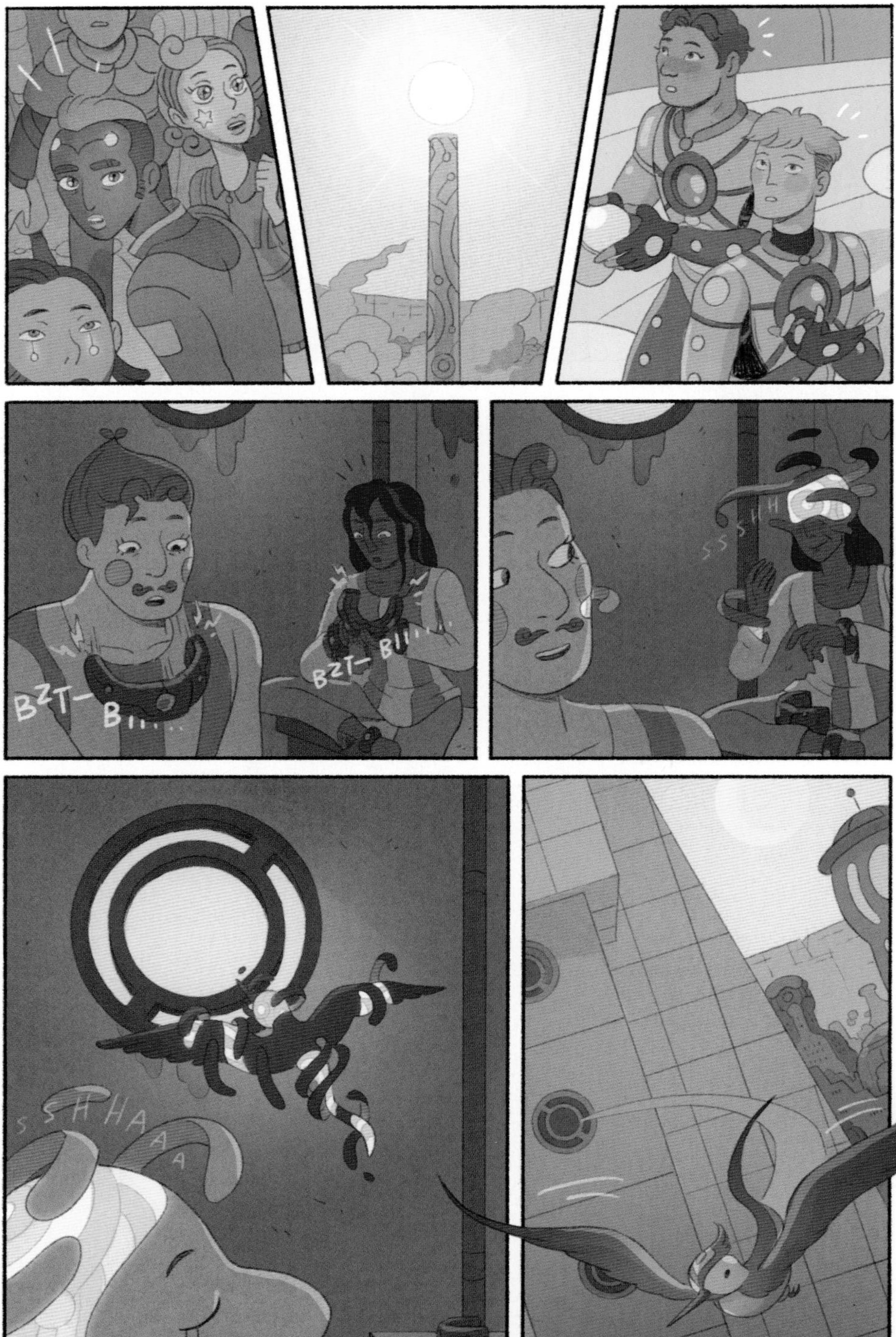
BZT—
BII...
BZT— BII...
SSSHH
SSHHAAAA

IT'S ABOUT TIME! WHERE HAVE YOU BEEN?

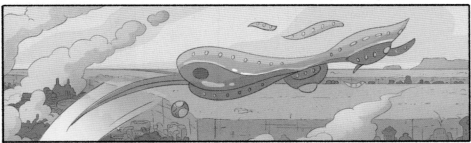

COME QUICKLY, *OONA!* *VECTOR SANDERSON* IS ON THE LINE!

I KNEW YOU'D DO IT, *LIGHTER OF BEACONS!*

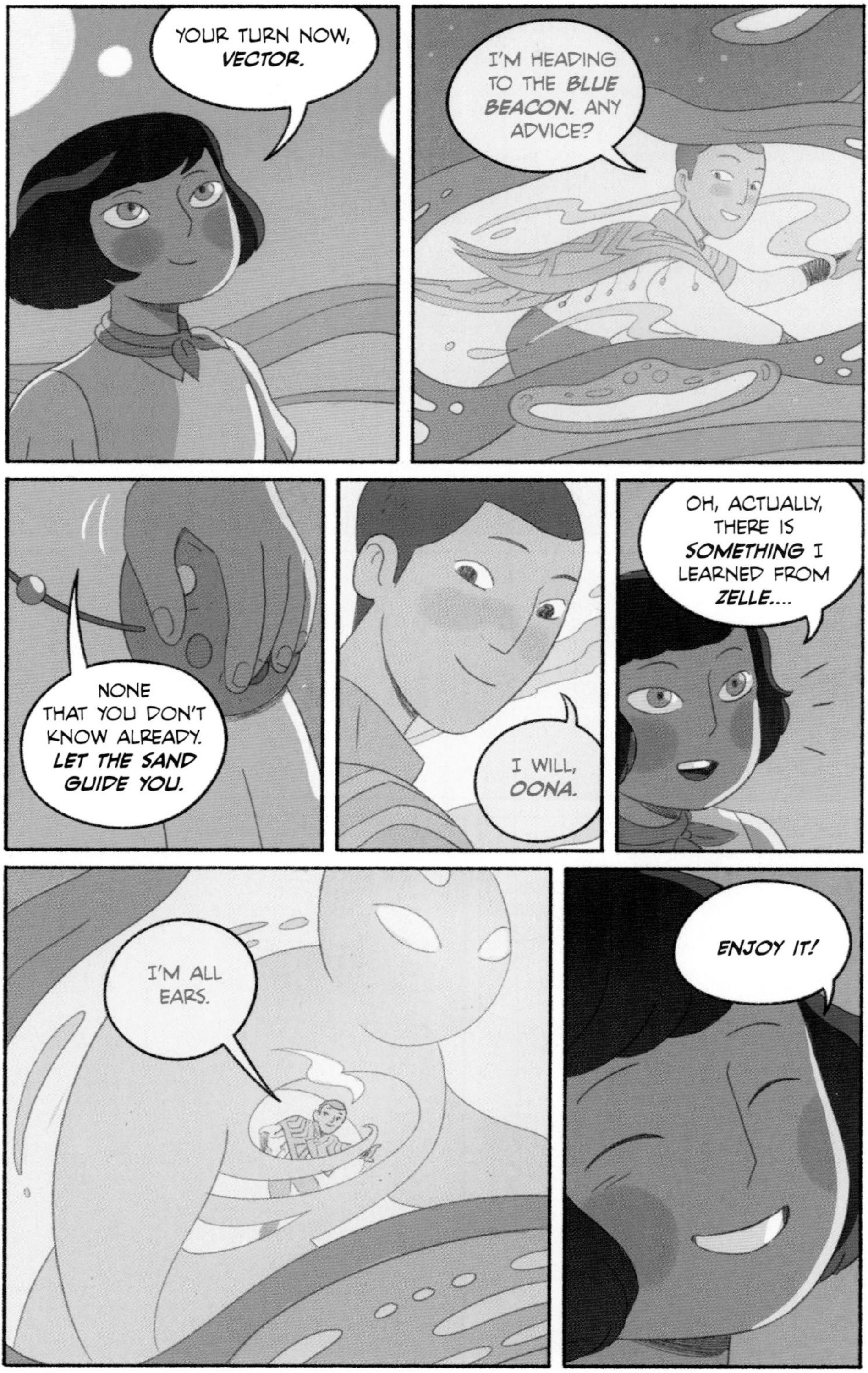
YOUR TURN NOW, VECTOR.
I'M HEADING TO THE BLUE BEACON. ANY ADVICE?
NONE THAT YOU DON'T KNOW ALREADY. LET THE SAND GUIDE YOU.
I WILL, OONA.
OH, ACTUALLY, THERE IS SOMETHING I LEARNED FROM ZELLE....
I'M ALL EARS.
ENJOY IT!

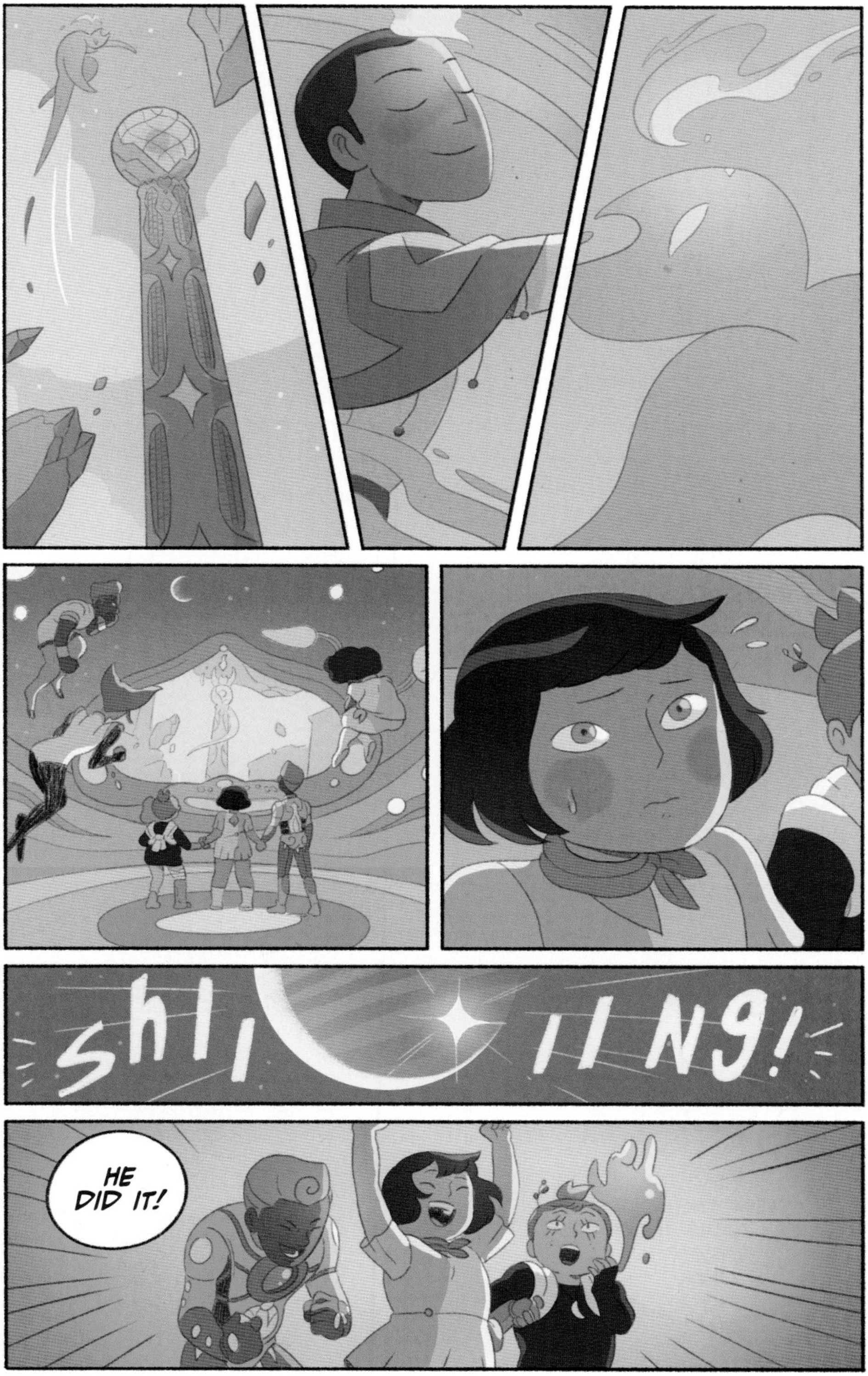
SHI ... IING!
HE DID IT!

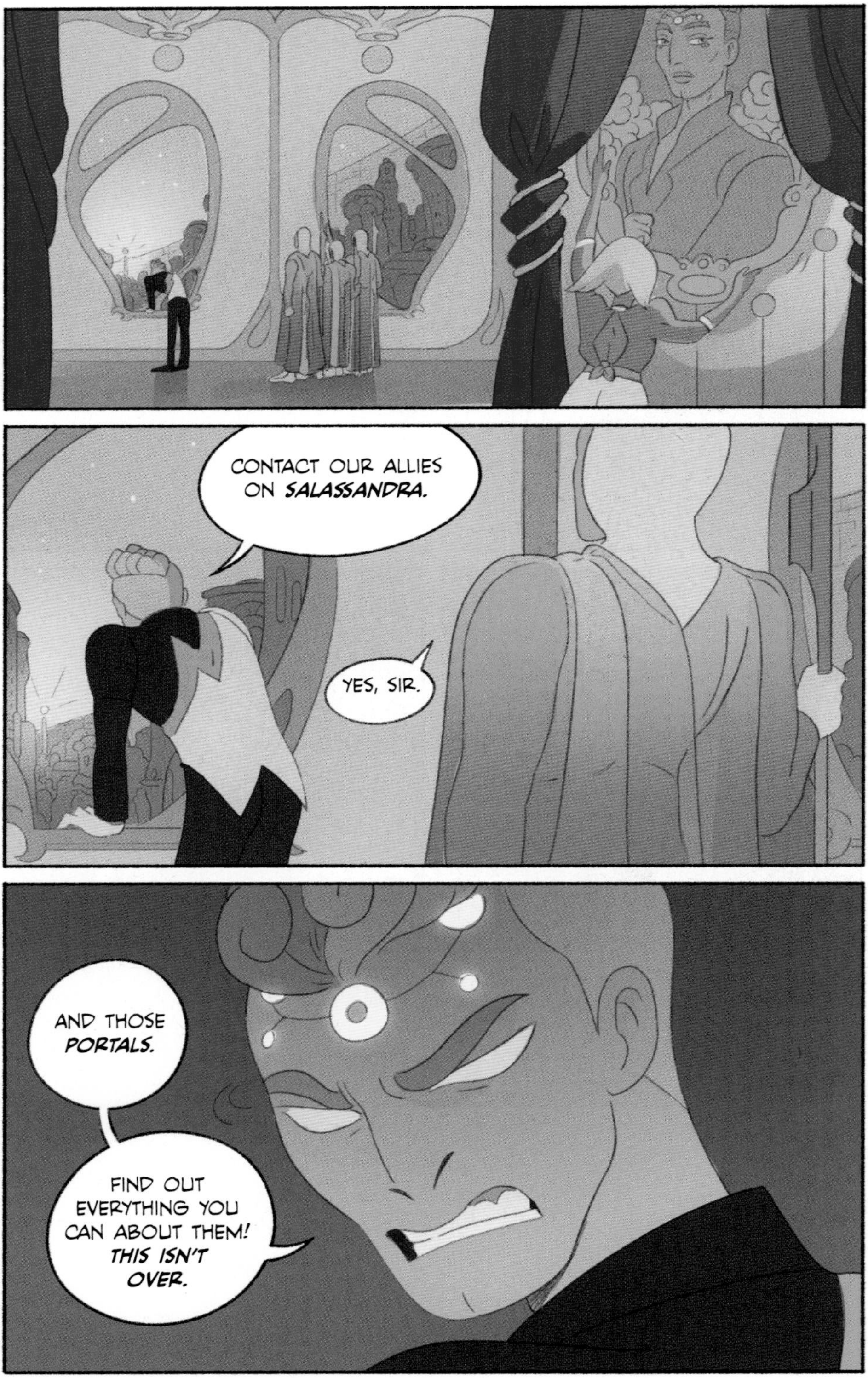
CONTACT OUR ALLIES ON SALASSANDRA.
YES, SIR.
AND THOSE PORTALS.
FIND OUT EVERYTHING YOU CAN ABOUT THEM! THIS ISN'T OVER.

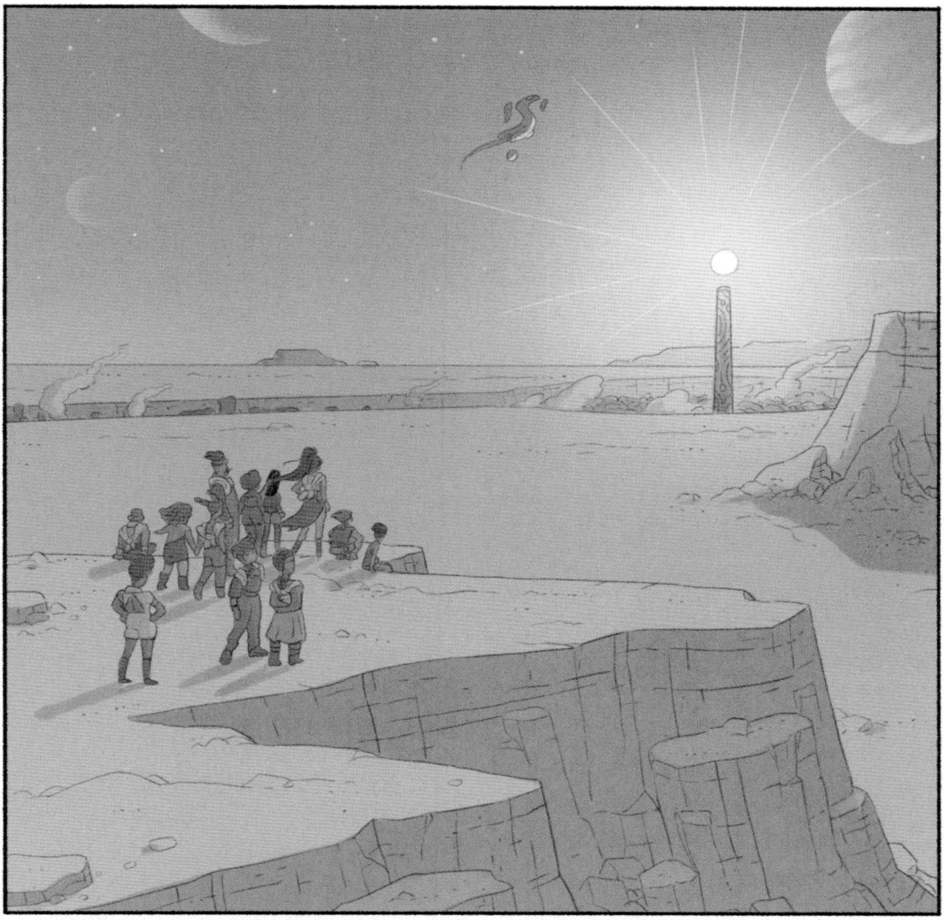

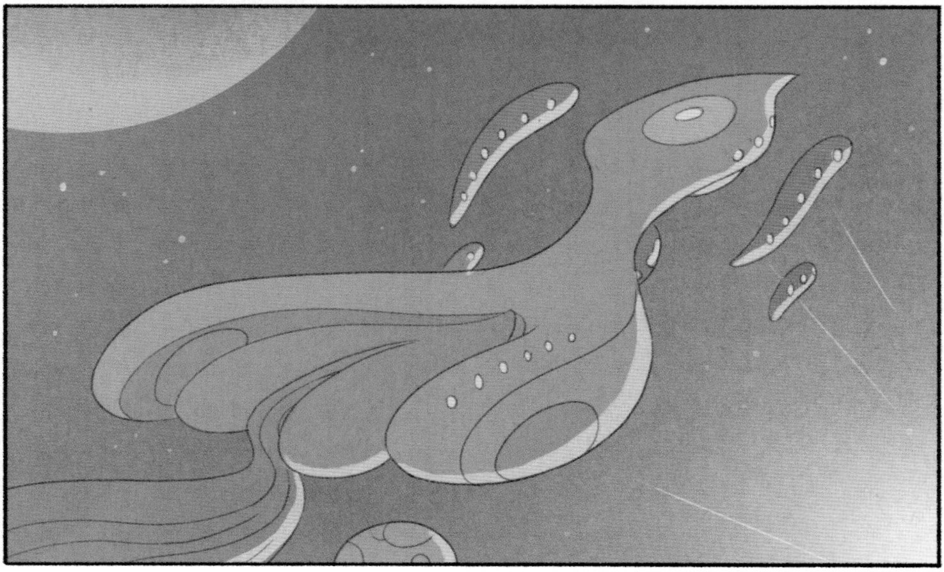

# EPILOGUE

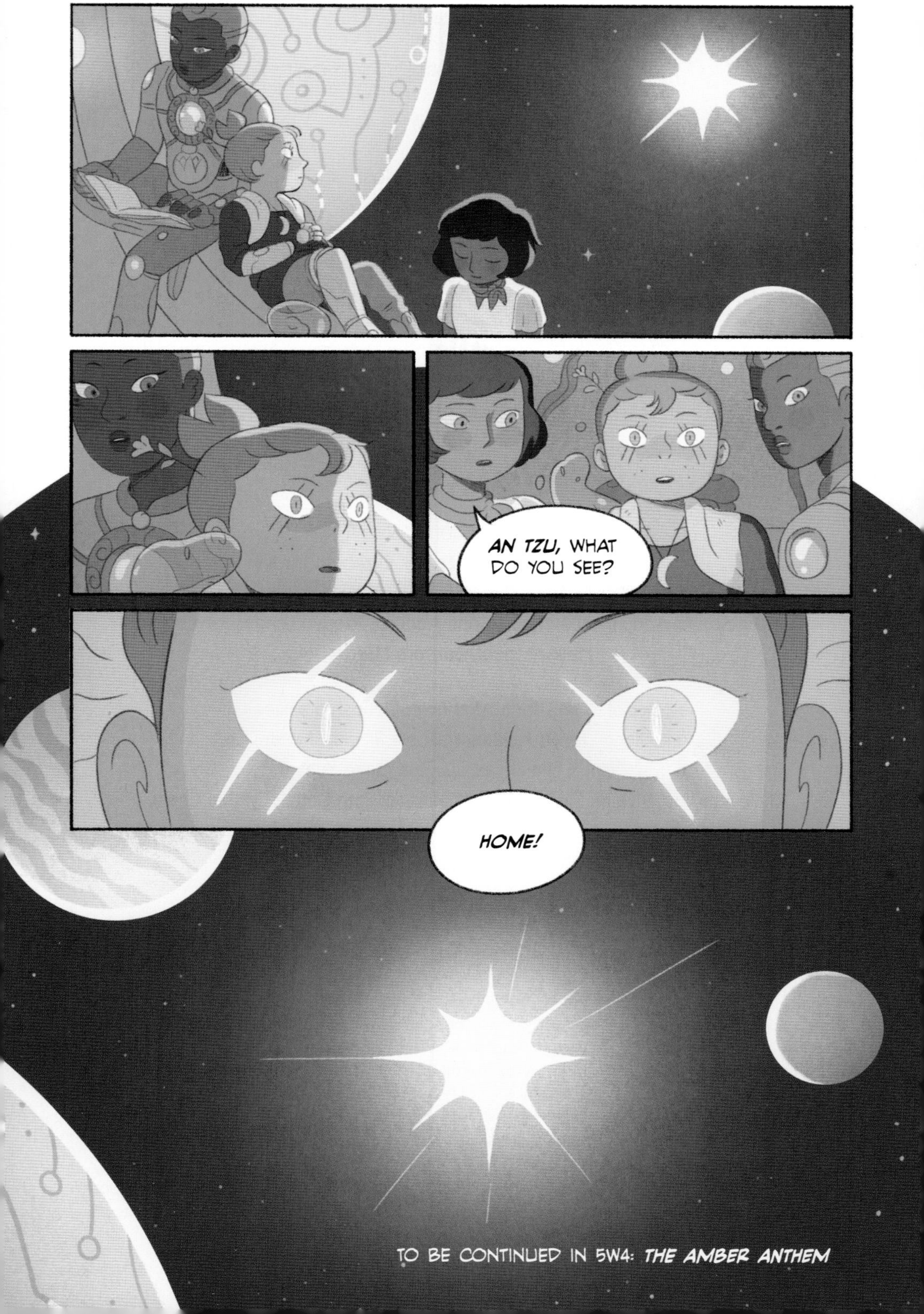
AN TZU, WHAT DO YOU SEE?
HOME!
TO BE CONTINUED IN 5W4: THE AMBER ANTHEM

To all our re-readers –MS

To all helpers, seen and unseen, with trust –AS

To Jo –XB

To anyone who has felt lost –MR

To Dad –BS

ACKNOWLEDGMENTS

Marie-Claire & Edward Siegel

Our amazing Random House team:
Michelle Nagler, Chelsea Eberly, Elizabeth Tardiff,
Kelly McGauley, Janine Perez, Aisha Cloud, Joshua Redlich, Alison Kolani, Lisa Nadel,
Kristin Schulz, Adrienne Waintraub, John Adamo, Jocelyn Lange, Joe English,
Mallory Loehr, Barbara Marcus

+ Special thanks for added help, friendship & magic:
Siena Siegel, Tanya McKinnon, Sonia Siegel, Shudan Yeh,
Felix & Elia Siegel, Julien & Clio Siegel,
Julie Sandfort, Viviana Simon, Hilde McKinnon, Sam Dutter, Cynthia Cheng,
Bryan Konietzko, and the Story Trust of Gene Luen Yang, Vera Brosgol,
Sam Bosma, Shelli Paroline & Braden Lamb

And the mighty inspirations of:
Stephen King, Lois McMaster Bujold, Naoki Urasawa & Rebecca Sugar

 Published in the United States by Random House Children's Books, a division of Penguin Random House LLC, New York. • Random House and the colophon are registered trademarks of Penguin Random House LLC. • Visit us on the Web! rhcbooks.com • Educators and librarians, for a variety of teaching tools, visit us at RHTeachersLibrarians.com Library of Congress Cataloging-in-Publication Data is available upon request. • ISBN 978-1-101-93592-7 (hc) ISBN 978-1-101-93594-1 (paperback) • ISBN 978-1-101-93593-4 (lib.bdg.) • ISBN 978-1-101-93606-1 (ebook) MANUFACTURED IN CHINA Random House Children's Books supports the First Amendment and celebrates the right to read. • 10 9 8 7 6 5 4 3 2 1 • First Edition

**MARK SIEGEL** has written and illustrated several award-winning picture books and graphic novels. He is also the editorial and creative director of First Second Books. He lives with his family in New York. Discover more at marksiegelbooks.com.

**ALEXIS SIEGEL** is a writer and translator based in Switzerland. He has translated a number of bestselling graphic novels, including Joann Sfar's *The Rabbi's Cat* and Pénélope Bagieu's *Exquisite Corpse* (both into English), and Gene Luen Yang's *American Born Chinese* (into French).

**XANTHE BOUMA** is an illustrator based in Southern California. When not working on picture books such as *Little Sid*, fashion illustration, and comics, Xanthe enjoys soaking up the beachside sun.

**MATT ROCKEFELLER** is an illustrator and comic artist living in the Pacific Northwest. He grew up in Tucson, Arizona, and draws inspiration from the desert's dramatic landscapes. His work has appeared in a variety of formats, including animation, book covers, and picture books such as *Train*, *Rocket*, and *Pop!*

**BOYA SUN** is an illustrator and coauthor of the graphic novel *Chasma Knights*. Originally from China, Boya has traveled from Canada to the United States and now lives in California.

# A Sneak Peek at the Making of 5W3

## Character Development

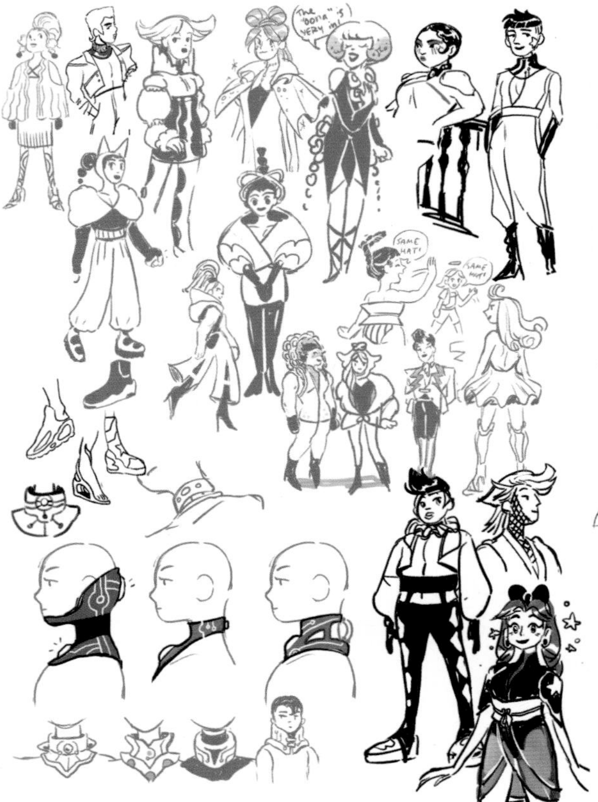
SAME HAT!
SAME HAT!

Early sketches for Yatta society

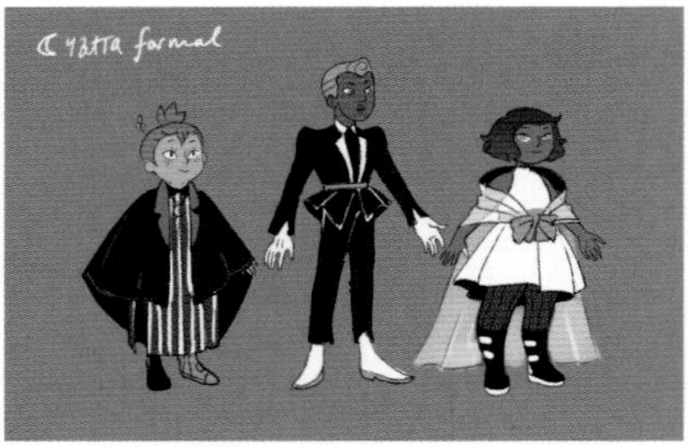
Yatta formal

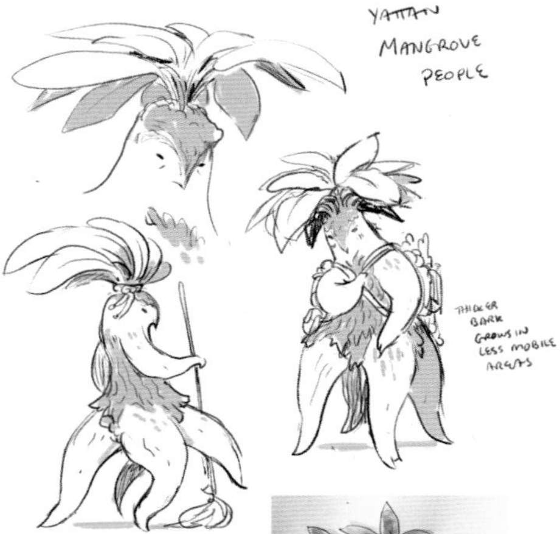
YATTAN MANGROVE PEOPLE
THICKER BARK GROWS IN LESS MOBILE AREAS

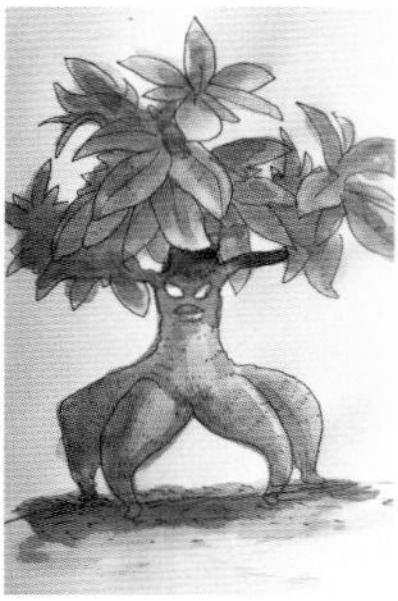

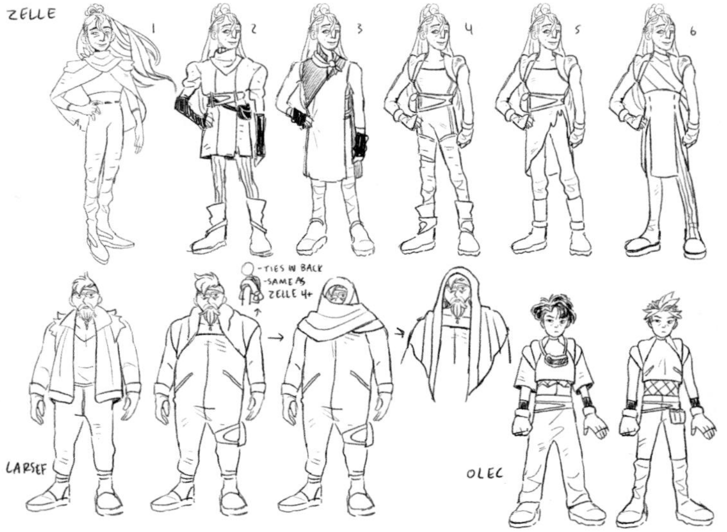
ZELLE
1
2
3
4
5
6
-TIES IN BACK
-SAME AS ZELLE 4+
LARSEF
OLEC

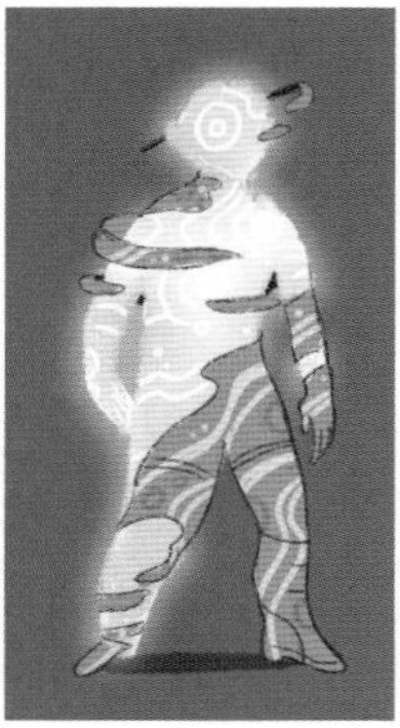

Shapeshifter study

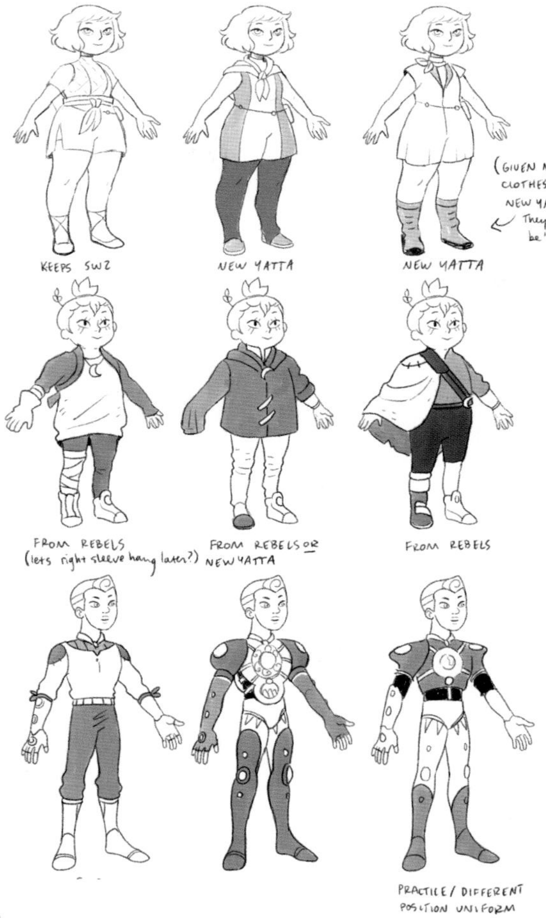
(GIVEN NICER CLOTHES ON NEW YATTA?)
They want her to be 'presentable'
KEEPS SWZ
NEW YATTA
NEW YATTA
FROM REBELS (lets right sleeve hang later?)
FROM REBELS OR NEW YATTA
FROM REBELS
PRACTICE / DIFFERENT POSITION UNIFORM

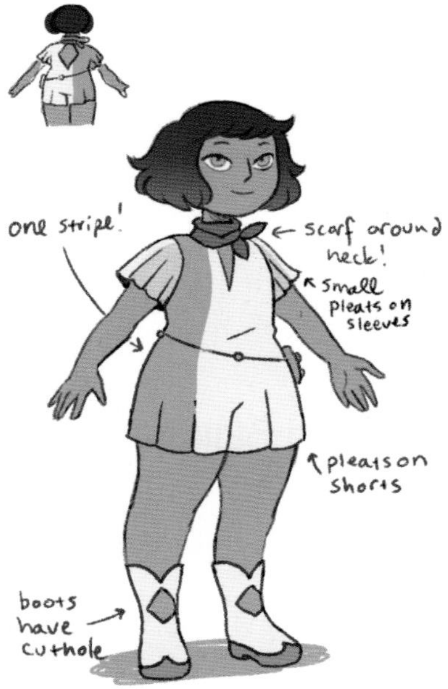
one stripe!
scarf around neck!
small pleats on sleeves
pleats on shorts
boots have cuthole

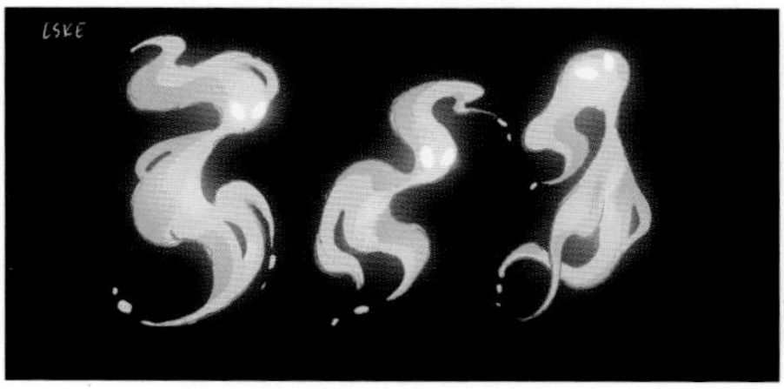

Salassi Devoti

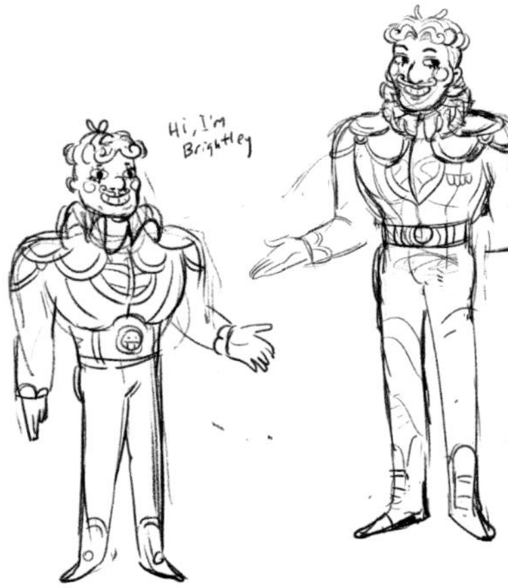
Hi, I'm Brightley

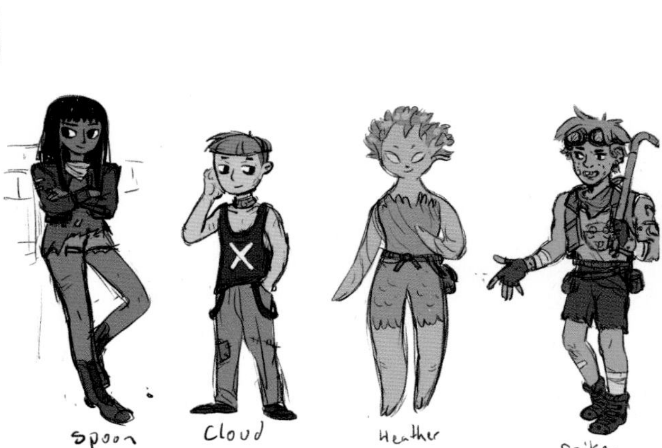
Spoon
Cloud
Heather
Spike

The Teen Rebels

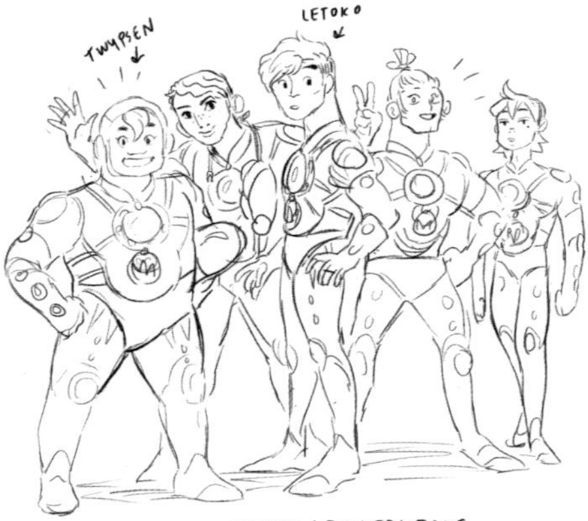
TWYPSEN
LETOKO

AMBER LEATHERHEADS

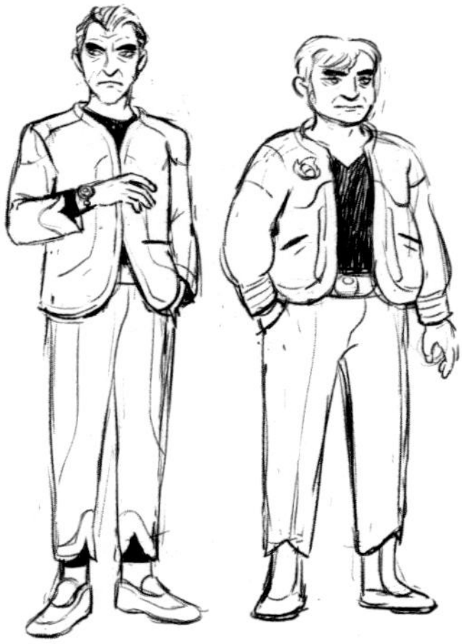

Eldridge Dearick

# World Building

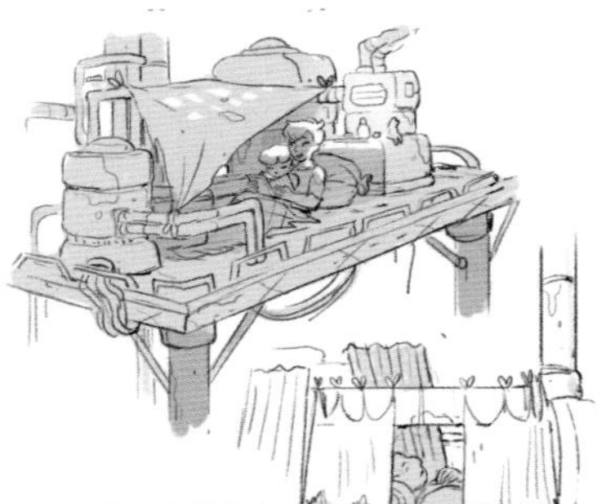

IN ADDITION TO RUN DOWN BUILDINGS, THE MAZE IS PEPPERED W/ MAKESHIFT SHELTERS FOR THE HOMELESS

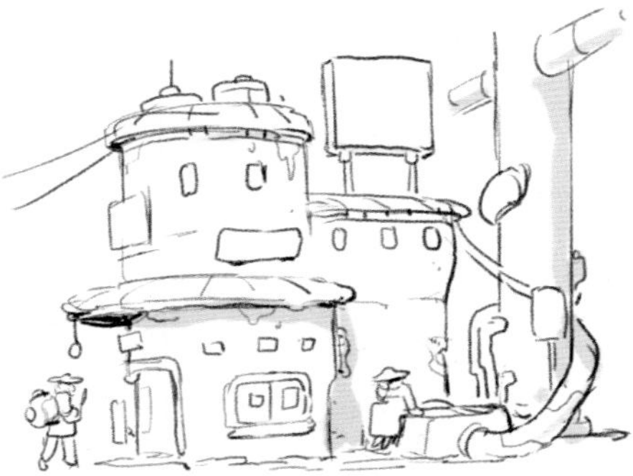

MOON YATTA, NEW YATTA CITY

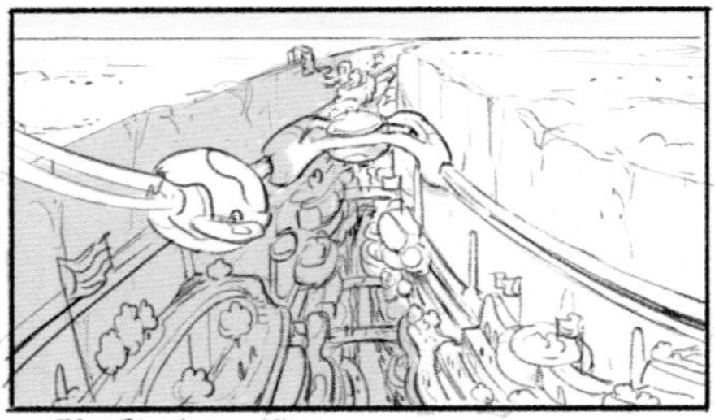

OUTER CITY "SUBURBS"

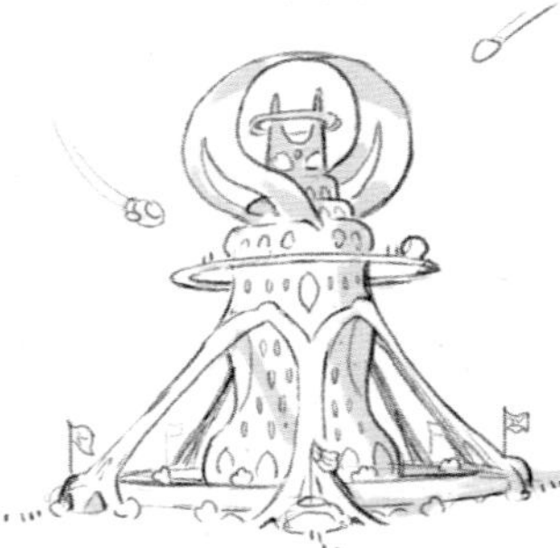

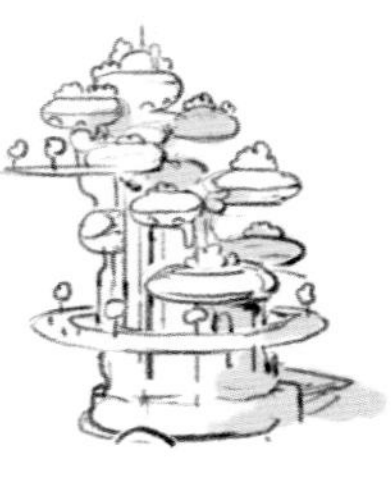

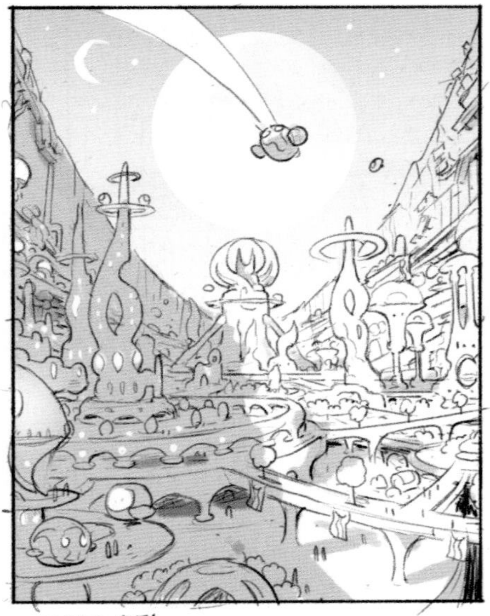

NEW YATTA CITY

MOON YATTA , FEDORA MESA

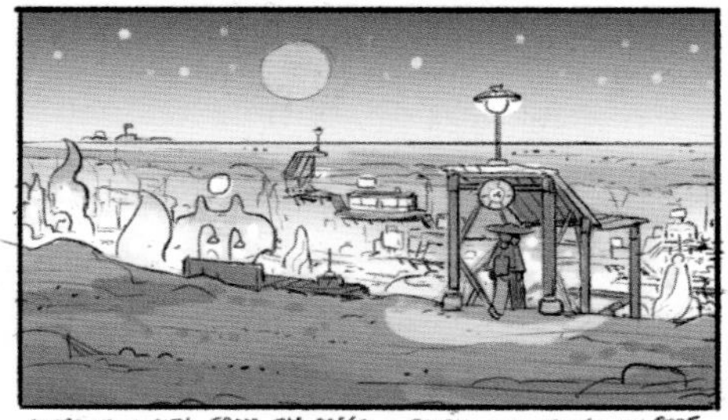

ENTERING A CITY FROM THE MESA – PEOPLE WHO TRAVEL ON FOOT ENTER FROM ABOVE. POORER, LOWER TECH SETTLEMENTS LINE THE UPPER WALLS

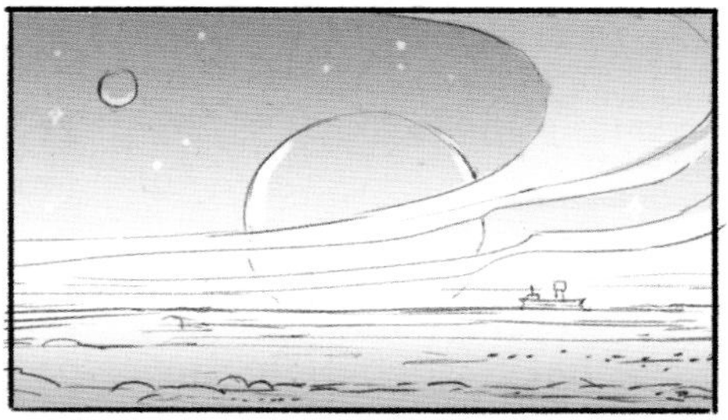

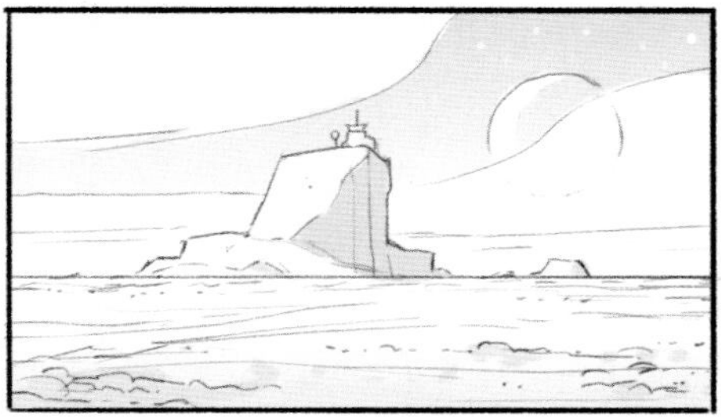

BUILDINGS OF THE MESA

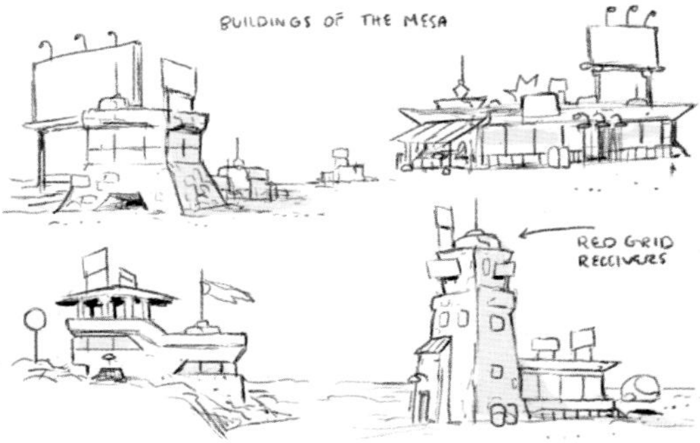
RED GRID RECEIVERS

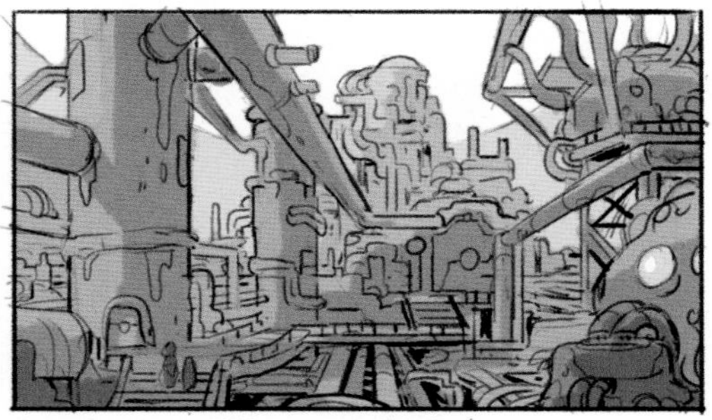

RED MAZE - UPPER LEVELS + BEACON

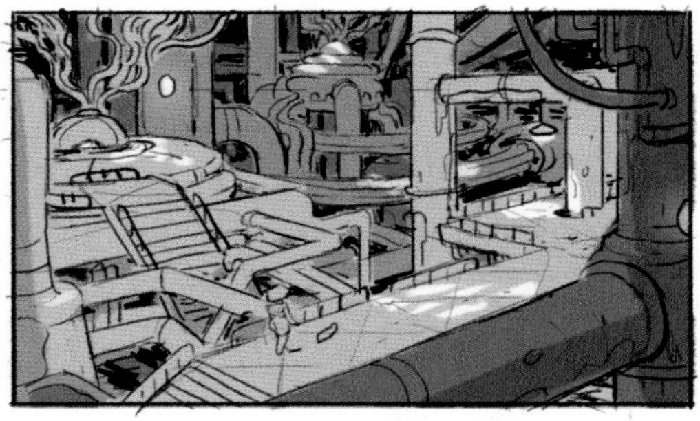

RED MAZE - LOWER LEVELS

SOME LIGHT COMES THROUGH FROM HIGH ABOVE

SAO SANGRE

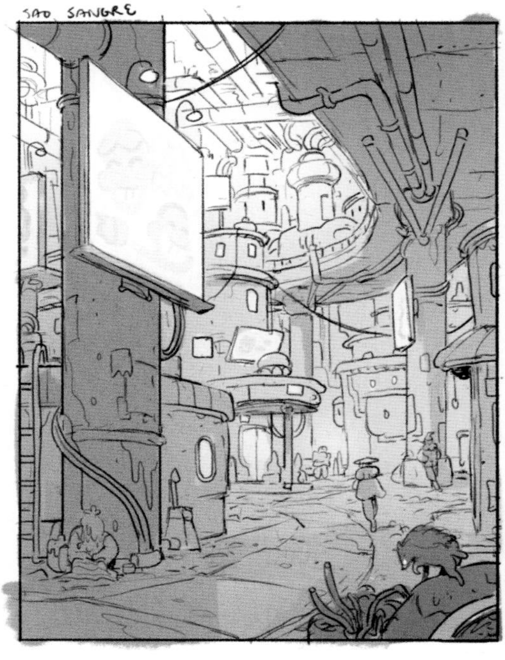

...and many sketchbooks more!

# Discover more  online!

@5WorldsTeam

POST YOUR **COSPLAY** PHOTOS AND SHARE YOUR BEST **FAN ART** WITH OTHER 5-WORLDERS, WITH HASHTAGS #DRAWOONA, #5WORLDS, AND #5WFANART.

## The Winners of the #DrawOona Fan Art Contest Are . . .

Kiara Rivera @Crybaby.kia

Hadley Griffin Johnson

Kristina Luu @stripeyworm

MOON YATTA, FEDORA MESA

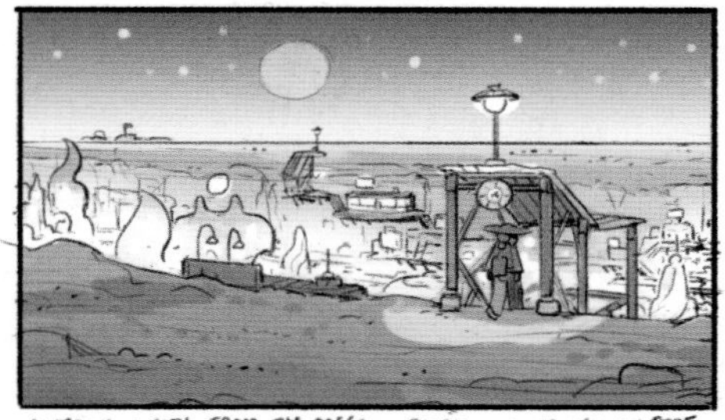

ENTERING A CITY FROM THE MESA - PEOPLE WHO TRAVEL ON FOOT ENTER FROM ABOVE. POORER, LOWER TECH SETTLEMENTS LINE THE UPPER WALLS

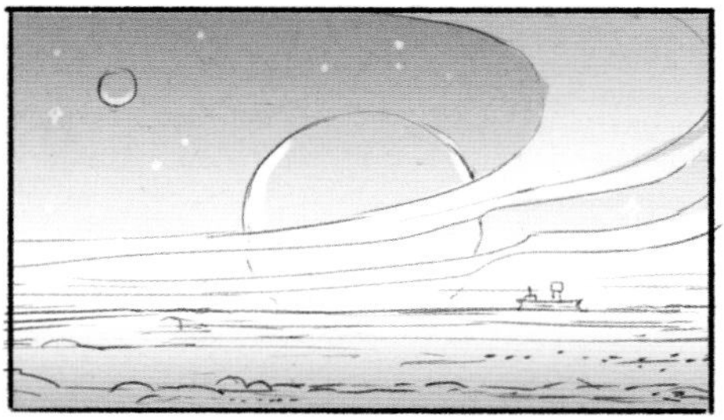

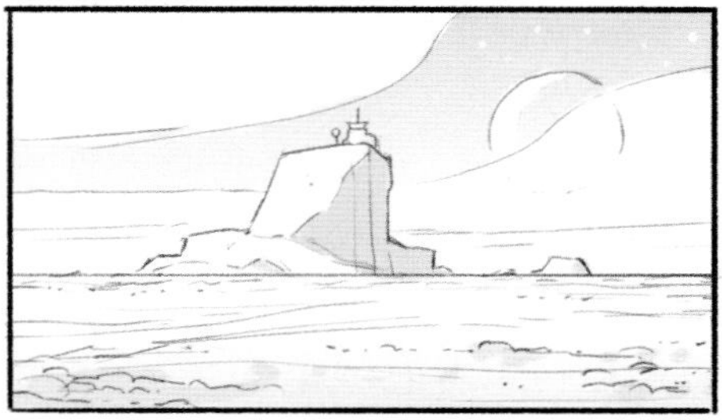

BUILDINGS OF THE MESA

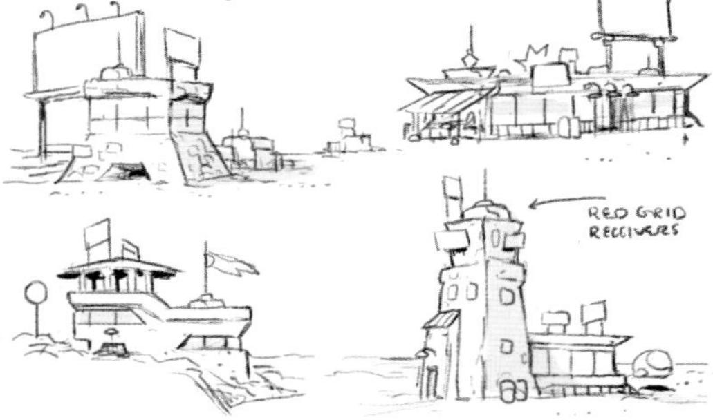
RED GRID RECEIVERS

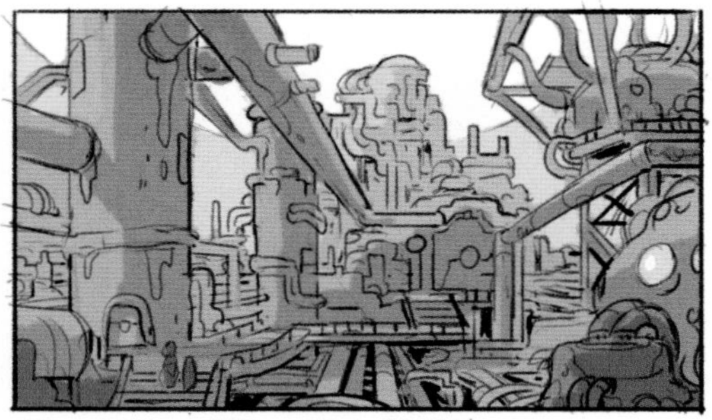

RED MAZE - UPPER LEVELS + BEACON

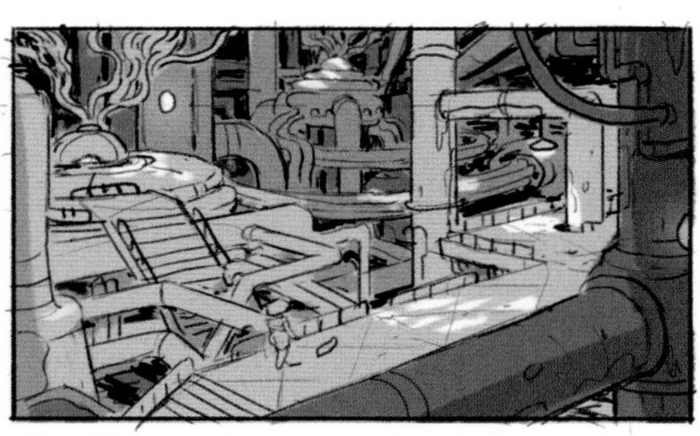

RED MAZE - LOWER LEVELS

SOME LIGHT COMES THROUGH FROM HIGH ABOVE

SAO SANGRE

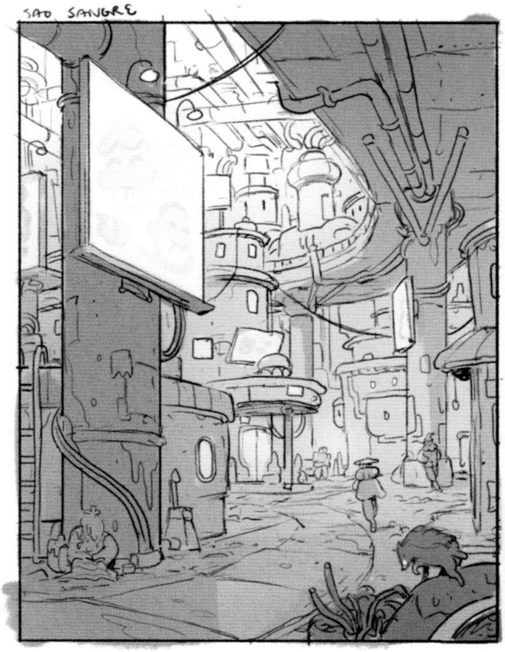

...and many sketchbooks more!

# Discover more  online!

@5WorldsTeam

POST YOUR **COSPLAY** PHOTOS AND SHARE YOUR BEST **FAN ART** WITH OTHER 5-WORLDERS, WITH HASHTAGS #DRAWOONA, #5WORLDS, AND #5WFANART.

## The Winners of the #DrawOona Fan Art Contest Are . . .

Kiara Rivera @Crybaby.kia

Hadley Griffin Johnson

Kristina Luu @stripeyworm

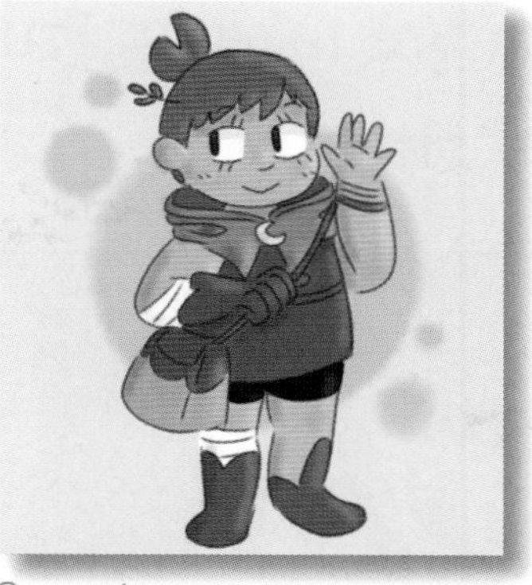

@_yumsty_

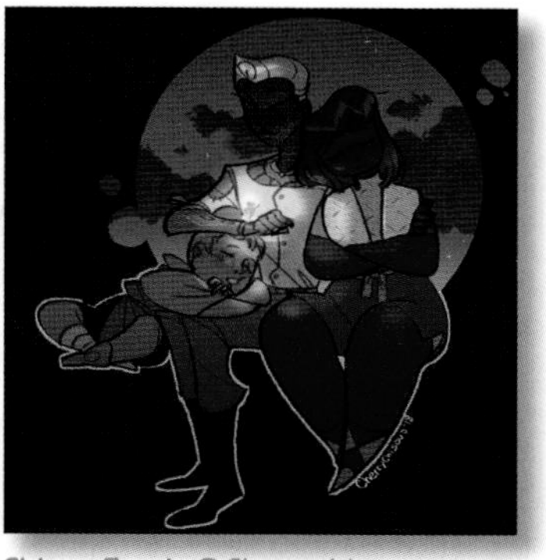

Chiara Farah @Cherrychisoup

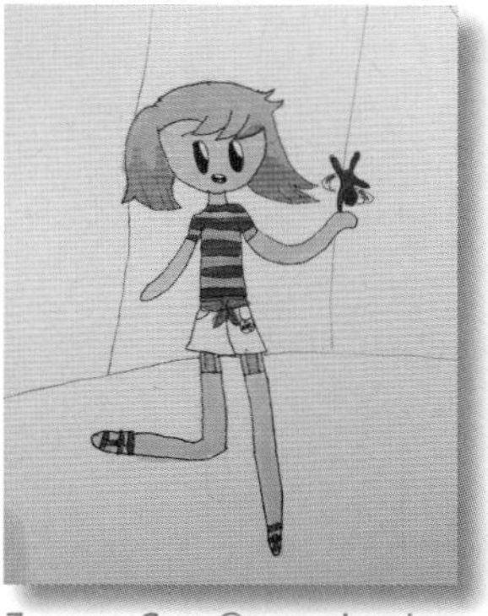

Zamora Cruz @paperbrarian

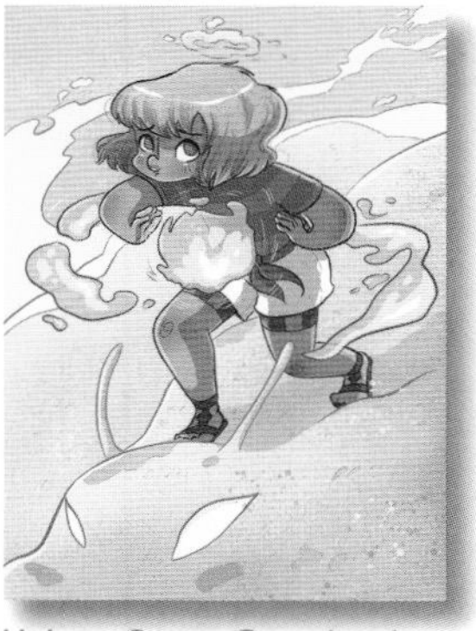

Helene Canac @poulpychoups

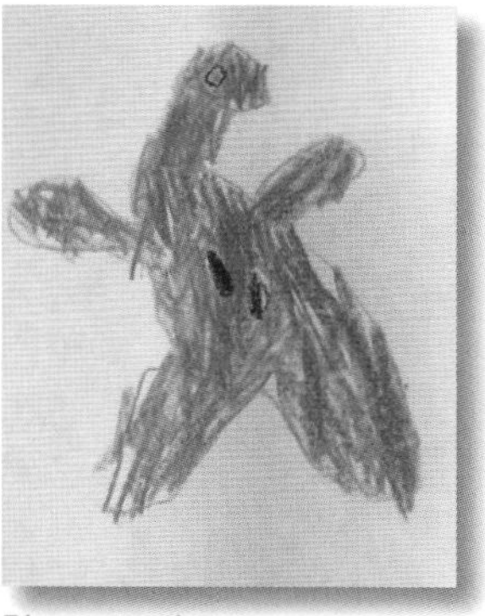

River, age 6

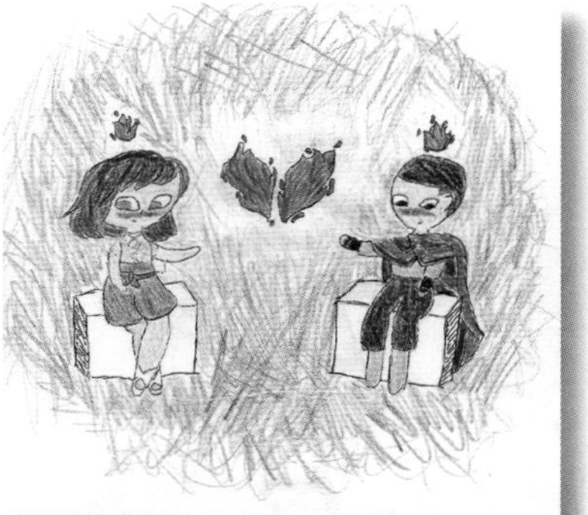

Fiona D. @bonjour_mes_amies

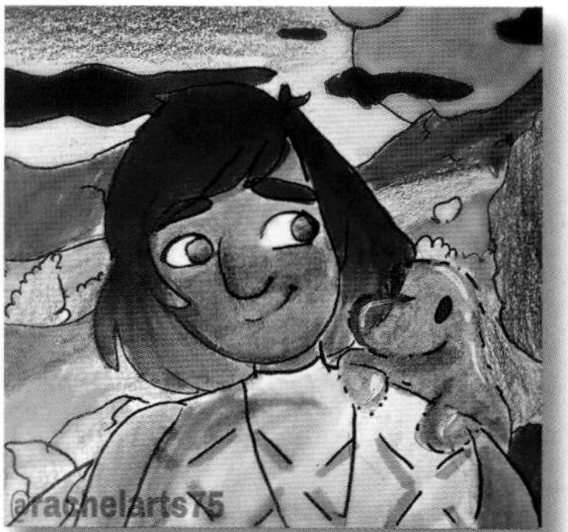
@rachelarts75

Rachel G @rachelarts75

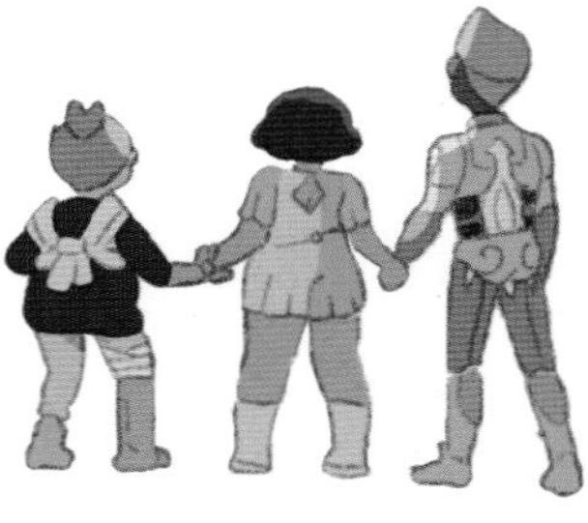

STAY TUNED
FOR CONTESTS
AND SPECIAL EVENTS
ON A PLANET NEAR YOU!

Where will the adventure take An Tzu, Jax, and Oona? Find out in

5 Worlds
THE AMBER ANTHEM
"Mind-blowingly beautiful.... A must-read."
—R.J. Palacio,
#1 New York Times bestselling author of Wonder
Mark Siegel
Alexis Siegel
Xanthe Bouma
Matt Rockefeller
Boya Sun

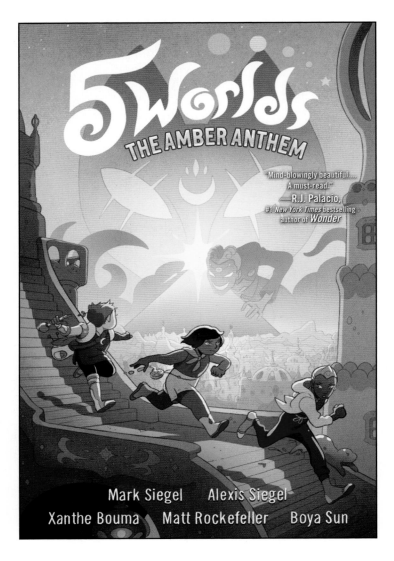

**5W4:**

**THE AMBER ANTHEM**

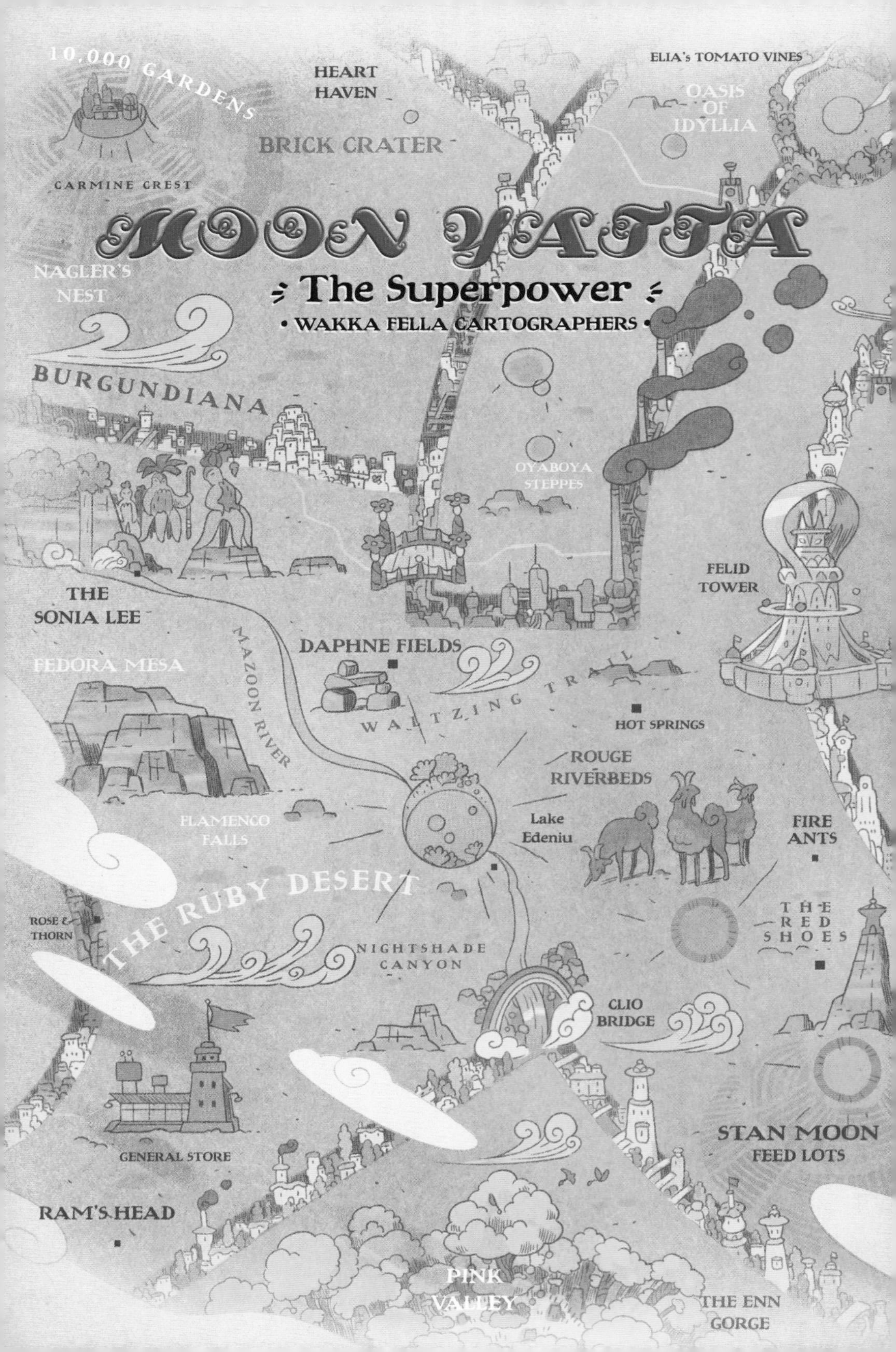
MOON YATTA
The Superpower
• WAKKA FELLA CARTOGRAPHERS •
10,000 GARDENS
HEART HAVEN
ELIA's TOMATO VINES
OASIS OF IDYLLIA
BRICK CRATER
CARMINE CREST
NAGLER'S NEST
BURGUNDIANA
OYABOYA STEPPES
FELID TOWER
THE SONIA LEE
MAZOON RIVER
DAPHNE FIELDS
FEDORA MESA
WALTZING TRAIL
HOT SPRINGS
ROUGE RIVERBEDS
Lake Edeniu
FLAMENCO FALLS
FIRE ANTS
THE RUBY DESERT
ROSE & THORN
THE RED SHOES
NIGHTSHADE CANYON
CLIO BRIDGE
GENERAL STORE
STAN MOON FEED LOTS
RAM'S HEAD
PINK VALLEY
THE ENN GORGE